I0818347

BETWEEN TWO WORLDS

The Weird Tales of Arthur Machen

Selected and introduced by Stephen Carver

TALES OF MYSTERY AND THE SUPERNATURAL

For
DAVID STUART DAVIES
In recognition of his huge contribution to the Wordsworth Mystery and the Supernatural series, the Wordsworth Blog and so much more

Readers who are interested in other titles from Wordsworth Editions are invited to visit our website at www.wordsworth-editions.com

This edition published 2024 by Wordsworth Editions Limited
PO Box 13147, Stansted CM21 1BT

ISBN 978 1 84022 848 9

Text © Wordsworth Editions Limited 2024
Wordsworth® and Wordsworth Editions are registered trade marks of Wordsworth Editions Limited

All rights reserved. This publication may not be reproduced, stored in a retrieval system or transmitted, in any form or by any means, electronic, mechanical, photocopying, recording or otherwise, without the prior permission of the publishers.

Typeset in Great Britain by Tom Griffith and RefineCatch Limited, Bungay, Suffolk

Printed and bound by Clays Ltd, Elcograf S.p.A.

'I stood here, and saw before me the unutterable, the unthinkable gulf that yawns profound between two worlds, the world of matter and the world of spirit; I saw the great empty deep stretch dim before me, and in that instant a bridge of light leapt from the earth to the unknown shore, and the abyss was spanned.'

— Arthur Machen, *The Great God Pan*

CONTENTS

INTRODUCTION

In the second volume of his autobiographical trilogy, *Things Near and Far* (1923), the Welsh author and reluctant journalist Arthur Machen calculated the income he had gained from 'forty-two years of toil' as a writer of supernatural, occult, and mystical fiction, 'this dismal old game of invention.' He also included his life writing and literary translations, most notably the *Memoirs of Casanova*. The amount he arrived at was £635.00: 'That is, I have been paid at the rate of fifteen pounds and a few shillings per annum.' And then, there was 'the debit of toil and endeavour and mortification and disappointment that these forty-two years of book-writing have cost me.' Machen's point was, of course, that he wasn't in it for the money. As he had written in his previous autobiography, *Far Off Things* (1922), 'I never have thought of it as a career, but only as a destiny.' As he got older, it seemed to feel more like a curse:

> Always, or almost always, I have had the horror of beginning a new book. I have burnt my fingers to the bone again and again in the last forty years and I dread the fire of literature. I know what will happen to me, just as the little boy knows what will happen to him when the dear old Head says: 'Come to my room after morning school.'

From his autobiographies, and, indeed, his pseudo-autobiographical novel *The Hill of Dreams* (1907), it is clear that Machen both suffered for his art and was totally committed. As an early career author in London, he once came close to starving to death in his Clarendon Road 'cell', working for a pittance as an indexer and cataloguer by day, writing by candlelight at night, running on dry bread, green tea, and 'plenty of tobacco by way of dessert.'

A modest inheritance from distant Scottish relatives passed down after the death of his father in 1887 allowed Machen an independent income until the money ran out around the turn of the century. During this period, he wrote some of his finest and most memorable works. *The Great God Pan* and 'The Inmost Light' (1894) were his first real forays into paganism, sexuality and folk horror. The episodic novel *The Three Impostors* (1895), loosely inspired by Robert Louis Stevenson's *The Dynamiter*, combines occult vengeance, secret societies, and debauched pagan rites, and includes framed stories that became famous in their own right, like 'The Novel of the White Powder'. Following 'The Novel of the Black Seal' in *The Three Impostors*, Machen wrote more stories of the 'Little People' structured around his fictional alter-ego and holistic detective 'Dyson' (from 'The Inmost Light' and *The Three Impostors*): 'The Shining Pyramid' and 'The Red Hand' (1895). His portrait of the artist, *The Hill of Dreams*, was completed in 1897 (but not published for ten years). He also wrote the stream-of- consciousness novella *The White People* in 1899 (published in 1904), and the prose-poems and flash fiction that would later be collected as *Ornaments in Jade* in 1924. By 1899 he was also working on two further novels, *A Fragment of Life* and *The Secret Glory*, as well as *Hieroglyphics: A Note upon Ecstasy in Literature*, although these were not completed or published until the new century. After this, the return to the struggle for economic survival necessitated that Machen took on the professional role of 'a wretched Fleet Street reporter', which he called a 'prostitution of the soul.' During this period, he wrote what is probably his most famous story, even if many people are completely unaware of the source or its author. 'The Bowmen' was a patriotic tale of the archers of Agincourt returning to defend the retreating British Expeditionary Force, written for the *London Evening News* in the dark days of 1914. Such was its impact, 'The Bowmen' led quickly to the legend of the 'Angels of Mons', a vision many soldiers vehemently claimed to have seen. This was much to Machen's annoyance, writing in another Great War story, 'Out of the Earth', 'my recent experience with "The Bowmen" has taught me that no tale is too idle to be believed.'

But, as Machen said himself, 'my literary activities cannot be adequately accounted for on the hypothesis of mere greed and money-grubbing.' A disciple of Coleridge, Machen's project was much more visionary. As he further argued in *Far Off Things*:

> The arts, then, are man's difference, that which makes him to be what he is; and when he speaks through them he is using

> the utterance which is proper to him, as man. For, if we once set aside the 'does it pay' nonsense, which is evidently nonsense and pestilent nonsense at that, we come clearly and freely to the truth that man is concerned with beauty, and with the ecstasy or rapture that proceeds from the creation of beauty and from the contemplation of it.

To quote his fictionalised self, Lucian Taylor, in *The Hill of Dreams*, the goal was always: 'To win the secret of words, to make a phrase that would murmur of summer and the bee, to summon the wind into a sentence, to conjure the odour of the night into the surge and fall and harmony of a line.' And if this did not always come to pass, 'It was better, he thought, to fail in attempting exquisite things than to succeed in the department of the utterly contemptible.'

This is not to say Machen *failed* at all, although his autobiographical writing is highly self-deprecating. In fact, the final volume, *The London Adventure*, is predominantly a book about his inability to write the book he wished to write about the psychogeography of London which was also to have been called *The London Adventure*. As he wrote in his introduction to the 1922 edition of *House of Souls*, 'he who adventures in London has a foretaste of infinity.' He also seemed to take a perverse pleasure in bad reviews, which he carefully preserved, and subsequently published in a strange little anthology of vituperative critical feedback directed at many of his major works entitled *Precious Balms* in 1924.

Though he always denied he was a gothic writer, Machen was initially a product of the Victorian gothic tradition, being a great admirer of Poe, Dickens, and Stevenson, as well as a devotee of the pagan connotations of the gothic revival in architecture. While working as a young man for the London publisher George Redway, Machen was also given the task of cataloguing a vast collection of esoteric and occult literature, which he read widely:

> There were the principal and the most obscure treatises on Alchemy or Astrology, on Magic; old Latin volumes most of them. Here were books about Witchcraft, Diabolical Possession, 'Fascination,' or the Evil Eye; here comments on the Kabbala. Ghosts and Apparitions were a large family, Secret Societies of all sorts hung on the skirts of the Rosicrucians and Freemasons, and so found a place in the collection. Then the semi-

> religious, semi-occult, semi-philosophical sects and schools were represented: we dealt in Gnostics and Mithraists, we harboured the Neoplatonists, we conversed with the Quietists and the Swedenborgians. These were the ancients; and beside them were the modern throng of Diviners and Stargazers and Psychometrists and Animal Magnetists and Mesmerists and Spiritualists and Psychic Researchers. In a word, the collection in the Catherine Street garret represented thoroughly enough that inclination of the human mind which may be a survival from the rites of the black swamp and the cave or – an anticipation of a wisdom and knowledge that are to come, transcending all the science of our day.

For Machen, modern science was always the enemy of the spiritual. As the reclusive Mansel exclaims in 'The Exalted Omega', 'Science deals with surfaces; what have I to do with surfaces?' Steeped in this ancient and curious lore, though still possessed of a healthy scepticism regarding the current trends in Spiritualism and Theosophy, Machen was well suited to the exoticism and general boundary-pushing of the *fin de siècle*. His short story 'A Double Return', published in *St. James's Gazette* in September 1890, with its implication that a *doppelgänger* had spent a night with the original's wife, was considered far too racy and got Machen kicked off the magazine though Oscar Wilde adored it for 'fluttering the dovecotes.' When *The Great God Pan and The Inmost Light* was published by John Lane in his Keynote series in 1894, with a yellow cover and art by Aubrey Beardsley, Machen was assumed to have gone full Decadent. *The Westminster Gazette* denounced *Pan* as, 'an incoherent nightmare of sex and the supposed horrible mysteries behind it, such as might conceivably possess a man who was given to a morbid brooding over these matters, but would soon lead to insanity if unrestrained.' For the *Manchester Guardian*, 'The book is, on the whole, the most acutely and intentionally disagreeable we have yet seen in English,' while *The Lady's Pictorial* found it 'gruesome, ghastly, and dull.' In a blistering attack in *The Contemporary Review*, art critic Harry Quilter described *Pan* as: 'a perfectly abominable story, in which the author has spared no endeavour to suggest loathsomeness and horror which he describes as beyond the reach of words.' John Lane was not spared either, Quilter adding that, 'Why should he be allowed, for the sake of a few miserable pounds, to cast into our midst these monstrous creations of his diseased brain?' For Quilter, such a book was a threat to the public, Christian morality (if not sanity), and the empire – a symptom of the then popular fear of Degeneration, that, like Imperial Rome, the British Empire could collapse into decadence and barbarism. Wilde, meanwhile, called it *un succès fou* – a runaway success – and sales were brisk, the book quickly going into a second edition. The reputational damage had, however, been done, which goes a long way to explaining Machen's subsequent near-constant streak of complaint from English literary critics, while after Wilde's trial the association of 'decadent horror' made it harder to find a publisher. Heinemann were to have originally published *The Three Impostors*, for example, but suddenly dropped it without explanation. It was instead again published by Lane.

Machen found a new generation of readers when *A Fragment of Life*, *The White People*, *The Great God Pan*, 'The Inmost Light', *The Three Impostors*, and 'The Red Hand' were republished collectively under the title of *The House of Souls* by E. Grant Richards in 1906 – although Machen again attracted critical ire for his introductory 'Note', a polemic against Puritanism and Non-Conformity. *The Athenæum*, which had critically annihilated *The Great God Pan and The Inmost Light* in 1894, seemed to get the point this time, writing that:

> Like Poe, Mr Machen sets himself to make the reader's flesh creep; like Hawthorne, he abounds with subtle and suggestive symbolism … He deals in ancient mysteries; he is for ever hinting at the macabre, the sinister, the unspeakable. His puppets peep and mutter through an atmosphere of forbidden knowledge and obscure rites of remote antiquity, which, however, he would seem to suggest are not so remote as they ought to be after all.

As Dyson explains in 'The Red Hand': 'There are sacraments of evil as well as of good about us, and we live and move to my belief in an unknown world, a place where there are caves and shadows and dwellers in twilight. It is possible that man may sometimes return on the track of evolution, and it is my belief that an awful lore is not yet dead.' And just as Dyson believed this, so did Machen, writing in *The London Adventure* that, 'For we, it is true, live in an illusory world, but there are other spheres of deception, beyond ours, and of a different order, into which we are scarcely meant to penetrate.' This is a recurrent theme in Machen's writing, which anticipates H.P. Lovecraft's definition of 'Weird' fiction, as opposed to more conventional horror, supernatural, or gothic tropes. As Lovecraft wrote in his seminal 1927 essay 'Supernatural Horror in Literature':

> The true weird tale has something more than secret murder, bloody bones, or a sheeted form clanking chains according to rule. A certain atmosphere of breathless and unexplainable dread of outer, unknown forces must be present; and there must be a hint, expressed with a seriousness and portentousness becoming its subject, of that most terrible conception of the human brain – a malign and particular suspension or defeat of those fixed laws of Nature which are our only safeguard against the assaults of chaos and the daemons of unplumbed space.

This concept of another world pushing against the boundaries of our perceived reality is the foundation of what we now know as the 'Cthulhu Mythos'. And Lovecraft was greatly influenced by Machen, writing in the same essay, 'Of living creators of cosmic fear raised to its most artistic pitch, few if any can hope to equal the versatile Arthur Machen, author of some dozen tales long and short, in which the elements of hidden horror and brooding fright attain an almost incomparable substance and realistic acuteness.' For Lovecraft, Machen was one of the 'Modern Masters' of horror (the others being Algernon Blackwood, Lord Dunsany, and M.R. James, all of whose work Machen's major texts predated). Only in his atheism does Lovecraft differ from the High Church Anglo-Catholicism that underpins Machen's layered realities, which have a spiritual dimension that Lovecraft eschews and Machen embraces: 'the sense of the eternal mysteries, the eternal beauty hidden beneath the crust of common and commonplace things; hidden and yet burning and glowing continually if you care to look with purged eyes.' This is the more optimistic side of Machen's world, which can be visionary and Romantic, like the phasing celestial gardens of Canon's Park in *N.* Yet in Machen's early and best-known fiction, the revelation is only rarely positive. More usually, it resembles the experience of Dr Black in 'The Inmost Light', and is isolating and terrible:

> There is a region of knowledge which you will never know, which wise men seeing from afar off shun like the plague, as

> well they may, but into that region I have gone. If you knew, if you could even dream of what may be done, of what one or two men have done in this quiet world of ours, your very soul would shudder and faint within you.

Like Stevenson's Dr Jekyll and Wells' Dr Moreau, Dr Black – and Dr Raymond in *The Great God Pan* – use science to release something ancient, primitive, and destructive. Not that this is conventional science which was, for Machen, 'always wrong,' as it removes mystery and magic from the universe. His 'mad scientists' are more akin to alchemists and shamans. Dr Raymond, for example, practices 'transcendental medicine' and both he and Black sacrifice innocent women in the pursuit of old gods and forbidden knowledge.

Lovecraft's enthusiasm for Machen is indicative of a wider appreciation in the United States in the 1920s, led by the American writers Vincent Starrett, James Branch Cabell, and Carl Van Vechten, Starrett producing an influential essay entitled 'Arthur Machen: A Novelist of Ecstasy and Sin', and editing two collections of his fiction. The twenties represented something of a renaissance for Machen on both sides of the Atlantic, with the publication of his novel *The Secret Glory* – in which a disaffected public schoolboy embarks on a quest for the holy grail – as well as his three-part autobiography and new editions of *The Hill of Dreams*, *The House of Souls*, and his Casanova translation. But as Lovecraft was celebrating him, this late bloom was mostly over, and Machen was forced to return to freelancing for magazines and newspapers, stabilising the family income with manuscript appraisal for the publisher Ernest Benn. By the time the American writer William Francis Gekle published his book *Arthur Machen: Weaver of Fantasy* in 1949, Machen was two-years' dead and his latest champion was, by his own admission, part of a tight huddle of what he called 'Machenites', comprising 'collectors and cultists … bibliographers and bibliophiles … anthologists and the zealots of the pulp press' (the 'horror boys'). And to a certain extent, that is where Machen remains to this day. His writing too dense and symbolic to yield its secrets easily, yet not part of the avant-garde and Modernist revolutions that dominated the period in which he was active, Machen is one of those authors that failed to join the literary canon. Instead, he is a cult figure much beloved by a hard core of readers who have found their way to his work and become enchanted. His legacy and influence is thus as arcane as his fiction, and wonderfully eclectic, with prominent fans as diverse as the comedian Stewart Lee, the former Archbishop of Canterbury, Rowan Williams, and Bob Dylan.

In addition to Lovecraft – whose story 'The Whisperer in Darkness' directly cites Machen, while 'The Call of Cthulhu' uses themes and textual devices from both 'The Novel of the Black Seal' and *The Great Return* – Machen influenced a generation of American pulp writers including Robert E. Howard, Clark Ashton Smith, and Frank Belknap Long, who wrote a sonnet entitled 'On Reading Arthur Machen'. Machen's work can, in fact, be read as a bridge between the later Victorian gothic of writers like Stevenson and J.S. Le Fanu, and the weird fiction of the Lovecraft circle, via the Decadent moment that produced dark, transgressive fantasies like Wilde's *The Picture of Dorian Gray* and Stoker's *Dracula*, the latter of which seems to look back to *The Great God Pan* as resolute English gentlemen face an ancient and inhuman force which dangerously sexualises women. W.B. Yeats and Sir Arthur Conan Doyle were fans, as was Aleister Crowley, though the admiration was not reciprocated. Jorge Luis Borges held Machen in high regard, and his writings can thus be said to have influenced the development of magic realism. At the same time, Poet Laureate Sir John Betjeman attributed his conversion to High Church Anglicanism to Machen. In more modern horror, Machen has been cited as a direct influence by Ramsey Campbell, Peter Straub, whose novel *Ghost Story* was inspired by *The Great God Pan*, and Stephen King, who described *Pan* as 'one of the best horror stories ever written. Maybe the best in the English language,' adding, 'And Machen was there first. He wrote "Pan" in 1895, when HPL was five years old.'

In other media, Machen's writings were an inspiration to Mark E. Smith, the sardonic wordsmith at the heart of the post-punk band The Fall. Smith referenced Machen in numerous songs, for example 'City Hobgoblins' ('Evil émigrés from old green glades' … 'Ten times my age/One-tenth my height' suggest the Little People); 'The Unutterable' ('the bastard offspring of Charles I and the Great God Pan'); and 'Leave The Capitol' ('Pan resides in Welsh green masquerades', while 'I live with cancer death wife' is a reference to Machen's first wife, Amelia 'Amy' Hogg). The sleeve notes for the Fall album *Dragnet*, meanwhile, claim the recording is the result of an experiment in the remote Welsh mountains. The iconic comic writer and novelist Alan Moore also took the death of Amy as the inspiration for his remarkable performance piece *Snakes and Ladders* (1999 – later illustrated by Eddie Campbell and published as *A Disease of Language*), with its focus on Machen's visionary experiences after her death in 1899. Machen attempted to describe the results of his cryptic spiritual 'experiment' in *Things Near and Far*:

> ...a peace of the spirit that was quite ineffable, a knowledge that all hurts and doles and wounds were healed, that that which was broken was reunited. Everything, of body and of mind, was resolved into an infinite and an exquisite delight; into a joy so great that – let this be duly noted – it became almost intolerable in its ecstasy.

As Moore put it, 'Amy died, but Arthur went to heaven.' Machen was a pioneer of psychogeography, the exploration of the interpersonal and historical connections to human spaces, later developed – particularly with regard to London – by writers such as Iain Sinclair, Peter Ackroyd, Michael Moorcock and, of course, Moore himself. As Machen explained in *The London Adventure*:

> I can look with a kind of pleasure on a very doorstep, on a doorstep approaching a shabby grey house of 1810 or thereabouts – if the stone be worn into a deep hollow by the feet of even a hundred years and a little over ... and that doorstep is to me sacramental, if not a sacrament, even though the neighbourhood round about Mount Pleasant is a very poor one. For, it seems to me that here you have the magic touch which redeems and exalts the dull mass of things, by tinging them with the soul of man.

'Caught in the crosshairs of geography and time,' and set and performed in Red Lion Square, *Snakes and Ladders* explores the disinterment of Oliver Cromwell and Elizabeth Siddal alongside Machen's response to Amy's death, all of which took place across time around the square. In Moore's latest novel, *The Great When* (2024), a hapless postwar bookseller's assistant discovers a copy of *A London Walk: Meditations in the Streets of the Metropolis* by 'the Reverend Thomas Hampole' among a pile of Machen's works, a book referenced in *N* which never existed outside the author's imagination. 'The experiments of the alchemists of the Dark Ages,' wrote Rev. Hampole, 'are, in fact, related, not to the transmutation of metals, but to the transmutation of the entire Universe.'

In film, John Carpenter makes the framing narrator of *The Fog* 'Mr Machen', while the subterranean troglodytes of *The Decent* (2005) directed by Neil Marshal recall the underground horrors of the 'The Novel of the Black Seal' and 'The Shining Pyramid'. More recently, a swarm of Machenesque 'fairies, banshees and baby stealers' assault a remote farmhouse in Corin Hardy's Irish horror film *The Hallow* (2015). Richard Stanley, who adapted Lovecraft's *Color Out of Space*, is a devotee, though the director most closely associated with Machen is the Academy Award winning Mexican filmmaker Guillermo del Toro. Machen's influence is particularly notable in del Toro's masterpiece, *Pan's Labyrinth*, but it is also on display in *Hellboy II: The Golden Army*, and *Don't Be Afraid of the Dark*, in which vanished fairy races rise, and grotesque and brutal 'Little People' steal children. Del Toro has written of Machen: 'It is a rare breed of fabulist who transcribes and records – rather than invents – a reality invisible to most of us. These scribes, like St. John the Divine, are possessed of a near-religious certainty that such worlds exist. Arthur Machen was one of these.'

Aside from Lovecraft, there has perhaps never been a writer whose preferred genre was predominantly horror whose work is so founded on a unifying philosophy as that of Arthur Machen. As S.T. Joshi wrote in his seminal study *The Weird Tale* (1990), 'Machen's tales are not merely outgrowths of his philosophy ... but are, like his essays, part and parcel of his grand attempt to promote his mystical view of life.' Joshi, I think rightly, distils Machen's 'philosophy' – and therefore his entire literary output – to a single idea: 'the awesome and unutterably unfathomable mystery of the universe,' which the author of *The Great God Pan* explores through the concepts of 'ecstasy, of the veil, and of the sacrament' (the state of grace, a mystical union with God). *Ecstasy* is a key word for Machen, and the core of his very personal literary theory, outlined in his 1902 book *Hieroglyphics: A Note upon Ecstasy in Literature*:

> If ecstasy be present, then I say there is fine literature, if it be absent, then, in spite of all the cleverness, all the talents, all the workmanship and observation and dexterity you may show me, then, I think, we have a product (possibly a very interesting one), which is not fine literature ... I have chosen this word as the

> representative of many. Substitute, if you like, rapture, beauty, adoration, wonder, awe, mystery, sense of the unknown, desire for the unknown. All and each will convey what I mean; for some particular case one term may be more appropriate than another, but in every case there will be that withdrawal from the common life and the common consciousness which justifies my choice of 'ecstasy' as the best symbol of my meaning.

The character of Ambrose echoes this terminology in the metaphysical discussion of 'sin' that frames *The White People*: 'Sorcery and sanctity, these are the only realities. Each is an ecstasy, a withdrawal from the common life.' It is this *withdrawal from the common life* that Machen's prose perpetually pursues, in tales both sacred and profane – the breach of the veil between the mundane and the marvellous, between ordinary existence and the spiritual realms that lie beyond. In the single recording of his sonorous voice that we have (a fragment of the BBC Radio *Welsh Programme* 'Points of View', broadcast on March 22, 1937), Machen explains the concept with a straightforward analogy:

> …the supreme artists have no interest in lifelike characters and don't depict them save perhaps in casual moments of fatigue and depression. The artist creates what neither he nor anybody else has ever seen or ever will see in actual life. The artificer, the secondary man, copies and compounds from the life about him. You remember the classic Turner story. The lady looks at a flaming canvas and says to the artist, 'Well I never saw a sunset like that.' Turner replies, 'No, but don't you wish you had?' There is the principle of it.

And in quest of this ecstatic vision, this piercing of the veil, Machen is drawn again and again to the hills, valleys, and ancient Romano-Celt ruins of his native Gwent, and the rookeries of London's East End. As John Simons wrote in 'The Case of Arthur Machen' (1993), 'the sinister world of fairy dovetails neatly with his sense of the strangeness of London.' As Julian's unnamed friend tells him in 'Nature': 'I always told you that the earth too, and the hills, and even the old walls are a language, hard to translate', while to Dyson in 'The Inmost Light', 'The science of the great city; the physiology of London' is 'literally and metaphysically the greatest subject that the mind of man can conceive.'

Machen's 'Little People' (fairy) mythopoeia can be likened to Lovecraft's 'Cthulhu Mythos', and it pervades many of his stories as well as his nonfiction. For Machen, this had an anthropological basis, which he outlined in his 1898 essay 'Folklore and Legends of the North':

> Of recent years abundant proof has been given that a short, non-Aryan race once dwelt beneath ground, in hillocks throughout Europe, their raths have been explored, and the weird old tales of green hills all lighted up at night have received confirmation. Much in the old legends may be explained by a reference to this primitive race. The stories of Changelings, and captive women, become clear on the supposition that the 'fairies' occasionally raided the houses of the invaders.

In *Things Near and Far*, he explained how he applied these legends to 'The Novel of the Black Seal' in *The Three Impostors*:

> I worked it all into my fairy tale, mixing up the old view that the fairy tales, the stories of Little People, are in fact traditions of the aborigines of these islands, small, dark men who took refuge under the hills from the invading Celt; with this view of the capacities of the human body, and my view, still newer, that the fairies may still be found under the hills, and that they are far from being pleasant little people.

This, of course, echos Professor Gregg in 'The Novel of the Black Seal':

> I became convinced that much of the folklore of the world is but an exaggerated account of events that really happened, and I was especially drawn to consider the stories of the fairies, the good folk of the Celtic races. Here I thought I could detect the fringe of embroidery and exaggeration, the fantastic guise, the little people dressed in green and gold sporting in the flowers, and I thought I saw a distinct analogy between the name given to this race (supposed to be imaginary) and the description of their

> appearance and manners. Just as our remote ancestors called the dreaded beings 'fair' and 'good' precisely because they dreaded them, so they had dressed them up in charming forms, knowing the truth to be the very reverse.

In an interview with *Cineaste* magazine in 2011, Guillermo del Toro explained how this had inspired *Don't Be Afraid of the Dark*: 'I love the Welsh author Arthur Machen and his idea that fairy lore comes from a dark place, that it's derived from little, pre-human creatures who are really, really nasty vermin but are magical in a way, living as they do for hundreds of years. His books are what compelled me to do this.' The Little People appear in several of Machen's stories. In 'The Novel of the Black Seal', for example, Professor Gregg finds a half-human hybrid and, possibly, the key to an underground kingdom; in 'The Shining Pyramid', Dyson investigates the disappearance of a farmer's daughter and mysterious signs marked out around a friend's desolate Welsh cottage, leading to the discovery of a terrible rite; in 'The Red Hand', Dyson discovers a murder committed with an ancient stone knife; in 'Change' a baby is swapped for a fairy changeling, and in 'Out of the Earth', the Little People approve of man's like-minded barbarity during the Great War: 'These little people of the earth rise up and rejoice in these times of ours. For they are glad, as the Welshman said, when they know that men follow their ways.' They are still hanging around in Machen's last novel, *The Green Round*, when one attaches itself to the reclusive protagonist. But terrible though they are, the Little People are also a symbol of 'ecstasy'; as Joshi argues, 'they have retained that primal sacrament (perverted, of course, by bestiality and violence) which links them with the Beyond.' As Ambrose explained in *The White People*, there is both 'sorcery and sanctity', and Machen's prose explores both. Thus, *The White People* – in which a young girl is indoctrinated into witchcraft and depravity – is thanatic and destructive, whereas ritual in the *Ornaments in Jade* stories is life-affirming and ecstatic.

Machen was born Arthur Llewellyn Jones in Caerleon on Usk, in the county of Gwent, South Wales, in 1863, the son of an Anglican priest. John Edward Jones was vicar of the church of Llandewi, near Caerleon, and Arthur, an only and bookish child, was raised at the rectory. Machen was his mother's maiden name, which Arthur later adopted as a penname. 'I shall always esteem it as the greatest piece of fortune that has fallen to me, that I was born in that noble, fallen Caerleon-on-Usk, in the heart of Gwent,' Machen wrote in *Far Off Things*, continuing:

> My greatest fortune, I mean, from that point of view which I now more especially have in mind, the career of letters. For the older I grow the more firmly am I convinced that anything which I may have accomplished in literature is due to the fact that when my eyes were first opened in earliest childhood they had before them the vision of an enchanted land. As soon as I saw anything I saw Twyn Barlwm, that mystic tumulus, the memorial of peoples that dwelt in that region before the Celts left the Land of Summer. This guarded the southern limit of the great mountain wall in the west; a little northward was Mynydd Maen – the Mountain of the Stone – a giant, rounded billow; and still to the north mountains, and on fair, clear days one could see the pointed summit of the Holy Mountain by Abergavenny. It would shine, I remember, a pure blue in the far sunshine; it was a mountain peak in a fairy tale.

Machen was a boarder at Hereford Cathedral School (an experience that later formed the basis of *The Secret Glory*), receiving a middle-class classical education, although his parents could not afford to send him to Oxford, his father's *alma mater* – a situation he later passes on to the fictional hero of several of his major works, Dyson, in 'The Inmost Light'. When he was seventeen, Machen self-published *Eleusinia*, a poem about the Eleusinian mysteries, annual initiations for the cult of Demeter and Persephone. This is a work that already signals Machen's interest in the relationship between landscape and time, and of the return of hidden lore and ritual:

> So sweet a song they made, the music yet
> Is not all silenced, some clear notes remain,
> Though many waves of centuries have passed
> Upon those pleasant days: but hark awhile
> Unto the chorus, though the years have sped,
> And the dim twilight of the world is come.

On the strength of this, Machen's family decided that 'journalism was the career for me' and he moved to London with the vague idea of becoming a writer, living in poverty in a tiny room in Clarendon Road, Notting Hill Gate, reading voraciously and exploring the city, though well outside Literary London:

> So I read and meditated night after night, and I am amazed at the utter loneliness of it all, when I contrast this life of mine with the beginnings of other men of letters. These others have often gathered friends of all sorts, both useful and pleasant, at the University; they have come of well-known stocks, every step they take is eased for them, their way is pointed out, there are hands to help them over the rough and difficult places.

His first book, the philosophical pastiche *The Anatomy of Tobacco* by 'Liolinus Siluriensis' was published by George Redway in 1884. Machen's pseudonym indicates his preoccupation with Ancient Wales; the Silures were a powerful tribe in southeast Wales who fiercely resisted Roman occupation. Redway offered Machen a job, and it was through him that he catalogued *The Literature of Occultism and Archaeology*.

During this period, Machen translated the *Heptamerone* of Marguerite de Navarre, François Béroalde de Verville's *Le Moyen de Parvenir* (*Fantastic Tales*), and the *Memoirs of Casanova* from the Old French. Reading Balzac and Rabelais inspired his first work of fiction, *The Chronicle of Clemendy* (1888), a mock-heroic epic of nested narratives set in his native Wales, which Machen later described as 'the Great Romance which was neither great nor a romance.' Like *The Anatomy of Tobacco*, the book was written in archaic English. He had also by this time married Amy Hogg, a 'New Woman' and member of the literary London scene, and the death of his parents had facilitated the inheritance that would allow him the space to write unbothered by the need to earn a living through the 1890s – again, a turn of fate that also happens to Dyson – in which he produced much of his finest work, finding his voice as a mature author.

Amy died after a long battle with cancer in 1899, and in an aberrant mental state (more than once he claimed to have met characters from *The Three Impostors* in the street), Machen briefly joined the Hermetic Order of the Golden Dawn. Machen later noted that, 'I must confess that it did me a great deal of good – for the time,' but of the hope that the Order 'might give me some light and guidance and leading on these matters ... I was mistaken; the Twilight Star shed no ray of any kind on my path.' Machen's visionary state faded, and he continued to heal by changing career, becoming an actor in Sir Francis Robert Benson's Shakespearean touring company. In 1903 he married another middle-class bohemian, Dorothie Purefoy Hudleston, with whom he had two children, Hilary and Janet. Precariously surviving by writing and acting, Machen finally surrendered to journalism at the end of the decade, writing first for the *Daily Mail* before becoming a staff writer on its sister paper, the *London Evening News*. Here, he once more gained notoriety for 'The Bowmen', the irony being that the by then renowned Celtic mystic was forced by his own sense of decency to adopt the materialist stance that he hated in arguing that a supernatural event which he would have loved was pure invention. This experience did, however, inspire Machen to return to writing fiction.

The twenties were good years, with recognition in the US and a bounce in Britain that could be partly ascribed to the rather desperate re-embracing of Spiritualism and occultism by bereaved relatives after the Great War. As Professor Warburton laments in 'The Dover Road':

> But the War had changed everything. It was, no doubt, a very severe national shock. It has had all sorts of bad effects and repercussions; and one of the worst, in my opinion, is this hysterical credulity that one sees everywhere. There's no tale too monstrous to be believed. We're threatened with the return of the most childish superstitions of the Middle Ages.

Unfortunately, the wave broke and rolled back, and Machen's later years were no more financially secure than the 1880s. In *Things Near and Far* he wrote of how he must still 'beg my bread in my sixtieth year.' In 1932, he was granted a Civil List pension of £100.00 PA for his services to literature, but the following year lost his job with the publisher Ernest Benn, causing a return to genteel poverty. Only when a literary appeal was launched for him by friends on his eightieth birthday in 1943 did Machen's fortunes improve, allowing him to live out the remainder of his life in reasonable comfort. Those supporting included T. S. Eliot, John Masefield, Max Beerbohm, Walter de la Mare, Algernon Blackwood, and George Bernard Shaw. He died at his home in Amersham in December 1947, a few months after Dorothie.

His final work had been the novel *The Green Round* (1933), in which the 'claustrophilic' hero picks up something nasty after visiting a verdant natural amphitheatre on holiday in Wales, and two collections of short stories, both published in 1936. *The Cosy Room and Other Stories* mostly contains previously published material with some new stories tacked on to the end, including the beautiful novelette *N*, in which a fragment of Paradise occasionally and randomly manifests in Stoke Newington. The stories contained in *The Children of the Pool* were all new.

This present collection is unique in containing the majority of Arthur Machen's short weird fiction in a single, representative volume, ranging from an extract from *The Chronicle of Clemendy* (1888) that is already penetrating the veil, albeit humorously, to Machen's final story, 'Ritual', published in 1937. Though Machen's stories were frequently not published at the time that they were written, I have opted to order them according to date of publication. This collection includes Machen's notable early magazine stories, as well as all his major work from the 1890s, including three stories extracted from *The Three Impostors*. I have also selected the three notably supernatural stories from *The Angel of Mons: The Bowmen and Other Legends of War* (1915); and reproduced in its entirety Machen's famous Great War 'shilling shocker' novella *The Terror* – an early example of the eco-horror subgenre in which animals rise up against humanity. As *Ornaments in Jade* (1924) should be read as a series of inter-connected pieces, it is also reproduced in full here. The collection concludes with Machen's significant stories from the 1930s, which are rarely anthologised. I have also appended Machen's introduction to *The Angel of Mons*, in which he discusses the widespread belief that the story of 'The Bowmen' was actually true. Unfortunately, there is not the space to include the longer works *A Fragment of Life*, *The Hill of Dreams*, *The Secret Glory*, and *The Green Round*, but it is hoped that a further edition of these novels and novellas is not beyond the realms of possibility.

We cannot claim that this is the only anthology of Arthur Machen's short fiction, but it is certainly the most comprehensive in one volume. It is also one of very few presently in print. Towards the end of his life, Machen had written to William Francis Gekle that, 'I question whether what you call the neglect of my work is due to any fault of publishers or public – the real cause of it, I believe, is the fact that I have been interested as a writer in a variety of things which only interest a few people. This is a matter of individual constitution: it is incurable.' S.T.

Joshi has similarly written that he suspected that Machen 'would have wished to be read only by a small band of sympathetic followers.' I must confess that my ambitions as a literary historian are bolder; my belief – and, indeed, hope – is that Machen deserves to be canonised and celebrated as a major figure in English and Welsh literature, and as a horror pioneer whose writing matches the depth and complexity of H.P. Lovecraft.

If you are already a believer, I hope this new collection finds favour. If you are new to the weird world of Arthur Machen, then you are in for a treat. Lower the lights, imagine the desolate loneliness and strangeness of the Welsh hills and the dark alleys of Edwardian London, and prepare to withdraw from the common life…

STEPHEN CARVER

NOTE ON THE TEXT

In bringing together stories from a variety of sources published over several decades, my aim has been to create a smooth reading experience and a uniform text with a minimum of editorial interference. With this in mind, I have discreetly modernised and standardised hyphenated words that would look strange to the contemporary reader – for example 'to-day', 'arm-chair', and 'folk-lore' – and replaced the rather archaic 'shew' with 'show'. I have also standardised the italicisation of book titles and Latin script. Otherwise, I have only corrected minor typographical errors, and the misspelling of a few place names, such as 'Tibet' for 'Thibet' and 'Peking' for 'Pekin'. In *The Great God Pan*, I have also taken the liberty of changing 'Buenos Ayres' to 'Buenos Aires', as it is plain that the ill-fated artist Meyrick died in South America whereas 'Buenos Ayres' is a small village in Trinidad and Tobago.

Original printed sources have been used whenever possible. The text of 'Strange Story from a Red Jar' was extracted from the 1926 edition of *The Chronicle of Clemendy* published by Alfred A. Knopf. 'A Double Return', 'The Lost Club', and 'The Autophone' are reproduced from the original *St. James's Gazette* magazines. *The Great God Pan* and 'The Inmost Light' are taken from the John Lane first edition of 1904. 'The Shining Pyramid' is taken from *The Shining Pyramid*, published in 1925 by Martin Seeker, as are 'Out of the Earth' and 'The Happy Children'. The 'Novels' of 'The Black Seal', 'The Iron Maid', and 'The White Powder' are extracted (and slightly cut, the framing narratives being omitted) from the first edition of *The Three Impostors*, published by John Lane in 1905. 'The Red Hand' and *The White People* are taken from the first edition of *The House of Souls* (E. Grant Richards, 1906). 'The Bowmen' and its introduction, as well as 'The Soldier's Rest' and 'The Monstrance' are taken from *The Angel of Mons: The Bowmen and Other Legends of War* (Simpkin, Marshall, Hamilton, Kent & Co, 1915). *The Great Return* is reproduced from the original Faith Press

Edition of 1915. *The Terror* is the full text of the first edition published by Duckworth in 1917. *Ornaments in Jade* is reproduced in its entirety from the first edition published by Knopf in 1924. 'Opening the Door', 'The Cosy Room', and *N* are all taken from the first edition of *The Cosy Room and Other Stories* (Rich & Cowan, 1936). 'The Bright Boy', 'The Children of the Pool', 'The Exalted Omega', 'Out of the Picture', and 'Change' are all taken from the first edition of *The Children of the Pool and Other Stories* (Hutchinson, 1936). 'The Dover Road' is the original text from the anthology *Missing from Their Homes* (Hutchinson, 1936), and 'Ritual' is taken from *Path and Pavement: Twenty New Tales of Britain* (Eric Grant, 1937).

With many thanks to Tom Griffith, David Francis, and Gracie Carver for their patience and diligence in preparing this manuscript for publication.

SC

BIBLIOGRAPHY

The stories in this collection originally appeared in the following publications:

'Strange Story of a Red Jar' (From *The Chronicle of Clemendy*. London: Privately printed for the Society of Pantegruelists, 1888).

'The Autophone' (*St. James's Gazette*, August 21, 1890).

'A Double Return' (*St. James's Gazette*, September 11, 1890).

'The Lost Club' (*Whirlwind* 2, December 20, 1890).

The Great God Pan (First published in its complete form in *The Great God Pan and The Inmost Light*: London: John Lane, 1894. Chapter 1 only published in *Whirlwind* 2, December 13, 1890).

'The Inmost Light' (*The Great God Pan and The Inmost Light*, 1894).

'The Shining Pyramid' (*Unknown World* 2, May 15, 1895).

'Novel of The Black Seal' (*The Three Impostors*, London: John Lane, 1895).

'Novel of The Iron Maid' (*The Three Impostors*, 1895).

'Novel of The White Powder' (*The Three Impostors*, 1895).

'The Red Hand' (*Chapman's Magazine* 2, December 1895; *The House of Souls*, London: E. Grant Richards, 1906).

The White People (*Horlick's Magazine* 1, January 1904; *The House of Souls*, 1906).

'The Bowmen' (*London Evening News* Sept 29, 1914; *The Angel of Mons: The Bowmen and Other Legends of War*. London: Simpkin, Marshall, Hamilton, Kent & Co, 1915).

'The Soldier's Rest' (*The Angel of Mons*, 1915).

'The Monstrance' (*The Angel of Mons*, 1915).

The Great Return (*The Great Return*. London: Faith Press, 1915).

'Out of the Earth' (*T.P.'s Weekly*, 26 November 27, 1915; Vincent Starrett, ed. *The Shining Pyramid*. Chicago: Covici-McGee, 1923).

The Terror (*London Evening News* 16 October 1916 to 31 October, 1916; *The Terror*. London: Duckworth, 1917).

'The Happy Children' (Sir J.A. Hammerton, ed. *The Masterpiece Library of Short Stories*. Vol 20. London: Educational Book Co., 1920; *The Shining Pyramid*, London: Martin Secker, 1925).

Ornaments in Jade (New York: Alfred A. Knopf, 1924).

'Opening the Door' (Lady Cynthia Asquith, ed. *When Graveyards Yawn*. London: Hutchinson, 1931; *The Cosy Room and Other Stories*. London: Rich & Cowan, 1936).

'The Bright Boy' (*The Children of the Pool and Other Stories*. London: Hutchinson, 1936).

'The Children of the Pool' (*The Children of the Pool*, 1936).

'The Exalted Omega' (*The Children of the Pool*, 1936).

'Out of the Picture' (*The Children of the Pool*, 1936).

'Change' (*The Children of the Pool*, 1936).

'The Cosy Room' (*The Cosy Room*, 1936).

N (*The Cosy Room*, 1936).

'The Dover Road' (Anon, ed. *Missing from Their Homes*. London: Hutchinson, 1936).

'Ritual' (John Rowland, ed. *Path and Pavement: Twenty New Tales of Britain*. London: Eric Grant, 1937).

Introduction to 'The Bowmen' (*The Angel of Mons*, 1915).

FURTHER READING

Benson, Lady Constance. *Mainly Players: Bensonian Memories.* London: Thornton Butterworth, 1926.

Brangham, Godfrey, ed. *Where Memory Slept: The Memoirs of Purefoy Machen.* Caerleon, Gwent: Green Round Press, 1991.

Danielson, Henry. *Arthur Machen: A Bibliography. With notes biographical and critical by Arthur Machen.* London: Henry Danielson, 1923.

Gawsworth, John. *The Life of Arthur Machen.* Coverdale: Tartarus Press, in association with the Friends of Arthur Machen and Reino de Redonda, 2005.

Gekle, William Francis. *Arthur Machen: Weaver of Fantasy.* New York: Round Table Press, 1949.

Joshi, S.T. *The Weird Tale.* Holicong, PA: Wildside Press, 1990.

Lovecraft, H.P. 'Supernatural Horror in Literature', 1927. *The H.P. Lovecraft Archive.* Available at: https://www.hplovecraft.com/writings/texts/essays/shil.aspx

Moore, Alan, Campbell, Eddie. *A Disease of Language.* London: Knockabout, 2005.

Moore, Alan. *The Great When: The Long London Quintet*, Book 1. London: Bloomsbury, 2024.

Reynolds, Aidan, Charlton, William. *Arthur Machen: A Short Account of His Life and Work.* London: The Richards Press, 1963.

Sewell, Brocard, ed. *Arthur Machen.* Llandeilo, Wales: St. Albert's Press, 1960.

Simons, John. 'Horror in the 1890s: The Case of Arthur Machen'. In Bloom, Clive, ed. *Creepers: British Horror & Fantasy in the Twentieth Century.* London: Pluto Press, 1993.

Starrett, Vincent. *Arthur Machen: A Novelist of Ecstasy and Sin.* Chicago: Walter M. Hill, 1918.

Sweetser, Wesley D. *Arthur Machen.* New York: Twayne, 1964.

Tearle, Oliver. *Bewilderments of Vision: Hallucination and Literature, 1880–1914.* Brighton: Sussex Academic Press, 2014.

Valentine, Mark. *Arthur Machen.* Bridgend: Seren, 1994.

Valentine, Mark, Dobson, Roger. *Arthur Machen: Apostle of Wonder*. Oxford & Northampton: Caermaen Books, 1985.

Wagenknect, Edward. *Seven Masters of Supernatural Fiction.* Westport, CT: Greenwood Press, 1991.

For more information visit *The Friends of Arthur Machen*, a fellowship dedicated to celebrating Machen and his work at: https://arthurmachen.co.uk

BETWEEN TWO WORLDS

Strange Story of a Red Jar

If you ever chance to spend a few weeks in the County of Monmouth, and are one of those clever people who know where to look for what is good, you will not fail to roam over the hills and across the valleys till you come to a little town called Uske. This town lies beside the fair river of the same name, and is sheltered on every side by wooded hills and sweet, greeny slopes; and to the east you can see the enchanted forest of Wentwood, where there are deep dells, shady alleys, rocks with water everlastingly dripping from them, and the finest black cherries that anybody could wish to taste. But, if you once cross the bridge and get into Uske, you will have plenty to look at without thinking of Wentwood, that is, if you are fond of quaint houses, wild old-fashioned gardens, and odd nooks and corners of every sort. And, better than all, there are old tales and legends still lingering about the sunny streets, and sleeping on the settles next to the fire; but it is getting rather difficult to wake them up now, because you see they are very old. They are, in fact, the last vestiges of the good old monks, who had a Priory in Uske, and this tale I am going to tell is considered by experienced judges to be as pleasant a story as any of them, because it has such a fine moral, without which a story is no more use than a wasp without his sting.

You must know, then, that there was once a monk at the Priory, named Brother Drogo, who was regarded by everybody as a splendid specimen of a monk; and not without reason, for he stood six feet high, and had a waist like a wine tub. He had roving twinkling black eyes, a firm mouth, and a voice like the roar of the pedal pipes of the organ, and it must be confessed that in his quire habit he looked a well-proportioned man, and a pillar of the Church. As for his intellect, all the brethren allowed him to be an admirable logician, an orthodox divine, and the best judge of sauces, seasonings, hot relishes, sweetmeats, and preserved dainties of the whole convent, and this was saying a great deal. It was Brother Drogo's science and deep knowledge of the nature of things, and of how to mingle hot and sweet together, that made the pious brethren long for Lent and fast days, and desire to mortify their throats with curious dishes, of which none but himself and the cook ever understood the composition. But yet this was not Brother Drogo's greatest art; for he was the Cellarer of the Priory, and took care of the casks in the cellar, and of that pleasant vineyard on a southern slope, where the sun was nearly always to be found; and if he were great in the kitchen and the larder, he was far greater in the affairs of the fragrant world below. But here his one fault got the better of him, and sometimes played him queer tricks; for, to tell the truth, Brother Drogo used now and then to get very drunk. When in this state he usually saw visions, which made some esteem him a very holy man (since it is only such that are blessed in this fashion); but others said that his visions were of the wrong sort and should be kept out of the monastic Chronicle. However this may be, the last vision that he ever saw was such a wonderful one that it lasted him the rest of his life, since he never touched anything but water afterwards; and this was the manner of it.

It was a very hot drowsy sort of day in the beginning of September; a day when the sickles were busy in the cornfields round Uske, a day of blue dim mists over the woods and hills and the river, a day of mellowed golden sunlight good for the vines and apples and pears and plums, and all the autumn fruits that were ripening in those tangled gardens of Gwent. In the castle above the town the lords and ladies were lying in the shade upon the grass and listening to the ballads and love songs of the minstrel Master Jehan de Laune of Paris town; and the girls let the squires and pages tickle them and snatch sly kisses as much as ever they liked; because it was too hot to scream and they knew it was right to bear and forbear. In the Priory the monks were (most of them) asleep and dreaming holy dreams that made them smile as they slept; but Brother Drogo was wide awake and walking up and down the cloister. Why was this? Well, it was because he was terribly thirsty, and felt as if a Lollard were being roasted somewhere at the back of his throat, and the reason that he did not drink was that he had doubts whether he should ever stop if he once began. This was in fact a knotty case of conscience and it puzzled the good man and made him feel thirstier than ever; the which was natural since theology is known to be a dry and thirsty science. It is bad enough when two or three divines are muddling a question between them, but this unfortunate monk had to be Praeses, Opponent, and Respondent all at once; and he found that it was necessary for him to take a little wine to clear his brain, for being a conscientious man he wished to settle this point before doing anything else. He therefore picked his way past a dozen or so of monks, all smiling very hard, and went along a dark passage, and began to go down the steps to the cellar. Now the steps were many and by reason of their great age, uneven; so it was slow work getting to the bottom, and the Cellarer had to stop short very often and tap his skull, for the cool air from below seemed to make his blood hotter than before. And when he stopped he held up his lamp and looked at the walls, which had been decorated in rather a curious manner by an ancient monk who had been dead a good many hundred years. This artist's fancy had led him to suppose that views of Purgatory and warmer places would be a nice ornament to the cellar stair; but whether he intended all these flames, fagots, and streams of fire as a sort of whet for the wine, or whether he meant to say 'that's what'll come to you if you get drunk' is more than I can tell. But these pictures made Brother Drogo feel warmer and warmer, though he couldn't help looking at them; and in one place where a fine powerful demon was sousing a big monk in a cauldron of fire and poking him with a three-pronged fork to see if he were done, the Cellarer was forced to discern a huge resemblance between the monk's features and his own. However he trod the last step in due time, and stood in the vaulted cellar, the which had aisles, transepts, side chapels, and ambulatories in abundance, but there were casks everywhere of all shapes and sizes, and a few curious-looking jars with Greek letters cut on them. In this shadowy world of wine Brother Drogo stood awhile and gazed about in an abstracted kind of way, rolling his tongue in his mouth and telling his tale on his fingers as he thought of Burgundy, Beaune, Champagne, and all the vintages of the fair land of France, of Valdepenas and Amontillado, of the juice of the Rhine mountains, and of the famous wines of Italy, which are drawn from the very mouth of the fire below. But the Cellarer's thirst was such a stupendous one that he could not see his way to allaying it on any of these; so he just drew himself a pint of his own red wine of Uske, and sat down on a stone form to consider things. When he had finished his draught he began to walk about among the casks and to peer into odd shelves and crannies in out of the way recesses and blind corners of the cellar, muttering to himself all the time 'Burgundy, Beaune, Champagne, Valdepenas, Amontillado, Montepulciano' as if he were bidding the beads of St Bacchus. By chance he came to a nook in the darkest part of the cellar, in the which nothing was kept, nor had been for many a long day; and holding up his lamp and peering about the dim and shadowy wall he saw faintly a great red jar, of the most ancient and uncouth form imaginable, graved all over with ivy leaves, vine tendrils, pine cones and a pomp of nymphs and fauns dancing all around it. But there was no mark, nor label to say what this jar held; so Brother Drogo found it was his duty as Cellarer to look a little more closely into the matter. Indeed he had his doubts as to whether this jar was a good Christian, so he got on a stone step and began to use his tools on the jar's mouth, which was covered tightly with black pitch. And as he cut this pitch away faint odours of delicious fragrance began to steal out tickling Brother Drogo's weakest places. 'The Prior will thank me for this day's work' thought he; and thus he cut the last piece away and the soul of the jar poured its whole fragrance out upon him like a breeze from the Islands in the High Levant, and went past into the cellar, and up the stair into the cloister where the monks were asleep, and out into the town so that the townsfolk said to one another ' 'Tis a balmy day, indeed marvellously balmy.' As for the girls in the castle their gallants squeezed them a little more closely, and they smiled and seemed to think everything was being properly performed and going on nicely; but then it was a sweet gale that blew upon them.

But Brother Drogo said to himself 'one cup – one little cup – of this wonderful wine will quite quench my thirst; better than a hogshead of any other wine; indeed if I were now half-seas-over, it would be my duty to taste it; am I not Cellarer? How shall I bring the matter before the Prior without having tasted?' You see Brother Drogo had not read Aristotle for nothing, so he gently inclined the jar to his cup, and let a dark purple stream run slowly like oil into it, till it was quite full. And when he tasted he had drained the cup, and when he had drained the cup he knew that he, the Cellarer of the Convent of St Mary, was a sinful man that had gloried all his days in a nice discrimination of various juices, when in point of fact, he had that moment tasted wine for the first time in his life. But instead of running up the stairs and telling the Prior, Brother Drogo drank and drank again, cup after cup, till he got chimes in his ears, fire in his veins, and a miz-maze in his brain. This veracious history does not say how many cups Brother Drogo lifted out of the red jar; but it was certainly a great many for he was a man of large capabilities. However, as he was drawing down the jar to fill once more that little cup, he seemed suddenly to fall asleep, and to have down cushions laid under his head, but this strange circumstance happened so suddenly that he had no time to take notes; and it is not possible to give so full a description of the affair as I should have wished. But the really strange part of the tale is that when he had slept till he could sleep no more, and woke up again, he was no longer in the cellar of the Convent at Uske; how this happened neither he nor I nor anybody else have ever made out, but it is certainly a fact that Brother Drogo rubbed his eyes and found himself lying on green grass. And when he had rubbed his eyes a second time, had stood up and looked about him, he saw that he was standing on the highest point of a mountain girt around with woods of dark pine trees, and dwarf oak thickets, and brakes of tangled undergrowth. Below very far was a city of a strange fashion, and beyond the city mountains rising one above the other; and behind him was the sea of a very deep blue. Before the Cellarer had finished wondering where he was and how he got there, his ears caught a noise of jangling and clashing of brass on brass, with shrill flute notes, beating of drums, and loud cries and hails now from one quarter and now from another, gathering together and drawing towards him. I do not see what Brother Drogo could do but open his mouth; it is certain that he did so, for he could not recollect what passage it was that led out of the cellar to the top of this mountain. But while he was thinking the matter over, the drums, tambourines, cymbals, single flutes, double flutes, and loud calling grew loud enough to deafen one; and all at once he was surrounded on all sides by a company of girls whose clothes seemed to be at the wash, for there was not enough of linen (or of anything else) to make a kerchief on the whole company. And when they began to dance round the poor man, calling to him in a tongue he did not understand, he began to be afraid he had got into bad company, not suited for a monk of St Bennet's rule. But he could not help allowing that these girls had very nice figures and seemed to be able to make a great noise. 'If I were a layman,' thought he, 'it would be different, but these amusements are not quite proper for ecclesiastical persons.' Round, around they whirled in dancing and the din of cymbals clashed louder yet; but then the figures of the naked girls became shadows and their music was hushed to a dull murmur. The next thing Brother Drogo heard was the words of the Prior of his Convent, saying 'He will yet live, and drink another cup.' 'Of water only' answered the poor Cellarer, who began to think he was always to be moving, from cellar to mountain and from mountain to his bed. In fact, he had been found, after much seeking, lying on his back in the cellar, with a nasty cut on his head, a great wine jar lying in shards beside him, and a pool of dark red wine on the floor giving forth a fragrance that made the monks sniff eagerly. Some persons have said that Brother Drogo must have slipped backwards, knocking his skull against the edge of a stone ascent, and pulling the wine jar after him. These persons make out that he dreamt whatever he saw, but I am disposed to think them rather too clever for this dull world of ours. But as I said at the beginning of the tale the Cellarer kept to water for the rest of his life, and leaving the cellar to another hand became the chief gardener of the Priory, and grew such worts, and flowers, and fruits as were not to be seen elsewhere in all Gwent. Indeed he invented that great green plum, as big as an egg, that melts in the mouth as sweet as honey, and is rightly called 'Soif de Dru', or 'Drogo's Thirst'.

And the moral of this history is – Leave old jars on the shelf. It seems to me a good one.

The Autophone

In a small parlour – the pre-Ruskinite parlour of country lodgings – the Rev. Arthur Hammond was sitting before the rickety round table, his head upon his hands, and his eyes fixed upon an open book. For an hour or more he sat still, never turning a leaf of his volume, nor looking through the window as the sun slowly sank into a bank of clouds and the sea changed from blue to misty grey; and the far away wash of water and the dull roar of the rising wind among the trees never reached his ears. The Rev. Arthur Hammond read on as the sun went down, but he read only one sentence over and over again, till his brain was in a whirl, and the types seemed to dance before his eyes. The sentence ran as follows:

> Personality is not a permanent but a transient thing; it lives and dies, begins and ends continually; no one can remain one and the same person two moments together.

The day had been hot and close, with one of those burning suns that sometimes shine in June and the evening seemed still hotter. Hammond had felt all day as if a weight were pressing on his head, but still he had persevered in his reading, hardly stopping to eat or drink. The next day he was going to the cathedral city to undergo his examination for priest's orders: for the last three months every moment of his spare time had been given to hard grinding study and for a week he had scarcely stirred from his books. His information on the Early Heresies was extensive and peculiar. He knew all about the Ebienites, and could explain the teachings of Basilides. He was prepared to defend St Peter from the charge of writing 'Baboo Greek', he had a good working knowledge of the Canon Law, and the Fathers were at his fingers' ends – if it be respectful to say so. The last day or two had been devoted to Butler's Analogy. Hammond had grimly struggled for the third or fourth time through the crabbed style and involved argument, and at last read 'Conclusion'. He leant back in his chair, supremely happy that his work was at last done and he was free to rest or do what he would. Should he go for a sail, or take a brisk walk over the hills, or call at the rector's and have a pipe? He dallied and he hesitated, carelessly turning over the leaves of the book, and at last, in mere indecision, began to read the dissertation 'Of Personal Identity', a kind of philosophical appendix to the Analogy. He read carelessly, half filled his pipe and looked round for a light. The matchbox was on the mantelpiece between two shell encrusted boxes, 'Presents from Baybeach', and Hammond felt too lazy to get up, and so he turned again to his book and read on. The words and phrases made but little impression on his tired brain; he felt as if everything were slowly sinking into a haze; the four walls of the little parlour seemed to hover indistinctly around him and the hot air beat palpably, as in waves, upon his temples. Suddenly his eyes fell upon the words 'Personality is but a transient thing.' It was like a flash of lightning – bright and yet blinding. What personality was sitting in that chair, gazing on an open book? Was it a little boy roaming among the woods and meadows in summers long ago? Or whose joys and griefs were those that now surged up in his memory? Who was that, walking with other lads across the playground, or kneeling by a death-bed? And whose were those companions, singing songs and uttering jests that made him flush for very shame? He seemed to hear a voice, hard and toneless, like the crash of a falling bough, calling 'Ha ha! you have tasted the apple,' and a rough man with a flushed face and a strange light in his eyes came forth from a door in a dark narrow street and shut it behind him as a girl looked out from the window. Then he heard the words 'Lives and dies, begins and ends, lives and dies, begins and ends' repeated again and again, louder and louder, swelling tumultuously, and then an awful crash that burst in upon his brain.

Mr Hammond looked up; the room was growing dark; yet he could see the twinkle of the lustres on the mantel, and he could hear, quite distinctly, the noise of tapping at his door. 'Come in,' he cried; and the door opened and some one stood by the sofa and began speaking to him in a low voice, yet audibly enough.

'The Rev. Arthur Hammond, I believe? Pray excuse me for intruding at such an hour; I am well aware how scanty is the leisure of the clergy; but I hope that in my case I may plead . . . '

'Pray don't apologise. I am afraid I was quite absorbed in my book and kept you waiting. What can I do for you, may I ask?'

'I have ventured to call upon you to submit to your notice an invention of mine which I think I may call the great invention of the age. I have exhibited it before many of the bishops, deans, archdeacons, and canons of the church, including your reverend diocesan; and I should like to add your name – a name, I must say, second to none among the younger generation of the clergy.'

'You are very kind indeed,' said Mr Hammond dreamily. 'Thank you very much; really very kind of you. By the way, you didn't happen to notice a young fellow going out of the house as you came in – a fair complexioned young man, a little like myself, but younger and, well, rather odd looking?'

'No, sir, I saw no one. Shall I now have the pleasure of exhibiting my invention?'

'Ah, to be sure – your invention. What do you call it?'

'I have named it the Autophone, the title was suggested to me by a beloved prelate and a distinguished scholar.'

'Quite so; very good; the Autophone. What is the nature of the invention?'

'Allow me. You see this disk of delicate yellow metal? Kindly pass the point of your forefinger (the right hand) lightly over it from north to south. Thank you; the polarity is now established. The next thing is to set the current in action. Do you happen to have such a thing as a musical box?'

'Yes, said Hammond, growing interested and less dazed than at first, 'there is an old one in that corner belonging to my landlady.'

'It will answer our purpose admirably. You see I place it on the table thus. I next insert the polarised metal disk, so. Now, if you please, just give that little knob a turn; exactly!'

A babel, a tumult of voices, of voices that he knew and remembered; one striving with another, calling to him out of the deep past; and some the voices of the dead.

'Ha ha! Do you hear that, you fellows? Hammond's in luck. Didn't you see him with her? The old rascal thought it was too dark under the tree, but Davis spotted him. Didn't you, old boy?' 'I should think I did. How's Mary, Hammond?' 'Never you mind, Hammond. You couldn't do better. I only wish I had your luck.' 'Now, then, old fellow, let's have a song. Get out another bottle of whisky, Williams. Go ahead, Hammond.'

The song began, and Hammond heard it across the great bridge of years; heard his own voice singing those shameful lines, and heard the laughter and the voices joining in the chorus.

'Curse you!' he cried; 'whoever you are, take your infernal machine away. It's a lie; I never did this.'

But the man only laughed, and the song was singing all the while, and Hammond rushed forward headlong, and fell as the thunder burst at last above the house.

They found him lying full length upon the floor, his forehead cut and bleeding and the musical box upside down on the floor beside him. It was playing 'Pop goes the weasel.' When the doctor came his verdict was 'Brain fever.'

A Double Return

The express from the west rushed through Acton with a scream, whirling clouds of dust around it; and Frank Halswell knocked out the ashes from his pipe and proceeded to gather from various quarters of the carriage his newspapers, his hat box, his handbag, and, chief of all, a large portfolio carefully packed in brown paper. He looked at his watch, and said to himself: '6.30; we shall be at Paddington in five minutes; and only five minutes late, for a wonder.' But he congratulated himself and the railway company rather too soon: a few minutes later and the train began to slacken, the speed grew slower and slower, and at last came the grinding sound of the brakes and a dead stop. Halswell looked out of the window over the dreary expanse of Wormwood Scrubs, and heard some one in the next carriage explaining the cause of the delay with pardonable pride in his technical knowledge. 'You see, them there signals is against us, and if we was to go on we should jolly well go to kingdom come, we should.' Halswell looked at his watch again and drummed his heels against the floor, wondering impatiently when they would be at Paddington, when, with a sudden whirl, a down train swept by them and the western express once more moved on. Halswell rubbed his eyes; he had looked up as the down train passed, and in one of the carriages he thought he had seen his own face. It was only for a second, and he could not be sure. 'It must have been a reflection,' he kept on saying, 'from the glass of one window to the other. Still, I fancied I saw a black coat, and mine is light. But of course it was a reflection.'

The express rolled into the terminus with dignity – it was only ten minutes late, after all; and Frank Halswell bundled himself and his traps into a hansom, congratulating himself on the paucity of his bags and the absence of his trunks as he watched the excited mob rushing madly at a Redan of luggage. '153, the Mall, Kensington!' he shouted to the driver above the hubbub of the platform; and they were soon threading deftly along the dingy streets that looked so much dingier than usual after the blue mist upon the sea, the purple heather and the sunny fields. Frank (he was a very popular artist in those days – a rising man, indeed) had been on a sketching tour in Devon and Cornwall: he had wandered along the deep sheltered lanes from hill to hill, by the orchards already red and gold, by moorland and lowland, by the rocky coast and the combes sinking down to the wondrous sea.

On the Cornish roads he had seen those many ancient crosses, with their weird interlacing carving, which sometimes stand upon a mound and mark where two ways meet; and as he put his portfolio beside him he could not help feeling a glow of pride at its contents. 'I fancy I shall make a pretty good show by next spring,' he thought. Poor fellow! he was never to paint another picture; but he did not know it. Then, as the hansom verged westward, gliding with its ringing bells past the great mansions facing the park, Halswell's thoughts went back to the hotel at Plymouth and the acquaintance he had made there. 'Yes; Kerr was an amusing fellow,' he thought; 'glad I gave him my card. Louie is sure to get on with him. Curious thing, too, he was wonderfully like me, if he had been only clean shaven and not "bearded like the pard". Dare say we shall see him before long; he said he was going to pay a short visit to London. I fancy he must be an actor; I never saw such a fellow to imitate a man's voice and gestures. I wonder what made him go off in such a hurry yesterday. Hullo! here we are; hi, cabman! there's 153.'

The twin doors of the hansom banged open; the garden gate shrieked and clanged, and Halswell bounded up the steps and rapped loudly at the door. The maid opened it. Even as he said, 'Thank you, Jane; your mistress quite well, I suppose?' he thought he noticed a strange look, half questioning, half surprised, in her eyes; but he ran past her, up the stairs, and burst into the pretty drawingroom. His wife was lying on the sofa; but she rose with a cry as he came in.

'Frank! Back again so soon? I am so glad! I thought you said you might have to be away a week.'

'My dear Louie, what do you mean? I have been away three weeks, haven't I? I rather think I left for Devonshire in the first week of August.'

'Yes, of course, my dear; but then you came back late last night.'

'What! I came back last night? I slept last night at Plymouth. What are you talking about?'

'Don't be silly, Frank. You know very well you rang us all up at twelve o'clock. Just like you, to come home in the middle of the night when nobody expected you. You know you said in your last letter you were not coming until today.'

'Louise dear, you must be dreaming. I never came here last night. Here is my bill at the hotel; you see, it is dated this morning.'

Mrs Halswell stared blankly at the bill; then she got up and rang the bell. How hot it was! The close air of the London street seemed to choke her. Halswell walked a few paces across the room, then suddenly stopped and shuddered.

'Jane, I want to ask you whether your master did not come here last night at twelve o'clock; and whether you did not get him a cab early this morning?'

'Yes, mum, at least – '

'At least what? You let him in yourself.'

'Yes, mum, of course I did. But, begging your pardon, sir, I thought as how your voice didn't sound quite natural this morning when you called out to the cabman to drive to Stepney, because you had changed your mind, and didn't want to go to Waterloo.'

'Good God! What are you thinking about? I never came here. I was in Plymouth.'

'Frank! You are joking! Look here, you left this behind you.'

She showed him a little silver cigarette case with his initials engraved on it. It was a present from his wife, he had missed it one day when he was strolling with Kerr, and had regretted it deeply, searching in the grass in vain.

Halswell held the toy in his hand. He thought he was indeed in a dream, and through the open window came the shrieks of the newsboys, 'Extry speshal! extry speshal!' The light had faded; it was getting dark. But suddenly it all flashed upon him. He remembered Kerr and the face he had caught sight of in the passing train; he remembered the strange likeness; he knew who had found the cigarette case; he knew well who it was that had come to his house.

The maid was a good girl; she had stolen away. No one knows what manner of conversation Frank and his wife had together in the darkness; but that night he went away, as it was said, to America. Mrs Halswell was dead before the next summer.

The Lost Club

One hot afternoon in August a gorgeous young gentleman, one would say the last of his race in London, set out from the Circus end, and proceeded to stroll along the lonely expanse of Piccadilly Deserta. True to the traditions of his race, faithful even in the wilderness, he had not bated one jot or tittle of his regulation equipage; a glorious red and yellow blossom in his wholly and exquisitely-cut frock coat proclaimed him a true son of the carnation; hat and boots and chin were all polished to the highest pitch; though there had not been rain for many weeks his trouser-ends were duly turned up, and the poise of the gold-headed cane was in itself a liberal education, But ah! the heavy changes since June, when the leaves glanced green in the sunlit air, and the club windows were filled, and the hansoms flashed in long processions through the streets, and girls smiled from every carriage. The young man sighed; he thought of the quiet little evenings at the Phoenix, of encounters of the Row, of the drive to Hurlingham, and many pleasant dinners in joyous company. Then he glanced up and saw a 'bus, half empty, slowly lumbering along the middle of the street, and in front of the White Horse Cellars a fourwheeler had stopped still (the driver was asleep on his seat), and in the Badminton the blinds were down. He half expected to see the Briar Rose trailing gracefully over the Hotel Cosmopole; certainly the Beauty, if such a thing were left in Piccadilly, was fast asleep.

Absorbed in these mournful reflections the hapless Johnny strolled on without observing that an exact duplicate of himself was advancing on the same pavement from the opposite direction; save that the inevitable carnation was salmon colour, and the cane a silver-headed one, instruments of great magnifying power would have been required to discriminate between them. The two met; each raised his eyes simultaneously at the strange sight of a well-dressed man, and each adjured the same old-world deity.

'By Jove! old man, what the deuce are you doing here?'

The gentleman who had advanced from the direction of Hyde Park Corner was the first to answer.

'Well, to tell the truth, Austin, I am detained in town on – ah – legal business. But how is it you are not in Scotland?'

'Well, it's curious; but the fact is, I have legal business in town also.'

'You don't say so? Great nuisance, ain't it? But these things must be seen to, or a fellow finds himself in no end of a mess, don't you know?'

'He does, by Jove! That's what I thought.'

Mr Austin relapsed into silence for a few moments.

'And where are you off to, Phillipps?'

The conversation had passed with the utmost gravity on both sides; at the joint mention of legal business, it was true, a slight twinkle had passed across their eyes, but the ordinary observer would have said that the weight of ages rested on those unruffled brows.

'I really couldn't say. I thought of having a quiet dinner at Azario's. The Badminton is closed, you know, for repairs or somethin', and I can't stand the Junior Wilton. Come along with me, and let's dine together.'

'By Jove! I think I will. I thought of calling on my solicitor, but I dare say he can wait.'

'Ah! I should think he could. We'll have some of that Italian wine – stuff in salad oil flasks – you know what I mean.'

The pair solemnly wheeled around, and solemnly paced towards the Circus, meditating, doubtless, on many things. The dinner in the little restaurant pleased them with a grave pleasure, as did the Chianti, of which they drank a good deal too much; 'quite a light wine, you know,' said Phillipps, and Austin agreed with him, so they emptied a quart flask between them and finished up with a couple of glasses apiece of Green Chartreuse. As they came out into the quiet street smoking vast cigars, the two slaves to duty and 'legal business' felt a dreamy delight in all things, the streets seemed full of fantasy in the dim light of the lamps, and a single star shining in the clear sky above seemed to Austin exactly of the same colour as Green Chartreuse. Phillipps agreed with him. 'You know, old fellow,' he said, 'there are times when a fellow feels all sorts of strange things – you know, the sort of things they put in magazines, don't you know, and novels. By Jove, Austin, old man, I feel as if I could write a novel myself.'

The pair wandered aimlessly on, not quite knowing where they were going, turning from one street to another, and discoursing in a maudlin strain. A great cloud had been slowly moving up from the south, darkening the sky, and suddenly it began to rain, at first slowly with great heavy drops, and then faster and faster in a pitiless, hissing shower; the gutters flooded over, and the furious drops danced up from the stones. The two Johnnies walked on as fast as they could, whistling and calling 'Hansom!' in vain; they were really getting very wet.

'Where the dickens are we?' said Phillipps. 'Confound it all, I don't know. We ought to be in Oxford Street.'

They walked on a little farther, when suddenly, to their great joy, they found a dry archway, leading into a dark passage or courtyard. They took shelter silently, too thankful and too wet to say anything. Austin looked at his hat; it was a wreck; and Phillipps shook himself feebly, like a tired terrier.

'What a beastly nuisance this is,' he muttered: 'I only wish I could see a hansom.'

Austin looked into the street; the rain was still falling in torrents; he looked up the passage, and noticed for the first time that it led to a great house, which towered grimly against the sky. It seemed all dark and gloomy, except that from some chink in a shutter a light shone out. He pointed it out to Phillipps, who stared vacantly about him, then exclaimed:

'Hang it! I know where we are now. At least, I don't exactly know, you know, but I once came by here with Wylliams, and he told me there was some club or somethin' down this passage; I don't recollect exactly what he said. Hullo! why there goes Wylliams. I say, Wylliams, tell us where we are!'

A gentleman had brushed past them in the darkness and was walking fast down the passage. He heard his name and turned round, looking rather annoyed.

'Well, Phillipps, what do you want? Good evening, Austin; you seem rather wet, both of you.'

'I should think we were wet; got caught in the rain. Didn't you tell me once there was some club down here? I wish you'd take us in, if you're a member.'

Mr Wylliams looked steadfastly at the two forlorn young men for a moment, hesitated, and said: 'Well, gentlemen, you may come with me if you like. But I must impose a condition; that you both give me your word of honour never to mention the club, or anything that you see while you are in it, to any individual whatsoever.'

'Certainly not,' replied Austin; 'of course we shouldn't dream of doing so, should we, Phillipps?'

'No, no; go ahead, Wylliams, we'll keep it dark enough.'

The party moved slowly down the passage till they came to the house. It was a very large house and very old; it looked as though it might have been an embassy of the last century. Wylliams whistled, knocked twice at the door, and whistled again, and it was opened by a man in black.

'Friends of yours, Mr Wylliams?'

Wylliams nodded and they passed on.

'Now mind,' he whispered, as they paused at a door, 'you are not to recognise anybody, and nobody will recognise you.'

The two friends nodded, and the door was opened, and they entered a vast room, brilliantly lighted with electric lamps. Men were standing in knots, walking up and down, and smoking at little tables; it was just like any club smoking room. Conversation was going on, but in a low murmur, and every now and then some one would stop talking, and look anxiously at the door at the other end of the room, and then turn round again. It was evident that they were waiting for some one or somebody. Austin and Phillipps were sitting on a sofa, lost in amazement; nearly every face was familiar to them. The flower of the Row was in that strange club room; several young noblemen, a young fellow who had just come into an enormous fortune, three or four fashionable artists and literary men, an eminent actor, and a well-known canon. What could it mean? They were all supposed to be scattered far and wide over the habitable globe, and yet here they were. Suddenly there came a loud knock at the door; and every man started, and those who were sitting got up. A servant appeared.

'The President is awaiting you, gentlemen,' he said, and vanished.

One by one the members filed out, and Wylliams and the two guests brought up the rear. They found themselves in a room still larger than the first, but almost quite dark. The President sat at a long table and before him burned two candles, which barely lit up his face. It was the famous Duke of Dartington, the largest landowner in England. As soon as the members had entered he said in a cold, hard voice, 'Gentlemen, you know our rules; the book is prepared. Whoever opens it at the black page is at the disposal of the committee and myself. We had better begin.' Some one began to read out the names in a low distinct voice, pausing after each name, and the member called came up to the table and opened at random the pages of a big folio volume that lay between the two candles. The gloomy light made it difficult to distinguish features, but Phillipps heard a groan beside him, and recognised an old friend. His face was working fearfully, the man was evidently in an agony of terror. One by one the members opened the book; as each man did so he passed out by another door. At last there was only one left; it was Phillipps's friend. There was foam upon his lips as he passed up the table, and his hand shook as he opened up the leaves. Wylliams had passed out after whispering to the President, and had returned to his friends' side. He could hardly hold them back as the unfortunate man groaned in agony and leant against the table; he had opened the book at the black page. 'Kindly come with me, Mr D'Aubigny,' said the President, and they passed out together.

'We can go now,' said Wylliams, 'I think the rain has gone off. Remember your promise, gentlemen. You have been at a meeting of the Lost Club. You will never see that young man again. Goodnight.'

'It isn't murder, is it?' gasped Austin.

'Oh no, not at all. Mr D'Aubigny will, I hope, live for many years; he has disappeared, merely disappeared. Goodnight; there's a hansom that will do for you.'

The two friends went to their homes in dead silence. They did not meet again for three weeks, and each thought the other looked ill and shaken. They walked drearily, with grave averted faces, down Piccadilly, each afraid to begin the recollection of the terrible club. Of a sudden Phillipps stopped as if he had been shot. 'Look there, Austin,' he muttered, 'look at that.' The posters of the evening papers were spread out beside the pavement, and on one of them Austin saw in large blue letters, 'Mysterious disappearance of a Gentleman'. Austin bought a copy and turned over the leaves with shaking fingers till he found the brief paragraph:

> Mr St John D'Aubigny, of Stoke D'Aubigny, in Sussex, has disappeared under mysterious circumstances. Mr D'Aubigny was staying at Strathdoon, in Scotland, and came up to London, as is stated, on business, on August 16th. It has been ascertained that he arrived safely at King's Cross, and drove to Piccadilly Circus, where he got out. It is said that he was last seen at the corner of Glass House Street, leading from Regent Street into Soho. Since the above date the unfortunate gentleman, who was much liked in London society, has not been heard of. Mr D'Aubigny was

to have been married in September. The police are extremely reticent.

'Good God! Austin, this is dreadful. You remember the date. Poor fellow, poor fellow!'

'Phillipps, I think I shall go home, I feel sick.'

D'Aubigny was never heard of again. But the strangest part of the story remains to be told. The two friends called upon Wylliams, and charged him with being a member of the Lost Club, and an accomplice in the fate of D'Aubigny. The placid Mr Wylliams at first stared at the two pale, earnest faces, and finally roared with laughter.

'My dear fellows, what on earth are you talking about? I never heard such a cock-and-bull story in my life. As you say, Phillipps, I once pointed out to you a house said to be a club, as we were walking through Soho; but that was a low gambling club, frequented by German waiters. I am afraid the fact is that Azario's Chianti was rather too strong for you. However, I will try to convince you of your mistake.'

Wylliams forthwith summoned his man, who swore that he and his master were in Cairo during the whole of August, and offered to produce the hotel bills. Phillipps shook his head, and they went away. Their next step was to try and find the archway where they had taken shelter, and after a good deal of trouble they succeeded. They knocked at the door of the gloomy house, whistling as Wylliams had done. They were admitted by a respectable mechanic in a white apron, who was evidently astonished at the whistle; in fact he was inclined to suspect the influence of a 'drop too much'. The place was a billiard table factory, and had been so (as they learnt in the neighbourhood) for many years. The rooms must once have been large and magnificent, but most of them had been divided into three or four separate workshops by wooden partitions.

Phillipps sighed; he could do no more for his lost friend; but both he and Austin remained unconvinced. In justice to Mr Wylliams, it must be stated that Lord Henry Harcourt assured Phillipps that he had seen Wylliams in Cairo about the middle of August; he thought, but could not be sure, on the 16th; and also, that the recent disappearances of some well known men about town are patient of explanations which would exclude the agency of the Lost Club.

The Great God Pan

I
The Experiment

'I am glad you came, Clarke; very glad indeed. I was not sure you could spare the time.'

'I was able to make arrangements for a few days; things are not very lively just now. But have you no misgivings, Raymond? Is it absolutely safe?'

The two men were slowly pacing the terrace in front of Dr Raymond's house. The sun still hung above the western mountain line, but it shone with a dull red glow that cast no shadows, and all the air was quiet; a sweet breath came from the great wood on the hillside above, and with it, at intervals, the soft murmuring call of the wild doves. Below, in the long lovely valley, the river wound in and out between the lonely hills, and, as the sun hovered and vanished into the west, a faint mist, pure white, began to rise from the hills. Dr Raymond turned sharply to his friend.

'Safe? Of course it is. In itself the operation is a perfectly simple one; any surgeon could do it.'

'And there is no danger at any other stage?'

'None; absolutely no physical danger whatsoever, I give you my word. You are always timid, Clarke, always; but you know my history. I have devoted myself to transcendental medicine for the last twenty years. I have heard myself called quack and charlatan and impostor, but all the while I knew I was on the right path. Five years ago I reached the goal, and since then every day has been a preparation for what we shall do tonight.'

'I should like to believe it is all true.' Clarke knit his brows, and looked doubtfully at Dr Raymond. 'Are you perfectly sure, Raymond, that your theory is not a phantasmagoria – a splendid vision, certainly, but a mere vision after all?'

Dr Raymond stopped in his walk and turned sharply. He was a middle-aged man, gaunt and thin, of a pale yellow complexion, but as he answered Clarke and faced him, there was a flush on his cheek.

'Look about you, Clarke. You see the mountain, and hill following after hill, as wave on wave, you see the woods and orchard, the fields of ripe corn, and the meadows reaching to the reed-beds by the river. You see me standing here beside you, and hear my voice; but I tell you that all these things – yes, from that star that has just shone out in the sky to the solid ground beneath our feet – I say that all these are but dreams and shadows; the shadows that hide the real world from our eyes. There *is* a real world, but it is beyond this glamour and this vision, beyond these "chases in Arras, dreams in a career", beyond them all as beyond a veil. I do not know whether any human being has ever lifted that veil; but I do know, Clarke, that you and I shall see it lifted this very night from before another's eyes. You may think this all strange nonsense; it may be strange, but it is true, and the ancients knew what lifting the veil means. They called it seeing the god Pan.'

Clarke shivered; the white mist gathering over the river was chilly.

'It is wonderful indeed,' he said. 'We are standing on the brink of a strange world, Raymond, if what you say is true. I suppose the knife is absolutely necessary?'

'Yes; a slight lesion in the grey matter, that is all; a trifling rearrangement of certain cells, a microscopical alteration that would escape the attention of ninety-nine brain specialists out of a hundred. I don't want to bother you with "shop", Clarke; I might give you a mass of technical detail which would sound very imposing, and would leave you as enlightened as you are now. But I suppose you have read, casually, in out-of-the-way corners of your paper, that immense strides have been made recently in the physiology of the brain. I saw a paragraph the other day about Digby's theory, and Browne Faber's discoveries. Theories and discoveries! Where they are standing now, I stood fifteen years ago, and I need not tell you that I have not been standing still for the last fifteen years. It will be enough if I say that five years ago I made the discovery that I alluded to when I said that ten years ago I reached the goal. After years of labour, after years of toiling and groping in the dark, after days and nights of disappointments and sometimes of despair, in which I used now and then to tremble and grow cold with the thought that perhaps there were others seeking for what I sought, at last, after so long, a pang of sudden joy thrilled my soul, and I knew the long journey was at an end. By what seemed then and still seems a chance, the suggestion of a moment's idle thought followed up upon familiar lines and paths that I had tracked a hundred times already, the great truth burst upon me, and I saw, mapped out in lines of sight, a whole world, a sphere unknown; continents and islands, and great oceans in which no ship has sailed (to my belief) since a Man first lifted up his eyes and beheld the sun, and the stars of heaven, and the quiet earth beneath. You will think this all high-flown language, Clarke, but it is hard to be literal. And yet; I do not know whether what I am hinting at cannot be set forth in plain and lonely terms. For instance, this world of ours is pretty well girded now with the telegraph wires and cables; thought, with something less than the speed of thought, flashes from sunrise to sunset, from north to south, across the floods and the desert places. Suppose that an electrician of today were suddenly to perceive that he and his friends have merely been playing with pebbles and mistaking them for the foundations of the world; suppose that such a man saw uttermost space lie open before the current, and words of men flash forth to the sun and beyond the sun into the systems beyond, and the voice of articulate-speaking men echo in the waste void that bounds our thought. As analogies go, that is a pretty good analogy of what I have done; you can understand now a little of what I felt as I stood here one evening; it was a summer evening, and the valley looked much as it does now; I stood here, and saw before me the unutterable, the unthinkable gulf that yawns profound between two worlds, the world of matter and the world of spirit; I saw the great empty deep stretch dim before me, and in that instant a bridge of light leapt from the earth to the unknown shore, and the abyss was spanned. You may look in Browne Faber's book, if you like, and you will find that to the present day men of science are unable to account for the presence, or to specify the functions of a certain group of nerve cells in the brain. That group is, as it were, land to let, a mere waste place for fanciful theories. I am not in the position of Browne Faber and the specialists, I am perfectly instructed as to the possible functions of those nerve centers in the scheme of things. With a touch I can bring them into play, with a touch, I say, I can set free the current, with a touch I can complete the communication between this world of sense and – we shall be able to finish the sentence later on. Yes, the knife is necessary; but think what that knife will effect. It will level utterly the solid wall of sense, and probably, for the first time since man was made, a spirit will gaze on a spirit world. Clarke, Mary will see the god Pan!'

'But you remember what you wrote to me? I thought it would be requisite that she – '

He whispered the rest into the doctor's ear.

'Not at all, not at all. That is nonsense. I assure you. Indeed, it is better as it is; I am quite certain of that.'

'Consider the matter well, Raymond. It's a great responsibility. Something might go wrong; you would be a miserable man for the rest of your days.'

'No, I think not, even if the worst happened. As you know, I rescued Mary from the gutter, and from almost certain starvation, when she was a child; I think her life is mine, to use as I see fit. Come, it's getting late; we had better go in.'

Dr Raymond led the way into the house, through the hall, and down a long dark passage. He took a key from his pocket and opened a heavy door, and motioned Clarke into his laboratory. It had once been a billiard room, and was lighted by a glass dome in the centre of the ceiling, whence there still shone a sad grey light on the figure of the doctor as he lit a lamp with a heavy shade and placed it on a table in the middle of the room.

Clarke looked about him. Scarcely a foot of wall remained bare; there were shelves all around laden with bottles and phials of all shapes and colours, and at one end stood a little Chippendale bookcase. Raymond pointed to this.

'You see that parchment Oswald Crollius? He was one of the first to show me the way, though I don't think he ever found it himself. That is a strange saying of his: "In every grain of wheat there lies hidden the soul of a star."'

There was not much furniture in the laboratory. The table in the centre, a stone slab with a drain in one corner, the two armchairs on which Raymond and Clarke were sitting; that was all, except an odd-looking chair at the furthest end of the room. Clarke looked at it, and raised his eyebrows.

'Yes, that is the chair,' said Raymond. 'We may as well place it in position.' He got up and wheeled the chair to the light, and began raising and lowering it, letting down the seat, setting the back at various angles, and adjusting the foot rest. It looked comfortable enough, and Clarke passed his hand over the soft green velvet, as the doctor manipulated the levers.

'Now, Clarke, make yourself quite comfortable. I have a couple hours' work before me; I was obliged to leave certain matters to the last.'

Raymond went to the stone slab, and Clarke watched him drearily as he bent over a row of phials and lit the flame under the crucible. The doctor had a small hand lamp, shaded as the larger one, on a ledge above his apparatus, and Clarke, who sat in the shadows, looked down at the great shadowy room, wondering at the bizarre effects of brilliant light and undefined darkness contrasting with one another. Soon he became conscious of an odd odour, at first the merest suggestion of odour, in the room, and as it grew more decided he felt surprised that he was not reminded of the chemist's shop or the surgery. Clarke found himself idly endeavouring to analyse the sensation, and half conscious, he began to think of a day, fifteen years ago, that he had spent roaming through the woods and meadows near his own home. It was a burning day at the beginning of August, the heat had dimmed the outlines of all things and all distances with a faint mist, and people who observed the thermometer spoke of an abnormal register, of a temperature that was almost tropical. Strangely that wonderful hot day of the fifties rose up again in Clarke's imagination; the sense of dazzling all-pervading sunlight seemed to blot out the shadows and the lights of the laboratory, and he felt again the heated air beating in gusts about his face, saw the shimmer rising from the turf, and heard the myriad murmur of the summer.

'I hope the smell doesn't annoy you, Clarke; there's nothing unwholesome about it. It may make you a bit sleepy, that's all.'

Clarke heard the words quite distinctly, and knew that Raymond was speaking to him, but for the life of him he could not rouse himself from his lethargy. He could only think of the lonely walk he had taken fifteen years ago; it was his last look at the fields and woods he had known since he was a child, and now it all stood out in brilliant light, as a picture, before him. Above all there came to his nostrils the scent of summer, the smell of flowers mingled, and the odour of the woods, of cool shaded places, deep in the green depths, drawn forth by the sun's heat; and the scent of the good earth, lying as it were with arms stretched forth, and smiling lips, overpowered all. His fancies made him wander, as he had wandered long ago, from the fields into the wood, tracking a little path between the shining undergrowth of beech trees; and the trickle of water dropping from the limestone rock sounded as a clear melody in the dream. Thoughts began to go astray and to mingle with other thoughts; the beech alley was transformed to a path between ilex trees, and here and there a vine climbed from bough to bough, and sent up waving tendrils and drooped with purple grapes, and the sparse grey-green leaves of a wild olive tree stood out against the dark shadows of the ilex. Clarke, in the deep folds of dream, was conscious that the path from his father's house had led him into an undiscovered country, and he was wondering at the strangeness of it all, when suddenly, in place of the hum and murmur of the summer, an infinite silence seemed to fall on all things, and the wood was hushed, and for a moment in time he stood face to face there with a presence, that was neither man nor beast, neither the living nor the dead, but all things mingled, the form of all things but devoid of all form. And in that moment, the sacrament of body and soul was dissolved, and a voice seemed to cry 'Let us go hence,' and then the darkness of darkness beyond the stars, the darkness of everlasting.

When Clarke woke up with a start he saw Raymond pouring a few drops of some oily fluid into a green phial, which he stoppered tightly.

'You have been dozing,' he said; 'the journey must have tired you out. It is done now. I am going to fetch Mary; I shall be back in ten minutes.'

Clarke lay back in his chair and wondered. It seemed as if he had but passed from one dream into another. He half expected to see the walls of the laboratory melt and disappear, and to awake in London, shuddering at his own sleeping fancies. But at last the door opened, and the doctor returned, and behind him came a girl of about seventeen, dressed all in white. She was so beautiful that Clarke did not wonder at what the doctor had written to him. She was blushing now over face and neck and arms, but Raymond seemed unmoved.

'Mary,' he said, 'the time has come. You are quite free. Are you willing to trust yourself to me entirely?'

'Yes, dear.'

'Do you hear that, Clarke? You are my witness. Here is the chair, Mary. It is quite easy. Just sit in it and lean back. Are you ready?'

'Yes, dear, quite ready. Give me a kiss before you begin.'

The doctor stooped and kissed her mouth, kindly enough. 'Now shut your eyes,' he said. The girl closed her eyelids, as if she were tired, and longed for sleep, and Raymond placed the green phial to her nostrils. Her face grew white, whiter than her dress; she struggled faintly, and then with the feeling of submission strong within her, crossed her arms upon her breast as a little child about to say her prayers. The bright light of the lamp fell full upon her, and Clarke watched changes fleeting over her face as the changes of the hills when the summer clouds float across the sun. And then she lay all white and still, and the doctor turned up one of her eyelids. She was quite unconscious. Raymond pressed hard on one of the levers and the chair instantly sank back. Clarke saw him cutting away a circle, like a tonsure, from her hair, and the lamp was moved nearer. Raymond took a small glittering instrument from a little case, and Clarke turned away shudderingly. When he looked again the doctor was binding up the wound he had made.

'She will awake in five minutes.' Raymond was still perfectly cool. 'There is nothing more to be done; we can only wait.'

The minutes passed slowly; they could hear a slow, heavy, ticking. There was an old clock in the passage. Clarke felt sick and faint; his knees shook beneath him, he could hardly stand.

Suddenly, as they watched, they heard a long-drawn sigh, and suddenly did the colour that had vanished return to the girl's cheeks, and suddenly her eyes opened. Clarke quailed before them. They shone with an awful light, looking far away, and a great wonder fell upon her face, and her hands stretched out as if to touch what was invisible; but in an instant the wonder faded, and gave place to the most awful terror. The muscles of her face were hideously convulsed, she shook from head to foot; the soul seemed struggling and shuddering within the house of flesh. It was a horrible sight, and Clarke rushed forward, as she fell shrieking to the floor.

Three days later Raymond took Clarke to Mary's bedside. She was lying wide awake, rolling her head from side to side, and grinning vacantly.

'Yes,' said the doctor, still quite cool, 'it is a great pity; she is a hopeless idiot. However, it could not be helped; and, after all, she has seen the Great God Pan.'

II

Mr Clarke's Memoirs

Mr Clarke, the gentleman chosen by Dr Raymond to witness the strange experiment of the god Pan, was a person in whose character caution and curiosity were oddly mingled; in his sober moments he thought of the unusual and eccentric with undisguised aversion, and yet, deep in his heart, there was a wide-eyed inquisitiveness with respect to all the more recondite and esoteric elements in the nature of men. The latter tendency had prevailed when he accepted Raymond's invitation, for though his considered judgment had always repudiated the doctor's theories as the wildest nonsense, yet he secretly hugged a belief in fantasy, and would have rejoiced to see that belief confirmed. The horrors that he witnessed in the dreary laboratory were to a certain extent salutary; he was conscious of being involved in an affair not altogether reputable, and for many years afterwards he clung bravely to the commonplace, and rejected all occasions of occult investigation. Indeed, on some homeopathic principle, he for some time attended the séances of distinguished mediums, hoping that the clumsy tricks of these gentlemen would make him altogether disgusted with mysticism of every kind, but the remedy, though caustic, was not efficacious. Clarke knew that he still pined for the unseen, and little by little, the old passion began to reassert itself, as the face of Mary, shuddering and convulsed with an unknown terror, faded slowly from his memory. Occupied all day in pursuits both serious and lucrative, the temptation to relax in the evening was too great, especially in the winter months, when the fire cast a warm glow over his snug bachelor apartment, and a bottle of some choice claret stood ready by his elbow. His dinner digested, he would make a brief pretence of reading the evening paper, but the mere catalogue of news soon palled upon him, and Clarke would find himself casting glances of warm desire in the direction of an old Japanese bureau, which stood at a pleasant distance from the hearth. Like a boy before a jam closet, for a few minutes he would hover indecisive, but lust always prevailed, and Clarke ended by drawing up his chair, lighting a candle, and sitting down before the bureau. Its pigeonholes and drawers teemed with documents on the most morbid subjects, and in the well reposed a large manuscript volume, in which he had painfully entered the gems of his collection. Clarke had a fine contempt for published literature; the most ghostly story ceased to interest him if it happened to be printed; his sole pleasure was in the reading, compiling, and rearranging what he called his 'Memoirs to prove the Existence of the Devil', and engaged in this pursuit the evening seemed to fly and the night appeared too short.

On one particular evening, an ugly December night, black with fog, and raw with frost, Clarke hurried over his dinner, and scarcely deigned to observe his customary ritual of taking up the paper and laying it down again. He paced two or three times up and down the room, and opened the bureau, stood still a moment, and sat down. He leant back, absorbed in one of those dreams to which he was subject, and at length drew out his book, and opened it at the last entry. There were three or four pages densely covered with Clarke's round, set penmanship, and at the beginning he had written in a somewhat larger hand:

> Singular Narrative told me by my Friend, Dr Phillips. He assures me that all the facts related therein are strictly and wholly True, but refuses to give either the Surnames of the Persons Concerned, or the Place where these Extraordinary Events occurred.

Mr Clarke began to read over the account for the tenth time, glancing now and then at the pencil notes he had made when it was told him by his friend. It was one of his humours to pride himself on a certain literary ability; he thought well of his style, and took pains in arranging the circumstances in dramatic order. He read the following story: –

The persons concerned in this statement are Helen V., who, if she is still alive, must now be a woman of twenty-three, Rachel M., since deceased, who was a year younger than the above, and Trevor W., an imbecile, aged eighteen. These persons were at the period of the story inhabitants of a village on the borders of Wales, a place of some importance in the time of the Roman occupation, but now a scattered hamlet, of not more than five hundred souls. It is situated on rising ground, about six miles from the sea, and is sheltered by a large and picturesque forest.

Some eleven years ago, Helen V. came to the village under rather peculiar circumstances. It is understood that she, being an orphan, was adopted in her infancy by a distant relative, who brought her up in his own house until she was twelve years old. Thinking, however, that it would be better for the child to have playmates of her own age, he advertised in several local papers for a good home in a comfortable farmhouse for a girl of twelve, and this advertisement was answered by Mr R., a well-to-do farmer in the above-mentioned village. His references proving satisfactory, the gentleman sent his adopted daughter to Mr R., with a letter, in which he stipulated that the girl should have a room to herself, and stated that her guardians need be at no trouble in the matter of education, as she was already sufficiently educated for the position in life which she would occupy. In fact, Mr R. was given to understand that the girl be allowed to find her own occupations and to spend her time almost as she liked. Mr R. duly met her at the nearest station, a town seven miles away from his house, and seems to have remarked nothing extraordinary about the child except that she was reticent as to her former life and her adopted father. She was, however, of a very different type from the inhabitants of the village; her skin was a pale, clear olive, and her features were strongly marked, and of a somewhat foreign character. She appears to have settled down easily enough into farmhouse life, and became a favourite with the children, who sometimes went with her on her rambles in the forest, for this was her amusement. Mr R. states that he has known her to go out by herself directly after their early breakfast, and not return till after dusk, and that, feeling uneasy at a young girl being out alone for so many hours, he communicated with her adopted father, who replied in a brief note that Helen must do as she chose. In the winter, when the forest paths are impassable, she spent most of her time in her bedroom, where she slept alone, according to the instructions of her relative. It was on one of these expeditions to the forest that the first of the singular incidents with which this girl is connected occurred, the date being about a year after her arrival at the village. The preceding winter had been remarkably severe, the snow drifting to a great depth, and the frost continuing for an unexampled period, and the summer following was as noteworthy for its extreme heat. On one of the very hottest days in this summer, Helen V. left the farmhouse for one of her long rambles in the forest, taking with her, as usual, some bread and meat for lunch. She was seen by some men in the fields making for the old Roman Road, a green causeway which traverses the highest part of the wood, and they were astonished to observe that the girl had taken off her hat, though the heat of the sun was already tropical. As it happened, a labourer, Joseph W. by name, was working in the forest near the Roman Road, and at twelve o'clock his little son, Trevor, brought the man his dinner of bread and cheese. After the meal, the boy, who was about seven years old at the time, left his father at work, and, as he said, went to look for flowers in the wood, and the man, who could hear him shouting with delight at his discoveries, felt no uneasiness. Suddenly, however, he was horrified at hearing the most dreadful screams, evidently the result of great terror, proceeding from the direction in which his son had gone, and he hastily threw down his tools and ran to see what had happened. Tracing his path by the sound, he met the little boy, who was running headlong, and was evidently terribly frightened, and on questioning him the man elicited that after picking a posy of flowers he felt tired, and lay down on the grass and fell asleep. He was suddenly awakened, as he stated, by a peculiar noise, a sort of singing he called it, and on peeping through the branches he saw Helen V. playing on the grass with a 'strange naked man', who he seemed unable to describe more fully. He said he felt dreadfully frightened and ran away crying for his father. Joseph W. proceeded in the direction indicated by his son, and found Helen V. sitting on the grass in the middle of a glade or open space left by charcoal burners. He angrily charged her with frightening his little boy, but she entirely denied the accusation and laughed at the child's story of a 'strange man', to which he himself did not attach much credence. Joseph W. came to the conclusion that the boy had woke up with a sudden fright, as children sometimes do, but Trevor persisted in his story, and continued in such evident distress that at last his father took him home, hoping that his mother would be able to soothe him. For many weeks, however, the boy gave his parents much anxiety; he became nervous and strange in his manner, refusing to leave the cottage by himself, and constantly alarming the household by waking in the night with cries of 'The man in the wood! father! father!'

In course of time, however, the impression seemed to have worn off, and about three months later he accompanied his father to the home of a gentleman in the neighbourhood, for whom Joseph W. occasionally did work. The man was shown into the study, and the little boy was left sitting in the hall, and a few minutes later, while the gentleman was giving W. his instructions, they were both horrified by a piercing shriek and the sound of a fall, and rushing out they found the child lying senseless on the floor, his face contorted with terror. The doctor was immediately summoned, and after some examination he pronounced the child to be suffering form a kind of fit, apparently produced by a sudden shock. The boy was taken to one of the bedrooms, and after some time recovered consciousness, but only to pass into a condition described by the medical man as one of violent hysteria. The doctor exhibited a strong sedative, and in the course of two hours pronounced him fit to walk home, but in passing through the hall the paroxysms of fright returned and with additional violence. The father perceived that the child was pointing at some object, and heard the old cry, 'The man in the wood', and looking in the direction indicated saw a stone head of grotesque appearance, which had been built into the wall above one of the doors. It seems the owner of the house had recently made alterations in his premises, and on digging the foundations for some offices, the men had found a curious head, evidently of the Roman period, which had been placed in the manner described. The head is pronounced by the most experienced archaeologists of the district to be that of a faun or satyr.*

From whatever cause arising, this second shock seemed too severe for the boy Trevor, and at the present date he suffers from a weakness of intellect, which gives but little promise of amending. The matter caused a good deal of sensation at the time, and the girl Helen was closely questioned by Mr R., but to no purpose, she steadfastly denying that she had frightened or in any way molested Trevor.

The second event with which this girl's name is connected took place about six years ago, and is of a still more extraordinary character.

At the beginning of the summer of 1882, Helen contracted a friendship of a peculiarly intimate character with Rachel M., the daughter of a prosperous farmer in the neighbourhood. This girl, who was a year younger than Helen, was considered by most people to be the prettier of the two, though Helen's features had to a great extent softened as she became older. The two girls, who were together on every available opportunity, presented a singular contrast, the one with her clear, olive skin and almost Italian appearance, and the other of the proverbial red and white of our rural districts. It must be stated that the payments made to Mr R. for the maintenance of Helen were known in the village for their excessive liberality, and the impression was general that she would one day inherit a large sum of money from her relative. The parents of Rachel were therefore not averse from their daughter's friendship with the girl, and even encouraged the intimacy, though they now bitterly regret having done so. Helen still retained her extraordinary fondness for the forest, and on several

* Dr Phillips tells me that he has seen the head in question, and assures me that he has never received such a vivid presentment of intense evil.

occasions Rachel accompanied her, the two friends setting out early in the morning, and remaining in the wood until dusk. Once or twice after these excursions Mrs M. thought her daughter's manner rather peculiar; she seemed languid and dreamy, and as it has been expressed, 'different from herself', but these peculiarities seem to have been thought too trifling for remark. One evening, however, after Rachel had come home, her mother heard a noise which sounded like suppressed weeping in the girl's room, and on going in found her lying, half undressed, upon the bed, evidently in the greatest distress. As soon as she saw her mother, she exclaimed, 'Ah, mother, mother, why did you let me go to the forest with Helen?' Mrs M. was astonished at so strange a question, and proceeded to make inquiries. Rachel told her a wild story. She said –

Clarke closed the book with a snap, and turned his chair towards the fire. When his friend sat one evening in that very chair, and told his story, Clarke had interrupted him at a point a little subsequent to this, had cut short his words in a paroxysm of horror. 'My God!' he had exclaimed, 'think, think what you are saying. It is too incredible, too monstrous; such things can never be in this quiet world, where men and women live and die, and struggle, and conquer, or maybe fail, and fall down under sorrow, and grieve and suffer strange fortunes for many a year; but not this, Phillips, not such things as this. There must be some explanation, some way out of the terror. Why, man, if such a case were possible, our earth would be a nightmare.'

But Phillips had told his story to the end, concluding:

'Her flight remains a mystery to this day; she vanished in broad sunlight; they saw her walking in a meadow, and a few moments later she was not there.'

Clarke tried to conceive the thing again, as he sat by the fire, and again his mind shuddered and shrank back, appalled before the sight of such awful, unspeakable elements enthroned as it were, and triumphant in human flesh. Before him stretched the long dim vista of the green causeway in the forest, as his friend had described it; he saw the swaying leaves and the quivering shadows on the grass, he saw the sunlight and the flowers, and far away, far in the long distance, the two figures moved toward him. One was Rachel, but the other?

Clarke had tried his best to disbelieve it all, but at the end of the account, as he had written it in his book, he had placed the inscription:

ET DIABOLUS INCARNATUS EST. ET HOMO FACTUS EST.

III
The City of Resurrections

'Herbert! Good God! Is it possible?'

'Yes, my name's Herbert. I think I know your face, too, but I don't remember your name. My memory is very queer.'

'Don't you recollect Villiers of Wadham?'

'So it is, so it is. I beg your pardon, Villiers, I didn't think I was begging of an old college friend. Good night.'

'My dear fellow, this haste is unnecessary. My rooms are close by, but we won't go there just yet. Suppose we walk up Shaftesbury Avenue a little way? But how in heaven's name have you come to this pass, Herbert?'

'It's a long story, Villiers, and a strange one too, but you can hear it if you like.'

'Come on, then. Take my arm, you don't seem very strong.'

The ill-assorted pair moved slowly up Rupert Street; the one in dirty, evil-looking rags, and the other attired in the regulation uniform of a man about town, trim, glossy, and eminently well-to-do. Villiers had emerged from his restaurant after an excellent dinner of many courses, assisted by an ingratiating little flask of Chianti, and, in that frame of mind which was with him almost chronic, had delayed a moment by the door, peering round in the dimly-lighted street in search of those mysterious incidents and persons with which the streets of London teem in every quarter and every hour. Villiers prided himself as a practised explorer of such obscure mazes and byways of London life, and in this unprofitable pursuit he displayed an assiduity which was worthy of more serious employment. Thus he stood by the lamp post surveying the passers-by with undisguised curiosity, and with that gravity known only to the systematic diner, had just enunciated in his mind the formula: 'London has been called the city of encounters; it is more than that, it is the city of Resurrections,' when these reflections were suddenly interrupted by a piteous whine at his elbow, and a deplorable appeal for alms. He looked around in some irritation, and with a sudden shock found himself confronted with the embodied proof of his somewhat stilted fancies. There, close beside him, his face altered and disfigured by poverty and disgrace, his body barely covered by greasy ill-fitting rags, stood his old friend Charles Herbert, who had matriculated on the same day as himself, with whom he had been merry and wise for twelve revolving terms. Different occupations and varying interests had interrupted the friendship, and it was six years since Villiers had seen Herbert; and now he looked upon this wreck of a man with grief and dismay, mingled with a certain inquisitiveness as to what dreary chain of circumstances had dragged him down to such a doleful pass. Villiers felt together with compassion all the relish of the amateur in mysteries, and congratulated himself on his leisurely speculations outside the restaurant.

They walked on in silence for some time, and more than one passer-by stared in astonishment at the unaccustomed spectacle of a well-dressed man with an unmistakable beggar hanging on to his arm, and, observing this, Villiers led the way to an obscure street in Soho. Here he repeated his question.

'How on earth has it happened, Herbert? I always understood you would succeed to an excellent position in Dorsetshire. Did your father disinherit you? Surely not?'

'No, Villiers; I came into all the property at my poor father's death; he died a year after I left Oxford. He was a very good father to me, and I mourned his death sincerely enough. But you know what young men are; a few months later I came up to town and went a good deal into society. Of course I had excellent introductions, and I managed to enjoy myself very much in a harmless sort of way. I played a little, certainly, but never for heavy stakes, and the few bets I made on races brought me in money – only a few pounds, you know, but enough to pay for cigars and such petty pleasures. It was in my second season that the tide turned. Of course you have heard of my marriage?'

'No, I never heard anything about it.'

'Yes, I married, Villiers. I met a girl, a girl of the most wonderful and most strange beauty, at the house of some people whom I knew. I cannot tell you her age; I never knew it, but, so far as I can guess, I should think she must have been about nineteen when I made her acquaintance. My friends had come to know her at Florence; she told them she was an orphan, the child of an English father and an Italian mother, and she charmed them as she charmed me. The first time I saw her was at an evening party. I was standing by the door talking to a friend, when suddenly above the hum and babble of conversation I heard a voice which seemed to thrill to my heart. She was singing an Italian song. I was introduced to her that evening, and in three months I married Helen. Villiers, that woman, if I can call her woman, corrupted my soul. The night of the wedding I found myself sitting in her bedroom in the hotel, listening to her talk. She was sitting up in bed, and I listened to her as she spoke in her beautiful voice, spoke of things which even now I would not dare whisper in the blackest night, though I stood in the midst of a wilderness. You, Villiers, you may think you know life, and London, and what goes on day and night in this dreadful city; for all I can say you may have heard the talk of the vilest, but I tell you you can have no conception of what I know, not in your most fantastic, hideous dreams can you have imaged forth the faintest shadow of what I have heard – and seen. Yes, seen. I have seen the incredible, such horrors that even I myself sometimes stop in the middle of the street and ask whether it is possible for a man to behold such things and live. In a year, Villiers, I was a ruined man, in body and soul – in body and soul.'

'But your property, Herbert? You had land in Dorset.'

'I sold it all; the fields and woods, the dear old house – everything.'

'And the money?'

'She took it all from me.'

'And then left you?'

'Yes; she disappeared one night. I don't know where she went, but I am sure if I saw her again it would kill me. The rest of my story is of no interest; sordid misery, that is all. You may think, Villiers, that I have exaggerated and talked for effect; but I have not told you half. I could tell you certain things which would convince you, but you would never know a happy day again. You would pass the rest of your life, as I pass mine, a haunted man, a man who has seen hell.'

Villiers took the unfortunate man to his rooms, and gave him a meal. Herbert could eat little, and scarcely touched the glass of wine set before him. He sat moody and silent by the fire, and seemed relieved when Villiers sent him away with a small present of money.

'By the way, Herbert,' said Villiers, as they parted at the door, 'what was your wife's name? You said Helen, I think? Helen what?'

'The name she passed under when I met her was Helen Vaughan, but what her real name was I can't say. I don't think she had a name. No, no, not in that sense. Only human beings have names, Villiers; I can't say any more. Goodbye; yes, I will not fail to call if I see any way in which you can help me. Good night.'

The man went out into the bitter night, and Villiers returned to his fireside. There was something about Herbert which shocked him inexpressibly; not his poor rags nor the marks which poverty had set upon his face, but rather an indefinite terror which hung about him like a mist. He had acknowledged that he himself was not devoid of blame; the woman, he had avowed, had corrupted him body and soul, and Villiers felt that this man, once his friend, had been an actor in scenes evil beyond the power of words. His story needed no confirmation: he himself was the embodied proof of it. Villiers mused curiously over the story he had heard, and wondered whether he had heard both the first and the last of it. 'No,' he thought, 'certainly not the last, probably only the beginning. A case like this is like a nest of Chinese boxes; you open one after the other and find a quainter workmanship in every box. Most likely poor Herbert is merely one of the outside boxes; there are stranger ones to follow.'

Villiers could not take his mind away from Herbert and his story, which seemed to grow wilder as the night wore on. The fire seemed to burn low, and the chilly air of the morning crept into the room; Villiers got up with a glance over his shoulder, and, shivering slightly, went to bed.

A few days later he saw at his club a gentleman of his acquaintance, named Austin, who was famous for his intimate knowledge of London life, both in its tenebrous and luminous phases. Villiers, still full of his encounter in Soho and its consequences, thought Austin might possibly be able to shed some light on Herbert's history, and so after some casual talk he suddenly put the question:

'Do you happen to know anything of a man named Herbert – Charles Herbert?'

Austin turned round sharply and stared at Villiers with some astonishment.

'Charles Herbert? Weren't you in town three years ago? No; then you have not heard of the Paul Street case? It caused a good deal of sensation at the time.'

'What was the case?'

'Well, a gentleman, a man of very good position, was found dead, stark dead, in the area of a certain house in Paul Street, off Tottenham Court Road. Of course the police did not make the discovery; if you happen to be sitting up all night and have a light in your window, the constable will ring the bell, but if you happen to be lying dead in somebody's area, you will be left alone. In this instance, as in many others, the alarm was raised by some kind of vagabond; I don't mean a common tramp, or a public house loafer, but a gentleman, whose business or pleasure, or both, made him a spectator of the London streets at five o'clock in the morning. This individual was, as he said, "going home", it did not appear whence or whither, and had occasion to pass through Paul Street between four and five a.m. Something or other caught his eye at Number 20; he said, absurdly enough, that the house had the most unpleasant physiognomy he had ever observed, but, at any rate, he glanced down the area and was a good deal astonished to see a man lying on the stones, his limbs all huddled together, and his face turned up. Our gentleman thought his face looked peculiarly ghastly, and so set off at a run in search of the nearest policeman. The constable was at first inclined to treat the matter lightly, suspecting common drunkenness; however, he came, and after looking at the man's face, changed his tone, quickly enough. The early bird, who had picked up this fine worm, was sent off for a doctor, and the policeman rang and knocked at the door till a slatternly servant girl came down looking more than half asleep. The constable pointed out the contents of the area to the maid, who screamed loudly enough to wake up the street, but she knew nothing of the man; had never seen him at the house, and so forth. Meanwhile, the original discoverer had come back with a medical man, and the next thing was to get into the area. The gate was open, so the whole quartet stumped down the steps. The doctor hardly needed a moment's examination; he said the poor fellow had been dead for several hours, and it was then the case began to get interesting. The dead man had not been robbed, and in one of his pockets were papers identifying him as – well, as a man of good family and means, a favourite in society, and nobody's enemy, as far as could be known. I don't give his name, Villiers, because it has nothing to do with the story, and because it's no good raking up these affairs about the dead when there are no relations living. The next curious point was that the medical men couldn't agree as to how he met his death. There were some slight bruises on his shoulders, but they were so slight that it looked as if he had been pushed roughly out of the kitchen door, and not thrown over the railings from the street or even dragged down the steps. But there were positively no other marks of violence about him, certainly none that would account for his death; and when they came to the autopsy there wasn't a trace of poison of any kind. Of course the police wanted to know all about the people at

Number 20, and here again, so I have heard from private sources, one or two other very curious points came out. It appears that the occupants of the house were a Mr and Mrs Charles Herbert; he was said to be a landed proprietor, though it struck most people that Paul Street was not exactly the place to look for country gentry. As for Mrs Herbert, nobody seemed to know who or what she was, and, between ourselves, I fancy the divers after her history found themselves in rather strange waters. Of course they both denied knowing anything about the deceased, and in default of any evidence against them they were discharged. But some very odd things came out about them. Though it was between five and six in the morning when the dead man was removed, a large crowd had collected, and several of the neighbours ran to see what was going on. They were pretty free with their comments, by all accounts, and from these it appeared that Number 20 was in very bad odour in Paul Street. The detectives tried to trace down these rumours to some solid foundation of fact, but could not get hold of anything. People shook their heads and raised their eyebrows and thought the Herberts rather "queer", "would rather not be seen going into their house", and so on, but there was nothing tangible. The authorities were morally certain the man met his death in some way or another in the house and was thrown out by the kitchen door, but they couldn't prove it, and the absence of any indications of violence or poisoning left them helpless. An odd case, wasn't it? But curiously enough, there's something more that I haven't told you. I happened to know one of the doctors who was consulted as to the cause of death, and some time after the inquest I met him, and asked him about it. "Do you really mean to tell me," I said, "that you were baffled by the case, that you actually don't know what the man died of?" "Pardon me," he replied, "I know perfectly well what caused death. Blank died of fright, of sheer, awful terror; I never saw features so hideously contorted in the entire course of my practice, and I have seen the faces of a whole host of dead." The doctor was usually a cool customer enough, and a certain vehemence in his manner struck me, but I couldn't get anything more out of him. I suppose the Treasury didn't see their way to prosecuting the Herberts for frightening a man to death; at any rate, nothing was done, and the case dropped out of men's minds. Do you happen to know anything of Herbert?'

'Well,' replied Villiers, 'he was an old college friend of mine.'

'You don't say so? Have you ever seen his wife?'

'No, I haven't. I have lost sight of Herbert for many years.'

'It's queer, isn't it, parting with a man at the college gate or at Paddington, seeing nothing of him for years, and then finding him pop up his head in such an odd place. But I should like to have seen Mrs Herbert; people said extraordinary things about her.'

'What sort of things?'

'Well, I hardly know how to tell you. Everyone who saw her at the police court said she was at once the most beautiful woman and the most repulsive they had ever set eyes on. I have spoken to a man who saw her, and I assure you he positively shuddered as he tried to describe the woman, but he couldn't tell why. She seems to have been a sort of enigma; and I expect if that one dead man could have told tales, he would have told some uncommonly queer ones. And there you are again in another puzzle; what could a respectable country gentleman like Mr Blank (we'll call him that if you don't mind) want in such a very queer house as Number 20? It's altogether a very odd case, isn't it?'

'It is indeed, Austin; an extraordinary case. I didn't think, when I asked you about my old friend, I should strike on such strange metal. Well, I must be off; good day.'

Villiers went away, thinking of his own conceit of the Chinese boxes; here was quaint workmanship indeed.

IV
The Discovery in Paul Street

A few months after Villiers' meeting with Herbert, Mr Clarke was sitting, as usual, by his after dinner hearth, resolutely guarding his fancies from wandering in the direction of the bureau. For more than a week he had succeeded in keeping away from the 'Memoirs', and he cherished hopes of a complete self-reformation; but, in spite of his endeavours, he could not hush the wonder and the strange curiosity that the last case he had written down had excited within him. He had put the case, or rather the outline of it, conjecturally to a scientific friend, who shook his head, and thought Clarke getting queer, and on this particular evening Clarke was making an effort to rationalise the story, when a sudden knock at the door roused him from his meditations.

'Mr Villiers to see you sir.'

'Dear me, Villiers, it is very kind of you to look me up; I have not seen you for many months; I should think nearly a year. Come in, come in. And how are you, Villiers? Want any advice about investments?'

'No, thanks, I fancy everything I have in that way is pretty safe. No, Clarke, I have really come to consult you about a rather curious matter that has been brought under my notice of late. I am afraid you will think it all rather absurd when I tell my tale. I sometimes think so myself, and that's just why I made up my mind to come to you, as I know you're a practical man.'

Mr Villiers was ignorant of the 'Memoirs to prove the Existence of the Devil'.

'Well, Villiers, I shall be happy to give you my advice, to the best of my ability. What is the nature of the case?'

'It's an extraordinary thing altogether. You know my ways; I always keep my eyes open in the streets, and in my time I have chanced upon some queer customers, and queer cases too, but this, I think, beats all. I was coming out of a restaurant one nasty winter night about three months ago; I had had a capital dinner and a good bottle of Chianti, and I stood for a moment on the pavement, thinking what a mystery there is about London streets and the companies that pass along them. A bottle of red wine encourages these fancies, Clarke, and I dare say I should have thought a page of small type, but I was cut short by a beggar who had come behind me, and was making the usual appeals. Of course I looked round, and this beggar turned out to be what was left of an old friend of mine, a man named Herbert. I asked him how he had come to such a wretched pass, and he told me. We walked up and down one of those long and dark Soho streets, and there I listened to his story. He said he had married a beautiful girl, some years younger than himself, and, as he put it, she had corrupted him body and soul. He wouldn't go into details; he said he dare not, that what he had seen and heard haunted him by night and day, and when I looked in his face I knew he was speaking the truth. There was something about the man that made me shiver. I don't know why, but it was there. I gave him a little money and sent him away, and I assure you that when he was gone I gasped for breath. His presence seemed to chill one's blood.'

'Isn't this all just a little fanciful, Villiers? I suppose the poor fellow had made an imprudent marriage, and, in plain English, gone to the bad.'

'Well, listen to this.' Villiers told Clarke the story he had heard from Austin.

'You see,' he concluded, 'there can be but little doubt that this Mr Blank, whoever he was, died of sheer terror; he saw something so awful, so terrible, that it cut short his life. And what he saw, he most certainly saw in that house, which, somehow or other, had got a bad name in the neighbourhood. I had the curiosity to go and look at the place for myself. It's a saddening kind of street; the houses are old enough to be mean and dreary, but not old enough to be quaint. As far as I could see most of them are let in lodgings, furnished and unfurnished, and almost every door has three bells to it. Here and there the ground floors have been made into shops of the commonest kind; it's a dismal street in every way. I found Number 20 was to let, and I went to the agent's and got the key. Of course I should have heard nothing of the Herberts in that quarter, but I asked the man, fair and square, how long they had left the house and whether there had been other tenants in the meanwhile. He looked at me queerly for a minute, and told me the Herberts had left immediately after the unpleasantness, as he called it, and since then the house had been empty.'

Mr Villiers paused for a moment.

'I have always been rather fond of going over empty houses; there's a sort of fascination about the desolate empty rooms, with the nails sticking in the walls, and the dust thick upon the window sills. But I didn't enjoy going over Number 20, Paul Street. I had hardly put my foot inside the passage when I noticed a queer, heavy feeling about the air of the house. Of course all empty houses are stuffy, and so forth, but this was something quite different; I can't describe it to you, but it seemed to stop the breath. I went into the front room and the back room, and the kitchens downstairs; they were all dirty and dusty enough, as you would expect, but there was something strange about them all. I couldn't define it to you, I only know I felt queer. It was one of the rooms on the first floor, though, that was the worst. It was a largish room, and once on a time the paper must have been cheerful enough, but when I saw it, paint, paper, and everything were most doleful. But the room was full of horror; I felt my teeth grinding as I put my hand on the door, and when I went in, I thought I should have fallen fainting to the floor. However, I pulled myself together, and stood against the end wall, wondering what on earth there could be about the room to make my limbs tremble, and my heart beat as if I were at the hour of death. In one corner there was a pile of newspapers littered on the floor, and I began looking at them; they were papers of three or four years ago, some of them half torn, and some crumpled as if they had been used for packing. I turned the whole pile over, and amongst them I found a curious drawing; I will show it to you presently. But I couldn't stay in the room; I felt it was overpowering me. I was thankful to come out, safe and sound, into the open air. People stared at me as I walked along the street, and one man said I was drunk. I was staggering about from one side of the pavement to the other, and it was as much as I could do to take the key back to the agent and get home. I was in bed for a week, suffering from what my doctor called nervous shock and exhaustion. One of those days I was reading the evening paper, and happened to notice a paragraph headed: "Starved to Death". It was the usual style of thing; a model lodging house in Marylebone, a door locked for several days, and a dead man in his chair when they broke in. "The deceased," said the paragraph, "was known as Charles Herbert, and is believed to have been once a prosperous country gentleman. His name was familiar to the public three years ago in connection with the mysterious death in Paul Street, Tottenham Court Road, the deceased being the tenant of the house Number 20, in the area of which a gentleman of good position was found dead under circumstances not devoid of suspicion." A tragic ending, wasn't it? But after all, if what he told me were true, which I am sure it was, the man's life was all a tragedy, and a tragedy of a stranger sort than they put on the boards.'

'And that is the story, is it?' said Clarke musingly.

'Yes, that is the story.'

'Well, really, Villiers, I scarcely know what to say about it. There are, no doubt, circumstances in the case which seem peculiar, the finding of the dead man in the area of Herbert's house, for instance, and the extraordinary opinion of the physician as to the cause of death; but, after all, it is conceivable that the facts may be explained in a straightforward manner. As to your own sensations, when you went to see the house, I would suggest that they were due to a vivid imagination; you must have been brooding, in a semi-conscious way, over what you had heard. I don't exactly see what more can be said or done in the matter; you evidently think there is a mystery of some kind, but Herbert is dead; where then do you propose to look?'

'I propose to look for the woman; the woman whom he married.

She is the mystery.'

The two men sat silent by the fireside; Clarke secretly congratulating himself on having successfully kept up the character of advocate of the commonplace, and Villiers wrapped in his gloomy fancies.

'I think I will have a cigarette,' he said at last, and put his hand in his pocket to feel for the cigarette case.

'Ah!' he said, starting slightly, 'I forgot I had something to show you. You remember my saying that I had found a rather curious sketch amongst the pile of old newspapers at the house in Paul Street? Here it is.'

Villiers drew out a small thin parcel from his pocket. It was covered with brown paper, and secured with string, and the knots were troublesome. In spite of himself Clarke felt inquisitive; he bent forward on his chair as Villiers painfully undid the string, and unfolded the outer covering. Inside was a second wrapping of tissue, and Villiers took it off and handed the small piece of paper to Clarke without a word.

There was dead silence in the room for five minutes or more; the two men sat so still that they could hear the ticking of the tall old-fashioned clock that stood outside in the hall, and in the mind of one of them the slow monotony of sound woke up a far, far memory. He was looking intently at the small pen-and-ink sketch of the woman's head; it had evidently been drawn with great care, and by a true artist, for the woman's soul looked out of the eyes, and the lips were parted with a strange smile. Clarke gazed still at the face; it brought to his memory one summer evening, long ago; he saw again the long lovely valley, the river winding between the hills, the meadows and the cornfields, the dull red sun, and the cold white mist rising from the water. He heard a voice speaking to him across the waves of many years, and saying 'Clarke, Mary will see the god Pan!' and then he was standing in the grim room beside the doctor, listening to the heavy ticking of the clock, waiting and watching, watching the figure lying on the green chair beneath the lamplight. Mary rose up, and he looked into her eyes, and his heart grew cold within him.

'Who is this woman?' he said at last. His voice was dry and hoarse.

'That is the woman who Herbert married.'

Clarke looked again at the sketch; it was not Mary after all. There certainly was Mary's face, but there was something else, something he had not seen on Mary's features when the white-clad girl entered the laboratory with the doctor, nor at her terrible awakening, nor when she lay grinning on the bed. Whatever it was, the glance that came from those eyes, the smile on the full lips, or the expression of the whole face, Clarke shuddered before it at his inmost soul, and thought, unconsciously, of Dr Phillip's words, 'the most vivid presentment of evil I have ever seen'. He turned the paper over mechanically in his hand and glanced at the back.

'Good God! Clarke, what is the matter? You are as white as death.'

Villiers had started wildly from his chair, as Clarke fell back with a groan, and let the paper drop from his hands.

'I don't feel very well, Villiers, I am subject to these attacks. Pour me out a little wine; thanks, that will do. I shall feel better in a few minutes.'

Villiers picked up the fallen sketch and turned it over as Clarke had done.

'You saw that?' he said. 'That's how I identified it as being a portrait of Herbert's wife, or I should say his widow. How do you feel now?'

'Better, thanks, it was only a passing faintness. I don't think I quite catch your meaning. What did you say enabled you to identify the picture?'

'This word – "Helen" – was written on the back. Didn't I tell you her name was Helen? Yes; Helen Vaughan.'

Clarke groaned; there could be no shadow of doubt.

'Now, don't you agree with me,' said Villiers, 'that in the story I have told you tonight, and in the part this woman plays in it, there are some very strange points?'

'Yes, Villiers,' Clarke muttered, 'it is a strange story indeed; a strange story indeed. You must give me time to think it over; I may be able to help you or I may not. Must you be going now? Well, good night, Villiers, good night. Come and see me in the course of a week.'

V
The Letter of Advice

'Do you know, Austin,' said Villiers, as the two friends were pacing sedately along Piccadilly one pleasant morning in May, 'do you know I am convinced that what you told me about Paul Street and the Herberts is a mere episode in an extraordinary history? I may as well confess to you that when I asked you about Herbert a few months ago I had just seen him.'

'You had seen him? Where?'

'He begged of me in the street one night. He was in the most pitiable plight, but I recognised the man, and I got him to tell me his history, or at least the outline of it. In brief, it amounted to this – he had been ruined by his wife.'

'In what manner?'

'He would not tell me; he would only say that she had destroyed him, body and soul. The man is dead now.'

'And what has become of his wife?'

'Ah, that's what I should like to know, and I mean to find her sooner or later. I know a man named Clarke, a dry fellow, in fact a man of business, but shrewd enough. You understand my meaning; not shrewd in the mere business sense of the word, but a man who really knows something about men and life. Well, I laid the case before him, and he was evidently impressed. He said it needed consideration, and asked me to come again in the course of a week. A few days later I received this extraordinary letter.'

Austin took the envelope, drew out the letter, and read it curiously. It ran as follows: –

> 'MY DEAR VILLIERS, – I have thought over the matter on which you consulted me the other night, and my advice to you is this. Throw the portrait into the fire, blot out the story from your mind. Never give it another thought, Villiers, or you will be sorry. You will think, no doubt, that I am in possession of some secret information, and to a certain extent that is the case. But I only know a little; I am like a traveller who has peered over an abyss, and has drawn back in terror. What I know is strange enough and horrible enough, but beyond my knowledge there are depths and horrors more frightful still, more incredible than any tale told of winter nights about the fire. I have resolved, and nothing shall shake that resolve, to explore no whit farther, and if you value your happiness you will make the same determination.
>
> 'Come and see me by all means; but we will talk on more cheerful topics than this.'

Austin folded the letter methodically, and returned it to Villiers.

'It is certainly an extraordinary letter,' he said, 'what does he mean by the portrait?'

'Ah! I forgot to tell you I have been to Paul Street and have made a discovery.'

Villiers told his story as he had told it to Clarke, and Austin listened in silence. He seemed puzzled.

'How very curious that you should experience such an unpleasant sensation in that room!' he said at length. 'I hardly gather that it was a mere matter of the imagination; a feeling of repulsion, in short.'

'No, it was more physical than mental. It was as if I were inhaling at every breath some deadly fume, which seemed to penetrate to every nerve and bone and sinew of my body. I felt racked from head to foot, my eyes began to grow dim; it was like the entrance of death.'

'Yes, yes, very strange certainly. You see, your friend confesses that there is some very black story connected with this woman. Did you notice any particular emotion in him when you were telling your tale?'

'Yes, I did. He became very faint, but he assured me that it was a mere passing attack to which he was subject.'

'Did you believe him?'

'I did at the time, but I don't now. He heard what I had to say with a good deal of indifference, till I showed him the portrait. It was then that he was seized with the attack of which I spoke. He looked ghastly, I assure you.'

'Then he must have seen the woman before. But there might be another explanation; it might have been the name, and not the face, which was familiar to him. What do you think?'

'I couldn't say. To the best of my belief it was after turning the portrait in his hands that he nearly dropped from the chair. The name, you know, was written on the back.'

'Quite so. After all, it is impossible to come to any resolution in a case like this. I hate melodrama, and nothing strikes me as more commonplace and tedious than the ordinary ghost story of commerce; but really, Villiers, it looks as if there were something very queer at the bottom of all this.'

The two men had, without noticing it, turned up Ashley Street, leading northward from Piccadilly. It was a long street, and rather a gloomy one, but here and there a brighter taste had illuminated the dark houses with flowers, and gay curtains, and a cheerful paint on the doors. Villiers glanced up as Austin stopped speaking, and looked at one of these houses; geraniums, red and white, drooped from every sill, and daffodil-coloured curtains were draped back from each window.

'It looks cheerful, doesn't it?' he said.

'Yes, and the inside is still more cheery. One of the pleasantest houses of the season, so I have heard. I haven't been there myself, but I've met several men who have, and they tell me it's uncommonly jovial.'

'Whose house is it?'

'A Mrs Beaumont's.'

'And who is she?'

'I couldn't tell you. I have heard she comes from South America, but after all, who she is is of little consequence. She is a very wealthy woman, there's no doubt of that, and some of the best people have taken her up. I hear she has some wonderful claret, really marvellous wine, which must have cost a fabulous sum. Lord Argentine was telling me about it; he was there last Sunday evening. He assures me he has never tasted such a wine, and Argentine, as you know, is an expert. By the way, that reminds me, she must be an oddish sort of woman, this Mrs Beaumont. Argentine asked her how old the wine was, and what do you think she said? "About a thousand years, I believe." Lord Argentine thought she was chaffing him, you know, but when he laughed she said she was speaking quite seriously and offered to show him the jar. Of course, he couldn't say anything more after that; but it seems rather antiquated for a beverage, doesn't it? Why, here we are at my rooms. Come in, won't you?'

'Thanks, I think I will. I haven't seen the curiosity shop for a while.'

It was a room furnished richly, yet oddly, where every jar and bookcase and table, and every rug and jar and ornament seemed to be a thing apart, preserving each its own individuality.

'Anything fresh lately?' said Villiers after a while.

'No; I think not; you saw those queer jugs, didn't you? I thought so. I don't think I have come across anything for the last few weeks.'

Austin glanced around the room from cupboard to cupboard, from shelf to shelf, in search of some new oddity. His eyes fell at last on an odd chest, pleasantly and quaintly carved, which stood in a dark corner of the room.

'Ah,' he said, 'I was forgetting, I have got something to show you.' Austin unlocked the chest, drew out a thick quarto volume, laid it on the table, and resumed the cigar he had put down.

'Did you know Arthur Meyrick the painter, Villiers?'

'A little; I met him two or three times at the house of a friend of mine. What has become of him? I haven't heard his name mentioned for some time.'

'He's dead.'

'You don't say so! Quite young, wasn't he?'

'Yes; only thirty when he died.'

'What did he die of?'

'I don't know. He was an intimate friend of mine, and a thoroughly good fellow. He used to come here and talk to me for hours, and he was one of the best talkers I have met. He could even talk about painting, and that's more than can be said of most painters. About eighteen months ago he was feeling rather overworked, and partly at my suggestion he went off on a sort of roving expedition, with no very definite end or aim about it. I believe New York was to be his first port, but I never heard from him. Three months ago I got this book, with a very civil letter from an English doctor practising at Buenos Aires, stating that he had attended the late Mr Meyrick during his illness, and that the deceased had expressed an earnest wish that the enclosed packet should be sent to me after his death. That was all.'

'And haven't you written for further particulars?'

'I have been thinking of doing so. You would advise me to write to the doctor?'

'Certainly. And what about the book?'

'It was sealed up when I got it. I don't think the doctor had seen it.'

'It is something very rare? Meyrick was a collector, perhaps?'

'No, I think not, hardly a collector. Now, what do you think of these Ainu jugs?'

'They are peculiar, but I like them. But aren't you going to show me poor Meyrick's legacy?'

'Yes, yes, to be sure. The fact is, it's rather a peculiar sort of thing, and I haven't shown it to any one. I wouldn't say anything about it if I were you. There it is.'

Villiers took the book, and opened it at haphazard.

'It isn't a printed volume, then?' he said.

'No. It is a collection of drawings in black and white by my poor friend Meyrick.'

Villiers turned to the first page, it was blank; the second bore a brief inscription, which he read:

Silet per diem universus, nec sine horrore secretus est; lucet nocturnis ignibus, chorus Aegipanum undique personatur: audiuntur et cantus tibi-

arum, et tinnitus cymbalorum per oram maritimam.

On the third page was a design which made Villiers start and look up at Austin; he was gazing abstractedly out of the window. Villiers turned page after page, absorbed, in spite of himself, in the frightful Walpurgis Night of evil, strange monstrous evil, that the dead artist had set forth in hard black and white. The figures of Fauns and Satyrs and Aegipans danced before his eyes, the darkness of the thicket, the dance on the mountaintop, the scenes by lonely shores, in green vineyards, by rocks and desert places, passed before him: a world before which the human soul seemed to shrink back and shudder. Villiers whirled over the remaining pages; he had seen enough, but the picture on the last leaf caught his eye, as he almost closed the book.

'Austin!'

'Well, what is it?'

'Do you know who that is?'

It was a woman's face, alone on the white page.

'Know who it is? No, of course not.'

'I do.'

'Who is it?'

'It is Mrs Herbert.'

'Are you sure?'

'I am perfectly sure of it. Poor Meyrick! He is one more chapter in her history.'

'But what do you think of the designs?'

'They are frightful. Lock the book up again, Austin. If I were you I would burn it; it must be a terrible companion even though it be in a chest.'

'Yes, they are singular drawings. But I wonder what connection there could be between Meyrick and Mrs Herbert, or what link between her and these designs?'

'Ah, who can say? It is possible that the matter may end here, and we shall never know, but in my own opinion this Helen Vaughan, or Mrs Herbert, is only the beginning. She will come back to London, Austin; depend on it, she will come back, and we shall hear more about her then. I doubt it will be very pleasant news.'

VI
The Suicides

Lord Argentine was a great favourite in London Society. At twenty he had been a poor man, decked with the surname of an illustrious family, but forced to earn a livelihood as best he could, and the most speculative of moneylenders would not have entrusted him with fifty pounds on the chance of his ever changing his name for a title, and his poverty for a great fortune. His father had been near enough to the fountain of good things to secure one of the family livings, but the son, even if he had taken orders, would scarcely have obtained so much as this, and moreover felt no vocation for the ecclesiastical estate. Thus he fronted the world with no better armour than the bachelor's gown and the wits of a younger son's grandson, with which equipment he contrived in some way to make a very tolerable fight of it. At twenty-five Mr Charles Aubernon saw himself still a man of struggles and of warfare with the world, but out of the seven who stood before him and the high places of his family three only remained. These three, however, were 'good lives', but yet not proof against the Zulu assegais and typhoid fever, and so one morning Aubernon woke up and found himself Lord Argentine, a man of thirty who had faced the difficulties of existence, and had conquered. The situation amused him immensely, and he resolved that riches should be as pleasant to him as poverty had always been. Argentine, after some little consideration, came to the conclusion that dining, regarded as a fine art, was perhaps the most amusing pursuit open to fallen humanity, and thus his dinners became famous in London, and an invitation to his table a thing covetously desired. After ten years of lordship and dinners Argentine still declined to be jaded, still persisted in enjoying life, and by a kind of infection had become recognised as the cause of joy in others, in short, as the best of company. His sudden and tragical death therefore caused a wide and deep sensation. People could scarcely believe it, even though the newspaper was before their eyes, and the cry of 'Mysterious Death of a Nobleman' came ringing up from the street. But there stood the brief paragraph: 'Lord Argentine was found dead this morning by his valet under distressing circumstances. It is stated that there can be no doubt that his lordship committed suicide, though no motive can be assigned for the act. The deceased nobleman was widely known in society, and much liked for his genial manner and sumptuous hospitality. He is succeeded by,' etc., etc.

By slow degrees the details came to light, but the case still remained a mystery. The chief witness at the inquest was the deceased's valet, who said that the night before his death Lord Argentine had dined with a lady of good position, whose name was suppressed in the newspaper reports. At about eleven o'clock Lord Argentine had returned, and informed his man that he should not require his services till the next morning. A little later the valet had occasion to cross the hall and was somewhat astonished to see his master quietly letting himself out at the front door. He had taken off his evening clothes, and was dressed in a Norfolk coat and knickerbockers, and wore a low brown hat. The valet had no reason to suppose that Lord Argentine had seen him, and though his master rarely kept late hours, thought little of the occurrence till the next morning, when he knocked at the bedroom door at a quarter to nine as usual. He received no answer, and, after knocking two or three times, entered the room, and saw Lord Argentine's body leaning forward at an angle from the bottom of the bed. He found that his master had tied a cord securely to one of the short bedposts, and, after making a running noose and slipping it round his neck, the unfortunate man must have resolutely fallen forward, to die by slow strangulation. He was dressed in the light suit in which the valet had seen him go out, and the doctor who was summoned pronounced that life had been extinct for more than four hours. All papers, letters, and so forth seemed in perfect order, and nothing was discovered which pointed in the most remote way to any scandal either great or small. Here the evidence ended; nothing more could be discovered. Several persons had been present at the dinner party at which Lord Argentine had assisted, and to all these he seemed in his usual genial spirits. The valet, indeed, said he thought his master appeared a little excited when he came home, but confessed that the alteration in his manner was very slight, hardly noticeable, indeed. It seemed hopeless to seek for any clue, and the suggestion that Lord Argentine had been suddenly attacked by acute suicidal mania was generally accepted.

It was otherwise, however, when within three weeks, three more gentlemen, one of them a nobleman, and the two others men of good position and ample means, perished miserably in almost precisely the same manner. Lord Swanleigh was found one morning in his dressing room, hanging from a peg affixed to the wall, and Mr Collier-Stuart and Mr Herries had chosen to die as Lord Argentine. There was no explanation in either case; a few bald facts; a living man in the evening, and a body with a black swollen face in the morning. The police had been forced to confess themselves powerless to arrest or to explain the sordid murders of Whitechapel; but before the horrible suicides of Piccadilly and Mayfair they were dumbfounded, for not even the mere ferocity which did duty as an explanation of the crimes of the East End, could be of service in the West. Each of these men who had resolved to die a tortured shameful death was rich, prosperous, and to all appearances in love with the world, and not the acutest research could ferret out any shadow of a lurking motive in either case. There was a horror in the air, and men looked at one another's faces when they met, each wondering whether the other was to be the victim of the fifth nameless tragedy. Journalists sought in vain in their scrapbooks for materials whereof to concoct reminiscent articles; and the morning paper was unfolded in many a house with a feeling of awe; no man knew when or where the blow would next light.

A short while after the last of these terrible events, Austin came to see Mr Villiers. He was curious to know whether Villiers had succeeded in discovering any fresh traces of Mrs Herbert, either through Clarke or by other sources, and he asked the question soon after he had sat down.

'No,' said Villiers, 'I wrote to Clarke, but he remains obdurate, and I have tried other channels, but without any result. I can't find out what became of Helen Vaughan after she left Paul Street, but I think she must have gone abroad. But to tell the truth, Austin, I haven't paid much attention to the matter for the last few weeks; I knew poor Herries intimately, and his terrible death has been a great shock to me, a great shock.'

'I can well believe it,' answered Austin gravely, 'you know Argentine was a friend of mine. If I remember rightly, we were speaking of him that day you came to my rooms.'

'Yes; it was in connection with that house in Ashley Street, Mrs Beaumont's house. You said something about Argentine's dining there.'

'Quite so. Of course you know it was there Argentine dined the night before – before his death.'

'No, I had not heard that.'

'Oh, yes; the name was kept out of the papers to spare Mrs Beaumont. Argentine was a great favourite of hers, and it is said she was in a terrible state for some time after.'

A curious look came over Villiers's face; he seemed undecided whether to speak or not. Austin began again.

'I never experienced such a feeling of horror as when I read the account of Argentine's death. I didn't understand it at the time, and I don't now. I knew him well, and it completely passes my understanding for what possible cause he – or any of the others for the matter of that – could have resolved in cold blood to die in such an awful manner. You know how men babble away each other's characters in London, you may be sure any buried scandal or hidden skeleton would have been brought to light in such a case as this; but nothing of the sort has taken place. As for the theory of mania, that is very well, of course, for the coroner's jury, but everybody knows that it's all nonsense. Suicidal mania is not smallpox.'

Austin relapsed into gloomy silence. Villiers sat silent, also, watching his friend. The expression of indecision still fleeted across his face; he seemed as if weighing his thoughts in the balance, and the considerations he was resolving left him still silent. Austin tried to shake off the remembrance of tragedies as hopeless and perplexed as the labyrinth of Daedalus, and began to talk in an indifferent voice of the more pleasant incidents and adventures of the season.

'That Mrs Beaumont,' he said, 'of whom we were speaking, is a great success; she has taken London almost by storm. I met her the other night at Fulham's; she is really a remarkable woman.'

'You have met Mrs Beaumont?'

'Yes; she had quite a court around her. She would be called very handsome, I suppose, and yet there is something about her face which I didn't like. The features are exquisite, but the expression is strange. And all the time I was looking at her, and afterwards, when I was going home, I had a curious feeling that that very expression was in some way or another familiar to me.'

'You must have seen her in the Row.'

'No, I am sure I never set eyes on the woman before; it is that which makes it puzzling. And to the best of my belief I have never seen anyone like her; what I felt was a kind of dim far off memory, vague but persistent. The only sensation I can compare it to, is that odd feeling one sometimes has in a dream, when fantastic cities and wondrous lands and phantom personages appear familiar and accustomed.'

Villiers nodded and glanced aimlessly round the room, possibly in search of something on which to turn the conversation. His eyes fell on an old chest somewhat like that in which the artist's strange legacy lay hid beneath a Gothic scutcheon.

'Have you written to the doctor about poor Meyrick?' he asked.

'Yes; I wrote asking for full particulars as to his illness and death. I don't expect to have an answer for another three weeks or a month. I thought I might as well inquire whether Meyrick knew an Englishwoman named Herbert, and if so, whether the doctor could give me any information about her. But it's very possible that Meyrick fell in with her at New York, or Mexico, or San Francisco; I have no idea as to the extent or direction of his travels.'

'Yes, and it's very possible that the woman may have more than one name.'

'Exactly. I wish I had thought of asking you to lend me the portrait of her which you possess. I might have enclosed it in my letter to Dr Matthews.'

'So you might; that never occurred to me. We might send it now. Hark! what are those boys calling?'

While the two men had been talking together a confused noise of shouting had been gradually growing louder. The noise rose from the eastward and swelled down Piccadilly, drawing nearer and nearer, a very torrent of sound; surging up streets usually quiet, and making every window a frame for a face, curious or excited. The cries and voices came echoing up the silent street where Villiers lived, growing more distinct as they advanced, and, as Villiers spoke, an answer rang up from the pavement:

'The West End Horrors; Another Awful Suicide; Full Details!'

Austin rushed down the stairs and bought a paper and read out the paragraph to Villiers as the uproar in the street rose and fell. The window was open and the air seemed full of noise and terror.

'Another gentleman has fallen a victim to the terrible epidemic of suicide which for the last month has prevailed in the West End. Mr Sidney Crashaw, of Stoke House, Fulham, and King's Pomeroy, Devon, was found, after a prolonged search, hanging dead from the branch of a tree in his garden at one o'clock today. The deceased gentleman dined last night at the Carlton Club and seemed in his usual health and spirits. He left the club at about ten o'clock, and was seen walking leisurely up St James's Street a little later. Subsequent to this his movements cannot be traced. On the discovery of the body medical aid was at once summoned, but life had evidently been long extinct. So far as is known, Mr Crashaw had no trouble or anxiety of any kind. This painful suicide, it will be remembered, is the fifth of the kind in the last month. The authorities at Scotland Yard are unable to suggest any explanation of these terrible occurrences.'

Austin put down the paper in mute horror.

'I shall leave London tomorrow,' he said, 'it is a city of nightmares. How awful this is, Villiers!'

Mr Villiers was sitting by the window quietly looking out into the street. He had listened to the newspaper report attentively, and the hint of indecision was no longer on his face.

'Wait a moment, Austin,' he replied, 'I have made up my mind to mention a little matter that occurred last night. It stated, I think, that Crashaw was last seen alive in St James's Street shortly after ten?'

'Yes, I think so. I will look again. Yes, you are quite right.'

'Quite so. Well, I am in a position to contradict that statement at all events. Crashaw was seen after that; considerably later indeed.'

'How do you know?'

'Because I happened to see Crashaw myself at about two o'clock this morning.'

'You saw Crashaw? You, Villiers?'

'Yes, I saw him quite distinctly; indeed, there were but a few feet between us.'

'Where, in Heaven's name, did you see him?'

'Not far from here. I saw him in Ashley Street. He was just leaving a house.'

'Did you notice what house it was?'

'Yes. It was Mrs Beaumont's.'

'Villiers! Think what you are saying; there must be some mistake. How could Crashaw be in Mrs Beaumont's house at two o'clock in the morning? Surely, surely, you must have been dreaming, Villiers; you were always rather fanciful.'

'No; I was wide awake enough. Even if I had been dreaming as you say, what I saw would have roused me effectually.'

'What you saw? What did you see? Was there anything strange about Crashaw? But I can't believe it; it is impossible.'

'Well, if you like I will tell you what I saw, or if you please, what I think I saw, and you can judge for yourself.'

'Very good, Villiers.'

The noise and clamour of the street had died away, though now and then the sound of shouting still came from the distance, and the dull, leaden silence seemed like the quiet after an earthquake or a storm. Villiers turned from the window and began speaking.

'I was at a house near Regent's Park last night, and when I came away the fancy took me to walk home instead of taking a hansom. It was a clear pleasant night enough, and after a few minutes I had the streets pretty much to myself. It's a curious thing, Austin, to be alone in London at night, the gas lamps stretching away in perspective, and the dead silence, and then perhaps the rush and clatter of a hansom on the stones, and the fire starting up under the horse's hoofs. I walked along pretty briskly, for I was feeling a little tired of being out in the night, and as the clocks were striking two I turned down Ashley Street, which, you know, is on my way. It was quieter than ever there, and the lamps were fewer; altogether, it looked as dark and gloomy as a forest in winter. I had done about half the length of the street when I heard a door closed very softly, and naturally I looked up to see who was abroad like myself at such an hour. As it happens, there is a street lamp close to the house in question, and I saw a man standing on the step. He had just shut the door and his face was towards me, and I recognised Crashaw directly. I never knew him to speak to, but I had often seen him, and I am positive that I was not mistaken in my man. I looked into his face for a moment, and then – I will confess the truth – I set off at a good run, and kept it up till I was within my own door.'

'Why?'

'Why? Because it made my blood run cold to see that man's face. I could never have supposed that such an infernal medley of passions could have glared out of any human eyes; I almost fainted as I looked. I knew I had looked into the eyes of a lost soul, Austin, the man's outward form remained, but all hell was within it. Furious lust, and hate that was like fire, and the loss of all hope and horror that seemed to shriek aloud to the night, though his teeth were shut; and the utter blackness of despair. I am sure that he did not see me; he saw nothing that you or I can see, but what he saw I hope we never shall. I do not know when he died; I suppose in an hour, or perhaps two, but when I passed down Ashley Street and heard the closing door, that man no longer belonged to this world; it was a devil's face I looked upon.'

There was an interval of silence in the room when Villiers ceased speaking. The light was failing, and all the tumult of an hour ago was quite hushed. Austin had bent his head at the close of the story, and his hand covered his eyes.

'What can it mean?' he said at length.

'Who knows, Austin, who knows? It's a black business, but I think we had better keep it to ourselves, for the present at any rate. I will see if I cannot learn anything about that house through private channels of information, and if I do light upon anything I will let you know.'

VII

The Encounter in Soho

Three weeks later Austin received a note from Villiers, asking him to call either that afternoon or the next. He chose the nearer date, and found Villiers sitting as usual by the window, apparently lost in meditation on the drowsy traffic of the street. There was a bamboo table by his side, a fantastic thing, enriched with gilding and queer painted scenes, and on it lay a little pile of papers arranged and docketed as neatly as anything in Mr Clarke's office.

'Well, Villiers, have you made any discoveries in the last three weeks?'

'I think so; I have here one or two memoranda which struck me as singular, and there is a statement to which I shall call your attention.'

'And these documents relate to Mrs Beaumont? It was really Crashaw whom you saw that night standing on the doorstep of the house in Ashley Street?'

'As to that matter my belief remains unchanged, but neither my inquiries nor their results have any special relation to Crashaw. But my investigations have had a strange issue. I have found out who Mrs Beaumont is!'

'Who is she? In what way do you mean?'

'I mean that you and I know her better under another name.'

'What name is that?'

'Herbert.'

'Herbert!' Austin repeated the word, dazed with astonishment.

'Yes, Mrs Herbert of Paul Street, Helen Vaughan of earlier adventures unknown to me. You had reason to recognise the expression of her face; when you go home look at the face in Meyrick's book of horrors, and you will know the sources of your recollection.'

'And you have proof of this?'

'Yes, the best of proof; I have seen Mrs Beaumont, or shall we say

Mrs Herbert?'

'Where did you see her?'

'Hardly in a place where you would expect to see a lady who lives in Ashley Street, Piccadilly. I saw her entering a house in one of the meanest and most disreputable streets in Soho. In fact, I had made an appointment, though not with her, and she was precise to both time and place.'

'All this seems very wonderful, but I cannot call it incredible. You must remember, Villiers, that I have seen this woman, in the ordinary adventure of London society, talking and laughing, and sipping her coffee in a commonplace drawingroom with commonplace people. But you know what you are saying.'

'I do; I have not allowed myself to be led by surmises or fancies. It was with no thought of finding Helen Vaughan that I searched for Mrs Beaumont in the dark waters of the life of London, but such has been the issue.'

'You must have been in strange places, Villiers.'

'Yes, I have been in very strange places. It would have been useless, you know, to go to Ashley Street, and ask Mrs Beaumont to give me a short sketch of her previous history. No; assuming, as I had to assume, that her record was not of the cleanest, it would be pretty certain that at some previous time she must have moved in circles not quite so refined as her present ones. If you see mud at the top of a stream, you may be sure that it was once at the bottom. I went to the bottom. I have always been fond of diving into Queer Street for my amusement, and I found my knowledge of that locality and its inhabitants very useful. It is, perhaps, needless to say that my friends had never heard the name of Beaumont, and as I had never seen the lady, and was quite unable to describe her, I had to set to work in an indirect way. The people there know me; I have been able to do some of them a service now and again, so they made no difficulty about giving their information; they were aware I had no communication direct or indirect with Scotland Yard. I had to cast out a good many lines, though, before I got what I wanted, and when I landed the fish I did not for a moment suppose it was my fish. But I listened to what I was told out of a constitutional liking for useless information, and I found myself in possession of a very curious story, though, as I imagined, not the story I was looking for. It was to this effect. Some five or six years ago, a woman named Raymond suddenly made her appearance in the neighbourhood to which I am referring. She was described to me as being quite young, probably not more than seventeen or eighteen, very handsome, and looking as if she came from the country. I should be wrong in saying that she found her level in going to this particular quarter, or associating with these people, for from what I was told, I should think the worst den in London far too good for her. The person from whom I got my information, as you may suppose, no great Puritan, shuddered and grew sick in telling me of the nameless infamies which were laid to her charge. After living there for a year, or perhaps a little more, she disappeared as suddenly as she came, and they saw nothing of her till about the time of the Paul Street case. At first she came to her old haunts only occasionally, then more frequently, and finally took up her abode there as before, and remained for six or eight months. It's of no use my going into details as to the life that woman led; if you want particulars you can look at Meyrick's legacy. Those designs were not drawn from his imagination. She again disappeared, and the people of the place saw nothing of her till a few months ago. My informant told me that she had taken some rooms in a house which he pointed out, and these rooms she was in the habit of visiting two or three times a week and always at ten in the morning. I was led to expect that one of these visits would be paid on a certain day about a week ago, and I accordingly managed to be on the look-out in company with my cicerone at a quarter to ten, and the hour and the lady came with equal punctuality. My friend and I were standing under an archway, a little way back from the street, but she saw us, and gave me a glance that I shall be long in forgetting. That look was quite enough for me; I knew Miss Raymond to be Mrs Herbert; as for Mrs Beaumont, she had quite gone out of my head. She went into the house, and I watched it till four o'clock, when she came out, and then I followed her. It was a long chase, and I had to be very careful to keep a long way in the background, and yet not lose sight of the woman. She took me down to the Strand, and then to Westminster, and then up St James's Street, and along Piccadilly. I felt queerish when I saw her turn up Ashley Street; the thought that Mrs Herbert was Mrs Beaumont came into my mind, but it seemed too impossible to be true. I waited at the corner, keeping my eye on her all the time, and I took particular care to note the house at which she stopped. It was the house with the gay curtains, the home of flowers, the house out of which Crashaw came the night he hanged himself in his garden. I was just going away with my discovery, when I saw an empty carriage come round and draw up in front of the house, and I came to the conclusion that Mrs Herbert was going out for a drive, and I was right. There, as it happened, I met a man I know, and we stood talking together a little distance from the carriage-way, to which I had my back. We had not been there for ten minutes when my friend took off his hat, and I glanced round and saw the lady I had been following all day. "Who is that?" I said, and his answer was "Mrs Beaumont; lives in Ashley Street." Of course there could be no doubt after that. I don't know whether she saw me, but I don't think she did. I went home at once, and, on consideration, I thought that I had a sufficiently good case with which to go to Clarke.'

'Why to Clarke?'

'Because I am sure that Clarke is in possession of facts about this woman, facts of which I know nothing.'

'Well, what then?'

Mr Villiers leaned back in his chair and looked reflectively at Austin for a moment before he answered:

'My idea was that Clarke and I should call on Mrs Beaumont.'

'You would never go into such a house as that? No, no, Villiers, you cannot do it. Besides, consider; what result . . . '

'I will tell you soon. But I was going to say that my information does not end here; it has been completed in an extraordinary manner.

'Look at this neat little packet of manuscript; it is paginated, you see, and I have indulged in the civil coquetry of a ribbon of red tape. It has almost a legal air, hasn't it? Run your eye over it, Austin. It is an account of the entertainment Mrs Beaumont provided for her choicer guests. The man who wrote this escaped with his life, but I do not think he will live many years. The doctors tell him he must have sustained some severe shock to the nerves.'

Austin took the manuscript, but never read it. Opening the neat pages at haphazard his eye was caught by a word and a phrase that followed it; and, sick at heart, with white lips and a cold sweat pouring like water from his temples, he flung the paper down.

'Take it away, Villiers, never speak of this again. Are you made of stone, man? Why, the dread and horror of death itself, the thoughts of the man who stands in the keen morning air on the black platform, bound, the bell tolling in his ears, and waits for the harsh rattle of the bolt, are as nothing compared to this. I will not read it; I should never sleep again.'

'Very good. I can fancy what you saw. Yes; it is horrible enough;

but after all, it is an old story, an old mystery played in our day, and in dim London streets instead of amidst the vineyards and the olive gardens. We know what happened to those who chanced to meet the Great God Pan, and those who are wise know that all symbols are symbols of something, not of nothing. It was, indeed, an exquisite symbol beneath which men long ago veiled their knowledge of the most awful, most secret forces which lie at the heart of all things; forces before which the souls of men must wither and die and blacken, as their bodies blacken under the electric current. Such forces cannot be named, cannot be spoken, cannot be imagined except under a veil and a symbol, a symbol to the most of us appearing a quaint, poetic fancy, to some a foolish tale. But you and I, at all events, have known something of the terror that may dwell in the secret place of life, manifested under human flesh; that which is without form taking to itself a form. Oh, Austin, how can it be? How is it that the very sunlight does not turn to blackness before this thing, the hard earth melt and boil beneath such a burden?'

Villiers was pacing up and down the room, and the beads of sweat stood out on his forehead. Austin sat silent for a while, but Villiers saw him make a sign upon his breast.

'I say again, Villiers, you will surely never enter such a house as that? You would never pass out alive.'

'Yes, Austin, I shall go out alive – I, and Clarke with me.'

'What do you mean? You cannot, you would not dare . . . '

'Wait a moment. The air was very pleasant and fresh this morning; there was a breeze blowing, even through this dull street, and I thought I would take a walk. Piccadilly stretched before me a clear, bright vista, and the sun flashed on the carriages and on the quivering leaves in the park. It was a joyous morning, and men and women looked at the sky and smiled as they went about their work or their pleasure, and the wind blew as blithely as upon the meadows and the scented gorse. But somehow or other I got out of the bustle and the gaiety, and found myself walking slowly along a quiet, dull street, where there seemed to be no sunshine and no air, and where the few foot passengers loitered as they walked, and hung indecisively about corners and archways. I walked along, hardly knowing where I was going or what I did there, but feeling impelled, as one sometimes is, to explore still further, with a vague idea of reaching some unknown goal. Thus I forged up the street, noting the small traffic of the milk-shop, and wondering at the incongruous medley of penny pipes, black tobacco, sweets, newspapers, and comic songs which here and there jostled one another in the short compass of a single window. I think it was a cold shudder that suddenly passed through me that first told me that I had found what I wanted. I looked up from the pavement and stopped before a dusty shop, above which the lettering had faded, where the red bricks of two hundred years ago had grimed to black; where the windows had gathered to themselves the dust of winters innumerable. I saw what I required; but I think it was five minutes before I had steadied myself and could walk in and ask for it in a cool voice and with a calm face. I think there must even then have been a tremor in my words, for the old man who came out of the back parlour, and fumbled slowly amongst his goods, looked oddly at me as he tied the parcel. I paid what he asked, and stood leaning by the counter, with a strange reluctance to take up my goods and go. I asked about the business, and learnt that trade was bad and the profits cut down sadly; but then the street was not what it was before traffic had been diverted, but that was done forty years ago, "just before my father died," he said. I got away at last, and walked along sharply; it was a dismal street indeed, and I was glad to return to the bustle and the noise. Would you like to see my purchase?'

Austin said nothing, but nodded his head slightly; he still looked white and sick. Villiers pulled out a drawer in the bamboo table, and showed Austin a long coil of cord, hard and new; and at one end was a running noose.

'It is the best hempen cord,' said Villiers, 'just as it used to be made for the old trade, the man told me. Not an inch of jute from end to end.'

Austin set his teeth hard, and stared at Villiers, growing whiter as he looked.

'You would not do it,' he murmured at last. 'You would not have blood on your hands. My God!' he exclaimed, with sudden vehemence, 'you cannot mean this, Villiers, that you will make yourself a hangman?'

'No. I shall offer a choice, and leave Helen Vaughan alone with this cord in a locked room for fifteen minutes. If when we go in it is not done, I shall call the nearest policeman. That is all.'

'I must go now. I cannot stay here any longer; I cannot bear this. Good night.'

'Good night, Austin.'

The door shut, but in a moment it was open again, and Austin stood, white and ghastly, in the entrance.

'I was forgetting,' he said, 'that I too have something to tell. I have received a letter from Dr Harding of Buenos Aires. He says that he attended Meyrick for three weeks before his death.'

'And does he say what carried him off in the prime of life? It was not fever?'

'No, it was not fever. According to the doctor, it was an utter collapse of the whole system, probably caused by some severe shock. But he states that the patient would tell him nothing, and that he was consequently at some disadvantage in treating the case.'

'Is there anything more?'

'Yes. Dr Harding ends his letter by saying: "I think this is all the information I can give you about your poor friend. He had not been long in Buenos Aires, and knew scarcely any one, with the exception of a person who did not bear the best of characters, and has since left – a Mrs Vaughan."'

VIII
The Fragments

[Amongst the papers of the well-known physician, Dr Robert Matheson, of Ashley Street, Piccadilly, who died suddenly, of apoplectic seizure, at the beginning of 1892, a leaf of manuscript paper was found, covered with pencil jottings. These notes were in Latin, much abbreviated, and had evidently been made in great haste. The MS. was only deciphered with difficulty, and some words have up to the present time evaded all the efforts of the expert employed. The date, 'xxv Jul. 1888', is written on the right-hand corner of the MS. The following is a translation of Dr Matheson's manuscript.]

'Whether science would benefit by these brief notes if they could be published, I do not know, but rather doubt. But certainly I shall never take the responsibility of publishing or divulging one word of what is here written, not only on account of my oath given freely to those two persons who were present, but also because the details are too abominable. It is probable that, upon mature consideration, and after weighing the good and evil, I shall one day destroy this paper, or at least leave it under seal to my friend

D., trusting in his discretion, to use it or to burn it, as he may think fit.

'As was befitting, I did all that my knowledge suggested to make sure that I was suffering under no delusion. At first astounded, I could hardly think, but in a minute's time I was sure that my pulse was steady and regular, and that I was in my real and true senses. I then fixed my eyes quietly on what was before me.

'Though horror and revolting nausea rose up within me, and an odour of corruption choked my breath, I remained firm. I was then privileged or accursed, I dare not say which, to see that which was on the bed, lying there black like ink, transformed before my eyes. The skin, and the flesh, and the muscles, and the bones, and the firm structure of the human body that I had thought to be unchangeable, and permanent as adamant, began to melt and dissolve.

'I know that the body may be separated into its elements by external agencies, but I should have refused to believe what I saw. For here there was some internal force, of which I knew nothing, that caused dissolution and change.

'Here too was all the work by which man had been made repeated before my eyes. I saw the form waver from sex to sex, dividing itself from itself, and then again reunited. Then I saw the body descend to the beasts whence it ascended, and that which was on the heights go down to the depths, even to the abyss of all being. The principle of life, which makes organism, always remained, while the outward form changed.

'The light within the room had turned to blackness, not the darkness of night, in which objects are seen dimly, for I could see clearly and without difficulty. But it was the negation of light; objects were presented to my eyes, if I may say so, without any medium, in such a manner that if there had been a prism in the room I should have seen no colours represented in it.

'I watched, and at last I saw nothing but a substance as jelly. Then the ladder was ascended again . . . [*here the MS. is illegible*] . . . for one instant I saw a Form, shaped in dimness before me, which I will not farther describe. But the symbol of this form may be seen in ancient sculptures, and in paintings which survived beneath the lava, too foul to be spoken of . . . as a horrible and unspeakable shape, neither man nor beast, was changed into human form, there came finally death.

'I who saw all this, not without great horror and loathing of soul, here write my name, declaring all that I have set on this paper to be true.'

'Robert Matheson, Med. Dr.'

* * *

. . . Such, Raymond, is the story of what I know and what I have seen. The burden of it was too heavy for me to bear alone, and yet I could tell it to none but you. Villiers, who was with me at the last, knows nothing of that awful secret of the wood, of how what we both saw die, lay upon the smooth, sweet turf amidst the summer flowers, half in sun and half in shadow, and holding the girl Rachel's hand, called and summoned those companions, and shaped in solid form, upon the earth we tread upon, the horror which we can but hint at, which we can only name under a figure. I would not tell Villiers of this, nor of that resemblance, which struck me as with a blow upon my heart, when I saw the portrait, which filled the cup of terror at the end. What this can mean I dare not guess. I know that what I saw perish was not Mary, and yet in the last agony Mary's eyes looked into mine. Whether there be any one who can show the last link in this chain of awful mystery, I do not know, but if there be any one who can do this, you, Raymond, are the man. And if you know the secret, it rests with you to tell it or not, as you please.

I am writing this letter to you immediately on my getting back to town. I have been in the country for the last few days; perhaps you may be able to guess in which part. While the horror and wonder of London was at its height – for 'Mrs Beaumont', as I have told you, was well known in society – I wrote to my friend Dr Phillips, giving some brief outline, or rather hint, of what happened, and asking him to tell me the name of the village where the events he had related to me occurred. He gave me the name, as he said with the less hesitation, because Rachel's father and mother were dead, and the rest of the family had gone to a relative in the State of Washington six months before. The parents, he said, had undoubtedly died of grief and horror caused by the terrible death of their daughter, and by what had gone before that death. On the evening of the day on which I received Phillips's letter I was at Caermaen, and standing beneath the mouldering Roman walls, white with the winters of seventeen hundred years, I looked over the meadow where once had stood the older temple of the 'God of the Deeps', and saw a house gleaming in the sunlight. It was the house where Helen had lived. I stayed at Caermaen for several days. The people of the place, I found, knew little and had guessed less. Those whom I spoke to on the matter seemed surprised that an antiquarian (as I professed myself to be) should trouble about a village tragedy, of which they gave a very commonplace version, and, as you may imagine, I told nothing of what I knew. Most of my time was spent in the great wood that rises just above the village and climbs the hillside, and goes down to the river in the valley; such another long lovely valley, Raymond, as that on which we looked one summer night, walking to and fro before your house. For many an hour I strayed through the maze of the forest, turning now to right and now to left, pacing slowly down long alleys of undergrowth, shadowy and chill, even under the midday sun, and halting beneath great oaks; lying on the short turf of a clearing where the faint sweet scent of wild roses came to me on the wind and mixed with the heavy perfume of the elder, whose mingled odour is like the odour of the room of the dead, a vapour of incense and corruption. I stood at the edges of the wood, gazing at all the pomp and procession of the foxgloves towering amidst the bracken and shining red in the broad sunshine, and beyond them into deep thickets of close undergrowth where springs boil up from the rock and nourish the waterweeds, dank and evil. But in all my wanderings I avoided one part of the wood; it was not till yesterday that I climbed to the summit of the hill, and stood upon the ancient Roman road that threads the highest ridge of the wood. Here they had walked, Helen and Rachel, along this quiet causeway, upon the pavement of green turf, shut in on either side by high banks of red earth, and tall hedges of shining beech, and here I followed in their steps, looking out, now and again, through partings in the boughs, and seeing on one side the sweep of the wood stretching far to right and left, and sinking into the broad level, and beyond, the yellow sea, and the land over the sea. On the other side was the valley and the river and hill following hill as wave on wave, and wood and meadow, and cornfield, and white houses gleaming, and a great wall of mountain, and far blue peaks in the north. And so at last I came to the place. The track went up a gentle slope, and widened out into an open space with a wall of thick undergrowth around it, and then, narrowing again, passed on into the distance and the faint blue mist of summer heat. And into this pleasant summer glade Rachel passed a girl, and left it, who shall say what? I did not stay long there.

In a small town near Caermaen there is a museum, containing for the most part Roman remains which have been found in the neighbourhood at various times. On the day after my arrival in Caermaen I walked over to the town in question, and took the opportunity of inspecting the museum. After I had seen most of the sculptured stones, the coffins, rings, coins, and fragments of tessellated pavement which the place contains, I was shown a small square pillar of white stone, which had been recently discovered in the wood of which I have been speaking, and, as I found on inquiry, in that open space where the Roman road broadens out. On one side of the pillar was an inscription, of which I took a note. Some of the letters have been defaced, but I do not think there can be any doubt as to those which I supply. The inscription is as follows:

DEVOMNODENT*i*
FLA*v*IUSSENILISPOSSU*it*
PROPTERNUP*tias*
*qua*SVIDITSUBUMBRA

'To the great god Nodens (the god of the Great Deep or Abyss) Flavius Senilis has erected this pillar on account of the marriage which he saw beneath the shade.'

The custodian of the museum informed me that local antiquaries were much puzzled, not by the inscription, or by any difficulty in translating it, but as to the circumstance or rite to which allusion is made.

* * *

. . . And now, my dear Clarke, as to what you tell me about Helen Vaughan, whom you say you saw die under circumstances of the utmost and almost incredible horror. I was interested in your account, but a good deal, nay all, of what you told me I knew already. I can understand the strange likeness you remarked in both the portrait and in the actual face; you have seen Helen's mother. You remember that still summer night so many years ago, when I talked to you of the world beyond the shadows, and of the god Pan. You remember Mary. She was the mother of Helen Vaughan, who was born nine months after that night.

Mary never recovered her reason. She lay, as you saw her, all the while upon her bed, and a few days after the child was born she died. I fancy that just at the last she knew me; I was standing by the bed, and the old look came into her eyes for a second, and then she shuddered and groaned and died. It was an ill work I did that night when you were present; I broke open the door of the house of life, without knowing or caring what might pass forth or enter in. I recollect your telling me at the time, sharply enough, and rightly too, in one sense, that I had ruined the reason of a human being by a foolish experiment, based on an absurd theory. You did well to blame me, but my theory was not all absurdity. What I said Mary would see she saw, but I forgot that no human eyes can look on such a sight with impunity. And I forgot, as I have just said, that when the house of life is thus thrown open, there may enter in that for which we have no name, and human flesh may become the veil of a horror one dare not express. I played with energies which I did not understand, you have seen the ending of it. Helen Vaughan did well to bind the cord about her neck and die, though the death was horrible. The blackened face, the hideous form upon the bed, changing and melting before your eyes from woman to man, from man to beast, and from beast to worse than beast, all the strange horror that you witness, surprises me but little. What you say the doctor whom you sent for saw and shuddered at I noticed long ago; I knew what I had done the moment the child was born, and when it was scarcely five years old I surprised it, not once or twice but several times with a playmate, you may guess of what kind. It was for me a constant, an incarnate horror, and after a few years I felt I could bear it no more, and I sent Helen Vaughan away. You know now what frightened the boy in the wood. The rest of the strange story, and all else that you tell me, as discovered by your friend, I have contrived to learn from time to time, almost to the last chapter. And now Helen is with her companions . . .

Note. – Helen Vaughan was born on August 5th, 1865, at the Red House, Breconshire, and died on July 25th, 1888, in her house in a street off Piccadilly, called Ashley Street in the story.

The Inmost Light

I

One evening in autumn, when the deformities of London were veiled in faint blue mist, and its vistas and far-reaching streets seemed splendid, Mr Charles Salisbury was slowly pacing down Rupert Street, drawing nearer to his favourite restaurant by slow degrees. His eyes were downcast in study of the pavement, and thus it was that as he passed in at the narrow door a man who had come up from the lower end of the street jostled against him.

'I beg your pardon – wasn't looking where I was going. Why, it's Dyson!'

'Yes, quite so. How are you, Salisbury?'

'Quite well. But where have you been, Dyson? I don't think I can have seen you for the last five years?'

'No; I dare say not. You remember I was getting rather hard up when you came to my place at Charlotte Street?'

'Perfectly. I think I remember your telling me that you owed five weeks' rent, and that you had parted with your watch for a comparatively small sum.'

'My dear Salisbury, your memory is admirable. Yes, I was hard up. But the curious thing is that soon after you saw me I became harder up. My financial state was described by a friend as "stone broke". I don't approve of slang, mind you, but such was my condition. But suppose we go in; there might be other people who would like to dine – it's a human weakness, Salisbury.'

'Certainly; come along. I was wondering as I walked down whether the corner table were taken. It has a velvet back, you know.'

'I know the spot; it's vacant. Yes, as I was saying, I became even harder up.'

'What did you do then?' asked Salisbury, disposing of his hat, and settling down in the corner of the seat, with a glance of fond anticipation at the *menu*.

'What did I do? Why, I sat down and reflected. I had a good classical education, and a positive distaste for business of any kind: that was the capital with which I faced the world. Do you know, I have heard people describe olives as nasty! What lamentable Philistinism! I have often thought, Salisbury, that I could write genuine poetry under the influence of olives and red wine. Let us have Chianti; it may not be very good, but the flasks are simply charming.'

'It is pretty good here. We may as well have a big flask.'

'Very good. I reflected, then, on my want of prospects, and I determined to embark in literature.'

'Really; that was strange. You seem in pretty comfortable circumstances, though.'

'Though! What a satire upon a noble profession. I am afraid, Salisbury, you haven't a proper idea of the dignity of an artist. You see me sitting at my desk – or at least you can see me if you care to call – with pen and ink, and simple nothingness before me, and if you come again in a few hours you will (in all probability) find a creation!'

'Yes, quite so. I had an idea that literature was not remunerative.'

'You are mistaken; its rewards are great. I may mention, by the way, that shortly after you saw me I succeeded to a small income. An uncle died, and proved unexpectedly generous.'

'Ah, I see. That must have been convenient.'

'It was pleasant – undeniably pleasant. I have always considered it in the light of an endowment of my researches. I told you I was a man of letters; it would, perhaps, be more correct to describe myself as a man of science.'

'Dear me, Dyson, you have really changed very much in the last few years. I had a notion, don't you know, that you were a sort of idler about town, the kind of man one might meet on the north side of Piccadilly every day from May to July.'

'Exactly. I was even then forming myself, though all unconsciously. You know my poor father could not afford to send me to the University. I used to grumble in my ignorance at not having completed my education. That was the folly of youth, Salisbury; my University was Piccadilly. There I began to study the great science which still occupies me.'

'What science do you mean?'

'The science of the great city; the physiology of London; literally and metaphysically the greatest subject that the mind of man can conceive. What an admirable *salmi* this is; undoubtedly the final end of the pheasant. Yet I feel sometimes positively overwhelmed with the thought of the vastness and complexity of London. Paris a man may get to understand thoroughly with a reasonable amount of study; but London is always a mystery. In Paris you may say: "Here live the actresses, here the Bohemians, and the *Ratés*"; but it is different in London. You may point out a street, correctly enough, as the abode of washerwomen; but, in that second floor, a man may be studying Chaldee roots, and in the garret over the way a forgotten artist is dying by inches.'

'I see you are Dyson, unchanged and unchangeable,' said Salisbury, slowly sipping his Chianti. 'I think you are misled by a too fervid imagination; the mystery of London exists only in your fancy. It seems to me a dull place enough. We seldom hear of a really artistic crime in London, whereas I believe Paris abounds in that sort of thing.'

'Give me some more wine. Thanks. You are mistaken, my dear fellow, you are really mistaken. London has nothing to be ashamed of in the way of crime. Where we fail is for want of Homers, not Agamemnons. *Carent quia vate sacro*, you know.'

'I recall the quotation. But I don't think I quite follow you.'

'Well, in plain language, we have no good writers in London who make a speciality of that kind of thing. Our common reporter is a dull dog; every story that he has to tell is spoilt in the telling. His idea of horror and of what excites horror is so lamentably deficient. Nothing will content the fellow but blood, vulgar red blood, and when he can get it he lays it on thick, and considers that he has produced a telling article. It's a poor notion. And, by some curious fatality, it is the most commonplace and brutal murders which always attract the most attention and get written up the most. For instance, I dare say that you never heard of the Harlesden case?'

'No; no, I don't remember anything about it.'

'Of course not. And yet the story is a curious one. I will tell it you over our coffee. Harlesden, you know, or I expect you don't know, is quite on the out-quarters of London; something curiously different from your fine old crusted suburb like Norwood or Hampstead, different as each of these is from the other. Hampstead, I mean, is where you look for the head of your great China house with his three acres of land and pine houses, though of late there is the artistic substratum;

while Norwood is the home of the prosperous middle-class family who took the house "because it was near the Palace", and sickened of the Palace six months afterwards; but Harlesden is a place of no character. it's too new to have any character as yet. There are the rows of red houses and the rows of white houses and the bright green Venetians, and the blistering doorways, and the little backyards they call gardens, and a few feeble shops, and then, just as you think you're going to grasp the physiognomy of the settlement, it all melts away.'

'How the dickens is that? The houses don't tumble down before one's eyes, I suppose!'

'Well, no, not exactly that. But Harlesden as an entity disappears. Your street turns into a quiet lane, and your staring houses into elm trees, and the back gardens into green meadows. You pass instantly from town to country; there is no transition as in a small country town, no soft gradations of wider lawns and orchards, with houses gradually becoming less dense, but a dead stop. I believe the people who live there mostly go into the City. I have seen once or twice a laden 'bus bound thitherwards. But however that may be, I can't conceive a greater loneliness in a desert at midnight than there is there at midday. It is like a city of the dead; the streets are glaring and desolate, and as you pass it suddenly strikes you that this too is part of London. Well, a year or two ago there was a doctor living there; he had set up his brass plate and his red lamp at the very end of one of those shining streets, and from the back of the house, the fields stretched away to the north. I don't know what his reason was in settling down in such an out-of-the-way place, perhaps Dr Black, as we will call him, was a far-seeing man and looked ahead. His relations, so it appeared afterwards, had lost sight of him for many years and didn't even know he was a doctor, much less where he lived. However, there he was settled in Harlesden, with some fragments of a practice, and an uncommonly pretty wife. People used to see them walking out together in the summer evenings soon after they came to Harlesden, and, so far as could be observed, they seemed a very affectionate couple. These walks went on through the autumn, and then ceased; but, of course, as the days grew dark and the weather cold, the lanes near Harlesden might be expected to lose many of their attractions. All through the winter nobody saw anything of Mrs Black; the doctor used to reply to his patients' inquiries that she was a "little out of sorts, would be better, no doubt, in the spring." But the spring came, and the summer, and no Mrs

Black appeared, and at last people began to rumour and talk amongst themselves, and all sorts of queer things were said at "high teas", which you may possibly have heard are the only form of entertainment known in such suburbs. Dr Black began to surprise some very odd looks cast in his direction, and the practice, such as it was, fell off before his eyes. In short, when the neighbours whispered about the matter, they whispered that Mrs Black was dead, and that the doctor had made away with her. But this wasn't the case; Mrs Black was seen alive in June. It was a Sunday afternoon, one of those few exquisite days that an English climate offers, and half London had strayed out into the fields, north, south, east, and west to smell the scent of the white May, and to see if the wild roses were yet in blossom in the hedges. I had gone out myself early in the morning, and had had a long ramble, and somehow or other as I was steering homeward I found myself in this very Harlesden we have been talking about. To be exact, I had a glass of beer in the "General Gordon", the most flourishing house in the neighbourhood, and as I was wandering rather aimlessly about, I saw an uncommonly tempting gap in a hedgerow, and resolved to explore the meadow beyond. Soft grass is very grateful to the feet after the infernal grit strewn on suburban sidewalks, and after walking about for some time I thought I should like to sit down on a bank and have a smoke. While I was getting out my pouch, I looked up in the direction of the houses, and as I looked I felt my breath caught back, and my teeth began to chatter, and the stick I had in one hand snapped in two with the grip I gave it. It was as if I had had an electric current down my spine, and yet for some moment of time which seemed long, but which must have been very short, I caught myself wondering what on earth was the matter. Then I knew what had made my very heart shudder and my bones grind together in an agony. As I glanced up I had looked straight towards the last house in the row before me, and in an upper window of that house I had seen for some short fraction of a second a face. It was the face of a woman, and yet it was not human. You and I, Salisbury, have heard in our time, as we sat in our seats in church in sober English fashion, of a lust that cannot be satiated and of a fire that is unquenchable, but few of us have any notion what these words mean. I hope you never may, for as I saw that face at the window, with the blue sky above me and the warm air playing in gusts about me, I knew I had looked into another world – looked through the window of a commonplace, brand new house, and seen hell open before me. When the first shock was over, I thought once or twice that I should have fainted; my face streamed with a cold sweat, and my breath came and went in sobs, as if I had been half drowned. I managed to get up at last, and walked round to the street, and there I saw the name "Dr Black" on the post by the front gate. As fate or my luck would have it, the door opened and a man came down the steps as I passed by. I had no doubt it was the doctor himself. He was of a type rather common in London; long and thin, with a pasty face and a dull black moustache. He gave me a look as we passed each other on the pavement, and though it was merely the casual glance which one foot passenger bestows on another, I felt convinced in my mind that here was an ugly customer to deal with. As you may imagine, I went my way a good deal puzzled and horrified too by what I had seen; for I had paid another visit to the "General Gordon", and had got together a good deal of the common gossip of the place about the Blacks. I didn't mention the fact that I had seen a woman's face in the window; but I heard that Mrs Black had been much admired for her beautiful golden hair, and round what had struck me with such a nameless terror, there was a mist of flowing yellow hair, as it were an aureole of glory round the visage of a satyr. The whole thing bothered me in an indescribable manner; and when I got home I tried my best to think of the impression I had received as an illusion, but it was no use. I knew very well I had seen what I have tried to describe to you, and I was morally certain that I had seen Mrs Black. And then there was the gossip of the place, the suspicion of foul play, which I knew to be false, and my own conviction that there was some deadly mischief or other going on in that bright red house at the corner of Devon Road: how to construct a theory of a reasonable kind out of these two elements. In short, I found myself in a world of mystery; I puzzled my head over it and filled up my leisure moments by gathering together odd threads of speculation, but I never moved a step towards any real solution, and as the summer days went on the matter seemed to grow misty and indistinct, shadowing some vague terror, like a nightmare of last month. I suppose it would before long have faded into the background of my brain – I should not have forgotten it, for such a thing could never be forgotten – but one morning as I was looking over the paper my eye was caught by a heading over some two dozen lines of small type. The words I had seen were simply, "The Harlesden Case", and I knew what I was going to read. Mrs Black was dead. Black had called in another medical man to certify as to cause of death, and something or other had aroused the strange doctor's suspicions and there had been an inquest and *post-mortem*. And the result? That, I will confess, did astonish me considerably; it was the triumph of the unexpected. The two doctors who made the autopsy were obliged to confess that they could not discover the faintest trace of any kind of foul play; their most exquisite tests and reagents failed to detect the presence of poison in the most infinitesimal quantity. Death, they found, had been caused by a somewhat obscure and scientifically interesting form of brain disease. The tissue of the brain and the molecules of the grey matter had undergone a most extraordinary series of changes; and the younger of the two doctors, who has some reputation, I believe, as a specialist in brain trouble, made some remarks in giving his evidence which struck me deeply at the time, though I did not then grasp their full significance. He said: "At the commencement of the examination I was astonished to find appearances of a character entirely new to me, notwithstanding my somewhat large experience. I need not specify these appearances at present, it will be sufficient for me to state that as I proceeded in my task I could scarcely believe that the brain before me was that of a human being at all." There was some surprise at this statement, as you may imagine, and the coroner asked the doctor if he meant to say that the brain resembled that of an animal. "No," he replied, "I should not put it in that way. Some of the appearances I noticed seemed to point in that direction, but others, and these were the more surprising, indicated a nervous organization of a wholly different character from that either of man or the lower animals." It was a curious thing to say, but of course the jury brought in a verdict of death from natural causes, and, so far as the public was concerned, the case came to an end. But after I had read what the doctor said I made up my mind that I should like to know a good deal more, and I set to work on what seemed likely to prove an interesting investigation. I had really a good deal of trouble, but I was successful in a measure. Though why – my dear fellow, I had no notion at the time. Are you aware that we have been here nearly four hours? The waiters are staring at us. Let's have the bill and be gone.'

The two men went out in silence, and stood a moment in the cool air, watching the hurrying traffic of Coventry Street pass before them to the accompaniment of the ringing bells of hansoms and the cries of the newsboys; the deep far murmur of London surging up ever and again from beneath these louder noises.

'It is a strange case, isn't it?' said Dyson at length. 'What do you think of it?'

'My dear fellow, I haven't heard the end, so I will reserve my opinion. When will you give me the sequel?'

'Come to my rooms some evening; say next Thursday. Here's the address. Good night; I want to get down to the Strand.' Dyson hailed a passing hansom, and Salisbury turned northward to walk home to his lodgings.

II

Mr Salisbury, as may have been gathered from the few remarks which he had found it possible to introduce in the course of the evening, was a young gentleman of a peculiarly solid form of intellect, coy and retiring before the mysterious and the uncommon, with a constitutional dislike of paradox. During the restaurant dinner he had been forced to listen in almost absolute silence to a strange tissue of improbabilities strung together with the ingenuity of a born meddler in plots and mysteries, and it was with a feeling of weariness that he crossed Shaftesbury Avenue, and dived into the recesses of Soho, for his lodgings were in a modest neighbourhood to the north of Oxford Street. As he walked he speculated on the probable fate of Dyson, relying on literature, unbefriended by a thoughtful relative, and could not help concluding that so much subtlety united to a too vivid imagination would in all likelihood have been rewarded with a pair of sandwich boards or a super's banner. Absorbed in this train of thought, and admiring the perverse dexterity which could transmute the face of a sickly woman and a case of brain disease into the crude elements of romance, Salisbury strayed on through the dimly-lighted streets, not noticing the gusty wind which drove sharply round corners and whirled the stray rubbish of the pavement into the air in eddies, while black clouds gathered over the sickly yellow moon. Even a stray drop or two of rain blown into his face did not rouse him from his meditations, and it was only when with a sudden rush the storm tore down upon the street that he began to consider the expediency of finding some shelter. The rain, driven by the wind, pelted down with the violence of a thunderstorm, dashing up from the stones and hissing through the air, and soon a perfect torrent of water coursed along the kennels and accumulated in pools over the choked-up drains. The few stray passengers who had been loafing rather than walking about the street had scuttered away, like frightened rabbits, to some invisible places of refuge, and though

Salisbury whistled loud and long for a hansom, no hansom appeared. He looked about him, as if to discover how far he might be from the haven of Oxford Street, but strolling carelessly along, he had turned out of his way, and found himself in an unknown region, and one to all appearance devoid even of a public house where shelter could be bought for the modest sum of twopence. The street lamps were few and at long intervals, and burned behind grimy glasses with the sickly light of oil, and by this wavering glimmer Salisbury could make out the shadowy and vast old houses of which the street was composed. As he passed along, hurrying, and shrinking from the full sweep of the rain, he noticed the innumerable bell handles, with names that seemed about to vanish of old age graven on brass plates beneath them, and here and there a richly carved penthouse overhung the door, blackening with the grime of fifty years. The storm seemed to grow more and more furious; he was wet through, and a new hat had become a ruin, and still Oxford Street seemed as far off as ever; it was with deep relief that the dripping man caught sight of a dark archway which seemed to promise shelter from the rain if not from the wind. Salisbury took up his position in the driest corner and looked about him; he was standing in a kind of passage contrived under part of a house, and behind him stretched a narrow footway leading between blank walls to regions unknown. He had stood there for some time, vainly endeavouring to rid himself of some of his superfluous moisture, and listening for the passing wheel of a hansom, when his attention was aroused by a loud noise coming from the direction of the passage behind, and growing louder as it drew nearer. In a couple of minutes he could make out the shrill, raucous voice of a woman, threatening and renouncing, and making the very stones echo with her accents, while now and then a man grumbled and expostulated. Though to all appearance devoid of romance, Salisbury had some relish for street rows, and was, indeed, somewhat of an amateur in the more amusing phases of drunkenness; he therefore composed himself to listen and observe with something of the air of a subscriber to grand opera. To his annoyance, however, the tempest seemed suddenly to be composed, and he could hear nothing but the impatient steps of the woman and the slow lurch of the man as they came towards him. Keeping back in the shadow of the wall, he could see the two drawing nearer; the man was evidently drunk, and had much ado to avoid frequent collision with the wall as he tacked across from one side to the other, like some bark beating up against a wind. The woman was looking straight in front of her, with tears streaming from her eyes, but suddenly as they went by the flame blazed up again, and she burst forth into a torrent of abuse, facing round upon her companion.

'You low rascal, you mean, contemptible cur,' she went on, after an incoherent storm of curses, 'you think I'm to work and slave for you always, I suppose, while you're after that Green Street girl and drinking every penny you've got? But you're mistaken, Sam – indeed, I'll bear it no longer. Damn you, you dirty thief, I've done with you and your master too, so you can go your own errands, and I only hope they'll get you into trouble.'

The woman tore at the bosom of her dress, and taking something out that looked like paper, crumpled it up and flung it away. It fell at Salisbury's feet. She ran out and disappeared in the darkness, while the man lurched slowly into the street, grumbling indistinctly to himself in a perplexed tone of voice. Salisbury looked out after him and saw him maundering along the pavement, halting now and then and swaying indecisively, and then starting off at some fresh tangent. The sky had cleared, and white fleecy clouds were fleeting across the moon, high in the heaven. The light came and went by turns, as the clouds passed by, and, turning round as the clear, white rays shone into the passage, Salisbury saw the little ball of crumpled paper which the woman had cast down. Oddly curious to know what it might contain, he picked it up and put it in his pocket, and set out afresh on his journey.

III

Salisbury was a man of habit. When he got home, drenched to the skin, his clothes hanging lank about him, and a ghastly dew besmearing his hat, his only thought was of his health, of which he took studious care. So, after changing his clothes and encasing himself in a warm dressing-gown, he proceeded to prepare a sudorific in the shape of a hot gin and water, warming the latter over one of those spirit lamps which mitigate the austerities of the modern hermit's life. By the time this preparation had been exhibited, and Salisbury's disturbed feelings had been soothed by a pipe of tobacco, he was able to get into bed in a happy state of vacancy, without a thought of his adventure in the dark archway, or of the weird fancies with which Dyson had seasoned his dinner. It was the same at breakfast the next morning, for Salisbury made a point of not thinking of any thing until that meal was over; but when the cup and saucer were cleared away, and the morning pipe was lit, he remembered the little ball of paper, and began fumbling in the pockets of his wet coat. He did not remember into which pocket he had put it, and as he dived now into one and now into another, he experienced a strange feeling of apprehension lest it should not be there at all, though he could not for the life of him have explained the importance he attached to what was in all probability mere rubbish. But he sighed with relief when his fingers touched the crumpled surface in an inside pocket, and he drew it out gently and laid it on the little desk by his easy chair with as much care as if it had been some rare jewel. Salisbury sat smoking and staring at his find for a few minutes, an odd temptation to throw the thing in the fire and have done with it struggling with as odd a speculation as to its possible contents, and as to the reason why the infuriated woman should have flung a bit of paper from her with such vehemence. As might be expected, it was the latter feeling that conquered in the end, and yet it was with something like repugnance that he at last took the paper and unrolled it, and laid it out before him. It was a piece of common dirty paper, to all appearance torn out of a cheap exercise book, and in the middle were a few lines written in a queer cramped hand. Salisbury bent his head and stared eagerly at it for a moment, drawing a long breath, and then fell back in his chair gazing blankly before him, till at last with a sudden revulsion he burst into a peal of laughter, so long and loud and uproarious that the landlady's baby on the floor below awoke from sleep and echoed his mirth with hideous yells. But he laughed again and again, and took the paper up to read a second time what seemed such meaningless nonsense.

> 'Q. has had to go and see his friends in Paris,' it began. 'Traverse Handel S. "Once around the grass, and twice around the lass, and thrice around the maple tree."'

Salisbury took up the paper and crumpled it as the angry woman had done, and aimed it at the fire. He did not throw it there, however, but tossed it carelessly into the well of the desk, and laughed again. The sheer folly of the thing offended him, and he was ashamed of his own eager speculation, as one who pores over the high-sounding announcements in the agony column of the daily paper, and finds nothing but advertisement and triviality. He walked to the window, and stared out at the languid morning life of his quarter; the maids in slatternly print dresses washing doorsteps, the fishmonger and the butcher on their rounds, and the tradesmen standing at the doors of their small shops, drooping for lack of trade and excitement. In the distance a blue haze gave some grandeur to the prospect, but the view as a whole was depressing, and would only have interested a student of the life of London, who finds something rare and choice in its very aspect. Salisbury turned away in disgust, and settled himself in the easy chair, upholstered in a bright shade of green, and decked with yellow gimp, which was the pride and attraction of the apartments. Here he composed himself to his morning's occupation – the perusal of a novel that dealt with sport and love in a manner that suggested the collaboration of a stud groom and a ladies' college. In an ordinary way, however, Salisbury would have been carried on by the interest of the story up to lunchtime, but this morning he fidgeted in and out of his chair, took the book up and laid it down again, and swore at last to himself and at himself in mere irritation. In point of fact the jingle of the paper found in the archway had 'got into his head', and do what he would he could not help muttering over and over, 'Once around the grass, and twice around the lass, and thrice around the maple tree.' It became a positive pain, like the foolish burden of a music hall song, everlastingly quoted, and sung at all hours of the day and night, and treasured by the street boys as an unfailing resource for six months together. He went out into the streets, and tried to forget his enemy in the jostling of the crowds and the roar and clatter of the traffic, but presently he would find himself stealing quietly aside, and pacing some deserted byway, vainly puzzling his brains, and trying to fix some meaning to phrases that were meaningless. It was a positive relief when Thursday came, and he remembered that he had made an appointment to go and see Dyson; the flimsy reveries of the self-styled man of letters appeared entertaining when compared with this ceaseless iteration, this maze of thought from which there seemed no possibility of escape. Dyson's abode was in one of the quietest of the quiet streets that led down from the Strand to the river, and when Salisbury passed from the narrow stairway into his friend's room, he saw that the uncle had been beneficent indeed. The floor glowed and flamed with all the colours of the East; it was, as Dyson pompously remarked, 'a sunset in a dream', and the lamplight, the twilight of London streets, was shut out with strangely worked curtains, glittering here and there with threads of gold. In the shelves of an oak *armoire* stood jars and plates of old French china, and the black and white of etchings not to be found in the Haymarket or in Bond Street, stood out against the splendour of a Japanese paper. Salisbury sat down on the settle by the hearth, and sniffed the mingled fumes of incense and tobacco, wondering and dumb before all this splendour after the green rep and the oleographs, the gilt-framed mirror, and the lustres of his own apartment.

'I am glad you have come,' said Dyson. 'Comfortable little room, isn't it? But you don't look very well, Salisbury. Nothing disagreed with you, has it?'

'No; but I have been a good deal bothered for the last few days. The fact is I had an odd kind of – of – adventure, I suppose I may call it, that night I saw you, and it has worried me a good deal. And the provoking part of it is that it's the merest nonsense – but, however, I will tell you all about it, by and by. You were going to let me have the rest of that odd story you began at the restaurant.'

'Yes. But I am afraid, Salisbury, you are incorrigible. You are a slave to what you call matter of fact. You know perfectly well that in your heart you think the oddness in that case is of my making, and that it is all really as plain as the police reports. However, as I have begun, I will go on. But first we will have something to drink, and you may as well light your pipe.'

Dyson went up to the oak cupboard, and drew from its depths a rotund bottle and two little glasses, quaintly gilded.

'It's Benedictine,' he said. 'You'll have some, won't you?'

Salisbury assented, and the two men sat sipping and smoking reflectively for some minutes before Dyson began.

'Let me see,' he said at last, 'we were at the inquest, weren't we? No, we had done with that. Ah, I remember. I was telling you that on the whole I had been successful in my inquiries, investigation, or whatever you like to call it, into the matter. Wasn't that where I left off?'

'Yes, that was it. To be precise, I think "though" was the last word you said on the matter.'

'Exactly. I have been thinking it all over since the other night, and I have come to the conclusion that that "though" is a very big "though" indeed. Not to put too fine a point on it, I have had to confess that what I found out, or thought I found out, amounts in reality to nothing. I am as far away from the heart of the case as ever. However, I may as well tell you what I do know. You may remember my saying that I was impressed a good deal by some remarks of one of the doctors who gave evidence at the inquest. Well, I determined that my first step must be to try if I could get something more definite and intelligible out of that doctor. Somehow or other I managed to get an introduction to the man, and he gave me an appointment to come and see him. He turned out to be a pleasant, genial fellow; rather young and not in the least like the typical medical man, and he began the conference by offering me whisky and cigars. I didn't think it worth while to beat about the bush, so I began by saying that part of his evidence at the Harlesden inquest struck me as very peculiar, and I gave him the printed report, with the sentences in question underlined. He just glanced at the slip, and gave me a queer look. "It struck you as peculiar, did it?" said he. "Well, you must remember that the Harlesden case was very peculiar. In fact, I think I may safely say that in some features it was unique – quite unique." "Quite so," I replied, "and that's exactly why it interests me, and why I want to know more about it. And I thought that if anybody could give me any information it would be you. What is your opinion of the matter?"

'It was a pretty downright sort of question, and my doctor looked rather taken aback.

'"Well," he said, "as I fancy your motive in inquiring into the question must be mere curiosity, I think I may tell you my opinion with tolerable freedom. So, Mr, Mr Dyson? if you want to know my theory, it is this: I believe that Dr Black killed his wife."

'"But the verdict," I answered, "the verdict was given from your own evidence."

'"Quite so; the verdict was given in accordance with the evidence of my colleague and myself, and, under the circumstances, I think the jury acted very sensibly. In fact, I don't see what else they could have done. But I stick to my opinion, mind you, and I say this also. I don't wonder at Black's doing what I firmly believe he did. I think he was justified."

'"Justified! How could that be?" I asked. I was astonished, as you may imagine, at the answer I had got. The doctor wheeled round his chair and looked steadily at me for a moment before he answered.

'"I suppose you are not a man of science yourself? No; then it would be of no use my going into detail. I have always been firmly opposed myself to any partnership between physiology and psychology. I believe that both are bound to suffer. No one recognises more decidedly than I do the impassable gulf, the fathomless abyss that separates the world of consciousness from the sphere of matter. We know that every change of consciousness is accompanied by a rearrangement of the molecules in the grey matter; and that is all. What the link between them is, or why they occur together, we do not know, and most authorities believe that we never can know. Yet, I will tell you that as I did my work, the knife in my hand, I felt convinced, in spite of all theories, that what lay before me was not the brain of a dead woman – not the brain of a human being at all. Of course I saw the face; but it was quite placid, devoid of all expression. It must have been a beautiful face, no doubt, but I can honestly say that I would not have looked in that face when there was life behind it for a thousand guineas, no, nor for twice that sum."

'"My dear sir," I said, "you surprise me extremely. You say that it was not the brain of a human being. What was it then?"

'"The brain of a devil." He spoke quite coolly, and never moved a muscle. "The brain of a devil," he repeated, "and I have no doubt that Black found some way of putting an end to it. I don't blame him if he did. Whatever Mrs Black was, she was not fit to stay in this world. Will you have anything more? No? Good night, good night."

'It was a queer sort of opinion to get from a man of science, wasn't it? When he was saying that he would not have looked on that face when alive for a thousand guineas, or two thousand guineas, I was thinking of the face I had seen, but I said nothing. I went again to Harlesden, and passed from one shop to another, making small purchases, and trying to find out whether there was anything about the Blacks which was not already common property, but there was very little to hear. One of the tradesmen to whom I spoke said he had known the dead woman well; she used to buy of him such quantities of grocery as were required for their small household, for they never kept a servant, but had a charwoman in occasionally, and she had not seen Mrs Black for months before she died. According to this man Mrs Black was "a nice lady", always kind and considerate, and so fond of her husband and he of her, as every one thought. And yet, to put the doctor's opinion on one side, I knew what I had seen. And then after thinking it all over, and putting one thing with another, it seemed to me that the only person likely to give me much assistance would be Black himself, and I made up my mind to find him. Of course he wasn't to be found in Harlesden; he had left, I was told, directly after the funeral. Everything in the house had been sold, and one fine day Black got into the train with a small portmanteau, and went, nobody knew where. It was a chance if he were ever heard of again, and it was by a mere chance that

I came across him at last. I was walking one day along Gray's Inn Road, not bound for anywhere in particular, but looking about me, as usual, and holding on to my hat, for it was a gusty day in early March, and the wind was making the treetops in the Inn rock and quiver. I had come up from the Holborn end, and I had almost got to Theobald's Road when I noticed a man walking in front of me, leaning on a stick, and to all appearance very feeble. There was something about his look that made me curious, I don't know why, and I began to walk briskly with the idea of overtaking him, when of a sudden his hat blew off and came bounding along the pavement to my feet. Of course I rescued the hat, and gave it a glance as I went towards its owner. It was a biography in itself; a Piccadilly maker's name in the inside, but I don't think a beggar would have picked it out of the gutter. Then I looked up and saw Dr Black of Harlesden waiting for me. A queer thing, wasn't it? But, Salisbury, what a change! When I saw Dr Black come down the steps of his house at Harlesden he was an upright man, walking firmly with well-built limbs; a man, I should say, in the prime of his life. And now before me there crouched this wretched creature, bent and feeble, with shrunken cheeks, and hair that was whitening fast, and limbs that trembled and shook together, and misery in his eyes. He thanked me for bringing him his hat, saying, "I don't think I should ever have got it, I can't run much now. A gusty day, sir, isn't it?" and with this he was turning away, but by little and little I contrived to draw him into the current of conversation, and we walked together eastward. I think the man would have been glad to get rid of me; but I didn't intend to let him go, and he stopped at last in front of a miserable house in a miserable street. It was, I verily believe, one of the most wretched quarters I have ever seen: houses that must have been sordid and hideous enough when new, that had gathered foulness with every year, and now seemed to lean and totter to their fall. "I live up there," said Black, pointing to the tiles, "not in the front – in the back. I am very quiet there. I won't ask you to come in now, but perhaps some other day – " I caught him up at that, and told him I should be only too glad to come and see him. He gave me an odd sort of glance, as if he were wondering what on earth I or anybody else could care about him, and I left him fumbling with his latchkey. I think you will say I did pretty well when I tell you that within a few weeks I had made myself an intimate friend of Black's. I shall never forget the first time I went to his room; I hope I shall never see such abject, squalid misery again. The foul paper, from which all pattern or trace of a pattern had long vanished, subdued and penetrated with the grime of the evil street, was hanging in mouldering pennons from the wall. Only at the end of the room was it possible to stand upright, and the sight of the wretched bed and the odour of corruption that pervaded the place made me turn faint and sick. Here I found him munching a piece of bread; he seemed surprised to find that I had kept my promise, but he gave me his chair and sat on the bed while we talked. I used to go to see him often, and we had long conversations together, but he never mentioned Harlesden or his wife. I fancy that he supposed me ignorant of the matter, or thought that if I had heard of it, I should never connect the respectable Dr Black of Harlesden with a poor garreteer in the backwoods of London. He was a strange man, and as we sat together smoking, I often wondered whether he were mad or sane, for I think the wildest dreams of Paracelsus and the Rosicrucians would appear plain and sober fact compared with the theories I have heard him earnestly advance in that grimy den of his. I once ventured to hint something of the sort to him. I suggested that something he had said was in flat contradiction to all science and all experience. "No," he answered, "not all experience, for mine counts for something. I am no dealer in unproved theories; what I say I have proved for myself, and at a terrible cost. There is a region of knowledge which you will never know, which wise men seeing from afar off shun like the plague, as well they may, but into that region I have gone. If you knew, if you could even dream of what may be done, of what one or two men have done in this quiet world of ours, your very soul would shudder and faint within you. What you have heard from me has been but the merest husk and outer covering of true science – that science which means death, and that which is more awful than death, to those who gain it. No, when men say that there are strange things in the world, they little know the awe and the terror that dwell always with them and about them." There was a sort of fascination about the man that drew me to him, and I was quite sorry to have to leave London for a month or two; I missed his odd talk. A few days after I came back to town I thought I would look him up, but when I gave the two rings at the bell that used to summon him, there was no answer. I rang and rang again, and was just turning to go away, when the door opened and a dirty woman asked me what I wanted. From her look I fancy she took me for a plain clothes officer after one of her lodgers, but when I inquired if Mr Black were in, she gave me a stare of another kind. "There's no Mr Black lives here," she said. "He's gone. He's dead this six weeks. I always thought he was a bit queer in his head, or else had been and got into some trouble or other. He used to go out every morning from ten till one, and one Monday morning we heard him come in, and go into his room and shut the door, and a few minutes after, just as we was a-sitting down to our dinner, there was such a scream that I thought I should have gone right off. And then we heard a stamping, and down he came, raging and cursing most dreadful, swearing he had been robbed of something that was worth millions. And then he just dropped down in the passage, and we thought he was dead. We got him up to his room, and put him on his bed, and I just sat there and waited, while my 'usband he went for the doctor. And there was the winder wide open, and a little tin box he had lying on the floor open and empty, but of course nobody could possible have got in at the winder, and as for him having anything that was worth anything, it's nonsense, for he was often weeks and weeks behind with his rent, and my 'usband he threatened often and often to turn him into the street, for, as he said, we've got a living to myke like other people – and, of course, that's true; but, somehow, I didn't like to do it, though he was an odd kind of a man, and I fancy had been better off. And then the doctor came and looked at him, and said as he couldn't do nothing, and that night he died as I was a-sitting by his bed; and I can tell you that, with one thing and another, we lost money by him, for the few bits of clothes as he had were worth next to nothing when they came to be sold." I gave the woman half a sovereign for her trouble, and went home thinking of Dr Black and the epitaph she had made him, and wondering at his strange fancy that he had been robbed. I take it that he had very little to fear on that score, poor fellow; but I suppose that he was really mad, and died in a sudden access of his mania. His landlady said that once or twice when she had had occasion to go into his room (to dun the poor wretch for his rent, most likely), he would keep her at the door for about a minute, and that when she came in she would find him putting away his tin box in the corner by the window; I suppose he had become possessed with the idea of some great treasure, and fancied himself a wealthy man in the midst of all his misery. *Explicit*, my tale is ended, and you see that though I knew Black, I know nothing of his wife or of the history of her death. – That's the Harlesden case, Salisbury, and I think it interests me all the more deeply because there does not seem the shadow of a possibility that I or any one else will ever know more about it. What do you think of it?'

'Well, Dyson, I must say that I think you have contrived to surround the whole thing with a mystery of your own making. I go for the doctor's solution: Black murdered his wife, being himself in all probability an undeveloped lunatic.'

'What? Do you believe, then, that this woman was something too awful, too terrible to be allowed to remain on the earth? You will remember that the doctor said it was the brain of a devil?'

'Yes, yes, but he was speaking, of course, metaphorically. it's really quite a simple matter if you only look at it like that.'

'Ah, well, you may be right; but yet I am sure you are not. Well, well, it's no good discussing it any more. A little more Benedictine? That's right; try some of this tobacco. Didn't you say that you had been bothered by something – something which happened that night we dined together?'

'Yes, I have been worried, Dyson, worried a great deal. I – But it's such a trivial matter – indeed, such an absurdity – that I feel ashamed to trouble you with it.'

'Never mind, let's have it, absurd or not.'

With many hesitations, and with much inward resentment of the folly of the thing, Salisbury told his tale, and repeated reluctantly the absurd intelligence and the absurder doggerel of the scrap of paper, expecting to hear Dyson burst out into a roar of laughter.

'Isn't it too bad that I should let myself be bothered by such stuff as that?' he asked, when he had stuttered out the jingle of once, and twice, and thrice.

Dyson listened to it all gravely, even to the end, and meditated for a few minutes in silence.

'Yes,' he said at length, 'it was a curious chance, your taking shelter in that archway just as those two went by. But I don't know that I should call what was written on the paper nonsense; it is bizarre certainly, but I expect it has a meaning for somebody. Just repeat it again, will you, and I will write it down. Perhaps we might find a cipher of some sort, though I hardly think we shall.'

Again had the reluctant lips of Salisbury slowly to stammer out the rubbish that he abhorred, while Dyson jotted it down on a slip of paper.

'Look over it, will you?' he said, when it was done; 'it may be important that I should have every word in its place. Is that all right?'

'Yes; that is an accurate copy. But I don't think you will get much out of it. Depend upon it, it is mere nonsense, a wanton scribble. I must be going now, Dyson. No, no more; that stuff of yours is pretty strong. Good night.'

'I suppose you would like to hear from me, if I did find out anything?'

'No, not I; I don't want to hear about the thing again. You may regard the discovery, if it is one, as your own.'

'Very well. Good night.'

IV

A good many hours after Salisbury had returned to the company of the green rep chairs, Dyson still sat at his desk, itself a Japanese romance, smoking many pipes, and meditating over his friend's story. The bizarre quality of the inscription which had annoyed Salisbury was to him an attraction, and now and again he took it up and scanned thoughtfully what he had written, especially the quaint jingle at the end. It was a token, a symbol, he decided, and not a cipher, and the woman who had flung it away was in all probability entirely ignorant of its meaning; she was but the agent of the 'Sam' she had abused and discarded, and he too was again the agent of some one unknown, possibly of the individual styled Q, who had been forced to visit his French friends. But what to make of 'Traverse Handel S.' Here was the root and source of the enigma, and not all the tobacco of Virginia seemed likely to suggest any clue here. It seemed almost hopeless, but Dyson regarded himself as the Wellington of mysteries, and went to bed feeling assured that sooner or later he would hit upon the right track. For the next few days he was deeply engaged in his literary labours, labours which were a profound mystery even to the most intimate of his friends, who searched the railway bookstalls in vain for the result of so many hours spent at the Japanese bureau in company with strong tobacco and black tea. On this occasion Dyson confined himself to his room for four days, and it was with genuine relief that he laid down his pen and went out into the streets in quest of relaxation and fresh air. The gas lamps were being lighted, and the fifth edition of the evening papers was being howled through the streets, and Dyson, feeling that he wanted quiet, turned away from the clamorous Strand, and began to trend away to the north-west. Soon he found himself in streets that echoed to his footsteps, and crossing a broad new thoroughfare, and verging still to the west, Dyson discovered that he had penetrated to the depths of Soho. Here again was life; rare vintages of France and Italy, at prices which seemed contemptibly small, allured the passer-by; here were cheeses, vast and rich, here olive oil, and here a grove of Rabelaisian sausages; while in a neighbouring shop the whole Press of Paris appeared to be on sale. In the middle of the roadway a strange miscellany of nations sauntered to and fro, for there cab and hansom rarely ventured; and from window over window the inhabitants looked forth in pleased contemplation of the scene. Dyson made his way slowly along, mingling with the crowd on the cobblestones, listening to the queer babel of French and German, and Italian and English, glancing now and again at the shop windows with their levelled batteries of bottles, and had almost gained the end of the street, when his attention was arrested by a small shop at the corner, a vivid contrast to its neighbours. It was the typical shop of the poor quarter; a shop entirely English. Here were vended tobacco and sweets, cheap pipes of clay and cherry wood; penny exercise bookss and penholders jostled for precedence with comic songs, and story papers with appalling cuts showed that romance claimed its place beside the actualities of the evening paper, the bills of which fluttered at the doorway. Dyson glanced up at the name above the door, and stood by the kennel trembling, for a sharp pang, the pang of one who has made a discovery, had for a moment left him incapable of motion. The name over the shop was Travers. Dyson looked up again, this time at the corner of the wall above the lamp pose, and read in white letters on a blue ground the words 'Handel Street, W. C.,' and the legend was repeated in fainter letters just below. He gave a little sigh of satisfaction, and without more ado walked boldly into the shop, and stared full in the face the fat man who was sitting behind the counter. The fellow rose to his feet, and returned the stare a little curiously, and then began in stereotyped phrase –

'What can I do for you, sir?'

Dyson enjoyed the situation and a dawning perplexity on the man's face. He propped his stick carefully against the counter and leaning over it, said slowly and impressively –

'Once around the grass, and twice around the lass, and thrice around the maple tree.'

Dyson had calculated on his words producing an effect, and he was not disappointed. The vendor of miscellanies gasped, open-mouthed like a fish, and steadied himself against the counter. When he spoke, after a short interval, it was in a hoarse mutter, tremulous and unsteady.

'Would you mind saying that again, sir? I didn't quite catch it.'

'My good man, I shall most certainly do nothing of the kind. You heard what I said perfectly well. You have got a clock in your shop, I see; an admirable timekeeper, I have no doubt. Well, I give you a minute by your own clock.'

The man looked about him in a perplexed indecision, and Dyson felt that it was time to be bold.

'Look here, Travers, the time is nearly up. You have heard of Q, I think. Remember, I hold your life in my hands. Now!'

Dyson was shocked at the result of his own audacity. The man shrank and shrivelled in terror, the sweat poured down a face of ashy white, and he held up his hands before him.

'Mr Davies, Mr Davies, don't say that – don't for Heaven's sake. I didn't know you at first, I didn't indeed. Good God! Mr Davies, you wouldn't ruin me? I'll get it in a moment.'

'You had better not lose any more time.'

The man slunk piteously out of his own shop, and went into a back parlour. Dyson heard his trembling fingers fumbling with a bunch of keys, and the creak of an opening box. He came back presently with a small package neatly tied up in brown paper in his hands, and, still full of terror, handed it to Dyson.

'I'm glad to be rid of it,' he said. 'I'll take no more jobs of this sort.'

Dyson took the parcel and his stick, and walked out of the shop with a nod, turning round as he passed the door. Travers had sunk into his seat, his face still white with terror, with one hand over his eyes, and Dyson speculated a good deal as he walked rapidly away as to what queer chords those could be on which he had played so roughly. He hailed the first hansom he could see and drove home, and when he had lit his hanging lamp, and laid his parcel on the table, he paused for a moment, wondering on what strange thing the lamplight would soon shine. He locked his door, and cut the strings, and unfolded the paper layer after layer, and came at last to a small wooden box, simply but solidly made. There was no lock, and Dyson had simply to raise the lid, and as he did so he drew a long breath and started back. The lamp seemed to glimmer feebly like a single candle, but the whole room blazed with light – and not with light alone, but with a thousand colours, with all the glories of some painted window; and upon the walls of his room and on the familiar furniture, the glow flamed back and seemed to flow again to its source, the little wooden box. For there upon a bed of soft wool lay the most splendid jewel, a jewel such as Dyson had never dreamed of, and within it shone the blue of far skies, and the green of the sea by the shore, and the red of the ruby, and deep violet rays, and in the middle of all it seemed aflame as if a fountain of fire rose up, and fell, and rose again with sparks like stars for drops. Dyson gave a long deep sigh, and dropped into his chair, and put his hands over his eyes to think. The jewel was like an opal, but from a long experience of the shop windows he knew there was no such thing as an opal one-quarter or one-eighth of its size. He looked at the stone again, with a feeling that was almost awe, and placed it gently on the table under the lamp, and watched the wonderful flame that shone and sparkled in its centre, and then turned to the box, curious to know whether it might contain other marvels. He lifted the bed of wool on which the opal had reclined, and saw beneath, no more jewels, but a little old pocketbook, worn and shabby with use. Dyson opened it at the first leaf, and dropped the book again appalled. He had read the name of the owner, neatly written in blue ink:

Steven Black, M. D.
Oranmore
Devon Road
Harlesden

It was several minutes before Dyson could bring himself to open the book a second time; he remembered the wretched exile in his garret; and his strange talk, and the memory too of the face he had seen at the window, and of what the specialist had said, surged up in his mind, and as he held his finger on the cover, he shivered, dreading what might be written within. When at last he held it in his hand, and turned the pages, he found that the first two leaves were blank, but the third was covered with clear, minute writing, and Dyson began to read with the light of the opal flaming in his eyes.

V

'Ever since I was a young man' – the record began – 'I devoted all my leisure and a good deal of time that ought to have been given to other studies to the investigation of curious and obscure branches of knowledge. What are commonly called the pleasures of life had never any attractions for me, and I lived alone in London, avoiding my fellow students, and in my turn avoided by them as a man self-absorbed and unsympathetic. So long as I could gratify my desire of knowledge of a peculiar kind, knowledge of which the very existence is a profound secret to most men, I was intensely happy, and I have often spent whole nights sitting in the darkness of my room, and thinking of the strange world on the brink of which I trod. My professional studies, however, and the necessity of obtaining a degree, for some time forced my more obscure employment into the background, and soon after I had qualified I met Agnes, who became my wife. We took a new house in this remote suburb, and I began the regular routine of a sober practice, and for some months lived happily enough, sharing in the life about me, and only thinking at odd intervals of that occult science which had once fascinated my whole being. I had learnt enough of the paths I had begun to tread to know that they were beyond all expression difficult and dangerous, that to persevere meant in all probability the wreck of a life, and that they led to regions so terrible, that the mind of man shrinks appalled at the very thought. Moreover, the quiet and the peace I had enjoyed since my marriage had wiled me away to a great extent from places where I knew no peace could dwell. But suddenly – I think indeed it was the work of a single night, as I lay awake on my bed gazing into the darkness – suddenly, I say, the old desire, the former longing, returned, and returned with a force that had been intensified ten times by its absence; and when the day dawned and I looked out of the window, and saw with haggard eyes the sunrise in the east, I knew that my doom had been pronounced; that as I had gone far, so now I must go farther with unfaltering steps. I turned to the bed where my wife was sleeping peacefully, and lay down again, weeping bitter tears, for the sun had set on our happy life and had risen with a dawn of terror to us both. I will not set down here in minute detail what followed; outwardly I went about the day's labour as before, saying nothing to my wife. But she soon saw that I had changed; I spent my spare time in a room which I had fitted up as a laboratory, and often I crept upstairs in the grey dawn of the morning, when the light of many lamps still glowed over London; and each night I had stolen a step nearer to that great abyss which I was to bridge over, the gulf between the world of consciousness and the world of matter. My experiments were many and complicated in their nature, and it was some months before I realised whither they all pointed, and when this was borne in upon me in a moment's time, I felt my face whiten and my heart still within me. But the power to draw back, the power to stand before the doors that now opened wide before me and not to enter in, had long ago been absent; the way was closed, and I could only pass onward. My position was as utterly hopeless as that of the prisoner in an utter dungeon, whose only light is that of the dungeon above him; the doors were shut and escape was impossible. Experiment after experiment gave the same result, and I knew, and shrank even as the thought passed through my mind, that in the work I had to do there must be elements which no laboratory could furnish, which no scales could ever measure. In that work, from which even I doubted to escape with life, life itself must enter; from some human being there must be drawn that essence which men call the soul, and in its place (for in the scheme of the world there is no vacant chamber) – in its place would enter in what the lips can hardly utter, what the mind cannot conceive without a horror more awful than the horror of death itself. And when I knew this, I knew also on whom this fate would fall; I looked into my wife's eyes. Even at that hour, if I had gone out and taken a rope and hanged myself, I might have escaped, and she also, but in no other way. At last I told her all. She shuddered, and wept, and called on her dead mother for help, and asked me if I had no mercy, and I could only sigh. I concealed nothing from her; I told her what she would become, and what would enter in where her life had been; I told her of all the shame and of all the horror. You who will read this when I am dead – if indeed I allow this record to survive, – you who have opened the box and have seen what lies there, if you could understand what lies hidden in that opal! For one night my wife consented to what I asked of her, consented with the tears running down her beautiful face, and hot shame flushing red over her neck and breast, consented to undergo this for me. I threw open the window, and we looked together at the sky and the dark earth for the last time; it was a fine starlight night, and there was a pleasant breeze blowing, and I kissed her on her lips, and her tears ran down upon my face. That night she came down to my laboratory, and there, with shutters bolted and barred down, with curtains drawn thick and close, so that the very stars might be shut out from the sight of that room, while the crucible hissed and boiled over the lamp, I did what had to be done, and led out what was no longer a woman. But on the table the opal flamed and sparkled with such light as no eyes of man have ever gazed on, and the rays of the flame that was within it flashed and glittered, and shone even to my heart. My wife had only asked one thing of me; that when there came at last what I had told her, I would kill her. I have kept that promise.'

There was nothing more. Dyson let the little pocketbook fall, and turned and looked again at the opal with its flaming inmost light, and then with unutterable irresistible horror surging up in his heart, grasped the jewel, and flung it on the ground, and trampled it beneath his heel. His face was white with terror as he turned away, and for a moment stood sick and trembling, and then with a start he leapt across the room and steadied himself against the door. There was an angry hiss, as of steam escaping under great pressure, and as he gazed, motionless, a volume of heavy yellow smoke was slowly issuing from the very centre of the jewel, and wreathing itself in snake-like coils above it. And then a thin white flame burst forth from the smoke, and shot up into the air and vanished; and on the ground there lay a thing like a cinder, black and crumbling to the touch.

The Shining Pyramid

I
The Arrowhead Character

'Haunted, you said?'

'Yes, haunted. Don't you remember, when I saw you three years ago, you told me about your place in the west with the ancient woods hanging all about it, and the wild, domed hills, and the ragged land? It has always remained a sort of enchanted picture in my mind as I sit at my desk and hear the traffic rattling in the street in the midst of whirling London. But when did you come up?'

'The fact is, Dyson, I have only just got out of the train. I drove to the station early this morning and caught the 10.45.'

'Well, I am very glad you looked in on me. How have you been getting on since we last met? There is no Mrs Vaughan, I suppose?'

'No,' said Vaughan, 'I am still a hermit, like yourself. I have done nothing but loaf about.'

Vaughan had lit his pipe and sat in the elbow chair, fidgeting and glancing about him in a somewhat dazed and restless manner. Dyson had wheeled round his chair when his visitor entered and sat with one arm fondly reclining on the desk of his bureau, and touching the litter of manuscript.

'And you are still engaged in the old task?' said Vaughan, pointing to the pile of papers and the teeming pigeonholes.

'Yes, the vain pursuit of literature, as idle as alchemy, and as entrancing. But you have come to town for some time I suppose; what shall we do tonight?'

'Well. I rather wanted you to try a few days with me down in the west. It would do you a lot of good. I'm sure.'

'You are very kind, Vaughan, but London in September is hard to leave. Doré could not have designed anything more wonderful and mystic than Oxford Street as I saw it the other evening; the sunset flaming, the blue haze transmuting the plain street into a road "far in the spiritual city".'

'I should like you to come down though. You would enjoy roaming over our hills. Does this racket go on all day and night? It quite bewilders me; I wonder how you can work through it. I am sure you would revel in the great peace of my old home among the woods.'

Vaughan lit his pipe again, and looked anxiously at Dyson to see if his inducements had had any effect, but the man of letters shook his head, smiling, and vowed in his heart a firm allegiance to the streets.

'You cannot tempt me,' he said.

'Well, you may be right. Perhaps, after all, I was wrong to speak of the peace of the country. There, when a tragedy does occur, it is like a stone thrown into a pond; the circles of disturbance keep on widening, and it seems as if the water would never be still again.'

'Have you ever any tragedies where you are?'

'I can hardly say that. But I was a good deal disturbed about a month ago by something that happened; it may or may not have been a tragedy in the usual sense of the word.'

'What was the occurrence?'

'Well, the fact is a girl disappeared in a way which seems highly mysterious. Her parents, people of the name of Trevor, are well-to-do farmers, and their eldest daughter Annie was a sort of village beauty; she was really remarkably handsome. One afternoon she thought she would go and see her aunt, a widow who farms her own land, and as the two houses are only about five or six miles apart, she started off, telling her parents she would take the short cut over the hills. She never got to her aunt's, and she never was seen again. That's putting it in a few words.'

'What an extraordinary thing! I suppose there are no disused mines, are there, on the hills? I don't think you quite run to anything so formidable as a precipice?'

'No; the path the girl must have taken had no pitfalls of any description; it is just a track over wild, bare hillside, far, even from a by-road. One may walk for miles without meeting a soul, but it is perfectly safe.'

'And what do people say about it?'

'Oh, they talk nonsense – among themselves. You have no notion as to how superstitious English cottagers are in out-of-the-way parts like mine. They are as bad as the Irish, every whit, and even more secretive.'

'But what do they say?'

'Oh, the poor girl is supposed to have "gone with the fairies", or to have been "taken by the fairies". Such stuff!' he went on, 'one would laugh if it were not for the real tragedy of the case.'

Dyson looked somewhat interested.

'Yes,' he said, '"fairies" certainly strike a little curiously on the ear in these days. But what do the police say? I presume they do not accept the fairy tale hypothesis?'

'No; but they seem quite at fault. What I am afraid of is that Annie Trevor must have fallen in with some scoundrels on her way. Castletown is a large seaport, you know, and some of the worst of the foreign sailors occasionally desert their ships and go on the tramp up and down the country. Not many years ago a Spanish sailor named Garcia murdered a whole family for the sake of plunder that was not worth sixpence. They are hardly human, some of these fellows, and I am dreadfully afraid the poor girl must have come to an awful end.'

'But no foreign sailor was seen by anyone about the country?'

'No; there is certainly that; and of course country people are quick to notice anyone whose appearance and dress are a little out of the common. Still it seems as if my theory were the only possible explanation.'

'There are no data to go upon,' said Dyson, thoughtfully. 'There was no question of a love affair, or anything of the kind, I suppose?'

'Oh, no, not a hint of such a thing. I am sure if Annie were alive she would have contrived to let her mother know of her safety.'

'No doubt, no doubt. Still it is barely possible that she is alive and yet unable to communicate with her friends. But all this must have disturbed you a good deal.'

'Yes, it did; I hate a mystery, and especially a mystery which is probably the veil of horror. But frankly, Dyson, I want to make a clean breast of it; I did not come here to tell you all this.'

'Of course not,' said Dyson, a little surprised at Vaughan's uneasy manner. 'You came to have a chat on more cheerful topics.'

'No, I did not. What I have been telling you about happened a month ago, but something which seems likely to affect me more personally has taken place within the last few days, and to be quite plain, I came up to town with the idea that you might be able to help me. You recollect that curious case you spoke to me about on our last meeting; something about a spectacle maker.'

'Oh, yes, I remember that. I know I was quite proud of my acumen at the time; even to this day the police have no idea why those peculiar yellow spectacles were wanted. But, Vaughan, you really look quite put out; I hope there is nothing serious?'

'No, I think I have been exaggerating, and I want you to reassure me. But what has happened is very odd.'

'And what has happened?'

'I am sure that you will laugh at me, but this is the story. You must know there is a path, a right of way, that goes through my land, and to be precise, close to the wall of the kitchen garden. It is not used by many people; a woodman now and again finds it useful, and five or six children who go to school in the village pass twice a day. Well, a few days ago I was taking a walk about the place before breakfast, and I happened to stop to fill my pipe just by the large doors in the garden wall. The wood, I must tell you, comes to within a few feet of the wall, and the track I spoke of runs right in the shadow of the trees. I thought the shelter from a brisk wind that was blowing rather pleasant, and I stood there smoking with my eyes on the ground. Then something caught my attention. Just under the wall, on the short grass; a number of small flints were arranged in a pattern; something like this': and Mr Vaughan caught at a pencil and piece of paper, and dotted down a few strokes.

'You see,' he went on, 'there were, I should think, twelve little stones neatly arranged in lines, and spaced at equal distances, as I have shown it on the paper. They were pointed stones, and the points were very carefully directed one way.'

'Yes,' said Dyson, without much interest, 'no doubt the children you have mentioned had been playing there on their way from school. Children, as you know, are very fond of making such devices with oyster shells or flints or flowers, or with whatever comes in their way.'

'So I thought; I just noticed these flints were arranged in a sort of pattern and then went on. But the next morning I was taking the same round, which, as a matter of fact, is habitual with me, and again I saw at the same spot a device in flints. This time it was really a curious pattern; something like the spokes of a wheel, all meeting at a common centre, and this centre formed by a device which looked like a bowl; all, you understand, done in flints.'

'You are right,' said Dyson, 'that seems odd enough. Still it is reasonable that your half-a-dozen school children are responsible for these fantasies in stone.'

'Well, I thought I would set the matter at rest. The children pass the gate every evening at half-past five, and I walked by at six, and found the device just as I had left it in the morning. The next day I was up and about at a quarter to seven, and I found the whole thing had been changed. There was a pyramid outlined in flints upon the grass. The children I saw going by an hour and a half later, and they ran past the spot without glancing to right or left. In the evening I watched them going home, and this morning when I got to the gate at six o'clock there was a thing like a half moon waiting for me.'

'So then the series runs thus: firstly ordered lines, then, the device of the spokes and the bowl, then the pyramid, and finally, this morning, the half moon. That is the order, isn't it?'

'Yes; that is right. But do you know it has made me feel very uneasy? I suppose it seems absurd, but I can't help thinking that some kind of signalling is going on under my nose, and that sort of thing is disquieting.'

'But what have you to dread? You have no enemies?'

'No; but I have some very valuable old plate.'

'You are thinking of burglars then?' said Dyson, with an accent of considerable interest, 'but you must know your neighbours. Are there any suspicious characters about?'

'Not that I am aware of. But you remember what I told you of the sailors.'

'Can you trust your servants?'

'Oh, perfectly. The plate is preserved in a strong room; the butler, an old family servant, alone knows where the key is kept. There is nothing wrong there. Still, everybody is aware that I have a lot of old silver, and all country folks are given to gossip. In that way information may have got abroad in very undesirable quarters.'

'Yes, but I confess there seems something a little unsatisfactory in the burglar theory. Who is signalling to whom? I cannot see my way to accepting such an explanation. What put the plate into your head in connection with these flint signs, or whatever one may call them?'

'It was the figure of the Bowl,' said Vaughan. 'I happen to possess a very large and very valuable Charles II punch bowl. The chasing is really exquisite, and the thing is worth a lot of money. The sign I described to you was exactly the same shape as my punch bowl.'

'A queer coincidence certainly. But the other figures or devices: you have nothing shaped like a pyramid?'

'Ah, you will think that queerer. As it happens, this punch bowl of mine, together with a set of rare old ladles, is kept in a mahogany chest of a pyramidal shape. The four sides slope upwards, the narrow towards the top.'

'I confess all this interests me a good deal,' said Dyson. 'let us go on then. What about the other figures; how about the Army, as we may call the first sign, and the Crescent or Half moon?'

'Ah, there is no reference that I can make out of these two. Still, you see I have some excuse for curiosity at all events. I should be very vexed to lose any of the old plate; nearly all the pieces have been in the family for generations. And I cannot get it out of my head that some scoundrels mean to rob me, and are communicating with one another every night.'

'Frankly,' said Dyson, 'I can make nothing of it; I am as much in the dark as yourself. Your theory seems certainly the only possible explanation, and yet the difficulties are immense.'

He leaned back in his chair, and the two men faced each other, frowning, and perplexed by so bizarre a problem.

'By the way,' said Dyson, after a long pause, 'what is your geological formation down there?'

Mr Vaughan looked up, a good deal surprised by the question.

'Old red sandstone and limestone, I believe,' he said. 'We are just beyond the coal measures, you know.'

'But surely there are no flints either in the sandstone or the limestone?'

'No, I never see any flints in the fields. I confess that did strike me as a little curious.'

'I should think so! It is very important. By the way, what size were the flints used in making these devices?'

'I happen to have brought one with me; I took it this morning.'

'From the Half moon?'

'Exactly. Here it is.'

He handed over a small flint, tapering to a point, and about three inches in length.

Dyson's face blazed up with excitement as he took the thing from Vaughan.

'Certainly,' he said, after a moment's pause, 'you have some curious neighbours in your country. I hardly think they can harbour any designs on your punch bowl. Do you know this is a flint arrowhead of vast antiquity, and not only that, but an arrowhead of a unique kind? I have seen specimens from all parts of the world, but there are features about this thing that are quite peculiar.'

He laid down his pipe, and took out a book from a drawer.

'We shall just have time to catch the 5.45 to Castletown,' he said.

II
The Eyes on the Wall

Mr Dyson drew in a long breath of the air of the hills and felt all the enchantment of the scene about him. It was very early morning, and he stood on the terrace in the front of the house. Vaughan's ancestor had built on the lower slope of a great hill, in the shelter of a deep and ancient wood that gathered on three sides about the house, and on the fourth side, the southwest, the land fell gently away and sank to the valley, where a brook wound in and out in mystic esses, and the dark and gleaming alders tracked the stream's course to the eye. On the terrace in the sheltered place no wind blew, and far beyond, the trees were still. Only one sound broke in upon the silence, and Dyson heard the noise of the brook singing far below, the song of clear and shining water rippling over the stones, whispering and murmuring as it sank to dark deep pools. Across the stream, just below the house, rose a grey stone bridge, vaulted and buttressed, a fragment of the Middle Ages, and then beyond the bridge the hills rose again, vast and rounded like bastions, covered here and there with dark woods and thickets of undergrowth, but the heights were all bare of trees, showing only grey turf and patches of bracken, touched here and there with the gold of fading fronds; Dyson looked to the north and south, and still he saw the wall of the hills, and the ancient woods, and the stream drawn in and out between them; all grey and dim with morning mist beneath a grey sky in a hushed and haunted air.

Mr Vaughan's voice broke in upon the silence.

'I thought you would be too tired to be about so early,' he said. 'I see you are admiring the view. It is very pretty, isn't it, though I suppose old Meyrick Vaughan didn't think much about the scenery when he built the house. A queer grey, old place, isn't it?'

'Yes, and how it fits into the surroundings; it seems of a piece with the grey hills and the grey bridge below.'

'I am afraid I have brought you down on false pretences, Dyson,' said Vaughan, as they began to walk up and down the terrace. 'I have been to the place, and there is not a sign of anything this morning.'

'Ah, indeed. Well, suppose we go round together.'

They walked across the lawn and went by a path through the ilex shrubbery to the back of the house. There Vaughan pointed out the track leading down to the valley and up to the heights above the wood, and presently they stood beneath the garden wall, by the door.

'Here, you see, it was,' said Vaughan, pointing to a spot on the turf. 'I was standing just where you are now that morning I first saw the flints.'

'Yes, quite so. That morning it was the Army, as I call it; then the Bowl, then the Pyramid, and, yesterday, the Half moon. What a queer old stone that is,' he went on, pointing to a block of limestone rising out of the turf just beneath the wall. 'It looks like a sort of dwarf pillar, but I suppose it is natural.'

'Oh, yes, I think so. I imagine it was brought here, though, as we stand on the red sandstone. No doubt it was used as a foundation stone for some older building.'

'Very likely,' Dyson was peering about him attentively, looking from the ground to the wall, and from the wall to the deep wood that hung almost over the garden and made the place dark even in the morning.

'Look here,' said Dyson at length, 'it is certainly a case of children this time. Look at that.' He was bending down and staring at the dull red surface of the mellowed bricks of the wall.

Vaughan came up and looked hard where Dyson's finger was pointing, and could scarcely distinguish a faint mark in deeper red.

'What is it?' he said. 'I can make nothing of it.'

'Look a little more closely. Don't you see it is an attempt to draw the human eye?'

'Ah, now I see what you mean. My sight is not very sharp. Yes, so it is, it is meant for an eye, no doubt, as you say. I thought the children learnt drawing at school.'

'Well, it is an odd eye enough. Do you notice the peculiar almond shape; almost like the eye of a Chinaman?'

Dyson looked meditatively at the work of the undeveloped artist, and scanned the wall again, going down on his knees in the minuteness of his inquisition.

'I should like very much,' he said at length, 'to know how a child in this out of the way place could have any idea of the shape of the Mongolian eye. You see the average child has a very distinct impression of the subject; he draws a circle, or something like a circle, and puts a dot in the centre. I don't think any child imagines that the eye is really made like that; it's just a convention of infantile art. But this almond-shaped thing puzzles me extremely. Perhaps it may be derived from a gilt Chinaman on a tea canister in the grocer's shop. Still that's hardly likely.'

'But why are you so sure it was done by a child?'

'Why! Look at the height. These old-fashioned bricks are little more than two inches thick; there are twenty courses from the ground to the sketch if we call it so; that gives a height of three and a half feet. Now, just imagine you are going to draw something on this wall. Exactly; your pencil, if you had one, would touch the wall somewhere on the level with your eyes, that is, more than five feet from the ground. It seems, therefore, a very simple deduction to conclude that this eye on the wall was drawn by a child about ten years old.'

'Yes, I had not thought of that. Of course one of the children must have done it.'

'I suppose so; and yet as I said, there is something singularly unchildlike about those two lines, and the eyeball itself, you see, is almost an oval. To my mind, the thing has an odd, ancient air; and a touch that is not altogether pleasant. I cannot help fancying that if we could see a whole face from the same hand it would not be altogether agreeable. However, that is nonsense, after all, and we are not getting farther in our investigations. It is odd that the flint series has come to such an abrupt end.'

The two men walked away towards the house, and as they went in at the porch there was a break in the grey sky, and a gleam of sunshine on the grey hill before them.

All the day Dyson prowled meditatively about the fields and woods surrounding the house. He was thoroughly and completely puzzled by the trivial circumstances he proposed to elucidate, and now he again took the flint arrowhead from his pocket, turning it over and examining it with deep attention. There was something about the thing that was altogether different from the specimens he had seen at the museums and private collections; the shape was of a distinct type, and around the edge there was a line of little punctured dots, apparently a suggestion of ornament. Who, thought Dyson, could possess such things in so remote a place; and who, possessing the flints, could have put them to the fantastic use of designing meaningless figures under Vaughan's garden wall? The rank absurdity of the whole affair offended him unutterably; and as one theory after another rose in his mind only to be rejected, he felt strongly tempted to take the next train back to town. He had seen the silver plate which Vaughan treasured, and had inspected the punch-bowl, the gem of the collection, with close attention; and what he saw and his interview with the butler convinced him that a plot to rob the strong box was out of the limits of enquiry. The chest in which the bowl was kept, a heavy piece of mahogany, evidently dating from the beginning of the century, was certainly strongly suggestive of a pyramid, and Dyson was at first inclined to the inept manoeuvres of the detective, but a little sober thought convinced him of the impossibility of the burglary hypothesis, and he cast wildly about for something more satisfying. He asked Vaughan if there were any gipsies in the neighbourhood, and heard that the Romany had not been seen for years. This dashed him a good deal, as he knew the gipsy habit of leaving queer hieroglyphics on the line of march, and had been much elated when the thought occurred to him. He was facing Vaughan by the old-fashioned hearth when he put the question, and leaned back in his chair in disgust at the destruction of his theory.

'It is odd,' said Vaughan, 'but the gipsies never trouble us here. Now and then the farmers find traces of fires in the wildest part of the hills, but nobody seems to know who the firelighters are.'

'Surely that looks like gipsies?'

'No, not in such places as those. Tinkers and gipsies and wanderers of all sorts stick to the roads and don't go very far from the farmhouses.'

'Well, I can make nothing of it. I saw the children going by this afternoon, and, as you say, they ran straight on. So we shall have no more eyes on the wall at all events.'

'No, I must waylay them one of these days and find out who is the artist.'

The next morning when Vaughan strolled in his usual course from the lawn to the back of the house he found Dyson already awaiting him by the garden door, and evidently in a state of high excitement, for he beckoned furiously with his hand, and gesticulated violently.

'What is it?' asked Vaughan. 'The flints again?'

'No; but took here, look at the wall. There; don't you see it?'

'There's another of those eyes!'

'Exactly. Drawn, you see, at a little distance from the first, almost on the same level, but slightly lower.'

'What on earth is one to make of it? It couldn't have been done by the children; it wasn't there last night, and they won't pass for another hour. What can it mean?'

'I think the very devil is at the bottom of all this,' said Dyson. 'Of course, one cannot resist the conclusion that these infernal almond eyes are to be set down to the same agency as the devices in the arrowheads; and where that conclusion is to lead us is more than I can tell. For my part, I have to put a strong check on my imagination, or it would run wild.'

'Vaughan,' he said, as they turned away from the wall, 'has it struck you that there is one point – a very curious point – in common between the figures done in flints and the eyes drawn on the wall?'

'What is that?' asked Vaughan, on whose face there had fallen a certain shadow of indefinite dread.

'It is this. We know that the signs of the Army, the Bowl, the Pyramid, and the Half moon must have been done at night. Presumably they were meant to be seen at night. Well, precisely the same reasoning applies to those eyes on the wall.'

'I do not quite see your point.'

'Oh, surely. The nights are dark just now, and have been very cloudy, I know, since I came down. Moreover, those overhanging trees would throw that wall into deep shadow even on a clear night.'

'Well?'

'What struck me was this. What very peculiarly sharp eyesight, they, whoever "they" are, must have to be able to arrange arrowheads in intricate order in the blackest shadow of the wood, and then draw the eyes on the wall without a trace of bungling, or a false line.'

'I have read of persons confined in dungeons for many years who have been able to see quite well in the dark,' said Vaughan.

'Yes,' said Dyson, 'there was the abbé in *Monte Cristo*. But it is a singular point.'

III
The Search for the Bowl

'Who was that old man that touched his hat to you just now?' said Dyson, as they came to the bend of the lane near the house.

'Oh, that was old Trevor. He looks very broken, poor old fellow.'

'Who is Trevor?'

'Don't you remember? I told you the story that afternoon I came to your rooms – about a girl named Annie Trevor, who disappeared in the most inexplicable manner about five weeks ago. That was her father.'

'Yes, yes, I recollect now. To tell the truth I had forgotten all about it. And nothing has been heard of the girl?'

'Nothing whatever. The police are quite at fault.'

'I am afraid I did not pay very much attention to the details you gave me. Which way did the girl go?'

'Her path would take her right across those wild hills above the house: the nearest point in the track must be about two miles from here.'

'Is it near that little hamlet I saw yesterday?'

'You mean Croesyceiliog, where the children came from? No; it goes more to the north.'

'Ah, I have never been that way.'

They went into the house, and Dyson shut himself up in his room, sunk deep in doubtful thought, but yet with the shadow of a suspicion growing within him that for a while haunted his brain, all vague and fantastic, refusing to take definite form. He was sitting by the open window and looking out on the valley and saw, as if in a picture, the intricate winding of the brook, the grey bridge, and the vast hills rising beyond; all still and without a breath of wind to stir the mystic hanging woods, and the evening sunshine glowed warm on the bracken, and down below a faint mist, pure white, began to rise from the stream. Dyson sat by the window as the day darkened and the huge bastioned hills loomed vast and vague, and the woods became dim and more shadowy: and the fancy that had seized him no longer appeared altogether impossible. He passed the rest of the evening in a reverie, hardly hearing what Vaughan said; and when he took his candle in the hall, he paused a moment before bidding his friend good night.

'I want a good rest,' he said. 'I have got some work to do tomorrow.'

'Some writing, you mean?'

'No. I am going to look for the Bowl.'

'The Bowl! If you mean my punch bowl, that is safe in the chest.'

'I don't mean the punch bowl. You may take my word for it that your plate has never been threatened. No; I will not bother you with any suppositions. We shall in all probability have something much stronger than suppositions before long. Good night, Vaughan.'

The next morning Dyson set off after breakfast. He took the path by the garden wall, and noted that there were now eight of the weird almond eyes dimly outlined on the brick.

'Six days more,' he said to himself, but as he thought over the theory he had formed, he shrank, in spite of strong conviction, from such a wildly incredible fancy. He struck up through the dense shadows of the wood, and at length came out on the bare hillside, and climbed higher and higher over the slippery turf, keeping well to the north, and following the indications given him by Vaughan. As he went on, he seemed to mount ever higher above the world of human life and customary things; to his right he looked at a fringe of orchard and saw a faint blue smoke rising like a pillar; there was the hamlet from which the children came to school, and there the only sign of life, for the woods embowered and concealed Vaughan's old grey house. As he reached what seemed the summit of the hill, he realised for the first time the desolate loneliness and strangeness of the land; there was nothing but grey sky and grey hill, a high, vast plain that seemed to stretch on for ever and ever, and a faint glimpse of a blue-peaked mountain far away and to the north. At length he came to the path, a slight track scarcely noticeable, and from its position and by what Vaughan had told him he knew that it was the way the lost girl, Annie Trevor, must have taken. He followed the path on the bare hilltop, noticing the great limestone rocks that cropped out of the turf, grim and hideous, and of an aspect as forbidding as an idol of the South Seas; and suddenly he halted, astonished, although he had found what he searched for. Almost without warning the ground shelved suddenly away on all sides, and Dyson looked down into a circular depression, which might well have been a Roman amphitheatre, and the ugly crags of limestone rimmed it round as if with a broken wall. Dyson walked round the hollow, and noted the position of the stones, and then turned on his way home.

'This,' he thought to himself, 'is more than curious. The Bowl is discovered, but where is the Pyramid?'

'My dear Vaughan,' he said, when he got back, 'I may tell you that

I have found the Bowl, and that it is all I shall tell you for the present. We have six days of absolute inaction before us; there is really nothing to be done.'

IV
The Secret of the Pyramid

'I have just been round the garden,' said Vaughan one morning. 'I have been counting those infernal eyes, and I find there are fourteen of them. For heaven's sake, Dyson, tell me what the meaning of it all is.'

'I should be very sorry to attempt to do so. I may have guessed this or that, but I always make it a principle to keep my guesses to myself. Besides, it is really not worth while anticipating events; you will remember my telling you that we had six days of inaction before us? Well, this is the sixth day, and the last of idleness. Tonight, I propose we take a stroll.'

'A stroll! Is that all the action you mean to take?'

'Well, it may show you some very curious things. To be plain, I want you to start with me at nine o'clock this evening for the hills. We may have to be out all night, so you had better wrap up well, and bring some of that brandy.'

'Is it a joke?' asked Vaughan, who was bewildered with strange events and strange surmises.

'No, I don't think there is much joke in it. Unless I am much mistaken we shall find a very serious explanation of the puzzle. You will come with me, I am sure?'

'Very good. Which way do you want to go?'

'By the path you told me of; the path Annie Trevor is supposed to have taken.'

Vaughan looked white at the mention of the girl's name.

'I did not think you were on that track,' he said. 'I thought it was the affair of those devices in flint and of the eyes on the wall that you were engaged on. It's no good saying any more, but I will go with you.'

At a quarter to nine that evening the two men set out, taking the path through the wood, and up the hillside. It was a dark and heavy night, the sky was thick with clouds, and the valley full of mist, and all the way they seemed to walk in a world of shadow and gloom, hardly speaking, and afraid to break the haunted silence. They came out at last on the steep hillside, and instead of the oppression of the wood there was the long, dim sweep of the turf, and higher, the fantastic limestone rocks hinted horror through the darkness, and the wind sighed as it passed across the mountain to the sea, and in its passage beat chill about their hearts. They seemed to walk on and on for hours, and the dim outline of the hill still stretched before them, and the haggard rocks still loomed through the darkness, when suddenly Dyson whispered, drawing his breath quickly, and coming close to his companion:

'Here,' he said, 'we will lie down. I do not think there is anything yet.'

'I know the place,' said Vaughan, after a moment. 'I have often been by in the daytime. The country people are afraid to come here, I believe; it is supposed to be a fairies' castle, or something of the kind. But why on earth have we come here?'

'Speak a little lower,' said Dyson. 'It might not do us any good if we are overheard.'

'Overheard here! There is not a soul within three miles of us.'

'Possibly not; indeed, I should say certainly not. But there might be a body somewhat nearer.'

'I don't understand you in the least,' said Vaughan, whispering to humour Dyson, 'but why have we come here?'

'Well, you see this hollow before us is the Bowl. I think we better not talk even in whispers.'

They lay full length upon the turf; the rock between their faces and the Bowl, and now and again, Dyson, slouching his dark, soft hat over his forehead, put out the glint of an eye, and in a moment drew back, not daring to take a prolonged view. Again he laid an ear to the ground and listened, and the hours went by, and the darkness seemed to blacken, and the faint sigh of the wind was the only sound.

Vaughan grew impatient with this heaviness of silence, this watching for indefinite terror; for to him there was no shape or form of apprehension, and he began to think the whole vigil a dreary farce.

'How much longer is this to last?' he whispered to Dyson, and Dyson who had been holding his breath in the agony of attention put his mouth to Vaughan's ear and said:

'Will you listen?' with pauses between each syllable, and in the voice with which the priest pronounces the awful words.

Vaughan caught the ground with his hands, and stretched forward, wondering what he was to hear. At first there was nothing, and then a low and gentle noise came very softly from the Bowl, a faint sound, almost indescribable, but as if one held the tongue against the roof of the mouth and expelled the breath. He listened eagerly and presently the noise grew louder, and became a strident and horrible hissing as if the pit beneath boiled with fervent heat, and Vaughan, unable to remain in suspense any longer, drew his cap half over his face in imitation of Dyson, and looked down to the hollow below.

It did, in truth, stir and seethe like an infernal caldron. The whole of the sides and bottom tossed and writhed with vague and restless forms that passed to and fro without the sound of feet, and gathered thick here and there and seemed to speak to one another in those tones of horrible sibilance, like the hissing of snakes, that he had heard. It was as if the sweet turf and the cleanly earth had suddenly become quickened with some foul writhing growth. Vaughan could not draw back his face, though he felt Dyson's finger touch him, but he peered into the quaking mass and saw faintly that there were things like faces and human limbs, and yet he felt his inmost soul chill with the sure belief that no fellow soul or human thing stirred in all that tossing and hissing host. He looked aghast, choking back sobs of horror, and at length the loathsome forms gathered thickest about some vague object in the middle of the hollow, and the hissing of their speech grew more venomous, and he saw in the uncertain light the abominable limbs, vague and yet too plainly seen, writhe and intertwine, and he thought he heard, very faint, a low human moan striking through the noise of speech that was not of man. At his heart something seemed to whisper ever 'the worm of corruption, the worm that dieth not', and grotesquely the image was pictured to his imagination of a piece of putrid offal stirring through and through with bloated and horrible creeping things. The writhing of the dusky limbs continued, they seemed clustered round the dark form in the middle of the hollow, and the sweat dripped and poured off Vaughan's forehead, and fell cold on his hand beneath his face.

Then, it seemed done in an instant, the loathsome mass melted and fell away to the sides of the Bowl, and for a moment Vaughan saw in the middle of the hollow the tossing of human arms. But a spark gleamed beneath, a fire kindled, and as the voice of a woman cried out loud in a shrill scream of utter anguish and terror, a great pyramid of flame spired up like a bursting of a pent fountain, and threw a blaze of light upon the whole mountain. In that instant Vaughan saw the myriads beneath; the things made in the form of men but stunted like children hideously deformed, the faces with the almond eyes burning with evil and unspeakable lusts; the ghastly yellow of the mass of naked flesh and then as if by magic the place was empty, while the fire roared and crackled, and the flames shone abroad.

'You have seen the Pyramid,' said Dyson in his ear, 'the Pyramid of fire.'

V
The Little People

'Then you recognise the thing?'

'Certainly. It is a brooch that Annie Trevor used to wear on Sundays; I remember the pattern. But where did you find it? You don't mean to say that you have discovered the girl?'

'My dear Vaughan, I wonder you have not guessed where I found the brooch. You have not forgotten last night already?'

'Dyson,' said the other, speaking very seriously, 'I have been turning it over in my mind this morning while you have been out. I have thought about what I saw, or perhaps I should say about what I thought I saw, and the only conclusion I can come to is this, that the thing won't bear recollection. As men live, I have lived soberly and honestly, in the fear of God, all my days, and all I can do is believe that I suffered from some monstrous delusion, from some phantasmagoria of the bewildered senses. You know we went home together in silence, not a word passed between us as to what I fancied I saw; had we not better agree to keep silence on the subject? When I took my walk in the peaceful morning sunshine, I thought all the earth seemed full of praise, and passing by that wall I noticed there were no more signs recorded, and I blotted out those that remained. The mystery is over, and we can live quietly again. I think some poison has been working for the last few weeks; I have trod on the verge of madness, but I am sane now.'

Mr Vaughan had spoken earnestly, and bent forward in his chair and glanced at Dyson with something of entreaty.

'My dear Vaughan,' said the other, after a pause, 'what's the use of this? It is much too late to take that tone; we have gone too deep. Besides you know as well as I that there is no delusion in the case; I wish there were with all my heart. No, in justice to myself I must tell you the whole story, so far as I know it.'

'Very good,' said Vaughan with a sigh, 'if you must, you must.'

'Then,' said Dyson, 'we will begin with the end if you please. I found this brooch you have just identified in the place we have called the Bowl. There was a heap of grey ashes, as if a fire had been burning, indeed, the embers were still hot, and this brooch was lying on the ground, just outside the range of the flame. It must have dropped accidentally from the dress of the person who was wearing it. No, don't interrupt me; we can pass now to the beginning, as we have had the end. Let us go back to that day you came to see me in my rooms in London. So far as I can remember, soon after you came in you mentioned, in a somewhat casual manner, that an unfortunate and mysterious incident had occurred in your part of the country; a girl named Annie Trevor had gone to see a relative, and had disappeared. I confess freely that what you said did not greatly interest me; there are so many reasons which may make it extremely convenient for a man and more especially a woman to vanish from the circle of their relations and friends. I suppose, if we were to consult the police, one would find that in London somebody disappears mysteriously every other week, and the officers would, no doubt, shrug their shoulders, and tell you that by the law of averages it could not be otherwise. So I was very culpably careless to your story, and besides, here is another reason for my lack of interest; your tale was inexplicable. You could only suggest a blackguard sailor on the tramp, but I discarded the explanation immediately.

'For many reasons, but chiefly because the occasional criminal, the amateur in brutal crime, is always found out, especially if he selects the country as the scene of his operations. You will remember the case of that Garcia you mentioned; he strolled into a railway station the day after the murder, his trousers covered with blood, and the works of the Dutch clock, his loot, tied in a neat parcel. So rejecting this, your only suggestion, the whole tale became, as I say, inexplicable, and, therefore, profoundly uninteresting. Yes, *therefore*, it is a perfectly valid conclusion. Do you ever trouble your head about problems which you know to be insoluble? Did you ever bestow much thought on the old puzzle of Achilles and the tortoise? Of course not, because you knew it was a hopeless quest, and so when you told me the story of a country girl who had disappeared I simply placed the whole thing down in the category of the insoluble, and thought no more about the matter. I was mistaken, so it has turned out; but if you remember, you immediately passed on to an affair which interested you more intensely, because personally. I need not go over the very singular narrative of the flint signs; at first I thought it all trivial, probably some children's game, and if not that a hoax of some sort; but your showing me the arrow-head awoke my acute interest. Here, I saw, there was something widely removed from the commonplace, and matter of real curiosity; and as soon as I came here I set to work to find the solution, repeating to myself again and again the signs you had described. First came the sign we have agreed to call the Army; a number of serried lines of flints, all pointing in the same way. Then the lines, like the spokes of a wheel, all converging towards the figure of a Bowl, then the triangle or Pyramid, and last of all the Half moon. I confess that I exhausted conjecture in my efforts to unveil this mystery, and as you will understand it was a duplex or rather triplex problem. For I had not merely to ask myself: what do these figures mean? but also, who can possibly be responsible for the designing of them? And again, who can possibly possess such valuable things, and knowing their value thus throw them down by the wayside? This line of thought led me to suppose that the person or persons in question did not know the value of unique flint arrowheads, and yet this did not lead me far, for a well-educated man might easily be ignorant on such a subject. Then came the complication of the eye on the wall, and you remember that we could not avoid the conclusion that in the two cases the same agency was at work. The peculiar position of these eyes on the wall made me inquire if there was such a thing as a dwarf anywhere in the neighbourhood, but I found that there was not, and I knew that the children who pass by every day had nothing to do with the matter. Yet I felt convinced that whoever drew the eyes must be from three and a half to four feet high, since, as I pointed out at the time, any one who draws on a perpendicular surface chooses by instinct a spot about level with his face. Then again, there was the question of the peculiar shape of the eyes; that marked Mongolian character of which the English countryman could have no conception, and for a final cause of confusion the obvious fact that the designer or designers must be able practically to see in the dark. As you remarked, a man who has been confined for many years in an extremely dark cell or dungeon might acquire that power; but since the days of Edmond Dantès, where would such a prison be found in Europe? A sailor, who had been immured for a considerable period in some horrible Chinese *oubliette*, seemed the individual I was in search of, and though it looked improbable, it was not absolutely impossible that a sailor or, let us say, a man employed on shipboard, should be a dwarf. But how to account for my imaginary sailor being in possession of prehistoric arrowheads? And the possession granted, what was the meaning and object of these mysterious signs of flint, and the almond-shaped eyes? Your theory of a contemplated burglary I saw, nearly from the first, to be quite untenable, and I confess I was utterly at a loss for a working hypothesis. It was a mere accident which put me on the track; we passed poor old Trevor, and your mention of his name and of the disappearance of his daughter, recalled the story which I had forgotten, or which remained unheeded. Here, then, I said to myself, is another problem, uninteresting, it is true, by itself; but what if it prove to be in relation with all these enigmas which torture me? I shut myself in my room, and endeavoured to dismiss all prejudice from my mind, and I went over everything *de novo*, assuming for theory's sake that the disappearance of Annie Trevor had some connection with the flint signs and the eyes on the wall. This assumption did not lead me very far, and I was on the point of giving the whole problem up in despair, when a possible significance of the Bowl struck me. As you know there is a "Devil's Punch bowl" in Surrey, and I saw that the symbol might refer to some feature in the country. Putting the two extremes together, I determined to look for the Bowl near the path which the lost girl had taken, and you know how I found it. I interpreted the sign by what I knew, and read the first, the Army, thus: "there is to be a gathering or assembly at the Bowl in a fortnight (that is the Half moon) to see the Pyramid, or to build the Pyramid." The eyes, drawn one by one, day by day, evidently checked off the days, and I knew that there would be fourteen and no more. Thus far the way seemed pretty plain; I would not trouble myself to inquire as to the nature of the assembly, or as to who was to assemble in the loneliest and most dreaded place among these lonely hills. In Ireland or China or the West of America the question would have been easily answered; a muster of the disaffected, the meeting of a secret society; Vigilantes summoned to report: the thing would be simplicity itself; but in this quiet corner of England, inhabited by quiet folk, no such suppositions were possible for a moment. But I knew that I should have an opportunity of seeing and watching the assembly, and I did not care to perplex myself with hopeless research; and in place of reasoning a wild fancy entered into judgment: I remembered what people had said about Annie Trevor's disappearance, that she had been "taken by the fairies". I tell you, Vaughan, I am a sane man as you are, my brain is not, I trust, mere vacant space to let to any wild improbability, and I tried my best to thrust the fantasy away. And the hint came of the old name of fairies, "the little people", and the very probable belief that they represent a tradition of the prehistoric Turanian inhabitants of the country, who were cave dwellers: and then I realised with a shock that I was looking for a being under four feet in height, accustomed to live in darkness, possessing stone instruments, and familiar with the Mongolian cast of features! I say this, Vaughan, that I should be ashamed to hint at such visionary stuff to you, if it were not for that which you saw with your very eyes last night, and I say that I might doubt the evidence of my senses, if they were not confirmed by yours. But you and I cannot look each other in the face and pretend delusion; as you lay on the turf beside me I felt your flesh shrink and quiver, and I saw your eyes in the light of the flame. And so I tell you without any shame what was in my mind last night as we went through the wood and climbed the hill, and lay hidden beneath the rock.

'There was one thing that should have been most evident that puzzled me to the very last. I told you how I read the sign of the Pyramid; the assembly was to see a pyramid, and the true meaning of the symbol escaped me to the last moment. The old derivation from *πυρ*, fire, though false, should have set me on the track, but it never occurred to me.

'I think I need say very little more. You know we were quite helpless, even if we had foreseen what was to come. Ah, the particular place where these signs were displayed? Yes, that is a curious question. But this house is, so far as I can judge, in a pretty central situation amongst the hills; and possibly, who can say yes or no, that queer, old limestone pillar by your garden wall was a place of meeting before the Celt set foot in Britain. But there is one thing I must add: I don't regret our inability to rescue the wretched girl. You saw the appearance of those things that gathered thick and writhed in the Bowl; you may be sure that what lay bound in the midst of them was no longer fit for earth.'

'So?' said Vaughan.

'So she passed in the Pyramid of Fire,' said Dyson, 'and they passed again to the underworld, to the places beneath the hills.'

Novel of the Black Seal

I am the daughter of a civil engineer, Steven Lally by name, who was so unfortunate as to die suddenly at the outset of his career, and before he had accumulated sufficient means to support his wife and her two children. My mother contrived to keep the small household going on resources which must have been incredibly small; we lived in a remote country village, because most of the necessaries of life were cheaper than in a town, but even so we were brought up with the severest economy. My father was a clever and well-read man, and left behind him a small but select collection of books, containing the best Greek, Latin, and English classics, and these books were the only amusement we possessed. My brother, I remember, learned Latin out of Descartes' *Meditationes*, and I, in place of the little tales which children are usually told to read, had nothing more charming than a translation of the *Gesta Romanorum*. We grew up thus, quiet and studious children, and in course of time my brother provided for himself. I continued to live at home; my poor mother had become an invalid, and demanded my continual care, and about two years ago she died after many months of painful illness. My situation was a terrible one; the shabby furniture barely sufficed to pay the debts I had been forced to contract, and the books I despatched to my brother, knowing how he would value them. I was absolutely alone. I was aware how poorly my brother was paid; and though I came up to London in the hope of finding employment, with the understanding that he would defray my expenses, I swore it should only be for a month, and that if I could not in that time find some work, I would starve rather than deprive him of the few miserable pounds he had laid by for his day of trouble. I took a little room in a distant suburb, the cheapest that I could find. I lived on bread and tea, and I spent my time in vain answering of advertisements, and vainer walks to addresses I had noted. Day followed on day, and week on week, and still I was unsuccessful, till at last the term I had appointed drew to a close, and I saw before me the grim prospect of slowly dying of starvation. My landlady was good-natured in her way; she knew the slenderness of my means, and I am sure that she would not have turned me out of doors. It remained for me then to go away, and to try and die in some quiet place. It was winter then, and a thick white fog gathered in the early part of the afternoon, becoming more dense as the day wore on; it was a Sunday, I remember, and the people of the house were at chapel. At about three o'clock I crept out and walked away as quickly as I could, for I was weak from abstinence. The white mist wrapped all the streets in silence, and a hard frost had gathered thick upon the bare branches of the trees, and frost crystals glittered on the wooden fences, and on the cold cruel ground beneath my feet. I walked on, turning to right and left in utter haphazard, without caring to look up at the names of the streets, and all that I remember of my walk on that Sunday afternoon seems but the broken fragments of an evil dream. In a confused vision I stumbled on, through roads half town and half country; grey fields melting into the cloudy world of mist on one side of me, and on the other comfortable villas with a glow of firelight flickering on the walls; but all unreal, red brick walls, and lighted windows, vague trees, and glimmering country, gas lamps beginning to star the white shadows, the vanishing perspectives of the railway line beneath high embankments, the green and red of the signal lamps, – all these were but momentary pictures flashed on my tired brain and senses numbed by hunger. Now and then I would hear a quick step ringing on the iron road, and men would pass me well wrapped up, walking fast for the sake of warmth, and no doubt eagerly foretasting the pleasures of a glowing hearth, with curtains tightly drawn about the frosted panes, and the welcomes of their friends; but as the early evening darkened and night approached, foot passengers got fewer and fewer, and I passed through street after street alone. In the white silence I stumbled on, as desolate as if I trod the streets of a buried city; and as I grew more weak and exhausted, something of the horror of death was folding thickly round my heart. Suddenly, as I turned a corner, some one accosted me courteously beneath the lamp pose, and I heard a voice asking if I could kindly point the way to Avon Road. At the sudden shock of human accents I was prostrated and my strength gave way, and I fell all huddled on the sidewalk and wept and sobbed and laughed in violent hysteria. I had gone out prepared to die, and as I stepped across the threshold that had sheltered me, I consciously bade adieu to all hopes and all remembrances; the door clanged behind me with the noise of thunder, and I felt that an iron curtain had fallen on the brief passages of my life, and that henceforth I was to walk a little way in a world, of gloom and shadow; I entered on the stage of the first act of death. Then came my wandering in the mist, the whiteness wrapping all things, the void streets, and muffled silence, till when that voice spoke to me, it was as if I had died and life returned to me. In a few minutes I was able to compose my feelings, and as I rose I saw that I was confronted by a middle-aged gentleman of specious appearance, neatly and correctly dressed. He looked at me with an expression of great pity, but before I could stammer out my ignorance of the neighbourhood, for indeed I had not the slightest notion of where I had wandered, he spoke.

'My dear madam,' he said, 'you seem in some terrible distress. You cannot think how you alarmed me. But may I inquire the nature of your trouble? I assure you that you can safely confide in me.'

'You are very kind,' I replied; 'but, I fear there is nothing to be done. My condition seems a hopeless one.'

'Oh, nonsense, nonsense! You are too young to talk like that. Come, let us walk down here, and you must tell me your difficulty. Perhaps I may be able to help you.'

There was something very soothing and persuasive in his manner, and as we walked together, I gave him an outline of my story, and told of the despair that had oppressed me almost to death.

'You were wrong to give in so completely,' he said, when I was silent. 'A month is too short a time in which to feel one's way in London. London, let me tell you, Miss Lally, does not lie open and undefended; it is a fortified place, fossed and double-moated with curious intricacies. As must always happen in large towns, the conditions of life have become hugely artificial; no mere simple palisade is run up to oppose the man or woman who would take the place by storm, but serried lines of subtle contrivances, mines, and pitfalls which it needs a strange skill to overcome. You, in your simplicity, fancied you had only to shout for these walls to sink into nothingness, but the time is gone for such startling victories as these. Take courage; you will learn the secret of success before very long.'

'Alas, sir,' I replied, 'I have no doubt your conclusions are correct, but at the present moment I seem to be in a fair way to die of starvation. You spoke of a secret; for heaven's sake, tell it me, if you have any pity for my distress.'

He laughed genially. 'There lies the strangeness of it all. Those who know the secret cannot tell it if they would; it is positively as ineffable as the central doctrine of Freemasonry. But I may say this, that you yourself have penetrated at least the outer husk of the mystery,' and he laughed again.

'Pray do not jest with me,' I said. 'What have I done, *que sais-je*? I am so far ignorant that I have not the slightest idea of how my next meal is to be provided.'

'Excuse me. You ask what you have done? You have met me. Come, we will fence no longer. I see you have self-education, the only education which is not infinitely pernicious, and I am in want of a governess for my two children. I have been a widower for some years; my name is Gregg. I offer you the post I have named, and shall we say a salary of a hundred a year?'

I could only stutter out my thanks, and slipping a card with his address and a banknote by way of earnest into my hand, Mr Gregg bade me goodbye, asking me to call in a day or two.

Such was my introduction to Professor Gregg, and can you wonder that the remembrance of despair and the cold blast that had blown from the gates of death upon me, made me regard him as a second father? Before the close of the week I was installed in my new duties; the professor had leased an old brick manor house in a western suburb of London, and here, surrounded by pleasant lawns and orchards, and soothed with the murmur of the ancient elms that rocked their boughs above the roof, the new chapter of my life began. Knowing as you do the nature of the professor's occupations, you will not be surprised to hear that the house teemed with books; and cabinets full of strange and even hideous objects filled every available nook in the vast low rooms. Gregg was a man whose one thought was for knowledge, and I too before long caught something of his enthusiasm, and strove to enter into his passion for research. In a few months I was perhaps more his secretary than the governess of the two children, and many a night I have sat at the desk in the glow of the shaded lamp while he, pacing up and down in the rich gloom of the firelight, dictated to me the substance of his *Textbook of Ethnology*. But amidst these more sober and accurate studies I always detected a something hidden, a longing and desire for some object to which he did not allude, and now and then he would break short in what he was saying and lapse into reverie, entranced, as it seemed to me, by some distant prospect of adventurous discovery. The textbook was at last finished, and we began to receive proofs from the printers, which were intrusted to me for a first reading, and then underwent the final revision of the professor. All the while his weariness of the actual business he was engaged on increased, and it was with the joyous laugh of a schoolboy when term is over that he one day handed me a copy of the book. 'There,' he said, 'I have kept my word; I promised to write it, and it is done with. Now I shall be free to live for stranger things; I confess it, Miss Lally, I covet the renown of Columbus. You will, I hope, see me play the part of an explorer.'

'Surely,' I said, 'there is little left to explore. You have been born a few hundred years too late for that.'

'I think you are wrong,' he replied; 'there are still, depend upon it, quaint undiscovered countries and continents of strange extent. Ah, Miss Lally, believe me, we stand amidst sacraments and mysteries full of awe, and it doth not yet appear what we shall be. Life, believe me, is no simple thing, no mass of grey matter and congeries of veins and muscles to be laid naked by the surgeon's knife; man is the secret which I am about to explore, and before I can discover him I must cross over weltering seas indeed, and oceans and the mists of many thousand years. You know the myth of the lost Atlantis; what if it be true, and I am destined to be called the discoverer of that wonderful land?'

I could see excitement boiling beneath his words, and in his face was the heat of the hunter; before me stood a man who believed himself summoned to tourney with the unknown. A pang of joy possessed me when I reflected that I was to be in a way associated with him in the adventure, and I too burned with the lust of the chase, not pausing to consider that I knew not what we were to unshadow.

The next morning Professor Gregg took me into his inner study, where ranged against the wall stood a nest of pigeonholes, every drawer neatly labelled, and the results of years of toil classified in a few feet of space.

'Here,' he said, 'is my life; here are all the facts which I have gathered together with so much pains, and yet it is all nothing. No, nothing to what I am about to attempt. Look at this;' and he took me to an old bureau, a piece fantastic and faded, which stood in a corner of the room. He unlocked the front and opened one of the drawers.

'A few scraps of paper,' he went on, pointing to the drawer, 'and a lump of black stone, rudely annotated with queer marks and scratches, – that is all that drawer holds. Here you see is an old envelope with the dark red stamp of twenty years ago, but I have pencilled a few lines at the back; here is a sheet of manuscript, and here some cuttings from obscure local journals. And if you ask me the subject matter of the collection, it will not seem extraordinary. A servant girl at a farmhouse, who disappeared from her place and has never been heard of, a child supposed to have slipped down some old working on the mountains, some queer scribbling on a limestone rock, a man murdered with a blow from a strange weapon; such is the scent I have to go upon. Yes, as you say, there is a ready explanation for all this; the girl may have run away to London, or Liverpool, or New York; the child may be at the bottom of the disused shaft; and the letters on the rock may be the idle whims of some vagrant. Yes, yes, I admit all that; but I know I hold the true key. Look!' and he held me out a slip of yellow paper.

'*Characters found inscribed on a limestone rock on the Grey Hills*,' I read, and then there was a word erased, presumably the name of a county, and a date some fifteen years back. Beneath was traced a number of uncouth characters, shaped somewhat like wedges or daggers, as strange and outlandish as the Hebrew alphabet.

'Now the seal,' said Professor Gregg, and he handed me the black stone, a thing about two inches long, and something like an old-fashioned tobacco stopper, much enlarged.

I held it up to the light, and saw to my surprise the characters on the paper repeated on the seal.

'Yes,' said the professor, 'they are the same. And the marks on the limestone rock were made fifteen years ago, with some red substance. And the characters on the seal are four thousand years old at least. Perhaps much more.'

'Is it a hoax?' I said.

'No, I anticipated that. I was not to be led to give my life to a practical joke. I have tested the matter very carefully. Only one person besides myself knows of the mere existence of that black seal. Besides, there are other reasons which I cannot enter into now.'

'But what does it all mean?' I said. 'I cannot understand to what conclusion all this leads.'

'My dear Miss Lally, that is a question I would rather leave unanswered for some little time. Perhaps I shall never be able to say what secrets are held here in solution; a few vague hints, the outlines of village tragedies, a few marks done with red earth upon a rock, and an ancient seal. A queer set of data to go upon? Half-a-dozen pieces of evidence, and twenty years before even so much could be got together; and who knows what mirage or *terra incognita* may be beyond all this? I look across deep waters, Miss Lally, and the land beyond may be but a haze after all. But still I believe it is not so, and a few months will show whether I am right or wrong.'

He left me, and alone I endeavoured to fathom the mystery, wondering to what goal such eccentric odds and ends of evidence could lead. I myself am not wholly devoid of imagination, and I had reason to respect the professor's solidity of intellect; yet I saw in the contents of the drawer but the materials of fantasy, and vainly tried to conceive what theory could be founded on the fragments that had been placed before me. Indeed, I could discover in what I had heard and seen but the first chapter of an extravagant romance; and yet deep in my heart I burned with curiosity, and day after day I looked eagerly in Professor Gregg's face for some hint of what was to happen.

It was one evening after dinner that the word came.

'I hope you can make your preparations without much trouble,' he said suddenly to me. 'We shall be leaving here in a week's time.'

'Really!' I said in astonishment. 'Where are we going?'

'I have taken a country house in the west of England, not far from Caermaen, a quiet little town, once a city, and the headquarters of a Roman legion. It is very dull there, but the country is pretty, and the air is wholesome.'

I detected a glint in his eyes, and guessed that this sudden move had some relation to our conversation of a few days before.

'I shall just take a few books with me,' said Professor Gregg, 'that is all. Everything else will remain here for our return. I have got a holiday,' he went on, smiling at me, 'and I shan't be sorry to be quit for a time of my old bones and stones and rubbish. Do you know,' he went on, 'I have been grinding away at facts for thirty years; it is time for fancies.'

The days passed quickly; I could see that the professor was all quivering with suppressed excitement, and I could scarce credit the eager appetence of his glance as we left the old manor house behind us, and began our journey. We set out at midday, and it was in the dusk of the evening that we arrived at a little country station. I was tired and excited, and the drive through the lanes seems all a dream. First the deserted streets of a forgotten village, while I heard Professor Gregg's voice talking of the Augustan Legion and the clash of arms, and all the tremendous pomp that followed the eagles; then the broad river swimming to full tide with the last afterglow glimmering duskily in the yellow water, the wide meadows, and the cornfields whitening, and the deep lane winding on the slope between the hills and the water. At last we began to ascend, and the air grew rarer; I looked down and saw the pure white mist tracking the outline of the river like a shroud, and a vague and shadowy country, imaginations and fantasy of swelling hills and hanging woods, and half-shaped outlines of hills beyond, and in the distance the glare of the furnace fire on the mountain, growing by turns a pillar of shining flame, and fading to a dull point of red. We were slowly mounting a carriage drive, and then there came to me the cool breath and the scent of the great wood that was above us; I seemed to wander in its deepest depths, and there was the sound of trickling water, the scent of the green leaves, and the breath of the summer night. The carriage stopped at last, and I could scarcely distinguish the form of the house as I waited a moment at the pillared porch; and the rest of the evening seemed a dream of strange things bounded by the great silence of the wood and the valley and the river.

The next morning when I awoke and looked out of the bow window of the big old-fashioned bedroom, I saw under a grey sky a country that was still all mystery. The long, lovely valley, with the river winding in and out below, crossed, in mid vision by a mediaeval bridge of vaulted and buttressed stone, the clear presence of the rising ground beyond, and the woods that I had only seen in shadow the night before, seemed tinged with enchantment, and the soft breath of air that sighed in at the opened pane was like no other wind. I looked across the valley, and beyond, hill followed on hill as wave on wave, and here a faint blue pillar of smoke rose still in the morning air from the chimney of an ancient grey farmhouse, there was a rugged height crowned with dark firs, and in the distance I saw the white streak of a road that climbed and vanished into some unimagined country. But the boundary of all was a great wall of mountain, vast in the west, and ending like a fortress with a steep ascent and a domed tumulus clear against the sky.

I saw Professor Gregg walking up and down the terrace path below the windows, and it was evident that he was revelling in the sense of liberty, and the thought that he had, for a while, bidden goodbye to task-work. When I joined him there was exultation in his voice as he pointed out the sweep of valley and the river that wound beneath the lovely hills.

'Yes,' he said, 'it is a strangely beautiful country; and to me, at least, it seems full of mystery. You have not forgotten the drawer I showed you, Miss Lally? No; and you have guessed that I have come here not merely for the sake of the children and the fresh air?'

'I think I have guessed as much as that,' I replied; 'but you must remember I do not know the mere nature of your investigations; and as for the connection between the search and this wonderful valley, it is past my guessing.'

He smiled queerly at me. 'You must not think I am making a mystery for the sake of mystery,' he said. 'I do not speak out because, so far, there is nothing to be spoken, nothing definite I mean, nothing that can be set down in hard black and white, as dull and sure and irreproachable as any blue book. And then I have another reason: many years ago a chance paragraph in a newspaper caught my attention, and focused in an instant the vagrant thoughts and half-formed fancies of many idle and speculative hours into a certain hypothesis. I saw at once that I was treading on a thin crust; my theory was wild and fantastic in the extreme, and I would not for any consideration have written a hint of it for publication. But I thought that in the company of scientific men like myself, men who knew the course of discovery, and were aware that the gas that blazes and flares in the gin palace was once a wild hypothesis; I thought that with such men as these I might hazard my dream – let us say Atlantis, or the philosopher's stone, or what you like – without danger of ridicule. I found I was grossly mistaken; my friends looked blankly at me and at one another, and I could see something of pity, and something also of insolent contempt, in the glances they exchanged. One of them called on me next day, and hinted that I must be suffering from overwork and brain exhaustion. "In plain terms," I said, "you think I am going mad. I think not;" and I showed him out with some little appearance of heat. Since that day I vowed that I would never whisper the nature of my theory to any living soul; to no one but yourself have I ever shown the contents of that drawer. After all, I may be following a rainbow; I may have been misled by the play of coincidence; but as I stand here in this mystic hush and silence amidst the woods and wild hills, I am more than ever sure that I am hot on the scent. Come, it is time we went in.'

To me in all this there was something both of wonder and excitement; I knew how in his ordinary work Professor Gregg moved step by step, testing every inch of the way, and never venturing on assertion without proof that was impregnable. Yet I divined more from his glance and the vehemence of his tone than from the spoken word that he had in his every thought the vision of the almost incredible continually with him; and I, who was with some share of imagination no little of a sceptic, offended at a hint of the marvellous, could not help asking myself whether he was cherishing a monomania, and barring out from this one subject all the scientific method of his other life.

Yet, with this image of mystery haunting my thoughts, I surrendered wholly to the charm of the country. Above the faded house on the hillside began the great forest; a long dark line seen from the opposing hills, stretching above the river for many a mile from north to south, and yielding in the north to even wilder country, barren and savage hills, and ragged common land, a territory all strange and unvisited, and more unknown to Englishmen than the very heart of Africa. The space of a couple of steep fields alone separated the house from the wood, and the children were delighted to follow me up the long alleys of undergrowth, between smooth pleached walls of shining beech, to the highest point in the wood, whence one looked on one side across the river and the rise and fall of the country to the great western mountain wall, and on the other, over the surge and dip of the myriad trees of the forest, over level meadows and the shining yellow sea to the faint coast beyond. I used to sit at this point on the warm sunlit turf which marked the track of the Roman Road, while the two children raced about hunting for the whinberries that grew here and there on the banks. Here beneath the deep blue sky and the great clouds rolling, like olden galleons with sails full-bellied, from the sea to the hills, as I listened to the whispered charm of the great and ancient wood, I lived solely for delight, and only remembered strange things when we would return to the house, and find Professor Gregg either shut up in the little room he had made his study, or else pacing the terrace with the look, patient and enthusiastic, of the determined seeker.

One morning, some eight or nine days after our arrival, I looked out of my window and saw the whole landscape transmuted before me. The clouds had dipped low and hidden the mountain in the west, and a southern wind was driving the rain in shifting pillars up the valley, and the little brooklet that burst the hill below the house now raged, a red torrent, down to the river. We were perforce obliged to keep snug within doors, and when I had attended to my pupils, I sat down in the morning room where the ruins of a library still encumbered an old-fashioned bookcase. I had inspected the shelves once or twice, but their contents had failed to attract me; volumes of eighteenth century sermons, an old book on farriery, a collection of *Poems* by 'persons of quality', Prideaux's *Connection*, and an odd volume of Pope were the boundaries of the library, and there seemed little doubt that everything of interest or value had been removed. Now, however, in desperation, I began to re-examine the musty sheepskin and calf bindings, and found, much to my delight, a fine old quarto printed by the Stephani, containing the three books of Pomponius Mela, *De Situ Orbis*, and other of the ancient geographers. I knew enough of Latin to steer my way through an ordinary sentence, and I soon became absorbed in the odd mixture of fact and fancy – light shining on a little of the space of the world, and beyond mist and shadow and awful forms. Glancing over the clear-printed pages, my attention was caught by the heading of a chapter in Solinus, and I read the words: –

MIRA DE INTIMIS GENTIBUS LIBYAE,
DE LAPIDE HEXECONTALITHO

'The wonders of the people that inhabit the inner parts
of Libya, and of the stone called Sixtystone.'

The odd title attracted me and I read on: –

'Gens ista avia et secreta habitat, in montibus horrendis foeda mysteria celebrat. De hominibus nihil aliud illi praeferunt quam figuram, ab humano ritu prorsus exulant, oderunt deum lucis. Stridunt potius quam loquuntur; vox absona nec sine horrore auditur. Lapide quodam gloriantur, quem Hexecontalithon vocant, dicunt enim hunc lapidem sexaginta notas ostendere. Cujus lapidis nomen secretum ineffabile colunt: quod Ixaxar.'

'This folk,' I translated to myself, 'dwells in remote and secret places, and celebrates foul mysteries on savage hills. Nothing have they in common with men save the face, and the customs of humanity are wholly strange to them; and they hate the sun. They hiss rather than speak; their voices are harsh, and not to be heard without fear. They boast of a certain stone, which they call Sixtystone; for they say that it displays sixty characters. And this stone has a secret unspeakable name; which is Ixaxar.'

I laughed at the queer inconsequence of all this, and thought it fit for Sinbad the Sailor or other of the supplementary *Nights*. When I saw Professor Gregg in the course of the day, I told him of my find in the bookcase, and the fantastic rubbish I had been reading. To my surprise, he looked up at me with an expression of great interest.

'That is really very curious,' he said. 'I have never thought it worth while to look into the old geographers, and I dare say I have missed a good deal. Ah, that is the passage, is it? It seems a shame to rob you of your entertainment, but I really think I must carry off the book.'

The next day the professor called to me to come to the study. I found him sitting at a table in the full light of the window, scrutinising something very attentively with a magnifying glass.

'Ah, Miss Lally,' he began, 'I want to use your eyes. This glass is pretty good, but not like my old one that I left in town. Would you mind examining the thing yourself, and telling me how many characters are cut on it?'

He handed me the object in his hand, and I saw that it was the black seal he had shown me in London, and my heart began to beat with the thought that I was presently to know something. I took the seal, and holding it up to the light checked off the grotesque dagger-shaped characters one by one.

'I make sixty-two,' I said at last.

'Sixty-two? Nonsense; it's impossible. Ah, I see what you have done, you have counted that and that,' and he pointed to two marks which I had certainly taken as letters with the rest.

'Yes, yes,' Professor Gregg went on; 'but those are obvious scratches, done accidentally; I saw that at once. Yes, then that's quite right. Thank you very much, Miss Lally.'

I was going away, rather disappointed at my having been called in merely to count a number of marks on the black seal, when suddenly there flashed into my mind what I had read in the morning.

'But, Professor Gregg, I cried, breathless, the seal, the seal. Why, it is the stone Hexecontalithos that Solinus writes of; it is Ixaxar.'

'Yes,' he said, 'I suppose it is. Or it maybe a mere coincidence. It never does to be too sure, you know, in these matters. Coincidence killed the professor.'

I went away puzzled by what I had heard, and as much as ever at a loss to find the ruling clue in this maze of strange evidence. For three days the bad weather lasted, changing from driving rain to a dense mist, fine and dripping, and we seemed to be shut up in a white cloud that veiled all the world away from us. All the while Professor Gregg was darkling in his room, unwilling, it appeared, to dispense confidences or talk of any kind, and I heard him walking to and fro with a quick, impatient step, as if he were in some way wearied of inaction. The fourth morning was fine, and at breakfast the professor said briskly: –

'We want some extra help about the house; a boy of fifteen or sixteen, you know. There are a lot of little odd jobs that take up the maids' time, which a boy could do much better.'

'The girls have not complained to me in any way,' I replied. 'Indeed, Anne said there was much less work than in London, owing to there being so little dust.'

'Ah, yes, they are very good girls. But I think we shall do much better with a boy. In fact, that is what has been bothering me for the last two days.'

'Bothering you?' I said in astonishment, for as a matter of fact the professor never took the slightest interest in the affairs of the house.

'Yes,' he said, 'the weather, you know. I really couldn't go out in that Scotch mist; I don't know the country very well, and I should have lost my way. But I am going to get the boy this morning.'

'But how do you know there is such a boy as you want anywhere about?'

'Oh, I have no doubt as to that. I may have to walk a mile or two at the most, but I am sure to find just the boy I require.'

I thought the professor was joking, but though his tone was airy enough there was something grim and set about his features that puzzled me. He got his stick, and stood at the door looking meditatively before him, and as I passed through the hall he called to me.

'By the way, Miss Lally, there was one thing I wanted to say to you. I daresay you may have heard that some of these country lads are not over bright; idiotic would be a harsh word to use, and they are usually called "naturals", or something of the kind, I hope you won't mind if the boy I am after should turn out not too keen-witted; he will be perfectly harmless, of course, and blacking boots doesn't need much mental effort.'

With that he was gone, striding up the road that led to the wood; and I remained stupefied, and then for the first time my astonishment was mingled with a sudden note of terror, arising I knew not whence, and all unexplained even to myself, and yet I felt about my heart for an instant something of the chill of death, and that shapeless, formless dread of the unknown that is worse than death itself. I tried to find courage in the sweet air that blew up from the sea, and in the sunlight after rain, but the mystic woods seemed to darken around me; and the vision of the river coiling between the reeds, and the silver grey of the ancient bridge, fashioned in my mind symbols of vague dread, as the mind of a child fashions terror from things harmless and familiar.

Two hours later Professor Gregg returned. I met him as he came down the road, and asked quietly if he had been able to find a boy.

'Oh, yes,' he answered; 'I found one easily enough. His name is Jervase Cradock, and I expect he will make himself very useful. His father has been dead for many years, and the mother, whom I saw, seemed very glad at the prospect of a few shillings extra coming in on Saturday nights. As I expected, he is not too sharp, has fits at times, the mother said; but as he will not be trusted with the china, that doesn't much matter, does it? And he is not in any way dangerous, you know, merely a little weak.'

'When is he coming?'

'Tomorrow morning at eight o'clock. Anne will show him what he has to do, and how to do it. At first he will go home every night, but perhaps it may ultimately turn out more convenient for him to sleep here, and only go home for Sundays.'

I found nothing to say to all this. Professor Gregg spoke in a quiet tone of matter-of-fact, as indeed was warranted by the circumstance; and yet I could not quell my sensation of astonishment at the whole affair. I knew that in reality no assistance was wanted in the housework, and the professor's prediction that the boy he was to engage might prove a little 'simple', followed by so exact a fulfilment, struck me as bizarre in the extreme. The next morning I heard from the housemaid that the boy Cradock had come at eight, and that she had been trying to make him useful. 'He doesn't seem quite all there, I don't think, miss,' was her comment; and later in the day I saw him helping the old man who worked in the garden. He was a youth of about fourteen, with black hair and black eyes, and an olive skin, and I saw at once from the curious vacancy of his expression that he was mentally weak. He touched his forehead awkwardly as I went by, and I heard him answering the gardener in a queer, harsh voice that caught my attention;

it gave me the impression of some one speaking deep below under the earth, and there was a strange sibilance, like the hissing of the phonograph as the pointer travels over the cylinder. I heard that he seemed anxious to do what he could, and was quite docile and obedient, and Morgan the gardener, who knew his mother, assured me he was perfectly harmless. 'He's always been a bit queer,' he said, 'and no wonder, after what his mother went through before he was born. I did know his father, Thomas Cradock, well, and a very fine workman he was too, indeed. He got something wrong with his lungs owing to working in the wet woods, and never got over it, and went off quite sudden like. And they do say as how Mrs Cradock was quite off her head; anyhow, she was found by Mr Hillyer, Ty Coch, all crouched up on the Grey Hills, over there, crying and weeping like a lost soul. And Jervase he was born about eight months afterwards, and as I was saying, he was a bit queer always; and they do say when he could scarcely walk he would frighten the other children into fits with the noises he would make.'

A word in the story had stirred up some remembrance within me, and vaguely curious, I asked the old man where the Grey Hills were.

'Up there,' he said, with the same gesture he had used before; 'you go past the Fox and Hounds, and through the forest, by the old ruins. It's a good five mile from here, and a strange sort of a place. The poorest soil between this and Monmouth, they do say, though it's good feed for sheep. Yes, it was a sad thing for poor Mrs Cradock.'

The old man turned to his work, and I strolled on down the path between the espaliers, gnarled and gouty with age, thinking of the story I had heard, and groping for the point in it that had some key to my memory. In an instant it came before me; I had seen the phrase 'Grey Hills' on the slip of yellowed paper that Professor Gregg had taken from the drawer in his cabinet. Again I was seized with pangs of mingled curiosity and fear; I remembered the strange characters copied from the limestone rock, and then again their identity with the inscription on the age-old seal, and the fantastic fables of the Latin geographer. I saw beyond doubt that, unless coincidence had set all the scene and disposed all these bizarre events with curious art, I was to be a spectator of things far removed from the usual and customary traffic and jostle of life. Professor Gregg I noted day by day. He was hot on his trail, growing lean with eagerness; and in the evenings, when the sun was swimming on the verge of the mountain, he would pace the terrace to and fro with his eyes on the ground, while the mist grew white in the valley, and the stillness of the evening brought far voices near, and the blue smoke rose a straight column from the diamond-shaped chimney of the grey farmhouse, just as I had seen it on the first morning. I have told you I was of sceptical habit; but though I understood little or nothing, I began to dread, vainly proposing to myself the iterated dogmas of science that all life is material, and that in the system of things there is no undiscovered land even beyond the remotest stars, where the supernatural can find a footing. Yet there struck in on this the thought that matter is as really awful and unknown as spirit, that science itself but dallies on the threshold, scarcely gaining more than a glimpse of the wonders of the inner place.

There is one day that stands up from amidst the others as a grim red beacon, betokening evil to come. I was sitting on a bench in the garden, watching the boy Cradock weeding, when I was suddenly alarmed by a harsh and choking sound, like the cry of a wild beast in anguish, and I was unspeakably shocked to see the unfortunate lad standing in full view before me, his whole body quivering and shaking at short intervals as though shocks of electricity were passing through him, and his teeth grinding, and foam gathering on his lips, and his face all swollen and blackened to a hideous mask of humanity. I shrieked with terror, and Professor Gregg came running; and as I pointed to Cradock, the boy with one convulsive shudder fell face forward, and lay on the wet earth, his body writhing like a wounded blind worm, and an inconceivable babble of sounds bursting and rattling and hissing from his lips; he seemed to pour forth an infamous jargon, with words, or what seemed words, that might have belonged to a tongue dead since untold ages, and buried deep beneath Nilotic mud, or in the inmost recesses of the Mexican forest. For a moment the thought passed through my mind, as my ears were still revolted with that infernal clamour, 'Surely this is the very speech of hell,' and then I cried out again and again, and ran away shuddering to my inmost soul. I had seen Professor Gregg's face as he stooped over the wretched boy and raised him, and I was appalled by the glow of exultation that shone on every lineament and feature. As I sat in my room with drawn blinds, and my eyes hidden in my hands, I heard heavy steps beneath, and I was told afterwards that Professor Gregg had carried Cradock to his study, and had locked the door. I heard voices murmur indistinctly, and I trembled to think of what might be passing within a few feet of where I sat; I longed to escape to the woods and sunshine, and yet I dreaded the sights that might confront me on the way. And at last, as I held the handle of the door nervously, I heard Professor Gregg's voice calling to me with a cheerful ring: 'It's all right now, Miss Lally,' he said. 'The poor fellow has got over it, and I have been arranging for him to sleep here after tomorrow. Perhaps I may be able to do something for him.'

'Yes,' he said later, 'it was a very painful sight, and I don't wonder you were alarmed. We may hope that good food will build him up a little, but I am afraid he will never be really cured;' and he affected the dismal and conventional air with which one speaks of hopeless illness, and yet beneath it I detected the delight that leapt up rampant within him, and fought and struggled to find utterance. It was as if one glanced down on the even surface of the sea, clear and immobile, and saw beneath raging depths, and a storm of contending billows. It was indeed to me a torturing and offensive problem that this man, who had so bounteously rescued me from the sharpness of death, and showed himself in all the relations of life full of benevolence and pity and kindly forethought, should so manifestly be for once on the side of the demons, and take a ghastly pleasure in the torments of an afflicted fellow creature. Apart, I struggled with the horned difficulty, and strove to find the solution, but without the hint of a clue; beset by mystery and contradiction, I saw nothing that might help me, and began to wonder whether, after all, I had not escaped from the white mist of the suburb at too dear a rate. I hinted something of my thought to the professor; I said enough to let him know that I was in the most acute perplexity, but the moment after regretted what I had done, when I saw his face contort with a spasm of pain.

'My dear Miss Lally,' he said, 'you surely do not wish to leave us? No, no, you would not do it. You do not know how I rely on you; how confidently I go forward, assured that you are here to watch over my children. You, Miss Lally, are my rearguard; for, let me tell you, that the business in which I am engaged is not wholly devoid of peril. You have not forgotten what I said the first morning here; my lips are shut by an old and firm resolve, till they can open to utter no ingenious hypothesis or vague surmise but irrefragable fact, as certain as a demonstration in mathematics. Think over it, Miss Lally, not for a moment would I endeavour to keep you here against your own instincts, and yet I tell you frankly that I am persuaded that it is here, here amidst the woods, that your duty lies.'

I was touched by the eloquence of his tone, and by the remembrance that the man, after all, had been my salvation, and I gave him my hand on a promise to serve him loyally and without question. A few days later the rector of our church, a little church, grey and severe and quaint, that hovered on the very banks of the river and watched the tides swim and return, came to see us, and Professor Gregg easily persuaded him to stay and share our dinner. Mr Meyrick was a member of an antique family of squires, whose old manor house stood amongst the hills some seven miles away, and thus rooted in the soil, the rector was a living store of all the old fading customs and lore of the country. His manner, genial with a deal of retired oddity, won on Professor Gregg; and towards the cheese, when a curious Burgundy had begun its incantations, the two men glowed like the wine, and talked of philology with the enthusiasm of a burgess over the peerage. The parson was expounding the pronunciation of the Welsh *ll*, and producing sounds like the gurgle of his native brooks, when Professor Gregg struck in.

'By the way,' he said, 'that was a very odd word I met with the other day. You know my boy, poor Jervase Cradock. Well, he has got the bad habit of talking to himself, and the day before yesterday I was walking in the garden here and heard him; he was evidently quite unconscious of my presence. A lot of what he said I couldn't make out, but one word struck me distinctly. It was such an odd sound; half-sibilant, half-guttural, and as quaint as those double *l*s you have been demonstrating. I do not know whether I can give you an idea of the sound. "Ishakshar" is perhaps as near as I can get; but the *k* ought to be a Greek *chi* or a Spanish *j*. Now what does it mean in Welsh?'

'In Welsh?' said the parson. 'There is no such word in Welsh, nor any word remotely resembling it. I know the book-Welsh, as they call it, and the colloquial dialects as well as any man, but there's no word like that from Anglesea to Usk. Besides, none of the Cradocks speaks a word of Welsh; it's dying out about here.'

'Really. You interest me extremely, Mr Meyrick. I confess the word didn't strike me as having the Welsh ring. But I thought it might be some local corruption.'

'No, I never heard such a word, or anything like it. Indeed,' he added, smiling whimsically, 'if it belongs to any language, I should say it must be that of the fairies – the Tylwydd Têg, as we call them.'

The talk went on to the discovery of a Roman villa in the neighbourhood; and soon after I left the room, and sat down apart to wonder at the drawing together of such strange clues of evidence. As the professor had spoken of the curious word, I had caught the glint of his eye upon me; and though the pronunciation he gave was grotesque in the extreme, I recognised the name of the stone of sixty characters mentioned by Solinus, the black seal shut up in some secret drawer of the study, stamped forever by a vanished race with signs that no man could read, signs that might, for all I knew, be the veils of awful things done long ago, and forgotten before the hills were moulded into form.

When, the next morning, I came down, I found Professor Gregg pacing the terrace in his eternal walk.

'Look at that bridge,' he said when he saw me, 'observe the quaint and Gothic design, the angles between the arches, and the silvery grey of the stone in the awe of the morning light. I confess it seems to me symbolic; it should illustrate a mystical allegory of the passage from one world to another.'

'Professor Gregg,' I said quietly, 'it is time that I knew something of what has happened, and of what is to happen.'

For the moment he put me off, but I returned again with the same question in the evening, and then Professor Gregg flamed with excitement. 'Don't you understand yet?' he cried. 'But I have told you a good deal; yes, and shown you a good deal. You have heard pretty nearly all that I have heard, and seen what I have seen; or at least,' and his voice chilled as he spoke, 'enough to make a good deal clear as noonday. The servants told you, I have no doubt, that the wretched boy Cradock had another seizure the night before last; he awoke me with cries in that voice you heard in the garden, and I went to him, and God forbid you should see what I saw that night. But all this is useless; my time here is drawing to a close; I must be back in town in three weeks, as I have a course of lectures to prepare, and need all my books about me. In a very few days it will be all over, and I shall no longer hint, and no longer be liable to ridicule as a madman and a quack. No, I shall speak plainly, and I shall be heard with such emotions as perhaps no other man has ever drawn from the breasts of his fellows.'

He paused, and seemed to grow radiant with the joy of great and wonderful discovery.

'But all that is for the future, the near future certainly, but still the future,' he went on at length. 'There is something to be done yet; you will remember my telling you that my researches were not altogether devoid of peril? Yes, there is a certain amount of danger to be faced; I did not know how much when I spoke on the subject before, and to a certain extent I am still in the dark. But it will be a strange adventure, the last of all, the last demonstration in the chain.'

He was walking up and down the room as he spoke, and I could hear in his voice the contending tones of exultation and despondence, or perhaps I should say awe, the awe of a man who goes forth on unknown waters, and I thought of his allusion to Columbus on the night he had laid his book before me. The evening was a little chilly, and a fire of logs had been lighted in the study where we were, and the remittent flame and the glow on the walls reminded me of the old days. I was sitting silent in an armchair by the fire, wondering over all I had heard, and still vainly speculating as to the secret springs concealed from me under all the phantasmagoria I had witnessed, when I became suddenly aware of a sensation that change of some sort had been at work in the room, and that there was something unfamiliar in its aspect. For some time I looked about me, trying in vain to localise the alteration that I knew had been made; the table by the window, the chairs, the faded settee were all as I had known them. Suddenly, as a sought-for recollection flashes into the mind, I knew what was amiss. I was facing the professor's desk, which stood on the other side of the fire, and above the desk was a grimy looking bust of Pitt, that I had never seen there before. And then I remembered the true position of this work of art; in the furthest corner by the door was an old cupboard, projecting into the room, and on the top of the cupboard, fifteen feet from the floor, the bust had been, and there no doubt it had delayed, accumulating dirt since the early years of the century.

I was utterly amazed, and sat silent still, in a confusion of thought. There was, so far as I knew, no such thing as a stepladder in the house, for I had asked for one to make some alterations in the curtains of my room; and a tall man standing on a chair would have found it impossible to take down the bust. It had been placed not on the edge of the cupboard, but far back against the wall; and Professor Gregg was, if anything, under the average height.

'How on earth did you manage to get down Pitt?' I said at last.

The professor looked curiously at me, and seemed to hesitate a little.

'They must have found you a stepladder, or perhaps the gardener brought in a short ladder from outside.'

'No, I have had no ladder of any kind. Now, Miss Lally,' he went on with an awkward simulation of jest, 'there is a little puzzle for you; a problem in the manner of the inimitable Holmes; there are the facts, plain and patent; summon your acuteness to the solution of the puzzle. For Heaven's sake,' he cried with a breaking voice, 'say no more about it. I tell you, I never touched the thing,' and he went out of the room with horror manifest on his face, and his hand shook and jarred the door behind him.

I looked round the room in vague surprise, not at all realising what had happened, making vain and idle surmises by way of explanation, and wondering at the stirring of black waters by an idle word, and the trivial change of an ornament. 'This is some petty business, some whim on which I have jarred,' I reflected; 'the professor is perhaps scrupulous and superstitious over trifles, and my question may have outraged unacknowledged fears, as though one killed a spider or spilled the salt before the very eyes of a practical Scotchwoman.' I was immersed in these fond suspicions, and began to plume myself a little on my immunity from such empty fears, when the truth fell heavily as lead upon my heart, and I recognised with cold terror that some awful influence had been at work. The bust was simply inaccessible; without a ladder no one could have touched it.

I went out to the kitchen and spoke as quietly as I could to the housemaid.

'Who moved that bust from the top of the cupboard, Anne?' I said to her. 'Professor Gregg says he has not touched it. Did you find an old stepladder in one of the outhouses?'

The girl looked at me blankly.

'I never touched it,' she said. 'I found it where it is now the other morning when I dusted the room. I remember now, it was Wednesday morning, because it was the morning after Cradock was taken bad in the night. My room is next to his, you know, miss,' the girl went on piteously; 'and it was awful to hear how he cried and called out names that I couldn't understand. It made me feel all afraid, and then master came, and I heard him speak, and he took down Cradock to the study and gave him something.'

'And you found that bust moved the next morning?'

'Yes, miss, there was a queer sort of a smell in the study when I came down and opened the windows; a bad smell it was, and I wondered what it could be. Do you know, miss, I went a long time ago to the Zoo in London with my cousin Thomas Barker, one afternoon that I had off, when I was at Mrs Prince's in Stanhope Gate, and we went into the snake house to see the snakes, and it was just the same sort of a smell, very sick it made me feel, I remember, and I got Barker to take me out. And it was just the same kind of a smell in the study, as I was saying, and I was wondering what it could be from, when I see that bust with Pitt cut in it standing on the master's desk, and I thought to myself, now who has done that, and how have they done it? And when I came to dust the things, I looked at the bust, and I saw a great mark on it where the dust was gone, for I don't think it can have been touched with a duster for years and years, and it wasn't like finger-marks, but a large patch like, broad and spread out. So I passed my hand over it, without thinking what I was doing, and where that patch was it was all sticky and slimy, as if a snail had crawled over it. Very strange, isn't it, miss? and I wonder who can have done it, and how that mess was made.'

The well-meant gabble of the servant touched me to the quick. I lay down upon my bed, and bit my lip that I should not cry out loud in the sharp anguish of my terror and bewilderment. Indeed, I was almost mad with dread; I believe that if it had been daylight I should have fled hot foot, forgetting all courage and all the debt of gratitude that was due to Professor Gregg, not caring whether my fate were that I must starve slowly so long as I might escape from the net of blind and panic fear that every day seemed to draw a little closer round me. If I knew, I thought, if I knew what there were to dread, I could guard against it; but here, in this lonely house, shut in on all sides by the olden woods and the vaulted hills, terror seems to spring inconsequent from every covert, and the flesh is aghast at the half-heard murmurs of horrible things. All in vain I strove to summon scepticism to my aid, and endeavoured by cool common sense to buttress my belief in a world of natural order, for the air that blew in at the open window was a mystic breath, and in the darkness I felt the silence go heavy and sorrowful as a mass of requiem, and I conjured images of strange shapes gathering fast amidst the reeds, beside the wash of the river.

In the morning, from the moment that I set foot in the breakfast room I felt that the unknown plot was drawing to a crisis; the professor's face was firm and set, and he seemed hardly to hear our voices when we spoke.

'I am going out for rather a long walk,' he said, when the meal was over. 'You mustn't be expecting me, now, or thinking anything has happened if I don't turn up to dinner. I have been getting stupid lately, and I dare say a miniature walking tour will do me good. Perhaps I may even spend the night in some little inn, if I find any place that looks clean and comfortable.'

I heard this, and knew by my experience of Professor Gregg's manner that it was no ordinary business or pleasure that impelled him. I knew not, nor even remotely guessed, where he was bound, nor had I the vaguest notion of his errand, but all the fear of the night before returned; and as he stood, smiling, on the terrace, ready to set out, I implored him to stay, and to forget all his dreams of the undiscovered continent.

'No, no, Miss Lally,' he replied, still smiling, 'it's too late now. *Vestigia nulla retrorsum*, you know, is the device of all true explorers, though I hope it won't be literally true in my ease. But, indeed, you are wrong to alarm yourself so; I look upon my little expedition as quite commonplace; no more exciting than a day with the geological hammers. There is a risk, of course, but so there is on the commonest excursion. I can afford to be jaunty; I am doing nothing so hazardous as 'Arry does a hundred times over in the course of every Bank Holiday. Well, then, you must look more cheerfully; and so goodbye till tomorrow at latest.'

He walked briskly up the road, and I saw him open the gate that marks the entrance of the wood, and then he vanished in the gloom of the trees.

All the day passed heavily with a strange darkness in the air, and again I felt as if imprisoned amidst the ancient woods, shut in an olden land of mystery and dread, and as if all was long ago and forgotten by the living outside. I hoped and dreaded, and when the dinner hour came, I waited expecting to hear the professor's step in the hall, and his voice exulting at I knew not what triumph. I composed my face to welcome him gladly, but the night descended dark, and he did not come.

In the morning when the maid knocked at my door, I called out to her, and asked if her master had returned; and when she replied that his bedroom stood open and empty, I felt the cold clasp of despair. Still, I fancied he might have discovered genial company, and would return for luncheon, or perhaps in the afternoon, and I took the children for a walk in the forest, and tried my best to play and laugh with them, and to shut out the thoughts of mystery and veiled terror. Hour after hour I waited, and my thoughts grew darker; again the night came and found me watching, and at last, as I was making much ado to finish my dinner, I heard steps outside and the sound of a man's voice.

The maid came in and looked oddly at me.

'Please, miss,' she began, 'Mr Morgan the gardener wants to speak to you for a minute, if you didn't mind.'

'Show him in, please,' I answered, and I set my lips tight.

The old man came slowly into the room, and the servant shut the door behind him.

'Sit down, Mr Morgan,' I said; 'what is it that you want to say to me?'

'Well, miss, Mr Gregg he gave me something for you yesterday morning, just before he went off; and he told me particular not to hand it up before eight o'clock this evening exactly, if so be as he wasn't back again home before, and if he should come home before I was just to return it to him in his own hands. So, you see, as Mr Gregg isn't here yet, I suppose I'd better give you the parcel directly.'

He pulled out something from his pocket, and gave it to me, half rising. I took it silently, and seeing that Morgan seemed doubtful as to what he was to do next, I thanked him and bade him good night, and he went out. I was left alone in the room with the parcel in my hand – a paper parcel neatly sealed and directed to me, with the instructions Morgan had quoted all written in the professor's large loose hand. I broke the seals with a choking at my heart, and found an envelope inside, addressed also, but open, and I took the letter out.

'My dear Miss Lally,' it began, 'To quote the old logic manual, the case of your reading this note is a case of my having made a blunder of some sort, and, I am afraid, a blunder that turns these lines into a farewell. It is practically certain that neither you nor anyone else will ever see me again. I have made my will with provision for this eventuality, and I hope you will consent to accept the small remembrance addressed to you, and my sincere thanks for the way in which you joined your fortunes to mine. The fate which has come upon me is desperate and terrible beyond the remotest dreams of man; but this fate you have a right to know – if you please. If you look in the left-hand drawer of my dressing table, you will find the key of the escritoire, properly labelled. In the well of the escritoire is a large envelope sealed and addressed to your name. I advise you to throw it forthwith into the fire; you will sleep better of nights if you do so. But if you must know the history of what has happened, it is all written down for you to read.'

The signature was firmly written below, and again I turned the page and read out the words one by one, aghast and white to the lips, my hands cold as ice, and sickness choking me. The dead silence of the room, and the thought of the dark woods and hills closing me in on every side, oppressed me, helpless and without capacity, and not knowing where to turn for counsel. At last I resolved that though knowledge should haunt my whole life and all the days to come, I must know the meaning of the strange terrors that had so long tormented me, rising grey, dim, and awful, like the shadows in the wood at dusk. I carefully carried out Professor Gregg's directions, and not without reluctance broke the seal of the envelope, and spread out his manuscript before me. This, then, was what I read that night, sitting at the desk, with a shaded lamp beside me.

The Statement of William Gregg, F.R.S., etc.

It is many years since the first glimmer of the theory which is now almost, if not quite, reduced to fact dawned first on my mind. A somewhat extensive course of miscellaneous and obsolete reading had done a good deal to prepare the way, and, later, when I became somewhat of a specialist and immersed myself in the studies known as ethnological, I was now and then startled by facts that would not square with orthodox scientific opinion, and by discoveries that seemed to hint at something still hidden for all our research. More particularly I became convinced that much of the folklore of the world is but an exaggerated account of events that really happened, and I was especially drawn to consider the stories of the fairies, the good folk of the Celtic races. Here I thought I could detect the fringe of embroidery and exaggeration, the fantastic guise, the little people dressed in green and gold sporting in the flowers, and I thought I saw a distinct analogy between the name given to this race (supposed to be imaginary) and the description of their appearance and manners. Just as our remote ancestors called the dreaded beings 'fair' and 'good' precisely because they dreaded them, so they had dressed them up in charming forms, knowing the truth to be the very reverse. Literature, too, had gone early to work, and had lent a powerful hand in the transformation, so that the playful elves of Shakespeare are already far removed from the true original, and the real horror is disguised in a form of prankish mischief. But in the older tales, the stories that used to make men cross themselves as they sat round the burning logs, we tread a different stage; I saw a widely opposed spirit in certain histories of children and of men and women who vanished strangely from the earth. They would be seen by a peasant in the fields walking towards some green and rounded hillock, and seen no more on earth; and there are stories of mothers who have left a child quietly sleeping with the cottage door rudely barred with a piece of wood, and have returned, not to find the plump and rosy little Saxon, but a thin and wizened creature, with sallow skin and black piercing eyes, the child of another race. Then, again, there were myths darker still; the dread of witch and wizard, the lurid evil of the Sabbath, and the hint of demons who mingled with the daughters of men. And just as we have turned the terrible 'fair folk' into a company of benignant, if freakish, elves, so we have hidden from us the black foulness of the witch and her companions under a popular *diablerie* of old women and broomsticks and a comic cat with tail on end. So the Greeks called the hideous furies benevolent ladies, and thus the northern nations have followed their example. I pursued my investigations, stealing odd hours from other and more imperative labors, and I asked myself the question: Supposing these traditions to be true, who were the demons who are reported to have attended the Sabbaths? I need not say that I laid aside what I may call the supernatural hypothesis of the middle ages, and came to the conclusion that fairies and devils were of one and the same race and origin; invention, no doubt, and the Gothic fancy of old days had done much in the way of exaggeration and distortion; yet I firmly believed that beneath all this imagery there was a black background of truth. As for some of the alleged wonders, I hesitated. While I should be very loth to receive any one specific instance of modern spiritualism as containing even a grain of the genuine, yet I was not wholly prepared to deny that human flesh may now and then, once perhaps in ten million cases, be the veil of powers which seem magical to us; powers which, so far from proceeding from the heights and leading men thither, are in reality survivals from the depths of being. The amoeba and the snail have powers which we do not possess; and I thought it possible that the theory of reversion might explain many things which seem wholly inexplicable. Thus stood my position; I saw good reason to believe that much of the tradition, a vast deal of the earliest and uncorrupted tradition of the so-called fairies, represented solid fact, and I thought that the purely supernatural element in these traditions, was to be accounted for on the hypothesis that a race which had fallen out of the grand march of evolution might have retained, as a survival, certain powers which would be to us wholly miraculous. Such was my theory as it stood conceived in my mind; and working with this in view, I seemed to gather confirmation from every side, from the spoils of a tumulus or a barrow, from a local paper reporting an antiquarian meeting in the country, and from general literature of all kinds. Amongst other instances, I remember being struck by the phrase 'articulate-speaking men' in Homer, as if the writer knew or had heard of men whose speech was so rude that it could hardly be termed articulate; and on my hypothesis of a race who had lagged far behind the rest, I could easily conceive that such a folk would speak a jargon but little removed from the inarticulate noises of brute beasts.

Thus I stood, satisfied that my conjecture was at all events not far removed from fact, when a chance paragraph in a small country print one day arrested my attention. It was a short account of what was to all appearance the usual sordid tragedy of the village; a young girl unaccountably missing, and evil rumour blatant and busy with her reputation. Yet I could read between the lines that all this scandal was purely hypothetical, and in all probability invented to account for what was in any other manner unaccountable. A flight to London or Liverpool, or an undiscovered body lying with a weight about its neck in the foul depths of a woodland pool, of perhaps murder, – such were the theories of the wretched girl's neighbours. But as I idly scanned the paragraph, a flash of thought passed through me with the violence of an electric shock: What if the obscure and horrible race of the hills still survived, still remained haunting wild places, and barren hills, and now and then repeating the evil of Gothic legend, unchanged and unchangeable as the Turanian Shelta, or the Basques of Spain. I have said that the thought came with violence; and indeed I drew in my breath sharply, and clung with both hands to my elbow chair, in a strange confusion of horror and elation. It was as if one of my *confrères* of physical science, roaming in a quiet English wood, had been suddenly stricken aghast by the presence of the slimy and loathsome terror of the ichthyosaurus, the original of the stories of the awful worms killed by valorous knights, or had seen the sun darkened by the pterodactyl, the dragon of tradition. Yet as a resolute explorer of knowledge, the thought of such a discovery threw me into a passion of joy, and I cut out the slip from the paper, and put it in a drawer in my old bureau, resolved that it should be but the first piece in a collection of the strangest significance. I sat long that evening dreaming of the conclusions I should establish, nor did cooler reflection at first dash my confidence. Yet as I began to put the case fairly, I saw that I might be building on an unstable foundation; the facts might possibly be in accordance with local opinion; and I regarded the affair with a mood of some reserve. Yet I resolved to remain perched on the look-out, and I hugged to myself the thought that I alone was watching and wakeful, while the great crowd of thinkers and searchers stood heedless and indifferent, perhaps letting the most prerogative facts pass by unnoticed.

Several years elapsed before I was enabled to add to the contents of the drawer; and the second find was in reality not a valuable one, for it was a mere repetition of the first, with only the variation of another and distant locality. Yet I gained something; for in the second case, as in the first, the tragedy took place in a desolate and lonely country, and so far my theory seemed justified. But the third piece was to me far more decisive. Again, amongst outland hills, far even from a main road of traffic, an old man was found done to death, and the instrument of execution was left beside him. Here, indeed, there was rumour and conjecture, for the deadly tool was a primitive stone axe, bound by gut to the wooden handle, and surmises the most extravagant and improbable were indulged in. Yet, as I thought with a kind of glee, the wildest conjectures went far astray; and I took the pains to enter into correspondence with the local doctor, who was called at the inquest. He, a man of some acuteness, was dumbfounded. 'It will not do to speak of these things in country places, he wrote to me; but, frankly, Professor Gregg, there is some hideous mystery here. I have obtained possession of the stone axe, and have been so curious as to test its powers. I took it into the back garden of my house one Sunday afternoon when my family and the servants were all out, and there, sheltered by the poplar hedges, I made my experiments. I found the thing utterly unmanageable. Whether there is some peculiar balance, some nice adjustment of weights, which require incessant practice, or whether an effectual blow can be struck only by a certain trick of the muscles, I do not know; but I assure you that I went into the house with but a sorry opinion of my athletic capacities. It was like an inexperienced man trying "putting the hammer"; the force exerted seemed to return on oneself, and I found myself hurled backwards with violence, while the axe fell harmless to the ground. On another occasion I tried the experiment with a clever woodman of the place; but this man, who had handled his axe for forty years, could do nothing with the stone implement, and missed every stroke most ludicrously. In short, if it were not so supremely absurd, I should say that for four thousand years no one on earth could have struck an effective blow with the tool that undoubtedly was used to murder the old man.' This, as may be imagined, was to me rare news; and afterwards, when I heard the whole story, and learned that the unfortunate old man had babbled tales of what might be seen at night on a certain wild hillside, hinting at unheard-of wonders, and that he had been found cold one morning on the very hill in question, my exultation was extreme, for I felt I was leaving conjecture far behind me. But the next step was of still greater importance. I had possessed for many years an extraordinary stone seal, – a piece of dull black stone, two inches long from the handle to the stamp, and the stamping end a rough hexagon an inch and a quarter in diameter. Altogether, it presented the appearance of an enlarged tobacco stopper of an old-fashioned make. It had been sent to me by an agent in the East, who informed me that it had been found near the site of the ancient Babylon. But the characters engraved on the seal were to me an intolerable puzzle. Somewhat of the cuneiform pattern, there were yet striking differences, which I detected at the first glance, and all efforts to read the inscription on the hypothesis that the rules for deciphering the arrowheaded writing would apply proved futile. A riddle such as this stung my pride, and at odd moments I would take the Black Seal out of the cabinet, and scrutinise it with so much idle perseverance that every letter was familiar to my mind, and I could have drawn the inscription from memory without the slightest error. Judge then of my surprise, when I one day received from a correspondent in the west of England a letter and an enclosure that positively left me thunderstruck. I saw carefully traced on a large piece of paper the very characters of the Black Seal, without alteration of any kind, and above the inscription my friend had written: *Inscription found on a limestone rock on the Grey Hills, Monmouthshire. Done in some red earth and quite recent.* I turned to the letter. My friend wrote: 'I send you the enclosed inscription with all due reserve. A shepherd who passed by the stone a week ago swears that there was then no mark of any kind. The characters, as I have noted, are formed by drawing some red earth over the stone, and are of an average height of one inch. They look to me like a kind of cuneiform character, a good deal altered, but this of course is impossible. It may be either a hoax or more probably some scribble of the gypsies, who are plentiful enough in this wild country. They have, as you are aware, many hieroglyphics which they use in communicating with one another. I happened to visit the stone in question two days ago in connection with a rather painful incident which has occurred here.'

As may be supposed, I wrote immediately to my friend, thanking him for the copy of the inscription, and asking him in a casual manner, the history of the incident he mentioned. To be brief, I heard that a woman named Cradock, who had lost her husband a day before, had set out to communicate the sad news to a cousin who lived some five miles away. She took a short cut which led by the Grey Hills. Mrs Cradock, who was then quite a young woman, never arrived at her relative's house. Late that night a farmer who had lost a couple of sheep, supposed to have wandered from the flock, was walking over the Grey Hills, with a lantern and his dog. His attention was attracted by a noise, which he described as a kind of wailing, mournful and pitiable to hear; and, guided by the sound, he found the unfortunate Mrs Cradock crouched on the ground by the limestone rock, swaying her body to and fro, and lamenting and crying in so heart-rending a manner that the farmer was, as he says, at first obliged to stop his ears, or he would have run away. The woman allowed herself to be taken home, and a neighbour came to see to her necessities. All the night she never ceased her crying, mixing her lament with words of some unintelligible jargon, and when the doctor arrived he pronounced her insane. She lay on her bed for a week, now wailing, as people said, like one lost and damned for eternity, and now sunk in a heavy coma; it was thought that grief at the loss of her husband had unsettled her mind, and the medical man did not at one time expect her to live. I need not say that I was deeply interested in this story, and I made my friend write to me at intervals with all the particulars of the case. I heard then that in the course of six weeks the woman gradually recovered the use of her faculties and some months later she gave birth to a son, christened Jervase, who unhappily proved to be of weak intellect. Such were the facts known to the village; but to me while I whitened at the suggested thought of the hideous enormities that had doubtless been committed, all this was nothing short of conviction, and I incautiously hazarded a hint of something like the truth to some scientific friends. The moment the words had left my lips I bitterly regretted having spoken, and thus given away the great secret of my life, but with a good deal of relief mixed with indignation, I found my fears altogether misplaced, for my friends ridiculed me to my face, and I was regarded as a madman; and beneath a natural anger I chuckled to myself, feeling as secure amidst these blockheads, as if I had confided what I knew to the desert sands.

But now, knowing so much, I resolved I would know all, and I concentrated my efforts on the task of deciphering the inscription on the Black Seal. For many years I made this puzzle the sole object of my leisure moments; for the greater portion of my time was, of course, devoted to other duties, and it was only now and then that I could snatch a week of clear research. If I were to tell the full history of this curious investigation, this statement would be wearisome in the extreme, for it would contain simply the account of long and tedious failure. By what I knew already of ancient scripts I was well-equipped for the chase, as I always termed it to myself. I had correspondents amongst all the scientific men in Europe, and, indeed, in the world, and I could not believe that in these days any character, however ancient and however perplexed, could long resist the searchlight I should bring to bear upon it. Yet, in point of fact, it was fully fourteen years before I succeeded. With every year my professional duties increased, and my leisure became smaller. This no doubt retarded me a good deal; and yet, when I look back on those years I am astonished at the vast scope of my investigation of the Black Seal. I made my bureau a centre, and from all the world and from all the ages I gathered transcripts of ancient writing. Nothing, I resolved, should pass me unawares, and the faintest hint should be welcomed and followed up. But as one covert after another was tried and proved empty of result, I began in the course of years to despair, and to wonder whether the Black Seal were the sole relic of some race that had vanished from the world and left no other trace of its existence, – had perished, in fine, as Atlantis is said to have done, in some great cataclysm, its secrets perhaps drowned beneath the ocean or moulded into the heart of the hills. The thought chilled my warmth a little, and though I still persevered, it was no longer with the same certainty of faith. A chance came to the rescue. I was staying in a considerable town in the north of England, and took the opportunity of going over the very creditable museum that had for some time been established in the place. The curator was one of my correspondents; and, as we were looking through one of the mineral cases, my attention was struck by a specimen, a piece of black stone some four inches square, the appearance of which reminded me in a measure of the Black Seal. I took it up carelessly, and was turning it over in my hand, when I saw, to my astonishment, that the under side was inscribed. I said, quietly enough, to my friend the curator that the specimen interested me, and that I should be much obliged if he would allow me to take it with me to my hotel for a couple of days. He, of course, made no objection, and I hurried to my rooms, and found that my first glance had not deceived me. There were two inscriptions; one in the regular cuneiform character, another in the character of the Black Seal, and I realised that my task was accomplished. I made an exact copy of the two inscriptions; and when I got to my London study, and had the Seal before me, I was able seriously to grapple with the great problem. The interpreting inscription on the museum specimen, though in itself curious enough, did not bear on my quest, but the transliteration made me master of the secret of the Black Seal. Conjecture, of course, had to enter into my calculations; there was here and there uncertainty about a particular ideograph, and one sign recurring again and again on the Seal baffled me for many successive nights. But at last the secret stood open before me in plain English, and I read the key of the awful transmutation of the hills. The last word was hardly written, when with fingers all trembling and unsteady I tore the scrap of paper into the minutest fragments, and saw them flame and blacken in the red hollow of the fire, and then I crushed the grey films that remained into finest powder. Never since then have I written those words; never will I write the phrases which tell me how man can be reduced to the slime from which he came, and be forced to put on the flesh of the reptile and the snake. There was now but one thing remaining. I knew; but I desired to see, and I was after some time able to take a house in the neighbourhood of the Grey Hills, and not far from the cottage where Mrs Cradock and her son Jervase resided. I need not go into a full and detailed account of the apparently inexplicable events which have occurred here, where I am writing this. I knew that I should find in Jervase Cradock something of the blood of the 'Little People', and I found later that he had more than once encountered his kinsmen in lonely places in that lonely land. When I was summoned one day to the garden, and found him in a seizure speaking or hissing the ghastly jargon of the Black Seal, I am afraid that exultation prevailed over pity. I heard bursting from his lips the secrets of the underworld, and the word of dread, 'Ishakshar', the signification of which I must be excused from giving.

But there is one incident I cannot pass over unnoticed. In the waste hollow of the night I awoke at the sound of those hissing syllables I knew so well; and on going to the wretched boy's room, I found him convulsed and foaming at the mouth, struggling on the bed as if he strove to escape the grasp of writhing demons. I took him down to my room and lit the lamp, while he lay twisting on the floor, calling on the power within his flesh to leave him. I saw his body swell and become distended as a bladder, while the face blackened before my eyes; and then at the crisis I did what was necessary according to the directions on the Seal, and putting all scruple on one side, I became a man of science, observant of what was passing. Yet the sight I had to witness was horrible, almost beyond the power of human conception and the most fearful fantasy; something pushed out from the body there on the floor, and stretched forth, a slimy wavering tentacle, across the room, and grasped the bust upon the cupboard, and laid it down on my desk.

When it was over, and I was left to walk up and down all the rest of the night, white and shuddering, with sweat pouring from my flesh, I vainly tried to reason with myself; I said, truly enough, that I had seen nothing really supernatural, that a snail pushing out his horns and drawing them in was but an instance on a smaller scale of what I had witnessed; and yet horror broke through all such reasonings and left me shattered and loathing myself for the share I had taken in the night's work.

There is little more to be said. I am going now to the final trial and encounter; for I have determined that there shall be nothing wanting, and I shall meet the 'Little People' face to face. I shall have the Black Seal and the knowledge of its secrets to help me, and if I unhappily do not return from my journey, there is no need to conjure up here a picture of the awfulness of my fate.

Such was the almost incredible story that the professor had left behind him. When I had finished reading it, it was late at night, but the next morning I took Morgan with me, and we proceeded to search the Grey Hills for some trace of the lost professor. I will not weary you with a description of the savage desolation of that tract of country, a tract of utterest loneliness, of bare green hills dotted over with grey limestone boulders, worn by the ravage of time into fantastic semblances of men and beasts. Finally, after many hours of weary searching, we found his watch and chain, the purse, and the ring – wrapped in a piece of coarse parchment. When Morgan cut the gut that bound the parcel together, and I saw the professor's property, I burst into tears, but the sight of the dreaded characters of the Black Seal repeated on the parchment froze me to silent horror, and I think I understood for the first time the awful fate that had come upon my late employer.

I have only to add that Professor Gregg's lawyer treated my account of what had happened as a fairy tale, and refused even to glance at the documents I laid before him. It was he who was responsible for the statement that appeared in the public press, to the effect that Professor Gregg had been drowned, and that his body must have been swept into the open sea.

Novel of the Iron Maid

I think the most extraordinary event which I can recall took place about five years ago. I was then still feeling my way; I had declared for business, and attended regularly at my office, but I had not succeeded in establishing a really profitable connection, and consequently I had a good deal of leisure time on my hands. I must briefly say, however, that I had a numerous circle of acquaintance, and was never at a loss as to how to spend my evenings. I was so fortunate as to have friends in most of the ranks of the social order; there is nothing so unfortunate, to my mind, as a specialised circle, wherein a certain round of ideas is continually traversed and retraversed. I have always tried to find out new types and persons whose brains contained something fresh to me; one may chance to gain information even from the conversation of city men on an omnibus. Amongst my acquaintance I knew a young doctor who lived in a far outlying suburb, and I used often to brave the intolerably slow railway journey, to have the pleasure of listening to his talk. One night we conversed so eagerly together over our pipes and whisky that the clock passed unnoticed, and when I glanced up I realised with a shock that I had just five minutes in which to catch the last train. I made a dash for my hat and stick, and jumped out of the house and down the steps, and tore at full speed up the street. It was no good, however; there was a shriek of the engine whistle, and I stood there at the station door and saw far on the long dark line of the embankment a red light shine and vanish, and a porter came down and shut the door with a bang.

'How far to London?' I asked him.

'A good nine miles to Waterloo Bridge.' And with that he went off.

Before me was the long suburban street, its dreary distance marked by rows of twinkling lamps, and the air was poisoned by the faint sickly smell of burning bricks; it was not a cheerful prospect by any means, and I had to walk through nine miles of such streets, deserted as those of

Pompeii. I knew pretty well what direction to take; so I set out wearily, looking at the stretch of lamps vanishing in perspective; and as I walked, street after street branched off to right and left, some far-reaching, to distances that seemed endless, communicating with other systems of thoroughfare; and some mere protoplasmic streets, beginning in orderly fashion with serried two-storied houses, and ending suddenly in waste, and pits, and rubbish heaps, and fields whence the magic had departed. I have spoken of systems of thoroughfare, and I assure you that, walking alone through these silent places, I felt fantasy growing on me, and some glamour of the infinite. There was here, I felt, an immensity as in the outer void of the universe. I passed from unknown to unknown, my way marked by lamps like stars, and on either hand was an unknown world where myriads of men dwelt and slept, street leading into street, as it seemed to world's end. At first the road by which I was travelling was lined with houses of unutterable monotony, a wall of grey brick pierced by two stories of windows, drawn close to the very pavement. But by degrees I noticed an improvement: there were gardens, and these grew larger; the suburban builder began to allow himself a wider scope; and for a certain distance each flight of steps was guarded by twin lions of plaster, and scents of flowers prevailed over the fume of heated bricks. The road began to climb a hill, and, looking up a side street, I saw the half moon rise over plane trees, and there on the other side was as if a white cloud had fallen, and the air around it was sweetened as with incense; it was a may tree in full bloom. I pressed on stubbornly, listening for the wheels and the clatter of some belated hansom; but into that land of men who go to the city in the morning and return in the evening, the hansom rarely enters, and I had resigned myself once more to the walk, when I suddenly became aware that some one was advancing to meet me along the sidewalk. The man was strolling rather aimlessly; and though the time and the place would have allowed an unconventional style of dress, he was vested in the ordinary frock coat, black tie, and silk hat of civilization. We met each other under the lamp, and, as often happens in this great town, two casual passengers brought face to face found each in the other an acquaintance.

'Mr Mathias, I think?' I said.

'Quite so. And you are Frank Burton. You know you are a man with a Christian name, so I won't apologise for my familiarity. But may I ask where you are going?'

I explained the situation to him, saying I had traversed a region as unknown to me as the darkest recesses of Africa. 'I think I have only about five miles farther,' I concluded.

'Nonsense; you must come home with me. My house is close by; in fact, I was just taking my evening walk when we met. Come along; I dare say you will find a makeshift bed easier than a five-mile walk.'

I let him take my arm and lead me along, though I was a good deal surprised at so much geniality from a man who was, after all, a mere casual club acquaintance. I suppose I had not spoken to Mr Mathias half a dozen times; he was a man who would sit silent in an armchair for hours, neither reading nor smoking, but now and again moistening his lips with his tongue and smiling queerly to himself. I confess he had never attracted me, and on the whole I should have preferred to continue my walk. But he took my arm and led me up a side street, and stopped at a door in a high wall. We passed through the still moonlit garden, beneath the black shadow of an old cedar, and into an old red-brick house with many gables. I was tired enough, and I sighed with relief as I let myself fall into a great leather armchair. You know the infernal grit with which they strew the sidewalk in those suburban districts; it makes walking a penance, and I felt my four-mile tramp had made me more weary than ten miles on an honest country road. I looked about the room with some curiosity; there was a shaded lamp, which threw a circle of brilliant light on a heap of papers lying on an old brass-bound secretaire of the last century; but the room was all vague and shadowy, and I could only see that it was long and low, and that it was filled with indistinct objects which might be furniture. Mr Mathias sat down in a second armchair, and looked about him with that odd smile of his. He was a queer-looking man, clean shaven, and white to the lips. I should think his age was something between fifty and sixty.

'Now I have got you here,' he began, 'I must inflict my hobby on you. You knew I was a collector? Oh, yes, I have devoted many years to collecting curiosities, which I think are really curious. But we must have a better light.'

He advanced into the middle of the room, and lit a lamp which hung from the ceiling; and as the bright light flashed round the wick, from every corner and space there seemed to start a horror. Great wooden frames with complicated apparatus of ropes and pulleys, stood against the wall; a wheel of strange shape had a place beside a thing that looked like a gigantic gridiron; little tables glittered with bright steel instruments carelessly put down as if ready for use; a screw and vice loomed out, casting ugly shadows, and in another nook was a saw with cruel jagged teeth.

'Yes,' said Mr Mathias; 'they are, as you suggest, instruments of torture – of torture and death. Some – many, I may say – have been used; a few are reproductions after ancient examples. Those knives were used for flaying; that frame is a rack, and a very fine specimen. Look at this; it comes from Venice. You see that sort of collar, something like a big horseshoe? Well, the patient, let us call him, sat down quite comfortably, and the horseshoe was neatly fitted round his neck. Then the two ends were joined with a silken band, and the executioner began to turn a handle connected with the band. The horseshoe contracted very gradually as the band tightened, and the turning continued till the man was strangled. It all took place quietly, in one of those queer garrets under the leads. But these things are all European; the Orientals are, of course, much more ingenious. These are the Chinese contrivances. You have heard of the "Heavy Death"? It is my hobby, this sort of thing. Do you know, I often sit here, hour after hour, and meditate over the collection. I fancy I see the faces of the men who have suffered – faces lean with agony and wet with sweats of death – growing distinct out of the gloom, and I hear the echoes of their cries for mercy. But I must show you my latest acquisition. Come into the next room.'

I followed Mr Mathias out. The weariness of the walk, the late hour, and the strangeness of it all, made me feel like a man in a dream; nothing would have surprised me very much. The second room was as the first, crowded with ghastly instruments; but beneath the lamp was a wooden platform, and a figure stood on it. It was a large statue of a naked woman, fashioned in green bronze; the arms were stretched out, and there was a smile on the lips; it might well have been intended for a Venus, and yet there was about the thing an evil and a deadly look.

Mr Mathias looked at it complacently. 'Quite a work of art, isn't it?' he said. 'It's made of bronze, as you see, but it has long had the name of the Iron Maid. I got it from Germany, and it was only unpacked this afternoon; indeed, I have not yet had time to open the letter of advice. You see that very small knob between the breasts? Well, the victim was bound to the Maid, the knob was pressed, and the arms slowly tightened round the neck. You can imagine the result.'

As Mr Mathias talked, he patted the figure affectionately. I had turned away, for I sickened at the sight of the man and his loathsome treasure. There was a slight click, of which I took no notice – it was not much louder than the tick of a clock; and then I heard a sudden whir, the noise of machinery in motion, and I faced round. I have never forgotten the hideous agony on Mathias's face as those relentless arms tightened about his neck; there was a wild struggle as of a beast in the toils, and then a shriek that ended in a choking groan. The whirring noise had suddenly changed into a heavy droning. I tore with all my might at the bronze arms, and strove to wrench them apart, but I could do nothing. The head had slowly bent down, and the green lips were on the lips of Mathias.

Of course I had to attend at the inquest. The letter which had accompanied the figure was found unopened on the study table. The German firm of dealers cautioned their client to be most careful in touching the Iron Maid, as the machinery had been put in thorough working order.

Novel of the White Powder

My name is Leicester; my father, Major General Wyn Leicester, a distinguished officer of artillery, succumbed five years ago to a complicated liver complaint acquired in the deadly climate of India. A year later my only brother, Francis, came home after an exceptionally brilliant career at the University, and settled down with the resolution of a hermit to master what has been well called the great legend of the law. He was a man who seemed to live in utter indifference to everything that is called pleasure; and though he was handsomer than most men, and could talk as merrily and wittily as if he were a mere vagabond, he avoided society, and shut himself up in a large room at the top of the house to make himself a lawyer. Ten hours a day of hard reading was at first his allotted portion; from the first light in the east to the late afternoon he remained shut up with his books, taking a hasty half-hour's lunch with me as if he grudged the wasting of the moments, and going out for a short walk when it began to grow dusk. I thought that such relentless application must be injurious, and tried to cajole him from the crabbed textbooks; but his ardour seemed to grow rather than diminish, and his daily tale of hours increased. I spoke to him seriously, suggesting some occasional relaxation, if it were but an idle afternoon with a harmless novel; but he laughed, and said that he read about feudal tenures when he felt in need of amusement, and scoffed at the notion of theatres, or a month's fresh air. I confessed that he looked well, and seemed not to suffer from his labours; but I knew that such unnatural toil would take revenge at last, and I was not mistaken. A look of anxiety began to lurk about his eyes, and he seemed languid, and at last he avowed that he was no longer in perfect health; he was troubled, he said, with a sensation of dizziness, and awoke now and then of nights from fearful dreams, terrified and cold with icy sweats. 'I am taking care of myself,' he said; 'so you must not trouble. I passed the whole of yesterday afternoon in idleness, leaning back in that comfortable chair you gave me, and scribbling nonsense on a sheet of paper. No, no; I will not overdo my work. I shall be well enough in a week or two depend upon it.'

Yet, in spite of his assurances, I could see that he grew no better, but rather worse; he would enter the drawingroom with a face all miserably wrinkled and despondent, and endeavour to look gaily when my eyes fell on him, and I thought such symptoms of evil omen, and was frightened sometimes at the nervous irritation of his movements, and at glances which I could not decipher. Much against his will, I prevailed on him to have medical advice, and with an ill grace he called in our old doctor.

Dr Haberden cheered me after his examination of his patient.

'There is nothing really much amiss,' he said to me. 'No doubt he reads too hard, and eats hastily, and then goes back again to his books in too great a hurry; and the natural consequence is some digestive trouble, and a little mischief in the nervous system. But I think – I do, indeed, Miss Leicester – that we shall be able to set this all right. I have written him a prescription which ought to do great things. So you have no cause for anxiety.'

My brother insisted on having the prescription made up by a chemist in the neighbourhood; it was an odd old-fashioned shop, devoid of the studied coquetry and calculated glitter that make so gay a show on the counters and shelves of the modern apothecary; but Francis liked the old chemist, and believed in the scrupulous purity of his drugs. The medicine was sent in due course, and I saw that my brother took it regularly after lunch and dinner. It was an innocent-looking white powder, of which a little was dissolved in a glass of cold water. I stirred it in, and it seemed to disappear, leaving the water clear and colourless. At first Francis seemed to benefit greatly; the weariness vanished from his face, and he became more cheerful than he had ever been since the time when he left school; he talked gayly of reforming himself, and avowed to me that he had wasted his time.

'I have given too many hours to law,' he said, laughing; 'I think you have saved me in the nick of time. Come, I shall be Lord Chancellor yet, but I must not forget life. You and I will have a holiday together before long; we will go to Paris and enjoy ourselves, and keep away from the Bibliothèque Nationale.'

I confessed myself delighted with the prospect.

'When shall we go?' I said. 'I can start the day after tomorrow, if you like.'

'Ah, that is perhaps a little too soon; after all, I do not know London yet, and I suppose a man ought to give the pleasures of his own country the first choice. But we will go off together in a week or two, so try and furbish up your French. I only know law French myself, and I am afraid that wouldn't do.'

We were just finishing dinner, and he quaffed off his medicine with a parade of carousal as if it had been wine from some choicest bin.

'Has it any particular taste?' I said.

'No; I should not know I was not drinking water,' and he got up from his chair, and began to pace up and down the room as if he were undecided as to what he should do next.

'Shall we have coffee in the drawingroom,' I said, 'or would you like to smoke?'

'No; I think I will take a turn; it seems a pleasant evening. Look at the afterglow; why, it is as if a great city were burning in flames, and down there between the dark houses it is raining blood fast, fast. Yes, I will go out. I may be in soon, but I shall take my key, so good night, dear, if I don't see you again.'

The door slammed behind him, and I saw him walk lightly down the street, swinging his malacca cane, and I felt grateful to Dr Haberden for such an improvement.

I believe my brother came home very late that night; but he was in a merry mood the next morning.

'I walked on without thinking where I was going,' he said, 'enjoying the freshness of the air, and livened by the crowds as I reached more frequented quarters. And then I met an old college friend, Orford, in the press of the pavement, and then – well, we enjoyed ourselves. I have felt what it is to be young and a man, I find I have blood in my veins, as other men have. I made an appointment with Orford for tonight; there will be a little party of us at the restaurant. Yes, I shall enjoy myself for a week or two, and hear the chimes at midnight, and then we will go for our little trip together.'

Such was the transmutation of my brother's character that in a few days he became a lover of pleasure, a careless and merry idler of western pavements, a hunter out of snug restaurants, and a fine critic of fantastic dancing; he grew fat before my eyes, and said no more of Paris, for he had clearly found his paradise in London. I rejoiced, and yet wondered a little, for there was, I thought, something in his gaiety that indefinitely displeased me, though I could not have defined my feeling. But by degrees there came a change; he returned still in the cold hours of the morning, but I heard no more about his pleasures, and one morning as we sat at breakfast together, I looked suddenly into his eyes and saw a stranger before me.

'Oh, Francis!' I cried; 'Oh, Francis, Francis, what have you done?' and rending sobs cut the words short, and I went weeping out of the room, for though I knew nothing, yet I knew all, and by some odd play of thought I remembered the evening when he first went abroad to prove his manhood, and the picture of the sunset sky glowed before me; the clouds like a city in burning flames, and the rain of blood. Yet I did battle with such thoughts, resolving that perhaps, after all, no great harm had been done, and in the evening at dinner I resolved to press him to fix a day for our holiday in Paris. We had talked easily enough, and my brother had just taken his medicine, which he had continued all the while. I was about to begin my topic, when the words forming in my mind vanished, and I wondered for a second what icy and intolerable weight oppressed my heart and suffocated me as with the unutterable horror of the coffin lid nailed down on the living.

We had dined without candles; the room had slowly grown from twilight to gloom, and the walls and corners were indistinct in the shadow. But from where I sat I looked out into the street; and as I thought of what I would say to Francis, the sky began to flush and shine, as it had done on a well-remembered evening, and in the gap between two dark masses that were houses an awful pageantry of flame appeared – lurid whorls of writhed cloud, and utter depths burning, and grey masses like the fume blown from a smoking city, and an evil glory blazing far above shot with tongues of more ardent fire, and below as if there were a deep pool of blood. I looked down to where my brother sat facing me, and the words were shaped on my lips, when I saw his hand resting on the table. Between the thumb and forefinger of the closed hand, there was a mark, a small patch about the size of a sixpence, and somewhat of the colur of a bad bruise. Yet, by some sense I cannot define, I knew that what I saw was no bruise at all. Oh, if human flesh could burn with flame, and if flame could be black as pitch, such was that before me! Without thought or fashioning of words, grey horror shaped within me at the sight, and in an inner cell it was known to be a brand. For a moment the stained sky became dark as midnight, and when the light returned to me I was alone in the silent room, and soon after I heard my brother go out.

Late as it was, I put on my bonnet and went to Dr Haberden, and in his great consulting room, ill-lighted by a candle which the doctor brought in with him, with stammering lips, and a voice that would break in spite of my resolve, I told him all; from the day on which my brother began to take the medicine down to the dreadful thing I had seen scarcely half an hour before.

When I had done, the doctor looked at me for a minute with an expression of great pity on his face.

'My dear Miss Leicester,' he said, 'you have evidently been anxious about your brother; you have been worrying over him, I am sure. Come, now, is it not so?

'I have certainly been anxious,' I said. 'For the last week or two I have not felt at ease.'

'Quite so; you know, of course, what a queer thing the brain is?'

'I understand what you mean; but I was not deceived. I saw what I have told you with my own eyes.'

'Yes, yes, of course. But your eyes had been staring at that very curious sunset we had tonight. That is the only explanation. You will see it in the proper light tomorrow, I am sure. But, remember, I am always ready to give any help that is in my power; do not scruple to come to me, or to send for me if you are in any distress.'

I went away but little comforted, all confusion and terror and sorrow, not knowing where to turn. When my brother and I met the next day, I looked quickly at him, and noticed, with a sickening at heart, that the right hand, the hand on which I had clearly seen the patch as of a black fire, was wrapped up with a handkerchief.

'What is the matter with your hand, Francis?' I said in a steady voice.

'Nothing of consequence. I cut a finger last night, and it bled rather awkwardly, so I did it up roughly to the best of my ability.'

'I will do it neatly for you, if you like.'

'No, thank you, dear, this will answer very well. Suppose we have breakfast; I am quite hungry.'

We sat down, and I watched him. He scarcely ate or drank at all, but tossed his meat to the dog when he thought my eyes were turned away; and there was a look in his eyes that I had never yet seen, and the thought fled across my mind that it was a look that was scarcely human. I was firmly convinced that awful and incredible as was the thing I had seen the night before, yet it was no illusion, no glamour of bewildered sense, and in the course of the morning I went again to the doctor's house.

He shook his head with an air puzzled and incredulous, and seemed to reflect for a few minutes.

'And you say he still keeps up the medicine? But why? As I understand, all the symptoms he complained of have disappeared long ago; why should he go on taking the stuff when he is quite well? And by the by, where did he get it made up? At Sayce's? I never send any one there; the old man is getting careless. Suppose you come with me to the chemist's; I should like to have some talk with him.'

We walked together to the shop. Old Sayce knew Dr Haberden, and was quite ready to give any information.

'You have been sending that in to Mr Leicester for some weeks, I think, on my prescription,' said the doctor, giving the old man a pencilled scrap of paper.

The chemist put on his great spectacles with trembling uncertainty, and held up the paper with a shaking hand.

'Oh, yes,' he said, 'I have very little of it left; it is rather an uncommon drug, and I have had it in stock some time. I must get in some more, if Mr Leicester goes on with it.'

'Kindly let me have a look at the stuff,' said Haberden; and the chemist gave him a glass bottle. He took out the stopper and smelt the contents, and looked strangely at the old man.

'Where did you get this?' he said, 'and what is it? For one thing, Mr Sayce, it is not what I prescribed. Yes, yes, I see the label is right enough, but I tell you this is not the drug.'

'I have had it a long time,' said the old man, in feeble terror. 'I got it from Burbage's in the usual way. It is not prescribed often, and I have had it on the shelf for some years. You see there is very little left.'

'You had better give it to me,' said Haberden. 'I am afraid something wrong has happened.'

We went out of the shop in silence, the doctor carrying the bottle neatly wrapped in paper under his arm.

'Dr Haberden,' I said when we had walked a little way – 'Dr Haberden.'

'Yes,' he said, looking at me gloomily enough.

'I should like you to tell me what my brother has been taking twice a day for the last month or so.'

'Frankly, Miss Leicester, I don't know. We will speak of this when we get to my house.'

We walked on quickly without another word till we reached Dr Haberden's. He asked me to sit down, and began pacing up and down the room, his face clouded over, as I could see, with no common fears.

'Well,' he said at length, 'this is all very strange; it is only natural that you should feel alarmed, and I must confess that my mind is far from easy. We will put aside, if you please, what you told me last night and this morning, but the fact remains that for the last few weeks Mr Leicester has been impregnating his system with a drug which is completely unknown to me. I tell you, it is not what I ordered; and what that stuff in the bottle really is remains to be seen.'

He undid the wrapper, and cautiously tilted a few grains of the white powder on to a piece of paper, and peered curiously at it.

'Yes,' he said, 'it is like the sulphate of quinine, as you say; it is flaky. But smell it.'

He held the bottle to me, and I bent over it. It was a strange sickly smell, vaporous and overpowering, like some strong anaesthetic.

'I shall have it analysed,' said Haberden. 'I have a friend who has devoted his whole life to chemistry as a science. Then we shall have something to go upon. No, no, say no more about that other matter; I cannot listen to that, and take my advice and think no more about it yourself.'

That evening my brother did not go out as usual after dinner.

'I have had my fling,' he said with a queer laugh; 'and I must go back to my old ways. A little law will be quite a relaxation after so sharp a dose of pleasure,' and he grinned to himself, and soon after went up to his room. His hand was still all bandaged.

Dr Haberden called a few days later.

'I have no special news to give you,' he said. 'Chambers is out of town, so I know no more about that stuff than you do. But I should like to see Mr Leicester if he is in.'

'He is in his room,' I said; 'I will tell him you are here.'

'No, no, I will go up to him; we will have a little quiet talk together. I dare say that we have made a good deal of fuss about very little; for, after all, whatever the white powder may be, it seems to have done him good.'

The doctor went upstairs, and standing in the hall I heard his knock, and the opening and shutting of the door; and then I waited in the silent house for an hour, and the stillness grew more and more intense as the hands of the clock crept round. Then there sounded from above the noise of a door shut sharply, and the doctor was coming down the stairs. His footsteps crossed the hall, and there was a pause at the door; I drew a long sick breath with difficulty, and saw my face white in a little mirror, and he came in and stood at the door. There was an unutterable horror shining in his eyes; he steadied himself by holding the back of a chair with one hand, and his lower lip trembled like a horse's, and he gulped and stammered unintelligible sounds before he spoke.

'I have seen that man,' he began in a dry whisper. 'I have been sitting in his presence for the last hour. My God! and I am alive and in my senses! I, who have dealt with death all my life, and have dabbled with the melting ruins of the earthly tabernacle. But not this! Oh, not this,' and he covered his face with his hands as if to shut out the sight of something before him.

'Do not send for me again, Miss Leicester,' he said with more composure. 'I can do nothing in this house. Goodbye.'

As I watched him totter down the steps and along the pavement towards his house, it seemed to me that he had aged by ten years since the morning.

My brother remained in his room. He called out to me in a voice I hardly recognised, that he was very busy, and would like his meals brought to his door and left there, and I gave the order to the servants. From that day it seemed as if the arbitrary conception we call time had been annihilated for me. I lived in an ever-present sense of horror, going through the routine of the house mechanically, and only speaking a few necessary words to the servants. Now and then I went out and paced the streets for an hour or two and came home again; but whether I were without or within, my spirit delayed before the closed door of the upper room, and, shuddering, waited for it to open. I have said that I scarcely reckoned time, but I suppose it must have been a fortnight after Dr Haberden's visit that I came home from my stroll a little refreshed and lightened. The air was sweet and pleasant, and the hazy form of green leaves, floating cloud-like in the square, and the smell of blossoms, had charmed my senses, and I felt happier and walked more briskly. As I delayed a moment at the verge of the pavement, waiting for a van to pass by before crossing over to the house, I happened to look up at the windows, and instantly there was the rush and swirl of deep cold waters in my ears, and my heart leapt up, and fell down, down as into a deep hollow, and I was amazed with a dread and terror without form or shape. I stretched out a hand blindly through folds of thick darkness, from the black and shadowy valley, and held myself from falling, while the stones beneath my feet rocked and swayed and tilted, and the sense of solid things seemed to sink away from under me. I had glanced up at the window of my brother's study, and at that moment the blind was drawn aside, and something that had life stared out into the world. Nay, I cannot say I saw a face or any human likeness; a living thing, two eyes of burning flame glared at me, and they were in the midst of something as formless as my fear, the symbol and presence of all evil and all hideous corruption. I stood shuddering and quaking as with the grip of ague, sick with unspeakable agonies of fear and loathing, and for five minutes I could not summon force or motion to my limbs. When I was within the door, I ran up the stairs to my brother's room, and knocked.

'Francis, Francis,' I cried, 'for heaven's sake answer me. What is the horrible thing in your room? Cast it out, Francis, cast it from you!'

I heard a noise as of feet shuffling slowly and awkwardly, and a choking, gurgling sound, as if some one was struggling to find utterance, and then the noise of a voice, broken and stifled, and words that I could scarcely understand.

'There is nothing here,' the voice said, 'Pray do not disturb me. I am not very well today.'

I turned away, horrified and yet helpless. I could do nothing, and I wondered why Francis had lied to me, for I had seen the appearance beyond the glass too plainly to be deceived, though it was but the sight of a moment. And I sat still, conscious that there had been something else, something I had seen in the first flash of terror before those burning eyes had looked at me. Suddenly I remembered; as I lifted my face the blind was being drawn back, and I had had an instant's glance of the thing that was moving it, and in my recollection I knew that a hideous image was engraved forever on my brain. It was not a hand: there were no fingers that held the blind, but a black stump pushed it aside; the mouldering outline and the clumsy movement as of a beast's paw had glowed into my senses before the darkling waves of terror had overwhelmed me as I went down quick into the pit. My mind was aghast at the thought of this, and of the awful presence that dwelt with my brother in his room; I went to his door and cried to him again, but no answer came. That night one of the servants came up to me and told me in a whisper that for three days food had been regularly placed at the door and left untouched; the maid had knocked, but had received no answer; she had heard the noise of shuffling feet that I had noticed. Day after day went by, and still my brother's meals were brought to his door and left untouched; and though I knocked and called again and again, I could get no answer. The servants began to talk to me; it appeared they were as alarmed as I. The cook said that when my brother first shut himself up in his room, she used to hear him come out at night and go about the house; and once, she said, the hall door had opened and closed again, but for several nights she had heard no sound. The climax came at last. It was in the dusk of the evening, and I was sitting in the darkening dreary room when a terrible shriek jarred and rang harshly out of the silence, and I heard a frightened scurry of feet dashing down the stairs. I waited, and the servant maid staggered into the room and faced me, white and trembling.

'O Miss Helen,' she whispered. 'Oh, for the Lord's sake, Miss Helen, what has happened? Look at my hand, miss; look at that hand!' I drew her to the window, and saw there was a black wet stain upon her hand.

'I do not understand you,' I said. 'Will you explain to me?'

'I was doing your room just now,' she began. 'I was turning down the bedclothes, and all of a sudden there was something fell upon my hand wet, and I looked up, and the ceiling was black and dripping on me.'

I looked hard at her, and bit my lip. 'Come with me,' I said. 'Bring your candle with you.'

The room I slept in was beneath my brother's, and as I went in I felt I was trembling. I looked up at the ceiling, and saw a patch, all black and wet and a dew of black drops upon it, and a pool of horrible liquor soaking into the white bedclothes.

I ran upstairs and knocked loudly.

'O Francis, Francis, my dear brother,' I cried, 'what has happened to you?'

And I listened. There was a sound of choking, and a noise like water bubbling and regurgitating, but nothing else, and I called louder, but no answer came.

In spite of what Dr Haberden had said, I went to him, and with tears streaming down my cheeks, I told him of all that had happened, and he listened to me with a face set hard and grim.

'For your father's sake,' he said at last, 'I will go with you, though I can do nothing.'

We went out together; the streets were dark and silent, and heavy with heat and a drought of many weeks. I saw the doctor's face white under the gas lamps, and when we reached the house his hand was shaking.

We did not hesitate, but went upstairs directly. I held the lamp, and he called out in a loud, determined voice –

'Mr Leicester, do you hear me? I insist on seeing you. Answer me at once.'

There was no answer, but we both heard that choking noise I have mentioned.

'Mr Leicester, I am waiting for you. Open the door this instant, or I shall break it down.' And he called a third time in a voice that rang and echoed from the walls.

'Mr Leicester! For the last time I order you to open the door.'

'Ah!' he said, after a pause of heavy silence, 'we are wasting time here. Will you be so kind as to get me a poker, or something of the kind?'

I ran into a little room at the back where odd articles were kept, and found a heavy adze-like tool that I thought might serve the doctor's purpose.

'Very good,' he said, 'that will do, I dare say. I give you notice, Mr Leicester,' he cried loudly at the keyhole, 'that I am now about to break into your room.'

Then I heard the wrench of the adze, and the woodwork split and cracked under it, and with a loud crash the door suddenly burst open; and for a moment we started back aghast at a fearful screaming cry, no human voice, but as the roar of a monster, that burst forth inarticulate and struck at us out of the darkness.

'Hold the lamp,' said the doctor, and we went in and glanced quickly round the room. 'There it is,' said Dr Haberden, drawing a quick breath; 'look, in that corner.'

I looked, and a pang of horror seized my heart as with a white-hot iron. There upon the floor was a dark and putrid mass, seething with corruption and hideous rottenness, neither liquid nor solid, but melting and changing before our eyes, and bubbling with unctuous oily bubbles like boiling pitch. And out of the midst of it shone two burning points like eyes, and I saw a writhing and stirring as of limbs, and something moved and lifted up that might have been an arm. The doctor took a step forward, and raised the iron bar and struck at the burning points, and drove in the weapon, and struck again and again in a fury of loathing. At last the thing was quiet.

A week or two later, when I had to some extent recovered from the terrible shock, Dr Haberden came to see me.

'I have sold my practice,' he began, 'and tomorrow I am sailing on a long voyage. I do not know whether I shall ever return to England; in all probability I shall buy a little land in California, and settle there for the remainder of my life. I have brought you this packet, which you may open and read when you feel able to do so. It contains the report of Dr Chambers on what I submitted to him. Goodbye, Miss Leicester, goodbye.'

When he was gone, I opened the envelope; I could not wait, and proceeded to read the papers within.

'My dear Haberden,' the letter began, 'I have delayed inexcusably in answering your questions as to the white substance you sent me. To tell you the truth, I have hesitated for some time as to what course I should adopt, for there is a bigotry and an orthodox standard in physical science as in theology, and I knew that if I told you the truth I should offend rooted prejudices which I once held dear myself. However, I have determined to be plain with you, and first I must enter into a short personal explanation.

'You have known me, Haberden, for many years as a scientific man; you and I have often talked of our profession together, and discussed the hopeless gulf that opens before the feet of those who think to attain to truth by any means whatsoever, except the beaten way of experiment and observation, in the sphere of material things. I remember the scorn with which you have spoken to me of men of science who have dabbled a little in the unseen, and have timidly hinted that perhaps the senses are not, after all, the eternal, impenetrable bounds of all knowledge, the everlasting walls beyond which no human being has ever passed. We have laughed together heartily, and I think justly, at the "occult" follies of the day, disguised under various names – the mesmerisms, spiritualisms, materializations, theosophies, all the rabble rant of imposture, with their machinery of poor tricks and feeble conjuring, the true back parlour magic of shabby London streets. Yet, in spite of what I have said, I must confess to you that I am no materialist, taking the word of course in its usual signification. It is now many years since I have convinced myself – convinced myself, a sceptic, remember – that the old iron-bound theory is utterly and entirely false. Perhaps this confession will not wound you so sharply as it would have done twenty years ago; for I think you cannot have failed to notice that for some time hypotheses have been advanced by men of pure science which are nothing less than transcendental, and I suspect that most modern chemists and biologists of repute would not hesitate to subscribe the *dictum* of the old Schoolman, *Omnia exeunt in mysterium*, which means, I take it, that every branch of human knowledge if traced up to its source and final principles vanishes into mystery. I need not trouble you now with a detailed account of the painful steps which led me to my conclusions; a few simple experiments suggested a doubt as to my then standpoint, and a train of thought that rose from circumstances comparatively trifling brought me far. My old conception of the universe has been swept away, and I stand in a world that seems as strange and awful to me as the endless waves of the ocean seen for the first time, shining, from a peak in Darien. Now I know that the walls of sense that seemed so impenetrable, that seemed to loom up above the heavens and to be founded below the depths, and to shut us in for evermore, are no such everlasting impassable barriers as we fancied, but thinnest and most airy veils that melt away before the seeker, and dissolve as the early mist of the morning about the brooks. I know that you never adopted the extreme materialistic position: you did not go about trying to prove a universal negative, for your logical sense withheld you from that crowning absurdity; but I am sure that you will find all that I am saying strange and repellent to your habits of thought. Yet, Haberden, what I tell you is the truth, nay, to adopt our common language, the sole and scientific truth, verified by experience; and the universe is verily more splendid and more awful than we used to dream. The whole universe, my friend, is a tremendous sacrament; a mystic, ineffable force and energy, veiled by an outward form of matter; and man, and the sun and the other stars, and the flower of the grass, and the crystal in the test tube, are each and every one as spiritual, as material, and subject to an inner working.

'You will perhaps wonder, Haberden, whence all this tends; but I think a little thought will make it clear. You will understand that from such a standpoint the whole view of things is changed, and what we thought incredible and absurd may be possible enough. In short, we must look at legend and belief with other eyes, and be prepared to accept tales that had become mere fables. Indeed, this is no such great demand. After all, modern science will concede as much, in a hypocritical manner. You must not, it is true, believe in witchcraft, but you may credit hypnotism; ghosts are out of date, but there is a good deal to be said for the theory of telepathy. Give a superstition a Greek name, and believe in it, should almost be a proverb.

'So much for my personal explanation. You sent me, Haberden, a phial, stoppered and sealed, containing a small quantity of a flaky white powder, obtained from a chemist who has been dispensing it to one of your patients. I am not surprised to hear that this powder refused to yield any results to your analysis. It is a substance which was known to a few many hundred years ago, but which I never expected to have submitted to me from the shop of a modern apothecary. There seems no reason to doubt the truth of the man's tale; he no doubt got, as he says, the rather uncommon salt you prescribed from the wholesale chemist's; and it has probably remained on his shelf for twenty years, or perhaps longer. Here what we call chance and coincidence begins to work; during all these years the salt in the bottle was exposed to certain recurring variations of temperature, variations probably ranging from 40° to 80°. And, as it happens, such changes, recurring year after year at irregular intervals, and with varying degrees of intensity and duration, have constituted a process, and a process so complicated and so delicate, that I question whether modern scientific apparatus directed with the utmost precision could produce the same result. The white powder you sent me is something very different from the drug you prescribed; it is the powder from which the wine of the Sabbath, the *Vinum Sabbati* was prepared. No doubt you have read of the Witches' Sabbath, and have laughed at the tales which terrified our ancestors; the black cats, and the broomsticks, and dooms pronounced against some old woman's cow. Since I have known the truth I have often reflected that it is on the whole a happy thing that such burlesque as this is believed, for it serves to conceal much that it is better should not be known generally. However, if you care to read the appendix to Payne Knight's monograph, you will find that the true Sabbath was something very different, though the writer has very nicely refrained from printing all he knew. The secrets of the true Sabbath were the secrets of remote times surviving into the Middle Ages, secrets of an evil science which existed long before Aryan man entered Europe.

Men and women, seduced from their homes on specious pretences, were met by beings well qualified to assume, as they did assume, the part of devils, and taken by their guides to some desolate and lonely place, known to the initiate by long tradition and unknown to all else. Perhaps it was a cave in some bare and windswept hill; perhaps some inmost recess of a great forest, and there the Sabbath was held. There, in the blackest hour of night, the *Vinum Sabbati* was prepared, and this evil graal was poured forth and offered to the neophytes, and they partook of an infernal sacrament; *sumentes calicem principis inferorum*, as an old author well expresses it. And suddenly, each one that had drunk found himself attended by a companion, a shape of glamour and unearthly allurement, beckoning him apart to share in joys more exquisite, more piercing than the thrill of any dream, to the consummation of the marriage of the Sabbath. It is hard to write of such things as these, and chiefly because that shape that allured with loveliness was no hallucination, but, awful as it is to express, the man himself. By the power of that Sabbath wine, a few grains of white powder thrown into a glass of water, the house of life was riven asunder, and the human trinity dissolved, and the worm which never dies, that which lies sleeping within us all, was made tangible and an external thing, and clothed with a garment of flesh. And then in the hour of midnight, the primal fall was repeated and re-presented, and the awful thing veiled in the mythos of the Tree in the Garden was done anew. Such was the nuptiae Sabbati.

'I prefer to say no more; you, Haberden, know as well as I do that the most trivial laws of life are not to be broken with impunity; and for so terrible an act as this, in which the very inmost place of the temple was broken open and defiled, a terrible vengeance followed. What began with corruption ended also with corruption.'

Underneath is the following in Dr Haberden's writing: –

> 'The whole of the above is unfortunately strictly and entirely true. Your brother confessed all to me on that morning when I saw him in his room. My attention was first attracted to the bandaged hand, and I forced him to show it me. What I saw made me, a medical man of many years standing, grow sick with loathing; and the story I was forced to listen to was infinitely more frightful than I could have believed possible. It has tempted me to doubt the Eternal Goodness which can permit nature to

offer such hideous possibilities; and if you had not with your own eyes seen the end, I should have said to you – disbelieve it all. I have not, I think, many more weeks to live, but you are young, and may forget all this.'

'JOSEPH HABERDEN, M.D.'

In the course of two or three months I heard that Dr Haberden had died at sea, shortly after the ship left England.

The Red Hand

The Problem of the Fish Hooks

'There can be no doubt whatever,' said Mr Phillipps, 'that my theory is the true one; these flints are prehistoric fish hooks.'

'I dare say; but you know that in all probability the things were forged the other day with a door key.'

'Stuff!' said Phillipps; 'I have some respect, Dyson, for your literary abilities, but your knowledge of ethnology is insignificant, or rather non-existent. These fish hooks satisfy every test; they are perfectly genuine.'

'Possibly, but as I said just now, you go to work at the wrong end. You neglect the opportunities that confront you and await you, obvious, at every corner; you positively shrink from the chance of encountering primitive man in this whirling and mysterious city, and you pass the weary hours in your agreeable retirement of Red Lion Square fumbling with bits of flint, which are, as I said, in all probability, rank forgeries.'

Phillipps took one of the little objects, and held it up in exasperation.

'Look at that ridge,' he said. 'Did you ever see such a ridge as that on a forgery?'

Dyson merely grunted and lit his pipe, and the two sat smoking in rich silence, watching through the open window the children in the square as they flitted to and fro in the twilight of the lamps, as elusive as bats flying on the verge of a dark wood.

'Well,' said Phillipps at last, 'it is really a long time since you have been round. I suppose you have been working at your old task.'

'Yes,' said Dyson, 'always the chase of the phrase. I shall grow old in the hunt. But it is a great consolation to meditate on the fact that there are not a dozen people in England who know what style means.'

'I suppose not; for the matter of that, the study of ethnology is far from popular. And the difficulties! Primitive man stands dim and very far off across the great bridge of years.'

'By the way,' he went on after a pause, 'what was that stuff you were talking just now about shrinking from the chance of encountering primitive man at the corner, or something of the kind? There are certainly people about here whose ideas are very primitive.'

'I wish, Phillipps, you would not rationalise my remarks. If I recollect the phrase correctly, I hinted that you shrank from the chance of encountering primitive man in this whirling and mysterious city, and I meant exactly what I said. Who can limit the age of survival? The troglodyte and the lake-dweller, perhaps representatives of yet darker races, may very probably be lurking in our midst, rubbing shoulders with frock-coated and finely draped humanity, ravening like wolves at heart and boiling with the foul passions of the swamp and the black cave. Now and then as I walk in Holborn or Fleet Street I see a face which I pronounce abhorred, and yet I could not give a reason for the thrill of loathing that stirs within me.'

'My dear Dyson, I refuse to enter myself in your literary "trying-on" department. I know that survivals do exist, but all things have a limit, and your speculations are absurd. You must catch me your troglodyte before I will believe in him.'

'I agree to that with all my heart,' said Dyson, chuckling at the case with which he had succeeded in "drawing" Phillips. 'Nothing could be better. It's a fine night for a walk,' he added, taking up his hat.

'What nonsense you are talking, Dyson!' said Phillipps. 'However, I have no objection to taking a walk with you: as you say, it is a pleasant night.'

'Come along then,' said Dyson, grinning, 'but remember our bargain.'

The two men went out into the square, and threading one of the narrow passages that serve as exits, struck towards the north-east. As they passed along a flaring causeway they could hear at intervals between the clamour of the children and the triumphant *Gloria* played on a piano-organ the long deep hum and roll of the traffic in Holborn, a sound so persistent that it echoed like the turning of everlasting wheels. Dyson looked to right and left and conned the way, and presently they were passing through a more peaceful quarter, touching on deserted squares and silent streets black as midnight. Phillipps had lost all count of direction, and as by degrees the region of faded respectability gave place to the squalid, and dirty stucco offended the eye of the artistic observer, he merely ventured the remark that he had never seen a neighbourhood more unpleasant or more commonplace.

'More mysterious, you mean,' said Dyson. 'I warn you, Phillipps, we are now hot upon the scent.'

They dived yet deeper into the maze of brickwork; some time before they had crossed a noisy thoroughfare running east and west, and now the quarter seemed all amorphous, without character; here a decent house with sufficient garden, here a faded square, and here factories surrounded by high, blank walls, with blind passages and dark corners; but all ill-lighted and unfrequented and heavy with silence.

Presently, as they paced down a forlorn street of two-story houses, Dyson caught sight of a dark and obscure turning.

'I like the look of that,' he said; 'it seems to me promising.' There was a street lamp at the entrance, and another, a mere glimmer, at the further end. Beneath the lamp, on the pavement, an artist had evidently established his academy in the daytime, for the stones were all a blur of crude colours rubbed into each other, and a few broken fragments of chalk lay in a little heap beneath the wall.

'You see people do occasionally pass this way,' said Dyson, pointing to the ruins of the screever's work. 'I confess I should not have thought it possible. Come, let us explore.'

On one side of this byway of communication was a great timber-yard, with vague piles of wood looming shapeless above the enclosing wall; and on the other side of the road a wall still higher seemed to enclose a garden, for there were shadows like trees, and a faint murmur of rustling leaves broke the silence. It was a moonless night, and clouds that had gathered after sunset had blackened, and midway between the feeble lamps the passage lay all dark and formless, and when one stopped and listened, and the sharp echo of reverberant footsteps ceased, there came from far away, as from beyond the hills, a faint roll of the noise of London. Phillipps was bolstering up his courage to declare that he had had enough of the excursion, when a loud cry from Dyson broke in upon his thoughts.

'Stop, stop for Heaven's sake, or you will tread on it! There! almost under your feet!' Phillipps looked down, and saw a vague shape, dark, and framed in surrounding darkness, dropped strangely on the pavement, and then a white cuff glimmered for a moment as Dyson lit a match, which went out directly.

'It's a drunken man,' said Phillipps very coolly.

'It's a murdered man,' said Dyson, and he began to call for police with all his might, and soon from the distance running footsteps echoed and grew louder, and cries sounded.

A policeman was the first to come up.

'What's the matter?' he said, as he drew to a stand, panting. 'Anything amiss here?' for he had not seen what was on the pavement.

'Look!' said Dyson, speaking out of the gloom. 'Look there! My friend and I came down this place three minutes ago, and that is what we found.'

The man flashed his light on the dark shape and cried out.

'Why, it's murder,' he said; 'there's blood all about him, and a puddle of it in the gutter there. He's not dead long, either. Ah! there's the wound! It's in the neck.'

Dyson bent over what was lying there. He saw a prosperous gentleman, dressed in smooth, well-cut clothes. The neat whiskers were beginning to grizzle a little; he might have been forty-five an hour before; and a handsome gold watch had half slipped out of his waistcoat pocket. And there in the flesh of the neck, between chin and ear, gaped a great wound, clean cut, but all clotted with dry blood, and the white of the cheeks shone like a lighted lamp above the red.

Dyson turned, and looked curiously about him; the dead man lay across the path with his head inclined towards the wall, and the blood from the wound streamed away across the pavement, and lay a dark puddle, as the policeman had said, in the gutter. Two more policemen had come up, the crowd gathered, humming from all quarters, and the officers had as much as they could do to keep the curious at a distance. The three lanterns were flashing here and there, searching for more evidence, and in the gleam of one of them Dyson caught sight of an object in the road, to which he called the attention of the policeman nearest to him.

'Look, Phillipps,' he said, when the man had secured it and held it up. 'Look, that should be something in your way!'

It was a dark flinty stone, gleaming like obsidian, and shaped to a broad edge something after the manner of an adze. One end was rough, and easily grasped in the hand, and the whole thing was hardly five inches long. The edge was thick with blood.

'What is that, Phillipps?' said Dyson; and Phillipps looked hard at it.

'It's a primitive flint knife,' he said. 'It was made about ten thousand years ago. One exactly like this was found near Aubury, in Wiltshire, and all the authorities gave it that age.'

The policeman stared astonished at such a development of the case; and Phillipps himself was all aghast at his own words. But Mr Dyson did not notice him. An inspector who had just come up and was listening to the outlines of the case, was holding a lantern to the dead man's head. Dyson, for his part, was staring with a white heat of curiosity at something he saw on the wall, just above where the man was lying; there were a few rude marks done in red chalk.

'This is a black business,' said the inspector at length; 'does anybody know who it is?'

A man stepped forward from the crowd. 'I do, governor,' he said, 'he's a big doctor, his name's Sir Thomas Vivian; I was in the 'orspital abart six months ago, and he used to come round; he was a very kind man.'

'Lord,' cried the inspector, 'this is a bad job indeed. Why, Sir Thomas Vivian goes to the Royal Family. And there's a watch worth a hundred guineas in his pocket, so it isn't robbery.'

Dyson and Phillipps gave their cards to the authorities, and moved off, pushing with difficulty through the crowd that was still gathering, gathering fast; and the alley that had been lonely and desolate now swarmed with white staring faces and hummed with the buzz of rumour and horror, and rang with the commands of the officers of police. The two men, once free from this swarming curiosity, stepped out briskly, but for twenty minutes neither spoke a word.

'Phillipps,' said Dyson, as they came into a small but cheerful street, clean and brightly lit, 'Phillipps, I owe you an apology. I was wrong to have spoken as I did tonight. Such infernal jesting,' he went on, with heat, 'as if there were no wholesome subjects for a joke. I feel as if I had raised an evil spirit.'

'For Heaven's sake say nothing more,' said Phillipps, choking down horror with visible effort. 'You told the truth to me in my room; the troglodyte, as you said, is still lurking about the earth, and in these very streets around us, slaying for mere lust of blood.'

'I will come up for a moment,' said Dyson when they reached Red Lion Square, 'I have something to ask you. I think there should be nothing hidden between us at all events.'

Phillipps nodded gloomily, and they went up to the room, where everything hovered indistinct in the uncertain glimmer of the light from without. When the candle was lighted and the two men sat facing each other, Dyson spoke.

'Perhaps,' he began, 'you did not notice me peering at the wall just above the place where the head lay. The light from the inspector's lantern was shining full on it, and I saw something that looked queer to me, and I examined it closely. I found that some one had drawn in red chalk a rough outline of a hand – a human hand – upon the wall. But it was the curious position of the fingers that struck me; it was like this'; and he took a pencil and a piece of paper and drew rapidly, and then handed what he had done to Phillipps. It was a rough sketch of a hand seen from the back, with the fingers clenched, and the top of the thumb protruded between the first and second fingers, and pointed downwards, as if to something below.

'It was just like that,' said Dyson, as he saw Phillipps's face grow still whiter. 'The thumb pointed down as if to the body; it seemed almost a live hand in ghastly gesture. And just beneath there was a small mark with the powder of the chalk lying on it – as if some one had commenced a stroke and had broken the chalk in his hand. I saw the bit of chalk lying on the ground. But what do you make of it?'

'It's a horrible old sign,' said Phillipps – 'one of the most horrible signs connected with the theory of the evil eye. It is used still in Italy, but there can be no doubt that it has been known for ages. It is one of the survivals; you must look for the origin of it in the black swamp whence man first came.'

Dyson took up his hat to go.

'I think, jesting apart,' said he, 'that I kept my promise, and that we were and are hot on the scent, as I said. It seems as if I had really shown you primitive man, or his handiwork at all events.'

Incident of the Letter

About a month after the extraordinary and mysterious murder of Sir Thomas Vivian, the well-known and universally respected specialist in heart disease, Mr Dyson called again on his friend Mr Phillipps, whom he found, not, as usual, sunk deep in painful study, but reclining in his easy chair in an attitude of relaxation. He welcomed Dyson with cordiality.

'I am very glad you have come,' he began; 'I was thinking of looking you up. There is no longer the shadow of doubt about the matter.'

'You mean the case of Sir Thomas Vivian?'

'Oh, no, not at all. I was referring to the problem of the fish hooks. Between ourselves, I was a little too confident when you were here last, but since then other facts have turned up; and only yesterday I had a letter from a distinguished F.R.S. which quite settles the affair. I have been thinking what I should tackle next; and I am inclined to believe that there is a good deal to be done in the way of so-called undecipherable inscriptions.'

'Your line of study pleases me,' said Dyson. 'I think it may prove useful. But in the meantime, there was surely something extremely mysterious about the case of Sir Thomas Vivian.'

'Hardly, I think. I allowed myself to be frightened that night; but there can be no doubt that the facts are patient of a comparatively commonplace explanation.'

'Really! What is your theory then?'

'Well, I imagine that Vivian must have been mixed up at some period of his life in an adventure of a not very creditable description, and that he was murdered out of revenge by some Italian whom he had wronged.'

'Why Italian?'

'Because of the hand, the sign of the mano in fica. That gesture is now only used by Italians. So you see that what appeared the most obscure feature in the case turns out to be illuminant.'

'Yes, quite so. And the flint knife?'

'That is very simple. The man found the thing in Italy, or possibly stole it from some museum. Follow the line of least resistance, my dear fellow, and you will see there is no need to bring up primitive man from his secular grave beneath the hills.'

'There is some justice in what you say,' said Dyson. 'As I understand you, then, you think that your Italian, having murdered Vivian, kindly chalked up that hand as a guide to Scotland Yard?'

'Why not? Remember a murderer is always a madman. He may plot and contrive nine-tenths of his scheme with the acuteness and the grasp of a chess player or a pure mathematician; but somewhere or other his wits leave him and he behaves like a fool. Then you must take into account the insane pride or vanity of the criminal; he likes to leave his mark, as it were, upon his handiwork.'

'Yes, it is all very ingenious; but have you read the reports of the inquest?'

'No, not a word. I simply gave my evidence, left the court, and dismissed the subject from my mind.'

'Quite so. Then if you don't object I should like to give you an account of the case. I have studied it rather deeply, and I confess it interests me extremely.'

'Very good. But I warn you I have done with mystery. We are to deal with facts now.'

'Yes, it is fact that I wish to put before you. And this is fact the first. When the police moved Sir Thomas Vivian's body they found an open knife beneath him. It was an ugly-looking thing such as sailors carry, with a blade that the mere opening rendered rigid, and there the blade was all ready, bare and gleaming, but without a trace of blood on it, and the knife was found to be quite new; it had never been used. Now, at the first glance it looks as if your imaginary Italian were just the man to have such a tool. But consider a moment. Would he be likely to buy a new knife expressly to commit murder? And, secondly, if he had such a knife, why didn't he use it, instead of that very odd flint instrument?

'And I want to put this to you. You think the murderer chalked up the hand after the murder as a sort of "melodramatic Italian assassin his mark" touch. Passing over the question as to whether the real criminal ever does such a thing, I would point out that, on the medical evidence, Sir Thomas Vivian hadn't been dead for more than an hour. That would place the stroke at about a quarter to ten, and you know it was perfectly dark when we went out at 9.30. And that passage was singularly gloomy and ill-lighted, and the hand was drawn roughly, it is true, but correctly and without the bungling of strokes and the bad shots that are inevitable when one tries to draw in the dark or with shut eyes. Just try to draw such a simple figure as a square without looking at the paper, and then ask me to conceive that your Italian, with the rope waiting for his neck, could draw the hand on the wall so firmly and truly, in the black shadow of that alley. It is absurd. By consequence, then, the hand was drawn early in the evening, long before any murder was committed; or else – mark this, Phillipps – it was drawn by some one to whom darkness and gloom were familiar and habitual; by some one to whom the common dread of the rope was unknown!

'Again: a curious note was found in Sir Thomas Vivian's pocket. Envelope and paper were of a common make, and the stamp bore the West Central postmark. I will come to the nature of the contents later on, but it is the question of the handwriting that is so remarkable. The address on the outside was neatly written in a small clear hand, but the letter itself might have been written by a Persian who had learnt the English script. It was upright, and the letters were curiously contorted, with an affectation of dashes and backward curves which really reminded me of an Oriental manuscript, though it was all perfectly legible. But – and here comes the poser – on searching the dead man's waistcoat pockets a small memorandum book was found; it was almost filled with pencil jottings. These memoranda related chiefly to matters of a private as distinct from a professional nature; there were appointments to meet friends, notes of theatrical first nights, the address of a good hotel in Tours, and the title of a new novel – nothing in any way intimate. And the whole of these jottings were written in a hand nearly identical with the writing of the note found in the dead man's coat pocket! There was just enough difference between them to enable the expert to swear that the two were not written by the same person. I will just read you so much of Lady Vivian's evidence as bears on this point of the writing; I have the printed slip with me. Here you see she says: "I was married to my late husband seven years ago; I never saw any letter addressed him in a hand at all resembling that on the envelope produced, nor have I ever seen writing like that in the letter before me. I never saw my late husband using the memorandum book, but I am sure he did write everything in it; I am certain of that because we stayed last May at the Hotel du Faisan, Rue Royale, Tours, the address of which is given in the book; I remember his getting the novel 'A Sentinel' about six weeks ago. Sir Thomas Vivian never liked to miss the first nights at the theatres. His usual hand was perfectly different from that used in the notebook."

'And now, last of all, we come back to the note itself. Here it is in facsimile. My possession of it is due to the kindness of Inspector Cleeve, who is pleased to be amused at my amateur inquisitiveness. Read it, Phillipps; you tell me you are interested in obscure inscriptions; here is something for you to decipher.'

Mr Phillipps, absorbed in spite of himself in the strange circumstances Dyson had related, took the piece of paper, and scrutinised it closely. The handwriting was indeed bizarre in the extreme, and, as Dyson had noted, not unlike the Persian character in its general effect, but it was perfectly legible.

'Read it aloud,' said Dyson, and Phillipps obeyed.

' "Hand did not point in vain. The meaning of the stars is no longer obscure. Strangely enough, the black heaven vanished, or was stolen yesterday, but that does not matter in the least, as I have a celestial globe. Our old orbit remains unchanged; you have not forgotten the number of my sign, or will you appoint some other house? I have been on the other side of the moon, and can bring something to show you." '

'And what do you make of that?' said Dyson.

'It seems to me mere gibberish,' said Phillipps; 'you suppose it has a meaning?'

'Oh, surely; it was posted three days before the murder; it was found in the murdered man's pocket; it is written in a fantastic hand which the murdered man himself used for his private memoranda. There must be purpose under all this, and to my mind there is something ugly enough hidden under the circumstances of this case of Sir Thomas Vivian.'

'But what theory have you formed?'

'Oh, as to theories, I am still in a very early stage; it is too soon to state conclusions. But I think I have demolished your Italian. I tell you, Phillipps, again, the whole thing has an ugly look to my eyes. I cannot do as you do, and fortify myself with cast iron propositions to the effect that this or that doesn't happen, and never has happened. You note that the first word in the letter is "hand". That seems to me, taken with what we know about the hand on the wall, significant enough, and what you yourself told me of the history and meaning of the symbol, its connection with a world-old belief and faiths of dim far off years, all this speaks of mischief, for me at all events. No; I stand pretty well to what I said to you half in joke that night before we went out. There are sacraments of evil as well as of good about us, and we live and move to my belief in an unknown world, a place where there are caves and shadows and dwellers in twilight. It is possible that man may sometimes return on the track of evolution, and it is my belief that an awful lore is not yet dead.'

'I cannot follow you in all this,' said Phillipps; 'it seems to interest you strangely. What do you propose to do?'

'My dear Phillipps,' replied Dyson, speaking in a lighter tone, 'I am afraid I shall have to go down a little in the world. I have a prospect of visits to the pawnbrokers before me, and the publicans must not be neglected. I must cultivate a taste for four ale; shag tobacco I already love and esteem with all my heart.'

Search for the Vanished Heaven

For many days after the discussion with Phillipps, Mr Dyson was resolute in the line of research he had marked out for himself. A fervent curiosity and an innate liking for the obscure were great incentives, but especially in this case of Sir Thomas Vivian's death (for Dyson began to boggle a little at the word 'murder') there seemed to him an element that was more than curious. The sign of the red hand upon the wall, the tool of flint that had given death, the almost identity between the handwriting of the note and the fantastic script reserved religiously, as it appeared, by the doctor for trifling jottings, all these diverse and variegated threads joined to weave in his mind a strange and shadowy picture, with ghastly shapes dominant and deadly, and yet ill-defined, like the giant figures wavering in an ancient tapestry. He thought he had a clue to the meaning of the note, and in his resolute search for the 'black heaven', which had vanished, he beat furiously about the alleys and obscure streets of central London, making himself a familiar figure to the pawnbroker, and a frequent guest at the more squalid pothouses.

For a long time he was unsuccessful, and he trembled at the thought that the 'black heaven' might be hid in the coy retirements of Peckham, or lurk perchance in distant Willesden, but finally, improbability, in which he put his trust, came to the rescue. It was a dark and rainy night, with something in the unquiet and stirring gusts that savoured of approaching winter, and Dyson, beating up a narrow street not far from the Gray's Inn Road, took shelter in an extremely dirty 'public', and called for beer, forgetting for the moment his preoccupations, and only thinking of the sweep of the wind about the tiles and the hissing of the rain through the black and troubled air. At the bar there gathered the usual company: the frowsy women and the men in shiny black, those who appeared to mumble secretly together, others who wrangled in interminable argument, and a few shy drinkers who stood apart, each relishing his dose, and the rank and biting flavour of cheap spirit. Dyson was wondering at the enjoyment of it all, when suddenly there came a sharper accent. The folding doors swayed open, and a middle-aged woman staggered towards the bar, and clutched the pewter rim as if she stepped a deck in a roaring gale. Dyson glanced at her attentively as a pleasing specimen of her class; she was decently dressed in black, and carried a black bag of somewhat rusty leather, and her intoxication was apparent and far advanced. As she swayed at the bar, it was evidently all she could do to stand upright, and the barman, who had looked at her with disfavour, shook his head in reply to her thick-voiced demand for a drink. The woman glared at him, transformed in a moment to a fury, with bloodshot eyes, and poured forth a torrent of execration, a stream of blasphemies and early English phraseology.

'Get out of this,' said the man; 'shut up and be off, or I'll send for the police.'

'Police, you — — ,' bawled the woman, 'I'll — — well give you something to fetch the police for!' and with a rapid dive into her bag she pulled out some object which she hurled furiously at the barman's head.

The man ducked down, and the missile flew over his head and smashed a bottle to fragments, while the woman with a peal of horrible laughter rushed to the door, and they could hear her steps pattering fast over the wet stones.

The barman looked ruefully about him.

'Not much good going after her,' he said, 'and I'm afraid what she's left won't pay for that bottle of whisky.' He fumbled amongst the fragments of broken glass, and drew out something dark, a kind of square stone it seemed, which he held up.

'Valuable cur'osity,' he said, 'any gent like to bid?'

The *habitués* had scarcely turned from their pots and glasses during these exciting incidents; they gazed a moment, fishily, when the bottle smashed, and that was all, and the mumble of the confidential was resumed and the jangle of the quarrelsome, and the shy and solitary sucked in their lips and relished again the rank flavour of the spirit.

Dyson looked quickly at what the barman held before him.

'Would you mind letting me see it?' he said; 'it's a queer-looking thing, isn't it?'

It was a small black tablet, apparently of stone, about four inches long by two and a half broad, and as Dyson took it he felt rather than saw that he touched the secular with his flesh. There was some kind of carving on the surface, and, most conspicuous, a sign that made Dyson's heart leap.

'I don't mind taking it,' he said quietly. 'Would two shillings be enough?'

'Say half a dollar,' said the man, and the bargain was concluded.

Dyson drained his pot of beer, finding it delicious, and lit his pipe, and went out deliberately soon after. When he reached his apartment he locked the door, and placed the tablet on his desk, and then fixed himself in his chair, as resolute as an army in its trenches before a beleaguered city. The tablet was full under the light of the shaded candle, and scrutinising it closely, Dyson saw first the sign of the hand with the thumb protruding between the fingers; it was cut finely and firmly on the dull black surface of the stone, and the thumb pointed downward to what was beneath.

'It is a mere ornament,' said Dyson to himself, 'perhaps symbolical ornament, but surely not an inscription, or the signs of any words ever spoken.'

The hand pointed to a series of fantastic figures, spirals and whorls of the finest, most delicate lines, spaced at intervals over the remaining surface of the tablet. The marks were as intricate and seemed almost as much as without design as the pattern of a thumb impressed on a pane of glass.

'Is it some natural marking?' thought Dyson; 'there have been queer designs, likenesses of beasts and flowers, in stones with which man's hand had nothing to do'; and he bent over the stone with a magnifier, only to be convinced that no hazard of nature could have delineated those varied labyrinths of line. The whorls were different sizes; some were less than the twelfth of an inch in diameter, and the largest was a little smaller than a sixpence, and under the glass the regularity and accuracy of the cutting were evident, and in the smaller spirals the lines were graduated at intervals of a hundredth of an inch. The whole thing had a marvellous and fantastic look, and gazing at the mystic whorls beneath the hand, Dyson became subdued with an impression of vast and far off ages, and of a living being that had touched the stone with enigmas before the hills were formed, when the hard rocks still boiled with fervent heat.

'The "black heaven" is found again,' he said, 'but the meaning of the stars is likely to be obscure for everlasting so far as I am concerned.'

London stilled without, and a chill breath came into the room as Dyson sat gazing at the tablet shining duskily under the candlelight; and at last, as he closed the desk over the ancient stone, all his wonder at the case of Sir Thomas Vivian increased tenfold, and he thought of the well-dressed prosperous gentleman lying dead mystically beneath the sign of the hand, and the insupportable conviction seized him that between the death of this fashionable West End doctor and the weird spirals of the tablet there were most secret and unimaginable links.

For days he sat before his desk gazing at the tablet, unable to resist its lodestone fascination, and yet quite helpless, without ever the hope of solving the symbols so secretly inscribed. At last, desperate, he called in Mr Phillipps in consultation, and told in brief the story of the finding the stone.

'Dear me!' said Phillipps, 'this is extremely curious; you have had a find indeed. Why it looks to me even more ancient than the Hittite seal. I confess the character, if it is a character, is entirely strange to me. These whorls are really very quaint.'

'Yes, but I want to know what they mean. You must remember this tablet is the "black heaven" of the letter found in Sir Thomas Vivian's pocket; it bears directly on his death.'

'Oh, no, that is nonsense! This is, no doubt, an extremely ancient tablet, which has been stolen from some collection. Yes, the hand makes an odd coincidence, but only a coincidence after all.'

'My dear Phillipps, you are a living example of the truth of the axiom that extreme scepticism is mere credulity. But can you decipher the inscription?'

'I undertake to decipher anything,' said Phillipps. 'I do not believe in the insoluble. These characters are curious, but I cannot fancy them to be inscrutable.'

'Then take the thing away with you and make what you can of it. It has begun to haunt me; I feel as if I had gazed too long into the eyes of the Sphinx.'

Phillipps departed with the tablet in an inner pocket. He had not much doubt of success, for he had evolved thirty-seven rules for the solution of inscriptions. Yet when a week had passed and he called to see Dyson there was no vestige of triumph on his features. He found his friend in a state of extreme irritation, pacing up and down in the room like a man in a passion. He turned with a start as the door opened.

'Well,' said Dyson, 'you have got it? What is it all about?'

'My dear fellow, I am sorry to say I have completely failed. I have tried every known device in vain. I have even been so officious as to submit it to a friend at the Museum, but he, though a man of prime authority on the subject, tells me that he is quite at fault. It must be some wreckage of a vanished race, almost, I think – a fragment of another world than ours. I am not a superstitious man, Dyson, and you know that I have no truck with even the noble delusions, but I confess I yearn to be rid of this small square of blackish stone. Frankly, it has given me an ill week; it seems to me troglodytic and abhorred.'

Phillipps drew out the tablet and laid it on the desk before Dyson.

'By the way,' he went on, 'I was right at all events in one particular; it has formed part of some collection. There is a piece of grimy paper on the back that must have been a label.'

'Yes, I noticed that,' said Dyson, who had fallen into deepest disappointment; 'no doubt the paper is a label. But as I don't much care where the tablet originally came from, and only wish to know what the inscription means, I paid no attention to the paper. The thing is a hopeless riddle, I suppose, and yet it must surely be of the greatest importance.'

Phillipps left soon after, and Dyson, still despondent, took the tablet in his hand and carelessly turned it over. The label had so grimed that it seemed merely a dull stain, but as Dyson looked at it idly, and yet attentively, he could see pencil marks, and he bent over it eagerly, with his glass to his eye. To his annoyance, he found that part of the paper had been torn away, and he could only with difficulty make out odd words and pieces of words. First he read something that looked like 'inroad', and then beneath, 'stony-hearted step – ' and a tear cut off the rest. But in an instant a solution suggested itself, and he chuckled with huge delight.

'Certainly,' he said aloud, 'this is not only the most charming but the most convenient quarter in all London; here I am, allowing for the accidents of side streets, perched on a tower of observation.'

He glanced triumphantly out of the window across the street to the gate of the British Museum. Sheltered by the boundary wall of that agreeable institution, a 'screever', or artist in chalks, displayed his brilliant impressions on the pavement, soliciting the approval and the coppers of the gay and serious.

'This,' said Dyson, 'is more than delightful! An artist is provided to my hand.'

The Artist of the Pavement

Mr Phillipps, in spite of all disavowals – in spite of the wall of sense of whose enclosure and limit he was wont to make his boast – yet felt in his heart profoundly curious as to the case of Sir Thomas Vivian. Though he kept a brave face for his friend, his reason could not decently resist the conclusion that Dyson had enunciated, namely, that the whole affair had a look both ugly and mysterious. There was the weapon of a vanished race that had pierced the great arteries; the red hand, the symbol of a hideous faith, that pointed to the slain man; and then the tablet which Dyson declared he had expected to find, and had certainly found, bearing the ancient impress of the hand of malediction, and a legend written beneath in a character compared with which the most antique cuneiform was a thing of yesterday. Besides all this, there were other points that tortured and perplexed. How to account for the bare knife found unstained beneath the body? And the hint that the red hand upon the wall must have been drawn by some one whose life was passed in darkness thrilled him with a suggestion of dim and infinite horror. Hence he was in truth not a little curious as to what was to come, and some ten days after he had returned the tablet he again visited the 'mystery man', as he privately named his friend.

Arrived in the grave and airy chambers in Great Russell Street, he found the moral atmosphere of the place had been transformed. All Dyson's irritation had disappeared, his brow was smoothed with complacency, and he sat at a table by the window gazing out into the street with an expression of grim enjoyment, a pile of books and papers lying unheeded before him.

'My dear Phillipps, I am delighted to see you! Pray excuse my moving. Draw your chair up here to the table, and try this admirable shag tobacco.'

'Thank you,' said Phillipps, 'judging by the flavour of the smoke, I should think it is a little strong. But what on earth is all this? What are you looking at?'

'I am on my watchtower. I assure you that the time seems short while I contemplate this agreeable street and the classic grace of the Museum portico.'

'Your capacity for nonsense is amazing,' replied Phillipps, 'but have you succeeded in deciphering the tablet? It interests me.'

'I have not paid much attention to the tablet recently,' said Dyson. 'I believe the spiral character may wait.'

'Really! And how about the Vivian murder?'

'Ah, you do take an interest in that case? Well, after all, we cannot deny that it was a queer business. But is not "murder" rather a coarse word? It smacks a little, surely, of the police poster. Perhaps I am a trifle decadent, but I cannot help believing in the splendid word; "sacrifice", for example, is surely far finer than "murder".'

'I am all in the dark,' said Phillipps. 'I cannot even imagine by what track you are moving in this labyrinth.'

'I think that before very long the whole matter will be a good deal clearer for us both, but I doubt whether you will like hearing the story.'

Dyson lit his pipe afresh and leant back, not relaxing, however, in his scrutiny of the street. After a somewhat lengthy pause, he startled Phillipps by a loud breath of relief as he rose from the chair by the window and began to pace the floor.

'It's over for the day,' he said, 'and, after all, one gets a little tired.'

Phillipps looked with enquiry into the street. The evening was darkening, and the pile of the Museum was beginning to loom indistinct before the lighting of the lamps, but the pavements were thronged and busy. The artist in chalks across the way was gathering together his materials, and blurring all the brilliance of his designs, and a little lower down there was the clang of shutters being placed in position. Phillipps could see nothing to justify Mr Dyson's sudden abandonment of his attitude of surveillance, and grew a little irritated by all these thorny enigmas.

'Do you know, Phillipps,' said Dyson, as he strolled at ease up and down the room, 'I will tell you how I work. I go upon the theory of improbability. The theory is unknown to you? I will explain. Suppose I stand on the steps of St Paul's and look out for a blind man lame of the left leg to pass me, it is evidently highly improbable that I shall see such a person by waiting for an hour. If I wait two hours the improbability is diminished, but is still enormous, and a watch of a whole day would give little expectation of success. But suppose I take up the same position day after day, and week after week, don't you perceive that the improbability is lessening constantly – growing smaller day after day? Don't you see that two lines which are not parallel are gradually approaching one another, drawing nearer and nearer to a point of meeting, till at last they do meet, and improbability has vanished altogether? That is how I found the black tablet: I acted on the theory of improbability. It is the only scientific principle I know of which can enable one to pick out an unknown man from amongst five million.'

'And you expect to find the interpreter of the black tablet by this method?'

'Certainly.'

'And the murderer of Sir Thomas Vivian also?'

'Yes, I expect to lay my hands on the person concerned in the death of Sir Thomas Vivian in exactly the same way.'

The rest of the evening, after Phillipps had left, was devoted by Dyson to sauntering in the streets, and afterwards, when the night grew late, to his literary labours, or the chase of the phrase, as he called it. The next morning the station by the window was again resumed. His meals were brought to him at the table, and he ate with his eyes on the street. With briefest intervals, snatched reluctantly from time to time, he persisted in his survey throughout the day, and only at dusk, when the shutters were put up and the 'screever' ruthlessly deleted all his labour of the day, just before the gas lamps began to star the shadows, did he feel at liberty to quit his post. Day after day this ceaseless glance upon the street continued, till the landlady grew puzzled and aghast at such a profitless pertinacity.

But at last, one evening, when the play of lights and shadows was scarce beginning, and the clear cloudless air left all distinct and shining, there came the moment. A man of middle age, bearded and bowed, with a touch of grey about the ears, was strolling slowly along the northern pavement of Great Russell Street from the eastern end. He looked up at the Museum as he went by, and then glanced involuntarily at the art of the 'screever', and at the artist himself, who sat beside his pictures, hat in hand. The man with the beard stood still an instant, swaying slightly to and fro as if in thought, and Dyson saw his fists shut tight, and his back quivering, and the one side of his face in view twitched and grew contorted with the indescribable torment of approaching epilepsy. Dyson drew a soft hat from his pocket, and dashed the door open, taking the stair with a run.

When he reached the street the person he had seen so agitated had turned about, and, regardless of observation, was racing wildly towards Bloomsbury Square, with his back to his former course.

Mr Dyson went up to the artist of the pavement, and gave him some money, observing quietly, 'You needn't trouble to draw that thing again.' Then he too turned about, and strolled idly down the street in the opposite direction to that taken by the fugitive. So the distance between Dyson and the man with the bowed head grew steadily greater.

Story of the Treasure House

'There are many reasons why I chose your rooms for the meeting in preference to my own. Chiefly, perhaps, because I thought the man would be more at his ease on neutral ground.'

'I confess, Dyson,' said Phillipps, 'that I feel both impatient and uneasy. You know my standpoint: hard matter of fact, materialism if you like, in its crudest form. But there is something about all this affair of Vivian that makes me a little restless. And how did you induce the man to come?'

'He has an exaggerated opinion of my powers. You remember what I said about the doctrine of improbability? When it does work out, it gives results which seem very amazing to a person who is not in the secret. That is eight striking, isn't it? And there goes the bell.'

They heard footsteps on the stair, and presently the door opened, and a middle-aged man, with a bowed head, bearded, and with a good deal of grizzling hair about his ears, came into the room. Phillipps glanced at his features, and recognised the lineaments of terror.

'Come in, Mr Selby,' said Dyson. 'This is Mr Phillipps, my intimate friend and our host for this evening. Will you take anything? Then perhaps we had better hear your story – a very singular one, I am sure.'

The man spoke in a voice hollow and a little quavering, and a fixed stare that never left his eyes seemed directed to something awful that was to remain before him by day and night for the rest of his life.

'You will, I am sure, excuse preliminaries,' he began; 'what I have to tell is best told quickly. I will say, then, that I was born in a remote part of the west of England, where the very outlines of the woods and hills, and the winding of the streams in the valleys, are apt to suggest the mystical to any one strongly gifted with imagination. When I was quite a boy there were certain huge and rounded hills, certain depths of hanging wood, and secret valleys bastioned round on every side that filled me with fancies beyond the bourne of rational expression, and as I grew older and began to dip into my father's books, I went by instinct, like the bee, to all that would nourish fantasy. Thus, from a course of obsolete and occult reading, and from listening to certain wild legends in which the older people still secretly believe, I grew firmly convinced of the existence of treasure, the hoard of a race extinct for ages, still hidden beneath the hills, and my every thought was directed to the discovery of the golden heaps that lay, as I fancied, within a few feet of the green turf. To one spot, in especial, I was drawn as if by enchantment; it was a tumulus, the doomed memorial of some forgotten people, crowning the crest of a vast mountain range; and I have often lingered there on summer evenings, sitting on the great block of limestone at the summit, and looking out far over the yellow sea towards the Devonshire coast. One day as I dug heedlessly with the ferrule of my stick at the mosses and lichens which grew rank over the stone, my eye was caught by what seemed a pattern beneath the growth of green; there was a curving line, and marks that did not look altogether the work of nature. At first I thought I had bared some rare fossil, and I took out my knife and scraped away at the moss till a square foot was uncovered. Then I saw two signs which startled me; first, a closed hand, pointing downwards, the thumb protruding between the fingers, and beneath the hand a whorl or spiral, traced with exquisite accuracy in the hard surface of the rock. Here, I persuaded myself, was an index to the great secret, but I chilled at the recollection of the fact that some antiquarians had tunnelled the tumulus through and through, and had been a good deal surprised at not finding so much as an arrowhead within. Clearly, then, the signs on the limestone had no local significance; and I made up my mind that I must search abroad. By sheer accident I was in a measure successful in my quest. Strolling by a cottage, I saw some children playing by the roadside; one was holding up some object in his hand, and the rest were going through one of the many forms of elaborate pretence which make up a great part of the mystery of a child's life. Something in the object held by the little boy attracted me, and I asked him to let me see it. The plaything of these children consisted of an oblong tablet of black stone; and on it was inscribed the hand pointing downwards, just as I had seen it on the rock, while beneath, spaced over the tablet, were a number of whorls and spirals, cut, as it seemed to me, with the utmost care and nicety. I bought the toy for a couple of shillings; the woman of the house told me it had been lying about for years; she thought her husband had found it one day in the brook which ran in front of the cottage; it was a very hot summer, and the stream was almost dry, and he saw it amongst the stones. That day I tracked the brook to a well of water gushing up cold and clear at the head of a lonely glen in the mountains. That was twenty years ago, and I only succeeded in deciphering the mysterious inscription last August. I must not trouble you with irrelevant details of my life; it is enough for me to say that I was forced, like many another man, to leave my old home and come to London. Of money I had very little, and I was glad to find a cheap room in a squalid street off the Gray's Inn Road. The late Sir Thomas Vivian, then far poorer and more wretched than myself, had a garret in the same house, and before many months we became intimate friends, and I had confided to him the object of my life. I had at first great difficulty in persuading him that I was not giving my days and my nights to an enquiry altogether hopeless and chimerical; but when he was convinced he grew keener than myself, and glowed at the thought of the riches which were to be the prize of some ingenuity and patience. I liked the man intensely, and pitied his case; he had a strong desire to enter the medical profession, but he lacked the means to pay the smallest fees, and indeed he was, not once or twice, but often reduced to the very verge of starvation. I freely and solemnly promised that, under whatever chances, he should share in my heaped fortune when it came, and this promise to one who had always been poor, and yet thirsted for wealth and pleasure in a manner unknown to me, was the strongest incentive. He threw himself into the task with eager interest, and applied a very acute intellect and unwearied patience to the solution of the characters on the tablet. I, like other ingenious young men, was curious in the matter of handwriting, and I had invented or adapted a fantastic script which I used occasionally, and which took Vivian so strongly that he was at the pains to imitate it. It was arranged between us that if we were ever parted, and had occasion to write on the affair that was so close to out hearts, this queer hand of my invention was to be used, and we also contrived a semi-cypher for the same purpose. Meanwhile we exhausted ourselves in efforts to get at the heart of the mystery, and after a couple of years had gone by I could see that Vivian began to sicken a little of the adventure, and one night he told me with some emotion that he feared both our lives were being passed away in idle and hopeless endeavour. Not many months afterwards he was so happy as to receive a considerable legacy from an aged and distant relative whose very existence had been almost forgotten by him; and with money at the bank, he became at once a stranger to me. He had passed his preliminary examination many years before, and he forthwith decided to enter at St Thomas's Hospital, and he told me that he must look out for a more convenient lodging. As we said goodbye, I reminded him of the promise I had given, and solemnly renewed it; but Vivian laughed with something between pity and contempt in his voice and expression as he thanked me. I need not dwell on the long struggle and misery of my existence, now doubly lonely; I never wearied or despaired of final success, and every day saw me at work, the tablet before me, and only at dusk would I go out and take my daily walk along Oxford Street, which attracted me I think by the noise and motion and glitter of lamps.

'This walk grew with me to a habit; every night, and in all weathers, I crossed the Gray's Inn Road and struck westward, sometimes choosing a northern track, by the Euston Road and Tottenham Court Road, sometimes I went by Holborn, and sometimes by the way of Great Russell Street. Every night I walked for an hour to and fro on the northern pavement of Oxford Street, and the tale of De Quincey and his name for the Street, "Stony-hearted step-mother", often recurred to my memory. Then I would return to my grimy den and spend hours more in endless analysis of the riddle before me.

'The answer came to me one night a few weeks ago; it flashed into my brain in a moment, and I read the inscription, and saw that after all I had not wasted my days. "The place of the treasure house of them that dwell below", were the first words, I read, and then followed minute indications of the spot in my own country where the great works of gold were to be kept for ever. Such a track was to be followed, such a pitfall avoided; here the way narrowed almost to a fox's hole, and there it broadened, and so at last the chamber would be reached. I determined to lose no time in verifying my discovery – not that I doubted at that great moment, but I would not risk even the smallest chance of disappointing my old friend Vivian, now a rich and prosperous man. I took the train for the West, and one night, with chart in hand, traced out the passage of the hills, and went so far that I saw the gleam of gold before me. I would not go on; I resolved that Vivian must be with me; and I only brought away a strange knife of flint which lay on the path, as confirmation of what I had to tell. I returned to London, and was a good deal vexed to find the stone tablet had disappeared from my rooms. My landlady, an inveterate drunkard, denied all knowledge of the fact, but I have little doubt she had stolen the thing for the sake of the glass of whisky it might fetch. However, I knew what was written on the tablet by heart, and I had also made an exact facsimile of the characters, so the loss was not severe. Only one thing annoyed me: when I first came into possession of the stone, I had pasted a piece of paper on the back and had written down the date and place of finding, and later on I had scribbled a word or two, a trivial sentiment, the name of my street, and suchlike idle pencillings on the paper; and these memories of days that had seemed so hopeless were dear to me: I had thought they would help to remind me in the future of the hours when I had hoped against despair. However, I wrote at once to Sir Thomas Vivian, using the handwriting I have mentioned and also the quasi-cypher. I told him of my success, and after mentioning the loss of the tablet and the fact that I had a copy of the inscription, I reminded him once more of my promise, and asked him either to write or call. He replied that he would see me in a certain obscure passage in Clerkenwell well known to us both in the old days, and at seven o'clock one evening I went to meet him. At the corner of this byway, as I was walking to and fro, I noticed the blurred pictures of some street artist, and I picked up a piece of chalk he had left behind him, not much thinking what I was doing. I paced up and down the passage, wondering a good deal, as you may imagine, as to what manner of man I was to meet after so many years of parting, and the thoughts of the buried time coming thick upon me, I walked mechanically without raising my eyes from the ground. I was startled out of my reverie by an angry voice and a rough enquiry why I didn't keep to the right side of the pavement, and looking up I found I had confronted a prosperous and important gentleman, who eyed my poor appearance with a look of great dislike and contempt. I knew directly it was my old comrade, and when I recalled myself to him, he apologised with some show of regret, and began to thank me for my kindness, doubtfully, as if he hesitated to commit himself, and, as I could see, with the hint of a suspicion as to my sanity. I would have engaged him at first in reminiscences of our friendship, but I found Sir Thomas viewed those days with a good deal of distaste, and replying politely to my remarks, continually edged in "business matters", as he called them. I changed my topics, and told him in greater detail what I have told you. Then I saw his manner suddenly change; as I pulled out the flint knife to prove my journey "to the other side of the moon", as we called it in our jargon, there came over him a kind of choking eagerness, his features were somewhat discomposed, and I thought I detected a shuddering horror, a clenched resolution, and the efforts to keep quiet succeed one another in a manner that puzzled me. I had occasion to be a little precise in my particulars, and it being still light enough, I remembered the red chalk in my pocket, and drew the hand on thc wall. "Here, you see, is the hand," I said, as I explained its true meaning, "note where the thumb issues from between the first and second fingers," and I would have gone on, and had applied the chalk to the wall to continue my diagram, when he struck my hand down, much to my surprise. "No, no," he said, "I do not want all that. And this place is not retired enough; let us walk on, and do you explain everything to me minutely." I complied readily enough, and he led me away, choosing the most unfrequented byways, while I drove in the plan of the hidden house word by word. Once or twice as I raised my eyes I caught Vivian looking strangely about him; he seemed to give a quick glint up and down, and glance at the houses; and there was a furtive and anxious air about him that displeased me. "Let us walk on to the north," he said at length, "we shall come to some pleasant lanes where we can discuss these matters, quietly; my night's rest is at your service." I declined, on the pretext that I could not dispense with my visit to Oxford Street, and went on till he understood every turning and winding and the minutest detail as well as myself. We had returned on our footsteps, and stood again in the dark passage, just where I had drawn the red hand on the wall, for I recognised the vague shape of the trees whose branches hung above us. "We have come back to our starting point," I said; "I almost think I could put my finger on the wall where I drew the hand. And I am sure you could put your finger on the mystic hand in the hills as well as I. Remember between stream and stone."

'I was bending down, peering at what I thought must be my drawing, when I heard a sharp hiss of breath, and started up, and saw Vivian with his arm uplifted and a bare blade in his hand, and death threatening in his eyes. In sheer self-defence I caught at the flint weapon in my pocket, and dashed at him in blind fear of my life, and the next instant he lay dead upon the stones.

'I think that is all,' Mr Selby continued after a pause, 'and it only remains for me to say to you, Mr Dyson, that I cannot conceive what means enabled you to run me down.'

'I followed many indications,' said Dyson, 'and I am bound to disclaim all credit for acuteness, as I have made several gross blunders. Your celestial cypher did not, I confess, give me much trouble; I saw at once that terms of astronomy were substituted for common words and phrases. You had lost something black, or something black had been stolen from you; a celestial globe is a copy of the heavens, so I knew you meant you had a copy of what you had lost. Obviously, then, I came to the conclusion that you had lost a black object with characters or symbols written or inscribed on it, since the object in question certainly contained valuable information, and all information must be written or pictured. "Our old orbit remains unchanged"; evidently our old course or arrangement. "The number of my sign" must mean the number of my house, the allusion being to the signs of the zodiac. I need not say that "the other side of the moon" can stand for nothing but some place where no one else has been; and "some other house" is some other place of meeting, the "house" being the old term "house of the heavens". Then my next step was to find the "black heaven" that had been stolen, and by a process of exhaustion I did so.'

'You have got the tablet?'

'Certainly. And on the back of it, on the slip of paper you have mentioned, I read "inroad", which puzzled me a good deal, till I thought of Gray's Inn Road; you forgot the second *n*. "Stony-hearted step – " immediately suggested the phrase of De Quincey you have alluded to; and I made the wild but correct shot, that you were a man who lived in or near the Gray's Inn Road, and had the habit of walking in Oxford Street, for you remember how the opium eater dwells on his wearying promenades along that thoroughfare? On the theory of improbability, which I have explained to my friend here, I concluded that occasionally, at all events, you would choose the way Guilford Street, Russell Square, and Great Russell Street, and I knew that if I watched long enough I should see you. But how was I to recognise my man? I noticed the screever opposite my rooms, and got him to draw every day a large hand, in the gesture so familiar to us all, upon the wall behind him. I thought that when the unknown person did pass he would certainly betray some emotion at the sudden vision of the sign, to him the most terrible of symbols. You know the rest. Ah, as to catching you an hour later, that was, I confess, a refinement. From the fact of your having occupied the same rooms for so many years, in a neighbourhood moreover where lodgers are migratory to excess, I drew the conclusion that you were a man of fixed habit, and I was sure that after you had got over your fright you would return for the walk down Oxford Street. You did, by way of New Oxford Street, and I was waiting at the corner.'

'Your conclusions are admirable,' said Mr Selby. 'I may tell you that I had my stroll down Oxford Street the night Sir Thomas Vivian died. And I think that is all I have to say.'

'Scarcely,' said Dyson. 'How about the treasure?'

'I had rather we did not speak of that,' said Mr Selby, with a whitening of the skin about the temples.

'Oh, nonsense, sir, we are not blackmailers. Besides, you know you are in our power.'

'Then, as you put it like that, Mr Dyson, I must tell you I returned to the place. I went on a little farther than before.'

The man stopped short; his mouth began to twitch, his lips moved apart, and he drew in quick breaths, sobbing.

'Well, well,' said Dyson, 'I dare say you have done comfortably.'

'Comfortably,' Selby went on, constraining himself with an effort, 'yes, so comfortably that hell burns hot within me for ever. I only brought one thing away from that awful house within the hills; it was lying just beyond the spot where I found the flint knife.'

'Why did you not bring more?'

The whole bodily frame of the wretched man visibly shrank and wasted; his face grew yellow as tallow, and the sweat dropped from his brows. The spectacle was both revolting and terrible, and when the voice came, it sounded like the hissing of a snake.

'Because the keepers are still there, and I saw them, and because of this,' and he pulled out a small piece of curious gold-work and held it up.

'There,' he said, 'that is the Pain of the Goat.'

Phillipps and Dyson cried out together in horror at the revolting obscenity of the thing.

'Put it away, man; hide it, for Heaven's sake, hide it!'

'I brought that with me; that is all,' he said. 'You do not wonder that I did not stay long in a place where those who live are a little higher than the beasts, and where what you have seen is surpassed a thousandfold?'

'Take this,' said Dyson, 'I brought it with me in case it might be useful'; and he drew out the black tablet, and handed it to the shaking, horrible man.

'And now,' said Dyson, 'will you go out?'

The two friends sat silent a little while, facing one another with restless eyes and lips that quivered.

'I wish to say that I believe him,' said Phillipps.

'My dear Phillipps,' said Dyson as he threw the windows wide open, 'I do not know that, after all, my blunders in this queer case were so very absurd.'

The White People

Prologue

'Sorcery and sanctity,' said Ambrose, 'these are the only realities. Each is an ecstasy, a withdrawal from the common life.'

Cotgrave listened, interested. He had been brought by a friend to this mouldering house in a northern suburb, through an old garden to the room where Ambrose the recluse dozed and dreamed over his books.

'Yes,' he went on, 'magic is justified of her children. There are many, I think, who eat dry crusts and drink water, with a joy infinitely sharper than anything within the experience of the "practical" epicure.'

'You are speaking of the saints?'

'Yes, and of the sinners, too. I think you are falling into the very general error of confining the spiritual world to the supremely good; but the supremely wicked, necessarily, have their portion in it. The merely carnal, sensual man can no more be a great sinner than he can be a great saint. Most of us are just indifferent, mixed-up creatures; we muddle through the world without realising the meaning and the inner sense of things, and, consequently, our wickedness and our goodness are alike second-rate, unimportant.'

'And you think the great sinner, then, will be an ascetic, as well as the great saint?'

'Great people of all kinds forsake the imperfect copies and go to the perfect originals. I have no doubt but that many of the very highest among the saints have never done a "good action" (using the words in their ordinary sense). And, on the other hand, there have been those who have sounded the very depths of sin, who all their lives have never done an "ill deed".'

He went out of the room for a moment, and Cotgrave, in high delight, turned to his friend and thanked him for the introduction.

'He's grand,' he said. 'I never saw that kind of lunatic before.'

Ambrose returned with more whisky and helped the two men in a liberal manner. He abused the teetotal sect with ferocity, as he handed the seltzer, and pouring out a glass of water for himself, was about to resume his monologue, when Cotgrave broke in –

'I can't stand it, you know,' he said, 'your paradoxes are too monstrous. A man may be a great sinner and yet never do anything sinful! Come!'

'You're quite wrong,' said Ambrose. 'I never make paradoxes; I wish I could. I merely said that a man may have an exquisite taste in Romanée Conti, and yet never have even smelt four ale. That's all, and it's more like a truism than a paradox, isn't it? Your surprise at my remark is due to the fact that you haven't realised what sin is. Oh, yes, there is a sort of connexion between Sin with the capital letter, and actions which are commonly called sinful: with murder, theft, adultery, and so forth. Much the same connexion that there is between the A, B, C and fine literature. But I believe that the misconception – it is all but universal – arises in great measure from our looking at the matter through social spectacles. We think that a man who does evil to us and to his neighbours must be very evil. So he is, from a social standpoint; but can't you realise that Evil in its essence is a lonely thing, a passion of the solitary, individual soul? Really, the average murderer, *quâ* murderer, is not by any means a sinner in the true sense of the word. He is simply a wild beast that we have to get rid of to save our own necks from his knife. I should class him rather with tigers than with sinners.'

'It seems a little strange.'

'I think not. The murderer murders not from positive qualities, but from negative ones; he lacks something which non-murderers possess. Evil, of course, is wholly positive – only it is on the wrong side. You may believe me that sin in its proper sense is very rare; it is probable that there have been far fewer sinners than saints. Yes, your standpoint is all very well for practical, social purposes; we are naturally inclined to think that a person who is very disagreeable to us must be a very great sinner! It is very disagreeable to have one's pocket picked, and we pronounce the thief to be a very great sinner. In truth, he is merely an undeveloped man. He cannot be a saint, of course; but he may be, and often is, an infinitely better creature than thousands who have never broken a single commandment. He is a great nuisance to *us*, I admit, and we very properly lock him up if we catch him; but between his troublesome and unsocial action and evil – Oh, the connexion is of the weakest.'

It was getting very late. The man who had brought Cotgrave had probably heard all this before, since he assisted with a bland and judicious smile, but Cotgrave began to think that his 'lunatic' was turning into a sage.

'Do you know,' he said, 'you interest me immensely? You think, then, that we do not understand the real nature of evil?'

'No, I don't think we do. We overestimate it and we under-estimate it. We take the very numerous infractions of our social "bye-laws" – the very necessary and very proper regulations which keep the human company together – and we get frightened at the prevalence of "sin" and "evil". But this is really nonsense. Take theft, for example. Have you any horror at the thought of Robin Hood, of the Highland caterans of the seventeenth century, of the moss-troopers, of the company promoters of our day?

'Then, on the other hand, we underrate evil. We attach such an enormous importance to the "sin" of meddling with our pockets (and our wives) that we have quite forgotten the awfulness of real sin.'

'And what is sin?' said Cotgrave.

'I think I must reply to your question by another. What would your feelings be, seriously, if your cat or your dog began to talk to you, and to dispute with you in human accents? You would be overwhelmed with horror. I am sure of it. And if the roses in your garden sang a weird song, you would go mad. And suppose the stones in the road began to swell and grow before your eyes, and if the pebble that you noticed at night had shot out stony blossoms in the morning?

'Well, these examples may give you some notion of what sin really is.'

'Look here,' said the third man, hitherto placid, 'you two seem pretty well wound up. But I'm going home. I've missed my tram, and I shall have to walk.'

Ambrose and Cotgrave seemed to settle down more profoundly when the other had gone out into the early misty morning and the pale light of the lamps.

'You astonish me,' said Cotgrave. 'I had never thought of that. If that is really so, one must turn everything upside down. Then the essence of sin really is – '

'In the taking of heaven by storm, it seems to me,' said Ambrose. 'It appears to me that it is simply an attempt to penetrate into another and higher sphere in a forbidden manner. You can understand why it is so rare. There are few, indeed, who wish to penetrate into other spheres, higher or lower, in ways allowed or forbidden. Men, in the mass, are amply content with life as they find it. Therefore there are few saints, and sinners (in the proper sense) are fewer still, and men of genius, who partake sometimes of each character, are rare also. Yes; on the whole, it is, perhaps, harder to be a great sinner than a great saint.'

'There is something profoundly unnatural about sin? Is that what you mean?'

'Exactly. Holiness requires as great, or almost as great, an effort; but holiness works on lines that *were* natural once; it is an effort to recover the ecstasy that was before the Fall. But sin is an effort to gain the ecstasy and the knowledge that pertain alone to angels, and in making this effort man becomes a demon. I told you that the mere murderer is not *therefore* a sinner; that is true, but the sinner is sometimes a murderer. Gilles de Raiz is an instance. So you see that while the good and the evil are unnatural to man as he now is – to man the social, civilised being – evil is unnatural in a much deeper sense than good. The saint endeavours to recover a gift which he has lost; the sinner tries to obtain something which was never his. In brief, he repeats the Fall.'

'But are you a Catholic?' said Cotgrave.

'Yes; I am a member of the persecuted Anglican Church.'

'Then, how about those texts which seem to reckon as sin that which you would set down as a mere trivial dereliction?'

'Yes; but in one place the word "sorcerers" comes in the same sentence, doesn't it? That seems to me to give the key-note. Consider: can you imagine for a moment that a false statement which saves an innocent man's life is a sin? No; very good, then, it is not the mere liar who is excluded by those words; it is, above all, the "sorcerers" who use the material life, who use the failings incidental to material life as instruments to obtain their infinitely wicked ends. And let me tell you this: our higher senses are so blunted, we are so drenched with materialism, that we should probably fail to recognise real wickedness if we encountered it.'

'But shouldn't we experience a certain horror – a terror such as you hinted we would experience if a rose tree sang – in the mere presence of an evil man?'

'We should if we were natural: children and women feel this horror you speak of, even animals experience it. But with most of us convention and civilisation and education have blinded and deafened and obscured the natural reason. No, sometimes we may recognise evil by its hatred of the good – one doesn't need much penetration to guess at the influence which dictated, quite unconsciously, the "Blackwood" review of Keats – but this is purely incidental; and, as a rule, I suspect that the Hierarchs of Tophet pass quite unnoticed, or, perhaps, in certain cases, as good but mistaken men.'

'But you used the word "unconscious" just now, of Keats's reviewers. Is wickedness ever unconscious?'

'Always. It must be so. It is like holiness and genius in this as in other points; it is a certain rapture or ecstasy of the soul; a transcendent effort to surpass the ordinary bounds. So, surpassing these, it surpasses also the understanding, the faculty that takes note of that which comes before it. No, a man may be infinitely and horribly wicked and never suspect it. But I tell you, evil in this, its certain and true sense, is rare, and I think it is growing rarer.'

'I am trying to get hold of it all,' said Cotgrave. 'From what you say, I gather that the true evil differs generically from that which we call evil?'

'Quite so. There is, no doubt, an analogy between the two; a resemblance such as enables us to use, quite legitimately, such terms as the "foot of the mountain" and the "leg of the table". And, sometimes, of course, the two speak, as it were, in the same language. The rough miner, or "puddler", the untrained, undeveloped "tiger-man", heated by a quart or two above his usual measure, comes home and kicks his irritating and injudicious wife to death. He is a murderer. And Gilles de Raiz was a murderer. But you see the gulf that separates the two? The "word", if I may so speak, is accidentally the same in each case, but the "meaning" is utterly different. It is flagrant "Hobson Jobson" to confuse the two, or rather, it is as if one supposed that Juggernaut and the Argonauts had something to do etymologically with one another. And no doubt the same weak likeness, or analogy, runs between all the "social" sins and the real spiritual sins, and in some cases, perhaps, the lesser may be "schoolmasters" to lead one on to the greater – from the shadow to the reality. If you are anything of a Theologian, you will see the importance of all this.'

'I am sorry to say,' remarked Cotgrave, 'that I have devoted very little of my time to theology. Indeed, I have often wondered on what grounds theologians have claimed the title of Science of Sciences for their favourite study; since the "theological" books I have looked into have always seemed to me to be concerned with feeble and obvious pieties, or with the kings of Israel and Judah. I do not care to hear about those kings.'

Ambrose grinned.

'We must try to avoid theological discussion,' he said. 'I perceive that you would be a bitter disputant. But perhaps the "dates of the kings" have as much to do with theology as the hobnails of the murderous puddler with evil.'

'Then, to return to our main subject, you think that sin is an esoteric, occult thing?'

'Yes. It is the infernal miracle as holiness is the supernal. Now and then it is raised to such a pitch that we entirely fail to suspect its existence; it is like the note of the great pedal pipes of the organ, which is so deep that we cannot hear it. In other cases it may lead to the lunatic asylum, or to still stranger issues. But you must never confuse it with mere social misdoing. Remember how the Apostle, speaking of the "other side", distinguishes between "charitable" actions and charity. And as one may give all one's goods to the poor, and yet lack charity; so, remember, one may avoid every crime and yet be a sinner.'

'Your psychology is very strange to me,' said Cotgrave, 'but I confess I like it, and I suppose that one might fairly deduce from your premises the conclusion that the real sinner might very possibly strike the observer as a harmless personage enough?'

'Certainly; because the true evil has nothing to do with social life or social laws, or if it has, only incidentally and accidentally. It is a lonely passion of the soul – or a passion of the lonely soul – whichever you like. If, by chance, we understand it, and grasp its full significance, then, indeed, it will fill us with horror and with awe. But this emotion is widely distinguished from the fear and the disgust with which we regard the ordinary criminal, since this latter is largely or entirely founded on the regard which we have for our own skins or purses. We hate a murderer, because we know that we should hate to be murdered, or to have any one that we like murdered. So, on the "other side", we venerate the saints, but we don't "like" them as we like our friends. Can you persuade yourself that you would have "enjoyed" St Paul's company? Do you think that you and I would have "got on" with Sir Galahad?

'So with the sinners, as with the saints. If you met a very evil man, and recognised his evil; he would, no doubt, fill you with horror and awe; but there is no reason why you should "dislike" him. On the contrary, it is quite possible that if you could succeed in putting the sin out of your mind you might find the sinner capital company, and in a little while you might have to reason yourself back into horror. Still, how awful it is. If the roses and the lilies suddenly sang on this coming morning; if the furniture began to move in procession, as in De Maupassant's tale!'

'I am glad you have come back to that comparison,' said Cotgrave, 'because I wanted to ask you what it is that corresponds in humanity to these imaginary feats of inanimate things. In a word – what is sin? You have given me, I know, an abstract definition, but I should like a concrete example.'

'I told you it was very rare,' said Ambrose, who appeared willing to avoid the giving of a direct answer. 'The materialism of the age, which has done a good deal to suppress sanctity, has done perhaps more to suppress evil. We find the earth so very comfortable that we have no inclination either for ascents or descents. It would seem as if the scholar who decided to "specialise" in Tophet, would be reduced to purely antiquarian researches. No palaeontologist could show you a *live* pterodactyl.'

'And yet you, I think, have "specialised", and I believe that your researches have descended to our modern times.'

'You are really interested, I see. Well, I confess that I have dabbled a little, and if you like I can show you something that bears on the very curious subject we have been discussing.'

Ambrose took a candle and went away to a far, dim corner of the room. Cotgrave saw him open a venerable bureau that stood there, and from some secret recess he drew out a parcel, and came back to the window where they had been sitting.

Ambrose undid a wrapping of paper, and produced a green pocketbook.

'You will take care of it?' he said. 'Don't leave it lying about. It is one of the choicer pieces in my collection, and I should be very sorry if it were lost.'

He fondled the faded binding.

'I knew the girl who wrote this,' he said. 'When you read it, you will see how it illustrates the talk we have had tonight. There is a sequel, too, but I won't talk of that.'

'There was an odd article in one of the reviews some months ago,' he began again, with the air of a man who changes the subject. 'It was written by a doctor – Dr Coryn, I think, was the name. He says that a lady, watching her little girl playing at the drawingroom window, suddenly saw the heavy sash give way and fall on the child's fingers. The lady fainted, I think, but at any rate the doctor was summoned, and when he had dressed the child's wounded and maimed fingers he was summoned to the mother. She was groaning with pain, and it was found that three fingers of her hand, corresponding with those that had been injured on the child's hand, were swollen and inflamed, and later, in the doctor's language, purulent sloughing set in.'

Ambrose still handled delicately the green volume.

'Well, here it is,' he said at last, parting with difficulty, it seemed, from his treasure.

'You will bring it back as soon as you have read it,' he said, as they went out into the hall, into the old garden, faint with the odour of white lilies.

There was a broad red band in the east as Cotgrave turned to go, and from the high ground where he stood he saw that awful spectacle of London in a dream.

The Green Book

The morocco binding of the book was faded, and the colour had grown faint, but there were no stains nor bruises nor marks of usage. The book looked as if it had been bought 'on a visit to London' some seventy or eighty years ago, and had somehow been forgotten and suffered to lie away out of sight. There was an old, delicate, lingering odour about it, such an odour as sometimes haunts an ancient piece of furniture for a century or more. The end-papers, inside the binding, were oddly decorated with coloured patterns and faded gold. It looked small, but the paper was fine, and there were many leaves, closely covered with minute, painfully formed characters.

I found this book (the manuscript began) in a drawer in the old bureau that stands on the landing. It was a very rainy day and I could not go out, so in the afternoon I got a candle and rummaged in the bureau. Nearly all the drawers were full of old dresses, but one of the small ones looked empty, and I found this book hidden right at the back. I wanted a book like this, so I took it to write in. It is full of secrets. I have a great many other books of secrets I have written, hidden in a safe place, and I am going to write here many of the old secrets and some new ones; but there are some I shall not put down at all. I must not write down the real names of the days and months which I found out a year ago, nor the way to make the Aklo letters, or the Chian language, or the great beautiful Circles, nor the Mao Games, nor the chief songs. I may write something about all these things but not the way to do them, for peculiar reasons. And I must not say who the Nymphs are, or the Dôls, or Jeelo, or what voolas mean. All these are most secret secrets, and I am glad when I remember what they are, and how many wonderful languages I know, but there are some things that I call the secrets of the secrets of the secrets that I dare not think of unless I am quite alone, and then I shut my eyes, and put my hands over them and whisper the word, and the Alala comes. I only do this at night in my room or in certain woods that I know, but I must not describe them, as they are secret woods. Then there are the Ceremonies, which are all of them important, but some are more delightful than others – there are the White Ceremonies, and the Green Ceremonies, and the Scarlet Ceremonies. The Scarlet Ceremonies are the best, but there is only one place where they can be performed properly, though there is a very nice imitation which I have done in other places. Besides these, I have the dances, and the Comedy, and I have done the Comedy sometimes when the others were looking, and they didn't understand anything about it. I was very little when I first knew about these things.

When I was very small, and mother was alive, I can remember remembering things before that, only it has all got confused. But I remember when I was five or six I heard them talking about me when they thought I was not noticing. They were saying how queer I was a year or two before, and how nurse had called my mother to come and listen to me talking all to myself, and I was saying words that nobody could understand. I was speaking the Xu language, but I only remember a very few of the words, as it was about the little white faces that used to look at me when I was lying in my cradle. They used to talk to me, and I learnt their language and talked to them in it about some great white place where they lived, where the trees and the grass were all white, and there were white hills as high up as the moon, and a cold wind. I have often dreamed of it afterwards, but the faces went away when I was very little. But a wonderful thing happened when I was about five. My nurse was carrying me on her shoulder; there was a field of yellow corn, and we went through it, it was very hot. Then we came to a path through a wood, and a tall man came after us, and went with us till we came to a place where there was a deep pool, and it was very dark and shady. Nurse put me down on the soft moss under a tree, and she said: 'She can't get to the pond now.' So they left me there, and I sat quite still and watched, and out of the water and out of the wood came two wonderful white people, and they began to play and dance and sing. They were a kind of creamy white like the old ivory figure in the drawingroom; one was a beautiful lady with kind dark eyes, and a grave face, and long black hair, and she smiled such a strange sad smile at the other, who laughed and came to her. They played together, and danced round and round the pool, and they sang a song till I fell asleep. Nurse woke me up when she came back, and she was looking something like the lady had looked, so I told her all about it, and asked her why she looked like that. At first she cried, and then she looked very frightened, and turned quite pale. She put me down on the grass and stared at me, and I could see she was shaking all over. Then she said I had been dreaming, but I knew I hadn't. Then she made me promise not to say a word about it to anybody, and if I did I should be thrown into the black pit. I was not frightened at all, though nurse was, and I never forgot about it, because when I shut my eyes and it was quite quiet, and I was all alone, I could see them again, very faint and far away, but very splendid; and little bits of the song they sang came into my head, but I couldn't sing it.

I was thirteen, nearly fourteen, when I had a very singular adventure, so strange that the day on which it happened is always called the White Day. My mother had been dead for more than a year, and in the morning I had lessons, but they let me go out for walks in the afternoon. And this afternoon I walked a new way, and a little brook led me into a new country, but I tore my frock getting through some of the difficult places, as the way was through many bushes, and beneath the low branches of trees, and up thorny thickets on the hills, and by dark woods full of creeping thorns. And it was a long, long way. It seemed as if I was going on for ever and ever, and I had to creep by a place like a tunnel where a brook must have been, but all the water had dried up, and the floor was rocky, and the bushes had grown overhead till they met, so that it was quite dark. And I went on and on through that dark place; it was a long, long way. And I came to a hill that I never saw before. I was in a dismal thicket full of black twisted boughs that tore me as I went through them, and I cried out because I was smarting all over, and then I found that I was climbing, and I went up and up a long way, till at last the thicket stopped and I came out crying just under the top of a big bare place, where there were ugly grey stones lying all about on the grass, and here and there a little twisted, stunted tree came out from under a stone, like a snake. And I went up, right to the top, a long way. I never saw such big ugly stones before; they came out of the earth some of them, and some looked as if they had been rolled to where they were, and they went on and on as far as I could see, a long, long way. I looked out from them and saw the country, but it was strange. It was winter time, and there were black terrible woods hanging from the hills all round; it was like seeing a large room hung with black curtains, and the shape of the trees seemed quite different from any I had ever seen before. I was afraid. Then beyond the woods there were other hills round in a great ring, but I had never seen any of them; it all looked black, and everything had a voor over it. It was all so still and silent, and the sky was heavy and grey and sad, like a wicked voorish dome in Deep Dendo. I went on into the dreadful rocks. There were hundreds and hundreds of them. Some were like horrid-grinning men; I could see their faces as if they would jump at me out of the stone, and catch hold of me, and drag me with them back into the rock, so that I should always be there. And there were other rocks that were like animals, creeping, horrible animals, putting out their tongues, and others were like words that I could not say, and others like dead people lying on the grass. I went on among them, though they frightened me, and my heart was full of wicked songs that they put into it; and I wanted to make faces and twist myself about in the way they did, and I went on and on a long way till at last I liked the rocks, and they didn't frighten me any more. I sang the songs I thought of; songs full of words that must not be spoken or written down. Then I made faces like the faces on the rocks, and I twisted myself about like the twisted ones, and I lay down flat on the ground like the dead ones, and I went up to one that was grinning, and put my arms round him and hugged him. And so I went on and on through the rocks till I came to a round mound in the middle of them. It was higher than a mound, it was nearly as high as our house, and it was like a great basin turned upside down, all smooth and round and green, with one stone, like a post, sticking up at the top. I climbed up the sides, but they were so steep I had to stop or I should have rolled all the way down again, and I should have knocked against the stones at the bottom, and perhaps been killed. But I wanted to get up to the very top of the big round mound, so I lay down flat on my face, and took hold of the grass with my hands and drew myself up, bit by bit, till I was at the top. Then I sat down on the stone in the middle, and looked all round about. I felt I had come such a long, long way, just as if I were a hundred miles from home, or in some other country, or in one of the strange places I had read about in the *Tales of the Genie* and the *Arabian Nights*, or as if I had gone across the sea, far away, for years and I had found another world that nobody had ever seen or heard of before, or as if I had somehow flown through the sky and fallen on one of the stars I had read about where everything is dead and cold and grey, and there is no air, and the wind doesn't blow. I sat on the stone and looked all round and down and round about me. It was just as if I was sitting on a tower in the middle of a great empty town, because I could see nothing all around but the grey rocks on the ground. I couldn't make out their shapes any more, but I could see them on and on for a long way, and I looked at them, and they seemed as if they had been arranged into patterns, and shapes, and figures. I knew they couldn't be, because I had seen a lot of them coming right out of the earth, joined to the deep rocks below, so I looked again, but still I saw nothing but circles, and small circles inside big ones, and pyramids, and domes, and spires, and they seemed all to go round and round the place where I was sitting, and the more I looked, the more I saw great big rings of rocks, getting bigger and bigger, and I stared so long that it felt as if they were all moving and turning, like a great wheel, and I was turning, too, in the middle. I got quite dizzy and queer in the head, and everything began to be hazy and not clear, and I saw little sparks of blue light, and the stones looked as if they were springing and dancing and twisting as they went round and round and round. I was frightened again, and I cried out loud, and jumped up from the stone I was sitting on, and fell down. When I got up I was so glad they all looked still, and I sat down on the top and slid down the mound, and went on again. I danced as I went in the peculiar way the rocks had danced when I got giddy, and I was so glad I could do it quite well, and I danced and danced along, and sang extraordinary songs that came into my head. At last I came to the edge of that great flat hill, and there were no more rocks, and the way went again through a dark thicket in a hollow. It was just as bad as the other one I went through climbing up, but I didn't mind this one, because I was so glad I had seen those singular dances and could imitate them. I went down, creeping through the bushes, and a tall nettle stung me on my leg, and made me burn, but I didn't mind it, and I tingled with the boughs and the thorns, but I only laughed and sang. Then I got out of the thicket into a close valley, a little secret place like a dark passage that nobody ever knows of, because it was so narrow and deep and the woods were so thick round it. There is a steep bank with trees hanging over it, and there the ferns keep green all through the winter, when they are dead and brown upon the hill, and the ferns there have a sweet, rich smell like what oozes out of fir trees. There was a little stream of water running down this valley, so small that I could easily step across it. I drank the water with my hand, and it tasted like bright, yellow wine, and it sparkled and bubbled as it ran down over beautiful red and yellow and green stones, so that it seemed alive and all colours at once. I drank it, and I drank more with my hand, but I couldn't drink enough, so I lay down and bent my head and sucked the water up with my lips. It tasted much better, drinking it that way, and a ripple would come up to my mouth and give me a kiss, and I laughed, and drank again, and pretended there was a nymph, like the one in the old picture at home, who lived in the water and was kissing me. So I bent low down to the water, and put my lips softly to it, and whispered to the nymph that I would come again. I felt sure it could not be common water, I was so glad when I got up and went on; and I danced again and went up and up the valley, under hanging hills. And when I came to the top, the ground rose up in front of me, tall and steep as a wall, and there was nothing but the green wall and the sky. I thought of 'for ever and for ever, world without end, Amen'; and I thought I must have really found the end of the world, because it was like the end of everything, as if there could be nothing at all beyond, except the kingdom of Voor, where the light goes when it is put out, and the water goes when the sun takes it away. I began to think of all the long, long way I had journeyed, how I had found a brook and followed it, and followed it on, and gone through bushes and thorny thickets, and dark woods full of creeping thorns. Then I had crept up a tunnel under trees, and climbed a thicket, and seen all the grey rocks, and sat in the middle of them when they turned round, and then I had gone on through the grey rocks and come down the hill through the stinging thicket and up the dark valley, all a long, long way. I wondered how I should get home again, if I could ever find the way, and if my home was there any more, or if it were turned and everybody in it into grey rocks, as in the *Arabian Nights*. So I sat down on the grass and thought what I should do next. I was tired, and my feet were hot with walking, and as I looked about I saw there was a wonderful well just under the high, steep wall of grass. All the ground round it was covered with bright, green, dripping moss; there was every kind of moss there, moss like beautiful little ferns, and like palms and fir trees, and it was all green as jewellery, and drops of water hung on it like diamonds. And in the middle was the great well, deep and shining and beautiful, so clear that it looked as if I could touch the red sand at the bottom, but it was far below. I stood by it and looked in, as if I were looking in a glass. At the bottom of the well, in the middle of it, the red grains of sand were moving and stirring all the time, and I saw how the water bubbled up, but at the top it was quite smooth, and full and brimming. It was a great well, large like a bath, and with the shining, glittering green moss about it, it looked like a great white jewel, with green jewels all round. My feet were so hot and tired that I took off my boots and stockings, and let my feet down into the water, and the water was soft and cold, and when I got up I wasn't tired any more, and I felt I must go on, farther and farther, and see what was on the other side of the wall. I climbed up it very slowly, going sideways all the time, and when I got to the top and looked over, I was in the queerest country I had seen, stranger even than the hill of the grey rocks. It looked as if earth-children had been playing there with their spades, as it was all hills and hollows, and castles and walls made of earth and covered with grass. There were two mounds like big bee-hives, round and great and solemn, and then hollow basins, and then a steep mounting wall like the ones I saw once by the seaside where the big guns and the soldiers were. I nearly fell into one of the round hollows, it went away from under my feet so suddenly, and I ran fast down the side and stood at the bottom and looked up. It was strange and solemn to look up. There was nothing but the grey, heavy sky and the sides of the hollow; everything else had gone away, and the hollow was the whole world, and I thought that at night it must be full of ghosts and moving shadows and pale things when the moon shone down to the bottom at the dead of the night, and the wind wailed up above. It was so strange and solemn and lonely, like a hollow temple of dead heathen gods. It reminded me of a tale my nurse had told me when I was quite little; it was the same nurse that took me into the wood where I saw the beautiful white people. And I remembered how nurse had told me the story one winter night, when the wind was beating the trees against the wall, and crying and moaning in the nursery chimney.

She said there was, somewhere or other, a hollow pit, just like the one I was standing in, everybody was afraid to go into it or near it, it was such a bad place. But once upon a time there was a poor girl who said she would go into the hollow pit, and everybody tried to stop her, but she would go. And she went down into the pit and came back laughing, and said there was nothing there at all, except green grass and red stones, and white stones and yellow flowers. And soon after people saw she had most beautiful emerald earrings, and they asked how she got them, as she and her mother were quite poor. But she laughed, and said her earrings were not made of emeralds at all, but only of green grass. Then, one day, she wore on her breast the reddest ruby that any one had ever seen, and it was as big as a hen's egg, and glowed and sparkled like a hot burning coal of fire. And they asked how she got it, as she and her mother were quite poor. But she laughed, and said it was not a ruby at all, but only a red stone. Then one day she wore round her neck the loveliest necklace that any one had ever seen, much finer than the queen's finest, and it was made of great bright diamonds, hundreds of them, and they shone like all the stars on a night in June. So they asked her how she got it, as she and her mother were quite poor. But she laughed, and said they were not diamonds at all, but only white stones. And one day she went to the Court, and she wore on her head a crown of pure angel-gold, so nurse said, and it shone like the sun, and it was much more splendid than the crown the king was wearing himself, and in her ears she wore the emeralds, and the big ruby was the brooch on her breast, and the great diamond necklace was sparkling on her neck. And the king and queen thought she was some great princess from a long way off, and got down from their thrones and went to meet her, but somebody told the king and queen who she was, and that she was quite poor. So the king asked why she wore a gold crown, and how she got it, as she and her mother were so poor. And she laughed, and said it wasn't a gold crown at all, but only some yellow flowers she had put in her hair. And the king thought it was very strange, and said she should stay at the Court, and they would see what would happen next. And she was so lovely that everybody said that her eyes were greener than the emeralds, that her lips were redder than the ruby, that her skin was whiter than the diamonds, and that her hair was brighter than the golden crown. So the king's son said he would marry her, and the king said he might. And the bishop married them, and there was a great supper, and afterwards the king's son went to his wife's room. But just when he had his hand on the door, he saw a tall, black man, with a dreadful face, standing in front of the door, and a voice said –

> Venture not upon your life,
> This is mine own wedded wife.

Then the king's son fell down on the ground in a fit. And they came and tried to get into the room, but they couldn't, and they hacked at the door with hatchets, but the wood had turned hard as iron, and at last everybody ran away, they were so frightened at the screaming and laughing and shrieking and crying that came out of the room. But next day they went in, and found there was nothing in the room but thick black smoke, because the black man had come and taken her away. And on the bed there were two knots of faded grass and a red stone, and some white stones, and some faded yellow flowers. I remembered this tale of nurse's while I was standing at the bottom of the deep hollow; it was so strange and solitary there, and I felt afraid. I could not see any stones or flowers, but I was afraid of bringing them away without knowing, and I thought I would do a charm that came into my head to keep the black man away. So I stood right in the very middle of the hollow, and I made sure that I had none of those things on me, and then I walked round the place, and touched my eyes, and my lips, and my hair in a peculiar manner, and whispered some queer words that nurse taught me to keep bad things away. Then I felt safe and climbed up out of the hollow, and went on through all those mounds and hollows and walls, till I came to the end, which was high above all the rest, and I could see that all the different shapes of the earth were arranged in patterns, something like the grey rocks, only the pattern was different. It was getting late, and the air was indistinct, but it looked from where I was standing something like two great figures of people lying on the grass. And I went on, and at last I found a certain wood, which is too secret to be described, and nobody knows of the passage into it, which I found out in a very curious manner, by seeing some little animal run into the wood through it. So I went after the animal by a very narrow dark way, under thorns and bushes, and it was almost dark when I came to a kind of open place in the middle. And there I saw the most wonderful sight I have ever seen, but it was only for a minute, as I ran away directly, and crept out of the wood by the passage I had come by, and ran and ran as fast as ever I could, because I was afraid, what I had seen was so wonderful and so strange and beautiful. But I wanted to get home and think of it, and I did not know what might not happen if I stayed by the wood. I was hot all over and trembling, and my heart was beating, and strange cries that I could not help came from me as I ran from the wood. I was glad that a great white moon came up from over a round hill and showed me the way, so I went back through the mounds and hollows and down the close valley, and up through the thicket over the place of the grey rocks, and so at last I got home again. My father was busy in his study, and the servants had not told about my not coming home, though they were frightened, and wondered what they ought to do, so I told them I had lost my way, but I did not let them find out the real way I had been. I went to bed and lay awake all through the night, thinking of what I had seen. When I came out of the narrow way, and it looked all shining, though the air was dark, it seemed so certain, and all the way home I was quite sure that I had seen it, and I wanted to be alone in my room, and be glad over it all to myself, and shut my eyes and pretend it was there, and do all the things I would have done if I had not been so afraid. But when I shut my eyes the sight would not come, and I began to think about my adventures all over again, and I remembered how dusky and queer it was at the end, and I was afraid it must be all a mistake, because it seemed impossible it could happen. It seemed like one of nurse's tales, which I didn't really believe in, though I was frightened at the bottom of the hollow; and the stories she told me when I was little came back into my head, and I wondered whether it was really there what I thought I had seen, or whether any of her tales could have happened a long time ago. It was so queer; I lay awake there in my room at the back of the house, and the moon was shining on the other side towards the river, so the bright light did not fall upon the wall. And the house was quite still. I had heard my father come upstairs, and just after the clock struck twelve, and after the house was still and empty, as if there was nobody alive in it. And though it was all dark and indistinct in my room, a pale glimmering kind of light shone in through the white blind, and once I got up and looked out, and there was a great black shadow of the house covering the garden, looking like a prison where men are hanged; and then beyond it was all white; and the wood shone white with black gulfs between the trees. It was still and clear, and there were no clouds on the sky. I wanted to think of what I had seen but I couldn't, and I began to think of all the tales that nurse had told me so long ago that I thought I had forgotten, but they all came back, and mixed up with the thickets and the grey rocks and the hollows in the earth and the secret wood, till I hardly knew what was new and what was old, or whether it was not all dreaming. And then I remembered that hot summer afternoon, so long ago, when nurse left me by myself in the shade, and the white people came out of the water and out of the wood, and played, and danced, and sang, and I began to fancy that nurse told me about something like it before I saw them, only I couldn't recollect exactly what she told me. Then I wondered whether she had been the white lady, as I remembered she was just as white and beautiful, and had the same dark eyes and black hair; and sometimes she smiled and looked like the lady had looked, when she was telling me some of her stories, beginning with 'Once on a time', or 'In the time of the fairies'. But I thought she couldn't be the lady, as she seemed to have gone a different way into the wood, and I didn't think the man who came after us could be the other, or I couldn't have seen that wonderful secret in the secret wood. I thought of the moon: but it was afterwards when I was in the middle of the wild land, where the earth was made into the shape of great figures, and it was all walls, and mysterious hollows, and smooth round mounds, that I saw the great white moon come up over a round hill. I was wondering about all these things, till at last I got quite frightened, because I was afraid something had happened to me, and I remembered nurse's tale of the poor girl who went into the hollow pit, and was carried away at last by the black man. I knew I had gone into a hollow pit too, and perhaps it was the same, and I had done something dreadful. So I did the charm over again, and touched my eyes and my lips and my hair in a peculiar manner, and said the old words from the fairy language, so that I might be sure I had not been carried away. I tried again to see the secret wood, and to creep up the passage and see what I had seen there, but somehow I couldn't, and I kept on thinking of nurse's stories. There was one I remembered about a young man who once upon a time went hunting, and all the day he and his hounds hunted everywhere, and they crossed the rivers and went into all the woods, and went round the marshes, but they couldn't find anything at all, and they hunted all day till the sun sank down and began to set behind the mountain. And the young man was angry because he couldn't find anything, and he was going to turn back, when just as the sun touched the mountain, he saw come out of a brake in front of him a beautiful white stag. And he cheered to his hounds, but they whined and would not follow, and he cheered to his horse, but it shivered and stood stock still, and the young man jumped off the horse and left the hounds and began to follow the white stag all alone. And soon it was quite dark, and the sky was black, without a single star shining in it, and the stag went away into the darkness. And though the man had brought his gun with him he never shot at the stag, because he wanted to catch it, and he was afraid he would lose it in the night. But he never lost it once, though the sky was so black and the air was so dark, and the stag went on and on till the young man didn't know a bit where he was. And they went through enormous woods where the air was full of whispers and a pale, dead light came out from the rotten trunks that were lying on the ground, and just as the man thought he had lost the stag, he would see it all white and shining in front of him, and he would run fast to catch it, but the stag always ran faster, so he did not catch it. And they went through the enormous woods, and they swam across rivers, and they waded through black marshes where the ground bubbled, and the air was full of will-o'-the-wisps, and the stag fled away down into rocky narrow valleys, where the air was like the smell of a vault, and the man went after it. And they went over the great mountains and the man heard the wind come down from the sky, and the stag went on and the man went after. At last the sun rose and the young man found he was in a country that he had never seen before; it was a beautiful valley with a bright stream running through it, and a great, big round hill in the middle. And the stag went down the valley, towards the hill, and it seemed to be getting tired and went slower and slower, and though the man was tired, too, he began to run faster, and he was sure he would catch the stag at last. But just as they got to the bottom of the hill, and the man stretched out his hand to catch the stag, it vanished into the earth, and the man began to cry; he was so sorry that he had lost it after all his long hunting. But as he was crying he saw there was a door in the hill, just in front of him, and he went in, and it was quite dark, but he went on, as he thought he would find the white stag. And all of a sudden it got light, and there was the sky, and the sun shining, and birds singing in the trees, and there was a beautiful fountain. And by the fountain a lovely lady was sitting, who was the queen of the fairies, and she told the man that she had changed herself into a stag to bring him there because she loved him so much. Then she brought out a great gold cup, covered with jewels, from her fairy palace, and she offered him wine in the cup to drink. And he drank, and the more he drank the more he longed to drink, because the wine was enchanted. So he kissed the lovely lady, and she became his wife, and he stayed all that day and all that night in the hill where she lived, and when he woke he found he was lying on the ground, close to where he had seen the stag first, and his horse was there and his hounds were there waiting, and he looked up, and the sun sank behind the mountain. And he went home and lived a long time, but he would never kiss any other lady because he had kissed the queen of the fairies, and he would never drink common wine any more, because he had drunk enchanted wine. And sometimes nurse told me tales that she had heard from her great-grandmother, who was very old, and lived in a cottage on the mountain all alone, and most of these tales were about a hill where people used to meet at night long ago, and they used to play all sorts of strange games and do queer things that nurse told me of, but I couldn't understand, and now, she said, everybody but her great-grandmother had forgotten all about it, and nobody knew where the hill was, not even her great-grandmother. But she told me one very strange story about the hill, and I trembled when I remembered it. She said that people always went there in summer, when it was very hot, and they had to dance a good deal. It would be all dark at first, and there were trees there, which made it much darker, and people would come, one by one, from all directions, by a secret path which nobody else knew, and two persons would keep the gate, and every one as they came up had to give a very curious sign, which nurse showed me as well as she could, but she said she couldn't show me properly. And all kinds of people would come; there would be gentle folks and village folks, and some old people and boys and girls, and quite small children, who sat and watched. And it would all be dark as they came in, except in one corner where some one was burning something that smelt strong and sweet, and made them laugh, and there one would see a glaring of coals, and the smoke mounting up red. So they would all come in, and when the last had come there was no door any more, so that no one else could get in, even if they knew there was anything beyond. And once a gentleman who was a stranger and had ridden a long way, lost his path at night, and his horse took him into the very middle of the wild country, where everything was upside down, and there were dreadful marshes and great stones everywhere, and holes underfoot, and the trees looked like gibbet posts, because they had great black arms that stretched out across the way. And this strange gentleman was very frightened, and his horse began to shiver all over, and at last it stopped and wouldn't go any farther, and the gentleman got down and tried to lead the horse, but it wouldn't move, and it was all covered with a sweat, like death. So the gentleman went on all alone, going farther and farther into the wild country, till at last he came to a dark place, where he heard shouting and singing and crying, like nothing he had ever heard before. It all sounded quite close to him, but he couldn't get in, and so he began to call, and while he was calling, something came behind him, and in a minute his mouth and arms and legs were all bound up, and he fell into a swoon. And when he came to himself, he was lying by the roadside, just where he had first lost his way, under a blasted oak with a black trunk, and his horse was tied beside him. So he rode on to the town and told the people there what had happened, and some of them were amazed; but others knew. So when once everybody had come, there was no door at all for anybody else to pass in by. And when they were all inside, round in a ring, touching each other, some one began to sing in the darkness, and some one else would make a noise like thunder with a thing they had on purpose, and on still nights people would hear the thundering noise far, far away beyond the wild land, and some of them, who thought they knew what it was, used to make a sign on their breasts when they woke up in their beds at dead of night and heard that terrible deep noise, like thunder on the mountains. And the noise and the singing would go on and on for a long time, and the people who were in a ring swayed a little to and fro; and the song was in an old, old language that nobody knows now, and the tune was queer. Nurse said her great-grandmother had known some one who remembered a little of it, when she was quite a little girl, and nurse tried to sing some of it to me, and it was so strange a tune that I turned all cold and my flesh crept as if I had put my hand on something dead. Sometimes it was a man that sang and sometimes it was a woman, and sometimes the one who sang it did it so well that two or three of the people who were there fell to the ground shrieking and tearing with their hands. The singing went on, and the people in the ring kept swaying to and fro for a long time, and at last the moon would rise over a place they called the Tole Deol, and came up and showed them swinging and swaying from side to side, with the sweet thick smoke curling up from the burning coals, and floating in circles all around them. Then they had their supper. A boy and a girl brought it to them; the boy carried a great cup of wine, and the girl carried a cake of bread, and they passed the bread and the wine round and round, but they tasted quite different from common bread and common wine, and changed everybody that tasted them.

Then they all rose up and danced, and secret things were brought out of some hiding place, and they played extraordinary games, and danced round and round and round in the moonlight, and sometimes people would suddenly disappear and never be heard of afterwards, and nobody knew what had happened to them. And they drank more of that curious wine, and they made images and worshipped them, and nurse showed me how the images were made one day when we were out for a walk, and we passed by a place where there was a lot of wet clay. So nurse asked me if I would like to know what those things were like that they made on the hill, and I said yes. Then she asked me if I would promise never to tell a living soul a word about it, and if I did I was to be thrown into the black pit with the dead people, and I said I wouldn't tell anybody, and she said the same thing again and again, and I promised. So she took my wooden spade and dug a big lump of clay and put it in my tin bucket, and told me to say if any one met us that I was going to make pies when I went home. Then we went on a little way till we came to a little brake growing right down into the road, and nurse stopped, and looked up the road and down it, and then peeped through the hedge into the field on the other side, and then she said, 'Quick!' and we ran into the brake, and crept in and out among the bushes till we had gone a good way from the road. Then we sat down under a bush, and I wanted so much to know what nurse was going to make with the clay, but before she would begin she made me promise again not to say a word about it, and she went again and peeped through the bushes on every side, though the lane was so small and deep that hardly anybody ever went there. So we sat down, and nurse took the clay out of the bucket, and began to knead it with her hands, and do queer things with it, and turn it about. And she hid it under a big dock leaf for a minute or two and then she brought it out again, and then she stood up and sat down, and walked round the clay in a peculiar manner, and all the time she was softly singing a sort of rhyme, and her face got very red. Then she sat down again, and took the clay in her hands and began to shape it into a doll, but not like the dolls I have at home, and she made the queerest doll I had ever seen, all out of the wet clay, and hid it under a bush to get dry and hard, and all the time she was making it she was singing these rhymes to herself, and her face got redder and redder. So we left the doll there, hidden away in the bushes where nobody would ever find it. And a few days later we went the same walk, and when we came to that narrow, dark part of the lane where the brake runs down to the bank, nurse made me promise all over again, and she looked about, just as she had done before, and we crept into the bushes till we got to the green place where the little clay man was hidden. I remember it all so well, though I was only eight, and it is eight years ago now as I am writing it down, but the sky was a deep violet blue, and in the middle of the brake where we were sitting there was a great elder tree covered with blossoms, and on the other side there was a clump of meadowsweet, and when I think of that day the smell of the meadowsweet and elder blossom seems to fill the room, and if I shut my eyes I can see the glaring blue sky, with little clouds very white floating across it, and nurse who went away long ago sitting opposite me and looking like the beautiful white lady in the wood. So we sat down and nurse took out the clay doll from the secret place where she had hidden it, and she said we must 'pay our respects', and she would show me what to do, and I must watch her all the time. So she did all sorts of queer things with the little clay man, and I noticed she was all streaming with perspiration, though we had walked so slowly, and then she told me to 'pay my respects', and I did everything she did because I liked her, and it was such an odd game. And she said that if one loved very much, the clay man was very good, if one did certain things with it, and if one hated very much, it was just as good, only one had to do different things, and we played with it a long time, and pretended all sorts of things. Nurse said her great-grandmother had told her all about these images, but what we did was no harm at all, only a game. But she told me a story about these images that frightened me very much, and that was what I remembered that night when I was lying awake in my room in the pale, empty darkness, thinking of what I had seen and the secret wood. Nurse said there was once a young lady of the high gentry, who lived in a great castle. And she was so beautiful that all the gentlemen wanted to marry her, because she was the loveliest lady that anybody had ever seen, and she was kind to everybody, and everybody thought she was very good. But though she was polite to all the gentlemen who wished to marry her, she put them off, and said she couldn't make up her mind, and she wasn't sure she wanted to marry anybody at all. And her father, who was a very great lord, was angry, though he was so fond of her, and he asked her why she wouldn't choose a bachelor out of all the handsome young men who came to the castle. But she only said she didn't love any of them very much, and she must wait, and if they pestered her, she said she would go and be a nun in a nunnery. So all the gentlemen said they would go away and wait for a year and a day, and when a year and a day were gone, they would come back again and ask her to say which one she would marry. So the day was appointed and they all went away; and the lady had promised that in a year and a day it would be her wedding day with one of them. But the truth was, that she was the queen of the people who danced on the hill on summer nights, and on the proper nights she would lock the door of her room, and she and her maid would steal out of the castle by a secret passage that only they knew of, and go away up to the hill in the wild land. And she knew more of the secret things than any one else, and more than any one knew before or after, because she would not tell anybody the most secret secrets. She knew how to do all the awful things, how to destroy young men, and how to put a curse on people, and other things that I could not understand. And her real name was the Lady Avelin, but the dancing people called her Cassap, which meant somebody very wise, in the old language. And she was whiter than any of them and taller, and her eyes shone in the dark like burning rubies; and she could sing songs that none of the others could sing, and when she sang they all fell down on their faces and worshipped her. And she could do what they called shib-show, which was a very wonderful enchantment. She would tell the great lord, her father, that she wanted to go into the woods to gather flowers, so he let her go, and she and her maid went into the woods where nobody came, and the maid would keep watch. Then the lady would lie down under the trees and begin to sing a particular song, and she stretched out her arms, and from every part of the wood great serpents would come, hissing and gliding in and out among the trees, and shooting out their forked tongues as they crawled up to the lady. And they all came to her, and twisted round her, round her body, and her arms, and her neck, till she was covered with writhing serpents, and there was only her head to be seen. And she whispered to them, and she sang to them, and they writhed round and round, faster and faster, till she told them to go. And they all went away directly, back to their holes, and on the lady's breast there would be a most curious, beautiful stone, shaped something like an egg, and coloured dark blue and yellow, and red, and green, marked like a serpent's scales. It was called a glame stone, and with it one could do all sorts of wonderful things, and nurse said her great-grandmother had seen a glame stone with her own eyes, and it was for all the world shiny and scaly like a snake. And the lady could do a lot of other things as well, but she was quite fixed that she would not be married. And there were a great many gentlemen who wanted to marry her, but there were five of them who were chief, and their names were Sir Simon, Sir John, Sir Oliver, Sir Richard, and Sir Rowland. All the others believed she spoke the truth, and that she would choose one of them to be her man when a year and a day was done; it was only Sir Simon, who was very crafty, who thought she was deceiving them all, and he vowed he would watch and try if he could find out anything. And though he was very wise he was very young, and he had a smooth, soft face like a girl's, and he pretended, as the rest did, that he would not come to the castle for a year and a day, and he said he was going away beyond the sea to foreign parts. But he really only went a very little way, and came back dressed like a servant girl, and so he got a place in the castle to wash the dishes. And he waited and watched, and he listened and said nothing, and he hid in dark places, and woke up at night and looked out, and he heard things and he saw things that he thought were very strange. And he was so sly that he told the girl that waited on the lady that he was really a young man, and that he had dressed up as a girl because he loved her so very much and wanted to be in the same house with her, and the girl was so pleased that she told him many things, and he was more than ever certain that the Lady Avelin was deceiving him and the others. And he was so clever, and told the servant so many lies, that one night he managed to hide in the Lady Avelin's room behind the curtains. And he stayed quite still and never moved, and at last the lady came. And she bent down under the bed, and raised up a stone, and there was a hollow place underneath, and out of it she took a waxen image, just like the clay one that I and nurse had made in the brake. And all the time her eyes were burning like rubies. And she took the little wax doll up in her arms and held it to her breast, and she whispered and she murmured, and she took it up and she laid it down again, and she held it high, and she held it low, and she laid it down again. And she said, 'Happy is he that begat the bishop, that ordered the clerk, that married the man, that had the wife, that fashioned the hive, that harboured the bee, that gathered the wax that my own true love was made of.' And she brought out of an aumbry a great golden bowl, and she brought out of a closet a great jar of wine, and she poured some of the wine into the bowl, and she laid her mannikin very gently in the wine, and washed it in the wine all over. Then she went to a cupboard and took a small round cake and laid it on the image's mouth, and then she bore it softly and covered it up. And

Sir Simon, who was watching all the time, though he was terribly frightened, saw the lady bend down and stretch out her arms and whisper and sing, and then Sir Simon saw beside her a handsome young man, who kissed her on the lips. And they drank wine out of the golden bowl together, and they ate the cake together. But when the sun rose there was only the little wax doll, and the lady hid it again under the bed in the hollow place. So Sir Simon knew quite well what the lady was, and he waited and he watched, till the time she had said was nearly over, and in a week the year and a day would be done. And one night, when he was watching behind the curtains in her room, he saw her making more wax dolls. And she made five, and hid them away. And the next night she took one out, and held it up, and filled the golden bowl with water, and took the doll by the neck and held it under the water. Then she said –

> Sir Dickon, Sir Dickon, your day is done,
> You shall be drowned in the water wan.

And the next day news came to the castle that Sir Richard had been drowned at the ford. And at night she took another doll and tied a violet cord round its neck and hung it up on a nail. Then she said –

> Sir Rowland, your life has ended its span,
> High on a tree I see you hang.

And the next day news came to the castle that Sir Rowland had been hanged by robbers in the wood. And at night she took another doll, and drove her bodkin right into its heart. Then she said –

> Sir Noll, Sir Noll, so cease your life,
> Your heart piercèd with the knife.

And the next day news came to the castle that Sir Oliver had fought in a tavern, and a stranger had stabbed him to the heart. And at night she took another doll, and held it to a fire of charcoal till it was melted. Then she said –

> Sir John, return, and turn to clay,
> In fire of fever you waste away.

And the next day news came to the castle that Sir John had died in a burning fever. So then Sir Simon went out of the castle and mounted his horse and rode away to the bishop and told him everything. And the bishop sent his men, and they took the Lady Avelin, and everything she had done was found out. So on the day after the year and a day, when she was to have been married, they carried her through the town in her smock, and they tied her to a great stake in the marketplace, and burned her alive before the bishop with her wax image hung round her neck. And people said the wax man screamed in the burning of the flames. And I thought of this story again and again as I was lying awake in my bed, and I seemed to see the Lady Avelin in the marketplace, with the yellow flames eating up her beautiful white body. And I thought of it so much that I seemed to get into the story myself, and I fancied I was the lady, and that they were coming to take me to be burnt with fire, with all the people in the town looking at me. And I wondered whether she cared, after all the strange things she had done, and whether it hurt very much to be burned at the stake. I tried again and again to forget nurse's stories, and to remember the secret I had seen that afternoon, and what was in the secret wood, but I could only see the dark and a glimmering in the dark, and then it went away, and I only saw myself running, and then a great moon came up white over a dark round hill. Then all the old stories came back again, and the queer rhymes that nurse used to sing to me; and there was one beginning 'Halsy cumsy Helen musty', that she used to sing very softly when she wanted me to go to sleep. And I began to sing it to myself inside of my head, and I went to sleep.

The next morning I was very tired and sleepy, and could hardly do my lessons, and I was very glad when they were over and I had had my dinner, as I wanted to go out and be alone. It was a warm day, and I went to a nice turfy hill by the river, and sat down on my mother's old shawl that I had brought with me on purpose. The sky was grey, like the day before, but there was a kind of white gleam behind it, and from where I was sitting I could look down on the town, and it was all still and quiet and white, like a picture. I remembered that it was on that hill that nurse taught me to play an old game called 'Troy Town', in which one had to dance, and wind in and out on a pattern in the grass, and then when one had danced and turned long enough the other person asks you questions, and you can't help answering whether you want to or not, and whatever you are told to do you feel you have to do it. Nurse said there used to be a lot of games like that that some people knew of, and there was one by which people could be turned into anything you liked, and an old man her great-grandmother had seen had known a girl who had been turned into a large snake. And there was another very ancient game of dancing and winding and turning, by which you could take a person out of himself and hide him away as long as you liked, and his body went walking about quite empty, without any sense in it. But I came to that hill because I wanted to think of what had happened the day before, and of the secret of the wood. From the place where I was sitting I could see beyond the town, into the opening I had found, where a little brook had led me into an unknown country. And I pretended I was following the brook over again, and I went all the way in my mind, and at last I found the wood, and crept into it under the bushes, and then in the dusk I saw something that made me feel as if I were filled with fire, as if I wanted to dance and sing and fly up into the air, because I was changed and wonderful. But what I saw was not changed at all, and had not grown old, and I wondered again and again how such things could happen, and whether nurse's stories were really true, because in the daytime in the open air everything seemed quite different from what it was at night, when I was frightened, and thought I was to be burned alive. I once told my father one of her little tales, which was about a ghost, and asked him if it was true, and he told me it was not true at all, and that only common, ignorant people believed in such rubbish. He was very angry with nurse for telling me the story, and scolded her, and after that I promised her I would never whisper a word of what she told me, and if I did I should be bitten by the great black snake that lived in the pool in the wood. And all alone on the hill I wondered what was true. I had seen something very amazing and very lovely, and I knew a story, and if I had really seen it, and not made it up out of the dark, and the black bough, and the bright shining that was mounting up to the sky from over the great round hill, but had really seen it in truth, then there were all kinds of wonderful and lovely and terrible things to think of, so I longed and trembled, and I burned and got cold. And I looked down on the town, so quiet and still, like a little white picture, and I thought over and over if it could be true. I was a long time before I could make up my mind to anything; there was such a strange fluttering at my heart that seemed to whisper to me all the time that I had not made it up out of my head, and yet it seemed quite impossible, and I knew my father and everybody would say it was dreadful rubbish. I never dreamed of telling him or anybody else a word about it, because I knew it would be of no use, and I should only get laughed at or scolded, so for a long time I was very quiet, and went about thinking and wondering; and at night I used to dream of amazing things, and sometimes I woke up in the early morning and held out my arms with a cry. And I was frightened, too, because there were dangers, and some awful thing would happen to me, unless I took great care, if the story were true. These old tales were always in my head, night and morning, and I went over them and told them to myself over and over again, and went for walks in the places where nurse had told them to me; and when I sat in the nursery by the fire in the evenings I used to fancy nurse was sitting in the other chair, and telling me some wonderful story in a low voice, for fear anybody should be listening. But she used to like best to tell me about things when we were right out in the country, far from the house, because she said she was telling me such secrets, and walls have ears. And if it was something more than ever secret, we had to hide in brakes or woods; and I used to think it was such fun creeping along a hedge, and going very softly, and then we would get behind the bushes or run into the wood all of a sudden, when we were sure that none was watching us; so we knew that we had our secrets quite all to ourselves, and nobody else at all knew anything about them. Now and then, when we had hidden ourselves as I have described, she used to show me all sorts of odd things. One day, I remember, we were in a hazel brake, overlooking the brook, and we were so snug and warm, as though it was April; the sun was quite hot, and the leaves were just coming out. Nurse said she would show me something funny that would make me laugh, and then she showed me, as she said, how one could turn a whole house upside down, without anybody being able to find out, and the pots and pans would jump about, and the china would be broken, and the chairs would tumble over of themselves. I tried it one day in the kitchen, and I found I could do it quite well, and a whole row of plates on the dresser fell off it, and cook's little work table tilted up and turned right over 'before her eyes', as she said, but she was so frightened and turned so white that I didn't do it again, as I liked her. And afterwards, in the hazel copse, when she had shown me how to make things tumble about, she showed me how to make rapping noises, and I learnt how to do that, too. Then she taught me rhymes to say on certain occasions, and peculiar marks to make on other occasions, and other things that her great-grandmother had taught her when she was a little girl herself. And these were all the things I was thinking about in those days after the strange walk when I thought I had seen a great secret, and I wished nurse were there for me to ask her about it, but she had gone away more than two years before, and nobody seemed to know what had become of her, or where she had gone. But I shall always remember those days if I live to be quite old, because all the time I felt so strange, wondering and doubting, and feeling quite sure at one time, and making up my mind, and then I would feel quite sure that such things couldn't happen really, and it began all over again. But I took great care not to do certain things that might be very dangerous. So I waited and wondered for a long time, and though I was not sure at all, I never dared to try to find out. But one day I became sure that all that nurse said was quite true, and I was all alone when I found it out. I trembled all over with joy and terror, and as fast as I could I ran into one of the old brakes where we used to go – it was the one by the lane, where nurse made the little clay man – and I ran into it, and I crept into it; and when I came to the place where the elder was, I covered up my face with my hands and lay down flat on the grass, and I stayed there for two hours without moving, whispering to myself delicious, terrible things, and saying some words over and over again. It was all true and wonderful and splendid, and when I remembered the story I knew and thought of what I had really seen, I got hot and I got cold, and the air seemed full of scent, and flowers, and singing. And first I wanted to make a little clay man, like the one nurse had made so long ago, and I had to invent plans and stratagems, and to look about, and to think of things beforehand, because nobody must dream of anything that I was doing or going to do, and I was too old to carry clay about in a tin bucket. At last I thought of a plan, and I brought the wet clay to the brake, and did everything that nurse had done, only I made a much finer image than the one she had made; and when it was finished I did everything that I could imagine and much more than she did, because it was the likeness of something far better. And a few days later, when I had done my lessons early, I went for the second time by the way of the little brook that had led me into a strange country. And I followed the brook, and went through the bushes, and beneath the low branches of trees, and up thorny thickets on the hill, and by dark woods full of creeping thorns, a long, long way. Then I crept through the dark tunnel where the brook had been and the ground was stony, till at last I came to the thicket that climbed up the hill, and though the leaves were coming out upon the trees, everything looked almost as black as it was on the first day that I went there. And the thicket was just the same, and I went up slowly till I came out on the big bare hill, and began to walk among the wonderful rocks. I saw the terrible voor again on everything, for though the sky was brighter, the ring of wild hills all around was still dark, and the hanging woods looked dark and dreadful, and the strange rocks were as grey as ever; and when I looked down on them from the great mound, sitting on the stone, I saw all their amazing circles and rounds within rounds, and I had to sit quite still and watch them as they began to turn about me, and each stone danced in its place, and they seemed to go round and round in a great whirl, as if one were in the middle of all the stars and heard them rushing through the air. So I went down among the rocks to dance with them and to sing extraordinary songs; and I went down through the other thicket, and drank from the bright stream in the close and secret valley, putting my lips down to the bubbling water; and then I went on till I came to the deep, brimming well among the glittering moss, and I sat down. I looked before me into the secret darkness of the valley, and behind me was the great high wall of grass, and all around me there were the hanging woods that made the valley such a secret place. I knew there was nobody here at all besides myself, and that no one could see me. So I took off my boots and stockings, and let my feet down into the water, saying the words that I knew. And it was not cold at all, as I expected, but warm and very pleasant, and when my feet were in it I felt as if they were in silk, or as if the nymph were kissing them. So when I had done, I said the other words and made the signs, and then I dried my feet with a towel I had brought on purpose, and put on my stockings and boots. Then I climbed up the steep wall, and went into the place where there are the hollows, and the two beautiful mounds, and the round ridges of land, and all the strange shapes. I did not go down into the hollow this time, but I turned at the end, and made out the figures quite plainly, as it was lighter, and I had remembered the story I had quite forgotten before, and in the story the two figures are called Adam and Eve, and only those who know the story understand what they mean. So I went on and on till I came to the secret wood which must not be described, and I crept into it by the way I had found. And when I had gone about halfway I stopped, and turned round, and got ready, and I bound the handkerchief tightly round my eyes, and made quite sure that I could not see at all, not a twig, nor the end of a leaf, nor the light of the sky, as it was an old red silk handkerchief with large yellow spots, that went round twice and covered my eyes, so that I could see nothing. Then I began to go on, step by step, very slowly. My heart beat faster and faster, and something rose in my throat that choked me and made me want to cry out, but I shut my lips, and went on. Boughs caught in my hair as I went, and great thorns tore me; but I went on to the end of the path. Then I stopped, and held out my arms and bowed, and I went round the first time, feeling with my hands, and there was nothing. I went round the second time, feeling with my hands, and there was nothing. Then I went round the third time, feeling with my hands, and the story was all true, and I wished that the years were gone by, and that I had not so long a time to wait before I was happy for ever and ever.

Nurse must have been a prophet like those we read of in the Bible. Everything that she said began to come true, and since then other things that she told me of have happened. That was how I came to know that her stories were true and that I had not made up the secret myself out of my own head. But there was another thing that happened that day. I went a second time to the secret place. It was at the deep brimming well, and when I was standing on the moss I bent over and looked in, and then I knew who the white lady was that I had seen come out of the water in the wood long ago when I was quite little. And I trembled all over, because that told me other things. Then I remembered how some time after I had seen the white people in the wood, nurse asked me more about them, and I told her all over again, and she listened, and said nothing for a long, long time, and at last she said, 'You will see her again.' So I understood what had happened and what was to happen. And I understood about the nymphs; how I might meet them in all kinds of places, and they would always help me, and I must always look for them, and find them in all sorts of strange shapes and appearances. And without the nymphs I could never have found the secret, and without them none of the other things could happen. Nurse had told me all about them long ago, but she called them by another name, and I did not know what she meant, or what her tales of them were about, only that they were very queer. And there were two kinds, the bright and the dark, and both were very lovely and very wonderful, and some people saw only one kind, and some only the other, but some saw them both. But usually the dark appeared first, and the bright ones came afterwards, and there were extraordinary tales about them. It was a day or two after I had come home from the secret place that I first really knew the nymphs. Nurse had shown me how to call them, and I had tried, but I did not know what she meant, and so I thought it was all nonsense. But I made up my mind I would try again, so I went to the wood where the pool was, where I saw the white people, and I tried again. The dark nymph, Alanna, came, and she turned the pool of water into a pool of fire. . . .

Epilogue

'That's a very queer story,' said Cotgrave, handing back the green book to the recluse, Ambrose. 'I see the drift of a good deal, but there are many things that I do not grasp at all. On the last page, for example, what does she mean by "nymphs"?'

'Well, I think there are references throughout the manuscript to certain "processes" which have been handed down by tradition from age to age. Some of these processes are just beginning to come within the purview of science, which has arrived at them – or rather at the steps which lead to them – by quite different paths. I have interpreted the reference to "nymphs" as a reference to one of these processes.'

'And you believe that there are such things?'

'Oh, I think so. Yes, I believe I could give you convincing evidence on that point. I am afraid you have neglected the study of alchemy? It is a pity, for the symbolism, at all events, is very beautiful, and moreover if you were acquainted with certain books on the subject, I could recall to your mind phrases which might explain a good deal in the manuscript that you have been reading.'

'Yes; but I want to know whether you seriously think that there is any foundation of fact beneath these fancies. Is it not all a department of poetry; a curious dream with which man has indulged himself?'

'I can only say that it is no doubt better for the great mass of people to dismiss it all as a dream. But if you ask my veritable belief – that goes quite the other way. No; I should not say belief, but rather knowledge. I may tell you that I have known cases in which men have stumbled quite by accident on certain of these "processes", and have been astonished by wholly unexpected results. In the cases I am thinking of there could have been no possibility of "suggestion" or subconscious action of any kind. One might as well suppose a schoolboy "suggesting" the existence of Aeschylus to himself, while he plods mechanically through the declensions.

'But you have noticed the obscurity,' Ambrose went on, 'and in this particular case it must have been dictated by instinct, since the writer never thought that her manuscripts would fall into other hands. But the practice is universal, and for most excellent reasons. Powerful and sovereign medicines, which are, of necessity, virulent poisons also, are kept in a locked cabinet. The child may find the key by chance, and drink herself dead; but in most cases the search is educational, and the phials contain precious elixirs for him who has patiently fashioned the key for himself.'

'You do not care to go into details?'

'No, frankly, I do not. No, you must remain unconvinced. But you saw how the manuscript illustrates the talk we had last week?'

'Is this girl still alive?'

'No. I was one of those who found her. I knew the father well; he was a lawyer, and had always left her very much to herself. He thought of nothing but deeds and leases, and the news came to him as an awful surprise. She was missing one morning; I suppose it was about a year after she had written what you have read. The servants were called, and they told things, and put the only natural interpretation on them – a perfectly erroneous one.

'They discovered that green book somewhere in her room, and I found her in the place that she described with so much dread, lying on the ground before the image.'

'It was an image?'

'Yes, it was hidden by the thorns and the thick undergrowth that had surrounded it. It was a wild, lonely country; but you know what it was like by her description, though of course you will understand that the colours have been heightened. A child's imagination always makes the heights higher and the depths deeper than they really are; and she had, unfortunately for herself, something more than imagination. One might say, perhaps, that the picture in her mind which she succeeded in a measure in putting into words, was the scene as it would have appeared to an imaginative artist. But it is a strange, desolate land.'

'And she was dead?'

'Yes. She had poisoned herself – in time. No; there was not a word to be said against her in the ordinary sense. You may recollect a story I told you the other night about a lady who saw her child's fingers crushed by a window?'

'And what was this statue?'

'Well, it was of Roman workmanship, of a stone that with the centuries had not blackened, but had become white and luminous. The thicket had grown up about it and concealed it, and in the Middle Ages the followers of a very old tradition had known how to use it for their own purposes. In fact it had been incorporated into the monstrous mythology of the Sabbath. You will have noted that those to whom a sight of that shining whiteness had been vouchsafed by chance, or rather, perhaps, by apparent chance, were required to blindfold themselves on their second approach. That is very significant.'

'And is it there still?'

'I sent for tools, and we hammered it into dust and fragments.'

'The persistence of tradition never surprises me,' Ambrose went on after a pause. 'I could name many an English parish where such traditions as that girl had listened to in her childhood are still existent in occult but unabated vigour. No, for me, it is the "story", not the "sequel", which is strange and awful, for I have always believed that wonder is of the soul.'

The Bowmen

It was during the Retreat of the Eighty Thousand, and the authority of the Censorship is sufficient excuse for not being more explicit. But it was on the most awful day of that awful time, on the day when ruin and disaster came so near that their shadow fell over London far away; and, without any certain news, the hearts of men failed within them and grew faint; as if the agony of the army in the battlefield had entered into their souls.

On this dreadful day, then, when three hundred thousand men in arms with all their artillery swelled like a flood against the little English company, there was one point above all other points in our battle line that was for a time in awful danger, not merely of defeat, but of utter annihilation. With the permission of the Censorship and of the military expert, this corner may, perhaps, be described as a salient, and if this angle were crushed and broken, then the English force as a whole would be shattered, the Allied left would be turned, and Sedan would inevitably follow.

All the morning the German guns had thundered and shrieked against this corner, and against the thousand or so of men who held it. The men joked at the shells, and found funny names for them, and had bets about them, and greeted them with scraps of music hall songs. But the shells came on and burst, and tore good Englishmen limb from limb, and tore brother from brother, and as the heat of the day increased so did the fury of that terrific cannonade. There was no help, it seemed. The English artillery was good, but there was not nearly enough of it; it was being steadily battered into scrap iron.

There comes a moment in a storm at sea when people say to one another, 'It is at its worst; it can blow no harder,' and then there is a blast ten times more fierce than any before it. So it was in these British trenches.

There were no stouter hearts in the whole world than the hearts of these men; but even they were appalled as this seven-times-heated hell of the German cannonade fell upon them and overwhelmed them and destroyed them. And at this very moment they saw from their trenches that a tremendous host was moving against their lines. Five hundred of the thousand remained, and as far as they could see the German infantry was pressing on against them, column upon column, a grey world of men, ten thousand of them, as it appeared afterwards.

There was no hope at all. They shook hands, some of them. One man improvised a new version of the battlesong, 'Goodbye, goodbye to Tipperary', ending with 'And we shan't get there.' And they all went on firing steadily. The officers pointed out that such an opportunity for high-class, fancy shooting might never occur again; the Germans dropped line after line; the Tipperary humorist asked, 'What price Sidney Street?' And the few machine guns did their best. But everybody knew it was of no use. The dead grey bodies lay in companies and battalions, as others came on and on and on, and they swarmed and stirred and advanced from beyond and beyond.

'World without end. Amen,' said one of the British soldiers with some irrelevance as he took aim and fired. And then he remembered – he says he cannot think why or wherefore – a queer vegetarian restaurant in London where he had once or twice eaten eccentric dishes of cutlets made of lentils and nuts that pretended to be steak. On all the plates in this restaurant there was printed a figure of St George in blue, with the motto, *Adsit Anglis Sanctus Georgius* – May St George be a present help to the English. This soldier happened to know Latin and other useless things, and now, as he fired at his man in the grey advancing mass – 300 yards away – he uttered the pious vegetarian motto. He went on firing to the end, and at last Bill on his right had to clout him cheerfully over the head to make him stop, pointing out as he did so that the King's ammunition cost money and was not lightly to be wasted in drilling funny patterns into dead Germans.

For as the Latin scholar uttered his invocation he felt something between a shudder and an electric shock pass through his body. The roar of the battle died down in his ears to a gentle murmur; instead of it, he says, he heard a great voice and a shout louder than a thunder-peal crying, 'Array, array, array!'

His heart grew hot as a burning coal, it grew cold as ice within him, as it seemed to him that a tumult of voices answered to his summons. He heard, or seemed to hear, thousands shouting: 'St George! St George!'

'Ha! messire; ha! sweet Saint, grant us good deliverance!'

'St George for merry England!'

'Harow! Harow! Monseigneur St George, succour us.'

'Ha! St George! Ha! St George! a long bow and a strong bow.'

'Heaven's Knight, aid us!'

And as the soldier heard these voices he saw before him, beyond the trench, a long line of shapes, with a shining about them. They were like men who drew the bow, and with another shout their cloud of arrows flew singing and tingling through the air towards the German hosts.

* * *

The other men in the trench were firing all the while. They had no hope; but they aimed just as if they had been shooting at Bisley. Suddenly one of them lifted up his voice in the plainest English, 'Gawd help us!' he bellowed to the man next to him, 'but we're blooming marvels! Look at those grey . . . gentlemen, look at them! D'ye see them? They're not going down in dozens, nor in 'undreds; it's thousands, it is. Look! look! there's a regiment gone while I'm talking to ye.'

'Shut it!' the other soldier bellowed, taking aim, 'what are ye gassing about!'

But he gulped with astonishment even as he spoke, for, indeed, the grey men were falling by the thousands. The English could hear the guttural scream of the German officers, the crackle of their revolvers as they shot the reluctant; and still line after line crashed to the earth.

* * *

All the while the Latin-bred soldier heard the cry:

'Harow! Harow! Monseigneur, dear saint, quick to our aid! St George help us!'

'High Chevalier, defend us!'

The singing arrows fled so swift and thick that they darkened the air; the heathen horde melted from before them.

* * *

'More machine guns!' Bill yelled to Tom.

'Don't hear them,' Tom yelled back. 'But, thank God, anyway; they've got it in the neck.'

In fact, there were ten thousand dead German soldiers left before that salient of the English army, and consequently there was no Sedan. In Germany, a country ruled by scientific principles, the Great General Staff decided that the contemptible English must have employed shells containing an unknown gas of a poisonous nature, as no wounds were discernible on the bodies of the dead German soldiers. But the man who knew what nuts tasted like when they called themselves steak knew also that St George had brought his Agincourt Bowmen to help the English.

The Soldiers' Rest

The soldier with the ugly wound in the head opened his eyes at last, and looked about him with an air of pleasant satisfaction. He still felt drowsy and dazed with some fierce experience through which he had passed, but so far he could not recollect much about it. But – an agreeable glow began to steal about his heart – such a glow as comes to people who have been in a tight place and have come through it better than they had expected. In its mildest form this set of emotions may be observed in passengers who have crossed the Channel on a windy day without being sick. They triumph a little internally, and are suffused with vague, kindly feelings.

The wounded soldier was somewhat of this disposition as he opened his eyes, pulled himself together, and looked about him. He felt a sense of delicious ease and repose in bones that had been racked and weary, and deep in the heart that had so lately been tormented there was an assurance of comfort – of the battle won. The thundering, roaring waves were passed; he had entered into the haven of calm waters. After fatigues and terrors that as yet he could not recollect he seemed now to be resting in the easiest of all easy chairs in a dim, low room.

In the hearth there was a glint of fire and a blue, sweet-scented puff of wood smoke; a great black oak beam roughly hewn crossed the ceiling. Through the leaded panes of the windows he saw a rich glow of sunlight, green lawns, and against the deepest and most radiant of all blue skies the wonderful far-lifted towers of a vast, Gothic cathedral – mystic, rich with imagery.

'Good Lord!' he murmured to himself. 'I didn't know they had such places in France. It's just like Wells. And it might be the other day when I was going past the Swan, just as it might be past that window, and asked the ostler what time it was, and he says, "What time? Why, summertime"; and there outside it looks like summer that would last for ever. If this was an inn they ought to call it The Soldiers' Rest.'

He dozed off again, and when he opened his eyes once more a kindly looking man in some sort of black robe was standing by him.

'It's all right now, isn't it?' he said, speaking in good English.

'Yes, thank you, sir, as right as can be. I hope to be back again soon.'

'Well well; but how did you come here? Where did you get that?' He pointed to the wound on the soldier's forehead.

The soldier put his hand: up to his brow and looked dazed and puzzled.

'Well, sir,' he said at last, 'it was like this, to begin at the beginning. You know how we came over in August, and there we were in the thick of it, as you might say, in a day or two. An awful time it was, and I don't know how I got through it alive. My best friend was killed dead beside me as we lay in the trenches. By Cambrai, I think it was.

'Then things got a little quieter for a bit, and I was quartered in a village for the best part of a week. She was a very nice lady where I was, and she treated me proper with the best of everything. Her husband he was fighting; but she had the nicest little boy I ever knew, a little fellow of five, or six it might be, and we got on splendid. The amount of their lingo that kid taught me – "We, we" and "Bong swor" and "Commong voo porty voo" and all – and I taught him English. You should have heard that nipper say "'Arf a mo', old un!" It was a treat.

'Then one day we got surprised. There was about a dozen of us in the village, and two or three hundred Germans came down on us early one morning. They got us; no help for it. Before we could shoot.'

* * *

'Well there we were. They tied our hands behind our backs, and smacked our faces and kicked us a bit, and we were lined up opposite the house where I'd been staying.

'And then that poor little chap broke away from his mother, and he run out and saw one of the Boshes, as we call them, fetch me one over the jaw with his clenched fist. Oh dear! oh dear! he might have done it a dozen times if only that little child hadn't seen him.

'He had a poor bit of a toy I'd bought him at the village shop; a toy gun it was. And out he came running, as I say, Crying out something in French like "Bad man! bad man! don't hurt my Anglish or I shoot you"; and he pointed that gun at the German soldier. The

German, he took his bayonet, and he drove it right through the poor little chap's throat.'

The soldier's face worked and twitched and twisted itself into a sort of grin, and he sat grinding his teeth and staring at the man in the black robe. He was silent for a little. And then he found his voice, and the oaths rolled terrible, thundering from him, as he cursed that murderous wretch, and bade him go down and burn for ever in hell. And the tears were raining down his face, and they choked him at last.

'I beg your pardon, sir, I'm sure,' he said, 'especially you being a minister of some kind, I suppose; but I can't help it, he was such a dear little man.'

The man in black murmured something to himself: '*Pretiosa in conspectu Domini mors innocentium ejus*' – Dear in the sight of the Lord is the death of His innocents. Then he put a hand very gently on the soldier's shoulder.

'Never mind,' said he; 'I've seen some service in my time, myself. But what about that wound?'

'Oh, that; that's nothing. But I'll tell you how I got it. It was just like this. The Germans had us fair, as I tell you, and they shut us up in a barn in the village; just flung us on the ground and left us to starve seemingly. They barred up the big door of the barn, and put a sentry there, and thought we were all right.

'There were sort of slits like very narrow windows in one of the walls, and on the second day it was, I was looking out of these slits down the street, and I could see those German devils were up to mischief. They were planting their machine guns everywhere handy where an ordinary man coming up the street would never see them, but I see them, and I see the infantry lining up behind the garden walls. Then I had a sort of a notion of what was coming; and presently, sure enough, I could hear some of our chaps singing "Hullo, hullo, hullo!" in the distance; and I says to myself, "Not this time."

'So I looked about me, and I found a hole under the wall; a kind of a drain I should think it was, and I found I could just squeeze through. And I got out and crept, round, and away I goes running down the street, yelling for all I was worth, just as our chaps were getting round the corner at the bottom. "Bang, bang!" went the guns, behind me and in front of me, and on each side of me, and then – bash! something hit me on the head and over I went; and I don't remember anything more till I woke up here just now.'

The soldier lay back in his chair and closed his eyes for a moment. When he opened them he saw that there were other people in the room besides the minister in the black robes. One was a man in a big black cloak. He had a grim old face and a great beaky nose. He shook the soldier by the hand.

'By God! sir,' he said, 'you're a credit to the British Army; you're a damned fine soldier and a good man, and, by God! I'm proud to shake hands with you.'

And then some one came out of the shadow, some one in queer clothes such as the soldier had seen worn by the heralds when he had been on duty at the opening of Parliament by the King.

'Now, by *Corpus Domini*,' this man said, 'of all knights ye be noblest and gentlest, and ye be of fairest report, and now ye be a brother of the noblest brotherhood that ever was since this world's beginning, since ye have yielded dear life for your friends' sake.'

The soldier did not understand what the man was saying to him. There were others, too, in strange dresses, who came and spoke to him. Some spoke in what sounded like French. He could not make it out; but he knew that they all spoke kindly and praised him.

'What does it all mean?' he said to the minister. 'What are they talking about? They don't think I'd let down my pals?'

'Drink this,' said the minister, and he handed the soldier a great silver cup, brimming with wine.

The soldier took a deep draught, and in that moment all his sorrows passed from him.

'What is it?' he asked?

'*Vin nouveau du Royaume*,' said the minister. 'New Wine of the Kingdom, you call it.' And then he bent down and murmured in the soldier's ear.

'What,' said the wounded man, 'the place they used to tell us about in Sunday school? With such drink and such joy – '

His voice was hushed. For as he looked at the minister the fashion of his vesture was changed. The black robe seemed to melt away from him. He was all in armour, if armour be made of starlight, of the rose of dawn, and of sunset fires; and he lifted up a great sword of flame.

Full in the midst, his Cross of Red
Triumphant Michael brandishèd,
And trampled the Apostate's pride.

The Monstrance

Then it fell out in the sacring of the Mass that right as the priest heaved up the Host there came a beam redder than any rose and smote upon it, and then it was changed bodily into the shape and fashion of a Child having his arms stretched forth, as he had been nailed upon the Tree. – OLD ROMANCE.

So far things were going very well indeed. The night was thick and black and cloudy, and the German force had come three-quarters of their way or more without an alarm. There was no challenge from the English lines; and indeed the English were being kept busy by a high shellfire on their front. This had been the German plan; and it was coming off admirably. Nobody thought that there was any danger on the left; and so the Prussians, writhing on their stomachs over the ploughed field, were drawing nearer and nearer to the wood. Once there they could establish themselves comfortably and securely during what remained of the night; and at dawn the English left would be hopelessly enfiladed – and there would be another of those movements which people who really understand military matters call 'readjustments of our line'.

The noise made by the men creeping and crawling over the fields was drowned by the cannonade, from the English side as well as the German. On the English centre and right things were indeed very brisk; the big guns were thundering and shrieking and roaring, the machine guns were keeping up the very devil's racket; the flares and illuminating shells were as good as the Crystal Palace in the old days, as the soldiers said to one another. All this had been thought of and thought out on the other side. The German force was beautifully organised. The men who crept nearer and nearer to the wood carried quite a number of machine guns in bits on their backs; others of them had small bags full of sand; yet others big bags that were empty. When the wood was reached the sand from the small bags was to be emptied into the big bags; the machine gun parts were to be put together, the guns mounted behind the sandbag redoubt, and then, as Major Von und Zu pleasantly observed, 'the English pigs shall to gehenna-fire quickly come.'

The major was so well pleased with the way things had gone that he permitted himself a very low and guttural chuckle; in another ten minutes success would be assured. He half turned his head round to whisper a caution about some detail of the sandbag business to the big sergeant-major, Karl Heinz, who was crawling just behind him. At that instant Karl Heinz leapt into the air with a scream that rent through the night and through all the roaring of the artillery. He cried in a terrible voice, 'The Glory of the Lord!' and plunged and pitched forward, stone dead. They said that his face as he stood up there and cried aloud was as if it had been seen through a sheet of flame.

'They' were one or two out of the few who got back to the German lines. Most of the Prussians stayed in the ploughed field. Karl Heinz's scream had frozen the blood of the English soldiers, but it had also ruined the major's plans. He and his men, caught all unready, clumsy with the burdens that they carried, were shot to pieces; hardly a score of them returned. The rest of the force were attended to by an English burying party. According to custom the dead men were searched before they were buried, and some singular relics of the campaign were found upon them, but nothing so singular as Karl Heinz's diary.

He had been keeping it for some time. It began with entries about bread and sausage and the ordinary incidents of the trenches; here and there Karl wrote about an old grandfather, and a big china pipe, and pinewoods and roast goose. Then the diarist seemed to get fidgety about his health. Thus:

April 17. – Annoyed for some days by murmuring sounds in my head. I trust I shall not become deaf, like my departed uncle Christopher.

April 20. – The noise in my head grows worse; it is a humming sound. It distracts me; twice I have failed to hear the captain and have been reprimanded.

April 22. – So bad is my head that I go to see the doctor. He speaks of tinnitus, and gives me an inhaling apparatus that shall reach, he says, the middle ear.

April 25. – The apparatus is of no use. The sound is now become

like the booming of a great church bell. It reminds me of the bell at St Lambart on that terrible day of last August.
April 26. – I could swear that it is the bell of St Lambart that I hear all the time. They rang it as the procession came out of the church.

The man's writing, at first firm enough, begins to straggle unevenly over the page at this point. The entries show that he became convinced that he heard the bell of St Lambart's Church ringing, though (as he knew better than most men) there had been no bell and no church at St Lambart's since the summer of 1914. There was no village either – the whole place was a rubbish heap.

Then the unfortunate Karl Heinz was beset with other troubles.

May 2. – I fear I am becoming ill. Today Joseph Kleist, who is next to me in the trench, asked me why I jerked my head to the right so constantly. I told him to hold his tongue; but this shows that I am noticed. I keep fancying that there is something white just beyond the range of my sight on the right hand.
May 3. – This whiteness is now quite clear, and in front of me. All this day it has slowly passed before me. I asked Joseph Kleist if he saw a piece of newspaper just beyond the trench. He stared at me solemnly – he is a stupid fool – and said, 'There is no paper.'
May 4. – It looks like a white robe. There was a strong smell of incense today in the trench. No one seemed to notice it. There is decidedly a white robe, and I think I can see feet, passing very slowly before me at this moment while I write.

There is no space here for continuous extracts from Karl Heinz's diary. But to condense with severity, it would seem that he slowly gathered about himself a complete set of sensory hallucinations. First the auditory hallucination of the sound of a bell, which the doctor called tinnitus. Then a patch of white growing into a white robe, then the smell of incense. At last he lived in two worlds. He saw his trench, and the level before it, and the English lines; he talked with his comrades and obeyed orders, though with a certain difficulty; but he also heard the deep boom of St Lambart's bell, and saw continually advancing towards him a white procession of little children, led by a boy who was swinging a censer. There is one extraordinary entry: 'But in August those children carried no lilies; now they have lilies in their hands. Why should they have lilies?'

It is interesting to note the transition over the border line. After May 2 there is no reference in the diary to bodily illness, with two notable exceptions. Up to and including that date the sergeant knows that he is suffering from illusions; after that he accepts his hallucinations as actualities. The man who cannot see what he sees and hear what he hears is a fool. So he writes: 'I ask who is singing "Ave Maria Stella". That blockhead Friedrich Schumacher raises his crest and answers insolently that no one sings, since singing is strictly forbidden for the present.'

A few days before the disastrous night expedition the last figure in the procession appeared to those sick eyes.

> The old priest now comes in his golden robe, the two boys holding each side of it. He is looking just as he did when he died, save that when he walked in St Lambart there was no shining round his head. But this is illusion and contrary to reason, since no one has a shining about his head. I must take some medicine.

Note here that Karl Heinz absolutely accepts the appearance of the martyred priest of St Lambart as actual, while he thinks that the halo must be an illusion; and so he reverts again to his physical condition.

The priest held up both his hands, the diary states, 'as if there were something between them. But there is a sort of cloud or dimness over this object, whatever it may be. My poor Aunt Kathie suffered much from her eyes in her old age.'

* * *

One can guess what the priest of St Lambart carried in his hands when he and the little children went out into the hot sunlight to implore mercy, while the great resounding bell of St Lambart boomed over the plain. Karl Heinz knew what happened then; they said that it was he who killed the old priest and helped to crucify the little child against the church door. The baby was only three years old. He died calling piteously for 'mummy' and 'daddy'.

* * *

And those who will may guess what Karl Heinz saw when the mist cleared from before the monstrance in the priest's hands. Then he shrieked and died.

The Great Return

I
The Rumour of the Marvellous

There are strange things lost and forgotten in obscure corners of the newspaper. I often think that the most extraordinary item of intelligence that I have read in print appeared a few years ago in the London Press. It came from a well known and most respected news agency; I imagine it was in all the papers. It was astounding.

The circumstances necessary – not to the understanding of this paragraph, for that is out of the question – but, we will say, to the understanding of the events which made it possible, are these. We had invaded Tibet, and there had been trouble in the hierarchy of that country, and a personage known as the Tashai Lama had taken refuge with us in India. He went on pilgrimage from one Buddhist shrine to another, and came at last to a holy mountain of Buddhism, the name of which I have forgotten. And thus the morning paper.

> His Holiness the Tashai Lama then ascended the Mountain and was transfigured. – Reuter.

That was all. And from that day to this I have never heard a word of explanation or comment on this amazing statement.

* * *

There was no more, it seemed, to be said. 'Reuter', apparently, thought he had made his simple statement of the facts of the case, had thereby done his duty, and so it all ended. Nobody, so far as I know, ever wrote to any paper asking what Reuter meant by it, or what the Tashai Lama meant by it. I suppose the fact was that nobody cared twopence about the matter; and so this strange event – if there were any such event – was exhibited to us for a moment, and the lantern show revolved to other spectacles.

This is an extreme instance of the manner in which the marvellous is flashed out to us and then withdrawn behind its black veils and concealments; but I have known of other cases. Now and again, at intervals of a few years, there appear in the newspapers strange stories of the strange doings of what are technically called poltergeists. Some house, often a lonely farm, is suddenly subjected to an infernal bombardment. Great stones crash through the windows, thunder down the chimneys, impelled by no visible hand. The plates and cups and saucers are whirled from the dresser into the middle of the kitchen, no one can say how or by what agency. Upstairs the big bedstead and an old chest or two are heard bounding on the floor as if in a mad ballet. Now and then such doings as these excite a whole neighbourhood; sometimes a London paper sends a man down to make an investigation. He writes half a column of description on the Monday, a couple of paragraphs on the Tuesday, and then returns to town. Nothing has been explained, the matter vanishes away; and nobody cares. The tale trickles for a day or two through the Press, and then instantly disappears, like an Australian stream, into the bowels of darkness. It is possible, I suppose, that this singular incuriousness as to marvellous events and reports is not wholly unaccountable. It may be that the events in question are, as it were, psychic accidents and misadventures. They are not meant to happen, or, rather, to be manifested. They belong to the world on the other side of the dark curtain; and it is only by some queer mischance that a corner of that curtain is twitched aside for an instant. Then – for an instant – we see; but the personages whom Mr Kipling calls the Lords of Life and Death take care that we do not see too much. Our business is with things higher and things lower, with things different, anyhow; and on the whole we are not suffered to distract ourselves with that which does not really concern us. The Transfiguration of the Lama and the tricks of the poltergeist are evidently no affairs of ours; we raise an uninterested eyebrow and pass on – to poetry or to statistics.

* * *

Be it noted; I am not professing any fervent personal belief in the reports to which I have alluded. For all I know, the Lama, in spite of Reuter, was not transfigured, and the poltergeist, in spite of the late Mr Andrew Lang, may in reality be only mischievous Polly, the servant girl at the farm. And to go farther: I do not know that I should be justified in putting either of these cases of the marvellous in line with a chance paragraph that caught my eye last summer; for this had not, on the face of it at all events, anything wildly out of the common. Indeed, I dare say that I should not have read it, should not have seen it, if it had not contained the name of a place which I had once visited, which had then moved me in an odd manner that I could not understand. Indeed, I am sure that this particular paragraph deserves to stand alone, for even if the poltergeist be a real poltergeist, it merely reveals the psychic whimsicality of some region that is not our region. There were better things and more relevant things behind the few lines dealing with Llantrisant, the little town by the sea in Arfonshire.

Not on the surface, I must say, for the cutting – I have preserved it – reads as follows:

> LLANTRISANT – The season promises very favourably: temperature of the sea yesterday at noon, 65 deg. Remarkable occurrences are supposed to have taken place during the recent Revival. The lights have not been observed lately. 'The Crown'. 'The Fisherman's Rest'.

The style was odd certainly; knowing a little of newspapers. I could see that the figure called, I think, tmesis, or cutting, had been generously employed; the exuberances of the local correspondent had been pruned by a Fleet Street expert. And these poor men are often hurried; but what did those 'lights' mean? What strange matters had the vehement blue pencil blotted out and brought to naught?

That was my first thought, and then, thinking still of Llantrisant and how I had first discovered it and found it strange, I read the paragraph again, and was saddened almost to see, as I thought, the obvious explanation. I had forgotten for the moment that it was wartime, that scares and rumours and terrors about traitorous signals and flashing lights were current everywhere by land and sea; some one, no doubt, had been watching innocent farmhouse windows and thoughtless fanlights of lodging houses; these were the 'lights' that had not been observed lately.

I found out afterwards that the Llantrisant correspondent had no such treasonous lights in his mind, but something very different. Still; what do we know? He may have been mistaken, 'the great rose of fire' that came over the deep may have been the port light of a coasting ship. Did it shine at last from the old chapel on the headland? Possibly; or possibly it was the doctor's lamp at Sarnau, some miles away. I have had wonderful opportunities lately of analysing the marvels of lying, conscious and unconscious; and indeed almost incredible feats in this way can be performed. If I incline to the less likely explanation of the 'lights' at Llantrisant, it is merely because this explanation seems to me to be altogether congruous with the 'remarkable occurrences' of the newspaper paragraph.

After all, if rumour and gossip and hearsay are crazy things to be utterly neglected and laid aside: on the other hand, evidence is evidence, and when a couple of reputable surgeons assert, as they do assert in the case of Olwen Phillips, Croeswen, Llantrisant, that there has been a 'kind of resurrection of the body', it is merely foolish to say that these things don't happen. The girl was a mass of tuberculosis, she was within a few hours of death; she is now full of life. And so, I do not believe that the rose of fire was merely a ship's light, magnified and transformed by dreaming Welsh sailors.

* * *

But now I am going forward too fast. I have not dated the paragraph, so I cannot give the exact day of its appearance, but I think it was somewhere between the second and third week of June. I cut it out partly because it was about Llantrisant, partly because of the 'remarkable occurrences'. I have an appetite for these matters, though I also have this misfortune, that I require evidence before I am ready to credit them, and I have a sort of lingering hope that some day I shall be able to elaborate some scheme or theory of such things.

But in the meantime, as a temporary measure, I hold what I call the doctrine of the jigsaw puzzle. That is: this remarkable occurrence, and that, and the other may be, and usually are, of no significance. Coincidence and chance and unsearchable causes will now and again make clouds that are undeniable fiery dragons, and potatoes that resemble Eminent Statesmen exactly and minutely in every feature, and rocks that are like eagles and lions. All this is nothing; it is when you get your set of odd shapes and find that they fit into one another, and at last that they are but parts of a large design; it is then that research grows interesting and indeed amazing, it is then that one queer form confirms the other, that the whole plan displayed justifies, corroborates, explains each separate piece.

So; it was within a week or ten days after I had read the paragraph about Llantrisant and had cut it out that I got a letter from a friend who was taking an early holiday in those regions.

'You will be interested,' he wrote, 'to hear that they have taken to ritualistic practices at Llantrisant. I went into the church the other day, and instead of smelling like a damp vault as usual, it was positively reeking with incense.'

I knew better than that. The old parson was a firm Evangelical; he would rather have burnt sulphur in his church than incense any day. So I could not make out this report at all; and went down to Arfon a few weeks later determined to investigate this and any other remarkable occurrence at Llantrisant.

II
Odours of Paradise

I went down to Arfon in the very heat and bloom and fragrance of the wonderful summer that they were enjoying there. In London there was no such weather; it rather seemed as if the horror and fury of the war had mounted to the very skies and were there reigning. In the mornings the sun burnt down upon the city with a heat that scorched and consumed; but then clouds heavy and horrible would roll together from all quarters of the heavens, and early in the afternoon the air would darken, and a storm of thunder and lightning, and furious, hissing rain would fall upon the streets. Indeed, the torment of the world was in the London weather. The city wore a terrible vesture; within our hearts was dread; without we were clothed in black clouds and angry fire.

It is certain that I cannot show in any words the utter peace of that Welsh coast to which I came; one sees, I think, in such a change a figure of the passage from the disquiets and the fears of earth to the peace of paradise. A land that seemed to be in a holy, happy dream, a sea that changed all the while from olivine to emerald, from emerald to sapphire, from sapphire to amethyst, that washed in white foam at the bases of the firm, grey rocks, and about the huge crimson bastions that hid the western bays and inlets of the waters; to this land I came, and to hollows that were purple and odorous with wild thyme, wonderful with many tiny, exquisite flowers. There was benediction in centaury, pardon in eyebright, joy in lady's slipper; and so the weary eyes were refreshed, looking now at the little flowers and the happy bees about them, now on the magic mirror of the deep, changing from marvel to marvel with the passing of the great white clouds, with the brightening of the sun. And the ears, torn with jangle and racket and idle, empty noise, were soothed and comforted by the ineffable, unutterable, unceasing murmur, as the tides swam to and fro, uttering mighty, hollow voices in the caverns of the rocks.

* * *

For three or four days I rested in the sun and smelt the savour of the blossoms and of the salt water, and then, refreshed, I remembered that there was something queer about Llantrisant that I might as well investigate. It was no great thing that I thought to find, for, it will be remembered, I had ruled out the apparent oddity of the reporter's – or commissioner's? – reference to lights, on the ground that he must have been referring to some local panic about signalling to the enemy; who had certainly torpedoed a ship or two off Lundy in the Bristol Channel. All that I had to go upon was the reference to the 'remarkable occurrences' at some revival, and then that letter of Jackson's, which spoke of Llantrisant church as 'reeking' with incense, a wholly incredible and impossible state of things. Why, old Mr Evans, the rector, looked upon coloured stoles as the very robe of Satan and his angels, as things dear to the heart of the Pope of Rome. But as to incense! As I have already familiarly observed, I knew better.

But as a hard matter of fact, this may be worth noting: when I went over to Llantrisant on Monday, August 9th, I visited the church, and it was still fragrant and exquisite with the odour of rare gums that had fumed there.

* * *

Now I happened to have a slight acquaintance with the rector. He was a most courteous and delightful old man, and on my last visit he had come across me in the churchyard, as I was admiring the very fine Celtic cross that stands there. Besides the beauty of the interlaced ornament there is an inscription in Ogham on one of the edges, concerning which the learned dispute; it is altogether one of the more famous crosses of Celtdom. Mr Evans, I say, seeing me looking at the cross, came up and began to give me, the stranger, a résumé – somewhat of a shaky and uncertain résumé, I found afterwards – of the various debates and questions that had arisen as to the exact meaning of the inscription, and I was amused to detect an evident but underlying belief of his own: that the supposed Ogham characters were, in fact, due to boys' mischief and weather and the passing of the ages. But then I happened to put a question as to the sort of stone of which the cross was made, and the rector brightened amazingly. He began to talk geology, and, I think, demonstrated that the cross or the material for it must have been brought to Llantrisant from the south-west coast of Ireland. This struck me as interesting, because it was curious evidence of the migrations of the Celtic saints, whom the rector, I was delighted to find, looked upon as good Protestants, though shaky on the subject of crosses; and so, with concessions on my part, we got on very well. Thus, with all this to the good, I was emboldened to call upon him.

I found him altered. Not that he was aged; indeed, he was rather made young, with a singular brightening upon his face, and something of joy upon it that I had not seen before, that I have seen on very few faces of men. We talked of the war, of course, since that is not to be avoided; of the farming prospects of the county; of general things, till I ventured to remark that I had been in the church, and had been surprised, to find it perfumed with incense.

'You have made some alterations in the service since I was here last? You use incense now?'

The old man looked at me strangely, and hesitated.

'No,' he said, 'there has been no change. I use no incense in the church. I should not venture to do so.'

'But,' I was beginning, 'the whole church is as if High Mass had just been sung there, and – '

He cut me short, and there was a certain grave solemnity in his manner that struck me almost with awe.

'I know you are a railer,' he said, and the phrase coming from this mild old gentleman astonished, me unutterably. 'You are a railer and a bitter railer; I have read articles that you have written, and I know your contempt and your hatred for those you call Protestants in your derision; though your grandfather, the vicar of Caerleon-on-Usk, called himself Protestant and was proud of it, and your great-grand-uncle Hezekiah, *ffeiriad coch yr Castletown* – the Red Priest of Castletown – was a great man with the Methodists in his day, and the people flocked by their thousands when he administered the Sacrament. I was born and brought up in Glamorganshire, and old men have wept as they told me of the weeping and contrition that there was when the Red Priest broke the Bread and raised the Cup. But you are a railer, and see nothing but the outside and the show. You are not worthy of this mystery that has been done here.'

I went out from his presence rebuked indeed, and justly rebuked; but rather amazed. It is curiously true that the Welsh are still one people, one family almost, in a manner that the English cannot understand, but I had never thought that this old clergyman would have known anything of my ancestry or their doings. And as for my articles and suchlike, I knew that the country clergy sometimes read, but I had fancied my pronouncements sufficiently obscure, even in London, much more in Arfon.

But so it happened, and so I had no explanation from the rector of Llantrisant of the strange circumstance, that his church was full of incense and odours of paradise.

* * *

I went up and down the ways of Llantrisant wondering, and came to the harbour, which is a little place, with little quays where some small coasting trade still lingers. A brigantine was at anchor here, and very lazily in the sunshine they were loading it with anthracite; for it is one of the oddities of Llantrisant that there is a small colliery in the heart of the wood on the hillside. I crossed a causeway which parts the outer harbour from the inner harbour, and settled down on a rocky beach hidden under a leafy hill. The tide was going out, and some children were playing on the wet sand, while two ladies – their mothers, I suppose – talked together as they sat comfortably on their rugs at a little distance from me.

At first they talked of the war, and I made myself deaf, for of that talk one gets enough, and more than enough, in London. Then there was a period of silence, and the conversation had passed to quite a different topic when I caught the thread of it again. I was sitting on the further side of a big rock, and I do not think that the two ladies had noticed my approach. However, though they spoke of strange things, they spoke of nothing which made it necessary for me to announce my presence.

'And, after all,' one of them was saying, 'what is it all about? I can't make out what is come to the people.'

This speaker was a Welshwoman; I recognised the clear, over-emphasised consonants, and a faint suggestion of an accent. Her friend came from the Midlands, and it turned out that they had only known each other for a few days. Theirs was a friendship of the beach and of bathing; such friendships are common, at small seaside places.

'There is certainly something odd about the people here. I have never been to Llantrisant before, you know; indeed, this is the first time we've been in Wales for our holidays, and knowing nothing about the ways of the people and not being accustomed to hear Welsh spoken, I thought, perhaps, it must be my imagination. But you think there really is something a little queer?'

'I can tell you this: that I have been in two minds whether I should not write to my husband and ask him to take me and the children away. You know where I am at Mrs Morgan's, and the Morgans' sitting room is just the other side of the passage, and sometimes they leave the door open, so that I can hear what they say quite plainly. And you see I understand the Welsh, though they don't know it. And I hear them saying the most alarming things!'

'What sort of things?

'Well, indeed, it sounds like some kind of a religious service, but it's not Church of England, I know that. Old Morgan begins it, and the wife and children answer. Something like; "Blessed be God for the messengers of Paradise." "Blessed be His Name for Paradise in the meat and in the drink." "Thanksgiving for the old offering." "Thanksgiving for the appearance of the old altar." "Praise for the joy of the ancient garden." "Praise for the return of those that have been long absent." And all that sort of thing. It is nothing but madness.'

'Depend upon it,' said the lady from the Midlands, 'there's no real harm in it. They're Dissenters; some new sect, I dare say. You know some Dissenters are very queer in their ways.'

'All that is like no Dissenters that I have ever known in all my life whatever,' replied the Welsh lady somewhat vehemently, with a very distinct intonation of the land. 'And have you heard them speak of the bright light that shone at midnight from the church?'

III
A Secret in a Secret Place

Now here was I altogether at a loss and quite bewildered. The children broke into the conversation of the two ladies and cut it all short, just as the midnight lights from the church came on the field, and when the little girls and boys went back again to the sands whooping, the tide of talk had turned, and Mrs Harland and Mrs Williams were quite safe and at home with Janey's measles, and a wonderful treatment for infantile earache, as exemplified in the case of Trevor. There was no more to be got out of them, evidently, so I left the beach, crossed the harbour causeway, and drank beer at the 'Fishermen's Rest' till it was time to climb up two miles of deep lane and catch the train for Penvro, where I was staying. And I went up the lane, as I say, in a kind of amazement; and not so much, I think, because of evidences and hints of things strange to the senses, such as the savour of incense where no incense had smoked for three hundred and fifty years and more, or the story of bright light shining from the dark, closed church at dead of night, as because of that sentence of thanksgiving 'for paradise in meat and in drink'.

For the sun went down and the evening fell as I climbed the long hill through the deep woods and the high meadows, and the scent of all the green things rose from the earth and from the heart of the wood, and at a turn of the lane far below was the misty glimmer of the still sea, and from far below its deep murmur sounded as it washed on the little hidden, enclosed bay where Llantrisant stands. And I thought, if there be paradise in meat and in drink, so much the more is there paradise in the scent of the green leaves at evening and in the appearance of the sea and in the redness of the sky; and there came to me a certain vision of a real world about us all the while, of a language that was only secret because we would not take the trouble to listen to it and discern it.

It was almost dark when I got to the station, and here were the few feeble oil lamps lit, glimmering in that lonely land, where the way is long from farm to farm. The train came on its way, and I got into it; and just as we moved from the station I noticed a group under one of those dim lamps. A woman and her child had got out, and they were being welcomed by a man who had been waiting for them. I had not noticed his face as I stood on the platform, but now I saw it as he pointed down the hill towards Llantrisant, and I think I was almost frightened.

He was a young man, a farmer's son, I would say, dressed in rough brown clothes, and as different from old Mr Evans, the rector, as one man might be from another. But on his face, as I saw it in the lamplight, there was the like brightening that I had seen on the face of the rector.

It was an illuminated face, glowing with an ineffable joy, and I thought it rather gave light to the platform lamp than received light from it. The woman and her child, I inferred, were strangers to the place, and had come to pay a visit to the young man's family. They had looked about them in bewilderment, half alarmed, before they saw him; and then his face was radiant in their sight, and it was easy to see that all their troubles were ended and over. A wayside station and a darkening country, and it was as if they were welcomed by shining, immortal gladness – even into paradise.

* * *

But though there seemed in a sense light all about my ways, I was myself still quite bewildered. I could see, indeed, that something strange had happened or was happening in the little town hidden under the hill, but there was so far no clue to the mystery, or rather, the clue had been offered to me, and I had not taken it, I had not even known that it was there; since we do not so much as see what we have determined, without judging, to be incredible, even though it be held up before our eyes. The dialogue that the Welsh Mrs Williams had reported to her English friend might have set me on the right way; but the right way was outside all my limits of possibility, outside the circle of my thought. The palaeontologist might see monstrous, significant marks in the slime of a river bank, but he would never draw the conclusions that his own peculiar science would seem to suggest to him; he would choose any explanation rather than the obvious, since the obvious would also be the outrageous – according to our established habit of thought, which we deem final.

* * *

The next day I took all these strange things with me for consideration to a certain place that I knew of not far from Penvro. I was now in the early stages of the jigsaw process, or rather I had only a few pieces before me, and – to continue the figure my difficulty was this: that though the markings on each piece seemed to have design and significance, yet I could not make the wildest guess as to the nature of the whole picture, of which these were the parts. I had clearly seen that there was a great secret; I had seen that on the face of the young farmer on the platform of Llantrisant station; and in my mind there was all the while the picture of him going down the dark, steep, winding lane that led to the town and the sea, going down through the heart of the wood, with light about him.

But there was bewilderment in the thought of this, and in the endeavour to match it with the perfumed church and the scraps of talk that I had heard and the rumour of midnight brightness; and though Penvro is by no means populous, I thought I would go to a certain solitary place called the Old Camp Head, which looks towards Cornwall and to the great deeps that roll beyond Cornwall to the far ends of the world; a place where fragments of dreams – they seemed such then – might, perhaps, be gathered into the clearness of vision.

It was some years since I had been to the Head, and I had gone on that last time and on a former visit by the cliffs, a rough and difficult path. Now I chose a landward way, which the county map seemed to justify, though doubtfully, as regarded the last part of the journey. So I went inland and climbed the hot summer by-roads, till I came at last to a lane which gradually turned turfy and grass-grown, and then on high ground, ceased to be. It left me at a gate in a hedge of old thorns; and across the field beyond there seemed to be some faint indications of a track. One would judge that sometimes men did pass by that way, but not often.

It was high ground but not within sight of the sea. But the breath of the sea blew about the hedge of thorns, and came with a keen savour to the nostrils. The ground sloped gently from the gate and then rose again to a ridge, where a white farmhouse stood all alone. I passed by this farmhouse, threading an uncertain way, followed a hedgerow doubtfully; and saw suddenly before me the Old Camp, and beyond it the sapphire plain of waters and the mist where sea and sky met. Steep from my feet the hill fell away, a land of gorse blossom, red-gold and mellow, of glorious purple heather. It fell into a hollow that went down, shining with rich green bracken, to the glimmering sea; and before me and beyond the hollow rose a height of turf, bastioned at the summit with the awful, age-old walls of the Old Camp; green, rounded circumvallations, wall within wall, tremendous, with their myriad years upon them.

* * *

Within these smoothed, green mounds, looking across the shining and changing of the waters in the happy sunlight, I took out the bread and cheese and beer that I had carried in a bag, and ate and drank, and lit my pipe, and set myself to think over the enigmas of Llantrisant. And I had scarcely done so when, a good deal to my annoyance, a man came climbing up over the green ridges, and took up his stand close by, and stared out to sea. He nodded to me, and began with 'Fine weather for the harvest' in the approved manner, and so sat down and engaged me in a net of talk. He was of Wales, it seemed, but from a different part of the country, and was staying for a few days with relations – at the white farmhouse which I had passed on my way. His tale of nothing flowed on to his pleasure and my pain, till he fell suddenly on Llantrisant and its doings. I listened then with wonder, and here is his tale condensed. Though it must be clearly understood that the man's evidence was only second-hand; he had heard it from his cousin, the farmer.

So, to be brief, it appeared that there had been a long feud at Llantrisant between a local solicitor, Lewis Prothero (we will say), and a farmer named James. There had been a quarrel about some trifle, which had grown more and more bitter as the two parties forgot the merits of the original dispute, and by some means or other, which I could not well understand, the lawyer had got the small freeholder 'under his thumb'. James, I think, had given a bill of sale in a bad season, and Prothero had bought it up; and the end was that the farmer was turned out of the old house, and was lodging in a cottage. People said he would have to take a place on his own farm as a labourer; he went about in dreadful misery, piteous to see. It was thought by some that he might very well murder the lawyer, if he met him.

They did meet, in the middle of the marketplace at Llantrisant one Saturday in June. The farmer was a little black man, and he gave a shout of rage, and the people were rushing at him to keep him off Prothero.

'And then,' said my informant, 'I will tell you what happened. This lawyer, as they tell me, he is a great big brawny fellow, with a big jaw and a wide mouth, and a red face and red whiskers. And there he was in his black coat and his high hard hat, and all his money at his back, as you may say. And, indeed, he did fall down on his knees in the dust there in the street in front of Philip James, and every one could see that terror was upon him. And he did beg Philip James's pardon, and beg of him to have mercy, and he did implore him by God and man and the saints of paradise. And my cousin, John Jenkins, Penmawr, he do tell me that the tears were falling from Lewis Prothero's eyes like the rain. And he put his hand into his pocket and drew out the deed of Pantyreos, Philip James's old farm that was, and did give him the farm back and a hundred pounds for the stock that was on it, and two hundred pounds, all in notes of the bank, for amendment and consolation.

'And then, from what they do tell me, all the people did go mad, crying and weeping and calling out all manner of things at the top of their voices. And at last nothing would do but they must all go up to the churchyard, and there Philip James and Lewis Prothero they swear friendship to one another for a long age before the old cross, and everyone sings praises. And my cousin he do declare to me that there were men standing in that crowd that he did never see before in Llantrisant in all his life, and his heart was shaken within him as if it had been in a whirlwind.'

I had listened to all this in silence. I said then:

'What does your cousin mean by that? Men that he had never seen in Llantrisant? What men?'

'The people,' he said very slowly, 'call them the Fishermen.'

And suddenly there came into my mind the 'Rich Fisherman' who in the old legend guards the holy mystery of the Graal.

IV
The Ringing of the Bell

So far I have not told the story of the things of Llantrisant, but rather the story of how I stumbled upon them and among them, perplexed and wholly astray, seeking, but yet not knowing at all what I sought; bewildered now and again by circumstances which seemed to me wholly inexplicable; devoid, not so much of the key to the enigma, but of the key to the nature of the enigma. You cannot begin to solve a puzzle till you know what the puzzle is about. 'Yards divided by minutes,' said the mathematical master to me long ago, 'will give neither pigs, sheep, nor oxen.' He was right; though his manner on this and on all other occasions was highly offensive. This is enough of the personal process, as I may call it; and here follows the story of what happened at Llantrisant last summer, the story as I pieced it together at last.

It all began, it appears, on a hot day, early in last June; so far as I can make out, on the first Saturday in the month. There was a deaf old woman, a Mrs Parry, who lived by herself in a lonely cottage a mile or so from the town. She came into the marketplace early on the Saturday morning in a state of some excitement, and as soon as she had taken up her usual place on the pavement by the churchyard, with her ducks and eggs and a few very early potatoes, she began to tell her neighbours about her having heard the sound of a great bell. The good women on each side smiled at one another behind Mrs Parry's back, for one had to bawl into her ear before she could make out what one meant; and Mrs Williams, Penycoed, bent over and yelled: 'What bell should that be, Mrs Parry? There's no church near you up at Penrhiw. Do you hear what nonsense she talks?' said Mrs Williams in a low voice to Mrs Morgan. 'As if she could hear any bell, whatever.'

'What makes you talk nonsense your self?' said Mrs Parry, to the amazement of the two women. 'I can hear a bell as well as you, Mrs Williams, and as well as your whispers either.'

And there is the fact, which is not to be disputed; though the deductions from it may be open to endless disputations; this old woman who had been all but stone deaf for twenty years – the defect had always been in her family – could suddenly hear on this June morning as well as anybody else. And her two old friends stared at her, and it was some time before they had appeased her indignation, and induced her to talk about the bell.

It had happened in the early morning, which was very misty. She had been gathering sage in her garden, high on a round hill looking over the sea. And there came in her ears a sort of throbbing and singing and trembling, 'as if there were music coming out of the earth,' and then something seemed to break in her head, and all the birds began to sing and make melody together, and the leaves of the poplars round the garden fluttered in the breeze that rose from the sea, and the cock crowed far off at Twyn, and the dog barked down in Kemeys Valley. But above all these sounds, unheard for so many years, there thrilled the deep and chanting note of the bell, 'like the bell and a man's voice singing at once.'

They stared again at her and at one another. 'Where did it sound from?' asked one. 'It came sailing across the sea,' answered Mrs Parry quite composedly, 'and I did hear it coming nearer and nearer to the land.'

'Well, indeed,' said Mrs Morgan, 'it was a ship's bell then, though I can't make out why they would be ringing like that.'

'It was not ringing on any ship, Mrs Morgan,' said Mrs Parry.

'Then where do you think it was ringing?'

'*Ym Mharadwys*,' replied Mrs Parry. Now that means 'in Paradise', and the two others changed the conversation quickly. They thought that Mrs Parry had got back her hearing suddenly – such things did happen now and then – and that the shock had made her 'a bit queer'. And this explanation would no doubt have stood its ground, if it had not been for other experiences. Indeed, the local doctor (who had treated Mrs Parry for a dozen years, not for her deafness, which he took to be hopeless and beyond cure, but for a tiresome and recurrent winter cough), sent an account of the case to a colleague at Bristol, suppressing, naturally enough, the reference to Paradise. The Bristol physician gave it as his opinion that the symptoms were absolutely what mighty have been expected. 'You have here, in all probability,' he wrote, 'the sudden breaking down of an old obstruction in the aural passage, and I should quite expect this process to be accompanied by tinnitus of a pronounced and even violent character.'

* * *

But for the other experiences? As the morning wore on and drew to noon, high market, and to the utmost brightness of that summer day, all the stalls and the streets were full of rumours and of awed faces. Now from one lonely farm, now from another, men and women came and told the story of how they had listened in the early morning with thrilling hearts to the thrilling music of a bell that was like no bell ever heard before. And it seemed that many people in the town had been roused, they knew not how, from sleep; waking up, as one of them said, as if bells were ringing and the organ playing, and a choir of sweet voices singing all together: 'There were such melodies and songs that my heart was full of joy.'

And a little past noon some fishermen who had been out all night returned, and brought a wonderful story into the town of what they had heard in the mist and one of them said he had seen something go by at a little distance from his boat. 'It was all golden and bright,' he said, 'and there was glory about it.' Another fisherman declared 'there was a song upon the water that was like heaven.'

And here I would say in parenthesis that on returning to town I sought out a very old friend of mine, a man who has devoted a lifetime to strange and esoteric studies. I thought that I had a tale that would interest him profoundly, but I found that he heard me with a good deal of indifference. And at this very point of the sailors' stories I remember saying: 'Now what do you make of that? Don't you think it's extremely curious?' He replied: 'I hardly think so. Possibly the sailors were lying; possibly it happened as they say. Well; that sort of thing has always been happening.' I give my friend's opinion; I make no comment on it.

Let it be noted that there was something remarkable as to the manner in which the sound of the bell was heard – or supposed to be heard. There are, no doubt, mysteries in sound as in all else; indeed, I am informed that during one of the horrible outrages that have been perpetrated on London during this autumn there was an instance of a great block of workmen's dwellings in which the only person who heard the crash of a particular bomb falling was an old deaf woman, who had been fast asleep till the moment of the explosion. This is strange enough of a sound that was entirely in the natural (and horrible) order; and so it was at Llantrisant, where the sound was either a collective auditory hallucination or a manifestation of what is conveniently, if inaccurately, called the supernatural order.

For the thrill of the bell did not reach to all ears – or hearts. Deaf Mrs Parry heard it in her lonely cottage garden, high above the misty sea; but then, in a farm on the other or western side of Llantrisant, a little child, scarcely three years old, was the only one out of a household of ten people who heard anything. He called out in stammering baby Welsh something that sounded like '*Clychau fawr, clychau fawr*' – the great bells, the great bells – and his mother wondered what he was talking about. Of the crews of half a dozen trawlers that were swinging from side to side in the mist, not more than four men had any tale to tell. And so it was that for an hour or two the man who had heard nothing suspected his neighbour who had heard marvels of lying; and it was some time before the mass of evidence coming from all manner of diverse and remote quarters convinced the people that there was a true story here. A might suspect B, his neighbour, of making up a tale; but when C, from some place on the hills five miles away, and D, the fisherman on the waters, each had a like report, then it was clear that something had happened.

* * *

And even then, as they told me, the signs to be seen upon the people were stranger than the tales told by them and among them. It has struck me that many people in reading some of the phrases that I have reported, will dismiss them with laughter as very poor and fantastic inventions; fishermen, they will say, do not speak of 'a song like heaven' or of 'a glory about it'. And I darc say this would bc a just enough criticism if I were reporting English fishermen; but, odd though it may be, Wales has not yet lost the last shreds of the grand manner. And let it be remembered also that in most cases such phrases are translated from another language, that is, from the Welsh.

So, they come trailing, let us say, fragments of the cloud of glory in their common speech; and so, on this Saturday, they began to display, uneasily enough in many cases, their consciousness that the things that were reported were of their ancient right and former custom. The comparison is not quite fair; but conceive Hardy's old Durbeyfield suddenly waking from long slumber to find himself in a noble thirteenth-century hall, waited on by kneeling pages, smiled on by sweet ladies in silken côtehardies.

So by evening time there had come to the old people the recollection of stories that their fathers had told them as they sat round the hearth of winter nights, fifty, sixty, seventy years; ago; stories of the wonderful bell of Teilo Sant, that had sailed across the glassy seas from Syon, that was called a portion of Paradise, 'and the sound of its ringing was like the perpetual choir of the angels.'

Such things were remembered by the old and told to the young that evening, in the streets of the town and in the deep lanes that climbed far hills. The sun went down to the mountain red with fire like a burnt offering, the sky turned violet, the sea was purple, as one told another of the wonder that had returned to the land after long ages.

V
The Rose of Fire

It was during the next nine days, counting from that Saturday early in June – the first Saturday in June, as I believe – that Llantrisant and all the regions about became possessed either by an extraordinary set of hallucinations or by a visitation of great marvels.

This is not the place to strike the balance between the two possibilities. The evidence is, no doubt, readily available; the matter is open to systematic investigation.

But this may be said: the ordinary man, in the ordinary passages of his life, accepts in the main the evidence of his senses, and is entirely right in doing so. He says that he sees a cow, that he sees a stone wall, and that the cow and the stone wall are 'there'. This is very well for all the practical purposes of life, but I believe that the metaphysicians are by no means so easily satisfied as to the reality of the stone wall and the cow. Perhaps they might allow that both objects are 'there' in the sense that one's reflection is in a glass; there is an actuality, but is there a reality external to oneself? In any event, it is solidly agreed that, supposing a real existence, this much is certain – it is not in the least like our conception of it. The ant and the microscope will quickly convince us that we do not see things as they really are, even supposing that we see them at all. If we could 'see' the real cow she would appear utterly incredible, as incredible as the things I am to relate.

Now, there is nothing that I know much more unconvincing than the stories of the red light on the sea. Several sailors, men on small coasting ships, who were working up or down the Channel on that Saturday night, spoke of 'seeing' the red light, and it must be said that there is a very tolerable agreement in their tales. All make the time as between midnight of the Saturday and one o'clock on the Sunday morning. Two of those sailormen are precise as to the time of the apparition; they fix it by elaborate calculations of their own as occurring at 12.20 a.m. And the story?

A red light, a burning spark seen far away in the darkness, taken at the first moment of seeing for a signal, and probably an enemy signal. Then it approached at a tremendous speed, and one man said he took it to be the port light of some new kind of navy motorboat which was developing a rate hitherto unheard of, a hundred or a hundred and fifty knots an hour. And then, in the third instant of the sight, it was clear that this was no earthly speed. At first a red spark in the farthest distance; then a rushing lamp; and then, as if in an incredible point of time, it swelled into a vast rose of fire that filled all the sea and all the sky and hid the stars and possessed the land. 'I thought the end of the world had come,' one of the sailors said.

And then, an instant more, and it was gone from them, and four of them say that there was a red spark on Chapel Head, where the old grey chapel of St Teilo stands, high above the water, in a cleft of the limestone rocks.

And thus the sailors; and thus their tales are incredible; but *they* are not incredible. I believe that men of the highest eminence in physical science have testified to the occurrence of phenomena every whit as marvellous, to things as absolutely opposed to all natural order, as we conceive it; and it may be said that nobody minds them. 'That sort of thing has always been happening,' as my friend remarked to me. But the men, whether or no the fire had ever been without them, there was no doubt that it was now within them, for it burned in their eyes. They were purged as if they had passed through the Furnace of the Sages governed with Wisdom that the alchemists know. They spoke without much difficulty of what they had seen, or had seemed to see, with their eyes, but hardly at all of what their hearts had known when for a moment the glory of the fiery rose had been about them.

For some weeks afterwards they were still, as it were, amazed; almost, I would say, incredulous. If there had been nothing more than the splendid and fiery appearance, showing and vanishing, I do believe that they themselves would have discredited their own senses and denied the truth of their own tales. And one does not dare to say whether they would not have been right. Men like Sir William Crookes and Sir Oliver Lodge are certainly to be heard with respect, and they bear witness to all manner of apparent eversions of laws which we, or most of us, consider far more deeply founded than the ancient hills. They may be justified; but in our hearts we doubt. We cannot wholly believe in inner sincerity that the solid table did rise, without mechanical reason or cause, into the air, and so defy that which we name the 'law of gravitation'. I know what may be said on the other side; I know that there is no true question of 'law' in the case; that the law of gravitation really means just this: that I have never seen a table rising without mechanical aid, or an apple, detached from the bough, soaring to the skies instead of falling to the ground. The so-called law is just the sum of common observation and nothing more; yet I say, in our hearts we do not believe that the tables rise; much less do we believe in the rose of fire that for a moment swallowed up the skies and seas and shores of the Welsh coast last June.

And the men who saw it would have invented fairy tales to account for it, I say again, if it had not been for that which was within them.

They said, all of them, and it was certain now that they spoke the truth, that in the moment of the vision, every pain and ache and malady in their bodies had passed away. One man had been vilely drunk on venomous spirit, procured at 'Jobson's Hole' down by the Cardiff Docks. He was horribly ill; he had crawled up from his bunk for a little fresh air; and in an instant his horrors and his deadly nausea had left him. Another man was almost desperate with the raging hammering pain of an abscess on a tooth; he says that when the red flame came near he felt as if a dull, heavy blow had fallen on his jaw, and then the pain was quite gone; he could scarcely believe that there had been any pain there.

And they all bear witness to an extraordinary exaltation of the senses. It is indescribable, this; for they cannot describe it. They are amazed, again; they do not in the least profess to know what happened; but there is no more possibility of shaking their evidence than there is a possibility of shaking the evidence of a man who says that water is wet and fire hot.

'I felt a bit queer afterwards,' said one of them, 'and I steadied myself by the mast, and I can't tell how I felt as I touched it. I didn't know that touching a thing like a mast could be better than a big drink when you're thirsty, or a soft pillow when you're sleepy.'

I heard other instances of this state of things, as I must vaguely call it, since I do not know what else to call it. But I suppose we can all agree that to the man in average health, the average impact of the external world on his senses is a matter of indifference. The average impact; a harsh scream, the bursting of a motor tyre, any violent assault on the aural nerves will annoy him, and he may say 'damn'. Then, on the other hand, the man who is not 'fit' will easily be annoyed and irritated by some one pushing past him in a crowd, by the ringing of a bell, by the sharp closing of a book.

But so far as I could judge from the talk of these sailors, the average impact of the external world had become to them a fountain of pleasure. Their nerves were on edge, but an edge to receive exquisite sensuous impressions. The touch of the rough mast, for example; that was a joy far greater than is the joy of fine silk to some luxurious skins; they drank water and stared as if they had been *fins gourmets* tasting an amazing wine; the creak and whine of their ship on its slow way were as exquisite as the rhythm and song of a Bach fugue to an amateur of music.

And then, within; these rough fellows have their quarrels and strifes and variances and envyings like the rest of us; but that was all over between them that had seen the rosy light; old enemies shook hands heartily, and roared with laughter as they confessed one to another what fools they had been.

'I can't exactly say how it has happened or what has happened at all,' said one, 'but if you have all the world and the glory of it, how can you fight for fivepence?'

* * *

The church of Llantrisant is a typical example of a Welsh parish church, before the evil and horrible period of 'restoration'.

This lower world is a palace of lies, and of all foolish lies there is none more insane than a certain vague fable about the mediaeval freemasons, a fable which somehow imposed itself upon the cold intellect of Hallam the historian. The story is, in brief, that throughout the Gothic period, at any rate, the art and craft of church building were executed by wandering guilds of 'freemasons', possessed of various secrets of building and adornment, which they employed wherever they went. If this nonsense were true, the Gothic of Cologne would be as the Gothic of Colne, and the Gothic of Arles like to the Gothic of Abingdon. It is so grotesquely untrue that almost every county, let alone every country, has its distinctive style in Gothic architecture. Arfon is in the west of Wales; its churches have marks and features which distinguish them from the churches in the east of Wales.

The Llantrisant church has that primitive division between nave and chancel which only very foolish people decline to recognise as equivalent to the Oriental iconostasis and as the origin of the Western roodscreen. A solid wall divided the church into two portions; in the centre was a narrow opening with a rounded arch, through which those who sat towards the middle of the church could see the small, red-carpeted altar and the three roughly shaped lancet windows above it.

The 'reading pew' was on the outer side of this wall of partition, and here the rector did his service, the choir being grouped in seats about him. On the inner side were the pews of certain privileged houses of the town and district.

On the Sunday morning the people were all in their accustomed places, not without a certain exultation in their eyes, not without a certain expectation of they knew not what. The bells stopped ringing, the rector, in his old-fashioned, ample surplice, entered the reading desk, and gave out the hymn: 'My God, and is Thy Table spread'.

And, as the singing began, all the people who were in the pews within the wall came out of them and streamed through the archway into the nave. They took what places they could find up and down the church, and the rest of the congregation looked at them in amazement.

Nobody knew what had happened. Those whose seats were next to the aisle tried to peer into the chancel, to see what had happened or what was going on there. But somehow the light flamed so brightly from the windows above the altar, those being the only windows in the chancel, one small lancet in the south wall excepted, that no one could see anything at all.

'It was as if a veil of gold adorned with jewels was hanging there,' one man said; and indeed there are a few odds and scraps of old painted glass left in the eastern lancets.

But there were few in the church who did not hear now and again voices speaking beyond the veil.

VI
Olwen's Dream

The well-to-do and dignified personages who left their pews in the chancel of Llantrisant Church and came hurrying into the nave could give no explanation of what they had done. They felt, they said, that they 'had to go', and to go quickly; they were driven out, as it were, by a secret, irresistible command. But all who were present in the church that morning were amazed, though all exulted in their hearts; for they, like the sailors who saw the rose of fire on the waters, were filled with a joy that was literally ineffable, since they could not utter it or interpret it to themselves.

And they too, like the sailors, were transmuted, or the world was transmuted for them. They experienced what the doctors call a sense of *bien être* but a *bien être* raised to the highest power. Old men felt young again, eyes that had been growing dim now saw clearly, and saw a world that was like Paradise, the same world, it is true, but a world rectified and glowing, as if an inner flame shone in all things, and behind all things.

And the difficulty in recording this state is this, that it is so rare an experience that no set language to express it is in existence. A shadow of its raptures and ecstasies is found in the highest poetry; there are phrases in ancient books telling of the Celtic saints that dimly hint at it; some of the old Italian masters of painting had known it, for the light of it shines in their skies and about the battlements of their cities that are founded on magic hills. But these are but broken hints.

It is not poetic to go to Apothecaries' Hall for similes. But for many years I kept by me an article from the *Lancet* or the *British Medical Journal* – I forget which – in which a doctor gave an account of certain experiments he had conducted with a drug called the Mescal Button, or *Anhelonium Lewinii*. He said that while under the influence of the drug he had but to shut his eyes, and immediately before him there would rise incredible Gothic cathedrals, of such majesty and splendour and glory that no heart had ever conceived. They seemed to surge from the depths to the very heights of heaven, their spires swayed amongst the clouds and the stars, they were fretted with admirable imagery. And as he gazed, he would presently become aware that all the stones were living stones, that they were quickening and palpitating, and then that they were glowing jewels, say, emeralds, sapphires, rubies, opals, but of hues that the mortal eye had never seen.

That description gives, I think, some faint notion of the nature of the transmuted world into which these people by the sea had entered, a world quickened and glorified and full of pleasures. Joy and wonder were on all faces; but the deepest joy and the greatest wonder were on the face of the rector. For he had heard through the veil the Greek word for 'holy', three times repeated. And he, who had once been a horrified assistant at High Mass in a foreign church, recognised the perfume of incense that filled the place from end to end.

* * *

It was on that Sunday night that Olwen Phillips of Croeswen dreamed her wonderful dream. She was a girl of sixteen, the daughter of small farming people, and for many months she had been doomed to certain death. Consumption, which flourishes in that damp, warm climate, had laid hold of her; not only her lungs but her whole system was a mass of tuberculosis. As is common enough, she had enjoyed many fallacious brief recoveries in the early stages of the disease, but all hope had long been over, and now for the last few weeks she had seemed to rush vehemently to death. The doctor had come on the Saturday morning, bringing with him a colleague. They had both agreed that the girl's case was in its last stages. 'She cannot possibly last more than a day or two,' said the local doctor to her mother. He came again on the Sunday morning and found his patient perceptibly worse, and soon afterwards she sank into a heavy sleep, and her mother thought that she would never wake from it.

The girl slept in an inner room communicating with the room occupied by her father and mother. The door between was kept open, so that Mrs Phillips could hear her daughter if she called to her in the night. And Olwen called to her mother that night, just as the dawn was breaking. It was no faint summons from a dying bed that came to the mother's ears, but a loud cry that rang through the house, a cry of great gladness. Mrs Phillips started up from sleep in wild amazement, wondering what could have happened. And then she saw Olwen, who had not been able to rise from her bed for many weeks past, standing in the doorway in the faint light of the growing day. The girl called to her mother: 'Mam! mam! It is all over. I am quite well again.'

Mrs Phillips roused her husband, and they sat up in bed staring, not knowing on earth, as they said afterwards, what had been done with the world. Here was their poor girl wasted to a shadow, lying on her deathbed, and the life sighing from her with every breath, and her voice, when she last uttered it, so weak that one had to put one's ear to her mouth. And here in a few hours she stood up before them; and even in that faint light they could see that she was changed almost beyond knowing. And, indeed, Mrs Phillips said that for a moment or two she fancied that the Germans must have come and killed them in their sleep, and so they were all dead together. But Olwen called out again, so the mother lit a candle and got up and went tottering across the room, and there was Olwen all gay and plump again, smiling with shining eyes. Her mother led her into her own room, and set down the candle there, and felt her daughter's flesh, and burst into prayers and tears of wonder and delight, and thanksgivings, and held the girl again to be sure that she was not deceived. And then Olwen told her dream, though she thought it was not a dream.

She said she woke up in the deep darkness, and she knew the life was fast going from her. She could not move so much as a finger, she tried to cry out, but no sound came from her lips. She felt that in another instant the whole world would fall from her – her heart was full of agony. And as the last breath was passing her lips, she heard a very faint, sweet sound, like the tinkling of a silver bell. It came from far away, from over by Ty-newydd. She forgot her agony and listened, and even then, she says, she felt the swirl of the world as it came back to her. And the sound of the bell swelled and grew louder, and it thrilled all through her body, and the life was in it. And as the bell rang and trembled in her ears, a faint light touched the wall of her room and reddened, till the whole room was full of rosy fire. And then she saw standing before her bed three men in blood-coloured robes with shining faces. And one man held a golden bell in his hand. And the second man held up something shaped like the top of a table. It was like a great jewel, and it was of a blue colour, and there were rivers of silver and of gold running through it and flowing as quick streams flow, and there were pools in it as if violets had been poured out into water, and then it was green as the sea near the shore, and then it was the sky at night with all the stars shining, and then the sun and the moon came down and washed in it. And the third man held up high above this a cup that was like a rose on fire; 'there was a great burning in it, and a dropping of blood in it, and a red cloud above it, and I saw a great secret. And I heard a voice that sang nine times: "Glory and praise to the Conqueror of Death, to the Fountain of Life immortal." Then the red light went from the wall, and it was all darkness, and the bell rang faint again by Capel Teilo, and then I got up and called to you.'

The doctor came on the Monday morning with the death certificate in his pocketbook, and Olwen ran out to meet him. I have quoted his phrase in the first chapter of this record: 'A kind of resurrection of the body.' He made a most careful examination of the girl; he has stated that he found that every trace of disease had disappeared. He left on the Sunday morning a patient entering into the coma that precedes death, a body condemned utterly and ready for the grave. He met at the garden gate on the Monday morning a young woman in whom life sprang up like a fountain, in whose body life laughed and rejoiced as if it had been a river flowing from an unending well.

* * *

Now this is the place to ask one of those questions – there are many such – which cannot be answered. The question is as to the continuance of tradition; more especially as to the continuance of tradition among the Welsh Celts of today. On the one hand, such waves and storms have gone over them. The wave of the heathen Saxons went over them, then the wave of Latin mediaevalism, then the waters of Anglicanism; last of all the flood of their queer Calvinistic Methodism, half Puritan, half pagan. It may well be asked whether any memory can possibly have survived such a series of deluges. I have said that the old people of Llantrisant had their tales of the Bell of Teilo Sant; but these were but vague and broken recollections. And then there is the name by which the 'strangers' who were seen in the marketplace were known; that is more precise. Students of the Graal legend know that the keeper of the Graal in the romances is the 'King Fisherman', or the 'Rich Fisherman'; students of Celtic hagiology know that it was prophesied before the birth of Dewi (or David) that he should be 'a man of aquatic life,' that another legend tells how a little child, destined to be a saint, was discovered on a stone in the river, how through his childhood a fish for his nourishment was found on that stone every day, while another saint, Ilar, if I remember, was expressly known as 'The Fisherman'. But has the memory of all this persisted in the church-going and chapel-going people of Wales at the present day? It is difficult to say. There is the affair of the Healing Cup of Nant Eos, or Tregaron Healing Cup, as it is also called. It is only a few years ago since it was shown to a wandering harper, who treated it lightly, and then spent a wretched night, as he said, and came back penitently and was left alone with the sacred vessel to pray over it, till 'his mind was at rest'. That was in 1887.

Then for my part – I only know modern Wales on the surface, I am sorry to say – I remember three or four years ago speaking to my temporary landlord of certain relics of Saint Teilo, which are supposed to be in the keeping of a particular family in that country. The landlord is a very jovial, merry fellow, and I observed with some astonishment that his ordinary, easy manner was completely altered as he said, gravely, 'That will be over there, up by the mountain,' pointing vaguely to the north. And he changed the subject, as a Freemason changes the subject.

There the matter lies, and its appositeness to the story of Llantrisant is this: that the dream of Olwen Phillips was, in fact, the Vision of the Holy Graal.

VII
The Mass of the Sangraal

'Ffeiriadwyr Melcisidec! Ffeiriadwyr Melcisidec!' shouted the old Calvinistic Methodist deacon with the grey beard. 'Priesthood of Melchizedek!

Priesthood of Melchizedek!'

And he went on:

'The Bell that is like *y glwys yr angel ym mharadwys* – the joy of the angels in Paradise – is returned; the Altar that is of a colour that no men can discern is returned, the Cup that came from Syon is returned, the ancient Offering is restored, the Three Saints have come back to the church of the *tri sant*, the Three Holy Fishermen are amongst us, and their net is full. *Gogoniant, gogoniant* – glory, glory!'

Then another Methodist began to recite in Welsh a verse from Wesley's hymn.

> God still respects Thy sacrifice,
> Its savour sweet doth always please;
> The Offering smokes through earth and skies,
> Diffusing life and joy and peace;
> To these Thy lower courts it comes
> And fills them with Divine perfumes.

The whole church was full, as the old books tell, of the odour of the rarest spiceries. There were lights shining within the sanctuary, through the narrow archway.

This was the beginning of the end of what befell at Llantrisant. For it was the Sunday after that night on which Olwen Phillips had been restored from death to life. There was not a single chapel of the Dissenters open in the town that day. The Methodists with their minister and their deacons and all the Nonconformists had returned on this Sunday morning to 'the old hive'. One would have said, a church of the Middle Ages, a church in Ireland today. Every seat – save those in the chancel – was full, all the aisles were full, the churchyard was full; everyone on his knees, and the old rector kneeling before the door into the holy place.

Yet they can say but very little of what was done beyond the veil. There was no attempt to perform the usual service; when the bells had stopped the old deacon raised his cry, and priest and people fell down on their knees as they thought they heard a choir within singing 'Alleluya, alleluya, alleluya.' And as the bells in the tower ceased ringing, there sounded the thrill of the bell from Syon, and the golden veil of sunlight fell across the door into the altar, and the heavenly voices began their melodies.

A voice like a trumpet cried from within the brightness.

Agyos, Agyos, Agyos.

And the people, as if an age-old memory stirred in them, replied:

Agyos yr Tâd, agyos yr Mab, agyos yr Yspryd Glan. Sant, sant, sant, Drindod sant vendigeid. Sanctus Arglwydd Dduw Sabaoth, Dominus Deus.

There was a voice that cried and sang from within the altar; most of the people had heard some faint echo of it in the chapels; a voice rising and falling and soaring in awful modulations that rang like the trumpet of the Last Angel. The people beat upon their breasts, the tears were like rain of the mountains on their cheeks; those that were able fell down flat on their faces before the glory of the veil. They said afterwards that men of the hills, twenty miles away, heard that cry and that singing, roaring upon them on the wind, and they fell down on their faces, and cried, 'The offering is accomplished,' knowing nothing of what they said.

There were a few who saw three come out of the door of the sanctuary, and stand for a moment on the pace before the door. These three were in dyed vesture, red as blood. One stood before two, looking to the west, and he rang the bell. And they say that all the birds of the wood, and all the waters of the sea, and all the leaves of the trees, and all the winds of the high rocks uttered their voices with the ringing of the bell. And the second and the third; they turned their faces one to another. The second held up the lost altar that they once called Sapphirus, which was like the changing of the sea and of the sky, and like the immixture of gold and silver. And the third heaved up high over the altar a cup that was red with burning and the blood of the offering.

And the old rector cried aloud then before the entrance:

Bendigeid yr Offeren yn oes oesoedd – blessed be the Offering unto the age of ages.

And then the Mass of the Sangraal was ended, and then began the passing out of that land of the holy persons and holy things that had returned to it after the long years. It seemed, indeed, to many that the thrilling sound of the bell was in their ears for days, even for weeks after that Sunday morning. But thenceforth neither bell nor altar nor cup was seen by any one; not openly, that is, but only in dreams by day and by night. Nor did the people see Strangers again in the market of Llantrisant, nor in the lonely places where certain persons oppressed by great affliction and sorrow had once or twice encountered them.

* * *

But that time of visitation will never be forgotten by the people. Many things happened in the nine days that have not been set down in this record – or legend. Some of them were trifling matters, though strange enough in other times. Thus a man in the town who had a fierce dog that was always kept chained up found one day that the beast had become mild and gentle.

And this is stranger: Edward Davies, of Lanafon, a farmer, was roused from sleep one night by a queer yelping and barking in his yard. He looked out of the window and saw his sheepdog playing with a big fox; they were chasing each other by turns, rolling over and over one another, 'cutting such capers as I did never see the like', as the astonished farmer put it. And some of the people said that during this season of wonder the corn shot up, and the grass thickened, and the fruit was multiplied on the trees in a very marvellous manner.

More important, it seemed, was the case of Williams, the grocer; though this may have been a purely natural deliverance. Mr Williams was to marry his daughter Mary to a smart young fellow from Carmarthen, and he was in great distress over it. Not over the marriage itself, but because things had been going very badly with him for some time, and he could not see his way to giving anything like the wedding entertainment that would be expected of him. The wedding was to be on the Saturday – that was the day on which the lawyer, Lewis Prothero, and the farmer, Philip James, were reconciled – and this John Williams, without money or credit, could not think how shame would not be on him for the meagreness and poverty of the wedding feast. And then on the Tuesday came a letter from his brother, David Williams, Australia, from whom he had not heard for fifteen years. And David, it seemed, had been making a great deal of money, and was a bachelor, and here was with his letter a paper good for a thousand pounds: 'You may as well enjoy it now as wait till I am dead.' This was enough, indeed, one might say; but hardly an hour after the letter had come the lady from the big house (Plas Mawr) drove up in all her grandeur, and went into the shop and said, 'Mr Williams, your daughter Mary has always been a very good girl, and my husband and I feel that we must give her some little thing on her wedding, and we hope she'll be very happy.' It was a gold watch worth fifteen pounds. And after Lady Watcyn, advances the old doctor with a dozen of port, forty years upon it, and a long sermon on how to decant it. And the old rector's old wife brings to the beautiful dark girl two yards of creamy lace, like an enchantment, for her wedding veil, and tells Mary how she wore it for her own wedding fifty years ago; and the squire, Sir Watcyn, as if his wife had not been already with a fine gift, calls from his horse, and brings out Williams and barks like a dog at him, 'Goin' to have a weddin', eh, Williams? Can't have a weddin' without champagne, y' know; wouldn't be legal, don't y' know. So look out for a couple of cases.' So Williams tells the story of the gifts; and certainly there was never so famous a wedding in Llantrisant before.

All this, of course, may have been altogether in the natural order; the 'glow,' as they call it, seems more difficult to explain. For they say that all through the nine days, and indeed after the time had ended, there never was a man weary or sick at heart in Llantrisant, or in the country round it. For if a man felt that his work of the body or the mind was going to be too much for his strength, then there would come to him of a sudden a warm glow and a thrilling all over him and he felt as strong as a giant, and happier than he had ever been in his life before, so that lawyer and hedger each rejoiced in the task that was before him, as if it were sport and play.

And much more wonderful than this or any other wonders was forgiveness, with love to follow it. There were meetings of old enemies in the marketplace and in the street that made the people lift up their hands and declare that it was as if one walked the miraculous streets of Syon.

* * *

But as to the 'phenomena', the occurrences for which, in ordinary talk, we should reserve the word 'miraculous'? Well, what do we know? The question that I have already stated comes up again, as to the possible survival of old tradition in a kind of dormant, or torpid, semi-conscious state. In other words, did the people 'see' and 'hear' what they expected to see and hear? This point, or one similar to it, occurred in a debate between Andrew Lang and Anatole France as to the visions of Joan of Arc. M. France stated that when Joan saw St Michael, she saw the traditional archangel of the religious art of her day, but to the best of my belief Andrew Lang proved that the visionary figure Joan described was not in the least like the fifteenth-century conception of St Michael. So, in the case of Llantrisant, I have stated that there was a sort of tradition about the Holy Bell of Teilo Sant; and it is, of course, barely possible that some vague notion of the Graal Cup may have reached even Welsh country folks through Tennyson's *Idylls*. But so far I see no reason to suppose that these people had ever heard of the portable altar (called Sapphirus in William of Malmesbury) or of its changing colours 'that no man could discern'.

And then there are the other questions of the distinction between hallucination and vision, of the average duration of one and the other, and of the possibility of collective hallucination. If a number of people all see (or think they see) the same appearances, can this be merely hallucination? I believe there is a leading case on the matter, which concerns a number of people seeing the same appearance on a church wall in Ireland; but there is, of course, this difficulty, that one may be hallucinated and communicate his impression to the others, telepathically.

But at the last, what do we know?

Out of the Earth

There was some sort of confused complaint during last August of the ill behaviour of the children at certain Welsh watering places. Such reports and vague rumours are most difficult to trace to their heads and fountains; none has better reason to know that than myself. I need not go over the old ground here, but I am afraid that many people are wishing by this time that they had never heard my name; again, a considerable number of estimable persons are concerning themselves gloomily enough, from my point of view, with my everlasting welfare. They write me letters, some in kindly remonstrance, begging me not to deprive poor, sick-hearted souls of what little comfort they possess amidst their sorrows. Others send me tracts and pink leaflets with allusions to 'the daughter of a well-known canon'; others again are violently and anonymously abusive. And then in open print, in fair book form, Mr Begbie has dealt with me righteously but harshly, as I cannot but think.

Yet, it was all so entirely innocent, nay casual, on my part. A poor linnet of prose, I did but perform my indifferent piping in the *Evening News* because I wanted to do so, because I felt that the story of 'The Bowmen' ought to be told. An inventor of fantasies is a poor creature, heaven knows, when all the world is at war; but I thought that no harm would be done, at any rate, if I bore witness, after the fashion of the fantastic craft, to my belief in the heroic glory of the English host who went back from Mons fighting and triumphing.

And then, somehow or other, it was as if I had touched a button and set in action a terrific, complicated mechanism of rumours that pretended to be sworn truth, of gossip that posed as evidence, of wild tarradiddles that good men most firmly believed. The supposed testimony of that 'daughter of a well-known canon' took parish magazines by storm, and equally enjoyed the faith of dissenting divines. The 'daughter' denied all knowledge of the matter, but people still quoted her supposed sure word; and the issues were confused with tales, probably true, of painful hallucinations and deliriums of our retreating soldiers, men fatigued and shattered to the very verge of death. It all became worse than the Russian myths, and as in the fable of the Russians, it seemed impossible to follow the streams of delusion to their fountainhead – or heads. Who was it who said that 'Miss M. knew two officers who, etc., etc.'? I suppose we shall never know his lying, deluding name.

And so, I dare say, it will be with this strange affair of the troublesome children of the Welsh seaside town, or rather of a group of small towns and villages lying within a certain section or zone, which I am not going to indicate more precisely than I can help, since I love that country, and my recent experience with 'The Bowmen' has taught me that no tale is too idle to be believed. And, of course, to begin with, nobody knew how this odd and malicious piece of gossip originated. So far as I know, it was more akin to the Russian myth than to the tale of 'The Angels of Mons'. That is, rumour preceded print; the thing was talked of here and there and passed from letter to letter long before the papers were aware of its existence. And – here it resembles rather the Mons affair – London and Manchester, Leeds and Birmingham were muttering vague unpleasant things while the little villages concerned basked innocently in the sunshine of an unusual prosperity.

In this last circumstance, as some believe, is to be sought the root of the whole matter. It is well known that certain east coast towns suffered from the dread of air raids, and that a good many of their usual visitors went westward for the first time. So there is a theory that the east coast was mean enough to circulate reports against the west coast out of pure malice and envy. It may be so; I do not pretend to know. But here is a personal experience, such as it is, which illustrated the way in which the rumour was circulated. I was lunching one day at my Fleet Street tavern – this was early in July – and a friend of mine, a solicitor, of Serjeants' Inn, came in and sat at the same table. We began to talk of holidays and my friend Eddis asked me where I was going. 'To the same old place,' I said. 'Manavon. You know we always go there.' 'Are you really?' said the lawyer; 'I thought that coast had gone off a lot. My wife has a friend who's heard that it's not at all that it was.'

I was astonished to hear this, not seeing how a little village like Manavon could have 'gone off'. I had known it for ten years as having accommodation for about twenty visitors, and I could not believe that rows of lodging houses had sprung up since the August of 1914. Still I put the question to Eddis: 'Trippers?' I asked, knowing firstly that trippers hate the solitudes of the country and the sea; secondly, that there are no industrial towns within cheap and easy distance, and thirdly, that the railways were issuing no excursion tickets during the war.

'No, not exactly trippers,' the lawyer replied. 'But my wife's friend knows a clergyman who says that the beach at Tremaen is not at all pleasant now, and Tremaen's only a few miles from Manavon, isn't it?'

'In what way not pleasant?' I carried on my examination. 'Pierrots and shows, and that sort of thing?' I felt that it could not be so, for the solemn rocks of Tremaen would have turned the liveliest Pierrot to stone. He would have frozen into a crag on the beach, and the seagulls would carry away his song and make it a lament by lonely, booming caverns that look on Avalon. Eddis said he had heard nothing about showmen; but he understood that since the war the children of the whole district had gone quite out of hand.

'Bad language, you know,' he said, 'and all that sort of thing, worse than London slum children. One doesn't want one's wife and children to hear foul talk at any time, much less on their holiday. And they say that Castell Coch is quite impossible; no decent woman would be seen there!'

I said: 'Really, that's a great pity,' and changed the subject. But I could not make it out at all. I knew Castell Coch well – a little bay bastioned by dunes and red sandstone cliffs, rich with greenery. A stream of cold water runs down there to the sea; there is the ruined Norman Castle, the ancient church and the scattered village; it is altogether a place of peace and quiet and great beauty. The people there, children and grown-ups alike, were not merely decent but courteous folk: if one thanked a child for opening a gate, there would come the inevitable response: 'And welcome kindly, sir.' I could not make it out at all. I didn't believe the lawyer's tales; for the life of me I could not see what he could be driving at. And, for the avoidance of all unnecessary mystery, I may as well say that my wife and child and myself went down to Manavon last August and had a most delightful holiday. At the time we were certainly conscious of no annoyance or unpleasantness of any kind. Afterwards, I confess, I heard a story that puzzled and still puzzles me, and this story, if it be received, might give its own interpretation to one or two circumstances which seemed in themselves quite insignificant.

But all through July I came upon traces of evil rumours affecting this most gracious corner of the earth. Some of these rumours were repetitions of Eddis's gossip; others amplified his vague story and made it more definite. Of course, no first-hand evidence was available. There never is any first-hand evidence in these cases. But A knew B who had heard from C that her second cousin's little girl had been set upon and beaten by a pack of young Welsh savages. Then people quoted 'a doctor in large practice in a well-known town in the Midlands', to the effect that Tremaen was a sink of juvenile depravity. They said that a responsible medical man's evidence was final and convincing; but they didn't bother to find out who the doctor was, or whether there was any doctor at all – or any doctor relevant to the issue. Then the thing began to get into the papers in a sort of oblique, by-the-way sort of manner. People cited the case of these imaginary bad children in support of their educational views. One side said that 'these unfortunate little ones' would have been quite well behaved if they had had no education at all; the opposition declared that continuation schools would speedily reform them and make them into admirable citizens. Then the poor Arfonshire children seemed to become involved in quarrels about Welsh disestablishment and in the question of the miners; and all the while they were going about behaving politely and admirably as they always do behave. I knew all the time that it was all nonsense, but I couldn't understand in the least what it meant, or who was pulling the wires of rumour, or their purpose in so pulling. I began to wonder whether the pressure and anxiety and suspense of a terrible war had unhinged the public mind, so that it was ready to believe any fable, to debate the reasons for happenings which had never happened. At last, quite incredible things began to be whispered: visitors' children had not only been beaten, they had been tortured; a little boy had been found impaled on a stake in a lonely field near Manavon; another child had been lured to destruction over the cliffs at Castell Coch. A London paper sent a good man down quietly to Arfon to investigate. He was away for a week, and at the end of that period returned to his office and in his own phrase, 'threw the whole story down'. There was not a word of truth, he said, in any of these rumours; no vestige of a foundation for the mildest forms of all this gossip. He had never seen such a beautiful country; he had never met pleasanter men, women or children; there was not a single case of anyone having been annoyed or troubled in any sort or fashion.

Yet all the while the story grew, and grew more monstrous and incredible. I was too much occupied in watching the progress of my own mythological monster to pay much attention. The town clerk of Tremaen, to which the legend had at length penetrated, wrote a brief letter to the press indignantly denying that there was the slightest foundation for 'the unsavoury rumours' which, he understood, were being circulated; and about this time we went down to Manavon and, as I say, enjoyed ourselves extremely. The weather was perfect: blues of paradise in the skies, the seas all a shimmering wonder, olive greens and emeralds, rich purples, glassy sapphires changing by the rocks; far away a haze of magic lights and colours at the meeting of sea and sky. Work and anxiety had harried me; I found nothing better than to rest on the thymy banks by the shore, finding an infinite balm and refreshment in the great sea before me, in the tiny flowers beside me. Or we would rest all the summer afternoon on a 'shelf' high on the grey cliffs and watch the tide creaming and surging about the rocks, and listen to it booming in the hollows and caverns below. Afterwards, as I say, there were one or two things that struck cold. But at the time those were nothing. You see a man in an odd white hat pass by and think little or nothing about it. Afterwards, when you hear that a man wearing just such a hat had committed murder in the next street five minutes before, then you find in that hat a certain interest and significance. 'Funny children,' was the phrase my little boy used; and I began to think they were 'funny' indeed.

If there be a key at all to this queer business, I think it is to be found in a talk I had not long ago with a friend of mine named Morgan. He is a Welshman and a dreamer, and some people say he is like a child who has grown up and yet has not grown up like other children of men. Though I did not know it, while I was at Manavon, he was spending his holiday time at Castell Coch. He was a lonely man and he liked lonely places, and when we met in the autumn he told me how, day after day, he would carry his bread and cheese and beer in a basket to a remote headland on that coast known as the Old Camp. Here, far above the waters, are solemn, mighty walls, turf-grown; circumvallations rounded and smooth with the passing of many thousand years. At one end of this most ancient place there is a tumulus, a tower of observation, perhaps, and underneath it slinks the green, deceiving ditch that seems to wind into the heart of the camp, but in reality rushes down to sheer rock and a precipice over the waters.

Here came Morgan daily, as he said, to dream of Avalon, to purge himself from the fuming corruption of the streets.

And so, as he told me, it was with singular horror that one afternoon as he dozed and dreamed and opened his eyes now and again to watch the miracle and magic of the sea, as he listened to the myriad murmurs of the waves, his meditation was broken by a sudden burst of horrible raucous cries – and the cries of children, too, but children of the lowest type. Morgan says that the very tones made him shudder – 'They were to the ear what slime is to the touch,' and then the words: every foulness, every filthy abomination of speech; blasphemies that struck like blows at the sky, that sank down into the pure, shining depths, defiling them! He was amazed. He peered over the green wall of the fort, and there in the ditch he saw a swarm of noisome children, horrible little stunted creatures with old men's faces, with bloated faces, with little sunken eyes, with leering eyes. It was worse than uncovering a brood of snakes or a nest of worms.

No; he would not describe what they were about. 'Read about Belgium,' said Morgan, 'and think they couldn't have been more than five or six years old.' There was no infamy, he said, that they did not perpetrate; they spared no horror of cruelty. 'I saw blood running in streams, as they shrieked with laughter, but I could not find the mark of it on the grass afterwards.'

Morgan said he watched them and could not utter a word; it was as if a hand held his mouth tight. But at last he found his voice and shrieked at them, and they burst into a yell of obscene laughter and shrieked back at him, and scattered out of sight. He could not trace them; he supposes that they hid in the deep bracken behind the Old Camp.

'Sometimes I can't understand my landlord at Castell Coch,' Morgan went on. 'He's the village postmaster and has a little farm of his own – a decent, pleasant, ordinary sort of chap. But now and again he will talk oddly. I was telling him about these beastly children and wondering who they could be when he broke into Welsh, something like "the battle that is for age unto ages; and the People take delight in it."'

So far Morgan, and it was evident that he did not understand at all. But this strange tale of his brought back an odd circumstance or two that I recollected: a matter of our little boy straying away more than once, and getting lost among the sand dunes and coming back screaming, evidently frightened horribly, and babbling about 'funny children'. We took no notice; did not trouble, I think, to look whether there were any children wandering about the dunes or not. We were accustomed to his small imaginations.

But after hearing Morgan's story I was interested and I wrote an account of the matter to my friend, old Doctor Duthoit, of Hereford. And he:

'They were only visible, only audible to children and the childlike. Hence the explanation of what puzzled you at first; the rumours, how did they arise? They arose from nursery gossip, from scraps and odds and ends of half-articulate children's talk of horrors that they didn't understand, of words that shamed their nurses and their mothers.

'These little people of the earth rise up and rejoice in these times of ours. For they are glad, as the Welshman said, when they know that men follow their ways.'

The Terror

I
The Coming of the Terror

After two years we are turning once more to the morning's news with a sense of appetite and glad expectation. There were thrills at the beginning of the war; the thrill of horror and of a doom that seemed at once incredible and certain; this was when Namur fell and the German host swelled like a flood over the French fields, and drew very near to the walls of Paris. Then we felt the thrill of exultation when the good news came that the awful tide had been turned back, that Paris and the world were safe; for a while at all events.

Then for days we hoped for more news as good as this or better. Has Von Kluck been surrounded? Not today, but perhaps he will be surrounded tomorrow. But the days became weeks, the weeks drew out to months; the battle in the West seemed frozen. Now and again things were done that seemed hopeful, with promise of events still better. But Neuve Chapelle and Loos dwindled into disappointments as their tale was told fully; the lines in the West remained, for all practical purposes of victory, immobile. Nothing seemed to happen; there was nothing to read save the record of operations that were clearly trifling and insignificant. People speculated as to the reason of this inaction; the hopeful said that Joffre had a plan, that he was 'nibbling', others declared that we were short of munitions, others again that the new levies were not yet ripe for battle. So the months went by, and almost two years of war had been completed before the motionless English line began to stir and quiver as if it awoke from a long sleep, and began to roll onward, overwhelming the enemy.

The secret of the long inaction of the British Armies has been well kept. On the one hand it was rigorously protected by the censorship, which severe, and sometimes severe to the point of absurdity – 'the captains and the . . . depart,' for instance – became in this particular matter ferocious. As soon as the real significance of that which was happening, or beginning to happen, was perceived by the authorities, an underlined circular was issued to the newspaper proprietors of Great Britain and Ireland. It warned each proprietor that he might impart the contents of this circular to one other person only, such person being the responsible editor of his paper, who was to keep the communication secret under the severest penalties. The circular forbade any mention of certain events that had taken place, that might take place; it forbade any kind of allusion to these events or any hint of their existence, or of the possibility of their existence, not only in the Press, but in any form whatever. The subject was not to be alluded to in conversation, it was not to be hinted at, however obscurely, in letters; the very existence of the circular, its subject apart, was to be a dead secret.

These measures were successful. A wealthy newspaper proprietor of the North, warmed a little at the end of the Throwsters' Feast (which was held as usual, it will be remembered), ventured to say to the man next to him: 'How awful it would be, wouldn't it, if . . . ' His words were repeated, as proof, one regrets to say, that it was time for 'old Arnold' to 'pull himself together'; and he was fined a thousand pounds. Then, there was the case of an obscure weekly paper published in the county town of an agricultural district in Wales. The *Meiros Observer* (we will call it) was issued from a stationer's back premises, and filled its four pages with accounts of local flower shows, fancy fairs at vicarages, reports of parish councils, and rare bathing fatalities. It also issued a visitors' list, which has been known to contain six names.

This enlightened organ printed a paragraph, which nobody noticed, which was very like paragraphs that small country newspapers have long been in the habit of printing, which could hardly give so much as a hint to any one – to any one, that is, who was not fully instructed in the secret. As a matter of fact, this piece of intelligence got into the paper because the proprietor, who was also the editor, incautiously left the last processes of this particular issue to the staff, who was the Lord-High-Everything-Else of the establishment; and the staff put in a bit of gossip he had heard in the market to fill up two inches on the back page. But the result was that the *Meiros*

Observer ceased to appear, owing to 'untoward circumstances' as the proprietor said; and he would say no more. No more, that is, by way of explanation, but a great deal more by way of execration of 'damned, prying busybodies'.

Now a censorship that is sufficiently minute and utterly remorseless can do amazing things in the way of hiding . . . what it wants to hide. Before the war, one would have thought otherwise; one would have said that, censor or no censor, the fact of the murder at X or the fact of the bank robbery at Y would certainly become known; if not through the Press, at all events through rumour and the passage of the news from mouth to mouth. And this would be true – of England three hundred years ago, and of savage tribelands of today. But we have grown of late to such a reverence for the printed word and such a reliance on it, that the old faculty of disseminating news by word of mouth has become atrophied. Forbid the Press to mention the fact that Jones has been murdered, and it is marvellous how few people will hear of it, and of those who hear how few will credit the story that they have heard. You meet a man in the train who remarks that he has been told something about a murder in Southwark; there is all the difference in the world between the impression you receive from such a chance communication and that given by half a dozen lines of print with name, and street and date and all the facts of the case. People in trains repeat all sorts of tales, many of them false; newspapers do not print accounts of murders that have not been committed.

Then another consideration that has made for secrecy. I may have seemed to say that the old office of rumour no longer exists; I shall be reminded of the strange legend of 'the Russians' and the mythology of the 'Angels of Mons'. But let me point out, in the first place, that both these absurdities depended on the papers for their wide dissemination. If there had been no newspapers or magazines Russians and Angels would have made but a brief, vague appearance of the most shadowy kind – a few would have heard of them, fewer still would have believed in them, they would have been gossiped about for a bare week or two, and so they would have vanished away.

And, then, again, the very fact of these vain rumours and fantastic tales having been so widely believed for a time was fatal to the credit of any stray mutterings that may have got abroad. People had been taken in twice; they had seen how grave persons, men of credit, had preached and lectured about the shining forms that had saved the British Army at Mons, or had testified to the trains, packed with gray-coated Muscovites, rushing through the land at dead of night: and now there was a hint of something more amazing than either of the discredited legends. But this time there was no word of confirmation to be found in daily paper, or weekly review, or parish magazine, and so the few that heard either laughed, or, being serious, went home and jotted down notes for essays on 'Wartime Psychology: Collective Delusions'.

I followed neither of these courses. For before the secret circular had been issued my curiosity had somehow been aroused by certain paragraphs concerning a 'Fatal Accident to Well-known Airman'. The propeller of the airplane had been shattered, apparently by a collision with a flight of pigeons; the blades had been broken and the machine had fallen like lead to the earth. And soon after I had seen this account, I heard of some very odd circumstances relating to an explosion in a great munition factory in the Midlands. I thought I saw the possibility of a connection between two very different events.

It has been pointed out to me by friends who have been good enough to read this record, that certain phrases I have used may give the impression that I ascribe all the delays of the war on the Western front to the extraordinary circumstances which occasioned the issue of the Secret Circular. Of course this is not the case, there were many reasons for the immobility of our lines from October 1914 to July 1916. These causes have been evident enough and have been openly discussed and deplored. But behind them was something of infinitely greater moment. We lacked men, but men were pouring into the new army; we were short of shells, but when the shortage was proclaimed the nation set itself to mend this matter with all its energy. We could undertake to supply the defects of our army both in men and munitions – if the new and incredible danger could be overcome. It has been overcome; rather, perhaps, it has ceased to exist; and the secret may now be told.

I have said my attention was attracted by an account of the death of a well-known airman. I have not the habit of preserving cuttings, I am sorry to say, so that I cannot be precise as to the date of this event. To the best of my belief it was either towards the end of May or the beginning of June 1915. The newspaper paragraph announcing the death of Flight-Lieutenant Western-Reynolds was brief enough; accidents, and fatal accidents, to the men who are storming the air for us are, unfortunately, by no means so rare as to demand an elaborated notice. But the manner in which Western-Reynolds met his death struck me as extraordinary, inasmuch as it revealed a new danger in the element that we have lately conquered. He was brought down, as I said, by a flight of birds; of pigeons, as appeared by what was found on the bloodstained and shattered blades of the propeller. An eye-witness of the accident, a fellow officer, described how Western-Reynolds set out from the aerodrome on a fine afternoon, there being hardly any wind. He was going to France; he had made the journey to and fro half a dozen times or more, and felt perfectly secure and at ease.

'"Wester" rose to a great height at once, and we could scarcely see the machine. I was turning to go when one of the fellows called out, "I say! What's this?" He pointed up, and we saw what looked like a black cloud coming from the south at a tremendous rate. I saw at once it wasn't a cloud; it came with a swirl and a rush quite different from any cloud I've ever seen. But for a second I couldn't make out exactly what it was. It altered its shape and turned into a great crescent, and wheeled and veered about as if it was looking for something. The man who had called out had got his glasses, and was staring for all he was worth. Then he shouted that it was a tremendous flight of birds, "thousands of them". They went on wheeling and beating about high up in the air, and we were watching them, thinking it was interesting, but not supposing that they would make any difference to "Wester", who was just about out of sight. His machine was just a speck. Then the two arms of the crescent drew in as quick as lightning, and these thousands of birds shot in a solid mass right up there across the sky, and flew away somewhere about nor'-nor'-by-west. Then Henley, the man with the glasses, called out, "He's down!" and started running, and I went after him. We got a car and as we were going along Henley told me that he'd seen the machine drop dead, as if it came out of that cloud of birds. He thought then that they must have mucked up the propeller somehow. That turned out to be the case. We found the propeller blades all broken and covered with blood and pigeon feathers, and carcasses of the birds had got wedged in between the blades, and were sticking to them.'

This was the story that the young airman told one evening in a small company. He did not speak 'in confidence', so I have no hesitation in reproducing what he said. Naturally, I did not take a verbatim note of his conversation, but I have something of a knack of remembering talk that interests me, and I think my reproduction is very near to the tale that I heard. And let it be noted that the flying man told his story without any sense or indication of a sense that the incredible, or all but the incredible, had happened. So far as he knew, he said, it was the first accident of the kind. Airmen in France had been bothered once or twice by birds – he thought they were eagles – flying viciously at them, but poor old 'Wester' had been the first man to come up against a flight of some thousands of pigeons.

'And perhaps I shall be the next,' he added, 'but why look for trouble? Anyhow, I'm going to see *Toodle-oo* tomorrow afternoon.'

Well, I heard the story, as one hears all the varied marvels and terrors of the air; as one heard some years ago of 'air pockets', strange gulfs or voids in the atmosphere into which airmen fell with great peril; or as one heard of the experience of the airman who flew over the Cumberland mountains in the burning summer of 1911, and as he swam far above the heights was suddenly and vehemently blown upwards, the hot air from the rocks striking his plane as if it had been a blast from a furnace chimney. We have just begun to navigate a strange region; we must expect to encounter strange adventures, strange perils. And here a new chapter in the chronicles of these perils and adventures had been opened by the death of Western-Reynolds; and no doubt invention and contrivance would presently hit on some way of countering the new danger.

It was, I think, about a week or ten days after the airman's death that my business called me to a northern town, the name of which, perhaps, had better remain unknown. My mission was to inquire into certain charges of extravagance which had been laid against the working people, that is, the munition workers of this especial town. It was said that the men who used to earn £2 10s. a week were now getting from seven to eight pounds, that 'bits of girls' were being paid two pounds instead of seven or eight shillings, and that, in consequence, there was an orgy of foolish extravagance. The girls, I was told, were eating chocolates at four, five, and six shillings a pound, the women were ordering thirty-pound pianos which they couldn't play, and the men bought gold chains at ten and twenty guineas apiece.

I dived into the town in question and found, as usual, that there was a mixture of truth and exaggeration in the stories that I had heard. Gramophones, for example: they cannot be called in strictness necessaries, but they were undoubtedly finding a ready sale, even in the more expensive brands. And I thought that there were a great many very spick and span perambulators to be seen on the pavement; smart perambulators, painted in tender shades of colour and expensively fitted.

'And how can you be surprised if people will have a bit of a fling?' a worker said to me. 'We're seeing money for the first time in our lives, and it's bright. And we work hard for it, and we risk our lives to get it. You've heard of the explosion yonder?'

He mentioned certain works on the outskirts of the town. Of course, neither the name of the works nor of the town had been printed; there had been a brief notice of 'Explosion at Munition Works in the Northern District: Many Fatalities'. The working man told me about it, and added some dreadful details.

'They wouldn't let their folks see bodies; screwed them up in coffins as they found them in shop. The gas had done it.'

'Turned their faces black, you mean?'

'Nay. They were all as if they had been bitten to pieces.'

This was a strange gas.

I asked the man in the northern town all sorts of questions about the extraordinary explosion of which he had spoken to me. But he had very little more to say. As I have noted already, secrets that may not be printed are often deeply kept; last summer there were very few people outside high official circles who knew anything about the 'Tanks', of which we have all been talking lately, though these strange instruments of war were being exercised and tested in a park not far from London. So the man who told me of the explosion in the munition factory was most likely genuine in his profession that he knew nothing more of the disaster. I found out that he was a smelter employed at a furnace on the other side of the town to the ruined factory; he didn't know even what they had been making there; some very dangerous high explosive, he supposed. His information was really nothing more than a bit of gruesome gossip, which he had heard probably at third or fourth or fifth hand. The horrible detail of faces 'as if they had been bitten to pieces' had made its violent impression on him, that was all.

I gave him up and took a tram to the district of the disaster; a sort of industrial suburb, five miles from the centre of the town. When I asked for the factory, I was told that it was no good my going to it as there was nobody there. But I found it; a raw and hideous shed with a walled yard about it, and a shut gate. I looked for signs of destruction, but there was nothing. The roof was quite undamaged; and again it struck me that this had been a strange accident. There had been an explosion of sufficient violence to kill workpeople in the building, but the building itself showed no wounds or scars.

A man came out of the gate and locked it behind him. I began to ask him some sort of question, or rather, I began to 'open' for a question with 'A terrible business here, they tell me,' or some such phrase of convention. I got no farther. The man asked me if I saw a policeman walking down the street. I said I did, and I was given the choice of getting about my business forthwith or of being instantly given in charge as a spy. 'Th'ast better be gone and quick about it,' was, I think, his final advice, and I took it.

Well, I had come literally up against a brick wall. Thinking the problem over, I could only suppose that the smelter or his informant had twisted the phrases of the story. The smelter had said the dead men's faces were 'bitten to pieces'; this might be an unconscious perversion of 'eaten away'. That phrase might describe well enough the effect of strong acids, and, for all I knew of the processes of munition-making, such acids might be used and might explode with horrible results in some perilous stage of their admixture.

It was a day or two later that the accident to the airman, Western-Reynolds, came into my mind. For one of those instants which are far shorter than any measure of time there flashed out the possibility of a link between the two disasters. But here was a wild impossibility, and I drove it away. And yet I think that the thought, mad as it seemed, never left me; it was the secret light that at last guided me through a sombre grove of enigmas.

It was about this time, so far as the date can be fixed, that a whole district, one might say a whole county, was visited by a series of extraordinary and terrible calamities, which were the more terrible inasmuch as they continued for some time to be inscrutable mysteries. It is, indeed, doubtful whether these awful events do not still remain mysteries to many of those concerned; for before the inhabitants of this part of the country had time to join one link of evidence to another the circular was issued, and thenceforth no one knew how to distinguish undoubted fact from wild and extravagant surmise.

The district in question is in the far west of Wales; I shall call it, for convenience, Meirion. In it there is one seaside town of some repute with holidaymakers for five or six weeks in the summer, and dotted about the county there are three or four small old towns that seem drooping in a slow decay, sleepy and grey with age and forgetfulness. They remind me of what I have read of towns in the west of Ireland. Grass grows between the uneven stones of the pavements, the signs above the shop windows decline, half the letters of these signs are missing, here and there a house has been pulled down, or has been allowed to slide into ruin, and wild greenery springs up through the fallen stones, and there is silence in all the streets. And, it is to be noted, these are not places that were once magnificent. The Celts have never had the art of building, and so far as I can see, such towns as Towy and Merthyr Tegveth and Meiros must have been always much as they are now, clusters of poorish, meanly-built houses, ill-kept and down at heel.

And these few towns are thinly scattered over a wild country where north is divided from south by a wilder mountain range. One of these places is sixteen miles from any station; the others are doubtfully and deviously connected by single-line railways served by rare trains that pause and stagger and hesitate on their slow journey up mountain passes, or stop for half an hour or more at lonely sheds called stations, situated in the midst of desolate marshes. A few years ago I travelled with an Irishman on one of these queer lines, and he looked to right and saw the bog with its yellow and blue grasses and stagnant pools, and he looked to left and saw a ragged hillside, set with gray stone walls. 'I can hardly believe,' he said, 'that I'm not still in the wilds of Ireland.'

Here, then, one sees a wild and divided and scattered region, a land of outland hills and secret and hidden valleys. I know white farms on this coast which must be separate by two hours of hard, rough walking from any other habitation, which are invisible from any other house. And inland, again, the farms are often ringed about by thick groves of ash, planted by men of old days to shelter their roof trees from rude winds of the mountain and stormy winds of the sea; so that these places, too, are hidden away, to be surmised only by the wood smoke that rises from the green surrounding leaves. A Londoner must see them to believe in them; and even then he can scarcely credit their utter isolation.

Such, then in the main is Meirion, and on this land in the early summer of last year terror descended – a terror without shape, such as no man there had ever known.

It began with the tale of a little child who wandered out into the lanes to pick flowers one sunny afternoon, and never came back to the cottage on the hill.

II
Death in the Village

The child who was lost came from a lonely cottage that stands on the slope of a steep hillside called the Allt, or the height. The land about it is wild and ragged; here the growth of gorse and bracken, here a marshy hollow of reeds and rushes, marking the course of the stream from some hidden well, here thickets of dense and tangled undergrowth, the outposts of the wood. Down through this broken and uneven ground a path leads to the lane at the bottom of the valley; then the land rises again and swells up to the cliffs over the sea, about a quarter of a mile away. The little girl, Gertrude Morgan, asked her mother if she might go down to the lane and pick the purple flowers – these were orchids – that grew there, and her mother gave her leave, telling her she must be sure to be back by teatime, as there was apple tart for tea.

She never came back. It was supposed that she must have crossed the road and gone to the cliff's edge, possibly in order to pick the sea pinks that were then in full blossom. She must have slipped, they said, and fallen into the sea, two hundred feet below. And, it may be said at once, that there was no doubt some truth in this conjecture, though it stopped very far short of the whole truth. The child's body must have been carried out by the tide, for it was never found.

The conjecture of a false step or of a fatal slide on the slippery turf that slopes down to the rocks was accepted as being the only explanation possible. People thought the accident a strange one because, as a rule, country children living by the cliffs and the sea become wary at an early age, and Gertrude Morgan was almost ten years old. Still, as the neighbours said, 'that's how it must have happened, and it's a great pity, to be sure.' But this would not do when in a week's time a strong young labourer failed to come to his cottage after the day's work. His body was found on the rocks six or seven miles from the cliffs where the child was supposed to have fallen; he was going home by a path that he had used every night of his life for eight or nine years, that he used of dark nights in perfect security, knowing every inch of it. The police asked if he drank, but he was a teetotaller; if he were subject to fits, but he wasn't. And he was not murdered for his wealth, since agricultural labourers are not wealthy. It was only possible again to talk of slippery turf and a false step; but people began to be frightened. Then a woman was found with her neck broken at the bottom of a disused quarry near Llanfihangel, in the middle of the county. The 'false step' theory was eliminated here, for the quarry was guarded with a natural hedge of gorse bushes. One would have to struggle and fight through sharp thorns to destruction in such a place as this; and indeed the gorse bushes were broken as if some one had rushed furiously through them, just above the place where the woman's body was found. And this was strange: there was a dead sheep lying beside her in the pit, as if the woman and the sheep together had been chased over the brim of the quarry. But chased by whom, or by what? And then there was a new form of terror.

This was in the region of the marshes under the mountain. A man and his son, a lad of fourteen or fifteen, set out early one morning to work and never reached the farm where they were bound. Their way skirted the marsh, but it was broad, firm and well metalled, and it had been raised about two feet above the bog. But when search was made in the evening of the same day Phillips and his son were found dead in the marsh, covered with black slime and pondweed. And they lay some ten yards from the path, which, it would seem, they must have left deliberately. It was useless of course, to look for tracks in the black ooze, for if one threw a big stone into it a few seconds removed all marks of the disturbance. The men who found the two bodies beat about the verges and purlieus of the marsh in hope of finding some trace of the murderers; they went to and fro over the rising ground where the black cattle were grazing, they searched the alder thickets by the brook; but they discovered nothing.

Most horrible of all these horrors, perhaps, was the affair of the Highway, a lonely and unfrequented by-road that winds for many miles on high and lonely land. Here, a mile from any other dwelling, stands a cottage on the edge of a dark wood. It was inhabited by a labourer named Williams, his wife, and their three children. One hot summer's evening, a man who had been doing a day's gardening at a rectory three or four miles away, passed the cottage, and stopped for a few minutes to chat with Williams, the labourer, who was pottering about his garden, while the children were playing on the path by the door. The two talked of their neighbours and of the potatoes till Mrs Williams appeared at the doorway and said supper was ready, and Williams turned to go into the house. This was about eight o'clock, and in the ordinary course the family would have their supper and be in bed by nine, or by half-past nine at latest. At ten o'clock that night the local doctor was driving home along the Highway. His horse shied violently and then stopped dead just opposite the gate to the cottage. The doctor got down, frightened at what he saw; and there on the roadway lay Williams, his wife, and the three children, stone dead, all of them. Their skulls were battered in as if by some heavy iron instrument; their faces were beaten into a pulp.

III
The Doctor's Theory

It is not easy to make any picture of the horror that lay dark on the hearts of the people of Meirion. It was no longer possible to believe or to pretend to believe that these men and women and children had met their deaths through strange accidents. The little girl and the young labourer might have slipped and fallen over the cliffs, but the woman who lay dead with the dead sheep at the bottom of the quarry, the two men who had been lured into the ooze of the marsh, the family who were found murdered on the Highway before their own cottage door; in these cases there could be no room for the supposition of accident. It seemed as if it were impossible to frame any conjecture or outline of a conjecture that would account for these hideous and, as it seemed, utterly purposeless crimes. For a time people said that there must be a madman at large, a sort of country variant of Jack the Ripper, some horrible pervert who was possessed by the passion of death, who prowled darkling about that lonely land, hiding in woods and in wild places, always watching and seeking for the victims of his desire.

Indeed, Dr Lewis, who found poor Williams, his wife and children miserably slaughtered on the Highway, was convinced at first that the presence of a concealed madman in the countryside offered the only possible solution to the difficulty.

'I felt sure,' he said to me afterwards, 'that the Williamses had been killed by a homicidal maniac. It was the nature of the poor creatures' injuries that convinced me that this was the case. Some years ago – thirty-seven or thirty-eight years ago as a matter of fact – I had something to do with a case which on the face of it had a strong likeness to the Highway murder. At that time I had a practice at Usk, in Monmouthshire. A whole family living in a cottage by the roadside were murdered one evening; it was called, I think, the Llangibby murder; the cottage was near the village of that name. The murderer was caught in Newport; he was a Spanish sailor, named Garcia, and it appeared that he had killed father, mother, and the three children for the sake of the brass works of an old Dutch clock, which were found on him when he was arrested.

'Garcia had been serving a month's imprisonment in Usk Jail for some small theft, and on his release he set out to walk to Newport, nine or ten miles away; no doubt to get another ship. He passed the cottage and saw the man working in his garden. Garcia stabbed him with his sailor's knife. The wife rushed out; he stabbed her. Then he went into the cottage and stabbed the three children, tried to set the place on fire, and made off with the clockworks. That looked like the deed of a madman, but Garcia wasn't mad – they hanged him, I may say – he was merely a man of a very low type, a degenerate who hadn't the slightest value for human life. I am not sure, but I think he came from one of the Spanish islands, where the people are said to be degenerates, very likely from too much interbreeding.

'But my point is that Garcia stabbed to kill and did kill, with one blow in each case. There was no senseless hacking and slashing. Now those poor people on the Highway had their heads smashed to pieces by what must have been a storm of blows. Any one of them would have been fatal, but the murderer must have gone on raining blows with his iron hammer on people who were already stone dead. And *that* sort of thing is the work of a madman, and nothing but a madman. That's how I argued the matter out to myself just after the event.

'I was utterly wrong, monstrously wrong. But who could have suspected the truth?'

Thus Dr Lewis, and I quote him, or the substance of him, as representative of most of the educated opinion of the district at the beginnings of the terror. People seized on this theory largely because it offered at least the comfort of an explanation, and any explanation, even the poorest, is better than an intolerable and terrible mystery. Besides, Dr Lewis's theory was plausible; it explained the lack of purpose that seemed to characterise the murders. And yet – there were difficulties even from the first. It was hardly possible that a strange madman should be able to keep hidden in a countryside where any stranger is instantly noted and noticed; sooner or later he would be seen as he prowled along the lanes or across the wild places. Indeed, a drunken, cheerful, and altogether harmless tramp was arrested by a farmer and his man in the fact and act of sleeping off beer under a hedge; but the vagrant was able to prove complete and undoubted alibis, and was soon allowed to go on his wandering way.

Then another theory, or rather a variant of Dr Lewis's theory, was started. This was to the effect that the person responsible for the outrages was, indeed, a madman; but a madman only at intervals. It was one of the members of the Porth Club, a certain Mr Remnant, who was supposed to have originated this more subtle explanation. Mr Remnant was a middle-aged man, who, having nothing particular to do, read a great many books by way of conquering the hours. He talked to the club – doctors, retired colonels, parsons, lawyers – about 'personality', quoted various psychological textbooks in support of his contention that personality was sometimes fluid and unstable, went back to 'Dr Jekyll and Mr Hyde' as good evidence of this proposition, and laid stress on Dr Jekyll's speculation that the human soul, so far from being one and indivisible, might possibly turn out to be a mere polity, a state in which dwelt many strange and incongruous citizens, whose characters were not merely unknown but altogether unsurmised by that form of consciousness which so rashly assumed that it was not only the president of the republic but also its sole citizen.

'The long and the short of it is,' Mr Remnant concluded, 'that any one of us may be the murderer, though he hasn't the faintest notion of the fact. Take Llewelyn there.'

Mr Payne Llewelyn was an elderly lawyer, a rural Tulkinghorn. He was the hereditary solicitor to the Morgans of Pentwyn. This does not sound anything tremendous to the Saxons of London; but the style is far more than noble to the Celts of West Wales; it is immemorial; Teilo Sant was of the collaterals of the first known chief of the race. And Mr Payne Llewelyn did his best to look like the legal adviser of this ancient house. He was weighty, he was cautious, he was sound, he was secure. I have compared him to Mr Tulkinghorn of Lincoln's Inn Fields; but

Mr Llewelyn would most certainly never have dreamed of employing his leisure in peering into the cupboards where the family skeletons were hidden. Supposing such cupboards to have existed, Mr Payne Llewelyn would have risked large out-of-pocket expenses to furnish them with double, triple, impregnable locks. He was a new man, an *advena*, certainly; for he was partly of the Conquest, being descended on one side from Sir Payne Turberville; but he meant to stand by the old stock.

'Take Llewelyn now,' said Mr Remnant. 'Look here, Llewelyn, can you produce evidence to show where you were on the night those people were murdered on the Highway? I thought not.'

Mr Llewelyn, an elderly man, as I have said, hesitated before speaking.

'I thought not,' Remnant went on. 'Now I say that it is perfectly possible that Llewelyn may be dealing death throughout Meirion, although in his present personality he may not have the faintest suspicion that there is another Llewelyn within him, a Llewelyn who follows murder as a fine art.'

Mr Payne Llewelyn did not at all relish Mr Remnant's suggestion that he might well be a secret murderer, ravening for blood, remorseless as a wild beast. He thought the phrase about his following murder as a fine art was both nonsensical and in the worst taste, and his opinion was not changed when Remnant pointed out that it was used by De Quincey in the title of one of his most famous essays.

'If you had allowed me to speak,' he said with some coldness of manner, 'I would have told you that on Tuesday last, the night on which those unfortunate people were murdered on the Highway, I was staying at the Angel Hotel, Cardiff. I had business in Cardiff, and I was detained till Wednesday afternoon.'

Having given this satisfactory alibi, Mr Payne Llewelyn left the club, and did not go near it for the rest of the week.

Remnant explained to those who stayed in the smoking room that, of course, he had merely used Mr Llewelyn as a concrete example of his theory, which, he persisted, had the support of a considerable body of evidence.

'There are several cases of double personality on record,' he declared. 'And I say again that it is quite possible that these murders may have been committed by one of us in his secondary personality. Why, I may be the murderer in my Remnant B. state, though Remnant A. knows nothing whatever about it, and is perfectly convinced that he could not kill a fowl, much less a whole family. Isn't it so, Lewis?'

Dr Lewis said it was so, in theory, but he thought not in fact.

'Most of the cases of double or multiple personality that have been investigated,' he said, 'have been in connection with the very dubious experiments of hypnotism, or the still more dubious experiments of spiritualism. All that sort of thing, in my opinion, is like tinkering with the works of a clock – amateur tinkering, I mean. You fumble about with the wheels and cogs and bits of mechanism that you don't really know anything about; and then you find your clock going backwards or striking 240 at teatime. And I believe it's just the same thing with these psychical research experiments; the secondary personality is very likely the result of the tinkering and fumbling with a very delicate apparatus that we know nothing about. Mind, I can't say that it's impossible for one of us to be the Highway murderer in his B. state, as Remnant puts it. But I think it's extremely improbable. Probability is the guide of life, you know, Remnant,' said Dr Lewis, smiling at that gentleman, as if to say that he also had done a little reading in his day. 'And it follows, therefore, that improbability is also the guide of life. When you get a very high degree of probability, that is, you are justified in taking it as a certainty; and on the other hand, if a supposition is highly improbable, you are justified in treating it as an impossible one. That is, in nine hundred and ninety-nine cases out of a thousand.'

'How about the thousandth case?' said Remnant. 'Supposing these extraordinary crimes constitute the thousandth case?'

The doctor smiled and shrugged his shoulders, being tired of the subject. But for some little time highly respectable members of Porth society would look suspiciously at one another wondering whether, after all, there mightn't be 'something in it'. However, both Mr Remnant's somewhat crazy theory and Dr Lewis's plausible theory became untenable when two more victims of an awful and mysterious death were offered up in sacrifice, for a man was found dead in the Llanfihangel quarry, where the woman had been discovered. And on the same day a girl of fifteen was found broken on the jagged rocks under the cliffs near Porth. Now, it appeared that these two deaths must have occurred at about the same time, within an hour of one another, certainly; and the distance between the quarry and the cliffs by Black

Rock is certainly twenty miles.

'A motor could do it,' one man said.

But it was pointed out that there was no high road between the two places; indeed, it might be said that there was no road at all between them. There was a network of deep, narrow, and tortuous lanes that wandered into one another at all manner of queer angles for, say, seventeen miles; this in the middle, as it were, between Black Rock and the quarry at Llanfihangel. But to get to the high land of the cliffs one had to take a path that went through two miles of fields; and the quarry lay a mile away from the nearest by-road in the midst of gorse and bracken and broken land. And, finally, there was no track of motor-car or motor-bicycle in the lanes which must have been followed to pass from one place to the other.

'What about an airplane, then?' said the man of the motor-car theory. Well, there was certainly an aerodrome not far from one of the two places of death; but somehow, nobody believed that the Flying Corps harboured a homicidal maniac. It seemed clear, therefore, that there must be more than one person concerned in the terror of Meirion. And Dr Lewis himself abandoned his own theory.

'As I said to Remnant at the Club,' he remarked, 'improbability is the guide of life. I can't believe that there are a pack of madmen or even two madmen at large in the country. I give it up.'

And now a fresh circumstance or set of circumstances became manifest to confound judgment and to awaken new and wild surmises. For at about this time people realised that none of the dreadful events that were happening all about them was so much as mentioned in the Press. I have already spoken of the fate of the *Meiros Observer*. This paper was suppressed by the authorities because it had inserted a brief paragraph about some person who had been 'found dead under mysterious circumstances'; I think that paragraph referred to the first death of Llanfihangel quarry. Thenceforth, horror followed on horror, but no word was printed in any of the local journals. The curious went to the newspaper offices – there were two left in the county – but found nothing save a firm refusal to discuss the matter. And the Cardiff papers were drawn and found blank; and the London Press was apparently ignorant of the fact that crimes that had no parallel were terrorising a whole countryside. Everybody wondered what could have happened, what was happening; and then it was whispered that the coroner would allow no inquiry to be made as to these deaths of darkness.

'In consequence of instructions received from the Home Office,' one coroner was understood to have said, 'I have to tell the jury that their business will be to hear the medical evidence and to bring in a verdict immediately in accordance with that evidence. I shall disallow all questions.'

One jury protested. The foreman refused to bring in any verdict at all.

'Very good,' said the coroner. 'Then I beg to inform you, Mr Foreman and gentlemen of the jury, that under the Defence of the Realm Act, I have power to supersede your functions, and to enter a verdict according to the evidence which has been laid before the Court as if it had been the verdict of you all.'

The foreman and jury collapsed and accepted what they could not avoid. But the rumours that got abroad of all this, added to the known fact that the terror was ignored in the Press, no doubt by official command, increased the panic that was now arising, and gave it a new direction. Clearly, people reasoned, these Government restrictions and prohibitions could only refer to the war, to some great danger in connection with the war. And that being so, it followed that the outrages which must be kept so secret were the work of the enemy, that is of concealed German agents.

IV
The Spread of the Terror

It is time, I think, for me to make one point clear. I began this history with certain references to an extraordinary accident to an airman whose machine fell to the ground after collision with a huge flock of pigeons; and then to an explosion in a northern munition factory, an explosion, as I noted, of a very singular kind. Then I deserted the neighbourhood of London, and the northern district, and dwelt on a mysterious and terrible series of events which occurred in the summer of 1915 in a Welsh county, which I have named, for convenience, Meirion.

Well, let it be understood at once that all this detail that I have given about the occurrences in Meirion does not imply that the county in the far west was alone or especially afflicted by the terror that was over the land. They tell me that in the villages about Dartmoor the stout Devonshire hearts sank as men's hearts used to sink in the time of plague and pestilence. There was horror, too, about the Norfolk Broads, and far up by Perth no one would venture on the path that leads by Scone to the wooded heights above the Tay. And in the industrial districts: I met a man by chance one day in an odd London corner who spoke with horror of what a friend had told him.

'"Ask no questions, Ned," he says to me, "but I tell yow a' was in Bairnigan t'other day, and a' met a pal who'd seen three hundred coffins going out of a works not far from there."'

And then the ship that hovered outside the mouth of the Thames with all sails set and beat to and fro in the wind, and never answered any hail, and showed no light! The forts shot at her and brought down one of the masts, but she went suddenly about with a change of wind under what sail still stood, and then veered down Channel, and drove ashore at last on the sandbanks and pinewoods of Arcachon, and not a man alive on her, but only rattling heaps of bones! That last voyage of the *Semiramis* would be something horribly worth telling; but I only heard it at a distance as a yarn, and only believed it because it squared with other things that I knew for certain.

This, then, is my point; I have written of the terror as it fell on Meirion, simply because I have had opportunities of getting close there to what really happened. Third or fourth or fifth hand in the other places; but round about Porth and Merthyr Tegveth I have spoken with people who have seen the tracks of the terror with their own eyes.

Well, I have said that the people of that far western county realised, not only that death was abroad in their quiet lanes and on their peaceful hills, but that for some reason it was to be kept all secret. Newspapers might not print any news of it, the very juries summoned to investigate it were allowed to investigate nothing. And so they concluded that this veil of secrecy must somehow be connected with the war; and from this position it was not a long way to a further inference: that the murderers of innocent men and women and children were either Germans or agents of Germany. It would be just like the Huns, everybody agreed, to think out such a devilish scheme as this; and they always thought out their schemes beforehand. They hoped to seize Paris in a few weeks, but when they were beaten on the Marne they had their trenches on the Aisne ready to fall back on: it had all been prepared years before the war. And so, no doubt, they had devised this terrible plan against England in case they could not beat us in open fight: there were people ready, very likely, all over the country, who were prepared to murder and destroy everywhere as soon as they got the word. In this way the Germans intended to sow terror throughout England and fill our hearts with panic and dismay, hoping so to weaken their enemy at home that he would lose all heart over the war abroad. It was the Zeppelin notion, in another form; they were committing these horrible and mysterious outrages thinking that we should be frightened out of our wits.

It all seemed plausible enough; Germany had by this time perpetrated so many horrors and had so excelled in devilish ingenuities that no abomination seemed too abominable to be probable, or too ingeniously wicked to be beyond the tortuous malice of the Hun. But then came the questions as to who the agents of this terrible design were, as to where they lived, as to how they contrived to move unseen from field to field, from lane to lane. All sorts of fantastic attempts were made to answer these questions; but it was felt that they remained unanswered. Some suggested that the murderers landed from submarines, or flew from hiding places on the West Coast of Ireland, coming and going by night; but there were seen to be flagrant impossibilities in both these suggestions. Everybody agreed that the evil work was no doubt the work of Germany; but nobody could begin to guess how it was done. Somebody at the Club asked Remnant for his theory.

'My theory,' said that ingenious person, 'is that human progress is simply a long march from one inconceivable to another. Look at that airship of ours that came over Porth yesterday: ten years ago that would have been an inconceivable sight. Take the steam engine, take printing, take the theory of gravitation: they were all inconceivable till somebody thought of them. So it is, no doubt, with this infernal dodgery that we're talking about: the Huns have found it out, and we haven't; and there you are. We can't conceive how these poor people have been murdered, because the method's inconceivable to us.'

The club listened with some awe to this high argument. After Remnant had gone, one member said: 'Wonderful man, that.'

'Yes,' said Dr Lewis. 'He was asked whether he knew something. And his reply really amounted to 'No, I don't.' But I have never heard it better put.'

It was, I suppose, at about this time when the people were puzzling their heads as to the secret methods used by the Germans or their agents to accomplish their crimes that a very singular circumstance became known to a few of the Porth people. It related to the murder of the Williams family on the Highway in front of their cottage door. I do not know that I have made it plain that the old Roman road called the Highway follows the course of a long, steep hill that goes steadily westward till it slants down and droops towards the sea. On either side of the road the ground falls away, here into deep shadowy woods, here to high pastures, now and again into a field of corn, but for the most part into the wild and broken land that is characteristic of Arfon. The fields are long and narrow, stretching up the steep hillside; they fall into sudden dips and hollows, a well springs up in the midst of one and a grove of ash and thorn bends over it, shading it; and beneath it the ground is thick with reeds and rushes. And then may come on either side of such a field territories glistening with the deep growth of bracken, and rough with gorse and rugged with thickets of blackthorn, green lichen hanging strangely from the branches; such are the lands on either side of the Highway.

Now on the lower slopes of it, beneath the Williams's cottage, some three or four fields down the hill, there is a military camp. The place has been used as a camp for many years, and lately the site has been extended and huts have been erected. But a considerable number of the men were under canvas here in the summer of 1915.

On the night of the Highway murder this camp, as it appeared afterwards, was the scene of the extraordinary panic of the horses.

A good many men in the camp were asleep in their tents soon after 9:30, when the Last Post was sounded. They woke up in panic. There was a thundering sound on the steep hillside above them, and down upon the tents came half a dozen horses, mad with fright, trampling the canvas, trampling the men, bruising dozens of them and killing two.

Everything was in wild confusion, men groaning and screaming in the darkness, struggling with the canvas and the twisted ropes, shouting out, some of them, raw lads enough, that the Germans had landed, others wiping the blood from their eyes, a few, roused suddenly from heavy sleep, hitting out at one another, officers coming up at the double roaring out orders to the sergeants, a party of soldiers who were just returning to camp from the village seized with fright at what they could scarcely see or distinguish, at the wildness of the shouting and cursing and groaning that they could not understand, bolting out of the camp again and racing for their lives back to the village: everything in the maddest confusion of wild disorder.

Some of the men had seen the horses galloping down the hill as if terror itself was driving them. They scattered off into the darkness, and somehow or another found their way back in the night to their pasture above the camp. They were grazing there peacefully in the morning, and the only sign of the panic of the night before was the mud they had scattered all over themselves as they pelted through a patch of wet ground. The farmer said they were as quiet a lot as any in Meirion; he could make nothing of it.

'Indeed,' he said, 'I believe they must have seen the devil himself to be in such a fright as that: save the people!'

Now all this was kept as quiet as might be at the time when it happened; it became known to the men of the Porth Club in the days when they were discussing the difficult question of the German outrages, as the murders were commonly called. And this wild stampede of the farm horses was held by some to be evidence of the extraordinary and unheard of character of the dreadful agency that was at work. One of the members of the club had been told by an officer who was in the camp at the time of the panic that the horses that came charging down were in a perfect fury of fright, that he had never seen horses in such a state, and so there was endless speculation as to the nature of the sight or the sound that had driven half a dozen quiet beasts into raging madness.

Then, in the middle of this talk, two or three other incidents, quite as odd and incomprehensible, came to be known, borne on chance trickles of gossip that came into the towns from outland farms, or were carried by cottagers tramping into Porth on market day with a fowl or two and eggs and garden stuff; scraps and fragments of talk gathered by servants from the country folk and repeated – to their mistresses. And in such ways it came out that up at Plas Newydd there had been a terrible business over swarming the bees; they had turned as wild as wasps and much more savage. They had come about the people who were taking the swarms like a cloud. They settled on one man's face so that you could not see the flesh for the bees crawling all over it, and they had stung him so badly that the doctor did not know whether he would get over it, and they had chased a girl who had come out to see the swarming, and settled on her and stung her to death. Then they had gone off to a brake below the farm and got into a hollow tree there, and it was not safe to go near it, for they would come out at you by day or by night.

And much the same thing had happened, it seemed, at three or four farms and cottages where bees were kept. And there were stories, hardly so clear or so credible, of sheepdogs, mild and trusted beasts, turning as savage as wolves and injuring the farm boys in a horrible manner – in one case it was said with fatal results. It was certainly true that old Mrs Owen's favourite Brahma-Dorking cock had gone mad; she came into Porth one Saturday morning with her face and her neck all bound up and plastered. She had gone out to her bit of a field to feed the poultry the night before, and the bird had flown at her and attacked her most savagely, inflicting some very nasty wounds before she could beat it off.

'There was a stake handy, lucky for me,' she said, 'and I did beat him and beat him till the life was out of him. But what is come to the world, whatever?'

Now Remnant, the man of theories, was also a man of extreme leisure. It was understood that he had succeeded to ample means when he was quite a young man, and after tasting the savours of the law, as it were, for half a dozen terms at the board of the Middle Temple, he had decided that it would be senseless to bother himself with passing examinations for a profession which he had not the faintest intention of practising. So he turned a deaf ear to the call of 'Manger' ringing through the Temple Courts, and set himself out to potter amiably through the world. He had pottered all over Europe, he had looked at Africa, and had even put his head in at the door of the East, on a trip which included the Greek isles and Constantinople. Now getting into the middle fifties, he had settled at Porth for the sake, as he said, of the Gulf Stream and the fuchsia hedges, and pottered over his books and his theories and the local gossip. He was no more brutal than the general public, which revels in the details of mysterious crime; but it must be said that the terror, black though it was, was a boon to him. He peered and investigated and poked about with the relish of a man to whose life a new zest has been added. He listened attentively to the strange tales of bees and dogs and poultry that came into Porth with the country baskets of butter, rabbits, and green peas; and he evolved at last a most extraordinary theory.

Full of this discovery, as he thought it, he went one night to see Dr

Lewis and take his view of the matter.

'I want to talk to you,' said Remnant to the doctor, 'about what I have called provisionally, the Z Ray.'

V
The Incident of the Unknown Tree

Dr Lewis, smiling indulgently, and quite prepared for some monstrous piece of theorising, led Remnant into the room that overlooked the terraced garden and the sea.

The doctor's house, though it was only a ten minutes' walk from the centre of the town, seemed remote from all other habitations. The drive to it from the road came through a deep grove of trees and a dense shrubbery, trees were about the house on either side, mingling with neighbouring groves, and below, the garden fell down, terrace by green terrace, to wild growth, a twisted path amongst red rocks, and at last to the yellow sand of a little cove. The room to which the doctor took Remnant looked over these terraces and across the water to the dim boundaries of the bay. It had French windows that were thrown wide open, and the two men sat in the soft light of the lamp – this was before the days of severe lighting regulations in the Far West – and enjoyed the sweet odours and the sweet vision of the summer evening. Then Remnant began:

'I suppose, Lewis, you've heard these extraordinary stories of bees and dogs and things that have been going about lately?'

'Certainly I have heard them. I was called in at Plas Newydd, and treated Thomas Trevor, who's only just out of danger, by the way. I certified for the poor child, Mary Trevor. She was dying when I got to the place. There was no doubt she was stung to death by bees, and I believe there were other very similar cases at Llantarnam and Morwen; none fatal, I think. What about them?'

'Well: then there are the stories of good-tempered old sheepdogs turning wicked and "savaging" children?'

'Quite so. I haven't seen any of these cases professionally; but I believe the stories are accurate enough.'

'And the old woman assaulted by her own poultry?'

'That's perfectly true. Her daughter put some stuff of their own concoction on her face and neck, and then she came to me. The wounds seemed going all right, so I told her to continue the treatment, whatever it might be.'

'Very good,' said Mr Remnant. He spoke now with an italic impressiveness. '*Don't you see the link between all this and the horrible things that have been happening about here for the last month*?'

Lewis stared at Remnant in amazement. He lifted his red eyebrows and lowered them in a kind of scowl. His speech showed traces of his native accent.

'Great burning!' he exclaimed. 'What on earth are you getting at now? It is madness. Do you mean to tell me that you think there is some connection between a swarm or two of bees that have turned nasty, a cross dog, and a wicked old barn door cock and these poor people that have been pitched over the cliffs and hammered to death on the road? There's no sense in it, you know.'

'I am strongly inclined to believe that there is a great deal of sense in it,' replied Remnant, with extreme calmness. 'Look here, Lewis, I saw you grinning the other day at the club when I was telling the fellows that in my opinion all these outrages had been committed, certainly by the Germans, but by some method of which we have no conception. But what I meant to say when I talked about inconceivables was just this: that the Williamses and the rest of them have been killed in some way that's not in theory at all, not in our theory, at all events, some way we've not contemplated, not thought of for an instant. Do you see my point?'

'Well, in a sort of way. You mean there's an absolute originality in the method? I suppose that is so. But what next?'

Remnant seemed to hesitate, partly from a sense of the portentous nature of what he was about to say, partly from a sort of half-unwillingness to part with so profound a secret.

'Well,' he said, 'you will allow that we have two sets of phenomena of a very extraordinary kind occurring at the same time. Don't you think that it's only reasonable to connect the two sets with one another.'

'So the philosopher of Tenterden steeple and the Goodwin Sands thought, certainly,' said Lewis. 'But what is the connection? Those poor folks on the Highway weren't stung by bees or worried by a dog. And horses don't throw people over cliffs or stifle them in marshes.'

'No; I never meant to suggest anything so absurd. It is evident to me that in all these cases of animals turning suddenly savage the cause has been terror, panic, fear. The horses that went charging into the camp were mad with fright, we know. And I say that in the other instances we have been discussing the cause was the same. The creatures were exposed to an infection of fear, and a frightened beast or bird or insect uses its weapons, whatever they may be. If, for example, there had been anybody with those horses when they took their panic they would have lashed out at him with their heels.'

'Yes, I dare say that that is so. Well.'

'Well; my belief is that the Germans have made an extraordinary discovery. I have called it the Z Ray. You know that the ether is merely an hypothesis; we have to suppose that it's there to account for the passage of the Marconi current from one place to another. Now, suppose that there is a psychic ether as well as a material ether, suppose that it is possible to direct irresistible impulses across this medium, suppose that these impulses are towards murder or suicide; then I think that you have an explanation of the terrible series of events that have been happening in Meirion for the last few weeks. And it is quite clear to my mind that the horses and the other creatures have been exposed to this Z Ray, and that it has produced on them the effect of terror, with ferocity as the result of terror. Now what do you say to that? Telepathy, you know, is well established; so is hypnotic suggestion. You have only to look in the *Encyclopaedia Britannica* to see that, and suggestion is so strong in some cases as to be an irresistible imperative. Now don't you feel that putting telepathy and suggestion together, as it were, you have more than the elements of what I call the Z Ray? I feel myself that I have more to go on in making my hypothesis than the inventor of the steam engine had in making his hypothesis when he saw the lid of the kettle bobbing up and down. What do you say?'

Dr Lewis made no answer. He was watching the growth of a new, unknown tree in his garden.

The doctor made no answer to Remnant's question. For one thing, Remnant was profuse in his eloquence – he has been rigidly condensed in this history – and Lewis was tired of the sound of his voice. For another thing, he found the Z Ray theory almost too extravagant to be bearable, wild enough to tear patience to tatters. And then as the tedious argument continued Lewis became conscious that there was something strange about the night.

It was a dark summer night. The moon was old and faint, above the Dragon's Head across the bay, and the air was very still. It was so still that Lewis had noted that not a leaf stirred on the very tip of a high tree that stood out against the sky; and yet he knew that he was listening to some sound that he could not determine or define. It was not the wind in the leaves, it was not the gentle wash of the water of the sea against the rocks; that latter sound he could distinguish quite easily. But there was something else. It was scarcely a sound; it was as if the air itself trembled and fluttered, as the air trembles in a church when they open the great pedal pipes of the organ.

The doctor listened intently. It was not an illusion, the sound was not in his own head, as he had suspected for a moment; but for the life of him he could not make out whence it came or what it was. He gazed down into the night over the terraces of his garden, now sweet with the scent of the flowers of the night; tried to peer over the treetops across the sea towards the Dragon's Head. It struck him suddenly that this strange fluttering vibration of the air might be the noise of a distant aeroplane or airship; there was not the usual droning hum, but this sound might be caused by a new type of engine. A new type of engine? Possibly it was an enemy airship; their range, it had been said, was getting longer; and Lewis was just going to call Remnant's attention to the sound, to its possible cause, and to the possible danger that might be hovering over them, when he saw something that caught his breath and his heart with wild amazement and a touch of terror.

He had been staring upward into the sky, and, about to speak to Remnant, he had let his eyes drop for an instant. He looked down towards the trees in the garden, and saw with utter astonishment that one had changed its shape in the few hours that had passed since the setting of the sun. There was a thick grove of ilexes bordering the lowest terrace, and above them rose one tall pine, spreading its head of sparse, dark branches dark against the sky.

As Lewis glanced down over the terraces he saw that the tall pine tree was no longer there. In its place there rose above the ilexes what might have been a greater ilex; there was the blackness of a dense growth of foliage rising like a broad and far-spreading and rounded cloud over the lesser trees.

Here, then was a sight wholly incredible, impossible. It is doubtful whether the process of the human mind in such a case has ever been analysed and registered; it is doubtful whether it ever can be registered. It is hardly fair to bring in the mathematician, since he deals with absolute truth (so far as mortality can conceive absolute truth);

but how would a mathematician feel if he were suddenly confronted with a two-sided triangle? I suppose he would instantly become a raging madman; and Lewis, staring wide-eyed and wild-eyed at a dark and spreading tree which his own experience informed him was not there, felt for an instant that shock which should affront us all when we first realise the intolerable antinomy of Achilles and the Tortoise. Common sense tells us that Achilles will flash past the tortoise almost with the speed of the lightning; the inflexible truth of mathematics assures us that till the earth boils and the heavens cease to endure the Tortoise must still be in advance; and thereupon we should, in common decency, go mad. We do not go mad, because, by special grace, we are certified that, in the final court of appeal, all science is a lie, even the highest science of all; and so we simply grin at Achilles and the Tortoise, as we grin at Darwin, deride Huxley, and laugh at Herbert Spencer.

Dr Lewis did not grin. He glared into the dimness of the night, at the great spreading tree that he knew could not be there. And as he gazed he saw that what at first appeared the dense blackness of foliage was fretted and starred with wonderful appearances of lights and colours.

Afterwards he said to me: 'I remember thinking to myself: "Look here, I am not delirious; my temperature is perfectly normal. I am not drunk; I only had a pint of Graves with my dinner, over three hours ago. I have not eaten any poisonous fungus; I have not taken *Anhelonium Lewinii* experimentally. So, now then! What is happening?"'

The night had gloomed over; clouds obscured the faint moon and the misty stars. Lewis rose, with some kind of warning and inhibiting gesture to Remnant, who, he was conscious, was gaping at him in astonishment. He walked to the open French window, and took a pace forward on the path outside, and looked, very intently, at the dark shape of the tree, down below the sloping garden, above the washing of the waves. He shaded the light of the lamp behind him by holding his hands on each side of his eyes.

The mass of the tree – the tree that couldn't be there – stood out against the sky, but not so clearly, now that the clouds had rolled up. Its edges, the limits of its leafage, were not so distinct. Lewis thought that he could detect some sort of quivering movement in it; though the air was at a dead calm. It was a night on which one might hold up a lighted match and watch it burn without any wavering or inclination of the flame.

'You know,' said Lewis, 'how a bit of burnt paper will sometimes hang over the coals before it goes up the chimney, and little worms of fire will shoot through it. It was like that, if you should be standing some distance away. Just threads and hairs of yellow light I saw, and specks and sparks of fire, and then a twinkling of a ruby no bigger than a pin point, and a green wandering in the black, as if an emerald were crawling, and then little veins of deep blue. "Woe is me!" I said to myself in Welsh, "What is all this colour and burning?"

'And, then, at that very moment there came a thundering rap at the door of the room inside, and there was my man telling me that I was wanted directly up at the Garth, as old Mr Trevor Williams had been taken very bad. I knew his heart was not worth much, so I had to go off directly, and leave Remnant to make what he could of it all.'

VI
Mr. Remnant's Z Ray

Dr Lewis was kept some time at the Garth. It was past twelve when he got back to his house. He went quickly to the room that overlooked the garden and the sea and threw open the French window and peered into the darkness. There, dim indeed against the dim sky but unmistakable, was the tall pine with its sparse branches, high above the dense growth of the ilex trees. The strange boughs which had amazed him had vanished; there was no appearance now of colours or of fires.

He drew his chair up to the open window and sat there gazing and wondering far into the night, till brightness came upon the sea and sky, and the forms of the trees in the garden grew clear and evident. He went up to his bed at last filled with a great perplexity, still asking questions to which there was no answer.

The doctor did not say anything about the strange tree to Remnant. When they next met, Lewis said that he had thought there was a man hiding amongst the bushes – this in explanation of that warning gesture he had used, and of his going out into the garden and staring into the night. He concealed the truth because he dreaded the Remnant doctrine that would undoubtedly be produced; indeed, he hoped that he had heard the last of the theory of the Z Ray. But Remnant firmly reopened this subject.

'We were interrupted just as I was putting my case to you,' he said. 'And to sum it all up, it amounts to this: that the Huns have made one of the great leaps of science. They are sending "suggestions" (which amount to irresistible commands) over here, and the persons affected are seized with suicidal or homicidal mania. The people who were killed by falling over the cliffs or into the quarry probably committed suicide; and so with the man and boy who were found in the bog. As to the Highway case, you remember that Thomas Evans said that he stopped and talked to Williams on the night of the murder. In my opinion Evans was the murderer. He came under the influence of the Ray, became a homicidal maniac in an instant, snatched Williams's spade from his hand and killed him and the others.'

'The bodies were found by me on the road.'

'It is possible that the first impact of the Ray produces violent nervous excitement, which would manifest itself externally. Williams might have called to his wife to come and see what was the matter with Evans. The children would naturally follow their mother. It seems to me simple. And as for the animals – the horses, dogs, and so forth, they as I say, were no doubt panic stricken by the Ray, and hence driven to frenzy.'

'Why should Evans have murdered Williams instead of Williams murdering Evans? Why should the impact of the Ray affect one and not the other?'

'Why does one man react violently to a certain drug, while it makes no impression on another man? Why is A able to drink a bottle of whisky and remain sober, while B is turned into something very like a lunatic after he has drunk three glasses?'

'It is a question of idiosyncrasy,' said the doctor.

'Is "idiosyncrasy" Greek for "I don't know" ?' asked Remnant.

'Not at all,' said Lewis, smiling blandly. 'I mean that in some diatheses whisky – as you have mentioned whisky – appears not to be pathogenic, or at all events not immediately pathogenic. In other cases, as you very justly observed, there seems to be a very marked cachexia associated with the exhibition of the spirit in question, even in comparatively small doses.'

Under this cloud of professional verbiage Lewis escaped from the Club and from Remnant. He did not want to hear any more about that Dreadful Ray, because he felt sure that the Ray was all nonsense. But asking himself why he felt this certitude in the matter he had to confess that he didn't know. An aeroplane, he reflected, was all nonsense before it was made; and he remembered talking in the early nineties to a friend of his about the newly discovered X Rays. The friend laughed incredulously, evidently didn't believe a word of it, till Lewis told him that there was an article on the subject in the current number of the *Saturday Review*; whereupon the unbeliever said, 'Oh, is that so? Oh, really. I see,' and was converted on the X Ray faith on the spot. Lewis, remembering this talk, marvelled at the strange processes of the human mind, its illogical and yet all-compelling ergos, and wondered whether he himself was only waiting for an article on the Z Ray in the *Saturday Review* to become a devout believer in the doctrine of Remnant.

But he wondered with far more fervour as to the extraordinary thing he had seen in his own garden with his own eyes. The tree that changed all its shape for an hour or two of the night, the growth of strange boughs, the apparition of secret fires among them, the sparkling of emerald and ruby lights: how could one fail to be afraid with great amazement at the thought of such a mystery?

Dr Lewis's thoughts were distracted from the incredible adventure of the tree by the visit of his sister and her husband. Mr and Mrs Merritt lived in a well-known manufacturing town of the Midlands, which was now, of course, a centre of munition work. On the day of their arrival at Porth, Mrs Merritt, who was tired after the long, hot journey, went to bed early, and Merritt and Lewis went into the room by the garden for their talk and tobacco. They spoke of the year that had passed since their last meeting, of the weary dragging of the war, of friends that had perished in it, of the hopelessness of an early ending of all this misery. Lewis said nothing of the terror that was on the land. One does not greet a tired man who is come to a quiet, sunny place for relief from black smoke and work and worry with a tale of horror. Indeed, the doctor saw that his brother-in-law looked far from well. And he seemed 'jumpy'; there was an occasional twitch of his mouth that Lewis did not like at all.

'Well,' said the doctor, after an interval of silence and port wine, 'I am glad to see you here again. Porth always suits you. I don't think you're looking quite up to your usual form. But three weeks of Meirion air will do wonders.'

'Well, I hope it will,' said the other. 'I am not up to the mark. Things are not going well at Midlingham.'

'Business is all right, isn't it?'

'Yes. Business is all right. But there are other things that are all wrong. We are living under a reign of terror. It comes to that.'

'What on earth do you mean?'

'Well, I suppose I may tell you what I know. It's not much. I didn't dare write it. But do you know that at every one of the munition works in Midlingham and all about it there's a guard of soldiers with drawn bayonets and loaded rifles day and night? Men with bombs, too. And machine guns at the big factories.'

'German spies?'

'You don't want Lewis guns to fight spies with. Nor bombs. Nor a platoon of men. I woke up last night. It was the machine gun at Benington's Army Motor Works. Firing like fury. And then bang! bang! bang! That was the hand bombs.'

'But what against?'

'Nobody knows.

'Nobody knows what is happening,' Merritt repeated, and he went on to describe the bewilderment and terror that hung like a cloud over the great industrial city in the Midlands, how the feeling of concealment, of some intolerable secret danger that must not be named, was worst of all.

'A young fellow I know,' he said, 'was on short leave the other day from the front, and he spent it with his people at Belmont – that's about four miles out of Midlingham, you know. "Thank God," he said to me, "I am going back tomorrow. It's no good saying that the Wipers salient is nice, because it isn't. But it's a damned sight better than this. At the front you know what you're up against anyhow." At Midlingham everybody has the feeling that we're up against something awful and we don't know what; it's that that makes people inclined to whisper. There's terror in the air.'

Merritt made a sort of picture of the great town cowering in its fear of an unknown danger.

'People are afraid to go about alone at nights in the outskirts. They make up parties at the stations to go home together if it's anything like dark, or if there are any lonely bits on their way.'

'But why? I don't understand. What are they afraid of?'

'Well, I told you about my being awakened up the other night with the machine guns at the motor works rattling away, and the bombs exploding and making the most terrible noise. That sort of thing alarms one, you know. It's only natural.'

'Indeed, it must be very terrifying. You mean, then, there is a general nervousness about, a vague sort of apprehension that makes people inclined to herd together?'

'There's that, and there's more. People have gone out that have never come back. There were a couple of men in the train to Holme, arguing about the quickest way to get to Northend, a sort of outlying part of Holme where they both lived. They argued all the way out of Midlingham, one saying that the high road was the quickest though it was the longest way. "It's the quickest going because it's the cleanest going," he said.'

'The other chap fancied a short cut across the fields, by the canal. "It's half the distance," he kept on. "Yes, if you don't lose your way," said the other. Well, it appears they put an even half-crown on it, and each was to try his own way when they got out of the train. It was arranged that they were to meet at the "Waggon" in Northend. "I shall be at the 'Waggon' first," said the man who believed in the short cut, and with that he climbed over the stile and made off across the fields. It wasn't late enough to be really dark, and a lot of them thought he might win the stakes. But he never turned up at the "Waggon" – or anywhere else for the matter of that.'

'What happened to him?'

'He was found lying on his back in the middle of a field – some way from the path. He was dead. The doctors said he'd been suffocated. Nobody knows how. Then there have been other cases. We whisper about them at Midlingham, but we're afraid to speak out.'

Lewis was ruminating all this profoundly. Terror in Meirion and terror far away in the heart of England; but at Midlingham, so far as he could gather from these stories of soldiers on guard, of crackling machine guns, it was a case of an organised attack on the munitioning of the army. He felt that he did not know enough to warrant his deciding that the terror of Meirion and of Stratfordshire were one.

Then Merritt began again:

'There's a queer story going about, when the door's shut and the curtain's drawn, that is, as to a place right out in the country over the other side of Midlingham; on the opposite side to Dunwich. They've built one of the new factories out there, a great red brick town of sheds they tell me it is, with a tremendous chimney. It's not been finished more than a month or six weeks. They plumped it down right in the middle of the fields, by the line, and they're building huts for the workers as fast as they can, but up to the present the men are billeted all about, up and down the line.

'About two hundred yards from this place there's an old footpath, leading from the station and the main road up to a small hamlet on the hillside. Part of the way this path goes by a pretty large wood, most of it thick undergrowth. I should think there must be twenty acres of wood, more or less. As it happens, I used this path once long ago; and I can tell you it's a black place of nights.

'A man had to go this way one night. He got along all right till he came to the wood. And then he said his heart dropped out of his body. It was awful to hear the noises in that wood. Thousands of men were in it, he swears that. It was full of rustling, and pattering of feet trying to go dainty, and the crack of dead boughs lying on the ground as some one trod on them, and swishing of the grass, and some sort of chattering speech going on, that sounded, so he said, as if the dead sat in their bones and talked! He ran for his life, anyhow; across fields, over hedges, through brooks. He must have run, by his tale, ten miles out of his way before he got home to his wife, and beat at the door, and broke in, and bolted it behind him.'

'There is something rather alarming about any wood at night,' said Dr Lewis.

Merritt shrugged his shoulders.

'People say that the Germans have landed, and that they are hiding in underground places all over the country.'

VII
The Case of the Hidden Germans

Lewis gasped for a moment, silent in contemplation of the magnificence of rumour. The Germans already landed, hiding underground, striking by night, secretly, terribly, at the power of England! Here was a conception which made the myth of 'The Russians' a paltry fable; before which the Legend of Mons was an ineffectual thing.

It was monstrous. And yet –

He looked steadily at Merritt; a square-headed, black-haired, solid sort of man. He had symptoms of nerves about him for the moment, certainly, but one could not wonder at that, whether the tales he told were true, or whether he merely believed them to be true. Lewis had known his brother-in-law for twenty years or more, and had always found him a sure man in his own small world. 'But then,' said the doctor to himself, 'those men, if they once get out of the ring of that little world of theirs, they are lost. Those are the men that believed in Madame Blavatsky.'

'Well,' he said, 'what do you think yourself? The Germans landed and hiding somewhere about the country: there's something extravagant in the notion, isn't there?'

'I don't know what to think. You can't get over the facts. There are the soldiers with their rifles and their guns at the works all over Stratfordshire, and those guns go off. I told you I'd heard them. Then who are the soldiers shooting at? That's what we ask ourselves at Midlingham.'

'Quite so; I quite understand. It's an extraordinary state of things.'

'It's more than extraordinary; it's an awful state of things. It's terror in the dark, and there's nothing worse than that. As that young fellow I was telling you about said, "At the front you do know what you're up against."'

'And people really believe that a number of Germans have somehow got over to England and have hid themselves underground?'

'People say they've got a new kind of poison gas. Some think that they dig underground places and make the gas there, and lead it by secret pipes into the shops; others say that they throw gas bombs into the factories. It must be worse than anything they've used in France, from what the authorities say.'

'The authorities? Do they admit that there are Germans in hiding about Midlingham?'

'No. They call it "explosions". But we know it isn't explosions. We know in the Midlands what an explosion sounds like and looks like. And we know that the people killed in these "explosions" are put into their coffins in the works. Their own relations are not allowed to see them.'

'And so you believe in the German theory?'

'If I do, it's because one must believe in something. Some say they've seen the gas. I heard that a man living in Dunwich saw it one night like a black cloud with sparks of fire in it floating over the tops of the trees by Dunwich Common.'

The light of an ineffable amazement came into Lewis's eyes. The night of Remnant's visit, the trembling vibration of the air, the dark tree that had grown in his garden since the setting of the sun, the strange leafage that was starred with burning, with emerald and ruby fires, and all vanished away when he returned from his visit to the Garth; and such a leafage had appeared as a burning cloud far in the heart of England: what intolerable mystery, what tremendous doom was signified in this? But one thing was clear and certain: that the terror of Meirion was also the terror of the Midlands.

Lewis made up his mind most firmly that if possible all this should be kept from his brother-in-law. Merritt had come to Porth as to a city of refuge from the horrors of Midlingham; if it could be managed he should be spared the knowledge that the cloud of terror had gone before him and hung black over the western land. Lewis passed the port and said in an even voice:

'Very strange, indeed; a black cloud with sparks of fire?'

'I can't answer for it, you know; it's only a rumour.'

'Just so; and you think or you're inclined to think that this and all the rest you've told me is to be put down to the hidden Germans?'

'As I say; because one must think something.'

'I quite see your point. No doubt, if it's true, it's the most awful blow that has ever been dealt at any nation in the whole history of man. The enemy established in our vitals! But is it possible, after all? How could it have been worked?'

Merritt told Lewis how it had been worked, or rather, how people said it had been worked. The idea, he said, was that this was a part, and a most important part, of the great German plot to destroy England and the British Empire.

The scheme had been prepared years ago, some thought soon after the Franco-Prussian War. Moltke had seen that the invasion of England (in the ordinary sense of the term invasion) presented very great difficulties. The matter was constantly in discussion in the inner military and high political circles, and the general trend of opinion in these quarters was that at the best, the invasion of England would involve Germany in the gravest difficulties, and leave France in the position of the *tertius gaudens*. This was the state of affairs when a very high Prussian personage was approached by the Swedish professor, Huvelius.

Thus Merritt, and here I would say in parenthesis that this Huvelius was by all accounts an extraordinary man. Considered personally and apart from his writings he would appear to have been a most amiable individual. He was richer than the generality of Swedes, certainly far richer than the average university professor in Sweden. But his shabby, green frock-coat, and his battered, furry hat were notorious in the university town where he lived. No one laughed, because it was well known that Professor Huvelius spent every penny of his private means and a large portion of his official stipend on works of kindness and charity. He hid his head in a garret, some one said, in order that others might be able to swell on the first floor. It was told of him that he restricted himself to a diet of dry bread and coffee for a month in order that a poor woman of the streets, dying of consumption, might enjoy luxuries in hospital.

And this was the man who wrote the treatise *De Facinore Humano*; to prove the infinite corruption of the human race.

Oddly enough, Professor Huvelius wrote the most cynical book in the world – Hobbes preaches rosy sentimentalism in comparison – with the very highest motives. He held that a very large part of human misery, misadventure, and sorrow was due to the false convention that the heart of man was naturally and in the main well disposed and kindly, if not exactly righteous. 'Murderers, thieves, assassins, violators, and all the host of the abominable,' he says in one passage, 'are created by the false pretense and foolish credence of human virtue. A lion in a cage is a fierce beast, indeed; but what will he be if we declare him to be a lamb and open the doors of his den? Who will be guilty of the deaths of the men, women and children whom he will surely devour, save those who unlocked the cage?' And he goes on to show that kings and the rulers of the peoples could decrease the sum of human misery to a vast extent by acting on the doctrine of human wickedness. 'War,' he declares, 'which is one of the worst of evils, will always continue to exist. But a wise king will desire a brief war rather than a lengthy one, a short evil rather than a long evil. And this not from the benignity of his heart towards his enemies, for we have seen that the human heart is naturally malignant, but because he desires to conquer, and to conquer easily, without a great expenditure of men or of treasure, knowing that if he can accomplish this feat his people will love him and his crown will be secure. So he will wage brief victorious wars, and not only spare his own nation, but the nation of the enemy, since in a short war the loss is less on both sides than in a long war. And so from evil will come good.'

And how, asks Huvelius, are such wars to be waged? The wise prince, he replies, will begin by assuming the enemy to be infinitely corruptible and infinitely stupid, since stupidity and corruption are the chief characteristics of man. So the prince will make himself friends in the very councils of his enemy, and also amongst the populace, bribing the wealthy by proffering to them the opportunity of still greater wealth, and winning the poor by swelling words. 'For, contrary to the common opinion, it is the wealthy who are greedy of wealth; while the populace are to be gained by talking to them about liberty, their unknown god. And so much are they enchanted by the words liberty, freedom, and suchlike, that the wise can go to the poor, rob them of what little they have, dismiss them with a hearty kick, and win their hearts and their votes for ever, if only they will assure them that the treatment which they have received is called liberty.'

Guided by these principles, says Huvelius, the wise prince will entrench himself in the country that he desires to conquer; 'nay, with but little trouble, he may actually and literally throw his garrisons into the heart of the enemy country before war has begun.'

This is a long and tiresome parenthesis; but it is necessary as explaining the long tale which Merritt told his brother-in-law, he having received it from some magnate of the Midlands, who had travelled in Germany. It is probable that the story was suggested in the first place by the passage from Huvelius which I have just quoted.

Merritt knew nothing of the real Huvelius, who was all but a saint; he thought of the Swedish professor as a monster of iniquity, 'worse,' as he said, 'than Neech' – meaning, no doubt, Nietzsche.

So he told the story of how Huvelius had sold his plan to the Germans; a plan for filling England with German soldiers. Land was to be bought in certain suitable and well-considered places, Englishmen were to be bought as the apparent owners of such land, and secret excavations were to be made, till the country was literally undermined. A subterranean Germany, in fact, was to be dug under selected districts of England; there were to be great caverns, underground cities, well drained, well ventilated, supplied with water, and in these places vast stores both of food and of munitions were to be accumulated, year after year, till 'the Day' dawned. And then, warned in time, the secret garrison would leave shops, hotels, offices, villas, and vanish underground, ready to begin their work of bleeding England at the heart.

'That's what Henson told me,' said Merritt at the end of his long story. 'Henson, head of the Buckley Iron and Steel Syndicate. He has been a lot in Germany.'

'Well,' said Lewis, 'of course, it may be so. If it is so, it is terrible beyond words.'

Indeed, he found something horribly plausible in the story. It was an extraordinary plan, of course; an unheard of scheme; but it did not seem impossible. It was the Trojan Horse on a gigantic scale; indeed, he reflected, the story of the horse with the warriors concealed within it which was dragged into the heart of Troy by the deluded Trojans themselves might be taken as a prophetic parable of what had happened to England – if Henson's theory were well founded. And this theory certainly squared with what one had heard of German preparations in Belgium and in France: emplacements for guns ready for the invader, German manufactories which were really German forts on Belgian soil, the caverns by the Aisne made ready for the cannon; indeed, Lewis thought he remembered something about suspicious concrete tennis courts on the heights commanding London. But a German army hidden under English ground! It was a thought to chill the stoutest heart.

And it seemed from that wonder of the burning tree, that the enemy mysteriously and terribly present at Midlingham, was present also in Meirion. Lewis, thinking of the country as he knew it, of its wild and desolate hillsides, its deep woods, its wastes and solitary places, could not but confess that no more fit region could be found for the deadly enterprise of secret men. Yet, he thought again, there was but little harm to be done in Meirion to the armies of England or to their munitionment. They were working for panic terror? Possibly that might be so; but the camp under the Highway? That should be their first object, and no harm had been done there.

Lewis did not know that since the panic of the horses men had died terribly in that camp; that it was now a fortified place, with a deep, broad trench, a thick tangle of savage barbed wire about it, and a machine gun planted at each corner.

VIII
What Mr. Merritt Found

Mr Merritt began to pick up his health and spirits a good deal. For the first morning or two of his stay at the doctor's he contented himself with a very comfortable deck chair close to the house, where he sat under the shade of an old mulberry tree beside his wife and watched the bright sunshine on the green lawns, on the creamy crests of the waves, on the headlands of that glorious coast, purple even from afar with the imperial glow of the heather, on the white farmhouses gleaming in the sunlight, high over the sea, far from any turmoil, from any troubling of men.

The sun was hot, but the wind breathed all the while gently, incessantly, from the east, and Merritt, who had come to this quiet place, not only from dismay, but from the stifling and oily airs of the smoky Midland town, said that that east wind, pure and clear and like well water from the rock, was new life to him. He ate a capital dinner at the end of his first day at Porth and took rosy views. As to what they had been talking about the night before, he said to Lewis, no doubt there must be trouble of some sort, and perhaps bad trouble; still, Kitchener would soon put it all right.

So things went on very well. Merritt began to stroll about the garden, which was full of the comfortable spaces, groves, and surprises that only country gardens know. To the right of one of the terraces he found an arbour or summer house covered with white roses, and he was as pleased as if he had discovered the Pole. He spent a whole day there, smoking and lounging and reading a rubbishy sensational story, and declared that the Devonshire roses had taken many years off his age. Then on the other side of the garden there was a filbert grove that he had never explored on any of his former visits; and again there was a find. Deep in the shadow of the filberts was a bubbling well, issuing from rocks, and all manner of green, dewy ferns growing about it and above it, and an angelica springing beside it. Merritt knelt on his knees, and hollowed his hand and drank the well water. He said (over his port) that night that if all water were like the water of the filbert well the world would turn to teetotalism. It takes a townsman to relish the manifold and exquisite joys of the country.

It was not till he began to venture abroad that Merritt found that something was lacking of the old rich peace that used to dwell in Meirion. He had a favourite walk which he never neglected, year after year. This walk led along the cliffs towards Meiros, and then one could turn inland and return to Porth by deep winding lanes that went over the Allt. So Merritt set out early one morning and got as far as a sentry box at the foot of the path that led up to the cliff. There was a sentry pacing up and down in front of the box, and he called on Merritt to produce his pass, or to turn back to the main road. Merritt was a good deal put out, and asked the doctor about this strict guard. And the doctor was surprised.

'I didn't know they had put their bar up there,' he said. 'I suppose it's wise. We are certainly in the far West here; still, the Germans might slip round and raid us and do a lot of damage just because Meirion is the last place we should expect them to go for.'

'But there are no fortifications, surely, on the cliff?'

'Oh, no; I never heard of anything of the kind there.'

'Well, what's the point of forbidding the public to go on the cliff, then? I can quite understand putting a sentry on the top to keep a look-out for the enemy. What I don't understand is a sentry at the bottom who can't keep a look-out for anything, as he can't see the sea. And why warn the public off the cliffs? I couldn't facilitate a German landing by standing on Pengareg, even if I wanted to.'

'It is curious,' the doctor agreed. 'Some military reasons, I suppose.'

He let the matter drop, perhaps because the matter did not affect him. People who live in the country all the year round, country doctors certainly, are little given to desultory walking in search of the picturesque.

Lewis had no suspicion that sentries whose object was equally obscure were being dotted all over the country. There was a sentry, for example, by the quarry at Llanfihangel, where the dead woman and the dead sheep had been found some weeks before. The path by the quarry was used a good deal, and its closing would have inconvenienced the people of the neighbourhood very considerably. But the sentry had his box by the side of the track and had his orders to keep everybody strictly to the path, as if the quarry were a secret fort.

It was not known till a month or two ago that one of these sentries was himself a victim of the terror. The men on duty at this place were given certain very strict orders, which from the nature of the case, must have seemed to them unreasonable. For old soldiers, orders are orders; but here was a young bank clerk, scarcely in training for a couple of months, who had not begun to appreciate the necessity of hard, literal obedience to an order which seemed to him meaningless. He found himself on a remote and lonely hillside, he had not the faintest notion that his every movement was watched; and he disobeyed a certain instruction that had been given him. The post was found deserted by the relief; the sentry's dead body was found at the bottom of the quarry.

This by the way; but Mr Merritt discovered again and again that things happened to hamper his walks and his wanderings. Two or three miles from Porth there is a great marsh made by the Afon river before it falls into the sea, and here Merritt had been accustomed to botanise mildly. He had learned pretty accurately the causeways of solid ground that lead through the sea of swamp and ooze and soft yielding soil, and he set out one hot afternoon determined to make a thorough exploration of the marsh, and this time to find that rare Bog Bean, that he felt sure, must grow somewhere in its wide extent.

He got into the by-road that skirts the marsh, and to the gate which he had always used for entrance.

There was the scene as he had known it always, the rich growth of reeds and flags and rushes, the mild black cattle grazing on the 'islands' of firm turf, the scented procession of the meadowsweet, the royal glory of the loosestrife, flaming pennons, crimson and golden, of the giant dock.

But they were bringing out a dead man's body through the gate.

A labouring man was holding open the gate on the marsh. Merritt, horrified, spoke to him and asked who it was, and how it had happened.

'They do say he was a visitor at Porth. Somehow he has been drowned in the marsh, whatever.'

'But it's perfectly safe. I've been all over it a dozen times.'

'Well, indeed, we did always think so. If you did slip by accident, like, and fall into the water, it was not so deep; it was easy enough to climb out again. And this gentleman was quite young, to look at him, poor man; and he has come to Meirion for his pleasure and holiday and found his death in it!'

'Did he do it on purpose? Is it suicide?'

'They say he had no reasons to do that.'

Here the sergeant of police in charge of the party interposed, according to orders, which he himself did not understand.

'A terrible thing, sir, to be sure, and a sad pity; and I am sure this is not the sort of sight you have come to see down in Meirion this beautiful summer. So don't you think, sir, that it would be more pleasant like, if you would leave us to this sad business of ours? I have heard many gentlemen staying in Porth say that there is nothing to beat the view from the hill over there, not in the whole of Wales.'

Every one is polite in Meirion, but somehow Merritt understood that, in English, this speech meant 'move on'.

Merritt moved back to Porth – he was not in the humour for any idle, pleasurable strolling after so dreadful a meeting with death. He made some inquiries in the town about the dead man, but nothing seemed known of him. It was said that he had been on his honeymoon, that he had been staying at the Porth Castle Hotel; but the people of the hotel declared that they had never heard of such a person. Merritt got the local paper at the end of the week; there was not a word in it of any fatal accident in the marsh. He met the sergeant of police in the street. That officer touched his helmet with the utmost politeness and a 'hope you are enjoying yourself, sir; indeed you do look a lot better already'; but as to the poor man who was found drowned or stifled in the marsh, he knew nothing.

The next day Merritt made up his mind to go to the marsh to see whether he could find anything to account for so strange a death. What he found was a man with an armlet standing by the gate. The armlet had the letters 'C.W.' on it, which are understood to mean Coast Watcher. The Watcher said he had strict instructions to keep everybody away from the marsh. Why? He didn't know, but some said that the river was changing its course since the new railway embankment was built, and the marsh had become dangerous to people who didn't know it thoroughly.

'Indeed, sir,' he added, 'it is part of my orders not to set foot on the other side of that gate myself, not for one scrag-end of a minute.'

Merritt glanced over the gate incredulously. The marsh looked as it had always looked; there was plenty of sound, hard ground to walk on; he could see the track that he used to follow as firm as ever. He did not believe in the story of the changing course of the river, and Lewis said he had never heard of anything of the kind. But Merritt had put the question in the middle of general conversation; he had not led up to it from any discussion of the death in the marsh, and so the doctor was taken unawares. If he had known of the connection in Merritt's mind between the alleged changing of the Afon's course and the tragical event in the marsh, no doubt he would have confirmed the official explanation. He was, above all things, anxious to prevent his sister and her husband from finding out that the invisible hand of terror that ruled at Midlingham was ruling also in Meirion.

Lewis himself had little doubt that the man who was found dead in the marsh had been struck down by the secret agency, whatever it was, that had already accomplished so much of evil; but it was a chief part of the terror that no one knew for certain that this or that particular event was to be ascribed to it. People do occasionally fall over cliffs through their own carelessness, and as the case of Garcia, the Spanish sailor, showed, cottagers and their wives and children are now and then the victims of savage and purposeless violence. Lewis had never wandered about the marsh himself; but Remnant had pottered round it and about it, and declared that the man who met his death there – his name was never known, in Porth at all events – must either have committed suicide by deliberately lying prone in the ooze and stifling himself, or else must have been held down in it. There were no details available, so it was clear that the authorities had classified this death with the others; still, the man might have committed suicide, or he might have had a sudden seizure and fallen in the slimy water face downwards. And so on: it was possible to believe that case A *or* B *or* C was in the category of ordinary accidents or ordinary crimes. But it was not possible to believe that A *and* B *and* C were all in that category. And thus it was to the end, and thus it is now. We know that the terror reigned, and how it reigned, but there were many dreadful events ascribed to its rule about which there must always be room for doubt.

For example, there was the case of the *Mary Ann*, the rowing boat which came to grief in so strange a manner, almost under Merritt's eyes. In my opinion he was quite wrong in associating the sorry fate of the boat and her occupants with a system of signalling by flashlights which he detected or thought that he detected, on the afternoon in which the *Mary Ann* was capsized. I believe his signalling theory to be all nonsense, in spite of the naturalised German governess who was lodging with her employers in the suspected house. But, on the other hand, there is no doubt in my own mind that the boat was overturned and those in it drowned by the work of the terror.

IX
The Light on the Water

Let it be noted carefully that so far Merritt had not the slightest suspicion that the terror of Midlingham was quick over Meirion. Lewis had watched and shepherded him carefully. He had let out no suspicion of what had happened in Meirion, and before taking his brother-in-law to the club he had passed round a hint among the members. He did not tell the truth about Midlingham – and here again is a point of interest, that as the terror deepened the general public cooperated voluntarily, and, one would say, almost subconsciously, with the authorities in concealing what they knew from one another – but he gave out a desirable portion of the truth: that his brother-in-law was 'nervy', not by any means up to the mark, and that it was therefore desirable that he should be spared the knowledge of the intolerable and tragic mysteries which were being enacted all about them.

'He knows about that poor fellow who was found in the marsh,' said Lewis, 'and he has a kind of vague suspicion that there is something out of the common about the case; but no more than that.'

'A clear case of suggested, or rather commanded suicide,' said Remnant. 'I regard it as a strong confirmation of my theory.'

'Perhaps so,' said the doctor, dreading lest he might have to hear about the Z Ray all over again. 'But please don't let anything out to him; I want him to get built up thoroughly before he goes back to Midlingham.'

Then, on the other hand, Merritt was as still as death about the doings of the Midlands; he hated to think of them, much more to speak of them; and thus, as I say, he and the men at the Porth Club kept their secrets from one another; and thus, from the beginning to the end of the terror, the links were not drawn together. In many cases, no doubt, A and B met every day and talked familiarly, it may be confidentially, on other matters of all sorts, each having in his possession half of the truth, which he concealed from the other. So the two halves were never put together to make a whole.

Merritt, as the doctor guessed, had a kind of uneasy feeling – it scarcely amounted to a suspicion – as to the business of the marsh; chiefly because he thought the official talk about the railway embankment and the course of the river rank nonsense. But finding that nothing more happened, he let the matter drop from his mind, and settled himself down to enjoy his holiday.

He found to his delight that there were no sentries or watchers to hinder him from the approach to Larnac Bay, a delicious cove, a place where the ashgrove and the green meadow and the glistening bracken sloped gently down to red rocks and firm yellow sands. Merritt remembered a rock that formed a comfortable seat, and here he established himself of a golden afternoon, and gazed at the blue of the sea and the crimson bastions and bays of the coast as it bent inward to Sarnau and swept out again southward to the odd-shaped promontory called the Dragon's Head. Merritt gazed on, amused by the antics of the porpoises who were tumbling and splashing and gambolling a little way out at sea, charmed by the pure and radiant air that was so different from the oily smoke that often stood for heaven at Midlingham, and charmed, too, by the white farmhouses dotted here and there on the heights of the curving coast.

Then he noticed a little row boat at about two hundred yards from the shore. There were two or three people aboard, he could not quite make out how many, and they seemed to be doing something with a line; they were no doubt fishing, and Merritt (who disliked fish) wondered how people could spoil such an afternoon, such a sea, such pellucid and radiant air by trying to catch white, flabby, offensive, evil-smelling creatures that would be excessively nasty when cooked. He puzzled over this problem and turned away from it to the contemplation of the crimson headlands. And then he says that he noticed that signalling was going on. Flashing lights of intense brilliance, he declares, were coming from one of those farms on the heights of the coast; it was as if white fire was spouting from it. Merritt was certain, as the light appeared and disappeared, that some message was being sent, and he regretted that he knew nothing of heliography. Three short flashes, a long and very brilliant flash, then two short flashes. Merritt fumbled in his pocket for pencil and paper so that he might record these signals, and, bringing his eyes down to the sea level, he became aware, with amazement and horror, that the boat had disappeared. All that he could see was some vague, dark object far to westward, running out with the tide.

Now it is certain, unfortunately, that the *Mary Ann* was capsized and that two schoolboys and the sailor in charge were drowned. The bones of the boat were found amongst the rocks far along the coast, and the three bodies were also washed ashore. The sailor could not swim at all, the boys only a little, and it needs an exceptionally fine swimmer to fight against the outward suck of the tide as it rushes past Pengareg Point.

But I have no belief whatever in Merritt's theory. He held (and still holds, for all I know), that the flashes of light which he saw coming from Penyrhaul, the farmhouse on the height, had some connection with the disaster to the *Mary Ann*. When it was ascertained that a family were spending their summer at the farm, and that the governess was a German, though a long-naturalised German, Merritt could not see that there was anything left to argue about, though there might be many details to discover. But, in my opinion, all this was a mere mare's nest; the flashes of brilliant light were caused, no doubt, by the sun lighting up one window of the farmhouse after the other.

Still, Merritt was convinced from the very first, even before the damning circumstance of the German governess was brought to light; and on the evening of the disaster, as Lewis and he sat together after dinner, he was endeavouring to put what he called the common sense of the matter to the doctor.

'If you hear a shot,' said Merritt, 'and you see a man fall, you know pretty well what killed him.'

There was a flutter of wild wings in the room. A great moth beat to and fro and dashed itself madly against the ceiling, the walls, the glass bookcase. Then a sputtering sound, a momentary dimming of the lamp. The moth had succeeded in its mysterious quest.

'Can you tell me,' said Lewis as if he were answering Merritt, 'why moths rush into the flame?'

Lewis had put his question as to the strange habits of the common moth to Merritt with the deliberate intent of closing the debate on death by heliograph. The query was suggested, of course, by the incident of the moth in the lamp, and Lewis thought that he had said, 'Oh, shut up!' in a somewhat elegant manner. And, in fact Merritt looked dignified, remained silent, and helped himself to port.

That was the end that the doctor had desired. He had no doubt in his own mind that the affair of the *Mary Ann* was but one more item in the long account of horrors that grew larger almost with every day; and he was in no humour to listen to wild and futile theories as to the manner in which the disaster had been accomplished. Here was a proof that the terror that was upon them was mighty not only on the land but on the waters; for Lewis could not see that the boat could have been attacked by any ordinary means of destruction. From Merritt's story, it must have been in shallow water. The shore of Larnac Bay shelves very gradually, and the Admiralty charts showed the depth of water two hundred yards out to be only two fathoms; this would be too shallow for a submarine. And it could not have been shelled, and it could not have been torpedoed; there was no explosion. The disaster might have been due to carelessness; boys, he considered, will play the fool anywhere, even in a boat; but he did not think so; the sailor would have stopped them. And, it may be mentioned, that the two boys were as a matter of fact extremely steady, sensible young fellows, not in the least likely to play foolish tricks of any kind.

Lewis was immersed in these reflections, having successfully silenced his brother-in-law; he was trying in vain to find some clue to the horrible enigma. The Midlingham theory of a concealed German force, hiding in places under the earth, was extravagant enough, and yet it seemed the only solution that approached plausibility; but then again even a subterranean German host would hardly account for this wreckage of a boat, floating on a calm sea. And then what of the tree with the burning in it that had appeared in the garden there a few weeks ago, and the cloud with a burning in it that had shown over the trees of the Midland village?

I think I have already written something of the probable emotions of the mathematician confronted suddenly with an undoubted two-sided triangle. I said, if I remember, that he would be forced, in decency, to go mad; and I believe that Lewis was very near to this point. He felt himself confronted with an intolerable problem that most instantly demanded solution, and yet, with the same breath, as it were, denied the possibility of there being any solution. People were being killed in an inscrutable manner by some inscrutable means, day after day, and one asked 'why' and 'how'; and there seemed no answer. In the Midlands, where every kind of munitionment was manufactured, the explanation of German agency was plausible; and even if the subterranean notion was to be rejected as savouring altogether too much of the fairytale, or rather of the sensational romance, yet it was possible that the backbone of the theory was true; the Germans might have planted their agents in some way or another in the midst of our factories. But here in Meirion, what serious effect could be produced by the casual and indiscriminate slaughter of a couple of schoolboys in a boat, of a harmless holidaymaker in a marsh? The creation of an atmosphere of terror and dismay? It was possible, of course, but it hardly seemed tolerable, in spite of the enormities of Louvain and of the *Lusitania*.

Into these meditations, and into the still dignified silence of Merritt broke the rap on the door of Lewis's man, and those words which harass the ease of the country doctor when he tries to take any ease: 'You're wanted in the surgery, if you please, sir.' Lewis bustled out, and appeared no more that night.

The doctor had been summoned to a little hamlet on the outskirts of Porth, separated from it by half a mile or three-quarters of road. One dignifies, indeed, this settlement without a name in calling it a hamlet; it was a mere row of four cottages, built about a hundred years ago for the accommodation of the workers in a quarry long since disused. In one of these cottages the doctor found a father and mother weeping and crying out to 'doctor bach, doctor bach', and two frightened children, and one little body, still and dead. It was the youngest of the three, little Johnnie, and he was dead.

The doctor found that the child had been asphyxiated. He felt the clothes; they were dry; it was not a case of drowning. He looked at the neck; there was no mark of strangling. He asked the father how it had happened, and father and mother, weeping most lamentably, declared they had no knowledge of how their child had been killed: 'unless it was the People that had done it.' The Celtic fairies are still malignant. Lewis asked what had happened that evening; where had the child been?

'Was he with his brother and sister? Don't they know anything about it?'

Reduced into some sort of order from its original piteous confusion, this is the story that the doctor gathered.

All three children had been well and happy through the day. They had walked in with the mother, Mrs Roberts, to Porth on a marketing expedition in the afternoon; they had returned to the cottage, had had their tea, and afterwards played about on the road in front of the house. John Roberts had come home somewhat late from his work, and it was after dusk when the family sat down to supper. Supper over, the three children went out again to play with other children from the cottage next door, Mrs Roberts telling them that they might have half an hour before going to bed.

The two mothers came to the cottage gates at the same moment and called out to their children to come along and be quick about it. The two small families had been playing on the strip of turf across the road, just by the stile into the fields. The children ran across the road; all of them except Johnnie Roberts. His brother Willie said that just as their mother called them he heard Johnnie cry out:

'Oh, what is that beautiful shiny thing over the stile?'

X
The Child and the Moth

The little Robertses ran across the road, up the path, and into the lighted room. Then they noticed that Johnnie had not followed them. Mrs Roberts was doing something in the back kitchen, and Mr Roberts had gone out to the shed to bring in some sticks for the next morning's fire. Mrs Roberts heard the children run in and went on with her work. The children whispered to one another that Johnnie would 'catch it' when their mother came out of the back room and found him missing; but they expected he would run in through the open door any minute. But six or seven, perhaps ten, minutes passed, and there was no Johnnie. Then the father and mother came into the kitchen together, and saw that their little boy was not there.

They thought it was some small piece of mischief – that the two other children had hidden the boy somewhere in the room: in the big cupboard perhaps.

'What have you done with him then?' said Mrs Roberts. 'Come out, you little rascal, directly in a minute.'

There was no little rascal to come out, and Margaret Roberts, the girl, said that Johnnie had not come across the road with them: he must be still playing all by himself by the hedge.

'What did you let him stay like that for?' said Mrs Roberts. 'Can't I trust you for two minutes together? Indeed to goodness, you are all of you more trouble than you are worth.' She went to the open door:

'Johnnie! Come you in directly, or you will be sorry for it. Johnnie!'

The poor woman called at the door. She went out to the gate and called there:

'Come you, little Johnnie. Come you, bachgen, there's a good boy. I do see you hiding there.'

She thought he must be hiding in the shadow of the hedge, and that he would come running and laughing – 'he was always such a happy little fellow' – to her across the road. But no little merry figure danced out of the gloom of the still, dark night; it was all silence.

It was then, as the mother's heart began to chill, though she still called cheerfully to the missing child, that the elder boy told how Johnnie had said there was something beautiful by the stile: 'and perhaps he did climb over, and he is running now about the meadow, and has lost his way.'

The father got his lantern then, and the whole family went crying and calling about the meadow, promising cakes and sweets and a fine toy to poor Johnnie if he would come to them.

They found the little body, under the ashgrove in the middle of the field. He was quite still and dead, so still that a great moth had settled on his forehead, fluttering away when they lifted him up.

Dr Lewis heard this story. There was nothing to be done; little to be said to these most unhappy people.

'Take care of the two that you have left to you,' said the doctor as he went away. 'Don't let them out of your sight if you can help it. It is dreadful times that we are living in.'

It is curious to record, that all through these dreadful times the simple little 'season' went through its accustomed course at Porth. The war and its consequences had somewhat thinned the numbers of the summer visitors; still a very fair contingent of them occupied the hotels and boarding houses and lodging houses and bathed from the old-fashioned machines on one beach, or from the new-fashioned tents on the other, and sauntered in the sun, or lay stretched out in the shade under the trees that grow down almost to the water's edge. Porth never tolerated Ethiopians or shows of any kind on its sands, but 'the Rockets' did very well during that summer in their garden entertainment, given in the castle grounds, and the fit-up companies that came to the Assembly Rooms are said to have paid their bills to a woman and to a man.

Porth depends very largely on its midland and northern custom, custom of a prosperous, well-established sort. People who think Llandudno overcrowded and Colwyn Bay too raw and red and new, come year after year to the placid old town in the southwest and delight in its peace; and as I say, they enjoyed themselves much as usual there in the summer of 1915. Now and then they became conscious, as Mr Merritt became conscious, that they could not wander about quite in the old way; but they accepted sentries and coast watchers and people who politely pointed out the advantages of seeing the view from this point rather than from that as very necessary consequences of the dreadful war that was being waged; nay, as a Manchester man said, after having been turned back from his favourite walk to Castell Coch, it was gratifying to think that they were so well looked after.

'So far as I can see,' he added, 'there's nothing to prevent a submarine from standing out there by Ynys Sant and landing half a dozen men in a collapsible boat in any of these little coves. And pretty fools we should look, shouldn't we, with our throats cut on the sands; or carried back to Germany in the submarine?' He tipped the coast watcher half-a-crown.

'That's right, lad,' he said, 'you give us the tip.'

Now here was a strange thing. The north-countryman had his thoughts on elusive submarines and German raiders; the watcher had simply received instructions to keep people off the Castell Coch fields, without reason assigned. And there can be no doubt that the authorities themselves, while they marked out the fields as in the 'terror zone', gave their orders in the dark and were themselves profoundly in the dark as to the manner of the slaughter that had been done there; for if they had understood what had happened, they would have understood also that their restrictions were useless.

The Manchester man was warned off his walk about ten days after Johnnie Roberts's death. The Watcher had been placed at his post because, the night before, a young farmer had been found by his wife lying in the grass close to the Castle, with no scar on him, nor any mark of violence, but stone dead.

The wife of the dead man, Joseph Cradock, finding her husband lying motionless on the dewy turf, went white and stricken up the path to the village and got two men who bore the body to the farm. Lewis was sent for, and knew at once when he saw the dead man that he had perished in the way that the little Roberts boy had perished – whatever that awful way might be. Cradock had been asphyxiated; and here again there was no mark of a grip on the throat. It might have been a piece of work by Burke and Hare, the doctor reflected; a pitch plaster might have been clapped over the man's mouth and nostrils and held there.

Then a thought struck him; his brother-in-law had talked of a new kind of poison gas that was said to be used against the munition workers in the Midlands: was it possible that the deaths of the man and the boy were due to some such instrument? He applied his tests but could find no trace of any gas having been employed. Carbonic acid gas? A man could not be killed with that in the open air; to be fatal that required a confined space, such a position as the bottom of a huge vat or of a well.

He did not know how Cradock had been killed; he confessed it to himself. He had been suffocated; that was all he could say.

It seemed that the man had gone out at about half-past nine to look after some beasts. The field in which they were was about five minutes' walk from the house. He told his wife he would be back in a quarter of an hour or twenty minutes. He did not return, and when he had been gone for three-quarters of an hour Mrs Cradock went out to look for him. She went into the field where the beasts were, and everything seemed all right, but there was no trace of Cradock. She called out; there was no answer.

Now the meadow in which the cattle were pastured is high ground; a hedge divides it from the fields which fall gently down to the castle and the sea. Mrs Cradock hardly seemed able to say why, having failed to find her husband among his beasts, she turned to the path which led to Castell Coch. She said at first that she had thought that one of the oxen might have broken through the hedge and strayed, and that Cradock had perhaps gone after it. And then, correcting herself, she said:

'There was that; and then there was something else that I could not make out at all. It seemed to me that the hedge did look different from usual. To be sure, things do look different at night, and there was a bit of sea mist about, but somehow it did look odd to me, and I said to myself, "have I lost my way, then?"'

She declared that the shape of the trees in the hedge appeared to have changed, and besides, it had a look 'as if it was lighted up, somehow', and so she went on towards the stile to see what all this could be, and when she came near everything was as usual. She looked over the stile and called and hoped to see her husband coming towards her or to hear his voice; but there was no answer, and glancing down the path she saw, or thought she saw, some sort of brightness on the ground, 'a dim sort of light like a bunch of glow-worms in a hedge-bank.

'And so I climbed over the stile and went down the path, and the light seemed to melt away; and there was my poor husband lying on his back, saying not a word to me when I spoke to him and touched him.'

So for Lewis the terror blackened and became altogether intolerable, and others, he perceived, felt as he did. He did not know, he never asked whether the men at the club had heard of these deaths of the child and the young farmer; but no one spoke of them. Indeed, the change was evident; at the beginning of the terror men spoke of nothing else; now it had become all too awful for ingenious chatter or laboured and grotesque theories. And Lewis had received a letter from his brother-in-law at Midlingham; it contained the sentence, 'I am afraid Fanny's health has not greatly benefited by her visit to Porth; there are still several symptoms I don't at all like.' And this told him, in a phraseology that the doctor and Merritt had agreed upon, that the terror remained heavy in the Midland town.

It was soon after the death of Cradock that people began to tell strange tales of a sound that was to be heard of nights about the hills and valleys to the northward of Porth. A man who had missed the last train from Meiros and had been forced to tramp the ten miles between Meiros and Porth seems to have been the first to hear it. He said he had got to the top of the hill by Tredonoc, somewhere between half-past ten and eleven, when he first noticed an odd noise that he could not make out at all; it was like a shout, a long, drawn-out, dismal wail coming from a great way off, faint with distance. He stopped to listen, thinking at first that it might be owls hooting in the woods; but it was different, he said, from that: it was a long cry, and then there was silence and then it began over again. He could make nothing of it, and feeling frightened, he did not quite know of what, he walked on briskly and was glad to see the lights of Porth station.

He told his wife of this dismal sound that night, and she told the neighbours, and most of them thought that it was 'all fancy' – or drink, or the owls after all. But the night after, two or three people, who had been to some small merrymaking in a cottage just off the Meiros road, heard the sound as they were going home, soon after ten. They, too, described it as a long, wailing cry, indescribably dismal in the stillness of the autumn night; 'like the ghost of a voice', said one; 'as if it came up from the bottom of the earth', said another.

XI
At Treff Loyne Farm

Let it be remembered, again and again, that, all the while that the terror lasted, there was no common stock of information as to the dreadful things that were being done. The press had not said one word upon it, there was no criterion by which the mass of the people could separate fact from mere vague rumour, no test by which ordinary misadventure or disaster could be distinguished from the achievements of the secret and awful force that was at work.

And so with every event of the passing day. A harmless commercial traveller might show himself in the course of his business in the tumbledown main street of Meiros and find himself regarded with looks of fear and suspicion as a possible worker of murder, while it is likely enough that the true agents of the terror went quite unnoticed. And since the real nature of all this mystery of death was unknown, it followed easily that the signs and warnings and omens of it were all the more unknown. Here was horror, there was horror; but there was no link to join one horror with another; no common basis of knowledge from which the connection between this horror and that horror might be inferred.

So there was no one who suspected at all that this dismal and hollow sound that was now heard of nights in the region to the north of Porth, had any relation at all to the case of the little girl who went out one afternoon to pick purple flowers and never returned, or to the case of the man whose body was taken out of the peaty slime of the marsh, or to the case of Cradock, dead in his fields, with a strange glimmering of light about his body, as his wife reported. And it is a question as to how far the rumour of this melancholy, nocturnal summons got abroad at all. Lewis heard of it, as a country doctor hears of most things, driving up and down the lanes, but he heard of it without much interest, with no sense that it was in any sort of relation to the terror. Remnant had been given the story of the hollow and echoing voice of the darkness in a coloured and picturesque form; he employed a Tredonoc man to work in his garden once a week. The gardener had not heard the summons himself, but he knew a man who had done so.

'Thomas Jenkins, Pentoppin, he did put his head out late last night to see what the weather was like, and he was cutting a field of corn the next day, and he did tell me that when he was with the Methodists in Cardigan he did never hear no singing eloquence in the chapels that was like to it. He did declare it was like a wailing of Judgment Day.'

Remnant considered the matter, and was inclined to think that the sound must be caused by a subterranean inlet of the sea; there might be, he supposed, an imperfect or half-opened or tortuous blowhole in the Tredonoc woods, and the noise of the tide, surging up below, might very well produce that effect of a hollow wailing, far away. But neither he nor any one else paid much attention to the matter; save the few who heard the call at dead of night, as it echoed awfully over the black hills.

The sound had been heard for three or perhaps four nights, when the people coming out of Tredonoc church after morning service on Sunday noticed that there was a big yellow sheepdog in the churchyard. The dog, it appeared, had been waiting for the congregation; for it at once attached itself to them, at first to the whole body, and then to a group of half a dozen who took the turning to the right. Two of these presently went off over the fields to their respective houses, and four strolled on in the leisurely Sunday morning manner of the country, and these the dog followed, keeping to heel all the time. The men were talking hay, corn and markets and paid no attention to the animal, and so they strolled along the autumn lane till they came to a gate in the hedge, whence a roughly made farm road went through the fields, and dipped down into the woods and to Treff Loyne farm.

Then the dog became like a possessed creature. He barked furiously. He ran up to one of the men and looked up at him, 'as if he were begging for his life', as the man said, and then rushed to the gate and stood by it, wagging his tail and barking at intervals. The men stared and laughed.

'Whose dog will that be?' said one of them.

'It will be Thomas Griffith's, Treff Loyne,' said another.

'Well, then, why doesn't he go home? Go home then!' He went through the gesture of picking up a stone from the road and throwing it at the dog. 'Go home, then! Over the gate with you.'

But the dog never stirred. He barked and whined and ran up to the men and then back to the gate. At last he came to one of them, and crawled and abased himself on the ground and then took hold of the man's coat and tried to pull him in the direction of the gate. The farmer shook the dog off, and the four went on their way; and the dog stood in the road and watched them and then put up its head and uttered a long and dismal howl that was despair.

The four farmers thought nothing of it; sheepdogs in the country are dogs to look after sheep, and their whims and fancies are not studied. But the yellow dog – he was a kind of degenerate collie – haunted the Tredonoc lanes from that day. He came to a cottage door one night and scratched at it, and when it was opened lay down, and then, barking, ran to the garden gate and waited, entreating, as it seemed, the cottager to follow him. They drove him away and again he gave that long howl of anguish. It was almost as bad, they said, as the noise that they had heard a few nights before. And then it occurred to somebody, so far as I can make out with no particular reference to the odd conduct of the Treff Loyne sheepdog, that Thomas Griffith had not been seen for some time past. He had missed market day at Porth, he had not been at Tredonoc church, where he was a pretty regular attendant on Sunday; and then, as heads were put together, it appeared that nobody had seen any of the Griffith family for days and days.

Now in a town, even in a small town, this process of putting heads together is a pretty quick business. In the country, especially in a countryside of wild lands and scattered and lonely farms and cottages, the affair takes time. Harvest was going on, everybody was busy in his own fields, and after the long day's hard work neither the farmer nor his men felt inclined to stroll about in search of news or gossip. A harvester at the day's end is ready for supper and sleep and for nothing else.

And so it was late in that week when it was discovered that Thomas Griffith and all his house had vanished from this world.

I have often been reproached for my curiosity over questions which are apparently of slight importance, or of no importance at all. I love to inquire, for instance, into the question of the visibility of a lighted candle at a distance. Suppose, that is, a candle lighted on a still, dark night in the country; what is the greatest distance at which you can see that there is a light at all? And then as to the human voice; what is its carrying distance, under good conditions, as a mere sound, apart from any matter of making out words that may be uttered?

They are trivial questions, no doubt, but they have always interested me, and the latter point has its application to the strange business of Treff Loyne. That melancholy and hollow sound, that wailing summons that appalled the hearts of those who heard it was, indeed, a human voice, produced in a very exceptional manner; and it seems to have been heard at points varying from a mile and a half to two miles from the farm. I do not know whether this is anything extraordinary; I do not know whether the peculiar method of production was calculated to increase or to diminish the carrying power of the sound.

Again and again I have laid emphasis in this story of the terror on the strange isolation of many of the farms and cottages in Meirion. I have done so in the effort to convince the townsman of something that he has never known. To the Londoner a house a quarter of a mile from the outlying suburban lamp, with no other dwelling within two hundred yards, is a lonely house, a place to fit with ghosts and mysteries and terrors. How can he understand then, the true loneliness of the white farmhouses of Meirion, dotted here and there, for the most part not even on the little lanes and deep winding byways, but set in the very heart of the fields, or alone on huge bastioned headlands facing the sea, and whether on the high verge of the sea or on the hills or in the hollows of the inner country, hidden from the sight of men, far from the sound of any common call. There is Penyrhaul, for example, the farm from which the foolish Merritt thought he saw signals of light being made: from seaward it is of course, widely visible; but from landward, owing partly to the curving and indented configuration of the bay, I doubt whether any other habitation views it from a nearer distance than three miles.

And of all these hidden and remote places, I doubt if any is so deeply buried as Treff Loyne. I have little or no Welsh, I am sorry to say, but I suppose that the name is corrupted from Trellwyn, or Tref-y-llwyn, 'the place in the grove', and, indeed, it lies in the very heart of dark, overhanging woods. A deep, narrow valley runs down from the high lands of the Allt, through these woods, through steep hillsides of bracken and gorse, right down to the great marsh, whence Merritt saw the dead man being carried. The valley lies away from any road, even from that by-road, little better than a bridlepath, where the four farmers, returning from church, were perplexed by the strange antics of the sheepdog. One cannot say that the valley is overlooked, even from a distance, for so narrow is it that the ash groves that rim it on either side seem to meet and shut it in. I, at all events, have never found any high place from which Treff Loyne is visible; though, looking down from the Allt, I have seen blue woodsmoke rising from its hidden chimneys.

Such was the place, then, to which one September afternoon a party went up to discover what had happened to Griffith and his family. There were half a dozen farmers, a couple of policemen, and four soldiers, carrying their arms; those last had been lent by the officer commanding at the camp. Lewis, too, was of the party; he had heard by chance that no one knew what had become of Griffith and his family; and he was anxious about a young fellow, a painter, of his acquaintance, who had been lodging at Treff Loyne all the summer.

They all met by the gate of Tredonoc churchyard, and tramped solemnly along the narrow lane; all of them, I think, with some vague discomfort of mind, with a certain shadowy fear, as of men who do not quite know what they may encounter. Lewis heard the corporal and the three soldiers arguing over their orders.

'The Captain says to me,' muttered the corporal, '"Don't hesitate to shoot if there's any trouble." "Shoot what, sir," I says. "The trouble," says he, and that's all I could get out of him.'

The men grumbled in reply; Lewis thought he heard some obscure reference to rat poison, and wondered what they were talking about.

They came to the gate in the hedge, where the farm road led down to Treff Loyne. They followed this track, roughly made, with grass growing up between its loosely laid stones, down by the hedge from field to wood, till at last they came to the sudden walls of the valley, and the sheltering groves of the ash trees. Here the way curved down the steep hillside, and bent southward, and followed henceforward the hidden hollow of the valley, under the shadow of the trees.

Here was the farm enclosure; the outlying walls of the yard and the barns and sheds and outhouses. One of the farmers threw open the gate and walked into the yard, and forthwith began bellowing at the top of his voice:

'Thomas Griffith! Thomas Griffith! Where be you, Thomas Griffith?'

The rest followed him. The corporal snapped out an order over his shoulder, and there was a rattling metallic noise as the men fixed their bayonets and became in an instant dreadful dealers out of death, in place of harmless fellows with a feeling for beer.

'Thomas Griffith!' again bellowed the farmer.

There was no answer to this summons. But they found poor Griffith lying on his face at the edge of the pond in the middle of the yard. There was a ghastly wound in his side, as if a sharp stake had been driven into his body.

XII
The Letter of Wrath

It was a still September afternoon. No wind stirred in the hanging woods that were dark all about the ancient house of Treff Loyne; the only sound in the dim air was the lowing of the cattle; they had wandered, it seemed, from the fields and had come in by the gate of the farmyard and stood there melancholy, as if they mourned for their dead master. And the horses: four great, heavy, patient-looking beasts; they were there too, and in the lower field the sheep were standing, as if they waited to be fed.

'You would think they all knew there was something wrong,' one of the soldiers muttered to another. A pale sun showed for a moment and glittered on their bayonets. They were standing about the body of poor, dead Griffith, with a certain grimness growing on their faces and hardening there. Their corporal snapped something at them again; they were quite ready. Lewis knelt down by the dead man and looked closely at the great gaping wound in his side.

'He's been dead a long time,' he said. 'A week, two weeks, perhaps. He was killed by some sharp pointed weapon. How about the family? How many are there of them? I never attended them.'

'There was Griffith, and his wife, and his son Thomas and Mary Griffith, his daughter. And I do think there was a gentleman lodging with them this summer.'

That was from one of the farmers. They all looked at one another, this party of rescue, who knew nothing of the danger that had smitten this house of quiet people, nothing of the peril which had brought them to this pass of a farmyard with a dead man in it, and his beasts standing patiently about him, as if they waited for the farmer to rise up and give them their food. Then the party turned to the house. It was an old, sixteenth century building, with the singular round, 'Flemish' chimney that is characteristic of Meirion. The walls were snowy with whitewash, the windows were deeply set and stone mullioned, and a solid, stone-tiled porch sheltered the doorway from any winds that might penetrate to the hollow of that hidden valley. The windows were shut tight. There was no sign of any life or movement about the place. The party of men looked at one another, and the churchwarden amongst the farmers, the sergeant of police, Lewis, and the corporal drew together.

'What is it to goodness, doctor?' said the churchwarden.

'I can tell you nothing at all – except that that poor man there has been pierced to the heart,' said Lewis.

'Do you think they are inside and they will shoot us?' said another farmer. He had no notion of what he meant by 'they', and no one of them knew better than he. They did not know what the danger was, or where it might strike them, or whether it was from without or from within. They stared at the murdered man, and gazed dismally at one another.

'Come!' said Lewis, 'we must do something. We must get into the house and see what is wrong.'

'Yes, but suppose they are at us while we are getting in,' said the sergeant. 'Where shall we be then, Doctor Lewis?'

The corporal put one of his men by the gate at the top of the farmyard, another at the gate by the bottom of the farmyard, and told them to challenge and shoot. The doctor and the rest opened the little gate of the front garden and went up to the porch and stood listening by the door. It was all dead silence. Lewis took an ash stick from one of the farmers and beat heavily three times on the old, black, oaken door studded with antique nails.

He struck three thundering blows, and then they all waited. There was no answer from within. He beat again, and still silence. He shouted to the people within, but there was no answer. They all turned and looked at one another, that party of quest and rescue who knew not what they sought, what enemy they were to encounter. There was an iron ring on the door. Lewis turned it but the door stood fast; it was evidently barred and bolted. The sergeant of police called out to open, but again there was no answer.

They consulted together. There was nothing for it but to blow the door open, and some one of them called in a loud voice to anybody that might be within to stand away from the door, or they would be killed. And at this very moment the yellow sheepdog came bounding up the yard from the woods and licked their hands and fawned on them and barked joyfully.

'Indeed now,' said one of the farmers; 'he did know that there was something amiss. A pity it was, Thomas Williams, that we did not follow him when he implored us last Sunday.'

The corporal motioned the rest of the party back, and they stood looking fearfully about them at the entrance to the porch. The corporal disengaged his bayonet and shot into the keyhole, calling out once more before he fired. He shot and shot again; so heavy and firm was the ancient door, so stout its bolts and fastenings. At last he had to fire at the massive hinges, and then they all pushed together and the door lurched open and fell forward. The corporal raised his left hand and stepped back a few paces. He hailed his two men at the top and bottom of the farmyard. They were all right, they said. And so the party climbed and struggled over the fallen door into the passage, and into the kitchen of the farmhouse.

Young Griffith was lying dead before the hearth, before a dead fire of white wood ashes. They went on towards the 'parlour', and in the doorway of the room was the body of the artist, Secretan, as if he had fallen in trying to get to the kitchen. Upstairs the two women, Mrs Griffith and her daughter, a girl of eighteen, were lying together on the bed in the big bedroom, clasped in each others' arms.

They went about the house, searched the pantries, the back kitchen and the cellars; there was no life in it.

'Look!' said Dr Lewis, when they came back to the big kitchen, 'look! It is as if they had been besieged. Do you see that piece of bacon, half gnawed through?'

Then they found these pieces of bacon, cut from the sides on the kitchen wall, here and there about the house. There was no bread in the place, no milk, no water.

'And,' said one of the farmers, 'they had the best water here in all Meirion. The well is down there in the wood; it is most famous water. The old people did use to call it Ffynnon Teilo; it was Saint Teilo's Well, they did say.'

'They must have died of thirst,' said Lewis. 'They have been dead for days and days.'

The group of men stood in the big kitchen and stared at one another, a dreadful perplexity in their eyes. The dead were all about them, within the house and without it; and it was in vain to ask why they had died thus. The old man had been killed with the piercing thrust of some sharp weapon; the rest had perished, it seemed probable, of thirst; but what possible enemy was this that besieged the farm and shut in its inhabitants? There was no answer.

The sergeant of police spoke of getting a cart and taking the bodies into Porth, and Dr Lewis went into the parlour that Secretan had used as a sitting room, intending to gather any possessions or effects of the dead artist that he might find there. Half a dozen portfolios were piled up in one corner, there were some books on a side table, a fishing rod and basket behind the door – that seemed all. No doubt there would be clothes and such matters upstairs, and Lewis was about to rejoin the rest of the party in the kitchen, when he looked down at some scattered papers lying with the books on the side table. On one of the sheets he read to his astonishment the words: 'Dr James Lewis, Porth'. This was written in a staggering trembling scrawl, and examining the other leaves he saw that they were covered with writing.

The table stood in a dark corner of the room, and Lewis gathered up the sheets of paper and took them to the window ledge and began to read, amazed at certain phrases that had caught his eye. But the manuscript was in disorder; as if the dead man who had written it had not been equal to the task of gathering the leaves into their proper sequence; it was some time before the doctor had each page in its place. This was the statement that he read, with ever-growing wonder, while a couple of the farmers were harnessing one of the horses in the yard to a cart, and the others were bringing down the dead women.

'I do not think that I can last much longer. We shared out the last drops of water a long time ago. I do not know how many days ago. We fall asleep and dream and walk about the house in our dreams, and I am often not sure whether I am awake or still dreaming, and so the days and nights are confused in my mind. I awoke not long ago, at least I suppose I awoke and found I was lying in the passage. I had a confused feeling that I had had an awful dream which seemed horribly real, and I thought for a moment what a relief it was to know that it wasn't true, whatever it might have been. I made up my mind to have a good long walk to freshen myself up, and then I looked round and found that I had been lying on the stones of the passage; and it all came back to me. There was no walk for me.

'I have not seen Mrs Griffith or her daughter for a long while. They said they were going upstairs to have a rest. I heard them moving about the room at first, now I can hear nothing. Young Griffith is lying in the kitchen, before the hearth. He was talking to himself about the harvest and the weather when I last went into the kitchen. He didn't seem to know I was there, as he went gabbling on in a low voice very fast, and then he began to call the dog, Tiger.

'There seems no hope for any of us. We are in the dream of death . . . '

Here the manuscript became unintelligible for half a dozen lines. Secretan had written the words 'dream of death' three or four times over. He had begun a fresh word and had scratched it out and then followed strange, unmeaning characters, the script, as Lewis thought, of a terrible language. And then the writing became clear, clearer than it was at the beginning of the manuscript, and the sentences flowed more easily, as if the cloud on Secretan's mind had lifted for a while. There was a fresh start, as it were, and the writer began again, in ordinary letter form:

'Dear Lewis,

'I hope you will excuse all this confusion and wandering. I intended to begin a proper letter to you, and now I find all that stuff that you have been reading – if this ever gets into your hands. I have not the energy even to tear it up. If you read it you will know to what a sad pass I had come when it was written. It looks like delirium or a bad dream, and even now, though my mind seems to have cleared up a good deal, I have to hold myself in tightly to be sure that the experiences of the last days in this awful place are true, real things, not a long nightmare from which I shall wake up presently and find myself in my rooms at Chelsea.

'I have said of what I am writing, "if it ever gets into your hands", and I am not at all sure that it ever will. If what is happening here is happening everywhere else, then I suppose, the world is coming to an end. I cannot understand it, even now I can hardly believe it. I know that I dream such wild dreams and walk in such mad fancies that I have to look out and look about me to make sure that I am not still dreaming.

'Do you remember that talk we had about two months ago when I dined with you? We got on, somehow or other, to space and time, and I think we agreed that as soon as one tried to reason about space and time one was landed in a maze of contradictions. You said something to the effect that it was very curious but this was just like a dream. "A man will sometimes wake himself from his crazy dream," you said, "by realising that he is thinking nonsense." And we both wondered whether these contradictions that one can't avoid if one begins to think of time and space may not really be proofs that the whole of life is a dream, and the moon and the stars bits of nightmare. I have often thought over that lately. I kick at the walls as Dr Johnson kicked at the stone, to make sure that the things about me are there. And then that other question gets into my mind – is the world really coming to an end, the world as we have always known it; and what on earth will this new world be like? I can't imagine it; it's a story like Noah's Ark and the Flood. People used to talk about the end of the world and fire, but no one ever thought of anything like this.

'And then there's another thing that bothers me. Now and then I wonder whether we are not all mad together in this house. In spite of what I see and know, or, perhaps, I should say, because what I see and know is so impossible, I wonder whether we are not all suffering from a delusion. Perhaps we are our own gaolers, and we are really free to go out and live. Perhaps what we think we see is not there at all. I believe I have heard of whole families going mad together, and I may have come under the influence of the house, having lived in it for the last four months. I know there have been people who have been kept alive by their keepers forcing food down their throats, because they are quite sure that their throats are closed, so that they feel they are unable to swallow a morsel. I wonder now and then whether we are all like this in Treff Loyne; yet in my heart I feel sure that it is not so.

'Still, I do not want to leave a madman's letter behind me, and so I will not tell you the full story of what I have seen, or believe I have seen. If I am a sane man you will be able to fill in the blanks for yourself from your own knowledge. If I am mad, burn the letter and say nothing about it. Or perhaps – and indeed, I am not quite sure – I may wake up and hear Mary Griffith calling to me in her cheerful sing-song that breakfast will be ready "directly, in a minute", and I shall enjoy it and walk over to Porth and tell you the queerest, most horrible dream that a man ever had, and ask what I had better take.

'I think that it was on a Tuesday that we first noticed that there was something queer about, only at the time we didn't know that there was anything really queer in what we noticed. I had been out since nine o'clock in the morning trying to paint the marsh, and I found it a very tough job. I came home about five or six o'clock and found the family at Treff Loyne laughing at old Tiger, the sheepdog. He was making short runs from the farmyard to the door of the house, barking, with quick, short yelps. Mrs Griffith and Miss Griffith were standing by the porch, and the dog would go to them, look in their faces, and then run up the farmyard to the gate, and then look back with that eager yelping bark, as if he were waiting for the women to follow him. Then, again and again, he ran up to them and tugged at their skirts as if he would pull them by main force away from the house.

'Then the men came home from the fields and he repeated this performance. The dog was running all up and down the farmyard, in and out of the barn and sheds yelping, barking; and always with that eager run to the person he addressed, and running away directly, and looking back as if to see whether we were following him. When the house door was shut and they all sat down to supper, he would give them no peace, till at last they turned him out of doors. And then he sat in the porch and scratched at the door with his claws, barking all the while. When the daughter brought in my meal, she said: "We can't think what is come to old Tiger, and indeed, he has always been a good dog, too."

'The dog barked and yelped and whined and scratched at the door all through the evening. They let him in once, but he seemed to have become quite frantic. He ran up to one member of the family after another; his eyes were bloodshot and his mouth was foaming, and he tore at their clothes till they drove him out again into the darkness. Then he broke into a long, lamentable howl of anguish, and we heard no more of him.'

XIII
The Last Words of Mr. Secretan

'I slept ill that night. I awoke again and again from uneasy dreams, and I seemed in my sleep to hear strange calls and noises and a sound of murmurs and beatings on the door. There were deep, hollow voices, too, that echoed in my sleep, and when I woke I could hear the autumn wind, mournful, on the hills above us. I started up once with a dreadful scream in my ears; but then the house was all still, and I fell again into uneasy sleep.

'It was soon after dawn when I finally roused myself. The people in the house were talking to each other in high voices, arguing about something that I did not understand.

'"It is those damned gipsies, I tell you," said old Griffith.

'"What would they do a thing like that for?" asked Mrs Griffith. "If it was stealing now – "

'"It is more likely that John Jenkins has done it out of spite," said the son. "He said that he would remember you when we did catch him poaching."

'They seemed puzzled and angry, so far as I could make out, but not at all frightened. I got up and began to dress. I don't think I looked out of the window. The glass on my dressing table is high and broad, and the window is small; one would have to poke one's head round the glass to see anything.

'The voices were still arguing downstairs. I heard the old man say, "Well, here's for a beginning anyhow," and then the door slammed.

'A minute later the old man shouted, I think, to his son. Then there was a great noise which I will not describe more particularly, and a dreadful screaming and crying inside the house and a sound of rushing feet. They all cried out at once to each other. I heard the daughter crying, "it is no good, mother, he is dead, indeed they have killed him," and Mrs Griffith screaming to the girl to let her go. And then one of them rushed out of the kitchen and shot the great bolts of oak across the door, just as something beat against it with a thundering crash.

'I ran downstairs. I found them all in wild confusion, in an agony of grief and horror and amazement. They were like people who had seen something so awful that they had gone mad.

'I went to the window looking out on the farmyard. I won't tell you all that I saw. But I saw poor old Griffith lying by the pond, with the blood pouring out of his side.

'I wanted to go out to him and bring him in. But they told me that he must be stone dead, and such things also that it was quite plain that any one who went out of the house would not live more than a moment. We could not believe it, even as we gazed at the body of the dead man; but it was there. I used to wonder sometimes what one would feel like if one saw an apple drop from the tree and shoot up into the air and disappear. I think I know now how one would feel.

'Even then we couldn't believe that it would last. We were not seriously afraid for ourselves. We spoke of getting out in an hour or two, before dinner anyhow. It couldn't last, because it was impossible. Indeed, at twelve o'clock young Griffith said he would go down to the well by the back way and draw another pail of water. I went to the door and stood by it. He had not gone a dozen yards before they were on him. He ran for his life, and we had all we could do to bar the door in time. And then I began to get frightened.

'Still we could not believe in it. Somebody would come along shouting in an hour or two and it would all melt away and vanish. There could not be any real danger. There was plenty of bacon in the house, and half the weekly baking of loaves and some beer in the cellar and a pound or so of tea, and a whole pitcher of water that had been drawn from the well the night before. We could do all right for the day and in the morning it would have all gone away.

'But day followed day and it was still there. I knew Treff Loyne was a lonely place – that was why I had gone there, to have a long rest from all the jangle and rattle and turmoil of London, that makes a man alive and kills him too. I went to Treff Loyne because it was buried in the narrow valley under the ash trees, far away from any track. There was not so much as a footpath that was near it; no one ever came that way. Young Griffith had told me that it was a mile and a half to the nearest house, and the thought of the silent peace and retirement of the farm used to be a delight to me.

'And now this thought came back without delight, with terror. Griffith thought that a shout might be heard on a still night up away on the Allt, "if a man was listening for it," he added, doubtfully. My voice was clearer and stronger than his, and on the second night I said I would go up to my bedroom and call for help through the open window. I waited till it was all dark and still, and looked out through the window before opening it. And then I saw over the ridge of the long barn across the yard what looked like a tree, though I knew there was no tree there. It was a dark mass against the sky, with wide-spread boughs, a tree of thick, dense growth. I wondered what this could be, and I threw open the window, not only because I was going to call for help, but because I wanted to see more clearly what the dark growth over the barn really was.

'I saw in the depth of the dark of it points of fire, and colours in light, all glowing and moving, and the air trembled. I stared out into the night, and the dark tree lifted over the roof of the barn and rose up in the air and floated towards me. I did not move till at the last moment when it was close to the house; and then I saw what it was and banged the window down only just in time. I had to fight, and I saw the tree that was like a burning cloud rise up in the night and sink again and settle over the barn.

'I told them downstairs of this. They sat with white faces, and Mrs Griffith said that ancient devils were let loose and had come out of the trees and out of the old hills because of the wickedness that was on the earth. She began to murmur something to herself, something that sounded to me like broken-down Latin.

'I went up to my room again an hour later, but the dark tree swelled over the barn. Another day went by, and at dusk I looked out, but the eyes of fire were watching me. I dared not open the window.

'And then I thought of another plan. There was the great old fireplace, with the round Flemish chimney going high above the house. If

I stood beneath it and shouted I thought perhaps the sound might be carried better than if I called out of the window; for all I knew the round chimney might act as a sort of megaphone. Night after night, then, I stood in the hearth and called for help from nine o'clock to eleven. I thought of the lonely place, deep in the valley of the ash trees, of the lonely hills and lands about it. I thought of the little cottages far away and hoped that my voice might reach to those within them. I thought of the winding lane high on the Allt, and of the few men that came there of nights; but I hoped that my cry might come to one of them.

'But we had drunk up the beer, and we would only let ourselves have water by little drops, and on the fourth night my throat was dry, and I began to feel strange and weak; I knew that all the voice I had in my lungs would hardly reach the length of the field by the farm.

'It was then we began to dream of wells and fountains, and water coming very cold, in little drops, out of rocky places in the middle of a cool wood. We had given up all meals; now and then one would cut a lump from the sides of bacon on the kitchen wall and chew a bit of it, but the saltness was like fire.

'There was a great shower of rain one night. The girl said we might open a window and hold out bowls and basins and catch the rain. I spoke of the cloud with burning eyes. She said "we will go to the window in the dairy at the back, and one of us can get some water at all events." She stood up with her basin on the stone slab in the dairy and looked out and heard the plashing of the rain, falling very fast. And she unfastened the catch of the window and had just opened it gently with one hand, for about an inch, and had her basin in the other hand. "And then," said she, "there was something that began to tremble and shudder and shake as it did when we went to the Choral Festival at St Teilo's, and the organ played, and there was the cloud and the burning close before me."

'And then we began to dream, as I say. I woke up in my sitting room one hot afternoon when the sun was shining, and I had been looking and searching in my dream all through the house, and I had gone down to the old cellar that wasn't used, the cellar with the pillars and the vaulted room, with an iron pike in my hand. Something said to me that there was water there, and in my dream I went to a heavy stone by the middle pillar and raised it up, and there beneath was a bubbling well of cold, clear water, and I had just hollowed my hand to drink it when I woke. I went into the kitchen and told young Griffith. I said I was sure there was water there. He shook his head, but he took up the great kitchen poker and we went down to the old cellar. I showed him the stone by the pillar, and he raised it up. But there was no well.

'Do you know, I reminded myself of many people whom I have met in life? I would not be convinced. I was sure that, after all, there was a well there. They had a butcher's cleaver in the kitchen and I took it down to the old cellar and hacked at the ground with it. The others didn't interfere with me. We were getting past that. We hardly ever spoke to one another. Each one would be wandering about the house, upstairs and downstairs, each one of us, I suppose, bent on his own foolish plan and mad design, but we hardly ever spoke. Years ago, I was an actor for a bit, and I remember how it was on first nights; the actors treading softly up and down the wings, by their entrance, their lips moving and muttering over the words of their parts, but without a word for one another. So it was with us. I came upon young Griffith one evening evidently trying to make a subterranean passage under one of the walls of the house. I knew he was mad, as he knew I was mad when he saw me digging for a well in the cellar; but neither said anything to the other.

'Now we are past all this. We are too weak. We dream when we are awake and when we dream we think we wake. Night and day come and go and we mistake one for another; I hear Griffith murmuring to himself about the stars when the sun is high at noonday, and at midnight I have found myself thinking that I walked in bright sunlit meadows beside cold, rushing streams that flowed from high rocks.

'Then at the dawn figures in black robes, carrying lighted tapers in their hands pass slowly about and about; and I hear great rolling organ music that sounds as if some tremendous rite were to begin, and voices crying in an ancient song shrill from the depths of the earth.

'Only a little while ago I heard a voice which sounded as if it were at my very ears, but rang and echoed and resounded as if it were rolling and reverberated from the vault of some cathedral, chanting in terrible modulations. I heard the words quite clearly.

'*Incipit liber irae Domini Dei nostri.* (Here beginneth The Book of the Wrath of the Lord our God.)

'And then the voice sang the word *Aleph*, prolonging it, it seemed through ages, and a light was extinguished as it began the chapter:

'*In that day, saith the Lord, there shall be a cloud over the land, and in the cloud a burning and a shape of fire, and out of the cloud shall issue forth my messengers; they shall run all together, they shall not turn aside; this shall be a day of exceeding bitterness, without salvation. And on every high hill, saith the Lord of Hosts, I will set my sentinels, and my armies shall encamp in the place of every valley; in the house that is amongst rushes I will execute judgment, and in vain shall they fly for refuge to the munitions of the rocks. In the groves of the woods, in the places where the leaves are as a tent above them, they shall find the sword of the slayer; and they that put their trust in walled cities shall be confounded. Woe unto the armed man, woe unto him that taketh pleasure in the strength of his artillery, for a little thing shall smite him, and by one that hath no might shall he be brought down into the dust. That which is low shall be set on high; I will make the lamb and the young sheep to be as the lion from the swellings of Jordan; they shall not spare, saith the Lord, and the doves shall be as eagles on the hill Engedi; none shall be found that may abide the onset of their battle.*

'Even now I can hear the voice rolling far away, as if it came from the altar of a great church and I stood at the door. There are lights very far away in the hollow of a vast darkness, and one by one they are put out. I hear a voice chanting again with that endless modulation that climbs and aspires to the stars, and shines there, and rushes down to the dark depths of the earth, again to ascend; the word is *Zain*.'

Here the manuscript lapsed again, and finally into utter, lamentable confusion. There were scrawled lines wavering across the page on which Secretan seemed to have been trying to note the unearthly music that swelled in his dying ears. As the scrapes and scratches of ink showed, he had tried hard to begin a new sentence. The pen had dropped at last out of his hand upon the paper, leaving a blot and a smear upon it.

Lewis heard the tramp of feet along the passage; they were carrying out the dead to the cart.

XIV
The End of the Terror

Dr Lewis maintained that we should never begin to understand the real significance of life until we began to study just those aspects of it which we now dismiss and overlook as utterly inexplicable, and therefore, unimportant.

We were discussing a few months ago the awful shadow of the terror which at length had passed away from the land. I had formed my opinion, partly from observation, partly from certain facts which had been communicated to me, and the passwords having been exchanged, I found that Lewis had come by very different ways to the same end.

'And yet,' he said, 'it is not a true end, or rather, it is like all the ends of human inquiry, it leads one to a great mystery. We must confess that what has happened might have happened at any time in the history of the world. It did not happen till a year ago as a matter of fact, and therefore we made up our minds that it never could happen; or, one would better say, it was outside the range even of imagination. But this is our way. Most people are quite sure that the Black Death – otherwise the Plague – will never invade Europe again. They have made up their complacent minds that it was due to dirt and bad drainage. As a matter of fact the Plague had nothing to do with dirt or with drains; and there is nothing to prevent its ravaging England tomorrow. But if you tell people so, they won't believe you. They won't believe in anything that isn't there at the particular moment when you are talking to them. As with the Plague, so with the Terror. We could not believe that such a thing could ever happen. Remnant said, truly enough, that whatever it was, it was outside theory, outside our theory. Flatland cannot believe in the cube or the sphere.'

I agreed with all this. I added that sometimes the world was incapable of seeing, much less believing, that which was before its own eyes.

'Look,' I said, 'at any eighteenth century print of a Gothic cathedral. You will find that the trained artistic eye even could not behold in any true sense the building that was before it. I have seen an old print of Peterborough Cathedral that looks as if the artist had drawn it from a clumsy model, constructed of bent wire and children's bricks.'

'Exactly; because Gothic was outside the aesthetic theory (and therefore vision) of the time. You can't believe what you don't see: rather, you can't see what you don't believe. It was so during the time of the Terror. All this bears out what Coleridge said as to the necessity of having the idea before the facts could be of any service to one. Of course, he was right; mere facts, without the correlating idea, are nothing and lead to no conclusion. We had plenty of facts, but we could make nothing of them. I went home at the tail of that dreadful procession from Treff Loyne in a state of mind very near to madness. I heard one of the soldiers saying to the other: "There's no rat that'll spike a man to the heart, Bill." I don't know why, but I felt that if

I heard any more of such talk as that I should go crazy; it seemed to me that the anchors of reason were parting. I left the party and took the short cut across the fields into Porth. I looked up Davies in the High Street and arranged with him that he should take on any cases I might have that evening, and then I went home and gave my man his instructions to send people on. And then I shut myself up to think it all out – if I could.

'You must not suppose that my experiences of that afternoon had afforded me the slightest illumination. Indeed, if it had not been that I had seen poor old Griffith's body lying pierced in his own farmyard, I think I should have been inclined to accept one of Secretan's hints, and to believe that the whole family had fallen a victim to a collective delusion or hallucination, and had shut themselves up and died of thirst through sheer madness. I think there have been such cases. It's the insanity of inhibition, the belief that you can't do something which you are really perfectly capable of doing. But; I had seen the body of the murdered man and the wound that had killed him.

'Did the manuscript left by Secretan give me no hint? Well, it seemed to me to make confusion worse confounded. You have seen it; you know that in certain places it is evidently mere delirium, the wanderings of a dying mind. How was I to separate the facts from the phantasms – lacking the key to the whole enigma. Delirium is often a sort of cloud-castle, a sort of magnified and distorted shadow of actualities, but it is a very difficult thing, almost an impossible thing, to reconstruct the real house from the distortion of it, thrown on the clouds of the patient's brain. You see, Secretan in writing that extraordinary document almost insisted on the fact that he was not in his proper sense; that for days he had been part asleep, part awake, part delirious. How was one to judge his statement, to separate delirium from fact? In one thing he stood confirmed; you remember he speaks of calling for help up the old chimney of Treff Loyne; that did seem to fit in with the tales of a hollow, moaning cry that had been heard upon the Allt: so far one could take him as a recorder of actual experiences. And I looked in the old cellars of the farm and found a frantic sort of rabbit hole dug by one of the pillars; again he was confirmed. But what was one to make of that story of the chanting voice, and the letters of the Hebrew alphabet, and the chapter out of some unknown Minor Prophet? When one has the key it is easy enough to sort out the facts, or the hints of facts from the delusions; but I hadn't the key on that

September evening. I was forgetting the "tree" with lights and fires in it; that, I think, impressed me more than anything with the feeling that Secretan's story was, in the main, a true story. I had seen a like appearance down there in my own garden; but what was it?

'Now, I was saying that, paradoxically, it is only by the inexplicable things that life can be explained. We are apt to say, you know, "a very odd coincidence" and pass the matter by, as if there were no more to be said, or as if that were the end of it. Well, I believe that the only real path lies through the blind alleys.'

'How do you mean?'

'Well, this is an instance of what I mean. I told you about Merritt, my brother-in-law, and the capsizing of that boat, the *Mary Ann*. He had seen, he said, signal lights flashing from one of the farms on the coast, and he was quite certain that the two things were intimately connected as cause and effect. I thought it all nonsense, and I was wondering how I was going to shut him up when a big moth flew into the room through that window, fluttered about, and succeeded in burning itself alive in the lamp. That gave me my cue; I asked Merritt if he knew why moths made for lamps or something of the kind; I thought it would be a hint to him that I was sick of his flashlights and his half-baked theories. So it was – he looked sulky and held his tongue.

'But a few minutes later I was called out by a man who had found his little boy dead in a field near his cottage about an hour before. The child was so still, they said, that a great moth had settled on his forehead and only fluttered away when they lifted up the body. It was absolutely illogical; but it was this odd "coincidence" of the moth in my lamp and the moth on the dead boy's forehead that first set me on the track. I can't say that it guided me in any real sense; it was more like a great flare of red paint on a wall; it rang up my attention, if I may say so; it was a sort of shock like a bang on the big drum. No doubt Merritt was talking great nonsense that evening so far as his particular instance went; the flashes of light from the farm had nothing to do with the wreck of the boat. But his general principle was sound; when you hear a gun go off and see a man fall it is idle to talk of "a mere coincidence". I think a very interesting book might be written on this question: I would call it "A Grammar of Coincidence".

'But as you will remember, from having read my notes on the matter, I was called in about ten days later to see a man named Cradock, who had been found in a field near his farm quite dead. This also was at night. His wife found him, and there were some very queer things in her story. She said that the hedge of the field looked as if it were changed; she began to be afraid that she had lost her way and got into the wrong field. Then she said the hedge was lighted up as if there were a lot of glow-worms in it, and when she peered over the stile there seemed to be some kind of glimmering upon the ground, and then the glimmering melted away, and she found her husband's body near where this light had been. Now this man Cradock had been suffocated just as the little boy Roberts had been suffocated, and as that man in the Midlands who took a short cut one night had been suffocated. Then I remembered that poor Johnnie Roberts had called out about "something shiny" over the stile just before he played truant. Then, on my part, I had to contribute the very remarkable sight I witnessed here, as I looked down over the garden; the appearance as of a spreading tree where I knew there was no such tree, and then the shining and burning of lights and moving colours. Like the poor child and Mrs Cradock, I had seen something shiny, just as some man in Stratfordshire had seen a dark cloud with points of fire in it floating over the trees. And Mrs Cradock thought that the shape of the trees in the hedge had changed.

'My mind almost uttered the word that was wanted; but you see the difficulties. This set of circumstances could not, so far as I could see, have any relation with the other circumstances of the Terror. How could I connect all this with the bombs and machine guns of the Midlands, with the armed men who kept watch about the munition shops by day and night. Then there was the long list of people here who had fallen over the cliffs or into the quarry; there were the cases of the men stifled in the slime of the marshes; there was the affair of the family murdered in front of their cottage on the Highway; there was the capsized *Mary Ann*. I could not see any thread that could bring all these incidents together; they seemed to me to be hopelessly disconnected. I could not make out any relation between the agency that beat out the brains of the Williamses and the agency that overturned the boat. I don't know, but I think it's very likely if nothing more had happened that I should have put the whole thing down as an unaccountable series of crimes and accidents which chanced to occur in Meirion in the summer of 1915. Well, of course, that would have been an impossible standpoint in view of certain incidents in Merritt's story. Still, if one is confronted by the insoluble, one lets it go at last. If the mystery is inexplicable, one pretends that there isn't any mystery. That is the justification for what is called free thinking.

'Then came that extraordinary business of Treff Loyne. I couldn't put that on one side. I couldn't pretend that nothing strange or out of the way had happened. There was no getting over it or getting round it. I had seen with my eyes that there was a mystery, and a most horrible mystery. I have forgotten my logic, but one might say that Treff Loyne demonstrated the existence of a mystery in the figure of Death.

'I took it all home, as I have told you, and sat down for the evening before it. It appalled me, not only by its horror, but here again by the discrepancy between its terms. Old Griffith, so far as I could judge, had been killed by the thrust of a pike or perhaps of a sharpened stake: how could one relate this to the burning tree that had floated over the ridge of the barn. It was as if I said to you: "here is a man drowned, and here is a man burned alive: show that each death was caused by the same agency!" And the moment that I left this particular case of Treff Loyne, and tried to get some light on it from other instances of the Terror, I would think of the man in the midlands who heard the feet of a thousand men rustling in the wood, and their voices as if dead men sat up in their bones and talked. And then I would say to myself, "and how about that boat overturned in a calm sea?" There seemed no end to it, no hope of any solution.

'It was, I believe, a sudden leap of the mind that liberated me from the tangle. It was quite beyond logic. I went back to that evening when Merritt was boring me with his flashlights, to the moth in the candle, and to the moth on the forehead of poor Johnnie Roberts. There was no sense in it; but I suddenly determined that the child and Joseph Cradock the farmer, and that unnamed Stratfordshire man, all found at night, all asphyxiated, had been choked by vast swarms of moths. I don't pretend even now that this is demonstrated, but I'm sure it's true.

'Now suppose you encounter a swarm of these creatures in the dark. Suppose the smaller ones fly up your nostrils. You will gasp for breath and open your mouth. Then, suppose some hundreds of them fly into your mouth, into your gullet, into your windpipe, what will happen to you? You will be dead in a very short time, choked, asphyxiated.'

'But the moths would be dead too. They would be found in the bodies.'

'The moths? Do you know that it is extremely difficult to kill a moth with cyanide of potassium? Take a frog, kill it, open its stomach. There you will find its dinner of moths and small beetles, and the "dinner" will shake itself and walk off cheerily, to resume an entirely active existence. No; that is no difficulty.

'Well, now I came to this. I was shutting out all the other cases. I was confining myself to those that came under the one formula. I got to the assumption or conclusion, whichever you like, that certain people had been asphyxiated by the action of moths. I had accounted for that extraordinary appearance of burning or coloured lights that I had witnessed myself, when I saw the growth of that strange tree in my garden. That was clearly the cloud with points of fire in it that the Stratfordshire man took for a new and terrible kind of poison gas, that was the shiny something that poor little Johnnie Roberts had seen over the stile, that was the glimmering light that had led Mrs Cradock to her husband's dead body, that was the assemblage of terrible eyes that had watched over Treff Loyne by night. Once on the right track I understood all this, for coming into this room in the dark, I have been amazed by the wonderful burning and the strange fiery colours of the eyes of a single moth, as it crept up the pane of glass, outside. Imagine the effect of myriads of such eyes, of the movement of these lights and fires in a vast swarm of moths, each insect being in constant motion while it kept its place in the mass: I felt that all this was clear and certain.

'Then the next step. Of course, we know nothing really about moths; rather, we know nothing of moth reality. For all I know there may be hundreds of books which treat of moth and nothing but moth. But these are scientific books, and science only deals with surfaces; it has nothing to do with realities – it is impertinent if it attempts to do with realities. To take a very minor matter; we don't even know why the moth desires the flame. But we do know what the moth does not do; it does not gather itself into swarms with the object of destroying human life. But here, by the hypothesis, were cases in which the moth had done this very thing; the moth race had entered, it seemed, into a malignant conspiracy against the human race. It was quite impossible, no doubt – that is to say, it had never happened before – but I could see no escape from this conclusion.

'These insects, then, were definitely hostile to man; and then I stopped, for I could not see the next step, obvious though it seems to me now. I believe that the soldiers' scraps of talk on the way to Treff Loyne and back flung the next plank over the gulf. They had spoken of "rat poison", of no rat being able to spike a man through the heart; and then, suddenly, I saw my way clear. If the moths were infected with hatred of men, and possessed the design and the power of combining against him; why not suppose this hatred, this design, this power shared by other non-human creatures?

'The secret of the Terror might be condensed into a sentence: the animals had revolted against men.

'Now, the puzzle became easy enough; one had only to classify. Take the cases of the people who met their deaths by falling over cliffs or over the edge of quarries. We think of sheep as timid creatures, who always ran away. But suppose sheep that don't run away; and, after all, in reason why should they run away? Quarry or no quarry, cliff or no cliff; what would happen to you if a hundred sheep ran after you instead of running from you? There would be no help for it; they would have you down and beat you to death or stifle you. Then suppose man, woman, or child near a cliff's edge or a quarry-side, and a sudden rush of sheep. Clearly there is no help; there is nothing for it but to go over. There can be no doubt that that is what happened in all these cases.

'And again; you know the country and you know how a herd of cattle will sometimes pursue people through the fields in a solemn, stolid sort of way. They behave as if they wanted to close in on you. Townspeople sometimes get frightened and scream and run; you or I would take no notice, or at the utmost, wave our sticks at the herd, which will stop dead or lumber off. But suppose they don't lumber off. The mildest old cow, remember, is stronger than any man. What can one man or half a dozen men do against half a hundred of these beasts no longer restrained by that mysterious inhibition, which has made for ages the strong the humble slaves of the weak? But if you are botanising in the marsh, like that poor fellow who was staying at Porth, and forty or fifty young cattle gradually close round you, and refuse to move when you shout and wave your stick, but get closer and closer instead, and get you into the slime. Again, where is your help? If you haven't got an automatic pistol, you must go down and stay down, while the beasts lie quietly on you for five minutes. It was a quicker death for poor Griffith of Treff Loyne – one of his own beasts gored him to death with one sharp thrust of its horn into his heart. And from that morning those within the house were closely besieged by their own cattle and horses and sheep; and when those unhappy people within opened a window to call for help or to catch a few drops of rain water to relieve their burning thirst, the cloud waited for them with its myriad eyes of fire. Can you wonder that Secretan's statement reads in places like mania? You perceive the horrible position of those people in Treff Loyne; not only did they see death advancing on them, but advancing with incredible steps, as if one were to die not only in nightmare but by nightmare. But no one in his wildest, most fiery dreams had ever imagined such a fate. I am not astonished that Secretan at one moment suspected the evidence of his own senses, at another surmised that the world's end had come.'

'And how about the Williamses who were murdered on the Highway near here?'

'The horses were the murderers; the horses that afterwards stampeded the camp below. By some means which is still obscure to me they lured that family into the road and beat their brains out; their shod hoofs were the instruments of execution. And, as for the *Mary Ann*, the boat that was capsized, I have no doubt that it was overturned by a sudden rush of the porpoises that were gambolling about in the water of Larnac Bay. A porpoise is a heavy beast – half a dozen of them could easily upset a light rowing boat. The munition works? Their enemy was rats. I believe that it has been calculated that in "greater London" the number of rats is about equal to the number of human beings, that is, there are about seven millions of them. The proportion would be about the same in all the great centres of population; and the rat, moreover, is, on occasion, migratory in its habits. You can understand now that story of the *Semiramis*, beating about the mouth of the Thames, and at last cast away by Arcachon, her only crew dry heaps of bones. The rat is an expert boarder of ships. And so one can understand the tale told by the frightened man who took the path by the wood that led up from the new munition works. He thought he heard a thousand men treading softly through the wood and chattering to one another in some horrible tongue; what he did hear was the marshalling of an army of rats – their array before the battle.

'And conceive the terror of such an attack. Even one rat in a fury is said to be an ugly customer to meet; conceive then, the irruption of these terrible, swarming myriads, rushing upon the helpless, unprepared, astonished workers in the munition shops.'

There can be no doubt, I think, that Dr Lewis was entirely justified in these extraordinary conclusions. As I say, I had arrived at pretty much the same end, by different ways; but this rather as to the general situation, while Lewis had made his own particular study of those circumstances of the Terror that were within his immediate purview, as a physician in large practice in the southern part of Meirion. Of some of the cases which he reviewed he had, no doubt, no immediate or first-hand knowledge; but he judged these instances by their similarity to the facts which had come under his personal notice. He spoke of the affairs of the quarry at Llanfihangel on the analogy of the people who were found dead at the bottom of the cliffs near Porth, and he was no doubt justified in doing so. He told me that, thinking the whole matter over, he was hardly more astonished by the Terror in itself than by the strange way in which he had arrived at his conclusions.

'You know,' he said, 'those certain evidences of animal malevolence which we knew of, the bees that stung the child to death, the trusted sheepdog's turning savage, and so forth. Well, I got no light whatever from all this; it suggested nothing to me – simply because I had not got that "idea" which Coleridge rightly holds necessary in all inquiry; facts *qua* facts, as we said, mean nothing and come to nothing. You do not believe, therefore you cannot see.

'And then, when the truth at last appeared it was through the whimsical "coincidence", as we call such signs, of the moth in my lamp and the moth on the dead child's forehead. This, I think, is very extraordinary.'

'And there seems to have been one beast that remained faithful; the dog at Treff Loyne. That is strange.'

'That remains a mystery.'

It would not be wise, even now, to describe too closely the terrible scenes that were to be seen in the munition areas of the north and the midlands during the black months of the Terror. Out of the factories issued at black midnight the shrouded dead in their coffins, and their very kinsfolk did not know how they had come by their deaths. All the towns were full of houses of mourning, were full of dark and terrible rumours; incredible, as the incredible reality. There were things done and suffered that perhaps never will be brought to light, memories and secret traditions of these things will be whispered in families, delivered from father to son, growing wilder with the passage of the years, but never growing wilder than the truth.

It is enough to say that the cause of the Allies was for a while in deadly peril. The men at the front called in their extremity for guns and shells. No one told them what was happening in the places where these munitions were made.

At first the position was nothing less than desperate; men in high places were almost ready to cry 'mercy' to the enemy. But, after the first panic, measures were taken such as those described by Merritt in his account of the matter. The workers were armed with special weapons, guards were mounted, machine guns were placed in position, bombs and liquid flame were ready against the obscene hordes of the enemy, and the 'burning clouds' found a fire fiercer than their own. Many deaths occurred amongst the airmen; but they, too, were given special guns, arms that scattered shot broadcast, and so drove away the dark flights that threatened the airplanes.

And, then, in the winter of 1915–16, the Terror ended suddenly as it had begun. Once more a sheep was a frightened beast that ran instinctively from a little child; the cattle were again solemn, stupid creatures, void of harm; the spirit and the convention of malignant design passed out of the hearts of all the animals. The chains that they had cast off for awhile were thrown again about them.

And, finally, there comes the inevitable 'why?' Why did the beasts who had been humbly and patiently subject to man, or affrighted by his presence, suddenly know their strength and learn how to league together, and declare bitter war against their ancient master?

It is a most difficult and obscure question. I give what explanation I have to give with very great diffidence, and an eminent disposition to be corrected, if a clearer light can be found.

Some friends of mine, for whose judgment I have very great respect, are inclined to think that there was a certain contagion of hate. They hold that the fury of the whole world at war, the great passion of death that seems driving all humanity to destruction, infected at last these lower creatures, and in place of their native instinct of submission, gave them rage and wrath and ravening.

This may be the explanation. I cannot say that it is not so, because I do not profess to understand the working of the universe. But I confess that the theory strikes me as fanciful. There may be a contagion of hate as there is a contagion of smallpox; I do not know, but I hardly believe it.

In my opinion, and it is only an opinion, the source of the great revolt of the beasts is to be sought in a much subtler region of inquiry. I believe that the subjects revolted because the king abdicated. Man has dominated the beasts throughout the ages, the spiritual has reigned over the rational through the peculiar quality and grace of spirituality that men possess, that makes a man to be that which he is. And when he maintained this power and grace, I think it is pretty clear that between him and the animals there was a certain treaty and alliance. There was supremacy on the one hand, and submission on the other; but at the same time there was between the two that cordiality which exists between lords and subjects in a well-organised state. I know a socialist who maintains that Chaucer's *Canterbury Tales* give a picture of true democracy. I do not know about that, but I see that knight and miller were able to get on quite pleasantly together, just because the knight knew that he was a knight and the miller knew that he was a miller. If the knight had had conscientious objections to his knightly grade, while the miller saw no reason why he should not be a knight, I am sure that their intercourse would have been difficult, unpleasant, and perhaps murderous.

So with man. I believe in the strength and truth of tradition. A learned man said to me a few weeks ago: 'When I have to choose between the evidence of tradition and the evidence of a document, I always believe the evidence of tradition. Documents may be falsified, and often are falsified; tradition is never falsified.' This is true; and, therefore, I think, one may put trust in the vast body of folklore which asserts that there was once a worthy and friendly alliance between man and the beasts. Our popular tale of Dick Whittington and his Cat no doubt represents the adaptation of a very ancient legend to a comparatively modern personage, but we may go back into the ages and find the popular tradition asserting that not only are the animals the subjects, but also the friends of man.

All that was in virtue of that singular spiritual element in man which the rational animals do not possess. Spiritual does not mean respectable, it does not even mean moral, it does not mean 'good' in the ordinary acceptation of the word. It signifies the royal prerogative of man, differentiating him from the beasts.

For long ages he has been putting off this royal robe, he has been wiping the balm of consecration from his own breast. He has declared, again and again, that he is not spiritual, but rational, that is, the equal of the beasts over whom he was once sovereign. He has vowed that he is not Orpheus but Caliban.

But the beasts also have within them something which corresponds to the spiritual quality in men – we are content to call it instinct. They perceived that the throne was vacant – not even friendship was possible between them and the self-deposed monarch. If he were not king he was a sham, an impostor, a thing to be destroyed.

Hence, I think, the Terror. They have risen once – they may rise again.

The Happy Children

A day after the Christmas of 1915, my professional duties took me up north; or to be as precise as our present conventions allow, to 'the north-eastern district'. There was some singular talk; mad gossip of the Germans having a 'dugout' somewhere by Malton Head. Nobody seemed to be quite clear as to what they were doing there or what they hoped to do there; but the report ran like wildfire from one foolish mouth to another, and it was thought desirable that the whole silly tale should be tracked down to its source and exposed or denied once and for all.

I went up, then, to that north-eastern district on Sunday, December 26th, 1915, and pursued my investigations from Helmsdale Bay, which is a small watering place within a couple of miles of Malton Head. The people of the dales and the moors had just heard of the fable, I found, and regarded it all with supreme and sour contempt. So far as I could make out, it originated from the games of some children who had stayed at Helmsdale Bay in the summer. They had acted a rude drama of German spies and their capture, and had used Helby Cavern, between Helmsdale and Malton Head, as the scene of their play. That was all; the fools apparently had done the rest; the fools who believed with all their hearts in 'the Russians', and got rough with anyone who expressed a doubt as to 'the Angels of Mons'.

'Gang oop to beasten and tell them sike a tale and they'll not believe it,' said one dalesman to me; and I have a suspicion that he thought that I, who had come so many hundred miles to investigate the story, was but little wiser than those who credited it. He could not be expected to understand that a journalist has two offices – to proclaim the truth and to denounce the lie.

I had finished with 'the Germans' and their dugout early in the afternoon of Monday, and I decided to break the journey home at Banwick, which I had often heard of as a beautiful and curious old place. So I took the one-thirty train, and went wandering inland, and stopped at many unknown stations in the midst of great levels, and changed at Marishes Ambo, and went on again through a strange land in the dimness of the winter afternoon. Somehow the train left the level and glided down into a deep and narrow dell, dark with winter woods, brown with withered bracken, solemn in its loneliness. The only thing that moved was the swift and rushing stream that foamed over the boulders and then lay still in brown pools under the bank.

The dark woods scattered and thinned into groups of stunted, ancient thorns; great grey rocks, strangely shaped, rose out of the ground; crenellated rocks rose on the heights on either side. The brooklet swelled and became a river, and always following this river we came to Banwick soon after the setting of the sun.

I saw the wonder of the town in the light of the afterglow that was red in the west. The clouds blossomed into rose gardens; there were seas of fairy green that swam about isles of crimson light; there were clouds like spears of flame, like dragons of fire. And under the mingling lights and colours of such a sky Banwick went down to the pools of its landlocked harbour and climbed again across the bridge towards the ruined abbey and the great church on the hill.

I came from the station by an ancient street, winding and narrow, with cavernous closes and yards opening from it on either side, and flights of uneven steps going upward to high terraced houses, or downward to the harbour and the incoming tide. I saw there many gabled houses, sunken with age far beneath the level of the pavement, with dipping roof trees and bowed doorways, with traces of grotesque carving on their walls. And when I stood on the quay, there on the other side of the harbour was the most amazing confusion of red-tiled roofs that I had ever seen, and the great grey Norman church high on the bare hill above them; and below them the boats swinging in the swaying tide, and the water burning in the fires of the sunset. It was the town of a magic dream. I stood on the quay till the shining had gone from the sky and the waterpools, and the winter night came down dark upon Banwick.

I found an old snug inn just by the harbour, where I had been standing. The walls of the rooms met each other at odd and unexpected angles; there were strange projections and juttings of masonry, as if one room were trying to force its way into another; there were indications as of unthinkable staircases in the corners of the ceilings.

But there was a bar where Tom Smart would have loved to sit, with a roaring fire and snug, old elbow chairs about it and pleasant indications that if 'something warm' were wanted after supper it could be generously supplied.

I sat in this pleasant place for an hour or two and talked to the pleasant people of the town who came in and out. They told me of the old adventures and industries of the town. It had once been, they said, a great whaling port, and then there had been a lot of shipbuilding, and later Banwick had been famous for its amber-cutting. 'And now there's nowt,' said one of the men in the bar; 'but we get on none so badly.'

I went out for a stroll before my supper. Banwick was now black, in thick darkness. For good reasons not a single lamp was lighted in the streets, hardly a gleam showed from behind the closely curtained windows. It was as if one walked a town of the Middle Ages, and with the ancient overhanging shapes of the houses dimly visible I was reminded of those strange, cavernous pictures of mediaeval Paris and Tours that Doré drew.

Hardly anyone was abroad in the streets; but all the courts and alleys seemed alive with children. I could just see little white forms fluttering to and fro as they ran in and out. And I never heard such happy children's voices. Some were singing, some were laughing; and peering into one black cavern, I made out a ring of children dancing round and round and chanting in clear voices a wonderful melody; some old tune of local tradition, as I supposed, for its modulations were such as I had never heard before.

I went back to my tavern and spoke to the landlord about the number of children who were playing about the dark streets and courts, and how delightfully happy they all seemed to be.

He looked at me steadily for a moment, and then said:

'Well, you see, sir, the children have got a bit out of hand of late; their fathers are out at the front, and their mothers can't keep them in order. So they're running a bit wild.'

There was something odd about his manner. I could not make out exactly what the oddity was, or what it meant. I could see that my remark had somehow made him uncomfortable; but I was at a loss to know what I had done. I had my supper, and then sat down for a couple of hours to settle 'the Germans' of Malton Head.

I finished my account of the German myth, and instead of going to bed, I determined that I would have one more look at Banwick in its wonderful darkness. So I went out and crossed the bridge, and began to climb up the street on the other side, where there was that strange huddle of red roofs mounting one above the other that I had seen in the afterglow. And to my amazement I found that these extraordinary Banwick children were still about and abroad, still revelling and carolling, dancing and singing, standing, as I supposed, on the top of the flights of steps that climbed from the courts up the hillside, and so having the appearance of floating in mid air. And their happy laughter rang out like bells on the night.

It was a quarter past eleven when I had left my inn, and I was just thinking that the Banwick mothers had indeed allowed indulgence to go too far, when the children began again to sing that old melody that I had heard in the evening. And now the sweet, clear voices swelled out into the night, and, I thought, must be numbered by hundreds. I was standing in a dark alleyway, and I saw with amazement that the children were passing me in a long procession that wound up the hill towards the abbey. Whether a faint moon now rose, or whether clouds passed from before the stars, I do not know; but the air lightened, and I could see the children plainly as they went by singing, with the rapture and exultation of them that sing in the woods in springtime.

They were all in white, but some of them had strange marks upon them which, I supposed, were of significance in this fragment of some traditional mystery play that I was beholding. Many of them had wreaths of dripping seaweed about their brows; one showed a painted scar on her throat; a tiny boy held open his white robe, and pointed to a dreadful wound above his heart, from which the blood seemed to flow; another child held out his hands wide apart and the palms looked torn and bleeding, as if they had been pierced. One of the children held up a little baby in her arms, and even the infant showed the appearance of a wound on its face.

The procession passed me by, and I heard it still singing as if in the sky as it went on its steep way up the hill to the ancient church. I went back to my inn, and as I crossed the bridge it suddenly struck me that this was the eve of the Holy Innocents. No doubt I had seen a confused relic of some mediaeval observance, and when I got back to the inn I asked the landlord about it.

Then I understood the meaning of the strange expression I had seen on the man's face. He was sick and shuddering with terror; he drew away from me as though I were a messenger from the dead.

Some weeks after this I was reading in a book called *The Ancient Rites of Banwick*. It was written in the reign of Queen Elizabeth by some anonymous person who had seen the glory of the old abbey, and then the desolation that had come to it. I found this passage:

'And on Childermas Day, at midnight, there was done there a marvellous solemn service. For when the monks had ended their singing of Te Deum at their Mattins, there came unto the altar the Lord Abbot, gloriously arrayed in a vestment of cloth of gold, so that it was a great marvel to behold him. And there came also into the church all the children that were of tender years of Banwick, and they were all clothed in white robes. And then began the lord abbot to sing the Mass of the Holy Innocents. And when the sacring of the Mass was ended, then there came up from the church into the quire the youngest child that there was present that might hold himself aright. And this child was borne up to the high altar, and the Lord Abbot set the little child upon a golden and glistering throne afore the high altar, and bowed down and worshipped him, singing, "*Talium Regnum Coelorum*, Alleluya. Of such is the Kingdom of Heaven. Alleluya", and all the quire answered singing, "*Amicti sunt stolis albis*, Alleluya, Alleluya; They are clad in white robes, Alleluya, Alleluya." And then the prior and all the monks in their order did like worship and reverence to the little child that was upon the throne.'

I had seen the White Order of the Innocents. I had seen those who came singing from the deep waters that are about the *Lusitania*; I had seen the innocent martyrs of the fields of Flanders and France rejoicing as they went up to hear their Mass in the spiritual place.

Ornaments in Jade

The Rose Garden

The Turanians

The Idealist

Witchcraft

The Ceremony

Psychology

Torture

Midsummer

Nature

The Holy Things

The Rose Garden

And afterwards she went very softly, and opened the window and looked out. Behind her, the room was in a mystical semi-darkness; chairs and tables were hovering, ill-defined shapes; there was but the faintest illusory glitter from the talc moons in the rich Indian curtain which she had drawn across the door. The yellow silk draperies of the bed were but suggestions of colour, and the pillow and the white sheets glimmered as a white cloud in a far sky at twilight.

She turned from the dusky room, and with dewy tender eyes gazed out across the garden towards the lake. She could not rest nor lay herself down to sleep; though it was late, and half the night had passed, she could not rest. A sickle moon was slowly drawing upwards through certain filmy clouds that stretched in a long band from east to west, and a pallid light began to flow from the dark water, as if there also some vague planet were rising. She looked with eyes insatiable for wonder; and she found a strange eastern effect in the bordering of reeds, in their spear-like shapes, in the liquid ebony that they shadowed, in the fine inlay of pearl and silver as the moon shone free; a bright symbol in the steadfast calm of the sky.

There were faint stirring sounds heard from the fringe of reeds, and now and then the drowsy, broken cry of the waterfowl, for they knew that the dawn was not far off. In the centre of the lake was a carved white pedestal, and on it shone a white boy, holding the double flute to his lips.

Beyond the lake the park began, and sloped gently to the verge of the wood, now but a dark cloud beneath the sickle moon. And then beyond, and farther still, undiscovered hills, grey bands of cloud, and the steep pale height of the heaven. She gazed on with her tender eyes, bathing herself, as it were, in the deep rest of the night, veiling her soul with the half-light and the half-shadow, stretching out her delicate hands into the coolness of the misty silvered air, wondering at her hands.

And then she turned from the window, and made herself a divan of cushions on the Persian carpet, and half sat, half lay there, as motionless, as ecstatic as a poet dreaming under roses, far in Ispahan. She had gazed out, after all, to assure herself that sight and the eyes showed nothing but a glimmering veil, a gauze of curious lights and figures: that in it there was no reality nor substance. He had always told her that there was only one existence, one science, one religion, that the external world was but a variegated shadow which might either conceal or reveal the truth; and now she believed.

He had shown her that bodily rapture might be the ritual and expression of the ineffable mysteries, of the world beyond sense, that must be entered by the way of sense; and now she believed. She had never much doubted any of his words, from the moment of their meeting a month before. She had looked up as she sat in the arbour, and her father was walking down through the avenue of roses, bringing to her the stranger, thin and dark, with a pointed beard and melancholy eyes. He murmured something to himself as they shook hands; she heard the rich, unknown words that sounded as the echo of far music. Afterwards he had told her what those words signified:

'How say ye that I was lost? I wandered among roses.
Can he go astray that enters the rose garden?
The Lover in the house of the Beloved is not forlorn.
I wandered among roses. How say ye that I was lost?'

His voice, murmuring the strange words, had persuaded her, and now she had the rapture of the perfect knowledge. She had looked out into the silvery uncertain night in order that she might experience the sense that for her these things no longer existed. She was not any more a part of the garden, or of the lake, or of the wood, or of the life that she had led hitherto. Another line that he had quoted came to her:

'The kingdom of I and We forsake
and your home in annihilation make.'

It had seemed at first almost nonsense – if it had been possible for him to talk nonsense; but now she was filled and thrilled with the meaning of it. Herself was annihilated; at his bidding she had destroyed all her old feelings and emotions, her likes and dislikes, all the inherited loves and hates that her father and mother had given her; the old life had been thrown utterly away.

It grew light, and when the dawn burned she fell asleep, murmuring:
'How say ye that I was lost?'

The Turanians

The smoke of the tinkers' camp rose a thin pale blue from the heart of the wood.

Mary had left her mother at work on 'things', and had gone out with a pale and languid face into the hot afternoon. She had talked of walking across the fields to the Green, and of having a chat with the doctor's daughter, but she had taken the other path that crept down towards the hollow and the dark thickets of the wood.

After all, she had felt too lazy to rouse herself, to make the effort of conversation, and the sunlight scorched the path that was ruled straight from stile to stile across the brown August fields, and she could see, even from far away, how the white dust clouds were smoking on the road by the Green. She hesitated, and at last went down under the far-spreading oak trees, by a winding way of grass that cooled her feet.

Her mother, who was very kind and good, used to talk to her sometimes on the evils of 'exaggeration', on the necessity of avoiding phrases violently expressed, words of too fierce an energy. She remembered how she had run into the house a few days before and had called her mother to look at a rose in the garden that 'burnt like a flame'. Her mother had said the rose was very pretty, and a little later had hinted her doubts as to the wisdom of 'such very strong expressions'.

'I know, my dear Mary,' she had said, 'that in your case it isn't affectation. You really *feel* what you say, don't you? Yes; but is it nice to feel like that? Do you think that it's quite *right*, even?'

The mother had looked at the girl with a curious wistfulness, almost as if she would say something more, and sought for the fit words, but could not find them. And then she merely remarked:

'You haven't seen Alfred Moorhouse since the tennis party, have you? I must ask him to come next Tuesday; you like him?'

The daughter could not quite see the link between her fault of 'exaggeration' and the charming young barrister, but her mother's warning recurred to her as she strayed down the shadowed path, and felt the long dark grass cool and refreshing about her feet. She would not have put this sensation into words, but she thought it was as though her ankles were gently, sweetly kissed as the rich grass touched them, and her mother would have said it was not right to think such things.

And what a delight there was in the colours all about her! It was as though she walked in a green cloud; the strong sunlight was filtered through the leaves, reflected from the grass, and made all visible things, the tree stems, the flowers, and her own hands seem new, transformed into another likeness. She had walked by the wood path over and over again, but today it had become full of mystery and hinting, and every turn brought a surprise.

Today the mere sense of being alone under the trees was an acute secret joy, and as she went down deeper and the wood grew dark about her, she loosened her brown hair, and when the sun shone over the fallen tree she saw her hair was not brown but bronze and golden, glowing on her pure white dress.

She stayed by the well in the rock, and dared to make the dark water her mirror, looking to right and left with shy glances and listening for the rustle of parted boughs, before she would match her gold with luminous ivory. She saw wonders in a glass as she leaned over the shadowed mysterious pool, and smiled at the smiling nymph, whose lips parted as if to whisper secrets.

As she went on her way, the thin blue smoke rose from a gap in the trees, and she remembered her childish dread of 'the gypsies'. She walked a little farther, and laid herself to rest on a smooth patch of turf, and listened to the strange intonations that sounded from the camp. 'Those horrible people' she had heard the yellow folk called, but she found now a pleasure in voices that sang and, indistinctly heard, were almost chanting, with a rise and fall of notes and a wild wail, and the solemnity of unknown speech. It seemed a fit music for the unknown woodland, in harmony with the drip of the well, and the birds' sharp notes, and the rustle and hurry of the wood creatures.

She rose again and went on till she could see the red fire between the boughs; and the voices thrilled into an incantation. She longed to summon up courage, and talk to these strange wood-folk, but she was afraid to burst into the camp. So she sat down under a tree and waited, hoping that one of them might happen to come her way.

There were six or seven men, as many women, and a swarm of fantastic children, lolling and squatting about the fire, gabbling to one another in their singsong speech. They were people of curious aspect, short and squat, high-cheekboned, with dingy yellow skin and long almond eyes; only in one or two of the younger men there was a suggestion of a wild, almost faun-like grace, as of creatures who always moved between the red fire and the green leaf. Though everybody called them gypsies, they were in reality Turanian metalworkers, degenerated into wandering tinkers; their ancestors had fashioned the bronze battleaxes, and they mended pots and kettles. Mary waited under the tree, sure that she had nothing to fear, and resolved not to run away if one of them appeared.

The sun sank into a mass of clouds and the air grew close and heavy; a mist steamed up about the trees, a blue mist like the smoke of a wood fire. A strange smiling face peered out from between the leaves, and the girl knew that her heart leapt as the young man walked towards her.

The Turanians moved their camp that night. There was a red glint, like fire, in the vast shadowy west, and then a burning paten floated up from a wild hill. A procession of weird bowed figures passed across the crimson disk, one stumbling after another in long single file, each bending down beneath his huge shapeless pack, and the children crawled last, goblin-like, fantastic.

The girl was lying in her white room, caressing a small green stone, a curious thing cut with strange devices, awful with age. She held it close to the luminous ivory, and the gold poured upon it.

She laughed for joy, and murmured and whispered to herself, asking herself questions in the bewilderment of her delight. She was afraid to say anything to her mother.

The Idealist

'Did you notice Symonds while Beever was telling that story just now?' said one clerk to the other.

'No. Why? Didn't he like it?'

The second clerk had been putting away his papers and closing his desk in a grave and businesslike manner, but when Beever's story was recalled to him he began to bubble anew, tasting the relish of the tale for a second time.

'He's a fair scorcher, old Beever,' he remarked between little gasps of mirth. 'But didn't Symonds like it?'

'Like it? He looked disgusted, I can tell you. Made a face, something in this style:' and the man drew his features into a design of sour disapproval, as he gave his hat the last polish with his coatsleeve.

'Well, I'm off now,' he said. 'I want to get home early, as there's tart for tea,' and he fashioned another grimace, an imitation of his favourite actor's favourite contortion.

'Well, goodbye,' said his friend. 'You are a hot 'un, you are. You're worse than Beever. See you on Monday. What will Symonds say?' and he shouted after him as the door swung to and fro.

Charles Symonds, who had failed to see the humour of Mr Beever's tale, had left the office a few minutes earlier and was now pacing slowly westward, mounting Fleet Street. His fellow clerk had not been much amiss in his observation. Symonds had heard the last phrases of Beever's story, and unconsciously had looked half round towards the group, angry and disgusted at their gross and stupid merriment. Beever and his friends seemed to him guilty of sacrilege; he likened them to ploughboys pawing and deriding an exquisite painted panel, blaring out their contempt and brutal ignorance. He could not control his features; in spite of himself he looked loathing at the three yahoos. He would have given anything if he could have found words and told them what he thought, but even to look displeasure was difficult. His shyness was a perpetual amusement to the other clerks, who often did little things to annoy him, and enjoyed the spectacle of Symonds inwardly raging and burning like Etna, but too hopelessly diffident to say a word. He would turn dead man's white, and grind his teeth at an insult, and pretend to join in the laugh, and pass it off as a joke. When he was a boy his mother was puzzled by him, not knowing whether he were sullen or insensible, or perhaps very good-tempered.

He climbed Fleet Street, still raw with irritation, partly from a real disgust at the profane coarseness of the clerks, and partly from a feeling that they talked so because they knew he hated such gross farces and novels. It was hideous to live and work with such foul creatures, and he glanced back fury at the City, the place of the stupid, the blatant, the intolerable.

He passed into the rush and flood of the Strand, into the full tide of a Saturday afternoon, still meditating the outrage, and constructing a cutting sentence for future use, heaping up words which should make Beever tremble. He was quite aware that he would never utter one of those biting phrases, but the pretence soothed him, and he began to remember other things. It was in late November and the clouds were already gathering for the bright solemnity of the sunset, flying to their places before the wind. They curled into fantastic shapes, high up there in the wind's whirlpool, and Symonds, looking towards the sky, was attracted by two grey writhing clouds that drew together in the west, in the far perspective of the Strand. He saw them as if they had been living creatures, noting every change and movement and transformation, till the shaking winds made them one and drove a vague form away to the south.

The curious interest he had taken in the cloud shapes had driven away the thought of the office, of the fetid talk which he so often heard. Beever and his friends ceased to exist, and Symonds escaped to his occult and private world which no one had ever divined. He lived far away down in Fulham, but he let the buses rock past him, and walked slowly, endeavouring to prolong the joys of anticipation. Almost with a visible gesture he drew himself apart, and went solitary, his eyes downcast, and gazing not on the pavement but on certain clear imagined pictures.

He quickened his steps as he passed along the northern pavement of Leicester Square, hurrying to escape the sight of the enamelled strange spectra who were already beginning to walk and stir abroad, issuing from their caves and waiting for the gaslight. He scowled as he looked up and chanced to see on a hoarding an icon with raddled cheeks and grinning teeth, at which some young men were leering; and one was recalling this creature's great song:

'And that's the way they do it.
How d'ye fink it's done?
Oh, *that's* the way they do it.
Doesn't it taike the bun?'

Symonds scowled at the picture of her, remembering how Beever had voted her 'good goods', how the boys bellowed the chorus under his windows of Saturday nights. Once he had opened the window as they passed by, and had sworn at them and cursed them, in a whisper, lest he should be overheard.

He peered curiously at the books in a Piccadilly shop; now and then when he could save a few pounds he had made purchases there, but the wares which the bookseller dealt in were expensive, and he was obliged to be rather neatly dressed at the office, and he had other esoteric expenses. He had made up his mind to learn Persian and he hesitated as to whether he should turn back now, and see if he could pick up a grammar in Great Russell Street at a reasonable price. But it was growing dark, and the mists and shadows that he loved were gathering and inviting him onwards to those silent streets near the river.

When he at last diverged from the main road he made his way by a devious and eccentric track, threading an intricate maze of streets which to most people would have been dull and gloomy and devoid of interest. But to Symonds these backwaters of London were as bizarre and glowing as a cabinet of Japanese curios; he found here his delicately chased bronzes, work in jade, the flush and flame of extraordinary colours. He delayed at a corner, watching a shadow on a lighted blind, watching it fade and blacken and fade, conjecturing its secrets, inventing dialogue for this drama in *Ombres Chinoises*. He glanced up at another window, and saw a room vivid, in a hard yellow light of flaming gas, and lurked in the shelter of an old elm till he was perceived and the curtains were drawn hastily. On the way he had chosen, it was his fortune to pass many well-ordered decent streets, by villas detached and semi-detached, half hidden behind flowering shrubs and evergreens. At this hour, on a Saturday in November, few were abroad, and Symonds was often able, crouching down by the fence, to peer into a lighted room, to watch persons who thought themselves utterly unobserved. As he came near to his home he went through meaner streets, and he stopped at a corner, observing two children at play, regarding them with the minute scrutiny of an entomologist at the microscope. A woman who had been out shopping crossed the road and drove the children home, and Symonds moved on, hastily, but with a long sigh of enjoyment.

His breath came quick, in gusts, as he drew out his latchkey. He lived in an old Georgian house, and he raced up the stairs, and locked the door of the great lofty room in which he lived. The evening was damp and chilly, but the sweat streamed down his face. He struck a match, and there was a strange momentary vision of the vast room, almost empty of furniture, a hollow space bordered by grave walls and the white glimmer of the corniced ceiling.

He lit a candle, opened a large box that stood in a corner, and set to work. He seemed to be fitting together some sort of lay figure; a vague hint of the human shape increased under his hands. The candle sparkled at the other end of the room, and Symonds was sweating over his task in a cavern of dark shadow. His nervous shaking fingers fumbled over that uncertain figure, and then he began to draw out incongruous monstrous things. In the dusk, white silk shimmered, laces and delicate frills hovered for a moment, as he bungled over the tying of knots, the fastening of bands. The old room grew rich, heavy, vaporous with subtle scents; the garments that were passing through his hands had been drenched with fragrance. Passion had contorted his face; he grinned stark in the candlelight.

When he had finished the work he drew it with him to the window, and lighted three more candles. In his excitement, for that night he forgot the effect of *Ombres Chinoises*, and those who passed and happened to look up at the white staring blind found singular matter for speculation.

Witchcraft

'Rather left the others behind, haven't we, Miss Custance?' said the captain, looking back to the gate and the larchwood.

'I'm afraid we have, Captain Knight. I hope you don't mind very much, do you?'

'Mind? Delighted, you know. Sure this damp air isn't bad for you, Miss Custance?'

'Oh, d'you think it's damp? I like it. Ever since I can remember I've enjoyed these quiet autumn days. I won't hear of father's going anywhere else.'

'Charmin' place, the Grange. Don't wonder you like comin' down here.'

Captain Knight glanced back again and suddenly chuckled.

'I say, Miss Custance,' he said, 'I believe the whole lot's lost their way. Don't see a sign of them. Didn't we pass another path on the left?'

'Yes, and don't you remember you wanted to turn off?'

'Yes, of course. I thought it looked more possible, don't you know. That's where they must have gone. Where does it lead?'

'Oh, nowhere exactly. It dwindles and twists about a lot, and I'm afraid the ground is rather marshy.'

'You don't say so?' The captain laughed out loud. 'How awfully sick Ferris will be. He hates crossing Piccadilly if there's a bit of mud about.'

'Poor Mr Ferris!' And the two went on, picking their way on the rough path, till they came in sight of a little old cottage sunken alone in a hollow amongst the woods.

'Oh, you must come and see Mrs Wise,' said Miss Custance. 'She's such a dear old thing, I'm sure you'd fall in love with her. And she'd never forgive me if she heard afterwards that we'd passed so close without coming in. Only for five minutes, you know.'

'Certainly, Miss Custance. Is that the old lady there at the door?'

'Yes. She's always been so good to us children, and I know she'll talk of our coming to see her for months. You don't mind, do you?'

'I shall be charmed, I'm sure,' and he looked back once more to see if there were any appearance of Ferris and his party.

'Sit down, Miss Ethel, sit down, please, miss,' said the old woman when they went in. 'And please to sit down here, sir, will you be so kind?'

She dusted the chairs, and Miss Custance enquired after the rheumatism and the bronchitis, and promised to send something from the Grange. The old woman had good country manners, and spoke well, and now and then politely tried to include Captain Knight in the conversation. But all the time she was quietly looking at him.

'Yes, sir, I be a bit lonely at times,' she said when her visitors rose. 'I do miss Nathan sorely; you can hardly remember my husband, can you, Miss Ethel? But I have the Book, sir, and good friends too.'

A couple of days later Miss Custance came alone to the cottage. Her hand trembled as she knocked at the door.

'Is it done?' she asked, when the old woman appeared.

'Come in, miss,' said Mrs Wise, and she shut the door, and put up the wooden bolt. Then she crept to the hearth, and drew out something from a hiding place in the stones.

'Look at that,' she said, showing it to the young lady. 'Isn't it a picture?'

Miss Custance took the object into her fine delicate hands, and glanced at it, and then flushed scarlet.

'How horrible!' she exclaimed. 'What did you do that for? You never told me.'

'It's the only way, miss, to get what you want.'

'It's a loathsome thing. I wonder you're not ashamed of yourself.'

'I be as much ashamed as you be, I think,' said Mrs Wise, and she leered at the pretty, shy-faced girl. Their eyes met and their eyes laughed at one another.

'Cover it up, please, Mrs Wise; I needn't look at it now, at all events. But are you sure?'

'There's never been a mishap since old Mrs Cradoc taught me, and she's been dead for sixty year and more. She used to tell of her grandmother's days when there were meetings in the wood over there.'

'And you're quite sure?'

'You do as I tell you. You must take it like this'; and the old woman whispered her instructions, and would have put out a hand in illustration, but the girl pushed it away.

'I understand now, Mrs Wise. No, don't do that. I quite see what you mean. Here's the money.'

'And whatever you do, don't you forget the ointment as I told you,' said Mrs Wise.

'I've been to read to poor old Mrs Wise,' Ethel said that evening to Captain Knight. 'She's over eighty and her eyesight is getting very bad.'

'Very good of you, Miss Custance, I'm sure,' said Captain Knight, and he moved away to the other end of the drawing room, and began to talk to a girl in yellow, with whom he had been exchanging smiles at a distance, ever since the men came in from the dining room.

That night, when she was alone in her room, Ethel followed Mrs Wise's instructions. She had hidden the object in a drawer, and as she drew it out, she looked about her, though the curtains were drawn close.

She forgot nothing, and when it was done she listened.

The Ceremony

From her childhood, from those early and misty days which began to seem unreal, she recollected the grey stone in the wood.

It was something between the pillar and the pyramid in shape, and its grey solemnity amidst the leaves and the grass shone and shone from those early years, always with some hint of wonder. She remembered how, when she was quite a little girl, she had strayed one day, on a hot afternoon, from her nurse's side, and only a little way in the wood the grey stone rose from the grass, and she cried out and ran back in panic terror.

'What a silly little girl,' the nurse had said. 'It's only the . . . stone.' She had quite forgotten the name that the servant had given, and she was always ashamed to ask as she grew older.

But always that hot day, that burning afternoon of her childhood when she had first looked consciously on the grey image in the wood, remained not a memory but a sensation. The wide wood swelling like the sea, the tossing of the bright boughs in the sunshine, the sweet smell of the grass and flowers, the beating of the summer wind upon her cheek, the gloom of the underglade rich, indistinct, gorgeous, significant as old tapestry; she could feel it and see it all, and the scent of it was in her nostrils. And in the midst of the picture, where the strange plants grew gross in shadow, was the old grey shape of the stone.

But there were in her mind broken remnants of another and far earlier impression. It was all uncertain, the shadow of a shadow, so vague that it might well have been a dream that had mingled with the confused waking thoughts of a little child. She did not know that she remembered, she rather remembered the memory. But again it was a summer day, and a woman, perhaps the same nurse, held her in her arms, and went through the wood. The woman carried bright flowers in one hand; the dream had in it a glow of bright red, and the perfume of cottage roses. Then she saw herself put down for a moment on the grass, and the red colour stained the grim stone, and there was nothing else – except that one night she woke up and heard the nurse sobbing.

She often used to think of the strangeness of very early life; one came, it seemed, from a dark cloud, there was a glow of light, but for a moment, and afterwards the night. It was as if one gazed at a velvet curtain, heavy, mysterious, impenetrable blackness, and then, for the twinkling of an eye, one spied through a pinhole a storied town that flamed, with fire about its walls and pinnacles. And then again the folding darkness, so that sight became illusion, almost in the seeing. So to her was that earliest, doubtful vision of the grey stone, of the red colour spilled upon it, with the incongruous episode of the nursemaid, who wept at night.

But the later memory was clear; she could feel, even now, the inconsequent terror that sent her away shrieking, running to the nurse's skirts. Afterwards, through the days of girlhood, the stone had taken its place amongst the vast array of unintelligible things which haunt every child's imagination. It was part of life, to be accepted and not questioned; her elders spoke of many things which she could not understand, she opened books and was dimly amazed, and in the Bible there were many phrases which seemed strange. Indeed, she was often puzzled by her parents' conduct, by their looks at one another, by their half-words, and amongst all these problems which she hardly recognised as problems was the grey ancient figure rising from dark grass.

Some semi-conscious impulse made her haunt the wood where shadow enshrined the stone. One thing was noticeable; that all through the summer months the passers-by dropped flowers there. Withered blossoms were always on the ground, amongst the grass, and on the stone fresh blooms constantly appeared. From the daffodil to the Michaelmas daisy there was marked the calendar of the cottage gardens, and in the winter she had seen sprays of juniper and box, mistletoe and holly. Once she had been drawn through the bushes by a red glow, as if there had been a fire in the wood, and when she came to the place, all the stone shone and all the ground about it was bright with roses.

In her eighteenth year she went one day into the wood, carrying with her a book that she was reading. She hid herself in a nook of hazel, and her soul was full of poetry, when there was a rustling, the rapping of parted boughs returning to their place. Her concealment was but a little way from the stone, and she peered through the net of boughs, and saw a girl timidly approaching. She knew her quite well; it was Annie Dolben, the daughter of a labourer, lately a promising pupil at Sunday school. Annie was a nice-mannered girl, never failing in her curtsy, wonderful for her knowledge of the Jewish Kings. Her face had taken an expression that whispered, that hinted strange things; there was a light and a glow behind the veil of flesh. And in her hand she bore lilies.

The lady hidden in hazels watched Annie come close to the grey image; for a moment her whole body palpitated with expectation, almost the sense of what was to happen dawned upon her. She watched Annie crown the stone with flowers, she watched the amazing ceremony that followed.

And yet, in spite of all her blushing shame, she herself bore blossoms to the wood a few months later. She laid white hothouse lilies upon the stone, and orchids of dying purple, and crimson exotic flowers. Having kissed the grey image with devout passion, she performed there all the antique immemorial rite.

Psychology

Mr Dale, who had quiet rooms in a western part of London, was very busily occupied one day with a pencil and little scraps of paper. He would stop in the middle of his writing, of his monotonous tramp from door to window, jot down a line of hieroglyphics, and turn again to his work. At lunch he kept his instruments on the table beside him, and a little notebook accompanied him on his evening walk about the

Green. Sometimes he seemed to experience a certain difficulty in the act of writing, as if the heat of shame or even incredulous surprise held his hand, but one by one the fragments of paper fell into the drawer, and a full feast awaited him at the day's close.

As he lit his pipe at dusk, he was standing by the window and looking out into the street. In the distance cab lights flashed to and fro, up and down the hill, on the main road. Across the way he saw the long line of sober grey houses, cheerfully lit up for the most part, displaying against the night the dining room and the evening meal. In one house, just opposite, there was brighter illumination, and the open windows showed a modest dinner party in progress, and here and there a drawing room on the first floor glowed ruddy, as the tall shaded lamp was lit. Everywhere Dale saw a quiet and comfortable respectability; if there were no gaiety there was no riot, and he thought himself fortunate to have got 'rooms' in so sane and meritorious a street.

The pavement was almost deserted. Now and again a servant would dart out from a side door and scurry off in the direction of the shops, returning in a few minutes in equal haste. But foot passengers were rare, and only at long intervals a stranger would drift from the highway and wander with slow speculation down Abingdon Road, as if he had passed its entrance a thousand times and had at last been piqued with curiosity and the desire of exploring the unknown. All the inhabitants of the quarter prided themselves on their quiet and seclusion, and many of them did not so much as dream that if one went far enough the road degenerated and became abominable, the home of the hideous, the mouth of a black purlieu. Indeed stories, ill and malodorous, were told of the streets parallel, to east and west, which perhaps communicated with the terrible sink beyond, but those who lived at the good end of Abingdon Road knew nothing of their neighbours.

Dale leant far out of his window. The pale London sky deepened to violet as the lamps were lit, and in the twilight the little gardens before the houses shone, seemed as if they grew more clear. The golden laburnum but reflected the last bright yellow veil that had fallen over the sky after sunset, the white hawthorn was a gleaming splendour, the red may a flameless fire in the dusk. From the open window, Dale could note the increasing cheerfulness of the diners opposite, as the moderate cups were filled and emptied; blinds in the higher stories brightened up and down the street when the nurses came up with the children. A gentle breeze that smelt of grass and woods and flowers fanned away the day's heat from the pavement stones, rustled through the blossoming boughs, and sank again, leaving the road to calm.

All the scene breathed the gentle domestic peace of the stories; there were regular lives, dull duties done, sober and common thoughts on every side. He felt that he needed not to listen at the windows, for he could divine all the talk, and guess the placid and usual channels in which the conversation flowed. Here there were no spasms, nor raptures, nor the red storms of romance, but a safe rest; marriage and birth and begetting were no more here than breakfast and lunch and afternoon tea.

And then he turned away from the placid transparency of the street, and sat down before his lamp and the papers he had so studiously noted. A friend of his, an 'impossible' man named Jenyns, had been to see him the night before, and they had talked about the psychology of the novelists, discussing their insight, and the depth of their probe.

'It is all very well as far as it goes,' said Jenyns. 'Yes, it is perfectly accurate. Guardsmen do like chorus girls, the doctor's daughter is fond of the curate, the grocer's assistant of the Baptist persuasion has sometimes religious difficulties, "smart" people no doubt think a great deal about social events and complications: the Tragic Comedians felt and wrote all that stuff, I dare say. But do you think that is all? Do you call a description of the gilt tools on the morocco here an exhaustive essay on Shakespeare?'

'But what more is there?' said Dale. 'Don't you think, then, that human nature has been fairly laid open? What more?'

'Songs of the frantic lupanar; delirium of the madhouse. Not extreme wickedness, but the insensate, the unintelligible, the lunatic passion and idea, the desire that must come from some other sphere that we cannot even faintly imagine. Look for yourself; it is easy.'

Dale looked now at the ends and scraps of paper. On them he had carefully registered all the secret thoughts of the day, the crazy lusts, the senseless furies, the foul monsters that his heart had borne, the maniac phantasies that he had harboured. In every note he found a rampant madness, the equivalents in thought of mathematical absurdity, of two-sided triangles, of parallel straight lines which met.

'And we talk of absurd dreams,' he said to himself. 'And these are wilder than the wildest visions. And our sins; but these are the sins of nightmare.

'And every day,' he went on, 'we lead two lives, and the half of our soul is madness, and half heaven is lit by a black sun. I say I am a man, but who is the other that hides in me?'

Torture

'I really do not know what to do with him,' said the father. 'He seems absolutely stupid.'

'Poor boy!' said his mother, 'I am afraid he is not well. He doesn't look in good health.'

'But what's the matter with him? He eats well enough; he had two helpings of meat, and two of pudding today at dinner, and a quarter of an hour afterwards he was munching some sweet stuff. His appetite's all right, you see, anyhow.'

'But he's very pale. He makes me feel anxious.'

'And he makes me feel anxious. Look at this letter from Wells, the headmaster. Here you see he says: "It seems almost impossible to get him to play games; he has had two or three thrashings, as I hear, for shirking cricket. And his form master gives me a very bad account of his work during the term, so that I fear the school is doing him little if any good." And you see, Mary, it isn't as if he were a little boy; he was fifteen last April. It's getting serious, you know.'

'What d'you think we had better do?'

'I wish I knew. Look at him here. He's only been home for a week, and you'd think he'd be in the best of spirits, enjoying himself with the squire's boys, and singing and racketing about all over the place. And you know the way he has been going on, almost from the day he came back; lounging and crawling from the house to the garden and back again, staying in bed half the day, and coming down with his eyes half open. I must insist on that being put a stop to, at all events. I shall trust to you to get him up at a proper time.'

'Very well, dear. I thought he looked so tired.'

'But he does nothing to make him tired! I wouldn't mind so much if the fellow were bookish, but you see what Wells says on that score. Why, I can't even get him to read a story book. I declare his face is enough to make one angry. One can see he's totally devoid of any interest in anything.'

'I am afraid he's unhappy, Robert.'

'Unhappy! A schoolboy unhappy! Well, I wish you'd see what you can do. I find it perfectly useless to talk to him myself.'

It was curious, but the father was quite right in laughing at the notion of his son's unhappiness. Harry was, in his quiet way, in the best of spirits. It was perfectly true that he hated cricket, and, the headmaster might have added, he hated other boys. He cared nothing for printed matter of any kind, whether fact or fiction, and he found *Treasure Island* as dull as Cicero. But all through the past term he had been pondering an idea; it had been with him in the early mornings in the dormitory, in schooltime and in playtime, and he watched with it at night, long after the other boys had gone to sleep. Before the coming of the idea he had found his existence unhappy enough. He had a puffy, unwholesome face and sandy hair, and his great wide mouth was made the subject of many jests. He was unpopular because he did not like games, and because he would not bathe unless he were flung into the water, and he was always in trouble over his lessons, which he could not understand. He burst out crying one night in the middle of preparation, and of course he would not say what was the matter. The fact was that he had been trying to extract the meaning from some weary nonsense about triangles, known by the absurd name of Euclid, and he had found it utterly impossible to learn the rabid stuff by heart. The impossibility of it, and the hopeless cloud in his mind, and the terror of the thrashing he would get in the morning, broke him down; the 'blubbering idiot', as they said.

Those were unhappy times, but that very night his idea came to him, and the holidays became indeed desirable, and ten times desirable. Every day and all the day he elaborated and re-elaborated his great thought, and though he was as stupid, unpopular, and unprofitable as ever, he was no longer wretched.

When he got home at the end of term he lost no time in setting about his task. It was true that he was sleepy and heavy in the mornings, but that was because he worked till late at night. He found it impossible to do much in the daytime; his parents spied out his ways, and he knew that he was much too dull to invent lies and explanations. The day after his return his father had come across him as he slunk into a dark corner of the shrubbery with something hidden under his coat. He could only stand and look hopeless, idiotic, when an empty beer bottle was drawn forth; he could not say what he was doing or what he wanted with a green glass bottle. His father had left him, telling him not to play the fool, and he felt that he was always watched. When he took the cord from the back kitchen one of the maids was peering after him down the passage, and his mother found him trying to bind a large log of wood to the trunk of one of the trees. She wanted to know what he was doing, and whether he could not find some more sensible amusement, and he stared at her with his heavy white face. He knew that he was under observation, and so he worked at night. The two servant girls who slept in the next room often awoke, fancying they heard a queer sort of noise, a 'chink-chink', as one of them described the sensation, but they could not make out what it was.

And at last he was ready. He was 'loafing about' one afternoon, and he happened to meet Charlotte Emery, a little girl of twelve, the daughter of a neighbour. Harry flushed to a dull burning red.

'Come for a walk with me to the Beeches?' he said. 'I wish you would.'

'Oh, I mustn't, Harry. Mother wouldn't like it.'

'Do come. I've got a new game; grand fun.'

'Is it really? What sort of game is it?'

'I can't show you here. Just walk on towards the Beeches, and I'll follow you directly. I knew you would.'

Harry ran full tilt to the hiding place where he had bestowed his apparatus. He soon overtook Charlotte, and the two went off together towards the Beeches, a lonely wooded hill a mile away. The boy's father would have been astonished if he could have seen him; Harry was glowing and burning with that dull red colour, but he laughed as he walked beside Charlotte.

When they were alone together in the wood, Charlotte said:

'Now you must show me the game. You promised.'

'I know. But you must do just as I tell you.'

'Yes, I will.'

'Even if it hurts?'

'Yes. But you wouldn't hurt me, Harry. I like you.'

The boy stared at her, gazed with his dull, fishy, light blue eyes; his white, unwholesome face glared at her almost in terror. She was a dark girl, olive-skinned, with black eyes and black hair, and the scent of her hair had already half intoxicated him, as they walked close together.

'You like me,' he said at last, stuttering.

'Yes, I like you very much. I love you, Harry dear. Won't you give me a kiss?' And she put her arm round his neck, round the neck of the ugly, pasty schoolboy. The leaden marks under his eyes seemed to grow darker.

He dropped the parcel that he held under one arm. It broke open and the contents fell to the ground. There were three or four fantastic instruments, ugly little knives made of green bottle glass, clumsily set into wooden handles. He had stolen a broom for this purpose. And there were some lengths of rope, fitted with running nooses. It was the idea that he had so long cherished.

But he threw himself full length upon the grass, and burst into tears – the 'blubbering idiot'.

Midsummer

The old farmhouse on the hill flushed rose in the afterglow, and then, as the dusk began to mount from the brook, faded and yet grew brighter, its whitewashed walls gleaming as though light flowed from them, as the moon gleams when the red clouds turn to grey.

The ancient hawthorn tree at the barn-end became a tall black stem and its leaves and boughs a black mass against the pale uncertain blue of the twilight sky. Leonard looked up with a great sigh of relief. He was perched on the stile by the bridge, and as the wind fell, the ripple of the water swelled into a sweeter song, and there was no other sound to be heard. His pipe was finished, and though he knew that his rooms up at the farm looked out on the red rose and the white, he could not make up his mind to leave the view of the shimmering unearthly walls, and the melody of clear running water.

The contrast of it all with London was almost too immense, hardly realised or credible. A few hours before, and his ears seemed bursting with the terrible battle of the streets, with the clangour and jangle of great waggons thundering over the stones, with the sharp rattle of hansoms, the heavy rumble of swaying omnibuses. And during the journey his eyes still saw the thronging crowds, the turbid, furious streams of men that pushed eastward and westward, hurrying and jostling one another, wearying the brain with their constant movement, the everlasting flux and reflux of white faces. And the air, a hot smoke, a faint sick breath as though from a fever-stricken city; the sky, all grey heat that beat upon weary men, as they looked up through the cloud of dust that went before and followed them.

And now he was soothed in the deep silence and soothed by the chanting water, his eyes saw the valley melting into soft shadow, and in his nostrils was the ineffable incense of a summer night, that as a medicine allayed all the trouble and pain of body and mind. He wet his hands in the dew of the long grass and bathed his forehead, as if all the defilement and anguish of the streets should thus be washed utterly away.

He tried to analyse the scent of the night. The green leaves that overshadowed the brook and made the water dark at noon, gave out their odour, and the deep meadow grass was fragrant, a gale of scent breathed from the huge elder-bush that lit up the vague hillside, hanging above the well. But the meadowsweet was bursting into blossom at his feet, and ah! the wild red roses drooped down from dreamland.

At last he began to climb the hillside towards those white magic walls that had charmed him. His two rooms were at the end of the long low farmhouse, and though there was a passage leading to the big kitchen, Leonard's sitting room opened immediately on the garden, on the crimson roses. He could go and come as he pleased without disturbing the household, or as the pleasant farmer had expressed it, he had a home of his own. He entered and locked the door, and lit the two candles that stood in bright brass candlesticks on the mantelpiece. The room had a low ceiling crossed by a whitewashed beam, the walls were bulging and uneven, decked with samplers, with faded prints, and in a corner stood a glass cupboard, displaying quaint flowery china of some forgotten local pattern.

The room was as quiet, as full of peace, as the air and the night, and Leonard knew that here, at the old bureau, he would find the treasure he had been long vainly seeking. He was tired, but he did not feel inclined to go to bed. He lit his pipe again, and began to arrange his papers, and idly sat down at the bureau, thinking of the task, or rather of the delight, before him. An idea flashed suddenly into his mind, and he began to write hurriedly, in an ecstasy, afraid lest he should lose what he had so happily found.

At midnight his window was still bright on the hill, and he laid down his pen with a sigh of pleasure at the accomplished work. And now he could not go to bed; he felt he must wander into the night, and summon sleep from the velvet air, from the scent of darkness, from the dew. He gently unlocked and locked the door, and walked slowly between the Persian roses, and climbed the stone stile in the garden wall. The moon was mounting to a throne, in full splendour; below, at a little distance, there seemed the painted scene of a village, and higher, beyond the farmhouse, a great wood began. And as he thought of the green retreats he had glanced at in the sunlit evening, he was filled with a longing for the wood-world at night, with a desire for its darkness, for the mystery of it beneath the moon. He followed the path he had noted, till on the wood's verge he looked back and found that the shape of the farmhouse had fallen into the night and vanished.

He entered the shadow, treading softly, and let the track lead him away from the world. The night became full of whisperings, of dry murmuring noises; it seemed soon as if a stealthy host were beneath the trees, every man tracking another. Leonard quite forgot his work, and its triumph, and felt as though his soul were astray in a new dark sphere that dreams had foretold. He had come to a place remote, without form or colour, made alone of shadow and overhanging gloom. Unconsciously he wandered from the path, and for a time he fought his way through the undergrowth, struggling with interlacing boughs and brambles that dragged back his feet.

At last he got free, and found that he had penetrated into a broad avenue, piercing, it seemed, through the heart of the wood. The moon shone bright from above the treetops, and gave a faint green colour to the track which ascended to an open glade; a great amphitheatre amidst the trees. He was tired, and lay down in the darkness beside the turfy road, and wondered whether he had lit on some forgotten way, on some great path that the legions had trodden. And as he lay there watching, gazing at the pale moonlight, he saw a shadow advancing on the grass before him.

'A breath of wind must be stirring some bough behind me,' he thought, but in the instant a woman went by, and then the shadows and white women followed thick.

Leonard gripped hard at a stick he was carrying, and drove his nails into the flesh. He saw the farmer's daughter, the girl who had waited on him a few hours before, and behind her came girls with like faces, no doubt the quiet modest girls of the English village, of the English farmhouse.

For a moment they fronted him, shameless, unabashed before one another, and then they had passed.

He had seen their smiles, he had seen their gestures, and things that he had thought the world had long forgotten.

The white writhing figures passed up towards the glade, and the boughs hid them, but he never doubted as to what he had seen.

Nature

'And there was a broad level by the river,' Julian went on, telling the story of his holiday. 'A broad level of misty meadows, divided by low banks, between the hills and the river. They say the Roman world is lost beneath the turf, that a whole city sleeps there, gold and marble and amber all buried for ever.'

'You did not see anything?'

'No, I suppose not. I used to get up early, and go out, and leave the little modern village behind me, hidden in the hot haze. And then I would stand in the misty meadows, and watch the green turf shimmer and lighten, as the grey halo rolled away. Oh! the silence. There was no sound except the lapping of the river, the wash of the water on the reeds.

'The banks are yellow mud,' he went on, 'but in the early morning, as the sun began to shine in the mist, they pearled and grew like silver. There was a low mound that hid something, and on it an old thorn tree bent towards the east; it was a little way from the tide's brim. I stood there and saw the woods swell out of the haze in the early morning, and that white sun seemed to encompass the town with gleaming walls. If I had stayed still, I think I should have seen the glittering legion and the eagles, I should have heard the sonorous trumpets pealing from the walls.'

'I expect you have seen and heard more than that,' said his friend. 'I always told you that the earth too, and the hills, and even the old walls are a language, hard to translate.'

'And I came upon a place that made me think of that,' said Julian. 'It was far from the town; I lost my way amongst those rolling hills, and strayed by footpaths from field to wood, and all that I saw of man was here and there a blue smoke that crawled up from the earth, from the tree, it might be, or the brook, for I could see no house. I went on, always with the sense that I was following an unknown object, and, suddenly, a shape rose from forgotten dreams. An old farmhouse, built of grey, silvering stones; a long barn wavering and dipping down to a black pool, pine trees overhanging the roof. It was all dim, as if it had been seen reflected in water. I went a little nearer, and I found that I was lifted free of the maze of hills. I fronted the mountain, looking across a deep broad valley, and all the year the mountain winds must blow upon the porch; they look from their deep windows and see the fleeting of the clouds and the sun, on that vast green hillside. Yellow flowers were shaking in the garden, for even on that still day the mountain wind swept across the valley. But those grey glistening walls! A light flowed from them, and they spoke of something beyond thought.

'I visited, too, the river valley, passing out to the north. The town was soon hidden behind trees, behind a curtain of Lombardy poplars, whispering of Italy, of the vine, the olive garden. The curving lane led me beneath orchards, their underboughs dark green, almost black, in the shadow, and the road winding between orchard and river led me into the long valley, where the forest is as a cloud upon the hill. I watched the yellow tide cease, and the water flow clear, and the breath of the wind was unearthly. It was there that I saw the burning pools.'

'You stayed for the sunset?'

'Yes, I stayed all day within the valley. The sky was grey, but not cloudy; rather it was a glowing of silver light that made the earth seem dim and yet shining. Indeed, I say that though the sun was hidden, you would have dreamed that white moons were floating through the air, for now and again I saw the misty hillside pale and lighten, and a tree would appear suddenly in mid-forest, and glitter as if it blossomed. Yes, and in the calm meadows by the riverside there were little points of brightness, as if tongues of white fire sparkled in the grey grass.'

'And the river itself?'

'It was all the day a hieroglyphic, winding in esses beneath those haunting banks, colourless, and yet alight like all the world around. At last, in the evening, I sat down beneath a wych elm on the slope, where I breathed the scent and knew the heavy stillness of the wood. Then a strong wind blew, high up in heaven, and the grey veil vanished. The sky was clear pale blue; in the west there was exhibited an opal burning green, and beneath a purple wall. Then, in the middle of the purple, a rent opened; there was a red glint, and red momentary rays, as if rose-hot metal were beaten and dinted on the anvil, and the sparks fled abroad. So the sun sank.

'I thought I would wait and see all the valley, the river, and the level, and the woods sink into twilight, become sombre, formless. The light went out from the river, the water paled as it flowed between the sad reeds and grasses. I heard a harsh melancholy cry, and above, in the dusky air, a flight of great birds passed seaward in changing, hieroglyphic order. The keen line of the hills by sunset home seemed to melt away, to become vague.

'Then I saw the sky was blossoming in the north. Rose gardens appeared there, with golden hedges, and bronze gates, and the great purple wall caught fire as it grew leaden. The earth was lit again, but with unnatural jewelled colours; the palest light was sardonyx, the darkness was amethyst. And then the valley was aflame. Fire in the wood, the fire of a sacrifice beneath the oaks. Fire in the level fields, a great burning in the north, and vehement flame to the south, above the town. And in the still river the very splendour of fire, yes, as if all precious things were cast into its furnace pools, as if gold and roses and jewels became flame.'

'And then?'

'Then, the shining of the evening star.'

'And you,' said his friend, 'perhaps without knowing, have told me the story of a wonderful and incredible passion.'

Julian stared at him, in amazement.

'You are quite right,' he said at length.

The Holy Things

The sky was blue above Holborn, and only one little cloud, half white, half golden, floated on the wind's way from west to east. The long aisle of the street was splendid in the full light of the summer, and away in the west, where the houses seemed to meet and join, it was as a rich tabernacle, mysterious, the carven house of holy things.

A man came into the great highway from a quiet court. He had been sitting under plane tree shade for an hour or more, his mind racked with perplexities and doubts, with the sense that all was without meaning or purpose, a tangle of senseless joys and empty sorrows. He had stirred in it and fought and striven, and now disappointment and success were alike tasteless. To struggle was weariness, to attain was weariness, to do nothing was weariness. He had felt, a little while before, that from the highest to the lowest things of life there was no choice, there was not one thing that was better than another: the savour of the cinders was no sweeter than the savour of the ashes. He had done work which some men liked and others disliked, and liking and disliking were equally tiresome to him. His poetry or his pictures or whatever it was that he worked at had utterly ceased to interest him, and he had tried to be idle, and found idleness as impossible as work. He had lost the faculty for making and he had lost the power of resting; he dozed in the daytime and started up and cried at night. Even that morning he had doubted and hesitated, wondering whether to stay indoors or to go out, sure that in either plan there was an infinite weariness and disgust.

When he at last went abroad he let the crowd push him into the quiet court, and at the same time cursed them in a low voice for doing so; he tried to persuade himself that he had meant to go somewhere else. When he sat down he desperately endeavoured to rouse himself, and as he knew that all the strong interests are egotistic, he made an effort to grow warm over the work he had done, to find a glow of satisfaction in the thought that he had accomplished something. It was nonsense; he had found out a clever trick and had made the most of it, and it was over. Besides, how would it interest him if afterwards he was praised when he was dead? And what was the use of trying to invent some new tricks? It was folly; and he ground his teeth as a new idea came into his mind and was rejected. To get drunk always made him so horribly ill, and other things were more foolish and tiresome than poesy or painting, whichever it was.

He could not even rest on the uncomfortable bench, beneath the dank, stinking plane tree. A young man and a girl came up and sat next to him, and the girl said, 'Oh, isn't it beautiful today?' and then they began to jabber to one another – the blasted fools! He flung himself from the seat and went out into Holborn.

As far as one could see, there were two processions of omnibuses, cabs, and vans that went east and west and west and east. Now the long line would move on briskly, now it stopped. The horses' feet rattled and pattered on the asphalt, the wheels ground and jarred, a bicyclist wavered in and out between the serried ranks, jangling his bell. The foot passengers went to and fro on the pavement, with an endless change of unknown faces; there was an incessant hum and murmur of voices. In the safety of a blind passage an Italian whirled round the handle of his piano-organ; the sound of it swelled and sank as the traffic surged and paused, and now and then one heard the shrill voices of the children who danced and shrieked in time to the music. Close to the pavement a coster pushed his barrow and proclaimed flowers in an odd intonation, reminding one of the Gregorian chant. The cyclist went by again with his jangling insistent bell, and a man who stood by the lamp post set fire to his pastille ribbon, and let the faint blue smoke rise into the sun. Away in the west, where the houses seemed to meet, the play of sunlight on the haze made, as it were, golden mighty shapes that paused and advanced, and paused again.

He had viewed the scene hundreds of times, and for a long while had found it a nuisance and a weariness. But now as he walked stupidly, slowly, along the southern side of Holborn, a change fell. He did not in the least know what it was, but there seemed to be a strange air, and a new charm that soothed his mind.

When the traffic was stopped, to his soul there was a solemn hush that summoned remnants of a far-off memory. The voices of the passengers sank away, the street was endued with a grave and reverent expectation. A shop that he passed had a row of electric lamps burning above the door, and the golden glow of them in the sunlight was, he felt, significant. The grind and jar of the wheels, as the procession moved on again, gave out a chord of music, the opening of some high service that was to be done, and now, in an ecstasy, he was sure that he heard the roll and swell and triumph of the organ, and shrill sweet choristers began to sing. So the music sank and swelled and echoed in the vast aisle – in Holborn.

What could these lamps mean, burning in the bright sunlight? The music was hushed in a grave close, and in the rattle of traffic he heard the last deep sonorous notes shake against the choir walls – he had passed beyond the range of the Italian's instrument. But then a rich voice began alone, rising and falling in monotonous but awful modulations, singing a longing triumphant song, bidding the faithful lift up their hearts, be joined in heart with the Angels and Archangels, with the Thrones and Dominations. He could see no longer, he could not see the man who passed close beside him, pushing his barrow, and calling flowers.

Ah! He could not be mistaken, he was sure now. The air was blue with incense, he smelt the adorable fragrance. The time had almost come. And then the silvery, reiterated, instant summons of a bell; and again, and again.

The tears fell from his eyes, in his weeping the tears poured a rain upon his cheeks. But he saw in the distance, in the far distance, the carven tabernacle, golden mighty figures moving slowly, imploring arms stretched forth.

There was a noise of a great shout; the choir sang in the tongue of his boyhood that he had forgotten:

SANT . . . SANT . . . SANT

Then the silvery bell tinkled anew; and again, and again. He looked and saw the Holy, White, and Shining Mysteries exhibited – in Holborn.

Opening the Door

The newspaper reporter, from the nature of the case, has generally to deal with the commonplaces of life. He does his best to find something singular and arresting in the spectacle of the day's doings; but, in spite of himself, he is generally forced to confess that whatever there may be beneath the surface, the surface itself is dull enough.

I must allow, however, that during my ten years or so in Fleet Street, I came across some tracks that were not devoid of oddity. There was that business of Campo Tosto, for example. That never got into the papers. Campo Tosto, I must explain, was a Belgian, settled for many years in England, who had left all his property to the man who looked after him.

My news editor was struck by something odd in the brief story that appeared in the morning paper, and sent me down to make enquiries. I left the train at Reigate; and there I found that Mr Campo Tosto had lived at a place called Burnt Green – which is a translation of his name into English – and that he shot at trespassers with a bow and arrows. I was driven to his house, and saw through a glass door some of the property which he had bequeathed to his servant: fifteenth-century triptychs, dim and rich and golden; carved statues of the saints; great spiked altar candlesticks; storied censers in tarnished silver; and much more of old church treasure. The legatee, whose name was Turk, would not let me enter; but, as a treat, he took my newspaper from my pocket and read it upside down with great accuracy and facility. I wrote this very queer story, but Fleet Street would not suffer it. I believe it struck them as too strange a thing for their sober columns.

And then there was the affair of the J.H.V.S. Syndicate, which dealt with a Cabalistic cipher, and the phenomenon, called in the Old Testament 'the Glory of the Lord', and the discovery of certain objects buried under the site of the Temple at Jerusalem; that story was left half told, and I never heard the ending of it. And I never understood the affair of the hoard of coins that a storm disclosed on the Suffolk coast near Aldeburgh. From the talk of the longshoremen, who were on the look-out amongst the dunes, it appeared that a great wave came in and washed away a slice of the sand cliff just beneath them. They saw glittering objects as the sea washed back, and retrieved what they could. I viewed the treasure – it was a collection of coins, the earliest of the twelfth century, the latest, pennies, three or four of them, of Edward VII, and a bronze medal of Charles Spurgeon. There are, of course, explanations of the puzzle; but there are difficulties in the way of accepting any one of them. It is very clear, for example, that the hoard was not gathered by a collector of coins; neither the twentieth-century pennies nor the medal of the great Baptist preacher would appeal to a numismatologist.

But perhaps the queerest story to which my newspaper connections introduced me was the affair of the Reverend Secretan Jones, the 'Canonbury Clergyman', as the headlines called him.

To begin with, it was a matter of sudden disappearance. I believe people of all sorts disappear by dozens in the course of every year, and nobody hears of them or their vanishings. Perhaps they turn up again, or perhaps they don't; anyhow, they never get so much as a line in the papers, and there is an end of it. Take, for example, that unknown man in the burning car, who cost the amorous commercial traveller his life. In a certain sense, we all heard of him; but he must have disappeared from somewhere in space, and nobody knew that he had gone from his world. So it is often; but now and then there is some circumstance that draws attention to the fact that A. or B. was in his place on Monday and missing from it on Tuesday and Wednesday, and then enquiries are made and usually the lost man is found, alive or dead, and the explanation is often simple enough.

But as to the case of Secretan Jones. This gentleman, a cleric as I have said, but seldom, it appeared, exercising his sacred office, lived retired in a misty, 1830–40 square in the recesses of Canonbury. He was understood to be engaged in some kind of scholarly research, was a well-known figure in the Reading Room of the British Museum, and looked anything between fifty and sixty. It seems probable that if he had been content with that achievement he might have disappeared as often as he pleased, and nobody would have troubled; but one night as he sat late over his books in the stillness of that retired quarter, a motor-lorry passed along a road not far from Tollit Square, breaking the silence with a heavy rumble and causing a tremor of the ground that penetrated into Secretan Jones's study. A teacup and saucer on a sidetable trembled slightly, and Secretan Jones's attention was taken from his authorities and notebooks.

This was in February or March of 1907, and the motor industry was still in its early stages. If you preferred a horse-bus, there were plenty left in the streets. Motor coaches were non-existent, hansom cabs still jogged and jingled on their cheerful way; and there were very few heavy motor-vans in use. But to Secretan Jones, disturbed by the rattle of his cup and saucer, a vision of the future, highly coloured, was vouchsafed, and he began to write to the papers. He saw the London streets almost as we know them today; streets where a horse-vehicle would be almost a matter to show one's children for them to remember in their old age; streets in which a great procession of huge omnibuses carrying fifty, seventy, a hundred people was continually passing; streets in which vans and trailers loaded far beyond the capacity of any manageable team of horses would make the ground tremble without ceasing.

The retired scholar, with the happy activity which does sometimes, oddly enough, distinguish the fish out of water, went on and spared nothing. Newton saw the apple fall, and built up a mathematical universe; Jones heard the teacup rattle, and laid the universe of London in ruins. He pointed out that neither the roadways nor the houses beside them were constructed to withstand the weight and vibration of the coming traffic. He crumbled all the shops in Oxford Street and Piccadilly into dust; he cracked the dome of St Paul's, brought down Westminster Abbey, reduced the Law Courts to a fine powder. What was left was dealt with by fire, flood and pestilence. The prophetic Jones demonstrated that the roads must collapse, involving the various services beneath them. Here, the water mains and the main drainage would flood the streets; there, huge volumes of gas would escape, and electric wires fuse; the earth would be rent with explosions, and the myriad streets of London would go up in a great flame of fire. Nobody really believed that it would happen, but it made good reading, and Secretan Jones gave interviews, started discussions, and enjoyed himself thoroughly. Thus he became the 'Canonbury Clergyman'. 'Canonbury Clergyman Says That Catastrophe Is Inevitable'; 'Doom of London Pronounced by Canonbury Clergyman'; 'Canonbury Clergyman's Forecast: London a Carnival of Flood, Fire and

Earthquake' – that sort of thing.

And thus Secretan Jones, though his main interests were liturgical, was able to secure a few newspaper paragraphs when he disappeared – rather more than a year after his great campaign in the press, which was not quite forgotten, but not very clearly remembered.

A few paragraphs, I said, and stowed away, most of them, in out-of-the-way corners of the papers. It seemed that Mrs Sedger, the woman who shared with her husband the business of looking after Secretan Jones, brought in tea on a tray to his study at four o'clock as usual, and came, again as usual, to take it away at five. And, a good deal to her astonishment, the study was empty. She concluded that her master had gone out for a stroll, though he never went out for strolls between tea and dinner. He didn't come back for dinner; and Sedger, inspecting the hall, pointed out that the master's hats and coats and sticks and umbrellas were all on their pegs and in their places. The Sedgers conjectured this, that, and the other, waited a week, and then went to the police, and the story came out and perturbed a few learned friends and correspondents: Prebendary Lincoln, author of *The Roman Canon in the Third Century*; Dr Brightwell, wise on the Rite of Malabar; and Stokes, the Mozarabic man. The rest of the populace did not take very much interest in the affair, and when, at the end of six weeks, there was a line or two stating that 'the Rev. Secretan Jones, whose disappearance at the beginning of last month from his house in Tollit Square, Canonbury, caused some anxiety to his friends, returned yesterday', there was neither enthusiasm nor curiosity. The last line of the paragraph said that the incident was supposed to be the result of a misunderstanding; and nobody even asked what that statement meant.

And there would have been the end of it – if Sedger had not gossiped to the circle in the private bar of The King of Prussia. Some mysterious and unofficial person, in touch with this circle, insinuated himself into the presence of my news editor and told him Sedger's tale. Mrs Sedger, a careful woman, had kept all the rooms tidy and well dusted. On the Tuesday afternoon she had opened the study door and saw, to her amazement and delight, her master sitting at his table with a great book open beside him and a pencil in his hand. She exclaimed:

'Oh, sir, I *am* glad to see you back again!'

'Back again?' said the clergyman. 'What do you mean? I think I should like some more tea.'

'I don't know in the least what it's all about,' said the news editor, 'but you might go and see Secretan Jones and have a chat with him. There may be a story in it.' There was a story in it, but not for my paper, or any other paper.

I got into the house in Tollit Square on some unhandsome pretext connected with Secretan Jones's traffic scare of the year before. He looked at me in a dim, abstracted way at first – the 'great book' of his servant's story, and other books, and many black quarto notebooks were about him – but my introduction of the proposed design for a 'mammoth carrier' clarified him, and he began to talk eagerly, and as it seemed to me lucidly, of the grave menace of the new mechanical transport.

'But what's the use of talking?' he ended. 'I tried to wake people up to the certain dangers ahead. I seemed to succeed for a few weeks; and then they forgot all about it. You would really say that the great majority are like dreamers, like sleepwalkers. Yes, like men walking in a dream, shutting out all the actualities, all the facts of life. They know that they are, in fact, walking on the edge of a precipice; and yet they are able to believe, it seems, that the precipice is a garden path; and they behave as if it were a garden path, as safe as that path you see down there, going to the door at the bottom of my garden.'

The study was at the back of the house, and looked on the long garden, heavily overgrown with shrubs run wild, mingling with one another, some of them flowering richly, and altogether and happily obscuring and confounding the rigid grey walls that doubtless separated each garden from its neighbours. Above the tall shrubs, taller elms and planes and ash trees grew unlopped and handsomely neglected; and under this deep concealment of green boughs the path went down to a green door, just visible under a cloud of white roses.

'As safe as that path you see there,' Secretan Jones repeated, and, looking at him, I thought his expression changed a little; very slightly, indeed, but to a certain questioning, one might say to a meditative doubt. He suggested to me a man engaged in an argument, who puts his case strongly, decisively; and then hesitates for the fraction of a second as a point occurs to him of which he had never thought before; a point as yet unweighed, unestimated; dimly present, but more as a shadow than a shape.

The newspaper reporter needs the gestures of the serpent as well as its wisdom. I forget how I glided from the safe topic of the traffic peril to the dubious territory which I had been sent to explore. At all events, my contortions were the most graceful that I could devise; but they were altogether vain. Secretan Jones's kind, lean, clean-shaven face took on an expression of distress. He looked at me as one in perplexity; he seemed to search his mind not for the answer that he should give me, but rather for some answer due to himself.

'I am extremely sorry that I cannot give you the information you want,' he said, after a considerable pause. 'But I really can't go any farther into the matter. In fact, it is quite out of the question to do so. You must tell your editor – or sub-editor; which is it? – that the whole business is due to a misunderstanding, a misconception, which I am not at liberty to explain. But I am really sorry that you have come all this way for nothing.'

There was real apology and regret, not only in his words, but in his tones and in his aspect. I could not clutch my hat and get on my way with a short word in the character of a disappointed and somewhat disgusted emissary; so we fell on general talk, and it came out that we both came from the Welsh borderland, and had long ago walked over the same hills and drunk of the same wells. Indeed, I believe we proved cousinship, in the seventh degree or so, and tea came in, and before long Secretan Jones was deep in liturgical problems, of which I knew just enough to play the listener's part. Indeed, when I had told him that the *hwyl*, or chanted eloquence, of the Welsh Methodists was, in fact, the Preface Tone of the Roman Missal, he overflowed with grateful interest, and made a note in one of his books, and said the point was most curious and important. It was a pleasant evening, and we strolled through the french windows into the green-shadowed, blossoming garden, and went on with our talk, till it was time – and high time – for me to go. I had taken up my hat as we left the study, and as we stood by the green door in the wall at the end of the garden, I suggested that I might use it.

'I'm so sorry,' said Secretan Jones, looking, I thought, a little worried, 'but I am afraid it's jammed, or something of that kind. It has always been an awkward door, and I hardly ever use it.'

So we went through the house, and on the doorstep he pressed me to come again, and was so cordial that I agreed to his suggestion of the Saturday sennight. And so at last I got an answer to the question with which my newspaper had originally entrusted me; but an answer by no means for newspaper use. The tale, or the experience, or the impression, or whatever it may be called, was delivered to me by very slow degrees, with hesitations, and in a manner of tentative suggestion that often reminded me of our first talk together. It was as if Jones were again and again questioning himself as to the matter of his utterances, as if he doubted whether they should not rather be treated as dreams, and dismissed as trifles without consequence.

He said once to me: 'People do tell their dreams, I know; but isn't it usually felt that they are telling nothing? That's what I am afraid of.'

I told him that I thought we might throw a great deal of light on very dark places if more dreams were told.

'But there,' I said, 'is the difficulty. I doubt whether the dreams that I am thinking of *can* be told. There are dreams that are perfectly lucid from beginning to end, and also perfectly insignificant. There are others which are blurred by a failure of memory, perhaps only on one point: you dream of a dead man as if he were alive. Then there are dreams which are prophetic: there seems, on the whole, no doubt of that. Then you may have sheer clotted nonsense; I once chased Julius Caesar all over London to get his recipe for curried eggs. But, besides these, there is a certain dream of another order: utter lucidity up to the moment of waking, and then perceived to be beyond the power of words to express. It is neither sense nor nonsense; it has, perhaps, a notation of its own, but . . . well, you can't play Euclid on the violin.'

Secretan Jones shook his head. 'I am afraid my experiences are rather like that,' he said. It was clear, indeed, that he found great difficulty in finding a verbal formula which should convey some hint of his adventures.

But that was later. To start with, things were fairly easy; but, characteristically enough, he began his story before I realised that the story was begun. I had been talking of the queer tricks a man's memory sometimes plays him. I was saying that a few days before, I was suddenly interrupted in some work I was doing. It was necessary that I should clear my desk in a hurry. I shuffled a lot of loose papers together and put them away, and awaited my caller with a fresh writing pad before me. The man came. I attended to the business with which he was concerned, and went back to my former affair when he had gone. But I could not find the sheaf of papers. I thought I had put them in a drawer. They were not in the drawer; they were not in any drawer, or in the blotting book, or in any place where one might reasonably expect to find them. They were found next morning by the servant who dusted the room, stuffed hard down into the crevice between the seat and the back of an armchair, and carefully hidden under a cushion.

'And,' I finished, 'I hadn't the faintest recollection of doing it. My mind was blank on the matter.'

'Yes,' said Secretan Jones, 'I suppose we all suffer from that sort of thing at times. About a year ago I had a very odd experience of the same kind. It troubled me a good deal at the time. It was soon after I had taken up that question of the new traffic and its probable – its certain – results. As you may have gathered, I have been absorbed for most of my life in my own special studies, which are remote enough from the activities and interests of the day. It hasn't been at all my way to write to the papers to say there are too many dogs in London, or to denounce street musicians. But I must say that the extraordinary dangers of using our present road system for a traffic for which it was not designed did impress themselves very deeply upon me; and I dare say I allowed myself to be over-interested and over-excited.

'There is a great deal to be said for the Apostolic maxim: "Study to be quiet and to mind your own business." I am afraid I got the whole thing on the brain, and neglected my own business, which at that particular time, if I remember, was the investigation of a very curious question – the validity or non-validity of the Consecration Formula of the *Grand Saint Graal: Car chou est li sanc di ma nouviele loy, li miens meismes*. Instead of attending to my proper work, I allowed myself to be drawn into the discussion I had started, and for a week or two I thought of very little else; even when I was looking up authorities at the British Museum, I couldn't get the rumble of the motor-van out of my head. So, you see, I allowed myself to get harried and worried and distracted, and I put down what followed to all the bother and excitement I was going through. The other day, when you had to leave your work in the middle and start on something else, I dare say you felt annoyed and put out, and shoved those papers of yours away without really thinking of what you were doing, and I suppose something of the same kind happened to me. Though it was still queerer, I think.'

He paused, and seemed to meditate doubtfully, and then broke out with an apologetic laugh, and: 'It really sounds quite crazy!' And then: 'I forgot where I lived.'

'Loss of memory, in fact, through overwork and nervous excitement?'

'Yes, but not quite in the usual way. I was quite clear about my name and my identity. And I knew my address perfectly well: Thirty-nine, Tollit Square, Canonbury.'

'But you said you forgot where you lived.'

'I know; but there's the difficulty of expression we were talking about the other day. I am looking for the notation, as you called it. But it was like this: I had been working till the morning in the Reading Room with the motor danger at the back of my mind, and as I left the Museum, feeling a sort of heaviness and confusion, I made up my mind to walk home. I thought the air might freshen me a little. I set out at a good pace. I knew every foot of the way, as I had often done the walk before, and I went ahead mechanically, with my mind wrapt up in a very important matter relating to my proper studies. As a matter of fact, I had found in a most unexpected quarter a statement that threw an entirely new light on the Rite of the Celtic Church, and I felt that I might be on the verge of an important discovery. I was lost in a maze of conjectures, and when I looked up I found myself standing on the pavement by the Angel, Islington, totally unaware of where I was to go next.

'Yes, quite so: I knew the Angel when I saw it, and I knew I lived in Tollit Square; but the relation between the two had entirely vanished from my consciousness. For me, there were no longer any points of the compass; there was no such thing as direction, neither north nor south, nor left nor right, an extraordinary sensation, which I don't feel I have made plain to you at all. I was a good deal disturbed, and felt that I must move somewhere, so I set off – and found myself at King's Cross railway station. Then I did the only thing there was to be done: took a hansom and got home, feeling shaky enough.'

I gathered that this was the first incident of significance in a series of odd experiences that befell this learned and amiable clergyman. His memory became thoroughly unreliable, or so he thought at first.

He began to miss important papers from his table in the study. A series of notes, on three sheets lettered A, B, and C, were placed by him on the table under a paperweight one night, just before he went up to bed. They were missing when he went into his study the next morning. He was certain that he had put them in that particular place, under the bulbous glass weight with the pink roses embedded in its depths, but they were not there. Then Mrs Sedger knocked at the door and entered with the papers in her hand. She said she had found them between the bed and the mattress in the master's bedroom, and thought they might be wanted.

Secretan Jones could not make it out at all. He supposed he must have put the papers where they were found and then forgotten all about it, and he was uneasy, feeling afraid that he was on the brink of a nervous breakdown. Then there were difficulties about his books, as to which he was very precise, every book having its own place. One morning he wanted to consult the *Missale de Arbuthnott*, a big red quarto, which lived at the end of a bottom shelf near the window. It was not there. The unfortunate man went up to his bedroom, and felt the bed all over and looked under his shirts in the chest of drawers, and searched all the room in vain. However, determined to get what he wanted, he went to the Reading Room, verified his reference, and returned to Canonbury: and there was the red quarto in its place. Now here, it seemed certain, there was no room for loss of memory; and Secretan Jones began to suspect his servants of playing tricks with his possessions, and tried to find a reason for their imbecility or villainy – he did not know what to call it. But it would not do at all. Papers and books disappeared and reappeared, or now and then vanished without return. One afternoon, struggling, as he told me, against a growing sense of confusion and bewilderment, he had with considerable difficulty filled two quarto sheets of ruled paper with a number of extracts necessary to the subject he had in hand. When this was done, he felt his bewilderment thickening like a cloud about him: 'It was, physically and mentally, as if the objects in the room became indistinct, were presented in a shimmering mist or darkness.' He felt afraid, and rose, and went out into the garden. The two sheets of paper he had left on his table were lying on the path by the garden door.

I remember he stopped dead at this point. To tell the truth, I was thinking that all these instances were rather matter for the ear of a mental specialist than for my hearing. There was evidence enough of a bad nervous breakdown, and it seemed to me, of delusions. I wondered whether it was my duty to advise the man to go to the best doctor he knew, and without delay. Then Secretan Jones began again:

'I won't tell you any more of these absurdities. I know they are drivel, pantomime tricks and traps, children's conjuring; contemptible, all of it.

'But it made me afraid. I felt like a man walking in the dark, beset with uncertain sounds and faint echoes of his footsteps that seem to come from a vast depth, till he begins to fear that he is treading by the edge of some awful precipice. There was something unknown about me; and I was holding on hard to what I knew, and wondering whether

I should be sustained.

'One afternoon I was in a very miserable and distracted state. I could not attend to my work. I went out into the garden, and walked up and down trying to calm myself. I opened the garden door and looked into the narrow passage which runs at the end of all the gardens on this side of the square. There was nobody there – except three children playing some game or other. They were queer, stunted little creatures, and I turned back into the garden and walked into the study. I had just sat down, and had turned to my work hoping to find relief in it, when Mrs Sedger, my servant, came into the room and cried out, in an excited sort of way, that she was glad to see me back again.

'I made up some story. I don't know whether she believes it. I suppose she thinks I have been mixed up in something disreputable.'

'And what had happened?'

'I haven't the remotest notion.'

We sat looking at each other for some time.

'I suppose what happened was just this,' I said at last. 'Your nervous system had been in a very bad way for some time. It broke down utterly; you lost your memory, your sense of identity – everything. You may have spent the six weeks in addressing envelopes in the City Road.'

He turned to one of the books on the table and opened it. Between the leaves there were the dimmed red and white petals of some flower that looked like an anemone.

'I picked this flower,' he said, 'as I was walking down the path that afternoon. It was the first of its kind to be in bloom – very early. It was still in my hand when I walked back into this room, six weeks later, as everybody declares. But it was quite fresh.'

There was nothing to be said. I kept silent for five minutes, I suppose, before I asked him whether his mind was an utter blank as to the six weeks during which no known person had set eyes on him; whether he had no sort of recollection, however vague.

'At first, nothing at all. I could not believe that more than a few seconds came between my opening the garden door and shutting it. Then in a day or two there was a vague impression that I had been somewhere where everything was absolutely right. I can't say more than that. No fairyland joys, or bowers of bliss, or anything of that kind; no sense of anything strange or unaccustomed. But there was no care there at all. *Est enim magnum chaos.*'

But that means 'For there is a great void', or 'a great gulf'.

We never spoke of the matter again. Two months later he told me that his nerves had been troubling him, and that he was going to spend a month or six weeks at a farm near Llanthony, in the Black Mountains, a few miles from his old home. In three weeks I got a letter, addressed in Secretan Jones's hand. Inside was a slip of paper on which he had written the words:

Est enim magnum chaos.

The day on which the letter was posted he had gone out in wild autumn weather, late one afternoon, and had never come back. No trace of him has ever been found.

The Bright Boy

I

Young Joseph Last, having finally gone down from Oxford, wondered a good deal what he was to do next and for the years following next. He was an orphan from early boyhood, both his parents having died of typhoid within a few days of each other when Joseph was ten years old, and he remembered very little of Dunham, where his father ended a long line of solicitors, practising in the place since 1707. The Lasts had once been very comfortably off. They had intermarried now and again with the gentry of the neighbourhood and did a good deal of the county business, managing estates, collecting rents, officiating as stewards for several manors, living generally in a world of quiet but snug prosperity, rising to their greatest height, perhaps, during the Napoleonic Wars and afterwards. And then they began to decline, not violently at all, but very gently, so that it was many years before they were aware of the process that was going on, slowly, surely. Economists, no doubt, understand very well how the country and the country town gradually became less important soon after the Battle of Waterloo; and the causes of the decay and change which vexed Cobbett so sadly, as he saw, or thought he saw, the life and strength of the land being sucked up to nourish the monstrous excrescence of London. Anyhow, even before the railways came, the assembly rooms of the country towns grew dusty and desolate, the county families ceased to come to their 'town houses' for the winter season, and the little theatres, where Mrs Siddons and Grimaldi had appeared in their divers parts, rarely opened their doors, and the skilled craftsmen, the clockmakers and the furniture makers and the like began to drift away to the big towns and to the capital city. So it was with Dunham. Naturally the fortunes of the Lasts sank with the fortunes of the town; and there had been speculations which had not turned out well, and people spoke of a heavy loss in foreign bonds. When Joseph's father died, it was found that there was enough to educate the boy and keep him in strictly modest comfort and not much more.

He had his home with an uncle who lived at Blackheath, and after a few years at Mr Jones's well-known preparatory school, he went to Merchant Taylors and thence to Oxford. He took a decent degree (2nd in Greats) and then began that wondering process as to what he was to do with himself. His income would keep him in chops and steaks, with an occasional roast fowl, and three or four weeks on the Continent once a year. If he liked, he could do nothing, but the prospect seemed tame and boring. He was a very decent classical scholar, with something more than the average schoolmaster's purely technical knowledge of Latin and Greek and professional interest in them: still, schoolmastering seemed his only clear and obvious way of employing himself. But it did not seem likely that he would get a post at any of the big public schools. In the first place, he had rather neglected his opportunities at Oxford. He had gone to one of the obscurer colleges, one of those colleges which you may read about in memoirs dealing with the first years of the nineteenth century as centres and fountains of intellectual life; which for some reason or no reason have fallen into the shadow. There is nothing against them in any way; but nobody speaks of them any more. In one of these places Joseph Last made friends with good fellows, quiet and cheerful men like himself; but they were not, in the technical sense of the term, the 'good friends' which a prudent young man makes at the university. One or two had the bar in mind, and two or three the civil service; but most of them were bound for country curacies and country offices. Generally, and for practical purposes, they were 'out of it': they were not the men whose whispers could lead to anything profitable in high quarters. And then, again, even in those days, games were getting important in the creditable schools; and there, young Last was very decidedly out of it. He wore spectacles with lenses divided in some queer manner: his athletic disability was final and complete.

He pondered, and thought at first of setting up a small preparatory school in one of the well-to-do London suburbs; a day school where parents might have their boys well grounded from the very beginning, for comparatively modest fees, and yet have their upbringing in their own hands. It had often struck Last that it was a barbarous business to send a little chap of seven or eight away from the comfortable and affectionate habit of his home to a strange place among cold strangers; to bare boards, an inky smell, and grammar on an empty stomach in the morning. But consulting with Jim Newman of his old college, he was warned by that sage to drop his scheme and leave it on the ground. Newman pointed out in the first place that there was no money in teaching unless it was combined with hotel keeping. That, he said, was all right, and more than all right; and he surmised that many people who kept hotels in the ordinary way would give a good deal to practise their art and mystery under housemaster's rules. 'You needn't pay so very much for your furniture, you know. You don't want to make the boys into young sybarites. Besides, there's nothing a healthy-minded boy hates more than stuffiness: what he likes is clean fresh air and plenty of it. And, you know, old chap, fresh air is cheap enough. And then with the food, there's apt to be trouble in the ordinary hotel if it's uneatable; but in the sort of hotel we're talking of, a little accident with the beef or mutton affords a very valuable opportunity for the exercise of the virtue of self-denial.'

Last listened to all this with a mournful grin.

'You seem to know all about it,' he said. 'Why don't you go in for it yourself?'

'I couldn't keep my tongue in my cheek. Besides, I don't think it's fair sport. I'm going out to India in the autumn. What about pig-sticking?'

'And there's another thing,' he went on after a meditative pause. 'That notion of yours about a day prep. school is rotten. The parents wouldn't say thank you for letting them keep their kids at home when they're all small and young. Some people go so far as to say that the chief purpose of schools is to allow parents a good excuse for getting rid of their children. That's nonsense. Most fathers and mothers are very fond of their children and like to have them about the house; when they're young, at all events. But somehow or other, they've got it into their heads that strange schoolmasters know more about bringing up a small boy than his own people; and there it is. So, on all counts, drop that scheme of yours.'

Last thought it over, and looked about him in the scholastic world, and came to the conclusion that Newman was right. For two or three years he took charge of reading parties in the long vacation. In the winter he found occupation in the coaching of backward boys, in preparing boys not so backward for scholarship examinations; and his little textbook, *Beginning Greek*, was found quite useful in lower school. He did pretty well on the whole, though the work began to bore him sadly, and such money as he earned, added to his income, enabled him to live in the way he liked, comfortably enough. He had a couple of rooms in one of the streets going down from the Strand to the river, for which he paid a pound a week, had bread and cheese and odds and ends for lunch, with beer from his own barrel in the cellar, and dined simply but sufficiently now in one, now in another of the snug taverns which then abounded in the quarter. And, now and again, once a month or so, perhaps, instead of the tavern dinners, there was the play at the Vaudeville or the Olympic, the Globe or the Strand, with supper and something hot to follow. The evening might turn into a little party: old Oxford friends would look him up in his rooms between six and seven; Zouch would gather from the Temple and Medwin from Buckingham Street, and possibly Garraway, taking the Yellow Albion bus, would descend from his remote steep in the northern parts of London, would knock at 14, Mowbray Street, and demand pipes, porter, and the pit at a good play. And, on rare occasions, another member of the little society, Noel, would turn up. Noel lived at Turnham Green in a red brick house which was then thought merely old-fashioned, which would now – but it was pulled down long ago – be distinguished as choice Queen Anne or Early Georgian. He lived there with his father, a retired official of the British Museum, and through a man whom he had known at Oxford, he had made some way in literary journalism, contributing regularly to an important weekly paper. Hence the consequence of his occasional descents on Buckingham Street, Mowbray Street, and the Temple. Noel, as in some sort a man of letters, or, at least, a professional journalist, was a member of Blacks Club, which in those days had exiguous premises in Maiden Lane. Noel would go round the haunts of his friends, and gather them to stout and oysters, and guide them into some neighbouring theatre pit, whence they viewed excellent acting and a cheerful, nonsensical play, enjoyed both, and were ready for supper at the Tavistock. This done, Noel would lead the party to Blacks, where they, very likely, saw some of the actors who had entertained them earlier in the evening, and Noel's friends, the journalists and men of letters, with a painter and a black-and-white man here and there. Here, Last enjoyed himself very much, more especially among the actors, who seemed to him more genial than the literary men. He became especially friendly with one of the players, old

Meredith Mandeville, who had talked with the elder Kean, was reliable in the smaller Shakespearean parts, and had engaging tales to tell of early days in county circuits. 'You had nine shillings a week to begin with. When you got to fifteen shillings you gave your landlady eight or nine shillings, and had the rest to play with. You felt a prince. And the county families often used to come and see us in the Green Room: most agreeable.'

With this friendly old gentleman, whose placid and genial serenity was not marred at all by incalculable quantities of gin, Last loved to converse, getting glimpses of a life strangely remote from his own: vagabondage, insecurity, hard times, and jollity; and against it all as a background, the lighted murmur of the stage, voices uttering tremendous things, and the sense of moving in two worlds. The old man, by his own account, had not been eminently prosperous or successful, and yet he had relished his life, and drew humours from its disadvantages, and made hard times seem an adventure. Last used to express his envy of the player's career, dwelling on the dull insignificance of his own labours, which, he said, were a matter of tinkering small boys' brains, teaching older boys the tricks of the examiners, and generally doing things that didn't matter.

'It's no more education than bricklaying is architecture,' he said one night. 'And there's no fun in it.'

Old Mandeville, on his side, listened with interest to these revelations of a world as strange and unknown to him as the life of the floats was to the tutor. Broadly speaking, he knew nothing of any books but play books. He had heard, no doubt, of things called examinations, as most people have heard of Red Indian initiations; but to him one was as remote as the other. It was interesting and strange to him to be sitting at Blacks and actually talking to a decent young fellow who was seriously engaged in this queer business. And there were – Last noted with amazement – points at which their two circles touched, or so it seemed. The tutor, wishing to be agreeable, began one night to talk about the origins of *King Lear*. The actor found himself listening to Celtic legends which to him sounded incomprehensible nonsense. And when it came to the Knight who fought the King of Fairyland for the hand of Cordelia till Doomsday, he broke in: '*Lear* is a pill; there's no doubt of that. You're too young to have seen Barry O'Brien's *Lear*: magnificent. The part has been attempted since his day. But it has never been played. I have depicted the Fool myself, and, I must say, not without some meed of applause. I remember once at Stafford . . . ' and Last was content to let him tell his tale, which ended, oddly enough, with a bullock's heart for supper.

But one night when Last was grumbling, as he often did, about the fragmentary, desultory, and altogether unsatisfactory nature of his occupation, the old man interrupted him in a wholly unexpected vein.

'It is possible,' he began, 'mark you, I say possible, that I may be the means of alleviating the tedium of your lot. I was calling some days ago on a cousin of mine, a Miss Lucy Pilliner, a very agreeable woman. She has a considerable knowledge of the world, and, I hope you will forgive the liberty, but I mentioned in the course of our conversation that I had lately became acquainted with a young gentleman of considerable scholastic distinction, who was somewhat dissatisfied with the too abrupt and frequent entrances and exits of his present tutorial employment. It struck me that my cousin received these remarks with a certain reflective interest, but I was not prepared to receive this letter.'

Mandeville handed Last the letter. It began: 'My dear Ezekiel,' and Last noted out of the corner of his eye a glance from the actor which pleaded for silence and secrecy on this point. The letter went on to say in a manner almost as dignified as Mandeville's, that the writer had been thinking over the circumstances of the young tutor, as related by her cousin in the course of their most agreeable conversation of Friday last, and she was inclined to think that she knew of an educational position shortly available in a private family, which would be of a more permanent and satisfactory nature. 'Should your friend feel interested,' Miss Pilliner ended, 'I should be glad if he would communicate with me, with a view to a meeting being arranged, at which the matter could be discussed with more exact particulars.'

'And what do you think of it?' said Mandeville, as Last returned Miss Pilliner's letter.

For a moment Last hesitated. There is an attraction and also a repulsion in the odd and the improbable, and Last doubted whether educational work obtained through an actor at Blacks and a lady at Islington – he had seen the name at the top of the letter – could be altogether solid or desirable. But brighter thoughts prevailed, and he assured Mandeville that he would be only too glad to go thoroughly into the matter, thanking him very warmly for his interest. The old man nodded benignly, gave him the letter again that he might take down Miss Pilliner's address, and suggested an immediate note asking for an appointment.

'And now,' he said, 'despite the carping objections of the Moody Prince, I propose to drink your jocund health tonight.'

And he wished Last all the good luck in the world with hearty kindliness.

In a couple of days Miss Pilliner presented her compliments to Mr Joseph Last and begged him to do her the favour of calling on her on a date three days ahead, at noon, 'if neither day nor hour were in any way incompatible with his convenience.' They might then, she proceeded, take advantage of the occasion to discuss a certain proposal, the nature of which, she believed, had been indicated to Mr Last by her good cousin, Mr Meredith Mandeville.

Corunna Square, where Miss Pilliner lived, was a small, almost a tiny, square in the remoter parts of Islington. Its two-storied houses of dim, yellowish brick were fairly covered with vines and clematis and all manner of creepers. In front of the houses were small paled gardens, gaily flowering, and the square enclosure held little else besides a venerable, wide-spreading mulberry, far older than the buildings about it. Miss Pilliner lived in the quietest corner of the square. She welcomed Last with some sort of compromise between a bow and a curtsy, and begged him to be seated in an upright armchair, upholstered in horsehair. Miss Pilliner, he noted, looked about sixty, and was, perhaps, a little older. She was spare, upright, and composed; and yet one might have suspected a lurking whimsicality. Then, while the weather was discussed, Miss Pilliner offered a choice of port or sherry, sweet biscuits or plum cake. And so to the business of the day.

'My cousin, Mr Mandeville, informed me,' she began, 'of a young friend of great scholastic ability, who was, nevertheless, dissatisfied with the somewhat casual and occasional nature of his employment. By a singular coincidence, I had received a letter a day or two before from a friend of mine, a Mrs Marsh. She is, in fact, a distant connection, some sort of cousin, I suppose, but not being a Highlander or a Welshwoman, I really cannot say how many times removed. She was a lovely creature; she is still a handsome woman. Her name was Manning, Arabella Manning, and what possessed her to marry Mr Marsh I really cannot say. I only saw the man once, and I thought him her inferior in every respect, and considerably older. However, she declares that he is a devoted husband and an excellent person in every respect. They first met, odd as it must seem, in Peking, where Arabella was governess in one of the legation families. Mr Marsh, I was given to understand, represented highly important commercial interests at the capital of the Flowery Land, and being introduced to my connection, a mutual attraction seems to have followed. Arabella Manning resigned her position in the attaché's family, and the marriage was solemnised in due course. I received this intelligence nine years ago in a letter from Arabella, dated at Peking, and my relative ended by saying that she feared it would be impossible to furnish an address for an immediate reply, as Mr Marsh was about to set out on a mission of an extremely urgent nature on behalf of his firm, involving a great deal of travelling and frequent changes of address. I suffered a good deal of uneasiness on Arabella's account, it seemed such an unsettled way of life, and so unhomelike. However, a friend of mine who is in the City assured me that there was nothing unusual in the circumstances, and that there was no cause for alarm. Still, as the years went on, and I received no further communication from my cousin, I made up my mind that she had probably contracted some tropical disease which had carried her off, and that Mr Marsh had heartlessly neglected to communicate to me the intelligence of the sad event. But a month ago, almost to the day' – Miss Pilliner referred to an almanac on the table beside her – 'I was astonished and delighted to receive a letter from Arabella. She wrote from one of the most luxurious and exclusive hotels in the West End of London, announcing the return of her husband and herself to their native land after many years of wandering. Mr Marsh's active concern in business had, it appeared, at length terminated in a highly prosperous and successful manner, and he was now in negotiation for the purchase of a small estate in the country, where he hoped to spend the remainder of his days in peaceful retirement.'

Miss Pilliner paused and replenished Last's glass.

'I am so sorry,' she continued, 'to trouble you with this long narrative, which, I am sure, must be a sad trial of your patience. But, as you will see presently, the circumstances are a little out of the common, and as you are, I trust, to have a particular interest in them, I think it is only right that you should be fully informed – fair and square, and all above board, as my poor father used to say in his bluff manner.

'Well, Mr Last, I received, as I have said, this letter from Arabella with its extremely gratifying intelligence. As you may guess, I was very much relieved to hear that all had turned out so felicitously. At the end of her letter, Arabella begged me to come and see them at Billing's Hotel, saying that her husband was most anxious to have the pleasure of meeting me.'

Miss Pilliner went to a drawer in a writing table by the window and took out a letter.

'Arabella was always considerate. She says: "I know that you have always lived very quietly, and are not accustomed to the turmoil of fashionable London. But you need not be alarmed. Billing's Hotel is no bustling modern caravanserai. Everything is very quiet, and, besides, we have our own small suite of apartments. Herbert" – her husband, Mr Last – "positively insists on your paying us a visit, and you must not disappoint us. If next Thursday, the 22nd, suits you, a carriage shall be sent at four o'clock to bring you to the hotel, and will take you back to Corunna Square, after you have joined us in a little dinner."

'Very kind, most considerate; don't you agree with me, Mr Last? But look at the postscript.'

Last took the letter, and read in a tight, neat script: 'PS. We have a wonderful piece of news for you. It is too good to write, so I shall keep it for our meeting.'

Last handed back Mrs Marsh's letter. Miss Pilliner's long and ceremonious approach was lulling him into a mild stupor; he wondered faintly when she would come to the point, and what the point would be like when she came to it, and, chiefly, what on earth this rather dull family history could have to do with him.

Miss Pilliner proceeded.

'Naturally, I accepted so kindly and urgent an invitation. I was anxious to see Arabella once more after her long absence, and I was glad to have the opportunity of forming my own judgment as to her husband, of whom I knew absolutely nothing. And then, Mr Last, I must confess that I am not deficient in that spirit of curiosity, which gentlemen have scarcely numbered with female virtues. I longed to be made partaker in the wonderful news which Arabella had promised to impart on our meeting, and I wasted many hours in speculating as to its nature.

'The day came. A neat brougham with its attendant footman arrived at the appointed hour, and I was driven in smooth luxury to Billing's Hotel in Manners Street, Mayfair. There a major-domo led the way to the suite of apartments on the first floor occupied by Mr and Mrs

Marsh. I will not waste your valuable time, Mr Last, by expatiating on the rich but quiet luxury of their apartments; I will merely mention that my relative assured me that the Sèvres ornaments in their drawing room had been valued at nine hundred guineas. I found Arabella still a beautiful woman, but I could not help seeing that the tropical countries in which she had lived for so many years had taken their toll of her once resplendent beauty; there was a weariness, a lassitude in her appearance and demeanour which I was distressed to observe. As to her husband, Mr Marsh, I am aware that to form an unfavourable judgment after an acquaintance which has only lasted a few hours is both uncharitable and unwise; and I shall not soon forget the discourse which dear Mr Venn delivered at Emmanuel Church on the very Sunday after my visit to my relative: it really seemed, and I confess it with shame, that Mr Venn had my own case in mind, and felt it his bounden duty to warn me while it was yet time. Still, I must say that I did not take at all to Mr Marsh. I really can't say why. To me he was most polite; he could not have been more so. He remarked more than once on the extreme pleasure it gave him to meet at last one of whom he had heard so much from his dear Bella; he trusted that now his wandering days were over, the pleasure might be frequently repeated; he omitted nothing that the most genial courtesy might suggest. And yet, I cannot say that the impression I received was a favourable one. However; I dare say that I was mistaken.'

There was a pause. Last was resigned. The point of the long story seemed to recede into some far distance, into vanishing perspective.

'There was nothing definite?' he suggested.

'No; nothing definite. I may have thought that I detected a lack of candour, a hidden reserve behind all the generosity of Mr Marsh's expressions. Still; I hope I was mistaken.

'But I am forgetting in these trivial and I trust erroneous observations, the sole matter that is of consequence; to you, at least, Mr Last. Soon after my arrival, before Mr Marsh had appeared, Arabella confided to me her great piece of intelligence. Her marriage had been blessed by offspring. Two years after her union with Mr Marsh, a child had been born, a boy. The birth took place at a town in South America, Santiago de Chile – I have verified the place in my atlas – where Mr Marsh's visit had been more protracted than usual. Fortunately, an English doctor was available, and the little fellow throve from the first, and as Arabella, his proud mother, boasted, was now a beautiful little boy, both handsome and intelligent to a remarkable degree. Naturally,

I asked to see the child, but Arabella said that he was not in the hotel with them. After a few days it was thought that the dense and humid air of London was not suiting little Henry very well; and he had been sent with a nurse to a resort in the Isle of Thanet, where he was reported to be in the best of health and spirits.

'And now, Mr Last, after this tedious but necessary preamble, we arrive at that point where you, I trust, may be interested. In any case, as you may suppose, the life which the exigencies of business compelled the Marshes to lead, involving as it did almost continual travel, would have been little favourable to a course of systematic education for the child. But this obstacle apart, I gathered that Mr Marsh holds very strong views as to the folly of premature instruction. He declared to me his conviction that many fine minds had been grievously injured by being forced to undergo the process of early stimulation; and he pointed out that, by the nature of the case, those placed in charge of very young children were not persons of the highest acquirements and the keenest intelligence. "As you will readily agree, Miss Pilliner," he remarked to me, "great scholars are not employed to teach infants their alphabet, and it is not likely that the mysteries of the multiplication table will be imparted by a master of mathematics." In consequence, he urged, the young and budding intelligence is brought into contact with dull and inferior minds, and the damage may well be irreparable.'

There was much more, but gradually light began to dawn on the dazed man. Mr Marsh had kept the virgin intelligence of his son Henry undisturbed and uncorrupted by inferior and incompetent culture. The boy, it was judged, was now ripe for true education, and Mr and Mrs Marsh had begged Miss Pilliner to make enquiries, and to find, if she could, a scholar who would undertake the whole charge of little Henry's mental upbringing. If both parties were satisfied, the engagement would be for seven years at least, and the appointments, as Miss Pilliner called the salary, would begin with five hundred pounds a year, rising by an annual increment of fifty pounds. References, particulars of university distinctions would be required: Mr Marsh, long absent from England, was ready to proffer the names of his bankers. Miss Pilliner was quite sure, however, that Mr Last might consider himself engaged, if the position appealed to him.

Last thanked Miss Pilliner profoundly. He told her that he would like a couple of days in which to think the matter over. He would then write to her, and she would put him into communication with

Mr Marsh. And so he went away from Corunna Square in a mood of great bewilderment and doubt. Unquestionably, the position had many advantages. The pay was very good. And he would be well lodged and well fed. The people were wealthy, and Miss Pilliner had assured him: 'You will have no cause to complain of your entertainment.' And from the educational point of view, it would certainly be an improvement on the work he had been doing since he left the university. He had been an odd-job man, a tinker, a patcher, a cobbler of other people's work; here was a chance to show that he was a master craftsman. Very few people, if any, in the teaching profession had ever enjoyed such an opportunity as this. Even the sixth-form masters in the big public schools must sometimes groan at having to underpin and relay the bad foundations of the fifth and fourth. He was to begin at the beginning, with no false work to hamper him: 'from A B C to Plato, Aeschylus, and Aristotle,' he murmured to himself. Undoubtedly it was a big chance.

And on the other side? Well, he would have to give up London, and he had grown fond of the homely, cheerful London that he knew; his comfortable rooms in Mowbray Street, quiet enough down by the unfrequented Embankment, and yet but a minute or two from the ringing Strand. Then there were the meetings with the old Oxford friends, the nights at the theatre, the snug taverns with their curtained boxes, and their good chops and steaks and stout, and chimes of midnight and after, heard in cordial company at Blacks: all these would have to go. Miss Pilliner had spoken of Mr Marsh as looking for some place a considerable distance from town, 'in the real country'. He had his eye, she said, on a house on the Welsh border, which he thought of taking furnished, with the option of buying, if he eventually found it suited him. You couldn't look up old friends in London and get back the same night, if you lived somewhere on the Welsh border. Still, there would be the holidays, and a great deal might be done in the holidays.

And yet; there was still debate and doubt within his mind, as he sat eating his bread and cheese and potted meat, and drinking his beer in his sitting room in peaceful Mowbray Street. He was influenced, he thought, by Miss Pilliner's evident dislike of Mr Marsh, and though Miss Pilliner talked in the manner of Dr Johnson, he had a feeling that, like a lady of the Doctor's own day, she had a bottom of good sense. Evidently she did not trust Mr Marsh overmuch. Yet, what can the most cunning swindler do to his resident tutor? Give him cold mutton for dinner or forget to pay his salary? In either case, the remedy was simple: the resident tutor would swiftly cease to reside, and go back to London, and not be much the worse. After all, Last reflected, a man can't compel his son's tutor to invest in Uruguayan silver or Java spices or any other fallacious commercial undertaking, so what mattered the supposed trickiness of Marsh to him?

But again, when all had been summed up and considered, for and against, there was a vague objection remaining. To oppose this, Last could bring no argument, since it was without form of words, shapeless, and mutable as a cloud.

However, when the next morning came, there came with it a couple of letters inviting him to cram two young dunderheads with facts and figures and verbs in *mi*. The prospect was so terribly distasteful that he wrote to Miss Pilliner directly after breakfast, enclosing his college testimonials and certain other commendatory letters he had in his desk. In due course, he had an interview with Mr Marsh at Billing's Hotel. On the whole, each was well enough pleased with the other. Last found Marsh a lean, keen, dark man in later middle age; there was a grizzle in his black hair above the ears, and wrinkles seamed his face about the eyes. His eyebrows were heavy, and there was a hint of a threat in his jaw, but the smile with which he welcomed Last lit up his grimmish features into a genial warmth. There was an oddity about his accent and his tone in speaking; something foreign, perhaps? Last remembered that he had journeyed about the world for many years, and supposed that the echoes of many languages sounded in his speech. His manner and address were certainly suave, but Last had no prejudice against suavity, rather, he cherished a liking for the decencies of common intercourse. Still, no doubt, Marsh was not the kind of man Miss Pilliner was accustomed to meet in Corunna Square society or among Mr Venn's congregation. She probably suspected him of having been a pirate.

And Mr Marsh on his side was delighted with Last. As appeared from a letter addressed by him to Miss Pilliner – 'or, may I venture to say, Cousin Lucy?' – Mr Last was exactly the type of man he and Arabella had hoped to secure through Miss Pilliner's recommendation. They did not want to give their boy into the charge of a flashy man of the world with a substratum of learning. Mr Last was, it was evident, a quiet and unworldly scholar, more at home among books than among men; the very tutor Arabella and himself had desired for their little son. Mr Marsh was profoundly grateful to Miss Pilliner for the great service she had rendered to Arabella, to himself, and to Henry.

And, indeed, as Mr Meredith Mandeville would have said, Last looked the part. No doubt, the spectacles helped to create the remote, retired, Dominie Sampson impression.

In a week's time it was settled, he was to begin his duties. Mr Marsh wrote a handsome cheque, 'to defray any little matters of outfit, travelling expenses, and so forth; nothing to do with your salary.' He was to take train to a certain large town in the west, and there he would be met and driven to the house, where Mrs Marsh and his pupil were already established – 'beautiful country, Mr Last; I am sure you will appreciate it.'

There was a famous farewell gathering of the old friends. Zouch and Medwin, Garraway and Noel came from near and far. There was grilled sole before the mighty steak, and a roast fowl after it. They had decided that as it was the last time, perhaps, they would not go to the play, but sit and talk about the mahogany. Zouch, who was understood to be the ruler of the feast, had conferred with the head waiter, and when the cloth was removed, a rare and curious port was solemnly set before them. They talked of the old days when they were up at Wells together, pretended – though they knew better – that the undergraduate who had cut his own father in Piccadilly was a friend of theirs, retold jokes that must have been older than the wine, related tales of Moll and Meg, and the famous history of Melcombe, who screwed up the dean in his own rooms. And then there was the affair of the Poses Plastiques. Certain lewd fellows, as one of the dons of Wells College expressed it, had procured scandalous figures from the waxwork booth at the fair, and had disposed them by night about the fountain in the college garden in such a manner that their scandal was shamefully increased. The perpetrators of this infamy had never been discovered: the five friends looked knowingly at each other, pursed their lips, and passed the port.

The old wine and the old stories blended into a mood of gentle meditation; and then, at the right moment, Noel carried them off to Blacks and new company. Last sought out old Mandeville and related, with warm gratitude, the happy issue of his intervention.

The chimes sounded, and they all went their several ways.

II

Though Joseph Last was by no means a miracle of observation and deduction, he was not altogether the simpleton among his books that Mr Marsh had judged him. It was not so very long before a certain uneasiness beset him in his new employment. At first everything had seemed very well. Mr Marsh had been right in thinking that he would be charmed by the scene in which the White House was set. It stood, terraced on a hillside, high above a grey and silver river winding in esses through a lonely, lovely valley. Above it, to the east, was a vast and shadowy and ancient wood, climbing to the high ridge of the hill, and descending by height and by depth of green to the level meadows and to the sea. And, standing on the highest point of the wood above the White House, Last looked westward between the boughs and saw the lands across the river, and saw the country rise and fall in billow upon billow to the huge dim wall of the mountain, blue in the distance, and white farms shining in the sun on its vast side. Here was a man in a new world. There had been no such country as this about Dunham in the Midlands, or in the surroundings of Blackheath or Oxford; and he had visited nothing like it on his reading parties. He stood amazed, enchanted under the green shade, beholding a great wonder. Close beside him the well bubbled from the grey rocks, rising out of the heart of the hill.

And in the White House, the conditions of life were altogether pleasant. He had been struck by the dark beauty of Mrs Marsh, who was clearly, as Miss Pilliner had told him, a great many years younger than her husband. And he noted also that effect which her cousin had ascribed to years of living in the tropics, though he would hardly have called it weariness or lassitude. It was something stranger than that; there was the mark of flame upon her, but Last did not know whether it were the flame of the sun, or the stranger fires of places that she had entered, perhaps long ago.

But the pupil, little Henry, was altogether a surprise and a delight. He looked rather older than seven, but Last judged that this impression was not so much due to his height or physical make as to the bright alertness and intelligence of his glance. The tutor had dealt with many little boys, though with none so young as Henry; and he had found them as a whole a stodgy and podgy race, with faces that recorded a fixed abhorrence of learning and a resolution to learn as little as possible.

Last was never surprised at this customary expression. It struck him as eminently natural. He knew that all elements are damnably dull and difficult. He wondered why it was inexorably appointed that the unfortunate human creature should pass a great portion of its life from the very beginning in doing things that it detested; but so it was, and now for the syntax of the optative.

But there were no such obstinate entrenchments in the face or the manner of Henry Marsh. He was a handsome boy, who looked brightly and spoke brightly, and evidently did not regard his tutor as a hostile force that had been brought against him. He was what some people would have called, oddly enough, old-fashioned; childlike, but not at all childish, with now and then a whimsical turn of phrase more suggestive of a humorous man than a little boy. This older habit was no doubt to be put down partly to the education of travel, the spectacle of the changing scene and the changing looks of men and things, but very largely to the fact that he had always been with his father and mother, and knew nothing of the company of children of his own age.

'Henry has had no playmates,' his father explained. 'He's had to be content with his mother and myself. It couldn't be helped. We've been on the move all the time; on shipboard or staying at cosmopolitan hotels for a few weeks, and then on the road again. The little chap had no chance of making any small friends.'

And the consequence was, no doubt, that lack of childishness that Last had noted. It was, probably, a pity that it was so. Childishness, after all, was a wonder world, and Henry seemed to know nothing of it: he had lost what might be, perhaps, as valuable as any other part of human experience, and he might find the lack of it as he grew older. Still, there it was; and Last ceased to think of these possibly fanciful deprivations, when he began to teach the boy, as he had promised himself, from the very beginning. Not quite from the beginning; the small boy confessed with a disarming grin that he had taught himself to read a little: 'But please, sir, don't tell my father, as I know he wouldn't like it. You see, my father and mother had to leave me alone sometimes, and it was so dull, and I thought it would be such fun if I learnt to read books all by myself.'

Here, thought Last, is a lesson for schoolmasters. Can learning be made a desirable secret, an excellent sport, instead of a horrible penance? He made a mental note, and set about the work before him. He found an extraordinary aptitude, a quickness in grasping his indications and explanations such as he had never known before – 'not in boys twice his age, or three times his age, for the matter of that,' as he reflected. This child, hardly removed from strict infancy, had something almost akin to genius – so the happy tutor was inclined to believe. Now and again, with his, 'Yes, sir, I see. And then, of course . . . ' he would veritably take the coming words out of Last's mouth, and anticipate what was, no doubt, logically the next step in the demonstration. But Last had not been accustomed to pupils who anticipated anything – save the hour for putting the books back on the shelf. And above all, the instructor was captured by the eager and intense curiosity of the instructed. He was like a man reading *The Moonstone*, or some such sensational novel, and unable to put the book down till he had read to the very last page and found out the secret. This small boy brought just this spirit of insatiable curiosity to every subject put before him. 'I wish I had taught him to read,' thought Last to himself. 'I have no doubt he would have regarded the alphabet as we regard those entrancing and mysterious cyphers in Edgar Allan Poe's stories. And, after all, isn't that the right and rational way of looking at the alphabet?'

And then he went on to wonder whether curiosity, often regarded as a failing, almost a vice, is not, in fact, one of the greatest virtues of the spirit of man, the key to all knowledge and all the mysteries, the very sense of the secret that must be discovered.

With one thing and another: with this treasure of a pupil, with the enchantment of the strange and beautiful country about him, and with the extreme kindness and consideration shown him by Mr and Mrs Marsh, Last was in rich clover. He wrote to his friends in town, telling them of his happy experiences, and Zouch and Noel, meeting by chance at the Sun, the Dog, or the Triple Tun, discussed their friend's felicity.

'Proud of the pup,' said Zouch.

'And pleased with the prospect,' responded Noel, thinking of Last's lyrics about the woods and the waters, and the scene of the White House. 'Still, *timeo Hesperides et dona ferentes*. I mistrust the west. As one of its own people said, it is a land of enchantment and illusion. You never know what may happen next. It is a fortunate thing that Shakespeare was born within the safety line. If Stratford had been twenty or thirty miles farther west . . . I don't like to think of it. I am quite sure that only fairy gold is dug from Welsh gold mines. And you know what happens to that.'

Meanwhile, far from the lamps and rumours of the Strand, Last continued happy in his outland territory, under the great wood. But before long he received a shock. He was strolling in the terraced garden one afternoon between tea and dinner, his work done for the day; and feeling inclined for tobacco with repose, drifted towards the stone summer house – or, perhaps, gazebo – that stood on the verge of the lawn in a coolness of dark ilex trees. Here one could sit and look down on the silver winding of the river, crossed by a grey bridge of ancient stone. Last was about to settle down when he noticed a book on the table before him. He took it up, and glanced into it, and drew in his breath, and turning over a few more pages, sank aghast upon the bench. Mr Marsh had always deplored his ignorance of books. 'I knew how to read and write and not much more,' he would say, 'when I was thrown into business – at the bottom of the stairs. And I've been so busy ever since that I'm afraid it's too late now to make up for lost time.' Indeed, Last had noted that though Marsh usually spoke carefully enough, perhaps too carefully, he was apt to lapse in the warmth of conversation: he would talk of 'fax', meaning 'facts'. And yet, it seemed, he had not only found time for reading, but had acquired sufficient scholarship to make out the Latin of a terrible Renaissance treatise, not generally known even to collectors of such things. Last had heard of the book; and the few pages he had glanced at showed him that it thoroughly deserved its very bad character.

It was a disagreeable surprise. He admitted freely to himself that his employer's morals were no business of his. But why should the man trouble to tell lies? Last remembered queer old Miss Pilliner's account of her impressions of him; she had detected 'a lack of candour', something reserved behind a polite front of cordiality. Miss Pilliner was, certainly, an acute woman: there was an undoubted lack of candour about Marsh.

Last left the wretched volume on the summer house table, and walked up and down the garden, feeling a good deal perturbed. He knew he was awkward at dinner, and said he felt a bit seedy, inclined to a headache. Marsh was bland and pleasant as usual, and Mrs Marsh sympathised with Last. She had hardly slept at all last night, she complained, and felt heavy and tired. She thought there was thunder in the air. Last, admiring her beauty, confessed again that Miss Pilliner had been right. Apart from her fatigue of the moment, there was a certain tropical languor about her, something of still, burning nights and the odour of strange flowers.

Marsh brought out a very special brandy which he administered with the black coffee; he said it would do both the invalids good, and that he would keep them company. Indeed, Last confessed to himself that he felt considerably more at ease after the good dinner, the good wine, and the rare brandy. It was humiliating, perhaps, but it was impossible to deny the power of the stomach. He went to his room early and tried to convince himself that the duplicity of Marsh was no affair of his. He found an innocent, or almost innocent explanation of it before he had finished his last pipe, sitting at the open window, hearing faintly the wash of the river and gazing towards the dim lands beyond it.

'Here,' he meditated, 'we have a modified form of Bounderby's Disease. Bounderby said that he began life as a wretched, starved, neglected little outcast. Marsh says that he was made into an office boy or something of the sort before he had time to learn anything. Bounderby lied, and no doubt Marsh lies. It is the trick of wealthy men; to magnify their late achievements by magnifying their early disadvantages.'

By the time he went to sleep he had almost decided that the young Marsh had been to a good grammar school, and had done well.

The next morning, Last awoke almost at ease again. It was no doubt a pity that Marsh indulged in a subtle and disingenuous form of boasting, and his taste in books was certainly deplorable: but he must look after that himself. And the boy made amends for all. He showed so clean a grasp of the English sentence, that Last thought he might well begin Latin before very long. He mentioned this one night at dinner, looking at Marsh with a certain humorous intention. But Marsh gave no sign that the dart had pricked him.

'That shows I was right,' he remarked. 'I've always said there's no greater mistake than forcing learning on children before they're fit to take it in. People will do it, and in nine cases out of ten the children's heads are muddled for the rest of their lives. You see how it is with Henry; I've kept him away from books up to now, and you see for yourself that I've lost him no time. He's ripe for learning, and I shouldn't wonder if he got ahead better in six months than the ordinary, early-crammed child would in six years.'

It might be so, Last thought, but on the whole he was inclined to put down the boy's swift progress rather to his own exceptional intelligence than to his father's system, or no system. And in any case, it was a great pleasure to teach such a boy. And his application to his books had certainly no injurious effect on his spirits. There was not much society within easy reach of the White House, and, besides, people did not know whether the Marshes were to settle down or whether they were transient visitors: they were chary of paying their calls while there was this uncertainty. However, the rector had called; first of all the rector and his wife, she cheery, good-humoured and chatty; he somewhat dim and vague. It was understood that the rector, a high wrangler in his day, divided his time between his garden and the invention of a flying machine. He had the character of being slightly eccentric. He came not again, but Mrs Winslow would drive over by the forest road in the governess car with her two children; Nancy, a pretty fair girl of seventeen, and Ted, a boy of eleven or twelve, of that type which Last catalogued as 'stodgy and podgy', broad and thick set, with bulgy cheeks and eyes, and something of the determined expression of a young bulldog. After tea Nancy would organise games for the two boys in the garden and join in them herself with apparent relish. Henry, who had known few companions besides his parents, and had probably never played a game of any kind, squealed with delight, ran here and there and everywhere, hid behind the summer house and popped out from the screen of the French beans with the greatest gusto, and Ted Winslow joined in with an air of protest. He was on his holidays, and his expression signified that all that sort of thing was only fit for girls and kids. Last was delighted to see Henry so ready and eager to be amused; after all, he had something of the child in him. He seemed a little uncomfortable when Nancy Winslow took him on her knee after the sports were over; he was evidently fearful of Ted Winslow's scornful eye. Indeed, the young bulldog looked as if he feared that his character would be compromised by associating with so manifest and confessed a kid. The next time Mrs Winslow took tea at the White House, Ted had a diplomatic headache and stayed at home. But Nancy found games that two could play, and she and Henry were heard screaming with joy all over the gardens. Henry wanted to show Nancy a wonderful well that he had discovered in the forest; it came, he said, from under the roots of a great yew tree. But Mrs Marsh seemed to think that they might get lost.

Last had got over the uncomfortable incident of that villainous book in the summer house. Writing to Noel, he had remarked that he feared his employer was a bit of an old rascal in some respects, but all right so far as he was concerned; and there it was. He got on with his job and minded his own business. Yet, now and again, his doubtful uneasiness about the man was renewed. There was a bad business at a hamlet a couple of miles away, where a girl of twelve or thirteen, coming home after dusk from a visit to a neighbour, had been set on in the wood and very vilely misused. The unfortunate child, it would appear, had been left by the scoundrel in the black dark of the forest, at some distance from the path she must have taken on her way home. A man who had been drinking late at the Fox and Hounds heard crying and screaming, 'like someone in a fit', as he expressed it, and found the girl in a terrible state, and in a terrible state she had remained ever since. She was quite unable to describe the person who had so shamefully maltreated her; the shock had left her beside herself; she cried out once that something had come behind her in the dark, but she could say no more, and it was hopeless to try to get her to describe a person that, most likely, she had not even seen. Naturally, this very horrible story made something of a feature in the local paper, and one night, as Last and Marsh were sitting smoking after dinner, the tutor spoke of the affair; said something about the contrast between the peace and beauty and quiet of the scene and the villainous crime that had been done hard by. He was surprised to find that Marsh grew at once ill at ease. He rose from his chair and walked up and down the room, muttering 'horrible business, shameful business'; and when he sat down again, with the light full on him, Last saw the face of a frightened man. The hand that Marsh laid on the table was twitching uneasily; he beat with his foot on the floor as he tried to bring his lips to order, and there was a dreadful fear in his eyes.

Last was shocked and astonished at the effect he had produced with a few conventional phrases. Nervously, willing to tide over a painful situation, he began to utter something even more conventional to the effect that the loveliness of external nature had never conferred immunity from crime, or some stuff to the same inane purpose. But Marsh, it was clear, was not to be soothed by anything of the kind. He started again from his chair and struck his hand upon the table, with a fierce gesture of denial and refusal.

'Please, Mr Last, let it be. Say no more about it. It has upset Mrs Marsh and myself very much indeed. It horrifies us to think that we have brought our boy here, to this peaceful place as we thought, only to expose him to the contagion of this dreadful affair. Of course we have given the servants strict orders not to say a word about it in Henry's presence; but you know what servants are, and what very sharp ears children have. A chance word or two may take root in a child's mind and contaminate his whole nature. It is, really, a very terrible thought. You must have noticed how distressed Mrs Marsh has been for the last few days. The only thing we can do is to try and forget it all, and hope no harm has been done.'

Last murmured a word or two of apology and agreement, and the talk moved off into safer country. But when the tutor was alone, he considered what he had seen and heard very curiously. He thought that Marsh's looks did not match his words. He spoke as the devoted father, afraid that his little boy should overhear nauseous and offensive gossip and conjecture about a horrible and obscene crime. But he looked like a man who had caught sight of a gallows, and that, Last felt, was altogether a very different kind of fear. And, then, there was his reference to his wife. Last had noticed that since the crime in the forest there had been something amiss with her; but, again, he mistrusted Marsh's comment. Here was a woman whose usual habit was a rather lazy good humour; but of late there had been a look and an air of suppressed fury, the burning glance of a jealous woman, the rage of despised beauty. She spoke little, and then as briefly as possible; but one might suspect flames and fires within. Last had seen this and wondered, but not very much, being resolved to mind his own business. He had supposed there had been some difference of opinion between her and her husband; very likely about the rearrangement of the drawing room furniture and hiring a grand piano. He certainly had not thought of tracing Mrs Marsh's altered air to the villainous crime that had been committed. And now Marsh was telling him that these glances of concealed rage were the outward signs of tender maternal anxiety; and not one word of all that did he believe. He put Marsh's half-hidden terror beside his wife's half-hidden fury; he thought of the book in the summer house and things that were being whispered about the horror in the wood: and loathing and dread possessed him. He had no proof, it was true; merely conjecture, but he felt no doubt. There could be no other explanation. And what could he do but leave this terrible place?

Last could get no sleep. He undressed and went to bed, and tossed about in the half dark of the summer night. Then he lit his lamp and dressed again, and wondered whether he had better not steal away without a word, and walk the eight miles to the station, and escape by the first train that went to London. It was not merely loathing for the man and his works; it was deadly fear, also, that urged him to fly from the White House. He felt sure that if Marsh guessed at his suspicions of the truth, his life might well he in danger. There was no mercy or scruple in that evil man. He might even now be at his door, listening, waiting. There was cold terror in his heart, and cold sweat pouring at the thought. He paced softly up and down his room in his bare feet, pausing now and again to listen for that other soft step outside. He locked the door as silently as he could, and felt safer. He would wait till the day came and people were stirring about the house, and then he might venture to come out and make his escape.

And yet when he heard the servants moving over their work, he hesitated. The light of the sun was shining in the valley, and the white mist over the silver river floated upward and vanished; the sweet breath of the wood entered the window of his room. The black horror and fear were raised from his spirit. He began to hesitate, to suspect his judgment, to inquire whether he had not rushed to his black conclusions in a panic of the night. His logical deductions at midnight seemed to smell of nightmare in the brightness of that valley; the song of the aspiring lark confuted him. He remembered Garraway's great argument after a famous supper at the Turk's Head: that it was always unsafe to make improbability the guide of life. He would delay a little, and keep a sharp look-out, and be sure before taking sudden and violent action. And perhaps the truth was that Last was influenced very strongly by his aversion from leaving young Henry, whose extraordinary brilliance and intelligence amazed and delighted him more and more.

It was still early when at last he left his room, and went out into the pure morning air. It was an hour or more before breakfast time, and he set out on the path that led past the wall of the kitchen garden up the hill and into the heart of the wood. He paused a moment at the upper corner, and turned round to look across the river at the happy country showing its morning magic and delight. As he dawdled and gazed, he heard soft steps approaching on the other side of the wall, and low voices murmuring. Then, as the steps drew near, one of the voices was raised a little, and Last heard Mrs Marsh speaking:

'Too old, am I? And thirteen is too young. Is it to be seventeen next when you can get her into the wood? And after all I have done for you, and after what you have done to me.'

Mrs Marsh enumerated all these things without remission, and without any quiver of shame in her voice. She paused for a moment. Perhaps her rage was choking her; and there was a shrill piping cackle of derision, as if Marsh's voice had cracked in its contempt.

Very softly, but very swiftly, Last, the man with the grey face and the staring eyes, bolted for his life, down and away from the White House. Once in the road, free from the fields and brakes, he changed his run into a walk, and he never paused or stopped, till he came with a gulp of relief into the ugly streets of the big industrial town. He made his way to the station at once, and found that he was an hour too soon for the London express. So there was plenty of time for breakfast; which consisted of brandy.

III

The tutor went back to his old life and his old ways, and did his best to forget the strange and horrible interlude of the White House. He gathered his podgy pups once more about him; crammed and coached, read with undergraduates during the long vacation, and was moderately satisfied with the course of things in general. Now and then, when he was endeavouring to persuade the podges against their deliberate judgment that Latin and Greek were languages once spoken by human beings, not senseless enigmas invented by demons, he would think with a sigh of regret of the boy who understood and longed to understand. And he wondered whether he had not been a coward to leave that enchanting child to the evil mercies of his hideous parents. But what could he have done? But it was dreadful to think of Henry, slowly or swiftly corrupted by his detestable father and mother, growing up with the fat slime of their abominations upon him.

He went into no detail with his old friends. He hinted that there had been grave unpleasantness, which made it impossible for him to remain in the west. They nodded, and perceiving that the subject was a sore one, asked no questions, and talked of old books and the new steak instead. They all agreed, in fact, that the steak was far too new, and William was summoned to explain this horror. Didn't he know that beefsteak, beefsteak meant for the consumption of Christian men, as distinguished from Hottentots, required hanging just as much as game? William, the ponderous and benignant, tasted and tested, and agreed; with sorrowful regret. He apologised, and went on to say that as the gentlemen would not care to wait for a fowl, he would suggest a very special, tender, and juicy fillet of roast veal, then in cut. The suggestion was accepted, and found excellent. The conversation turned to Choric metres and Florence St John at the Strand. There was port later.

It was many years afterwards, when this old life, after crumbling for a long while, had come down with a final crash, that Last heard the real story of his tutorial engagement at the White House. Three dreadful people were put in the dock at the Old Bailey. There was an old man, with the look of a deadly snake; a fat, sloppy, deplorable woman with pendulous cheeks and a faint hint of perished beauty in her eyes; and to the utter blank amazement of those who did not know the story, a wonderful little boy. The people who saw him in court said he might have been taken for a child of nine or ten; no more. But the evidence that was given showed that he must be between fifty and sixty at the least; perhaps more than that.

The indictment charged these three people with an unspeakable and hideous crime. They were charged under the name of Mailey, the name which they had borne at the time of their arrest; but it turned out at the end of the trial that they had been known by many names in the course of their career: Mailey, Despasse, Lartigan, Delarue, Falcon, Lecossic, Hammond, Marsh, Haringworth. It was established that the apparent boy, whom Last had known as Henry Marsh, was no relation of any kind to the elder prisoners. 'Henry's' origins were deeply obscure. It was conjectured that he was the illegitimate son of a very high Englishman, a diplomatist, whose influence had counted for a great deal in the Far East. Nobody knew anything about the mother. The boy showed brilliant promise from very early years, and the father, a bachelor, and disliking what little he knew of his relations, left his very large fortune to his son. The diplomatist died when the boy was twelve years old; and he had been aged, and more than aged when the child was born. People remarked that Arthur Wesley, as he was then called, was very short for his years, and he remained short, and his face remained that of a boy of seven or eight. He could not be sent to a school, so he was privately educated, When he was of age, the trustees had the extraordinary experience of placing a very considerable property in the hands of a young man who looked like a little boy. Very soon afterwards, Arthur Wesley disappeared. Dubious rumours spoke of reappearances, now here, now there, in all quarters of the world. There were tales that he had 'gone fantee' in what was then unknown Africa, when the Mountains of the Moon still lingered on the older maps. It was reported, again, that he had gone exploring in the higher waters of the Amazon, and had never come back; but a few years later a personage that must have been Arthur Wesley was displaying unpleasant activities in Macao. It was soon after this period, according to the prosecution, that – in the words of counsel – he realised the necessity of 'taking cover'. His extraordinary personality, naturally enough, drew attention to him and his doings, and these doings being generally or always of an infamous kind, such attention was both inconvenient and dangerous. Somewhere in the East, and in very bad company, he came upon the two people who were charged with him. Arabella Manning, who was said to have respectable connections in Wiltshire, had gone out to the East as a governess, but had soon found other occupations. Meers had been a clerk in a house of business at Shanghai. His very ingenious system of fraud obtained his discharge, but, for some reason or other, the firm refused to prosecute, and Meers went – where Arthur Wesley found him. Wesley thought of his great plan. Manning and Meers were to pretend to be Mr and Mrs Marsh – that seemed to have been their original style – and he was to be their little boy. He paid them well for their various services: Arabella was his mistress-in-chief, the companion of his milder moments, for some years. Occasionally, a tutor was engaged to make the situation more plausible. In this state, the horrible trio peregrinated over the earth.

The court heard all this, and much more, after the jury had found the three prisoners guilty of the particular offence with which they were charged. This last crime – which the press had to enfold in paraphrase and periphrase – had been discovered, strange as it seemed, largely as a result of the woman's jealousy. Wesley's . . . affections, let us call them, were still apt to wander, and Arabella's jealous rage drove her beyond all caution and all control. She was the weak joint in Wesley's armour, the rent in his cover. People in court looked at the two; the debauched, deplorable woman with her flagging, sagging cheeks, and the dim fire still burning in her weary old eyes, and at Wesley, still, to all appearance, a bright and handsome little boy; they gasped with amazement at the grotesque, impossible horror of the scene. The judge raised his head from his notes, and gazed steadily at the convicted persons for some moments; his lips were tightly compressed.

The detective drew to the end of his portentous history. The track of these people, he said, had been marked by many terrible scandals, but till quite lately there had been no suspicion of their guilt. Two of these cases involved the capital charge, but formal evidence was lacking.

He drew to his close.

'In spite of his diminutive stature and juvenile appearance, the prisoner, Charles Mailey, *alias* Arthur Wesley, made a desperate resistance to his arrest. He is possessed of immense strength for his size, and almost choked one of the officers who arrested him.'

The formulas of the court were uttered. The judge, without a word of comment, sentenced Mailey, or Wesley, to imprisonment for life, John Meers to fifteen years' imprisonment, Arabella Manning to ten years' imprisonment.

The old world, it has been noted, had crashed down. Many, many years had passed since Last had been hunted out of Mowbray Street, that went down dingily, peacefully from the Strand. Mowbray Street was now all blazing office buildings. Later, he had been driven from one nook and corner and snug retreat after another as new London rose in majesty and splendour. But for a year or more he had lain hidden in a by-street that had the advantage of leading into a disused graveyard near the Gray's Inn Road. Medwin and Garraway were dead; but Last summoned the surviving Zouch and Noel to his abode one night; and then and there made punch, and good punch for them.

'It's so jolly it must be sinful,' he said, as he pared his lemons, 'but up to the present I believe it is not illegal. And I still have a few bottles of that port I bought in ninety-two.'

And then he told them for the first time all the whole story of his engagement at the White House.

The Children of the Pool

A couple of summers ago I was staying with old friends in my native county, on the Welsh border. It was in the heat and drought of a hot and dry year, and I came into those green, well-watered valleys with a sense of a great refreshment. Here was relief from the burning of London streets, from the close and airless nights, when all the myriad walls of brick and stone and concrete and the pavements that are endless give out into the heavy darkness the fires that all day long have been drawn from the sun. And from those roadways that have become like railways, with their changing lamps, and their yellow globes, and their bars and studs of steel; from the menace of instant death if your feet stray from the track: from all this what a rest to walk under the green leaf in quiet, and hear the stream trickling from the heart of the hill.

My friends were old friends, and they were urgent that I should go my own way. There was breakfast at nine, but it was equally serviceable and excellent at ten; and I could be in for something cold for lunch, if I liked; and if I didn't like I could stay away till dinner at half past seven; and then there was all the evening for talks about old times and about the changes, with comfortable drinks, and bed soothed by memories and tobacco, and by the brook that twisted under dark alders through the meadow below. And not a red bungalow to be seen for many a mile around! Sometimes, when the heat even in that green land was more than burning, and the wind from the mountains in the west ceased, I would stay all day under shade on the lawn, but more often I went afield and trod remembered ways, and tried to find new ones, in that happy and bewildered country. There, paths go wandering into undiscovered valleys, there from deep and narrow lanes with overshadowing hedges, still smaller tracks that I suppose are old bridlepaths, creep obscurely, obviously leading nowhere in particular.

It was on a day of cooler air that I went adventuring abroad on such an expedition. It was a 'day of the veil'. There were no clouds in the sky, but a high mist, grey and luminous, had been drawn all over it. At one moment, it would seem that the sun must shine through, and the blue appear; and then the trees in the wood would seem to blossom, and the meadows lightened; and then again the veil would be drawn. I struck off by the stony lane that led from the back of the house up over the hill; I had last gone that way a-many years ago, of a winter afternoon, when the ruts were frozen into hard ridges, and dark pines on high places rose above snow, and the sun was red and still above the mountain. I remembered that the way had given good sport, with twists to right and left, and unexpected descents, and then risings to places of thorn and bracken, till it darkened to the hushed stillness of a winter's night, and I turned homeward reluctant. Now I took another chance with all the summer day before me, and resolved to come to some end and conclusion of the matter.

I think I had gone beyond the point at which I had stopped and turned back as the frozen darkness and the bright stars came on me. I remembered the dip in the hedge, from which I saw the round tumulus on high at the end of the mountain wall; and there was the white farm on the hillside, and the farmer was still calling to his dog, as he – or his father – had called before, his voice high and thin in the distance. After this point, I seemed to be in undiscovered country; the ash trees grew densely on either side of the way and met above it: I went on and on into the unknown in the manner of the only good guidebooks, which are the tales of old knights.

The road went down, and climbed, and again descended, all through the deep of the wood. Then, on both sides, the trees ceased, though the hedges were so high that I could see nothing of the way of the land about me. And just at the wood's ending, there was one of those tracks or little paths of which I have spoken, going off from my lane on the right, and winding out of sight quickly under all its leafage of hazel and wild rose, maple and hornbeam, with a holly here and there, and honeysuckle golden, and dark briony shining and twining everywhere. I could not resist the invitation of a path so obscure and uncertain, and set out on its track of green and profuse grass, with the ground beneath still soft to the feet, even in the drought of that fiery summer. The way wound, as far as I could make out, on the slope of a hill, neither ascending nor descending, and after a mile or more of this rich walking, it suddenly ceased, and I found myself on a bare hillside, on a rough track that went down to a grey house. It was now a farm by its looks and surroundings, but there were signs of old state about it: good sixteenth-century mullioned windows and a Jacobean porch projecting from the centre, with dim armorial bearings mouldering above the door.

It struck me that bread and cheese and cider would be grateful, and I beat upon the door with my stick, and brought a pleasant woman to open it.

'Do you think,' I began, 'you could be so good as . . . '

And then came a shout from somewhere at the end of the stone passage, and a great voice called:

'Come in, then, come in, you old scoundrel, if your name is Meyrick, as I'm sure it is.'

I was amazed. The pleasant woman grinned and said: 'It seems you are well known here, sir, already. But perhaps you had heard that Mr Roberts was staying here.'

My old acquaintance, James Roberts, came tumbling out from his den at the back. He was a man whom I had known a long time, but not very well. Our affairs in London moved on different lines, and so we did not often meet. But I was glad to see him in that unexpected place: he was a round man, always florid and growing redder in the face with his years. He was a countryman of mine, but I had hardly known him before we both went to town, since his home had been at the northern end of the county.

He shook me cordially by the hand, and looked as if he would like to smack me on the back – he was, a little, that kind of man – and repeated his 'Come in, come in!' adding to the pleasant woman:

'And bring you another plate, Mrs Morgan, and all the rest of it. I hope you've not forgotten how to eat Caerphilly cheese, Meyrick. I can tell you, there is none better than Mrs Morgan's making. And, Mrs Morgan, another jug of cider, and *seidr dda*, mind you.'

I never knew whether he had been brought up as a boy to speak Welsh. In London he had lost all but the faintest trace of accent, but down here in Gwent the tones of the country had quickly returned to him; and he smacked as strongly of the land in his speech as the cheerful farmer's wife herself. I judged his accent was a part of his holiday.

He drew me into the little parlour with its old furniture and its pleasant old-fashioned ornaments and faintly flowering wallpaper, and set me in an elbow chair at the round table, and gave me, as I told him, exactly what I had meant to ask for; bread and cheese and cider. All very good; Mrs Morgan, it was clear, had the art of making a Caerphilly cheese that was succulent – a sort of white bel paese – far different from those dry and stony cheeses that often bring dishonour on the Caerphilly name. And afterwards there was gooseberry jam and cream. And the tobacco that the country uses: Shag-on-the-Back, from the Welsh Back, Bristol. And then there was gin.

This last we partook of out of doors, in an old stone summer house, in the garden at the side. A white rose had grown all over the summer house, and shaded and glorified it. The water in the big jug had just been drawn from the well in the limestone rock – and I told Roberts gratefully that I felt a great deal better than when I had knocked at the farmhouse door. I told him where I was staying – he knew my host by name – and he, in turn, informed me that it was his first visit to Lanypwll, as the farm was called. A neighbour of his at Lee had recommended Mrs Morgan's cooking very highly: and, as he said, you couldn't speak too well of her in that way or any other.

We sipped and smoked through the afternoon in that pleasant retreat under the white roses. I meditated gratefully on the fact that I should not dare to enjoy Shag-on-the-Back so freely in London: a potent tobacco, of full and ripe savour, but not for the hard streets,

'You say the farm is called Lanypwll,' I interjected, 'that means "by the pool", doesn't it? Where is the pool? I don't see it.'

'Come you,' said Roberts, 'and I will show you.'

He took me by a little gate through the garden hedge of laurels, thick and high, and round to the left of the house, the opposite side to that by which I had made my approach. And there we climbed a green rounded bastion of the old ages, and he pointed down to a narrow valley, shut in by steep wooded hills. There at the bottom was a level, half marshland and half black water lying in still pools, with green islands of iris and of all manner of rank and strange growths that love to have their roots in slime.

'There is your pool for you,' said Roberts.

It was the most strange place, I thought, hidden away under the hills as if it were a secret. The steeps that went down to it were a tangle of undergrowth, of all manner of boughs mingled with taller trees rising above the mass, and down at the edge of the marsh some of these had perished in the swampy water, and stood white and bare and ghastly, with leprous limbs.

'An ugly looking place,' I said to Roberts.

'I quite agree with you. It is an ugly place enough. They tell me at the farm it's not safe to go near it, or you may get fever and I don't know what else. And, indeed, if you didn't go down carefully and watch your steps, you might easily find yourself up to the neck in that black muck there.'

We turned back into the garden and to our summer house, and soon after, it was time for me to make my way home.

'How long are you staying with Nichol?' Roberts asked me as we parted. I told him, and he insisted on my dining with him at the end of the week.

'I will "send you",' he said. 'I will take you by a short cut across the fields and see that you don't lose your way. Roast duck and green peas,' he added alluringly, 'and something good for the digestion afterwards.'

It was a fine evening when I next journeyed to the farm, but indeed we got tired of saying 'fine weather' throughout that wonderful summer. I found Roberts cheery and welcoming, but, I thought, hardly in such rosy spirits as on my former visit. We were having a cocktail of his composition in the summer house, as the famous duck gained the last glow of brown perfection; and I noticed that his speech was not bubbling so freely from him as before. He fell silent once or twice and looked thoughtful. He told me he'd ventured down to the pool, the swampy place at the bottom. 'And it looks no better when you see it close at hand. Black, oily stuff that isn't like water, with a scum upon it, and weeds like a lot of monsters. I never saw such queer, ugly plants. There's one rank-looking thing down there covered with dull crimson blossoms, all bloated out and speckled like a toad.'

'You're no botanist,' I remarked.

'No, not I. I know buttercups and daisies and not much more. Mrs Morgan here was quite frightened when I told her where I'd been. She said she hoped I mightn't be sorry for it. But I feel as well as ever. I don't think there are many places left in the country now where you can get malaria.'

We proceeded to the duck and the green peas and rejoiced in their perfection. There was some very old ale that Mr Morgan had bought when an ancient tavern in the neighbourhood had been pulled down; its age and original excellence had combined to make a drink like a rare wine. The 'something good for the digestion' turned out to be a mellow brandy that Roberts had brought with him from town. I told him that I had never known a better hour. He warmed up with the good meat and drink and was cheery enough; and yet I thought there was a reserve, something obscure at the back of his mind that was by no means cheerful.

We had a second glass of the mellow brandy, and Roberts, after a moment's indecision, spoke out. He dropped his holiday game of Welsh countryman completely.

'You wouldn't think, would you,' he began, 'that a man would come down to a place like this to be blackmailed at the end of the journey?'

'Good Lord!' I gasped in amazement, 'I should think not indeed. What's happened?'

He looked very grave. I thought even that he looked frightened.

'Well, I'll tell you. A couple of nights ago, I went for a stroll after my dinner; a beautiful night, with the moon shining, and a nice, clean breeze. So I walked up over the hill, and then took the path that leads down through the wood to the brook. I'd got into the wood, fifty yards or so, when I heard my name called out: "Roberts! James Roberts!" in a shrill, piercing voice, a young girl's voice, and I jumped pretty well out of my skin, I can tell you. I stopped dead and stared all about me. Of course I could see nothing at all – bright moonlight and black shadow and all those trees – anybody could hide. Then it came to me that it was some girl of the place having a game with her sweetheart: James Roberts is a common enough name, especially in this part of the country. So I was just going on, not bothering my head about the local love affairs, when that scream came right in my ear: "Roberts! Roberts! James Roberts!" – and then half a dozen words that I won't trouble you with; not yet, at any rate.'

I have said that Roberts was by no means an intimate friend of mine. But I had always known him as a genial, cordial fellow, a thoroughly good-natured man; and I was sorry and shocked, too, to see him sitting there wretched and dismayed. He looked as if he had seen a ghost; he looked much worse than that. He looked as if he had seen terror.

But it was too early to press him closely. I said:

'What did you do then?'

'I turned about, and ran back through the wood, and tumbled over the stile. I got home here as quick as ever I could, and shut myself up in this room, dripping with fright and gasping for breath. I was almost crazy, I believe. I walked up and down. I sat down in the chair and got up again. I wondered whether I should wake up in my bed and find I'd been having a nightmare. I cried at last. I'll tell you the truth: I put my head in my hands, and the tears ran down my cheeks. I was quite broken.'

'But, look here,' I said, 'isn't this making a great to-do about very little? I can quite see it must have been a nasty shock. But, how long did you say you had been staying here; ten days, was it?'

'A fortnight, tomorrow.'

'Well; you know country ways as well as I do. You may be sure that everybody within three or four miles of Lanypwll knows about a gentleman from London, a Mr James Roberts, staying at the farm. And there are always unpleasant young people to be found, wherever you go. I gather that this girl used very abusive language when she hailed you. She probably thought it was a good joke. You had taken that walk through the wood in the evening a couple of times before? No doubt, you had been noticed going that way, and the girl and her friend or friends planned to give you a shock. I wouldn't think any more of it, if I were you.'

He almost cried out.

'Think any more of it! What will the world think of it?' There was an anguish of terror in his voice. I thought it was time to come to cues. I spoke up pretty briskly:

'Now, look here, Roberts, it's no good beating about the bush. Before we can do anything, we've got to have the whole tale, fair and square. What I've gathered is this: you go for a walk in a wood near here one evening, and a girl – you say it was a girl's voice – hails you by your name, and then screams out a lot of filthy language. Is there anything more in it than that?'

'There's a lot more than that. I was going to ask you not to let it go any further; but as far as I can see, there won't be any secret in it much longer. There's another end to the story, and it goes back a good many years – to the time when I first came to London as a young man. That's twenty-five years ago.'

He stopped speaking. When he began again, I could feel that he spoke with unutterable repugnance. Every word was a horror to him.

'You know as well as I do, that there are all sorts of turnings in London that a young fellow can take; good, bad, and indifferent. There was a good deal of bad luck about it, I do believe, and I was too young to know or care much where I was going; but I got into a turning with the black pit at the end of it.'

He beckoned me to lean forward across the table, and whispered for a minute or two in my ear. In my turn, I heard not without horror. I said nothing.

'That was what I heard shrieked out in the wood. What do you say?'

'You've done with all that long ago?'

'It was done with very soon after it was begun. It was no more than a bad dream. And then it all flashed back on me like deadly lightning. What do you say? What can I do?'

I told him that I had to admit that it was no good to try to put the business in the wood down to accident, the casual filthy language of a depraved village girl. As I said, it couldn't be a case of a bow drawn at a venture.

'There must be somebody behind it. Can you think of anybody?'

'There may be one or two left. I can't say. I haven't heard of any of them for years. I thought they had all gone; dead, or at the other side of the world.'

'Yes; but people can get back from the other side of the world pretty quickly in these days. Yokohama is not much farther off than Yarmouth. But you haven't heard of any of these people lately?'

'As I said, not for years. But the secret's out.'

'But, let's consider. Who is this girl? Where does she live? We must get at her, and try if we can't frighten the life out of her. And, in the first place, we'll find out the source of her information. Then we shall know where we are. I suppose you have discovered who she is?'

'I've not a notion of who she is or where she lives.'

'I dare say you wouldn't care to ask the Morgans any questions. But to go back to the beginning: you spoke of blackmail. Did this damned girl ask you for money to shut her mouth?'

'No; I shouldn't have called it blackmail. She didn't say anything about money.'

'Well; that sounds more helpful. Let's see; tonight is Saturday. You took this unfortunate walk of yours a couple of nights ago; on Thursday night. And you haven't heard anything more since. I should keep away from that wood, and try to find out who the young lady is. That's the first thing to be done, clearly.'

I was trying to cheer him up a little; but he only stared at me with his horror-stricken eyes.

'It didn't finish with the wood,' he groaned. 'My bedroom is next door to this room where we are. When I had pulled myself together a bit that night, I had a stiff glass, about double my allowance, and went off to bed and to sleep. I woke up with a noise of tapping at the window, just by the head of the bed. Tap, tap, tap, it went. I thought it might be a bough beating on the glass. And then I heard that voice calling me: "James Roberts: open, open!"

'I tell you, my flesh crawled on my bones. I would have cried out, but I couldn't make a sound. The moon had gone down, and there's a great old pear tree close to the window, and it was quite dark. I sat up in my bed, shaking for fear. It was dead still, and I began to think that the fright I had got in the wood had given me nightmare. Then the voice called again, and louder:

'"James Roberts! Open. Quick."

'And I had to open. I leaned half out of bed, and got at the latch, and opened the window a little. I didn't dare to look out. But it was too dark to see anything in the shadow of the tree. And then she began to talk to me. She told me all about it from the beginning. She knew all the names. She knew where my business was in London, and where I lived, and who my friends were. She said that they should all know. And she said: "And you yourself shall tell them, and you shall not be able to keep back a single word!"'

The wretched man fell back in his chair, shuddering and gasping for breath. He beat his hands up and down, with a gesture of hopeless fear and misery; and his lips grinned with dread.

I won't say that I began to see light. But I saw a hint of certain possibilities of light or – let us say – of a lessening of the darkness. I said a soothing word or two, and let him get a little more quiet. The telling of this extraordinary and very dreadful experience had set his nerves all dancing; and yet, having made a clean breast of it all, I could see that he felt some relief. His hands lay quiet on the table, and his lips ceased their horrible grimacing. He looked at me with a faint expectancy, I thought; as if he had begun to cherish a dim hope that I might have some sort of help for him. He could not see himself the possibility of rescue; still, one never knew what resources and freedoms the other man might bring.

That, at least, was what his poor, miserable face seemed to me to express; and I hoped I was right, and let him simmer a little, and gather to himself such twigs and straws of hope as he could. Then, I began again:

'This was on the Thursday night. And last night? Another visit?'

'The same as before. Almost word for word.'

'And it was all true, what she said? The girl was not lying?'

'Every word of it was true. There were some things that I had forgotten myself; but when she spoke of them, I remembered at once. There was the number of a house in a certain street, for example. If you had asked me for that number a week ago I should have told you, quite honestly, that I knew nothing about it. But when I heard it, I knew it in the instant: I could see that number in the light of a street lamp. The sky was dark and cloudy, and a bitter wind was blowing, and driving the leaves on the pavement – that November night.'

'When the fire was lit?'

'That night. When they appeared.'

'And you haven't seen this girl? You couldn't describe her?'

'I was afraid to look; I told you. I waited when she stopped speaking. I sat there for half an hour or an hour. Then I lit my candle and shut the window latch. It was three o'clock and growing light.'

I was thinking it over. I noted, that Roberts confessed that every word spoken by his visitant was true. She had sprung no surprises on him; there had been no suggestion of fresh details, names, or circumstances. That struck me as having a certain – possible – significance; and the knowledge of Roberts's present circumstances, his City address, and his home address, and the names of his friends: that was interesting, too.

There was a glimpse of a possible hypothesis. I could not be sure; but I told Roberts that I thought something might be done. To begin with, I said, I was going to keep him company for the night. Nichol would guess that I had shirked the walk home after nightfall; that would be quite all right. And in the morning he was to pay Mrs Morgan for the two extra weeks he had arranged to stay, with something by way of compensation. 'And it should be something handsome,' I added with emotion, thinking of the duck and the old ale. 'And then,' I finished, 'I shall pack you off to the other side of the island.'

Of that old ale I made him drink a liberal dose by way of sleeping draught. He hardly needed a hypnotic; the terror that he had endured and the stress of telling it had worn him out. I saw him fall into bed and fall asleep in a moment, and I curled up, comfortably enough, in a roomy armchair. There was no trouble in the night, and when I writhed myself awake, I saw Roberts sleeping peacefully. I let him alone, and wandered about the house and the shining morning garden, till I came upon Mrs Morgan, busy in the kitchen.

I broke the trouble to her. I told her that I was afraid that the place was not agreeing at all with Mr Roberts. 'Indeed,' I said, 'he was taken so ill last night that I was afraid to leave him. His nerves seem to be in a very bad way.'

'Indeed, then, I don't wonder at all,' replied Mrs Morgan, with a very grave face. But I wondered a good deal at this remark of hers, not having a notion as to what she meant.

I went on to explain what I had arranged for our patient, as I called him: east-coast breezes, and crowds of people, the noisier the better, and, indeed, that was the cure that I had in mind. I said that I was sure Mr Roberts would do the proper thing.

'That will be all right, sir, I am sure: don't you trouble yourself about that. But the sooner you get him away after I have given you both your breakfasts, the better I shall be pleased. I am frightened to death for him, I can tell you.'

And she went off to her work, murmuring something that sounded like '*Plant y pwll, plant y pwll.*'

I gave Roberts no time for reflection. I woke him up, bustled him out of bed, hurried him through his breakfast, saw him pack his suit-case, make his farewells to the Morgans, and had him sitting in the shade on Nichol's lawn well before the family were back from church. I gave Nichol a vague outline of the circumstances – nervous breakdown and so forth – introduced them to one another, and left them talking about the Black Mountains, Roberts's land of origin. The next day I saw him off at the station, on his way to Great Yarmouth, via London. I told him with an air of authority that he would have no more trouble, 'from any quarter,' I emphasised. And he was to write to me at my town address in a week's time.

'And, by the way,' I said, Just before the train slid along the platform, 'here's a bit of Welsh for you. What does "*plant y pwll*" mean? Something of the pool?'

'"*Plant y pwll*,"' he explained, 'means "children of the pool".'

When my holiday was ended, and I had got back to town, I began my investigations into the case of James Roberts and his nocturnal visitant. When he began his story I was extremely distressed – I made no doubt as to the bare truth of it, and was shocked to think of a very kindly man threatened with overwhelming disgrace and disaster. There seemed nothing impossible in the tale stated at large, and in the first outline. It is not altogether unheard of for very decent men to have had a black patch in their lives, which they have done their best to live down and atone for and forget. Often enough, the explanation of such misadventure is not hard to seek. You have a young fellow, very decently but very simply brought up among simple country people, suddenly pitched into the labyrinth of London, into a maze in which there are many turnings, as the unfortunate Roberts put it, which lead to disaster, or to something blacker than disaster. The more experienced man, the man of keen instincts and perceptions, knows the aspect of these tempting passages and avoids them; some have the wit to turn back in time; a few are caught in the trap at the end. And in some cases, though there may be apparent escape, and peace and security for many years, the teeth of the snare are about the man's leg all the while, and close at last on highly reputable chairmen and churchwardens and pillars of all sorts of seemly institutions. And then gaol, or at best, hissing and extinction.

So, on the first face of it, I was by no means prepared to pooh-pooh Roberts's tale. But when he came to detail, and I had time to think it over, that entirely illogical faculty, which sometimes takes charge of our thoughts and judgments, told me that there was some huge flaw in all this, that somehow or other, things had not happened so. This mental process, I may say, is strictly indefinable and unjustifiable by any laws of thought that I have ever heard of. It won't do to take our stand with Bishop Butler, and declare with him that probability is the guide of life; deducing from this premise the conclusion that the improbable doesn't happen. Any man who cares to glance over his experience of the world and of things in general is aware that the most wildly improbable events are constantly happening. For example, I take up today's paper, sure that I shall find something to my purpose, and in a minute I come across the headline: 'Damaging a Model Elephant'. A father, evidently a man of substance, accuses his son of this strange offence. Last summer, the father told the court, his son constructed in their front garden a large model of an elephant, the material being bought by witness. The skeleton of the elephant was made of tubing, and it was covered with soil and fibre, and held together with wire netting. Flowers were planted on it, and it cost £3 5s.

A photograph of the elephant was produced in court, and the clerk remarked: 'It is a fearsome-looking thing.'

And then the catastrophe. The son got to know a married woman much older than himself, and his parents frowned, and there were quarrels. And so, one night, the young man came to his father's house, jumped over the garden wall and tried to push the elephant over. Failing, he proceeded to disembowel the elephant with a pair of wire clippers.

There! Nothing can be much more improbable than that tale, but it all happened so, as the *Daily Telegraph* assures me, and I believe every word of it. And I have no doubt that if I care to look I shall find something as improbable, or even more improbable, in the newspaper columns three or perhaps four times a week. What about the old man, unknown, unidentified, found in the Thames: in one pocket, a stone Buddha; in the other, a leather wallet, with the inscription: 'The hen that sits on the china egg is best off.'

The improbable happens and is constantly happening; but, using that faculty which I am unable to define, I rejected Roberts's girl of the wood and the window. I did not suspect him for a moment of leg-pulling of an offensive and vicious kind. His misery and terror were too clearly manifest for that, and I was certain that he was suffering from a very serious and dreadful shock – and yet I didn't believe in the truth of the story he had told me. I felt convinced that there was no girl in the case; either in the wood or at the window. And when Roberts told me, with increased horror, that every word she spoke was true, that she had even reminded him of matters that he had himself forgotten, I was greatly encouraged in my growing surmise. For, it seemed to me at least probable that if the case had been such as he supposed it, there would have been new and damning circumstances in the story, utterly unknown to him and unsuspected by him. But, as it was, everything that he was told he accepted; as a man in a dream accepts without hesitation the wildest fantasies as matters and incidents of his daily experience. Decidedly, there was no girl there.

On the Sunday that he spent with me at the Wern, Nichol's place, I took advantage of his calmer condition – the night's rest had done him good – to get some facts and dates out of him, and when I returned to town, I put these to the test. It was not altogether an easy investigation since, on the surface, at least, the matters to be investigated were eminently trivial; the early days of a young man from the country up in London in a business house; and twenty-five years ago. Even really exciting murder trials and changes of ministries become blurred and uncertain in outline, if not forgotten, in twenty-five years, or in twelve years for that matter: and compared with such events, the affair of

James Roberts seemed perilously like nothing at all.

However, I had made the best use I could of the information that Roberts had given me; and I was fortified for the task by a letter I received from him. He told me that there had been no recurrence of the trouble (as he expressed it), that he felt quite well, and was enjoying himself immensely at Yarmouth. He said that the shows and entertainments on the sands were doing him 'no end of good. There's a retired executioner who does his old business in a tent, with the drop and everything. And there's a bloke who calls himself Archbishop of London, who fasts in a glass case, with his mitre and all his togs on.' Certainly, my patient was either recovered, or in a very fair way to recovery: I could set about my researches in a calm spirit of scientific curiosity, without the nervous tension of the surgeon called upon at short notice to perform a life-or-death operation.

As a matter of fact it was all more simple than I thought it would be. True, the results were nothing, or almost nothing, but that was exactly what I had expected and hoped. With the slight sketch of his early career in London, furnished me by Roberts, the horrors omitted by my request; with a name or two and a date or two, I got along very well. And what did it come to? Simply this: here was a lad – he was just seventeen – who had been brought up amongst lonely hills and educated at a small grammar school, furnished through a London uncle with a very small stool in a City office. By arrangement, settled after a long and elaborate correspondence, he was to board with some distant cousins, who lived in the Cricklewood-Kilburn-Brondesbury region, and with them he settled down, comfortably enough, as it seemed, though Cousin Ellen objected to his learning to smoke in his bedroom, and begged him to desist. The household consisted of Cousin Ellen, her husband, Henry Watts, and the two daughters, Helen and Justine. Justine was about Robert's own age; Helen three or four years older. Mr Watts had married rather late in life, and had retired from his office a year or so before. He interested himself chiefly in tuberous-rooted begonias, and in the season went out a few miles to his cricket club and watched the game on Saturday afternoons. Every morning there was breakfast at eight, every evening there was high tea at seven, and in the meantime young Roberts did his best in the City, and liked his job well enough. He was shy with the two girls at first, but Justine was lively, and couldn't help having a voice like a peacock, and Helen was adorable. And so things went on very pleasantly for a year or perhaps eighteen months; on this basis, that Justine was a great joke, and that Helen was adorable. The trouble was that Justine didn't think she was a great joke.

For, it must be said that Roberts's stay with his cousins ended in disaster. I rather gather that the young man and the quiet Helen were guilty of – shall, we say – amiable indiscretions, though without serious consequences. But it appeared that Cousin Justine, a girl with black eyes and black hair, made discoveries which she resented savagely, denouncing the offenders at the top of that piercing voice of hers, in the waste hours of the Brondesbury night, to the immense rage, horror, and consternation of the whole house. In fact, there was the devil to pay, and Mr Watts then and there turned young Roberts out of the house. And there is no doubt that he should have been thoroughly ashamed of himself. But young men . . .

Nothing very much happened. Old Watts had cried in his rage that he would let Roberts's chief in the City hear the whole story; but, on reflection, he held his tongue. Roberts roamed about London for the rest of the night, refreshing himself occasionally at coffee stalls. When the shops opened, he had a wash and brush-up, and was prompt and bright at his office. At midday, in the underground smoking room of the tea shop, he conferred with a fellow clerk over their dominoes, and arranged to share rooms with him out Norwood way. From that point onwards, the career of James Roberts had been eminently quiet, uneventful, successful.

Now, everybody, I suppose, is aware that in recent years the silly business of divination by dreams has ceased to be a joke and has become a very serious science. It is called 'Psychoanalysis'; and is compounded, I would say, by mingling one grain of sense with a hundred of pure nonsense. From the simplest and most obvious dreams, the Psychoanalyst deduces the most incongruous and extravagant results. A black savage tells him that he has dreamed of being chased by lions, or, maybe, by crocodiles: and the psycho man knows at once that the black is suffering from the Oedipus complex. That is, he is madly in love with his own mother, and is, therefore, afraid of the vengeance of his father. Everybody knows, of course, that 'lion' and 'crocodile' are symbols of 'father'. And I understand that there are educated people who believe this stuff.

It is all nonsense, to be sure; and so much the greater nonsense inasmuch as the true interpretation of many dreams – not by any means of all dreams – moves, it may be said, in the opposite direction to the method of psychoanalysis. The psychoanalyst infers the monstrous and abnormal from a trifle; it is often safe to reverse the process. If a man dreams that he has committed a sin before which the sun hid his face, it is often safe to conjecture that, in sheer forgetfulness, he wore a red tie, or brown boots with evening dress. A slight dispute with the vicar may deliver him in sleep into the clutches of the Spanish Inquisition, and the torment of a fiery death. Failure to catch the post with a rather important letter will sometimes bring a great realm to ruin in the world of dreams. And here, I have no doubt, we have the explanation of part of the explanation of the Roberts affair. Without question, he had been a bad boy; there was something more than a trifle at the heart of his trouble. But his original offence, grave as we may think it, had in his hidden consciousness, swollen and exaggerated itself into a monstrous mythology of evil. Some time ago, a learned and curious investigator demonstrated how Coleridge had taken a bald sentence from an old chronicler, and had made it the nucleus of *The Ancient Mariner*. With a vast gesture of the spirit, he had unconsciously gathered from all the four seas of his vast reading all manner of creatures into his net: till the bare hint of the old book glowed into one of the great masterpieces of the world's poetry. Roberts had nothing in him of the poetic faculty, nothing of the shaping power of the imagination, no trace of the gift of expression, by which the artist delivers his soul of its burden. In him, as in many men, there was a great gulf fixed between the hidden and the open consciousness; so that which could not come out into the light grew and swelled secretly, hugely, horribly in the darkness. If Roberts had been a poet or a painter or a musician; we might have had a masterpiece. As he was neither: we had a monster. And I do not at all believe that his years had consciously been vexed by a deep sense of guilt. I gathered in the course of my researches that not long after the flight from Brondesbury, Roberts was made aware of unfortunate incidents in the Watts saga – if we may use this honoured term – which convinced him that there were extenuating circumstances in his offence, and excuses for his wrongdoing. The actual fact had, no doubt, been forgotten or remembered very slightly, rarely, casually, without any sense of grave moment or culpability attached to it; while, all the while, a pageantry of horror was being secretly formed in the hidden places of the man's soul. And at last, after the years of growth and swelling in the darkness, the monster leapt into the light, and with such violence that to the victim it seemed an actual and objective entity.

And, in a sense, it had risen from the black waters of the pool. I was reading a few days ago, in a review of a grave book on psychology, the following very striking sentences:

> The things which we distinguish as qualities or values are inherent in the real environment to make the configuration that they do make with our sensory response to them. There is such a thing as a 'sad' landscape, even when we who look at it are feeling jovial; and if we think it is 'sad' only because we attribute to it something derived from our own past associations with sadness, Professor Koffka gives us good reason to regard the view as superficial. That is not imputing human attributes to what are described as 'demand characters' in the environment, but giving proper recognition to the other end of a nexus, of which only one end is organised in our own mind.

Psychology is, I am sure, a difficult and subtle science, which, perhaps naturally, must be expressed in subtle and difficult language. But so far as I can gather the sense of the passage which I have quoted, it comes to this: that a landscape, a certain configuration of wood, water, height and depth, light and dark, flower and rock, is, in fact, an objective reality, a thing; just as opium and wine are things, not clotted fancies, mere creatures of our make-believe, to which we give a kind of spurious reality and efficacy. The dreams of De Quincey were a synthesis of De Quincey, *plus* opium; the riotous gaiety of Charles Surface and his friends was the product and result of the wine they had drunk, *plus* their personalities. So, the profound Professor Koffka – his book is called *Principles of Gestalt Psychology* – insists that the 'sadness' which we attribute to a particular landscape is really and efficiently in the landscape and not merely in ourselves; and consequently that the landscape can affect us and produce results in us, in precisely the same manner as drugs and meat and drink affect us in their several ways. Poe, who knew many secrets, knew this, and taught that landscape gardening was as truly a fine art as poetry or painting; since it availed to communicate the mysteries to the human spirit.

And perhaps, Mrs Morgan of Lanypwll Farm put all this much better in the speech of symbolism, when she murmured about the children of the pool. For if there is a landscape of sadness, there is certainly also a landscape of a horror of darkness and evil; and that black and oily depth, overshadowed with twisted woods, with its growth of foul weeds and its dead trees and leprous boughs, was assuredly potent in terror. To Roberts it was a strong drug, a drug of evocation; the black deep without calling to the black deep within, and summoning the inhabitant thereof to come forth. I made no attempt to extract the legend of that dark place from Mrs Morgan; and I do not suppose that she would have been communicative if I had questioned her. But it has struck me as possible and even probable that Roberts was by no means the first to experience the power of the pool.

Old stories often turn out to be true.

The Exalted Omega

I

One darkening autumn evening, not long ago, a man stopped a moment in his quarterdeck walk up and down his sittingroom in Gray's Inn Square and gazed out of the window at the trees, tossing and restless before the west wind, with a look of vague perplexity, in which there was a hint of slight uneasiness. Not more than a hint; it was rather the air of a man who is confronted by a minor difficulty or obstacle in some little plans he is making, or in the train of thought he is following; and to be precise, with J. F. Mansel, the personage in question, it was hardly so large a matter as that. The fact was that Mansel had been a good deal struck by an odd book he had once read, the 'Adventure' of two English ladies in the gardens of Versailles. Most people, I suppose, have read the book in question, and have puzzled their heads over it, and tried to find some plausible explanation of its story: a day in the French Revolution returning over the gulf of years; the image of the lady sketching in the garden, the lady who must have been Marie Antoinette, the hurrying messengers, perturbed footmen, stolid gardeners; all, as it appeared, going about their affairs, quiet or unquiet, as they had gone about them on that October day in 1789.

But Mansel was not thinking, as he stared out of the window, of the men and women whose apparitions, as it seemed, had been called up to puzzle the two scholastic Englishwomen and their readers. For the moment, it was not the ghostly people, but the ghostly landscape of the vision – or whatever it was – that slightly troubled him. He recollected that either Miss Moberly or Miss Jourdain – or was it both ladies? – had noted at the time of the strange experience, as they walked by woods and groves that are not marked in the modern maps of Versailles, since they have long ceased to exist, that the scene had something unusual in its aspect, that the trees were more like the pictured trees in a tapestry, objects on the flat, than the stout growth of the common wood. And, as it happened, Mansel looking out of his window on that familiar scene – the plane trees of the Inn Garden, and the turf beneath, and a glimpse here and there of Raymond Buildings on the other side of the lawn – was reminded of the Versailles manifestation. There was, he hesitated, something not altogether solid and satisfactory in the sight before him. It looked, he felt, as though leafage and tree trunks, green turf and grey bricks of Raymond Buildings wavered together, as he had seen vistas and towers wavering on the theatre backcloth, in the old days when things, perhaps, were generally more cheerful, and he had been used to go to the play. He glanced again, and doubtfully supposed it was all right, because it must be all right; and then turned from the window to the fireplace, and sat down in the ugly, comfortable armchair, which he had brought up from his old home in the west, quite a long time ago. There was a little round table beside the chair, one of those papier mâché pieces of the 'thirties and 'forties, that people are beginning to esteem curious. It had a painting of woods, and a lake, and distant mountains on it, with an inlay of mother-of-pearl and a cusped and gilded edge. It had been in his Aunt Eleanor's drawing room at the Garth. Aunt Eleanor's workbox usually stood on it, and obstructed the view of the painted scene, somewhat to the distress of Johnny – as they called him then. He wanted to stand by the gleaming lake, where the sunset light shone on the water through a cleft in the trees. He desired also to track a path – he saw the entrance and the beginning of it – that wound through the dark, rich wood; there to gather unknown purple flowers that drooped in the shade, and at last, perhaps, to come out and ascend the shining mountaintops: which he called The Land that is Very Far Off.

The workbox had vanished long ago; he thought that Cousin Emma had taken it away with her after the funeral; and when Emma died thirty – or forty? – years ago, there had been a sale and everything was scattered. He rather missed the workbox now, and wished he had secured it; but Durham was a long journey. There was a book on the table, the *Secret Counsels of a Certain Exile*. He laid a hand on it as if to take it up, but let it stay beside the lake, and sat back in his chair, and half-dozed and half-waked, and scarcely distinguished between a broken dream and a confused waking. Outside, the September evening darkened, and the leaves stilled as the west wind sank to peace. The jangle of the 'buses, the cry of the newsboys, the traffic of Theobald's Road, sounded very faintly; now and again there was a dull thud as the last clerks to go banged the outer doors of the lawyers' offices on the stairs. The place grew heavy with silence, and the lamps began to flicker in the square.

Mansel lay back in the soft comfort of his armchair. When he woke, or half-woke, he found his room dark about him, and didn't trouble to light the candles – he had never used gas or electricity in his rooms. He would soon get up and light the two candles on the mantelshelf; but, as he considered, there was nothing particular to do, and he might have supper instead of dinner; there was a 'bus that would take him from the corner of Theobald's Road down to Shaftesbury Avenue. He thought of the jolly hours when, perhaps, 'things had been more cheerful', long ago, soon after he had come to live in the inn: great evenings at the Café de l'Europe in its golden days. Indeed; why shouldn't he go there tonight for his supper? It might be, likely enough, that he might meet Tom, or Dick, or Harry there; or, perhaps, all three of them; and the old quartet would be assembled again, and the old jokes and passwords recalled, and the band in its balcony would play the tunes from *The Belle of New York*. The recollection merged into a dream: there he was at the table in the corner, with his old friends about him, and nothing said about his long absence, and the band blared away as in the merry time. Then there was the question of a dream within the dream. For as he sat and talked and laughed with his friends, it suddenly struck him that, after all, it was not as it had been: there was a sad and heavy background, or a cloud that drifted across his happiness, that he had known nothing of long ago. Long ago: but, what if he had dreamed all those years of heaviness, as he slept in his chair in the inn? They had never been, perhaps; he had met Tom, and Dick, and Harry last night, and he would meet them tomorrow. He shook his head, as if to drive the shadow away, and rattled the lid of his *krug*, and left it open, to show the waiter that he wanted more Munich beer. He had quite forgotten that Tom, and Dick, and Harry had been dead for years, that friendship had failed before life failed; and that the Café de l'Europe had closed its doors twenty years before.

The scene of the café had dissolved, and formless sleep had come heavily upon him, when he started up, roused by a woman's voice, raw and raucous. As he woke, he heard the words:

'Quiet? Mahvlessly quiet, I'm sure. In fact, I should call it bloody quiet.' She shrieked like a macaw.

The voice burst through his head, like an express train whirling and thundering through a station. He staggered up out of his chair, and stared, distraught, about him. For a moment, swift and gone as a flash, though he had not lit those candles after all, the room seemed glaring bright, and all disturbed and quaking, till his chairs and tables and bookcases shivered and settled down into their accustomed places. They were his chairs and tables? The garden was in moonlight; and he crept cautiously about the room, and satisfied himself that each piece was in its accustomed place.

Mansel had long been aware that the sharp outlines of life and time and daily event were becoming blurred and indistinct for him. He was apt, he knew quite well, to confuse the years and those who passed through them. He would assign in thought this or that friend to a year long before the time when the two first met; he would think of men talking together who, in fact, had never encountered; a whole group of interests were antedated or post-dated. Edwardians wandered back into the Victorian years and sometimes a young countryman of his boyhood in the west would stray into the café and seem familiar with the place and with those other men whom he had never met, or even heard of. And, then, Mansel would question himself. 'After all, wasn't there a night when Vaughan joined us and came up to my rooms afterwards? He did come up to town once, I'm sure. Or, did I dream it all?' He was never quite sure. He felt that his lonely habit and silent days were more and more closing in upon him like a cloud; but by the time that he had realised the danger – if it were a danger – his resolution and will to live clearly and in the light of the day had weakened and dissolved. Once or twice, old friends had looked him up and tried to rouse him and to renew laughter and life within him. But it would not do. Mansel remembered very well who they were, or rather, who they had been; for they had become strangers, or ghosts that spoke of ghostly meetings that had lost all savour. The talk would die down, the man would feel his cheerful intent sink away from him, and go as quickly as he could, and hardly summon a conventional smile as Mansel closed his outer door.

'Poor Mansel!' he might say afterwards. 'I could do nothing with him. He's not interested in anything. I tried him with the sort of talk that used to set him on fire; but no good. He might as well be dead, it seems to me.'

So, one by one, his friends dropped away and left him alone, wondering what had happened to dry up all the springs of joy. Indeed, the question was an obscure one. There had been no tragedy, no violent disappointment or loss, no specific malady of mind or body, to be ascertained, defined, and encountered with remedies. He had been conscious of a savour gradually departing from the whole body of life, so that a grave book or a gay gathering had become alike flat and meaningless. Walking up and down his rooms, laying down the law, arguing, growing heated about the essence of poetry or the demerits of Meredith: that had been fine, relishing sport once on a time: and now it was nothing. He would look at old notebooks he had filled, and wonder what possessed him to write down all those futilities. And then; the last cheerful evening that he had attempted with his old friends, who drank a little and laughed a great deal; that held no cheerfulness for Mansel. He asked with Johnson: 'Where's the merriment?' and stole away home very sadly, and sat alone in the dark room. And one of these old friends talking to another, said: 'I don't know what's happened to Mansel. He may have sinned against the light or he may be suffering from some obscure form of liver. I feel sure he hasn't taken to drinking methylated.'

Mansel was a good deal vexed with that sudden shriek of a woman's voice that had made him start up from his dreams and drowsy recollections. He could not make it out. There was nobody in any one of his three rooms; he was sure of that. He found his outer door shut fast. The only other person to have a key was his laundress, and she only came in the morning. Besides; she did not talk like that. Her voice was soft and heavy and suety; and she was particular as to what she said, in the presence of her clients, at all events. The voice could not have come across the landing, where the rooms were inhabited by another lonely bachelor. It might have been somebody wandering about the place, looking for rooms, and standing on the landing itself. There was certainly that small opening contrived in the wall, by the door, to enable the tenant, summoned by a knock, to stand in the darkness and inspect his caller, displayed in the light of the window or the lamp. The raucous cry that had roused him might, perhaps, have penetrated through the hole in the wall. He hoped that no such company might come about his stairs again.

But here he was disappointed. Again and again, and constantly, his journeys into the past, and dreams and meditations were broken by a hubbub of voices, shouts of laughter, always accompanied by that glare of light in the moment of awakening, the sense of disturbance and confusion in the objects about him. He was perplexed and frightened, and wondered whether he were going mad, for it was clear that there was no ordinary explanation of the strange trouble. He thought of consulting a doctor, but he knew he could never summon up the resolution for such an encounter. And so he grew into the sense of being hemmed about by these dismal visitants, creatures, he supposed, of his own morbid fancies or diseased body. They were not real; he was sure of that. In the darkness of the night, as he came up from the wood of the purple flowers, and stood in the sunlight on a shining, happy hill – perhaps the true Land that was Very Far Off – a shriek of laughter would shatter his dreams, and he would start up in terror, and his gloomy bedroom would be ablaze.

And, then, the trouble began to beset his daydreams in another form, without the violence of the awaking. He heard the woman, her voice subdued, though it still grated on his ears, murmuring, murmuring, and a gruff man's tones, assenting or objecting or denying. It would seem that this muffled talk went on, day after day, night after night; and by degrees Mansel got the impression that he was listening to the plot of a deadly business. There were mysterious allusions to 'a bottle party', which conveyed nothing to him; and someone called 'Cousin Jerome' was to get a drink from the right bottle; and the man's voice, answering, it seemed, a question, said 'eighty thousand at least, perhaps more'. And, then, again the words came: 'No danger, no danger. No weed killer for me, no flypapers, or any damn childish tricks of that sort. You have only to hang the leg of mutton long enough; and the juice of it will have no taste or smell or colour. The place will be all shut while we are away in the country. If anything gets through closed doors and windows; I dare say rats die under the floor now and then.'

And one . . . night or day, he could hardly tell which; as if the low voice were speaking in his very ear: 'Old Mansel will never tell.' And then they laughed, quite quietly for once: and those five words struck through his soul with unutterable horror.

He thought that one misty evening he must have left his rooms and wandered out of the inn to escape that instant horror that beset him. He could not tell the way he took, but he thought he remembered crossing a bridge, and straying on through unknown places, till he found himself in a maze of streets almost deserted; streets of little houses; dismal, monotonous, and yet pretentious. There was one house with a great green bush growing up from the area, and here he stopped, and somehow found himself within it. He was in a small room on the ground floor; a shabby and flashy room with flaring, foolish ornaments above the empty grate, and a gaudy linoleum on the floor. At the gimcrack table there sat a party of seven people; there were six men and women; three on each side; and at one end, a stout, dark, middle-aged woman, with black and greasy hair elaborately done in a sort of structure on top of her head. She wore a black and shiny and belaced dress, shabby and pretentious like all else in that place. The others bent their heads in an attitude of profound attention; the woman at the head of the table seemed to gaze before her, as if she saw nothing. She held up her hands in the Jewish attitude of prayer; and began to sway gently to and fro. The light was dim, for there was only one gas jet burning, and that was turned low, but Mansel noted big rings studded with apparent emeralds, rubies, and diamonds thick on her fingers. One of the men at the table got up and sat down again, and a gramophone began to discourse, 'Abide With Me'.

The dark woman spoke in a thick, unctuous voice:

'I get a message for Sam. Is there anyone here named Samuel?'

A man looked up eagerly, and stuttered, as he answered.

'I haven't been called Samuel since I was a nipper nine years old. My name is Albert Samuel Morton, right enough, but I always call myself Albert Morton. Who can it be?'

'I get a message for Sam. Ask him if he remembers Aunt Clara. Clara? Clara? I am not certain about this name.'

'It's not Clara,' said the man, excitedly. 'I had an Aunt Sarah, all right.'

'It comes through clearly now. Ask him if he remembers his Aunt Sarah, and her china dogs.'

'So she had!' exclaimed the man. 'On her mantelpiece in the parlour. I can remember them. It's wonderful.'

'The message says: "Look after the pence, and the pounds will look after themselves!" '

'That's Aunt Sarah, right enough!' The man bubbled with amazement and delight. 'Why, that was a regular saying of hers. My dad always called her "Saving Sarah"! Isn't it wonderful? Well, I'm glad to think she's not forgotten me.'

There were more messages of much the same character. Most of them seemed to find an echo in the breasts of those present. There was one woman who could not remember any 'Cousin Joshua', who seemed distressed about some matter which he said she would understand. The woman reflected, and said: No. No, she couldn't recollect any Cousin Joshua.

'Perhaps,' said the lady at the head of the table, 'he died when you were very young. There may have been something painful, which prevented his friends talking about him.'

The woman's face was blank; then she started slightly, and kept silence; looking a little frightened.

There was a pause. The gramophone had run down. The dark woman had seemed to deliver her last message with a certain difficulty. Her voice faltered; she paled through her paint. There was silence in the dim room.

The woman shuddered as if an electric shock had passed through her. She shook from head to foot. Her face was twisted all awry. And then she suddenly bent forward, and began to scribble with a pencil on a piece of paper that lay on the table before her. Her crooked face was all ghastly and twitching, as she rather struck with the pencil than wrote; and in a few seconds, it seemed, there was a harsh noise in her throat, and she fell sideways from her chair to the floor, in some kind of fit or seizure, that was very dreadful to behold.

The clients started in alarm from their places. Someone turned up the gas, and the two women of the party approached the epileptic fearfully. A bell was rung, and a timid, shadowy little man came running upstairs and looked into the room, a sluttish servant following on his heels. Two or three of the party carried out the dark woman, still struggling and foaming. One of those who was left picked up the paper that had fallen to the floor. He scanned it curiously under the gas, now flaring.

'You can't get much out of that,' he said, in a disappointed tone. 'A lot of marks that don't look as if they meant anything, and something about "grows my spirit", and more marks. The fit was on her, no doubt.'

He laid down the paper on the table, and turned to go.

Mansel, vague as usual, supposed he must have found his way out with the rest of the party. No doubt, he mused and wondered over the strange ending of the evening as he made his way back to the inn, and took no note of the streets through which he passed; for his next impression was of the familiar room. It was silent at first; and then he caught once more the mutter of those evil voices.

II

There can be no doubt, I am afraid, that Mrs Ladislaw sometimes cheated. Her mediumship had often been assailed, and not merely by the incredulous outsiders who take a pleasure in turning on their torches at inopportune moments, and in grasping at ectoplasm and giving it another name. Eminent Spiritualists had exposed her in their papers. It is true, that other eminent Spiritualists had at first taken her part, and had called for justice and for the spirit of English fair play. There had been the spirit paintings, for example, which were supposed to blaze out suddenly on a blank sheet of paper. It seemed all right at first. There was the paper lying white and virgin, on the table before Mrs Ladislaw; and half a dozen coloured chalks beside it. She would lay a large, fat hand upon it and the chalks, and go into a mild trance: then, the hand was lifted, and a glowing work of art appeared on the page. But an elderly and honoured Spiritualist first of all recognised the picture submitted to him as an indifferent copy of a coloured plate that had appeared in a Christmas Number many years before. There was a controversy about this in the *Metapsychical Review* and in *Daybreak*. It was pointed out that the subject matter of the picture was beside the point: the question was, how it had appeared on a piece of blank paper in the course of a few seconds. How, if not through the agency of Red Bull, Mrs Ladislaw's control? This question was answered before long in a sense which seemed to make the aid of Red Bull superfluous and unnecessary. Then, there were questions on slips of paper, which were placed in a casket, and duly sealed by one of the sitters, who had brought with him an old armorial signet ring, with an elaborate coat engraved on it. At the next séance, the casket was passed round, and it was clear that the seal had not been tampered with in any way. It was then solemnly broken by the owner of the jewel; and inside the box, there were the slips of paper with the questions, and answers, more or less coherent, written beneath in scrawling, untidy script. This interesting manifestation was repeated several times and made a considerable impression. It seemed quite clear that on each occasion the seal was absolutely undisturbed; and people of some intelligence were beginning to be interested, when one of these thought of turning the mysterious casket upside down, and discovered the secret in the construction of the bottom of the box. It slid open, in response to judicious pressure on one of the four knobs or feet on which it rested. So, on the whole, it was felt in the higher circles of Spiritualism that Mrs Ladislaw must be dropped; that she must be seen no more at the College of Research, or at the Spiritualist Institute. So she carried on her business in some obscure street in south London, and, on the whole, satisfied her local clients very well. They were not critical; they had never heard of the *Metapsychical Review*, they accepted the messages they received, and when the lights were turned quite out, they enjoyed the marvellous things that happened. None of them carried an electric torch to the dark séance; none of them raised objections if the spirit of a Roman Cardinal uttered the blessed word 'Benedictine'. So Mrs Ladislaw sank to the lower levels of necromantic culture, and was heard of no more amongst literate Spiritualists. And yet, a few who had seen her in her more prosperous days maintained that, in spite of all, there was something strange about the woman, something not altogether explicable. They confessed that she was, beyond doubt, an arrant cheat: 'there can be no doubt that Eusapia Palladino cheated, and cheated almost openly at times,' one of them reminded me, and he went on: 'Mrs Ladislaw's childish tricks didn't deceive me for a moment. They were old tricks that were going in the 'sixties, as you can see if you look up the newspaper files of the time. They were exposed then, and were forgotten, and this woman, whose mother may have been in the business for anything I know, brought them up again, and ran them till they were exposed a second time. But it wasn't all cheating; not quite all. I remember sitting with her at the Institute, seven or eight years ago. It was a summer afternoon, and the séance room was in full light. There were about a dozen people there. Mrs Ladislaw was doing the Red Bull act. She had passed round the half-sheet of notepaper that was to show the picture in a minute or two, so that everybody might see that it was absolutely blank and clean. It went round from hand to hand, and people looked at it hard, and held it up to the light, and felt the texture of the paper to be sure that it was one piece, not two. One man pulled out a magnifying glass from his pocket, and went over the surface inch by inch. Two or three were trying what they could make of the coloured chalks, turning them over, and weighing them in their hands: I don't know what they thought that would do, I am sure. I wasn't bothering about the chalks or the paper myself, you see, because I know how it is done.

'Anyhow; pretty well everybody was busy investigating and testing and the rest of it, with their eyes fixed on the table, or the paper going its round, and two or three of them were arguing in low voices about the fluidity of matter.

'You don't know Séance Room 5 at the Institute? Well, the table runs down the room between the fireplace and the window. I was sitting halfway down with my back to the fireplace. I was looking at Mrs Ladislaw, dark and greasy, who was sitting straight up with her fat hands flat on the table before her. She was doing the dignified and impassive very fairly well: presently, as I knew, when those keen fellows had finished investigating, she would begin her trick.

'Her face changed. She turned her head a little, and I saw her staring at the wall behind me. She went white. Her mouth dropped open. She was glaring with terror at something that was happening at the back of my head. Naturally, I looked round to see what had frightened the woman.

'In the middle of the mantelshelf behind me was one of those infernal Greek Temple clocks, in black and green marble, with rows of pillars and gilding where it had no business; an ugly, heavy thing. It was at this clock that Mrs Ladislaw was staring: frozen with fright. And then I saw the clock rise high from the mantelpiece and sail gently down on to the floor. Mrs Ladislaw fell forward with her face on the table, in a faint.

'The sénce broke up in confusion. The women looked after Mrs Ladislaw. In the process, the picture was to have appeared if things had gone better, fluttered from somewhere on to the floor, and there was some argument as to what this proved. I got up, and looked at the clock, which was sitting on the carpet. I lifted it up – heavy goods – and put it back in its place. No; no wire, or thread, or anything of the sort, and if there had been, it wouldn't have accounted for anything. If that lumping thing had been twitched from the mantelpiece, it would have fallen with a crash. It *sailed* down, quite gently, like a feather. You can call it a *Poltergeist* case, if you think that makes it any clearer. I don't. I don't know in the least how it was done. But, as I was saying, I've always thought since then that there was something odd about the old swindler that she didn't understand herself. I never saw anybody look so frightened as she did.'

It is to be presumed that this tinge of interest in 'the old swindler' led this cautious and sceptical investigator of obscure things to keep in some sort of touch with her down in the lower levels to which she had drifted. Anyhow, it was through this man, Welling, that I was made acquainted with a very queer business, in which Mrs Ladislaw played a part – a principal part perhaps it might be called, but I don't know about that.

A month or so before, Welling had sent me a singular script, an example, as he said, of what is called 'automatic writing'. A lady living in a small town in Somerset had discovered that she possessed this gift. She had sat down at her desk with pencil and paper before her, intending to make a list of goods she required from the grocer. She took the pencil in her hand, and, as she declared, it 'ran away with her', and proceeded to scrawl and scribble away at a great rate. The slip of paper was soon exhausted, Miss Tuke supplied another, and again the pencil raced away. It had covered six or seven sheets before the impulse or whatever it is ceased. And this had happened several times when Miss Tuke communicated with my acquaintance, Welling, and asked his opinion: should she persist, or resist the impulse when it next occurred?

'I told her,' said Welling, 'to go on if she liked; provided she regarded it as a parlour game, without any consequence, and quite devoid of any sort of authority. The scripts? Oh, the usual thing: pious exclamations – I understand Miss Tuke is a Wesleyan – and moral maxims, and all sorts of vagueness, and words running into each other, and some repeated three or four times. But this last thing she sent me is a bit of a curiosity; it seems to be Latin tied into knots. I haven't time to disentangle them. But the lady assures me that she doesn't understand it, as she knows no language but her own.'

I took the slip home, and found it was much as Welling said: scraps of Latin that read as if they had been taken down from dictation by somebody ignorant of Latin. I corrected the text without much difficulty, and it gave up a number of admirable sentences that might have been extracted from the Fathers: 'Jordan was driven back that Israel might enter the land of promise: in like manner it is necessary that the river of our sins be turned back if we would come into that holy land of our inheritance': and a good deal more in that vein. How Miss Tuke came by it all, we never knew. I gathered from Welling that there was no reason to doubt her word, that she knew no Latin. He was inclined to think that she had read it all without understanding it when she was a child, and that it had been preserved, imperfectly enough, in her subconscious memory: a guess, nothing more. And soon after, Welling told me that Miss Tuke had written to him to say that she had given up her 'sittings' with pencil and paper, as she thought it was an unsuitable employment for a middle-aged woman.

And all this leads up to something much more significant; at least, so it strikes me. One day, not long ago, Welling called on me, and began at once on Miss Tuke's Latin script.

'You know how you made sense of that stuff. Well, look here. This is worse, and I wonder whether you will be able to make anything of it. Here you are; see what you can do.' And he handed me a sheet of paper that gave the effect of a child's scribble.

'And what is one to make of that trident thing or whatever it is?' He was evidently a good deal interested. And I was more than interested when I saw the device which he had called, 'that trident thing'.

It was the oddest looking document. At the head of the paper, the word 'quotient' was repeated six times. Then came 'poison' scrawled in large, loose letters. Then the word 'ore' was written twice, followed by 'or', and then 'oar' was written three times. Then 'quite' and finally, the words, 'grows my spirit'.

It was not difficult. It was, clearly, an attempt at a familiar phrase in Hamlet, 'the potent poison quite o'ercrows my spirit'; written, apparently, by a person in delirium. 'Quotient' for 'potent' was odd; but there were similar mistakes in the more subdued scripts of Miss Tuke: the effect being, as I noted in some of her communications, that of a dictation taken down by somebody who failed to catch the exact sound of individual words, and had no notion of the meaning of the complete sentence.

But all this was a very minor matter. It was the symbol that I found exciting. It was dashed all over the paper, sometimes obscuring the writing. It was not exactly a trident. I should have described it as a small Greek omega, at the end of a stick. The two outer lines of the letter were curved inwardly; the middle line, which in a trident is equal in length to the others, was barely indicated. The 'stick', as I have called it, was about an inch and a half long.

'Now,' said I to Welling, 'would you tell me all about it, and where it comes from?'

'Well, it's rather queer. You remember me talking to you about that medium, Mrs Ladislaw, and the clock business? Well, for that reason I kept something of an eye on her doings. You know she's been down in the world some time now. She lives somewhere in Stockwell, and has séances there, and makes what she can; the old game, the old tricks. There was one of these séances a week ago; and people were getting messages from Aunt This and Uncle That, and they were satisfied, and everything was going all right, when quite suddenly, Mrs Ladislaw began to twist her face about and scribble away on this bit of paper. And then she went into a fit, and a pretty bad one. A man I know was there, and brought this along, thinking it might interest me. What do you think of it?'

I told him that, apart from the Hamlet quotation, there were some interesting points that I should like to go into at leisure. I promised to let him know if there were anything of real consequence involved, and so sent him on his way.

It was the omega mark that concerned me. About twenty-five years ago, I was living in Verulam Buildings, Gray's Inn. In summer, it was often my habit to take a turn about the Square, on fine nights, after the gates were shut; and I soon became aware of a small nocturnal population, who were never seen about the inn in daytime. There were three or four – perhaps five or six – of them; and they prowled in a hapless, aimless, hesitating fashion; stopping now and then and looking vaguely about them, and then moving on, dragging one foot slowly after another. They never spoke to each other, or seemed aware of one another in any sort of way. It is a race that has long been familiar in the Inns of Court. Dickens, who knew all about them, thought that it was the gloom and isolation of the sets of the inns that had reduced them to their dismal apathy and misery. It may be so, or it is possible that the solemn air of antiquity and retirement in the heart of London appeals to men of retired and melancholy habit. I have been long absent from the courts and squares and buildings, and I do not know whether the silent men still resort in these places.

It was an accident that introduced me to one of them. One June night, about ten o'clock, when the sky was still luminous, I was strolling round the Square, and was just passing one of the brotherhood of the night, when he slipped on something on the pavement, and fell sideways, very awkwardly. I helped him up at once, and put him on his feet, and he gave a cry of pain as I did so. He had sprained or strained his ankle muscle, and was evidently in anguish when he tried to set the foot on the ground. I told him to lean on me, and I would see him home. He said his name was Mansel, and he gave me his number; one of the top sets on the west side of the Square. I got him up the stairs with a good deal of difficulty, took his key and supported him to his armchair by the fireplace. Then I suggested fetching the doctor from Warwick Place; but he wouldn't hear of that. 'We will see how it feels after a good night's rest. I don't like sending for thc doctor; you never know what they may say.'

I expressed my doubts as to the effects of the night's rest, and proposed that I should leave him in his candlelit room.

'I wish you would sit down and keep me company for an hour, if you can spare the time. Light your pipe – I've seen you smoking in the Square – and if you don't mind going to that cupboard, I think you'll find some whiskey there, and glasses, and a jug of water.'

The whiskey bottle was unopened and dusty, and I searched at his direction in a drawer for the corkscrew. I set a glass beside him, and was about to pour, when he checked me with a gesture, and a 'help yourself'. And then, relenting, he said: 'I think I will have a little to-night. I am still feeling rather shaky.' But he stopped me when about a tablespoonful had gone into the glass, and added water largely, and so made himself a ghostly and ineffectual drink.

We began to talk. He told me he had been living in the inn for four or five years; he didn't seem certain as to the precise duration of his residence.

'One gets a little vague, don't you think, living in these old rooms, looking down on the trees,' he apologised, 'and, somehow, I have rather fallen out of the way of seeing people, and getting about, and so forth, and so forth. One drifts along from day to day, rather sluggishly and ineffectually, I'm afraid . . . and, the edges get dulled, I suppose.'

He was a man in the early or middle thirties by his looks: a slight, dark man, with small features, and nothing very distinctive or distinguished about him.

He was difficult to talk to. He never read the papers, he told me. He spoke with a glint of fervour about his old home in the west, of waterbrooks in still hidden valleys, of the wild outlands where no one came, of the sun shining on the bracken on the mountainside, of the grove of ash trees and their magic.

'*Hic vox sine clamore sonat; hic saltat et cantat chorus nympharum eternus.*' He spoke as if he were quoting some familiar text.

He drifted on, in his own terms, rather sluggishly and ineffectually.

I noted that bookcases, well filled, took up a great part of the wall space.

'You have at least good company there,' I said, pointing to the shelves.

'Well, I have read a good deal in my time. Yes; I used to be a considerable reader – of a very unsystematic kind, I may say. I never read a book that I didn't want to read. Nobody shall shove books down my throat . . . But I find myself losing the habit of reading; I can't get the relish that I used to find in it. What did I say just now? The edges are dulled . . . When a man finds *Tristram Shandy* flat, you know? I remember when I first read it, and for long after that, it was pure sorcery to me; a spell, a spell.'

He took up the book from the little table by his chair, and handed it to me as if in illustration of what he had just said. It was an early nineteenth century edition, rather shabbily printed.

I turned over the leaves of the great fantasy, and something on the flyleaf caught my attention: an odd mark or symbol; the mark that I have described as an omega on a stick. We talked a little longer, and then I left him, with the hope that he might find the remedy of a night's rest efficient in the cure of the twisted ankle. He looked a disconsolate figure in his chair in the dim room, with the misty night in the plane trees of the inn garden as a background.

The next day my business took me up north, among the singing voices of Northumberland. I was away for nearly a week, and when I got back there were evening engagements and amusements to occupy me. It must have been ten days before leisure and a pale green sky led me to take my stroll about the Square. Three or four of the usual nocturnal company were dawdling and creeping round the pavement in the usual manner; but there was no sign of Mansel. I knew it would be of no use to ask about him from these men; it was not likely that any one of them would know his name. I went up his stair, and knocked at the black door. There was no reply, no sound. I waited and knocked again and louder: still, nothing. For a third time I beat my summons, and then there were slow footsteps sounding along the passage. The door was opened; and there stood Mansel, carrying a candle; and the light of it showed a face of strong distaste for the caller; for any caller. But he relaxed a little when he saw me, and asked me to follow him. He was still limping from the injury of ten days before. No doubt, he had tried neither care nor cure.

'It hasn't troubled me much,' he remarked when we sat down. 'If I had wanted to get about it would have been tiresome, I dare say. But then, I never do want to get about. I hardly ever go beyond the inn gates. I have seen it all, I don't want to see it again.'

He spoke a little of his reading, which had become, he repeated, distasteful to him.

'You get to the end of it all,' he murmured. 'Or, so I have found. Everywhere, you come to a blank wall. Every path and track you take ends with a blank wall. Not read everything? No indeed; I have neglected vast deserts of dulness. Would you advise me to try Mommsen, or Professor Freeman, or Darwin? Science deals with surfaces; what have I to do with surfaces?'

I was saying that Dickens knew about the solitaries of the Inns of Court. As Mansel was talking his weary nonsense, about coming to the end of everything, of being brought up by a blank wall whatever track he took, I was reminded very strongly of Mr Parkle's friend in 'Chambers'.

'One dry hot autumn evening at twilight, this man, being then turned of fifty, looked in upon Parkle in his usual lounging way, with his cigar in his mouth as usual, and said: "I am going out of town." As he never went out of town Parkle said: "Oh, indeed! At last?" "Yes," says he, "at last. For what is a man to do? London is so small! If you go west, you come to Hounslow. If you go east, you come to Bow. If you go south, there's Brixton or Norwood. If you go north, you can't get rid of Barnet."'

It struck me as odd that two such different people as the actual Mansel and the Dickens character should reach the same end by their varying ways. The blank wall loomed equally before them. I hoped that Mansel would not find at last the same end as Parkle's friend; the end of a suicide's rope.

I tried to stir the man a little out of his apathy. I misquoted a well-known passage of a well-known writer; and he flickered into a faint gleam of interest.

'Not quite that, is it? "We are all as God made us, and many of us a great deal worse." Surely, "and often a great deal worse"? Would you mind verifying? There's the book, at the end of the second shelf.'

I verified the *Don Quixote* quotation; and he nodded a very brief satisfaction at having the phrase correctly. I was putting the book back in its place, and it slipped from my hand to the floor. As I picked it up, I noticed again the mark of the omega; this time on the title page.

'May I ask,' I said, 'if this odd omega in your books has any particular meaning?'

He smiled faintly. 'That,' he explained, 'is a bit of schoolboy nonsense. I don't recollect whether it was because I was proud of having learnt the Greek alphabet; but I got into the way of putting that thing in my books instead of my name or initials, and I kept it up afterwards. You would find it in every book on the shelves, and sometimes I've used it to mark a passage, in the margin. Indeed, I used to sign my letters to old friends with the Omega Exalted, as I called it.'

I stayed on at Gray's Inn for the next six or seven months, and I suppose I repeated my visit to Mansel three or four times. I could not say that I was welcome, but I was not exactly unwelcome. It was a pang for him to open his door, but he was not displeased to let me in. There was no change in him, no sign that he would revive, and live again like other men. Then I left London, and remained away for many years, and I cannot say that Mansel was much more than a dim image in my memory. On my return, finding myself one day in Holborn, it struck me that I might make some enquiries. They told me in the inn that Mr Mansel was understood to be very infirm; that he had not been seen outside his chambers for years and years. I thought I had better not look him up; he would not remember me or desire to do so.

A year ago his laundress found him dead in his chair next to the fireplace. It appeared on examination that his heart had given out. He had left his money and his goods to a distant cousin in the west, who came up to town, did what was necessary, and went down again to some obscure retreat by the sunset. Mansel's books and furniture – there was nothing of value – were sold and dispersed.

The inn painted and papered the set of rooms on the top floor of the Square, and made them look as gay as they could look. But they did not let readily. There were plenty of applicants, but I gathered that people who came in a hurry to secure chambers giving on the Garden, drew back when they were taken into the set. Something seemed amiss; they could not say what. They didn't 'fancy' the place. Everything in the way of decoration, it was allowed, was extremely bright and cheerful; but . . . there was something, and that something was far from cheerful. One prospective tenant, a lady, was seized with a fit of shivering and said she felt as if icy water were trickling down her spine. It must have been nine or ten months after Mansel's death that the set was taken by a young couple, who seemed to think themselves lucky, and made no complaint as to 'something' or anything. The gentleman was connected with finance, and the lady was gaiety itself. She had a loud and cheerful voice, and a louder laugh, and expressed herself, so it was said, with considerable freedom. These people laid themselves out to brighten things. They gave frequent parties, a little on the loud side, it was thought, for the Inn, and the porters at the Holborn Gate were busy long after midnight.

And then, all this liveliness came to an end in a very tragic manner. In the middle of a 'bottle party', when everything was at a high pitch, one of the guests, a Mr Jerome Platt, understood to be a cousin of the host's, suddenly complained of agonising internal pains. He was taken to the hotel where he was staying, and doctors were summoned, and everything done that could be done. But Mr Platt died the next day; of acute ptomaine poisoning as the evidence at the inquest demonstrated. He had dined at a fashionable West End restaurant before going on to the party at Gray's Inn. There were no complaints from any other of the diners.

By the end of the month, old Mansel's rooms were again vacant, The bright tenants, very naturally, as people said, felt they could not go on living in a place where such a terrible thing had happened. They were supposed to have gone abroad within three weeks of the disastrous 'bottle party'.

And as to that very different party given by Mrs Ladislaw, and the end of it, and the scribble on the paper? So far as I can make out from what Welling has told me, the Ladislaw séance must have taken place a day, or perhaps two days, before that grim gathering in Gray's Inn. Mansel had been dead for many months: what are we to infer? Had he anything to do with the seizure of the medium, and with what was written by her?

There is one point that should not be forgotten. I noted that, in Welling's opinion, the corrupt Latin 'messages' written by Miss Tuke might very well be subconscious memories, imperfectly preserved, of something which she had read without understanding years before, and which had entirely disappeared from her conscious mind. So, perhaps, with the 'exalted omega'. Mansel's books had been dispersed. None of them was of any interest to the big second-hand booksellers, to the dealers in rarities; the volumes would therefore tend to find their way to the small shops and the poorer neighbourhoods. Mrs Ladislaw might very well have passed such shops on her marketing rounds; she might have turned over the books in the threepenny and sixpenny boxes – and she might easily have seen old Mansel's omega mark; very likely without consciously noting it.

It is distinctly possible that this is the solution of the problem; though here also there are lurking difficulties and obscurities.

Out of the Picture

I

In the old days – which means anything from ten to thirty years ago – there was a question which used to be asked now and then at studio parties and Chelsea pubs. The question was:

'But who was the twisted man?'

And it was often followed by another:

'But where did M'Calmont take himself off to?'

Neither interrogation ever got an answer; save that to the second query, a young man in very full dark green corduroy trousers is reported to have said once upon a time:

'Somebody told me he had been seen in Quito.'

But to this neither credit or attention was given. And it is probable from what follows that the double enigma is to be reckoned with that question as to what song the Sirens sang; if, indeed, it is not past all solution.

Going back, then, to those old days aforesaid, and rather to the earlier portion of them, when, as a journalist, I saw many strange things and people; I was once sent to view an exhibition of pictures at the Molyneux Galleries in Danby Place. Perhaps the event may be sufficiently dated by saying that the Exhibition was opened somewhere between the Battle of Sidney Street and the Coronation of King George V; and I have a feeling that it was a misty May morning when I went to see it. It was not a large exhibition: all the pictures were contained in two sizeable rooms, and as soon as I got into them I saw at once that I could make nothing of it – that is, from any serious standpoint. I cared nothing; my point of view in that instance, as in all others like it, was that if the paper chose to send an outsider and an ignoramus to criticise works of art – especially the works of a new and tentative and experimental school – then, on the head of the paper let the just doom fall. And the school represented on this particular occasion at the Molyneux Galleries evidently represented a fierce revolt against the traditions and conventions of the elders. To begin with, my eye was caught by 'The Old Harbour'. There were buildings in vertical perspective, their walls appearing to incline together and to aspire to meet in the upper part of the canvas, and with a sense about them as if the whole mass were unstable, impermanent, void of true solidity and settlement on the earth. A mystic once told me that after he had finished his meditation and gone out into the street, he had seen the grey bulk of the houses opposite suddenly melt, evaporate, go up like smoke, leaving void nothingness in their place. And so the painter with his art had made these warehouses and Customs buildings, or whatever they were, in such a fashion that they seemed as if they also were on the very point to turn to mist, to float into the air, and to disappear. And then, for the rest, there was grey water, and segments, and portions, and particles of keels, sails, masts, ropes, decks, and deck furniture, not cohering, or fitting together, but dispersed and apart. Here, I could see, was choice matter on which the expert and art critic could exercise their knowledge and judgement. As I had neither, I made an experiment or two, and was able to inform the readers of the paper that if you walked briskly past the picture, winking both eyes as fast as possible, you really got a sort of impression of movement and activity, of ships and boats coming into harbour and sailing out of it, of sails lowered and hoisted, of an uncertain background, now obscured, now left visible as a ship in full sail passed before it. It struck me that, in my hands, art criticism was in a fair way to become a popular sport.

And then there was another picture that both attracted and distracted me. It was a big canvas, and the subject was a number of geometrical figures of all kinds, most ingeniously fitted into one another, and rainbow painted, no doubt on some occult principle of contrast and complement and correspondence. It was called 'King Solomon's Cargoes'. I murmured: 'Gold and silver and ivory and apes and peacocks,' and looked for them. I could not see any of them, and I thought I would go back to Fleet Street, relying on my impressions of 'The Old Harbour', which would just fill the 'two sticks' that had been allotted to the story. It was, decidedly, a case of least said, soonest mended. In spite of the defence which, as I have mentioned, I had ready; I felt I was on unsafe and treacherous ground. Who was I to sit in judgment on the work of painters? No doubt, I might say that I had looked for apes and peacocks in that picture and had found none; and, likely enough, that remark might merely serve to display my utter ignorance of the subject I was pretending to treat. But it was not written that I should escape 'King Solomon's Cargoes' so easily.

It was some years after the exhibition at the Molyneux Galleries that I found myself in a various company one evening. I saw a few people that I knew, and was talking to one of them, when the friend who had brought me along came and said:

'Do you mind if I introduce you to a man? It's M'Calmont, the painter, who says he's been wanting to meet you for years. Some criticism of yours that he read seems to have made a great impression on him.'

He took me up to a dark, slight man with a black moustache, and left me. M'Calmont made room on the settee, and began at once:

'I've been wanting to thank you for a long time for that notice you wrote in your paper about the Exhibition in the Molyneux Galleries. You'll remember? It was in Coronation year.'

I told him I thought I did remember something about it. But I wondered, internally, what sort of thanks I was going to get from a painter for my vain ribaldry. He went on:

'I said to myself at the time: "This A.M., whoever he may be, has got an eye to detect the falsities and fallacies, and I'd like to have a talk with him." Then somebody told me your name, but I left town soon after, and this is the first chance I've had.'

And, finally, it came to this: that the falsities and fallacies were the picture of 'The Old Harbour', by Frank Guildford, and M'Calmont had enjoyed the way I had stuck my knife into the fellow.

I explained. I said I knew nothing about painting, and had been afraid that I had been guilty of ill-placed and unmannerly humour. He wouldn't hear of this.

'It was just instinct, pure instinct. You may not have the technical knowledge, but you know a silly man when you see him.'

I asked what had become of this unhappy man.

'He's what they call a fashionable painter, and makes his eight thousand a year by painting grocers and their wives – damn him!'

And he went on:

'I don't know whether you happened to see a thing I had in that Exhibition? I called it "King Solomon's Cargoes".'

I lied. I dwelt again and more forcibly on the utter unscrupulousness of my character when simulating an art critic. I said I had not seen his canvas. I had just dashed into the galleries, invented my silly game with the ships in the harbour, and run out again as soon as I had got material for my two or three paragraphs. But, in fact, I remembered those purple squares, scarlet triangles, sky blue circles very well.

M'Calmont nodded his head gloomily.

'I'm glad it didn't catch your eye. You might have had something to say to me too. You'd have been right, and you'd have been wrong. I was never a faker like Guildford. I never pretended that if you painted a bit of mast here and a scrap of a sail there and a deck in another part of the canvas you could call it painting a ship. But I did believe in abstract painting – and I do still in a way.'

I asked him to tell me all about it.

'I'd like to explain what I was after in those days. You say you know nothing about the technical side of painting. You won't want to know anything about it: it's not a technical question. It's behind all that and beyond it. But you can't talk sense in the middle of all these havers. Come away.'

I followed him out, and by devious and obscure ways he led me to an obscure tavern, where we sat down together in a quiet corner of a bulging and old-fashioned bar. They spoke his language there, since his order for 'two wee halfyins' was fulfilled without comment. But I looked at the stuff in my glass, and remembered how the poet had said that the half is greater than the whole – 'greater,' I corrected mentally, 'than the double.' I added water.

'Don't kill good drink,' M'Calmont said reproachfully. '*Scelus est jugulare Falernum*, and this is better. It's the genuine Lagavulin, not the trash they sell in London for whiskey. But you were asking about abstract painting. It will be necessary to go back and away a little if we're to see what we're after. They say distance lends enchantment to the view; I'd put it myself, "lends vision", *theoria*. It may turn out, of course, that when you do see, you see enchantment, but that is just secondary; a kind of by-product, you might say, of the proposition. I'll ask you, then, if you know anything about the Kabbala of the Hebrews?'

Whatever I knew of that matter, I dissembled. I am a lover of the rich improbabilities, and I would not check this rare manifestation of them.

'Well, I don't want you to feel like a cow in a fremd loaming; so we won't go too deeply into those dark mysteries. But the Kabbalists tell us that at the Fall of Man, the Serpent did not ascend to Kether in the Tree of Life. It stopped at Da'ath. And that's their way of saying that the nature of man was not entirely corrupted. The Serpent poisoned and infected the logical understanding, but there was a pure, spiritual region above that which remained untouched.

'Very good. You see that? And there you have the reason why a man that's sunk deep in the blackest mud of materialism may very possibly be overcome with delight at the Fugues of Bach. You see how that may be? That's absolute music. It has nothing to do with Da'ath, the logical understanding. I'm speaking, you understand, of the pattern of sounds that reaches the ears of the hearer; just the ordered noise that he hears, if you like to put it that way. In the making of the music, no doubt, in the technical part of the creation, the understanding had its share, as the slave of the spirit. If you want to build Jerusalem with its Temple you must have your hewers of wood and stone and drawers of water. You're a writer yourself, and you know you can't do much in that way without calling in the aid of the penmakers and the ink manufacturers and paper merchants; but you don't allow them to teach you how to turn the phrase.

'But the way the thing is fashioned is nothing to do with us. What we're concerned with is the thing we hear; and with that thing the logical understanding has just no concern at all. You'll note there's no tongue or language in which we can speak of it. There's no answer to the question: "But what does it mean?" when that question is asked of pure music. Bach, you may say, had the gift of tongues; but in his case there's no legitimate gift of the interpretation of tongues. It's impossible to translate the language of Kether into the speech of Da'ath. I remember well going to hear *Lohengrin*, and there was a manner of commentary attached to the bill of the opera. I just glanced at it and saw that when the overture began I was to picture to myself a blue sky, and then to watch the wee white clouds forming on it. There you have your music critic calling in nature, and I saw in the paper, there was another of them puzzling his head over Berlioz, and decided that he was a "pictural", not a "linear" composer – calling in the terms of another art. And you'll hear often enough of the "magnificent colour" of this or that passage of music. And I don't say they can do better. But it proves what I am telling you: that the understanding has nothing to do with absolute music, and nothing to say to it.

'Aye, and what about painting? That's the question I asked myself years ago. You know Aristotle says that all art is imitation. It's a very questionable pronouncement. If I'm not mistaken he had the drama chiefly in his mind when he made it. But the drama is just an impure or mixed development of the dance. In its primitive, original form, the dance was not an imitation of anything. It was, like music, an expression of something; but that's different. You may say that the drama of the Greeks was the dance set to words. And then, there's architecture. You can't say that the Parthenon is an imitation of anything, or that Rheims Cathedral is an imitation of anything. And literature. I shan't need to tell you that all the things we value most in the finest literature are just the things that soar above the sense – that is the logical understanding of it. If you turn to the Book and read Second Samuel, one, seventeen, you'll find a statement to the effect that David lamented the decease of Saul and Jonathan; but you'll not tell me that the vital interest and value of that proposition is to be discovered in the logical sense of it. And if you read Coleridge's *Kubla Khan*, I think you'll be puzzled to find out the logical sense in it and to tell me what it is. But there you have literature almost becoming music.

'And now you see what I've been getting at all the while.'

I did not; but I forbore to say so.

'It was just this: that I asked myself why should there not be abstract or absolute painting, as well as absolute music and architecture? In the past, painting has been almost entirely Aristotelian, imitative. Why should it continue wholly on those lines? And you'll have gathered that I don't consider you solve the problem by cracking an object up into bits and scraps and pieces, and then painting the bits as they lie abroad. And if you paint a man's hands three times their natural size and draw a jackass with five legs, I'm not thinking you're any nearer to a solution. And that's how I came to paint the picture that I sent into those Galleries, that I'm glad now you didn't see. I was on the wrong track.'

He lapsed at last into silence. I broke it by making a proposition remote from pure aesthetics. He declined to accede to it.

'No, no,' said M'Calmont, 'I'll not hear of it. In the "Crown and Thistle", I'm in Scotland, and you're my guest. Where's the Macfarlane creature?'

When we parted soon after, he wrote his address on a scrap of paper torn from his notebook, and begged me to come and see him one evening.

'I'd like to show you the new track I've found,' he said, and vanished into the night, as we came out together.

II

It may be as well to make it clear at once that I am not the man to be daunted by the unusual. I have seen too much of it for that. I know that there are quarters, and very influential quarters, in which it is considered improper to mention such things. Every age has its conventions of propriety and impropriety: every age and every race. The missionary's wife in Africa shocked her two black servants horribly and unspeakably when she said that she was afraid the fruit was too green for a tart. Her husband's name was Green, and every (black) body knows that for a wife to utter her husband's name is both impious and obscene in the highest degree. We talk quite freely in the drawing room in a style that would have made Dickens run out of the smoking room, and when we write books we set down boldly words that were only forced out of the policeman of yesterday by the strict order of the Bench. It is all a matter of convention and taboo, and perhaps it is idle to ask for reasons. Mrs Green, I dare say, couldn't understand why on earth she shouldn't utter the word 'green'; and I suppose I am in much the same case when I say that I have no notion why I shouldn't mention the unusual, the odd, the extraordinary when I come across it. At any rate, I propose to defy this particular convention, here and elsewhere and always. As I was saying, I have seen too much of it to affect disbelief in its existence. I heard from the brassfounders of Clerkenwell about a former member of their craft who had confuted Darwin by the Hebrew alphabet and by the stars, and had buried the pot of gold in a field, where it was found by the navvies who were making the cutting for the Midland Railway. I have discussed with a solicitor, in his London office, the affairs of the J.H.V.S. Syndicate, who were seeking for the Ark of the Covenant from the directions of a cypher contained in that chapter of the Prophet Ezekiel which is called Mercabah. I know all about Campo Tosto, of Burnt Green, near Reigate, who defended his treasures with the bow and arrow. Why, then, should I hush up M'Calmont the painter, who drew his artistic principles from the Hebrew Kabbala?

As a matter of fact, I thought him an interesting man, and determined that I would see more of him. And so, one windy night in October, a few weeks after our meeting, I set out from somewhere in the west and made up the Gray's Inn Road. I am not certain by which street I turned from it. I think, but I am not sure, that it was by Acton Street. I know that I had gone too far north, and that when I came to the bottom of the street, and traversed the King's Cross Road, I found out my mistake, and had to incline somewhat to the right in climbing the hill. It is a district both devious and obscure, and I suppose that its twisting streets and unexpected squares of dusty trees will all come to ruin before they are intelligently explored. I had trod these mazes before, and thought I knew them tolerably well, but it was some years since I had been in that region, and I found myself perplexed and at fault, while the great wind blew the leaves of shadowy trees about my head and at my feet. At last I entered a black passage at a venture, and came down a short flight of steps into an irregular open space, on which there abutted a chapel of the Countess of Huntingdon's Connexion. I went round and about this square or triangle or trapezium, which was sparsely lit, till I found the green door in a wall to which I was directed, and rang the bell under the name M'Calmont. It was M'Calmont who opened the door and, taking hold of my arm, led me down a passage, past a house all lit up, where they were singing, and so to his studio, with trees all about it, bending and tossing and straining in the wind. Inside, there was a hanging lamp, and though it was not cold, the blaze of the fire was cheerful; and lamplight and firelight glittered on the carved and gilded frames of the pictures that hung on the walls. We sat down on a big settee at a comfortable distance from the fire; and he pressed on my attention what he called 'Eela' – which is spelt, I found, 'Islay'.

And then there was more of it. Not of the spirit of the western isle, but of art, as he expounded it. It seemed that he had been forced to modify, one might say, to abandon his earlier views.

'I found out, and I was not so long about it, that you can't have absolute painting any more than you can have absolute literature. There are people, as you know, who are trying their hands at that – by writing gibberish without grammar. And *that* won't do. And I discovered that my endeavours in the direction of pure painting wouldn't do either. The principle of it is all right; but it's not for pigments. If you would carry it out, you must turn Eastern carpetmaker. And I'll maintain that there are Persian carpets as fine as any symphony of Beethoven's. They are the very analogy in colour and form of pure music.

'As it seemed that I couldn't go forward, I went back. And there, as you'll no doubt be well aware, I was in the height of the fashion. The sculptors and painters too have been trying back for the last quarter of a century. There are men who do their best to forget all the bare elements of their art, their drawing and their perspective and all the rest of it, that they may paint as if they were five years old. Another lot are off to Borrioboola-Gha, to learn the principles of sculpture from black savages. And I've no doubt there's a weary band trying to tramp back all the way to the Stone Age to see what they can find there. It's all very interesting. I'd like it fine – if they'd not call their imitations of barbarism Modern Art. And now I shall show you where I've gone back myself, so as to be in the movement.'

He barked derisively, and turning up the lamp a little, proceeded to guide me round the studio. And I felt as helpless and as futile as I had been in the old days, when I was an art critic *pour rire*.

For I was not at all sure where he had gone back, to use his own phrase. The pictures were all landscapes, painted, I conjecture, in the manner of the eighteenth century. There seemed to me, the uninstructed, as it were a dark shadow that hung over them all. Now and again there were patches of an intense and glowing blue in M'Calmont's skies; but these were contrasted with purple cloud masses rimmed with fire, with huge white clouds blown up into the sky by gathering thunder, with cloudy walls of black streaked with coppery flame. The green of the trees and of the grass was dark and livid, and the water of the pools and streams reflected something of the threat of the skies. M'Calmont had depicted open spaces in the midst of mysterious woods, narrow valleys edged with grim rocks, paths that wound in and out by lonely lands to shattered walls on a far height, trees of strange growth hanging over a well, glades glooming with twilight and the coming storm. There was an enchantment; but the incantation was of oppression and terror. There were three things that I noticed as curious: the first was that in every picture M'Calmont had introduced fire: logs burning under a broken wall, flames breaking out of yellowish smoke in the forest clearing, a fire by the well, a fire on the far hillside. Water, also, was represented in each canvas; well, or brook, or pool in the woods; and in every one of them there was the figure of a man, the same man, so far as I could judge. The figure was roughly dressed in the costume of an eighteenth-century countryman, in ragged clothes, with a scarlet cap on his head. He was depicted as tending the invariable fire, perhaps, or leaning on his staff, or half-hidden behind the trunk of a tree, or crouching among thorns on the border of a broken road. As I passed slowly from picture to picture, I noticed that the figure became more prominent. At first, it was barely seen in the background. Then it came forward into the middle distance, and at the end of the tour, the recently painted pictures, as M'Calmont told me, it was prominent in the foreground. In one picture he led a procession of torch bearers into a wood as the night came on; but mostly he was alone in these desolate places that M'Calmont had made. And there was about this figure an impression of distortion. There was no specific deformity, as of hunched back or misshapen limbs, but yet a distinct sense of a form twisted and awry. And the face, where it could be clearly seen, was at once piteous and malignant, as of a stricken snake, wounded and dying.

Whatever my feelings about this odd gallery of paintings may have been, I kept it to myself. I reminded M'Calmont that I was an outsider and (perhaps exaggerating a little) that I could never be an admirer of the famous slaughterhouse, since it told no story.

'You're an awful liar,' he said with engaging directness as we sat down again, 'but let that flea stick to the wa'. I told you I was going back, like the rest, but not to the ignorance of childhood or savagery. I'm returning to a great art, and exploring its possibilities. You know that the Gothic architecture was the result of the builders, first of the Dark Ages and then of the Middle Ages, exploring the possibilities of the architecture of the Romans?'

'I have heard that theory advanced,' I said, 'but I don't know that it holds the field so decisively as you seem to think. I believe that some authorities would tell you that the gothicosity of the Gothic derives, to a great extent at least, from the East.'

'I wouldn't believe a word of that tale – not that it signifies one way or the other in the argument. But I've seen churches down on the Rhône where the Gothic seems growing out of the Classic before your very eyes. There's one such at Valence: a regular Classic pediment, and all the detail of it one would call Norman, if one saw it in England. And anyone who will cast an eye over a First Pointed capital will see in a moment that it's a Corinthian capital in disguise; especially if it's got the square abacus.'

'Very good, then,' I assented, 'let us grant your doctrine of Gothic.

You're applying it to painting?'

'That is so. As I said; I'm exploring the possibilities of an old school of landscape. I don't know whether it's ever struck you; but there's no doubt that some of the painters of that age anticipated the world that came to Coleridge and Wordsworth. The eighteenth-century literature was Pope. It belonged to Da'ath, the region of the logical understanding. To the men of that age, the poetry of the sixteenth century and the first half of the seventeenth century was just Egyptian hieroglyphics. They could not interpret a single word of it; they'd forgotten what it meant. And, naturally, they could not dream of what was to come after them. But if you look at some of their painting, you'll see the landscapes of *Kubla Khan* – the awe, and the terror, and the hidden mysteries of earth and air, water and fire. And I just meant to find out what's beyond the turn of those paths they made.'

He paused for a moment. 'But that's not painter's talk,' he went on. 'I mean, of course, that I've taken a certain school of landscape painting as my starting point; and I will see if I can't develop it on its own lines. I hope to draw something new out of the old.'

'You have a figure, I notice, in all your pictures.'

'You must have the human figure. Without that all your scenery would dissolve and melt away. It would be just nothing at all.'

I did not ask if it was necessary that this human figure should be abhorrent of aspect. For that, I was certain, would not be painter's talk. And soon after, I went out into the labyrinth on the hillside. It was late, and the night had grown misty, and the sound of the streets below came faintly, with strange voices.

III

I remember being told a good many years ago in the course of a cheerful evening that the one thing fatal to an actor was intelligence.

'Or if you like it better,' said the speaker, 'I will say intellect. Or, better still, that something or other in a man that can pick a character to pieces, and analyse it, and find out why it does this, that, or the other, and relate it to the plot and the other parts in the cast; and then, continuing the process, build up by careful reasoning, the impersonation out of tones of the voice, facial expression, gesture, habit of body, and so forth.'

'But,' said a gentleman in the company, 'isn't that the way to act? I thought that was how it was done.'

'That's how I do it,' replied the lecturer. 'But I haven't any illusions. The man who depicts by that method will never be a "feerst actor", as the German producer called it when I was in *Old Heidelberg* with Alexander. You know the story of Irving and poor Bill Terriss. Bill was ponging away for all he was worth as Henry VIII. Irving stopped him.

'"Very good, Terriss; very good indeed. I suppose you don't understand the meaning of one single word that you have uttered?"

'"No, guv'nor," said Terriss, not in the least put out. "But it'll go all right on the night."

'That's the way to act.'

'But, excuse me,' said the man who wanted to know, 'I'm afraid I don't quite grasp your meaning. *What* is the way to act?'

'You begin by not being able to give a single reason for anything you do or for your particular style of doing it. The rest comes along by itself. And I think I will help myself to another drink ere I go to that bourne . . . I don't want to miss the twelve-forty.'

It was probable, I considered, that the old actor – a dignified Priest in *Hamlet* – was right in the main. Creative work, even such secondary creative work as the actor's, is not achieved by theories or by taking thought. A man must know the grammar of his business, whatever it is; the rest, if it is to be of the first order, must be the work of the hidden flame within. And, therefore, I had grave doubts of the validity of M'Calmont's art, when I thought of the elaboration of his theories. I remembered Claude Lantier in *L'Oeuvre*. He made up his mind to be a stark realist, to paint bunches of carrots with sincerity. But he listened to theories, and ended by hanging himself before his symbolical picture of Paris as a nude woman, whose flesh glowed with jewels, like a Byzantine icon. It was some time before I went to see him again in that retired and secret studio. I met him in Holborn a few weeks after my visit, and he asked me in a very cheerful manner whether I was recovering from his pictures by degrees – giving his short bark of laughter. I told him that I had been allowed out for the last week.

'But,' said I, willing to continue the vein of mild facetiousness, 'you know art without a story is no good to me. Do tell me the story of that figure in all your paintings – the figure of the twisted man.'

He stared at me blankly as if he hadn't a notion what I was talking about. Then he caught sight of an east-bound 'bus in a slowly moving press of traffic, ran for it, and shook a jocular fist at me from the top of the stair. And that was the last I saw of M'Calmont for a considerable time.

I was occupied as a matter of fact all through that winter with affairs and interests of my own. What is generally and conveniently known as psychical research has always had a strong attraction for me, in spite, or perhaps because, of the obscurities, difficulties and drawbacks of the pursuit. I must say, that the usual demand of the men of physical science does not strike me as in the least rational. This demand is, I believe, that psychical phenomena should be made to conform to the laws of the laboratory experiment. The man of science says: 'I can make hydrogen by a simple process of mixing acid and water and zinc. If you don't believe me, come along now to my laboratory, and I will make hydrogen in three or four minutes, and show you how it is done, so that you can make it yourself – and blow yourself up, too, if you don't follow the directions. Or, if you like, I will make hydrogen tomorrow morning at eleven, or tomorrow night at twelve, or on Saturday by written appointment.' You confess your belief in the validity and efficacy of the hydrogen process; and your scientific friend goes on: 'Very good; but you were telling me of a woman who looked in a crystal one morning, and saw and foretold correctly certain things that happened fifty miles away four hours later. Then, find that woman and bring her along to the laboratory, and let me see and hear her doing it again, and let her explain to me how she does it.' And here, I say, physical science strikes me as profoundly irrational. A great poet cannot guarantee a masterpiece to be written on demand, under the eye of an observer, by 6.50 p.m. Shillaker, the famous bat, would never undertake to reproduce his 250 not out and no chances given, against the Patagonians. He knows that when he next meets that famous eleven, he may be out for a duck in the first over. And what painter can explain how he does it? Can Dick, Tom, and Harry go to the Master, listen to a demonstration, and come away, fully prepared to equal his immortal works? Clearly, men are capable of all sorts of performances of body and spirit which are not in the least amenable to the law of the laboratory. Let us remember the historic case of one of whom it is recorded: 'at tip-cheese, or odd and even, his hand is out.' If Master Tommy Bardell had been required to demonstrate his skill at tip-cheese then and there in Court, under the immediate eye of Mr Justice Stareleigh, he would, very likely, have made a miserable fiasco.

So I have always ruled out the scientific demand and its implied conclusion as void and vain and foolish. The real difficulties in these enquiries are to be found, partly in the exquisite skill to which the art of the conjurer is sometimes brought, partly to the rarity of the faculty of keen and clear observation, partly to inaccurate and unreliable memory, a little to the commonness of lying: but most of all to the vast and bottomless credulity of the race of men. It is not a case of a plausible tale deceiving a simpleton; it is a case of homely strangers going to a hotel in a busy seaside town, telling the managing director of the concern that they are leaving him a couple of million in their wills, and living at the hotel free of payment for eight or nine months. What is to be expected when the managing director – the type is common – devotes his talents to psychical research?

Still, with all this in my mind, I persevered; perhaps not altogether displeased at the thought that, so far as clear and final and general conclusions were concerned, the quest was a hopeless one. After all, there is something eminently human in the desire of impossible things. To seek for possibilities is rather the business of the lower animals than of man. To be more specific: it had often struck me that from the singular phenomena grouped together under the heading of *poltergeist* there might, possibly or even probably, emerge a good deal of light on the doings and showings of modern spiritualism. In both cases, naturally, a huge discount has to be made. No doubt, the *poltergeist* was often a bad child, delighting in annoying, alarming, and humbugging its elders, delighting also in playing the leading part in the comedy. Sometimes, hysteria was to be expected; and hysteria is capable of anything. But it seems to me that there was a very considerable remnant of *poltergeist* cases in which mischief and trickery and ordinary hysteria were necessarily excluded from consideration. As to the other end of the enquiry, spiritualism; its history might, in a sense, be called a sad one. The last time I looked into the leading spiritualist journal I saw on one page a description of the unpleasing methods by which the medium had hidden the flowers that were to drop later from the spirit world on to the séance table; on another page was a brief announcement that an eminent spiritualist had declared the equally eminent Mr X, the spirit photographer, to be a highly fraudulent person. For the time, at all events, I decided on occupying myself with the manifestations of the simple *poltergeist*.

And, as it happened, a favourable opportunity came in my way. Soon after my encounter with M'Calmont in Holborn, I ran across an old acquaintance of mine, Manning, who was something in the British Museum. A few years before, when he had been a lodger in a Bloomsbury street, I had been accustomed to see a good deal of him; but he had married and gone to live with his wife on some remote heights up at Hornsey, and we had not encountered one another for some time. We found a nook in which we could exchange such news as we had, and I heard a good deal about the fine old garden, 'above the London smoke', and of great success with roses. Then came something interesting.

'Six months ago,' Manning began, 'we took a boarder. He's a boy of fifteen, and his father, Richards, an old friend of mine, has got a job in the East, which will keep him there for some years. He asked me if my wife and I would take charge of the lad for the next year or two, anyhow. The mother is dead, and, as Richards put it, he didn't want to leave his son with strangers. The young fellow is a day boy at Westminster, so we don't see too much of him, in term time at all events.

'Well, he came along and seemed a decent young chap enough, and didn't give any trouble – till the last week or so. And now we don't know what to do about him.'

'What's wrong?' I asked. 'Stays out late at night and comes home drunk? That sort of thing?'

'Not a bit of it. He sticks to his work all of the evening and goes to bed soon after ten. But, wherever he is, things go smash. It began with a stone coming through the dining room window. I thought, naturally, some hooligan had thrown it from the street, and rushed out. The only people near enough to have done it were a couple of quiet old ladies walking along and chatting to each other about the vicar. Another night the clock jumped from the shelf onto the table. Then he went into the kitchen to get me a box of matches, and the plates on the dresser began falling about. It worries my wife – and it bothers me too. Young Richards says he doesn't do it. No doubt he does, all the same, but I haven't succeeded in catching him at it, so far. I suppose I shall have to write to his father, and that won't be pleasant.'

I saw my chance. I told Manning that young Richards must be regarded, not as an infernal nuisance, but as an interesting case. On my earnest petition, Mrs Manning being, I believe, rather glad to have another man on the premises, I became the second paying guest at the Hornsey house, promising myself important and first-hand evidence. And I had better say at once that I was disappointed. As young Richards pored over his homework at a side table, I saw a small piece of Samian ware rise up from the table at the other end of the room, hover, or seem to hover, for an instant, and then fall to the floor, breaking into fragments. I could not see how Richards could possibly be the conscious agent in this event. There was, certainly, no apparatus of threads or wires concerned in the destruction of the Samian bowl. The boy looked frightened and furious; and I found out that he had been thrashed at his preparatory school for 'wilful destruction'. But, from the enquirer's point of view, 'what next?' It seemed that one was reduced to posit an unknown force, devoid of conscious or intelligent direction, and wholly outside and beyond the sphere of physical science. And yet, this was something.

Richards in himself was an entirely ordinary and normal boy, a very decent fellow, I should say, neither too stupid nor too intelligent. It was only in his appearance that there was something not quite ordinary. I do not know that he was short for his age, but his breadth of chest made him appear short, and gave a certain vague impression of deformity, and also of considerable strength.

I had been staying with the Mannings for six or seven weeks, and it was drawing towards the darkest and shortest days in the year. There was a succession of heavy fogs, and it was after one of these that the 'Horrible Dwarf' scare began its course in the papers. A small child, living with its parents in a back street of Westminster, had been sent on some errand to a shop round the corner. The fog was thick down there by the river, but the distance was short, the little girl went to the shop for her mother every other day, and there were no roads to be crossed. She came back crying, and evidently badly frightened, having dropped the sixpenn'orth of tea, or whatever it was. When she had been soothed into coherence, she told a tale of a 'dreadful little man', who came out of a passage, and bent down with all his teeth showing, and put out his hands as if he would take her by the throat and kill her – and then disappeared into the fog, without saying a word. Of course the neighbours came swarming to hear all about it, and deafened each other with conjectures of an impossible kind, and proposed moves and measures which led nowhere. On the whole, it was to be gathered that the horrible little man must be a stranger, since no dwarfs were known to inhabit the neighbourhood. The police were called in, and made very little of the business, ranking the offender with those tiresome but not dangerous semi-lunatics who cut off girls' hair on the 'bus, or slash their clothes in the street. The paragraphs in the press were brief, and some people were inclined to think that the small messenger had let the tea or sugar spill into the gutter and had invented the dwarf in order to escape punishment. But, then, in a couple of days, there was something more serious. Late on a dismal afternoon, a man who was taking a short cut through an unfrequented bystreet off the Tottenham Court Road, felt, as he said, a violent punch in the back, and found himself at the bottom of a flight of area stairs. He was bruised and shaken, but conscious, and as he looked up, he saw an ugly little man grinning at him through the railings. He struggled to his feet, and ran up the steps, shouting: 'Stop, thief!' There were two or three people about, who came running; but they had seen nothing. Then, on another evening, five or six days later, a girl looking into a shop window in Camden Town became aware that there was a short man, 'with a nasty look on his face', standing beside her, and the next moment she felt a piercing pain in her arm, screamed out in agony and fear, and fainted. There was hurry and bustle, shouting and confusion, running here and there from all quarters, but by the time the girl had come to herself and was able to say what had happened to her, the assailant had disappeared. A doctor came up and found a long needle almost buried in her arm. The newspaper paragraphs had become half-columns, and people began to be afraid. And the next outrage of the 'Horrible Dwarf' was again at Westminster, and close to the place where the small messenger had been frightened. Again there was a dense fog; rather a thick white mist, deadening to sound, so that in those narrow streets where there is little wheeled traffic on the brightest days, such noises as these were could hardly be heard, and seemed dull and muffled as if they came from a place far off. But through this thick, stilled silence there broke a lamentable complaint. A man, making his way homeward, cautiously, warily, and slowly, passed through one of these by-streets where, for some years, there had been a patch of wretched and wasted land. Four or five cottages had been pulled down, and for some reason or another the plans for rebuilding had fallen through, and the plot where the houses stood lay as the housebreakers had left it. There were cavernous remains of underground rooms or cellars, brickbat mountains, plaster valleys, all scattered over with fragments of mouldering beams and jagged with slates; a very dismal and ruined place, separated from the pavement by a line of broken-down palings. As the homeward-bound man felt his way along the street, he thought he heard a noise of crying, a very faint, sad sound. He stopped and listened by a window, where the light from within was barely apparent through the thick, white folds of mist, and wondered whether the sound came from a child, shut up alone and frightened. He could not satisfy himself that this was so, and walked on a few paces, still listening, and thinking that he was drawing nearer to the noise of crying. He was now by the palings that hedged off the waste land, and he became sure that here was the scene of the trouble. He broke through the rotten fence, and went prowling and stumbling about, well aware, as he had often passed that way, that he might very well come to grief himself in the broken-down ruin and confusion of the place. But, with good fortune, he came without disaster to a wretched child lying on his back amidst the rubbish, sobbing and wailing most piteously. The man gave him a cheerful 'What's the matter, Tommy? Come along, and we'll make it all right,' and tried to lift the child to his feet. But the poor misery cried out in sharper anguish, and the man raised him as gently as he could and bore him away, dreadfully afraid all the while that he might stumble and fall and, as he said afterwards, do the poor little beggar in.

However, he brought his burden safely out of the horrible pits, and rang the bell at the first house he came to. The rescuer and the people of the house saw a terrible sight. It was a poor place, with a bed in the sitting room, and on this they laid the wreckage. It was a boy of nine or ten. One leg seemed bent under him, and when they tried to straighten it the child screamed with pain. But it was the boy's face that frightened them. It was all swollen and bloody, and black with bruises, and the blood was still gushing from the nostrils, which were as if they had been stamped on by the hoof of a horse. One went out and shouted through the fog for the police; and in time the poor boy was taken in an ambulance to the hospital. In a day or two, a little mended and recovered, he told his tale of a twisted man that came out of the mist, and took him up as if he would have broken him, and carried him over the fence and threw him down, and then stamped with his feet on his face.

The newspapers altered their headline to 'Devilish Dwarf', and cursed the police – and so forth.

And it was after this most detestable outrage that Manning horrified me one night, as we sat by the fire with the rest of the house abed. He told me that he was seriously afraid that young Richards was guilty of these abominations. He urged that they had all taken place at a time when the boy was on his way from Westminster to Hornsey, that he had certainly been late home on the occasions of the first and last of the outrages. He dwelt on his dwarfish appearance, on his great strength, but above all on those abnormal activities which had interested me in the first place.

'You know yourself there's something queer about the fellow. Upon my word, I'm afraid he's the man. And if we don't do something, it will come to murder.'

I was, indeed, horrified for a moment when he began, but at the end I laughed, I am glad to remember. I told him that the fog would amply account for Richards's late return on the two occasions he had mentioned; that to the best of my recollection he had been back in good time on the other two evenings of outrage; and finally, and most conclusively, that he was talking nonsense. 'Excepting only that singular faculty or fatality of his, he's a very ordinary boy, and a good sort.'

In short, I laughed him out of it. Happily, there were no more horrors of the 'Devilish Dwarf' order for the rest of the winter. They stopped as suddenly as they had begun; and in the succeeding calm somebody found sense enough to write an article pointing out the helplessness of the police when confronted with the motiveless outrages of a maniac. The new generation heard all about the doings of Jack the Ripper, and the analogy seemed fair enough. And at the same time – it was, of course, pure coincidence – the *poltergeist* activity, or possession, or whatever it was, of young Richards dwindled and ceased. The house on the Hornsey heights was in all respects at peace with itself when I left it for the valley of London in the early spring.

IV

Extract from a letter received about eighteen months after 'the early spring' mentioned above.

> ... Now, as to this M'Calmont business. In your place, I should certainly go no farther – or 'further' – I never know which is right and which is wrong. There's no question of bringing the story to its logical conclusion, because there isn't one. Your theories and conjectures and the rest of it may be all right – and they may be all wrong. And just remember that for all we know M'Calmont

may turn up any day, and that might be a nasty business for you. I remember Sandy M'Calmont very well, and he always struck me as a man who would be extremely (shall we say) tenacious, if he got in a temper.

I note what you say about your visit to his studio in the spring of last year. In the first place; as to the man himself. You say he struck you as very much changed: 'silent, morose, and apparently not in the least glad to see me'. And I gather that the Lagavulin touch was conspicuous by its absence. I don't think there's much significance in that. There are genial Scotchmen and frozen Scotchmen, and sometimes and naturally enough you have samples of both temperaments in one man. And, as I've just said, he always struck me as having a reserve of grimness. One of his race gave me a most cordial invitation to dine with him at his club, and when the evening came, I was going to say, he didn't speak half a dozen words. That's a figure of speech; but, to be strictly accurate, if he had been 'measured up', I don't think his remarks all through the evening would have exceeded a hundred words. He was all right the next time we met. Some of them are like that.

You say that all the pictures you had seen when you went to the studio the autumn before had been cleared away, and that there was a new lot on the walls. The change you noticed is certainly interesting: the seduction of the elaborate landscapes into mere backgrounds, the trees barely indicated, the detail shadowy, and so forth: the Twisted Man promoted from a sort of super to be the real subject of the picture – 'a devilish figure', as you say, with, I gather, minor demons grouped about him, being instructed in strange traps and chases, in obscure employments, in pastimes that did not strike you as too agreeable. I was rather reminded of an old lacquer bureau I grew up with. I remember one of the drawers was decorated with a design of a golden garden of unearthly trees, in which Chinamen in golden robes tormented a porcupine with long wands of gold. All this was certainly very odd. You didn't like M'Calmont's manner when he said: 'You asked me for the story of the Twisted Man and here it is'? I don't see much in that. But that particular gesture in one of the pictures: the man pointing to an indistinct figure on the ground, and lifting up his foot above it: well . . . Still, as you can see for yourself, there's nothing you can fasten on in that. You can't charge a painter with the crimes he chooses to paint. And that's the fatal flaw in the whole of your case; if you think you have a case.

Of course I remember that awful business of the poor girl in the July following. It was one of the most hideous and revolting things that have happened in my time; and I think that we should both agree that Fleet Street, with all its faults, rendered a public service by its suppression of most of the facts. I knew Selwyn of the *Gazette*, who was put on the country end of the story. He managed to see a sort of diary the girl had kept – about her visits to London and all that. I don't care to recall what he told me. But there again, when you try to put two and two together, you'll find it can't be done. There was nothing in those papers that Selwyn looked at to connect the unfortunate wretch with the studio. As you say, that square in Bloomsbury where the body was found is not a great distance off, but that's nothing to go on.

And, after all, it seems to me that either way, you would be well advised to let it alone. The man has gone away, and it seems likely that he will stay away, so there's no fear of any recurrence of these abominations. But, on the other hand, he may come back, and if he did, you might find yourself in the dock on a charge of criminal libel. And I don't think that such evidence as you have is anything like strong enough for you to put up a good defence. I say again: drop it.

I took this advice, so far as making any representations to the police authorities was concerned. After some years – nine, getting on for ten – nothing has been heard of M'Calmont. A cousin of his eventually received authority to deal with the pictures in the studio. Some of the earlier canvases appeared in due course in the dealers' shops round St James's and Bond Street, and others went to the auction rooms and realised very fair prices. There is a movement, I have gathered, in certain circles of art criticism, to appreciate M'Calmont's work very highly. One critic wrote lately: 'It is all old school, if you like, but there is something there that the old school never had; and I don't think that any of us quite know what it is. And I am convinced that collectors, public and private, will do well to keep a very keen eye on M'Calmont. At the present prices they are undoubted bargains.'

And the studios are still asking where M'Calmont got his model for the wonderful Twisted Man.

There was one circumstance which I failed to mention, when I consulted the friend who wrote me the letter of advice. I am not sure why I left it out of my story; possibly from a whimsical dislike of making the case too complete, possibly from a feeling, equally whimsical, that it was as well to keep one card at least safe and secret in my own hand.

But, two nights after the discovery of the package in Irving Square, when horror was still black and raging, I felt that I must visit that secret studio on the hillside. It was a clear night with a red moon, just past the full, rising out of a low band of clouds, and this time I found my way without any difficulty. And just as I came down the flight of steps that led into the open square, I saw the green door of M'Calmont's studio open, very cautiously at first, inch by inch, and then wider, and a figure, vague against the darkness behind it, seemed to peer about for a moment. Then, the door was opened wide, and as quickly shut, and I saw a man, all twisted and bent so as to be dwarflike, go capering with fantastic and extravagant gestures across the scene of light, and vanish into a narrow passage which led down the hill between garden walls and the shadowy boughs of trees. I stood still, beaten back into the shelter of my steps, drawing a long breath. I had recognised very well that dancing and terrible figure, and I was quite overcome by the utter impossibility of that which I had certainly seen, I had been living for some time with gathering suspicions of some dreadful and mysterious connection between the work of the studio and the horror of the waste place in Westminster; but they had been vague surmises and unshapen fears. But this was delirium; nightmare walking visibly abroad. I shook myself out of my terror and went briskly up to the studio door and rang the bell.

The door was opened by M'Calmont's handy man whom I had seen pottering about on my last visit. I asked him if Mr M'Calmont were at home.

'Not at the moment, sir,' he replied. 'But please to step in. Mr M'Calmont told me he'd be back in a minute; he's only gone to post a letter – and I'm sure he'd be very sorry to miss you.'

I followed the man to the studio, which was all lit up. I stood there in a great bewilderment.

'But, William,' I said, 'I saw somebody come out by that door just as I was coming down the steps. But it was a twisted sort of man, like that man in all Mr M'Calmont's pictures. I thought it must be the model.' The notion had flashed into my mind that moment, as with a deep sigh of relief.

William looked puzzled.

'It must have been Mr M'Calmont, sir. There's nobody else been here tonight. He went out a couple of minutes ago.'

'But the man I saw was twisted, crooked. And he was dancing about like a lunatic.'

'Then, sir, I think that was Mr M'Calmont all right. I expect he was doing what he calls his Physical Jerks, thinking there would be nobody about to see him. He says it's strongly recommended by the doctors. But do be seated, sir, if you please.'

I was staring at a great sheet of paper on an easel. It was covered with black charcoal outlines, to me significant and most awful. I had heard something of the contents of the package that had been found under the bushes of Irving Square.

I told the man I really could not wait. I hurried out of the place, and struck away up to the north, and made as quickly as I could for the broad and jangling streets, and so got home at last, avoiding dark narrows and short cuts all the way.

I do not know how long William waited for his master to return. But he waited vainly.

Change

'Here,' said old Mr Vincent Rimmer, fumbling in the pigeonholes of his great ancient bureau, 'is an oddity which may interest you.'

He drew a sheet of paper out of the dark place where it had been hidden, and handed it to Reynolds, his curious guest. The oddity was an ordinary sheet of notepaper, of a sort which has long been popular; a bluish grey with slight flecks and streaks of a darker blue embedded in its substance. It had yellowed a little with age at the edges. The outer page was blank; Reynolds laid it open and spread it out on the table beside his chair. He read something like this:

a aa e ee i e ee
aa i i o e ee o
ee ee i aa o oo o
a o a a e i ee
e o i ee a e i

Reynolds scanned it with stupefied perplexity.

'What on earth is it?' he said. 'Does it mean anything? Is it a cypher, or a silly game, or what?'

Mr Rimmer chuckled. 'I thought it might puzzle you,' he remarked. 'Do you happen to notice anything about the writing; anything out of the way at all?'

Reynolds scanned the document more closely.

'Well, I don't know that there is anything out of the way in the script itself. The letters are rather big, perhaps, and they are rather clumsily formed. But it's difficult to judge handwriting by a few letters, repeated again and again. But, apart from the writing, what is it?'

'That's a question that must wait a bit. There are many strange things related to that bit of paper. But one of the strangest things about it is this; that it is intimately connected with the Darren Mystery.'

'What Mystery did you say? The Darren Mystery? I don't think I ever heard of it.'

'Well, it was a little before your time. And, in any case, I don't see how you could have heard of it. There were, certainly, some very curious and unusual circumstances in the case, but I don't think that they were generally known, and if they were known, they were not understood. You won't wonder at that, perhaps, when you considered that the bit of paper before you was one of those circumstances.'

'But what exactly happened?'

'That is largely a matter of conjecture. But, anyhow, here's the outside of the case, for a beginning. Now, to start with, I don't suppose you've ever been to Meirion? Well, you should go. It's a beautiful county, in West Wales, with a fine sea coast, and some very pleasant places to stay at, and none of them too large or too popular. One of the smallest of these places, Trenant, is just a village. There is a wooded height above it called the Allt; and down below, the church, with a Celtic cross in the churchyard, a dozen or so of cottages, a row of lodging houses on the slope round the corner, a few more cottages dotted along the road to Meiros, and that's all. Below the village are marshy meadows where the brook that comes from the hills spreads abroad, and then the dunes, and the sea, stretching away to the Dragon's Head in the far east and enclosed to the west by the beginnings of the limestone cliffs. There are fine, broad sands all the way between Trenant and Porth, the market town, about a mile and a half away, and it's just the place for children.

'Well, just forty-five years ago, Trenant was having a very successful season. In August there must have been eighteen or nineteen visitors in the village. I was staying in Porth at the time, and, when I walked over, it struck me that the Trenant beach was quite crowded – eight or nine children castle-building and learning to swim, and looking for shells, and all the usual diversions. The grown-up people sat in groups on the edge of the dunes and read and gossiped, or took a turn towards Porth, or perhaps tried to catch prawns in the rock pools at the other end of the sands. Altogether a very pleasant, happy scene in its simple way, and, as it was a beautiful summer, I have no doubt they all enjoyed themselves very much. I walked to Trenant and back three or four times, and I noticed that most of the children were more or less in charge of a very pretty dark girl, quite young, who seemed to advise in laying out the ground plan of the castle, and to take off her stockings and tuck up her skirts – we thought a lot of Legs in those days – when the bathers required supervision. She also indicated the kinds of shells which deserved the attention of collectors: an extremely serviceable girl.

'It seemed that this girl, Alice Hayes, was really in charge of the children – or of the greater part of them. She was a sort of nursery-governess or lady of all work to Mrs Brown, who had come down from London in the early part of July with Miss Hayes and little Michael, a child of eight, who refused to recover nicely from his attack of measles. Mr Brown had joined them at the end of the month with the two elder children, Jack and Rosamund. Then, there were the Smiths, with their little family, and the Robinsons with their three; and the fathers and mothers, sitting on the beach every morning, got to know each other very easily. Mrs Smith and Mrs Robinson soon appreciated Miss Hayes's merits as a child-herd; they noticed that Mrs Brown sat placid and went on knitting in the sun, quite safe and unperturbed, while they suffered from recurrent alarms. Jack Smith, though barely fourteen, would be seen dashing through the waves to swim to the Dragon's Head, about twenty miles away, or Jane Robinson, in bright pink, would reappear suddenly right way among the rocks of the points, ready to vanish into the perilous unknown round the corner. Hence, alarums and excursions, tiresome expeditions of rescue and remonstrance, through soft sand or over slippery rocks under a hot sun. And then these ladies would discover that certain of their offspring had entirely disappeared or were altogether missing from the landscape; and dreadful and true tales of children who had driven tunnels into the sand and had been overwhelmed therein rushed to the mind. And all the while Mrs Brown sat serene, confident in the overseership of her Miss Hayes. So, as was to be gathered, the other two took counsel together. Mrs Brown was approached, and something called an arrangement was made, by which Miss Hayes undertook the joint mastership of all three packs, greatly to the ease of Mrs Smith and Mrs Robinson.

'It was about this time, I suppose, that I got to know this group of holidaymakers. I had met Smith, whom I knew slightly in town, in the streets of Porth, just as I was setting out for one of my morning walks. We strolled together to Trenant on the firm sand down by the water's edge, and introductions went round, and so I joined the party, and sat with them, watching the various diversions of the children and the capable superintendence of Miss Hayes.

'"Now there's a queer thing about his little place," said Brown, a genial man, connected, I believe, with Lloyd's. "Wouldn't you say this was as healthy a spot as any you could find? Well sheltered from the north, southern aspect, never too cold in winter, fresh sea breeze in summer: what could you have more?"

'"Well," I replied, "it always agrees with me very well: a little relaxing, perhaps, but I like being relaxed. Isn't it a healthy place, then? What makes you think so?"

'"I'll tell you. We have rooms on Govan Terrace, up there on the hillside. The other night I woke up with a coughing fit. I got out of bed to get a drink of water, and then had a look out of the window to see what sort of night it was. I didn't like the look of those clouds in the south-west after sunset the night before. As you can see, the upper windows of Govan Terrace command a good many of the village houses. And, do you know, there was a light in almost every house? At two o'clock in the morning. Apparently the village is full of sick people. But who would have thought it?"

'We were sitting a little apart from the rest. Smith had brought a London paper from Porth and he and Robinson had their heads together over the City article. The three women were knitting and talking hard, and down by the blue, creaming water Miss Hayes and her crew were playing happily in the sunshine.

'"Do you mind," I said to Brown, "if I swear you to secrecy? A limited secrecy: I don't want you to speak of this to any of the village people. They wouldn't like it. And have you told your wife or any of the party about what you saw?"

'"As a matter of fact, I haven't said a word to anybody. Illness isn't a very cheerful topic for a holiday, is it? But what's up? You don't mean to say there's some sort of epidemic in the place that they're keeping dark? I say! That would be awful. We should have to leave at once. Think of the children."

'"Nothing of the kind. I don't think that there's a single case of illness in the place unless you count old Thomas Evans, who has been in what he calls a decline for thirty years. You won't say anything? Then I'm going to give you a shock. The people have a light burning in their houses all night to keep out the fairies."

'I must say it was a success. Brown looked frightened. Not of the fairies; most certainly not; rather at the reversion of his established order of things. He occupied his business in the City; he lived in an extremely comfortable house at Addiscombe; he was a keen though sane adherent of the Liberal Party; and in the world between these points there was no room at all either for fairies or for people who believed in fairies. The latter were almost as fabulous to him as the former, and still more objectionable.

'"Look here!" he said at last. "You're pulling my leg. Nobody believes in fairies. They haven't for hundreds of years. Shakespeare didn't believe in fairies. He says so."

'I let him run on. He implored me to tell him whether it was typhoid, or only measles, or even chicken pox. I said at last:

'"You seem very positive on the subject of fairies. Are you sure there are no such things?"

'"Of course I am," said Brown, very crossly.

'"How do you know?"

'It is a shocking thing to be asked a question like that, to which, be it observed, there is no answer. I left him seething dangerously.

'"Remember," I said, "not a word of lit windows to anybody; but if you are uneasy as to epidemics, ask the doctor about it."

'He nodded his head glumly. I knew he was drawing all sorts of false conclusions; and for the rest of our stay I would say that he did not seek me out – until the last day of his visit. I had no doubt that he put me down as a believer in fairies and a maniac; but it is, I consider, good for men who live between the City and Liberal Politics and Addiscombe to be made to realise that there is a world elsewhere. And, as it happens, it was quite true that most of the Trenant people believed in the fairies and were horribly afraid of them.

'But this was only an interlude. I often strolled over and joined the party. And I took up my freedom with the young members by contributing posts and a tennis net to the beach sports. They had brought down rackets and balls, in the vague idea that they might be able to get a game somehow and somewhere, and my contribution was warmly welcomed. I helped Miss Hayes to fix the net, and she marked out the court, with the help of many suggestions from the elder children, to which she did not pay the slightest attention. I think the constant disputes as to whether the ball was 'in' or 'out' brightened the game, though Wimbledon would not have approved. And sometimes the elder children accompanied their parents to Porth in the evening and watched the famous Japanese Jugglers or Pepper's Ghost at the Assembly Rooms, or listened to the Mysterious Musicians at the De Barry Gardens – and altogether everybody had, you would say, a very jolly time.

'It all came to a dreadful end. One morning when I had come out on my usual morning stroll from Porth, and had got to the camping ground of the party at the end of the dunes, I found somewhat to my surprise that there was nobody there. I was afraid that Brown had been in part justified in his dread of concealed epidemics, and that some of the children had 'caught something' in the village. So I walked up in the direction of Govan Terrace, and found Brown standing at the bottom of his flight of steps, and looking very much upset.

'I hailed him.

'"I say," I began, "I hope you weren't right, after all. None of the children down with measles, or anything of that sort?"

'"It's something worse than measles. We none of us know what has happened. The doctor can make nothing of it. Come in, and we can talk it over."

'Just then a procession came down the steps leading from a house a few doors further on. First of all there was the porter from the station, with a pile of luggage on his truck. Then there came the two elder Smith children, Jack and Millicent, and finally, Mr and Mrs Smith. Mr Smith was carrying something wrapped in a bundle in his arms.

'"Where's Bob?" He was the youngest; a brave, rosy little man of five or six.

'"Smith's carrying him," murmured Brown.

'"What's happened? Has he hurt himself on the rocks? I hope it's nothing serious."

'I was going forward to make my enquiries, but Brown put a hand on my arm and checked me. Then I looked at the Smith party more closely, and I saw at once that there was something very much amiss. The two elder children had been crying, though the boy was doing his best to put up a brave face against disaster – whatever it was. Mrs Smith had drawn her veil over her face, and stumbled as she walked, and on Smith's face there was a horror as of ill dreams.

'"Look," said Brown in his low voice.

'Smith had half-turned, as he set out with his burden to walk down the hill to the station. I don't think he knew we were there; I don't think any of the party had noticed us as we stood on the bottom step, half hidden by a blossoming shrub. But as he turned uncertainly, like a man in the dark, the wrappings fell away a little from what he carried, and I saw a little wizened, yellow face peering out; malignant, deplorable.

'I turned helplessly to Brown, as that most wretched procession went on its way and vanished out of sight.

'"What on earth has happened? That's not Bobby. Who is it?"

'"Come into the house," said Brown, and he went before me up the long flight of steps that led to the terrace.

'There was a shriek and a noise of thin, shrill, high-pitched laughter as we came into the lodging house.

'"That's Miss Hayes in blaspheming hysterics," said Brown grimly, My wife's looking after her. The children are in the room at the back. I daren't let them go out by themselves in this awful place." He beat with his foot on the floor and glared at me, awestruck, a solid man shaken.

'"Well," he said at last, "I'll tell you what we know; and as far as I can make out, that's very little. However . . . You know Miss Hayes, who helps Mrs Brown with the children, had more or less taken over the charge of the lot; the young Robinsons and the Smiths, too. You've seen how well she looks after them all on the sands in the morning. In the afternoon she's been taking them inland for a change. You know there's beautiful country if you go a little way inland; rather wild and woody; but still very nice; pleasant and shady. Miss Hayes thought that the all-day glare of the sun on the sands might not be very good for the small ones, and my wife agreed with her. So they took their teas with them and picnicked in the woods and enjoyed themselves very much, I believe. They didn't go more than a couple of miles or three at the outside; and the little ones used to take turns in a go-cart. They never seemed too tired.

'"Yesterday at lunch they were talking about some caves at a place called the Darren, about two miles away. My children seemed very anxious to see them, and Mrs Probert, our landlady, said they were quite safe, so the Smiths and Robinsons were called in, and they were enthusiastic, too; and the whole party set off with their tea baskets, and candles and matches, in Miss Hayes's charge. Somehow they made a later start than usual, and from what I could make out they enjoyed themselves so much in the cool dark cave, first of all exploring, and then looking for treasure, and winding up with tea by candlelight, that they didn't notice how the time was going – nobody had a watch – and by the time they'd packed up their traps and come out from underground, it was quite dark. They had a little trouble making out the way at first, but not very much, and came along in high spirits, tumbling over molehills and each other, and finding it all quite an adventure.

'"They had got down in the road there, and were sorting themselves out into the three parties, when somebody called out: 'Where's Bobby Smith?' Well, he wasn't there. The usual story; everybody thought he was with somebody else. They were all mixed up in the dark, talking and laughing and shrieking at the top of their voices, and taking everything for granted – I suppose it was like that. But poor little Bob was missing. You can guess what a scene there was. Everybody was much too frightened to scold Miss Hayes, who had no doubt been extremely careless, to say the least of it – not like her. Robinson pulled us together. He told Mrs Smith that the little chap would be perfectly all right: there were no precipices to fall over and no water to fall into, the way they'd been, that it was a warm night, and the child had had a good stuffing tea, and he would be as right as rain when they found him. So we got a man from the farm, with a lantern, and Miss Hayes to show us exactly where they'd been, and Smith and Robinson and I went off to find poor Bobby, feeling a good deal better than at first. I noticed that the farm man seemed a good deal put out when we told him what had happened and where we were going. 'Got lost in the Darren,' he said, 'indeed that is a pity.' That set Smith off at once; and he asked Williams what he meant; what was the matter with the place? Williams said there was nothing the matter with it at all whatever but it was 'a tiresome place to be in after dark'. That reminded me of what you were saying a couple of weeks ago about the people here. 'Some damned superstitious nonsense,' I said to myself, and thanked God it was nothing worse. I thought the fellow might be going to tell us of a masked bog or something like that. I gave Smith a hint in a whisper as to where the land lay; and we went on, hoping to come on little Bob any minute. Nearly all the way we were going through open fields without any cover or bracken or anything of that sort, and Williams kept twirling his lantern, and Miss Hayes and the rest of us called out the child's name; there didn't seem much chance of missing him.

'"However, we saw nothing of him – till we got to the Darren. It's an odd sort of place, I should think. You're in an ordinary field, with a gentle upward slope, and you come to a gate, and down you go into a deep, narrow valley; a regular nest of valleys as far as I could make out in the dark, one leading into another, and the sides covered with trees. The famous caves were on one of these steep slopes, and, of course, we all went in. They didn't stretch far; nobody could have got lost in them, even if the candles gave out. We searched the place thoroughly, and saw where the children had had their tea; no signs of Bobby. So we went on down the valley between the woods, till we came to where it opens out into a wide space, with one tree growing all alone in the middle. And then we heard a miserable whining noise, like some little creature that's got hurt. And there under the tree was – what you saw poor Smith carrying in his arms this morning.

'"It fought like a wild cat when Smith tried to pick it up, and jabbered some unearthly sort of gibberish. Then Miss Hayes came along and seemed to soothe it; and it's been quiet ever since. The man with the lantern was shaking with terror; the sweat was pouring down his face."

'I stared hard at Brown. "And," I thought to myself, "'You are very much in the same condition as Williams." Brown was obviously overcome with dread.

'We sat there in silence.

'"Why do you say 'it'?" I asked. "Why don't you say 'him'?"

'"You saw."

'"Do you mean to tell me seriously that you don't believe that child you helped to bring home was Bobby? What does Mrs Smith say?"

'"She says the clothes are the same. I suppose it must be Bobby. The doctor from Porth says the child must have had a severe shock. I don't think he knows anything about it."

'He stuttered over his words, and said at last:

'"I was thinking of what you said about the lighted windows. I hoped you might be able to help. Can you do anything? We are leaving this afternoon; all of us. Is there nothing to be done?"

'"I'm afraid not."

'I had nothing else to say. We shook hands and parted without more words.'

'The next day I walked over to the Darren. There was something fearful about the place, even in the haze of a golden afternoon. As Brown had said, the entrance and the disclosure of it were sudden and abrupt. The fields of the approach held no hint of what was to come. Then, past the gate, the ground fell violently away on every side, grey rocks of an ill shape pierced through it, and the ash trees on the steep slopes overshadowed all. The descent was into silence, without the singing of a bird, into a wizard shade. At the farther end, where the wooded heights retreated somewhat, there was the open space, or circus, of turf; and in the middle of it a very ancient, twisted thorn tree, beneath which the party in the dark had found the little creature that whined and cried out in unknown speech. I turned about, and on my way back I entered the caves, and lit the carriage candle I had brought with me. There was nothing much to see – I never think there is much to see in caves. There was the place where the children and others before them had taken their tea, with a ring of blackened stones within which many fires of twigs had been kindled. In caves or out of caves, townsfolk in the country are always alike in leaving untidy and unseemly litter behind; and here were the usual scraps of greasy paper, daubed with smears of jam and butter, the half-eaten sandwich, and the gnawed crust. Amidst all this nastiness I saw a piece of folded note-paper, and in sheer idleness picked it up and opened it. You have just seen it. When I asked you if you saw anything peculiar about the writing, you said that the letters were rather big and clumsy. The reason of that is that they were written by a child. I don't think you examined the back of the second leaf. Look: "Rosamund" – Rosamund Brown, that is. And beneath; there, in the corner.'

Reynolds looked, and read, and gaped aghast.

'That was – her other name; her name in the dark.'

'Name in the dark?'

'In the dark night of the Sabbath. That pretty girl had caught them all. They were in her hands, those wretched children, like the clay images she made. I found one of those things, hidden in a cleft of the rocks, near the place where they had made their fire. I ground it into dust beneath my feet.'

'And I wonder what her name was?'

'They called her, I think, the Bridegroom and the Bride.'

'Did you ever find out who she was, or where she came from?'

'Very little. Only that she had been a mistress at the Home for Christian Orphans in North Tottenham, where there was a hideous scandal some years before.'

'Then she must have been older than she looked, according to your description.'

'Possibly.'

They sat in silence for a few minutes. Then Reynolds said:

'But I haven't asked you about this formula, or whatever you may call it – all these vowels, here. Is it a cypher?'

'No. But it is really a great curiosity, and it raises some extraordinary questions, which are outside this particular case. To begin with – and I am sure I could go much farther back than my beginning, if I had the necessary scholarship – I once read an English rendering of a Greek manuscript of the second or third century – I won't be certain which. It's a long time since I've seen the thing. The translator and editor of it was of the opinion that it was a Mithraic Ritual; but I have gathered that weightier authorities are strongly inclined to discredit this view. At any rate, it was no doubt an initiation rite into some mystery; possibly it had Gnostic connections; I don't know. But our interest lies in this, that one of the stages or portals, or whatever you call them, consisted, almost exactly, of that formula you have in your hand. I don't say that the vowels and double vowels are in the same order; I don't think the Greek manuscript has any *ae*s or *aa*s. But it is perfectly clear that the two documents are of the same kind and have the same purpose. And, advancing a little in time from the Greek manuscript, I don't think it is very surprising that the final operation of an incantation in mediaeval and later magic consisted of this wailing on vowels arranged in a certain order.

'But here is something that is surprising. A good many years ago I strolled one Sunday morning into a church in Bloomsbury, the headquarters of a highly respectable sect. And in the middle of a very dignified ritual, there rose quite suddenly, without preface or warning, this very sound, a wild wail on vowels. The effect was astounding, anyhow; whether it was terrifying or merely funny, is a matter of taste. You'll have guessed what I heard: they call it "speaking with tongues", and they believe it to be a heavenly language. And I need scarcely say that they mean very well. But the problem is: how did a congregation of solid Scotch Presbyterians hit upon that queer, ancient and not over-sanctified method of expressing spiritual emotion? It is a singular puzzle.

'And that woman? That is not by any means so difficult. The good Scotchmen – I can't think how they did it – got hold of something that didn't belong to them: she was in her own tradition. And, as they say down there: *asakai dasa*: the darkness is undying.'

The Cosy Room

I

And he found to his astonishment that he came to the appointed place with a sense of profound relief. It was true that the window was somewhat high up in the wall, and that, in case of fire, it might be difficult, for many reasons, to get out that way; it was barred like the basement windows that one sees now and then in London houses, but as for the rest it was an extremely snug room. There was a gay flowering paper on the walls, a hanging bookshelf – his stomach sickened for an instant – a little table under the window with a board and draughtsmen on it, two or three good pictures, religious and ordinary, and the man who looked after him was arranging the tea things on the table in the middle of the room. And there was a nice wicker chair by a bright fire. It was a thoroughly pleasant room; cosy you would call it. And, thank God, it was all over, anyhow.

II

It had been a horrible time for the last three months, up to an hour ago. First of all there was the trouble; all over in a minute, that was, and couldn't be helped, though it was a pity, and the girl wasn't worth it. But then there was the getting out of the town. He thought at first of just going about his ordinary business and knowing nothing about it; he didn't think that anybody had seen him following Joe down to the river. Why not loaf about as usual, and say nothing, and go into the Ringland Arms for a pint? It might be days before they found the body under the alders; and there would be an inquest, and all that. Would it be the best plan just to stick it out, and hold his tongue if the police came asking him questions? But then, how could he account for himself and his doings that evening? He might say he went for a stroll in Bleadon Woods and home again without meeting anybody. There was nobody who could contradict him that he could think of.

And now, sitting in the snug room with the bright wallpaper, sitting in the cosy chair by the fire – all so different from the tales they told of such places – he wished he had stuck it out and faced it out, and let them come on and find out what they could. But, then, he had got frightened. Lots of men had heard him swearing it would be outing does for Joe if he didn't leave the girl alone. And he had shown his revolver to Dick Haddon, and 'Lobster' Carey, and Finniman, and others, and then they would be fitting the bullet into the revolver, and it would be all up. He got into a panic and shook with terror, and knew he could never stay in Ledham, not another hour.

III

Mrs Evans, his landlady, was spending the evening with her married daughter at the other side of the town, and would not be back till eleven. He shaved off his stubbly black beard and moustache, and slunk out of the town in the dark and walked all through the night by a lonely by-road, and got to Darnley, twenty miles away, in the morning in time to catch the London excursion. There was a great crowd of people, and, so far as he could see, nobody that he knew, and the carriages packed full of Darnleyites and Lockwood weavers all in high spirits and taking no notice of him. They all got out at King's Cross, and he strolled about with the rest, and looked round here and there as they did and had a glass of beer at a crowded bar. He didn't see how anybody was to find out where he had gone.

IV

He got a back room in a quiet street off the Caledonian Road, and waited. There was something in the evening paper that night, something that you couldn't very well make out. By the next day Joe's body was found, and they got to Murder – the doctor said it couldn't be suicide. Then his own name came in, and he was missing and was asked to come forward. And then he read that he was supposed to have gone to London, and he went sick with fear. He went hot and he went cold. Something rose in his throat and choked him. His hands shook as he held the paper, his head whirled with terror. He was afraid to go home to his room, because he knew he could not stay still in it; he would be tramping up and down, like a wild beast, and the landlady would wonder. And he was afraid to be in the streets, for fear a policeman would come behind him and put a hand on his shoulder. There was a kind of small square round the corner and he sat down on one of the benches there and held up the paper before his face, with the children yelling and howling and playing all about him on the asphalt paths. They took no notice of him, and yet they were company of a sort; it was not like being all alone in that little, quiet room. But it soon got dark and the man came to shut the gates.

V

And after that night; nights and days of horror and sick terrors that he never had known a man could suffer and live. He had brought enough money to keep him for a while, but every time he changed a note he shook with fear, wondering whether it would be traced. What could he do? Where could he go? Could he get out of the country? But there were passports and papers of all sorts; that would never do. He read that the police held a clue to the Ledham Murder Mystery; and he trembled to his lodgings and locked himself in and moaned in his agony, and then found himself chattering words and phrases at random, without meaning or relevance; strings of gibbering words: 'all right, all right, all right . . . yes, yes, yes, yes . . . there, there, there . . . well, well, well, well . . . ' just because he must utter something, because he could not bear to sit still and silent, with that anguish tearing his heart, with that sick horror choking him, with that weight of terror pressing on his breast. And then, nothing happened; and a little, faint, trembling hope fluttered in his breast for a while, and for a day or two he felt he might have a chance after all.

One night he was in such a happy state that he ventured round to the little public house at the corner, and drank a bottle of Old Brown Ale with some enjoyment, and began to think of what life might be again, if by a miracle – he recognised even then that it would be a miracle – all this horror passed away, and he was once more just like other men, with nothing to be afraid of. He was relishing the Brown Ale, and quite plucking up a spirit, when a chance phrase from the bar caught him: 'looking for him not far from here, so they say'. He left the glass of beer half full, and went out wondering whether he had the courage to kill himself that night. As a matter of fact the men at the bar were talking about a recent and sensational cat burglar; but every such word was doom to this wretch. And ever and again, he would check himself in his horrors, in his mutterings and gibberings, and wonder with amazement that the heart of a man could suffer such bitter agony, such rending torment. It was as if he had found out and discovered, he alone of all men living, a new world of which no man before had ever dreamed, in which no man could believe, if he were told the story of it. He had woken up in his past life from such nightmares, now and again, as most men suffer. They were terrible, so terrible that he remembered two or three of them that had oppressed him years before; but they were pure delight to what he now endured. Not endured, but writhed under as a worm twisting amidst red, burning coals.

He went out into the streets, some noisy, some dull and empty, and considered in his panic-stricken confusion which he should choose. They were looking for him in that part of London; there was deadly peril in every step. The streets where people went to and fro and laughed and chattered might be the safer; he could walk with the others and seem to be of them, and so be less likely to be noticed by those who were hunting on his track. But then, on the other hand, the great electric lamps made these streets almost as bright as day, and every feature of the passers-by was clearly seen. True, he was clean-shaven now, and the pictures of him in the papers showed a bearded man, and his own face in the glass still looked strange to him. Still, there were sharp eyes that could penetrate such disguises; and they might have brought down some man from Ledham who knew him well, and knew the way he walked; and so he might be hailed and held at any moment. He dared not walk under the clear blaze of the electric lamps. He would be safe in the dark, quiet by-ways.

He was turning aside, making for a very quiet street close by, when he hesitated. This street, indeed, was still enough after dark, and not over well lighted. It was a street of low, two-storied houses of grey brick that had grimed, with three or four families in each house. Tired men came home here after working hard all day, and people drew their blinds early and stirred very little abroad, and went early to bed; footsteps were rare in this street and in other streets into which it led, and the lamps were few and dim compared with those in the big thoroughfares. And yet, the very fact that few people were about made such as were all the more noticeable and conspicuous. And the police went slowly on their beats in the dark streets as in the bright, and with few people to look at no doubt they looked all the more keenly at such as passed on the pavement. In his world, that dreadful world that he had discovered and dwelt in, alone, the darkness was brighter than the daylight, and solitude more dangerous than a multitude of men. He dared not go into the light, he feared the shadows, and went trembling to his room and shuddered there as the hours of the night went by; shuddered and gabbled to himself his infernal rosary: 'all right, all right, all right . . . splendid, splendid . . . that's the way, that's the way, that's the way, that's the way . . . yes, yes, yes . . . first rate, first rate . . . all right . . . one, one, one, one' – gabbled in a low mutter to keep himself from howling like a wild beast.

VI

It was somewhat in the manner of a wild beast that he beat and tore against the cage of his fate. Now and again it struck him as incredible. He would not believe that it was so. It was something that he would wake from, as he had waked from those nightmares that he remembered, for things did not really happen so. He could not believe it, he would not believe it. Or, if it were so indeed, then all these horrors must be happening to some other man into whose torments he had mysteriously entered. Or he had got into a book, into a tale which one read and shuddered at, but did not for one moment credit; all make-believe, it must be, and presumably everything would be all right again. And then the truth came down on him like a heavy hammer, and beat him down, and held him down – on the burning coals of his anguish.

Now and then he tried to reason with himself. He forced himself to be sensible, as he put it; not to give way, to think of his chances. After all, it was three weeks since he had got into the excursion train at Darnley, and he was still a free man, and every day of freedom made his chances better. These things often die down. There were lots of cases in which the police never got the man they were after. He lit his pipe and began to think things over quietly. It might be a good plan to give his landlady notice, and leave at the end of the week, and make for somewhere in South London, and try to get a job of some sort: that would help to put them off his track. He got up and looked thoughtfully out of the window; and caught his breath. There, outside the little newspaper shop opposite, was the bill of the evening paper: New Clue in Ledham Murder Mystery.

VII

The moment came at last. He never knew the exact means by which he was hunted down. As a matter of fact, a woman who knew him well happened to be standing outside Darnley station on the Excursion Day morning, and she had recognised him, in spite of his beardless chin. And then, at the other end, his landlady, on her way upstairs, had heard his mutterings and gabblings, though the voice was low. She was interested, and curious, and a little frightened, and wondered whether her lodger might be dangerous, and naturally she talked to her friends. So the story trickled down to the ears of the police, and the police asked about the date of the lodger's arrival. And there you were. And there was our nameless friend, drinking a good, hot cup of tea, and polishing off the bacon and eggs with rare appetite; in the cosy room with the cheerful paper; otherwise the Condemned Cell.

N

I

They were talking about old days and old ways and all the changes that have come on London in the last weary years; a little party of three of them, gathered for a rare meeting in Perrott's rooms.

One man, the youngest of the three, a lad of fifty-five or so, had begun to say:

'I know every inch of that neighbourhood, and I tell you there's no such place.'

His name was Harliss; and he was supposed to have something to do with chemicals and carboys and crystals.

They had been recalling many London vicissitudes, these three; and it must be noted that the boy of the party, Harliss, could remember very well the Strand as it used to be, before they spoilt it all. Indeed, if he could not have gone as far back as the years of those doings, it is doubtful whether Perrott would have let him into the meeting in Mitre Place, an alley which was an entrance of the inn by day, but was blind after nine o'clock at night, when the iron gates were shut, and the pavement grew silent. The rooms were on the second floor, and from the front windows could be seen the elms in the inn garden, where the rooks used to build before the war. Within, the large, low room was softly, deeply carpeted from wall to wall; the winter night, with a bitter dry wind rising, and moaning even in the heart of London, was shut out by thick crimson curtains, and the three then sat about a blazing fire in an old fireplace, a fireplace that stood high from the hearth, with hobs on each side of it, and a big kettle beginning to murmur on one of them. The armchairs on which the three sat were of the sort that Mr Pickwick sits on for ever in his frontispiece. The round table of dark mahogany stood on one leg, very deeply and profusely carved, and Perrott said it was a George IV table, though the third friend, Arnold, held that William IV, or even very early Victoria, would have been nearer the mark. On the dark red wallpaper there were eighteenth-century engravings of Durham Cathedral and Peterborough Cathedral, which showed that, in spite of Horace Walpole and his friend Mr Gray, the eighteenth century couldn't draw a Gothic building when its towers and traceries were before its eyes: 'because they couldn't see it,' Arnold had insisted, late one night, when the gliding signs were far on in their course, and the punch in the jar had begun to thicken a little on its spices. There were other engravings of a later date about the walls, things of the thirties and forties by forgotten artists, known well enough in their day; landscapes of the Valley of the Usk, and the Holy Mountain, and Llanthony: all with a certain enchantment and vision about them, as if their domed hills and solemn woods were more of grace than of nature. Over the hearth was *Bolton Abbey in the Olden Time*.

Perrott would apologise for it.

'I know,' he would say. 'I know all about it. It is a pig, and a goat, and a dog, and a damned nonsense' – he was quoting a Welsh story – 'but it used to hang over the fire in the dining room at home. And I often wish I had brought along *Te Deum Laudamus* as well.'

'What's that?' Harliss asked.

'Ah, you're too young to have lived with it. It depicts three choirboys in surplices; one singing for his life, and the other two looking about them – just like choirboys. And we were always told that the busy boy was hanged at last. The companion picture showed three charity girls, also singing. This was called *Te Dominum Confitemur*. I never heard their story.'

'I know.' Harliss brightened. 'I came upon them both in lodgings near the station at Brighton, in Mafeking year. And, a year or two later, I saw *Sherry, Sir* in an hotel at Tenby.'

'The finest wax fruit I ever saw,' Arnold joined in, 'was in a window in the King's Cross Road.'

So they would maunder along, about the old-fashioned rather than the old. And so on this winter night of the cold wind they lingered about the London streets of forty, forty-five, fifty-five years ago.

One of them dilated on Bloomsbury, in the days when the bars were up, and the Duke's porters had boxes beside the gates, and all was peace, not to say profound dullness, within those solemn boundaries. Here was the high vaulted church of a strange sect, where, they said, while the smoke of incense fumed about a solemn rite, a wailing voice would suddenly rise up with the sound of an incantation in magic. Here, another church, where Christina Rossetti bowed her head; all about, dim squares where no one walked, and the leaves of the trees were dark with smoke and soot.

'I remember one spring,' said Arnold, 'when they were the brightest green I ever saw. In Bloomsbury Square. Long ago.'

'That wonderful little lion stood on the iron posts in the pavement in front of the British Museum,' Perrott put in. 'I believe they have kept a few and hidden them in museums. That's one of the reasons why the streets grow duller and duller. If there is anything curious, anything beautiful in a street, they take it away and stick it in a museum. I wonder what has become of that odd little figure, I think it was in a cocked hat, that stood by the bar parlour door in the courtyard of the bell in Holborn.'

They worked their way down by Fetter Lane, and lamented Dryden's house – 'I think it was in '87 that they pulled it down' – and lingered on the site of Clifford's Inn – 'you could walk into the seventeenth century' – and so at last into the Strand.

'Some one said it was the finest street in Europe.'

'Yes, no doubt – in a sense. Not at all in the obvious sense; it wasn't belle architecture de ville. It was of all ages and all sizes and heights and styles: a unique enchantment of a street; an incantation, full of words that meant nothing to the uninitiated.'

A sort of Litany followed.

'The Shop of the Pale Puddings, where little David Copperfield might have bought his dinner.'

'That was close to Bookseller's Row – sixteenth-century houses.'

'And "Chocolate as in Spain"; opposite Charing Cross.'

'The *Globe* office, where one sent one's early turnovers.'

'The narrow alleys with steps going down to the river.'

'The smell of making soap from the scent shop.'

'Nutt's bookshop, near the Welsh mutton butcher's, where the street was narrow.'

'The *Family Herald* office; with a picture in the window of an early typesetting machine, showing the operator working a contraption with long arms, that hovered over the case.'

'And Garden House in the middle of a lawn, in Clement's Inn.'

'And the flicker of those old yellow gas lamps, when the wind blew up the street, and the people were packing into that passage that led to the Lyceum pit.'

One of them, his ear caught by a phrase that another had used, began to murmur verses from 'Oh, plump head waiter at the Cock.'

'What chops they were!' sighed Perrott. And he began to make the punch, grating first of all the lumps of sugar against the lemons; drawing forth thereby the delicate, aromatic oils from the rind of the Mediterranean fruit. Matters were brought forth from cupboards at the dark end of the room: rum from the Jamaica Coffee House in the City, spices in blue china boxes, one or two old bottles containing secret essences. The kettle boiled, the ingredients were dusted in and poured into the red-brown jar, which was then muffled and set to digest on the hearth, in the heat of the fire.

'*Misce, fiat mistura,*' said Harliss.

'Very well,' answered Arnold. 'But remember that all the true matters of the work are invisible.'

Nobody minded him or his alchemy; and after a due interval, the glasses were held over the fragrant steam of the jar, and then filled. The three sat round the fire, drinking and sipping with grateful hearts.

II

Let it be noted that the glasses in question held no great quantity of the hot liquor. Indeed, they were what used to be called rummers; round, and of a bloated aspect, but of comparatively small capacity. Therefore, nothing injurious to the clearness of those old heads is to be inferred, when it is said that between the third and fourth filling, the talk drew away from central London and the lost, beloved Strand and began to go farther afield, into stranger, less-known territories. Perrott began it, by tracing a curious passage he had once made northward, dodging by the Globe and the Olympic theatres into the dark labyrinth of Clare Market, under arches and by alleys, till he came into Great Queen Street, near the Freemason's Tavern and Inigo Jones's red pilasters. Another took up the tale, and drifting into Holborn by Whetstone's Park, and going astray a little to visit Kingsgate Street – 'just like Phiz's plate: mean, low, deplorable; but I wish they hadn't pulled it down' – finally reached Theobald's Road. There, they delayed a little, to consider curiously decorated leaden water cisterns that were once to be seen in the areas of a few of the older houses, and also to speculate on the legend that an ancient galleried inn, now used as a warehouse, had survived till quite lately at the back of Tibbles Road – for so they called it. And thence, northward and eastward, up the Gray's Inn Road, crossing the King's Cross Road, and going up the hill.

'And here,' said Arnold, 'we begin to touch on the conjectured. We have left the known world behind us.'

Indeed, it was he who now had the party in charge.

'Do you know,' said Perrott, 'that sounds awful rot, but it's true; at least so far as I am concerned. I don't think I ever went beyond Holborn Town Hall, as it used to be – I mean walking. Of course, I've driven in a hansom to King's Cross Railway Station, and I went once or twice to the Military Tournament, when it was at the Agricultural Hall, in Islington; but I don't remember how I got there.'

Harliss said he had been brought up in North London, but much farther north – Stoke Newington way.

'I once knew a man,' said Perrott, 'who knew all about Stoke Newington; at least he ought to have known about it. He was a Poe enthusiast, and he wanted to find out whether the school where Poe boarded when he was a little boy was still standing. He went again and again; and the odd thing is that, in spite of his interest in the matter, he didn't seem to know whether the school was still there, or whether he had seen it. He spoke of certain survivals of the Stoke Newington that Poe indicates in a phrase or two in "William Wilson": the dreamy village, the misty trees, the old rambling red-brick houses, standing in their gardens, with high walls all about them. But though he declared that he had gone so far as to interview the vicar, and could describe the old church with the dormer windows, he could never make up his mind whether he had seen Poe's school.'

'I never heard of it when I lived there,' said Harliss. 'But I came of business stock. We didn't gossip much about authors. I have a vague sort of notion that I once heard somebody speak of Poe as a notorious drunkard – and that's about all I ever heard of him till a good deal later.'

'It is queer, but it's true,' Arnold broke in, 'that there's a general tendency to seize on the accidental, and ignore the essential. You may be vague enough about the treble works, the vast designs of the laboured rampart lines; but at least you knew that the Duke of Wellington had a very big nose. I remember it on the tins of knife polish.'

'But that fellow I was speaking of,' said Perrott, going back to his topic, 'I couldn't make him out. I put it to him; "Surely you know one way or the other: this old school is still standing – or was still standing – or not: you either saw it or you didn't: there can't be any doubt about the matter." But we couldn't get to negative or positive. He confessed that it was strange; "But upon my word I don't know. I went once, I think, about '95, and then, again, in '99 – that was the time I called on the vicar; and I have never been since." He talked like a man who had gone into a mist, and could not speak with any certainty of the shapes he had seen in it.

'And that reminds me. Long after my talk with Hare – that was the man who was interested in Poe – a distant cousin of mine from the country came up to town to see about the affairs of an old aunt of his who had lived all her life somewhere Stoke Newington way, and had just died. He came in here one evening to look me up – we had not met for many years – and he was saying, truly enough, I am sure, how little the average Londoner knew of London, when you once took him off his beaten track. "For example," he said to me, "have you ever been in Stoke Newington?" I confessed that I hadn't, that I had never had any reason to go there. "Exactly; and I don't suppose you've ever even heard of Canon's Park?" I confessed ignorance again. He said it was an extraordinary thing that such a beautiful place as this, within four or five miles of the centre of London, seemed absolutely unknown and unheard of by nine Londoners out of ten.'

'I know every inch of that neighbourhood,' broke in Harliss. 'I was born there and lived there till I was sixteen. There's no such place anywhere near Stoke Newington.'

'But, look here, Harliss,' said Arnold. 'I don't know that you're really an authority.'

'Not an authority on a place I knew backwards for sixteen years? Besides, I represented Crosbies in that district later, soon after I went into business.'

'Yes, of course. But – I suppose you know the Haymarket pretty well, don't you?'

'Of course I do; both for business and pleasure. Everybody knows the Haymarket.'

'Very good. Then tell me the way to St James's Market.'

'There's no such market.'

'We have him,' said Arnold, with bland triumph. 'Literally, he is correct: I believe it's all pulled down now. But it was standing during the war: a small open space with old, low buildings in it, a stone's throw from the back of the tube station. You turned to the right, as you walked down the Haymarket.'

'Quite right,' confirmed Perrott. 'I went there, only once, on the business of an odd magazine that was published in one of those low buildings. But I was talking of Canon's Park, Stoke Newington – '

'I beg your pardon,' said Harliss. 'I remember now. There is a part in Stoke Newington or near it called Canon's Park. But it isn't a park at all; nothing like a park. That's only a builder's name. It's just a lot of streets. I think there's a Canon's Square, and a Park Crescent, and an Esplanade: there are some decent shops there. But it's all quite ordinary; there's nothing beautiful about it.'

'But my cousin said it was an amazing place. Not a bit like the ordinary London parks or anything of the kind he'd seen abroad. You go in through a gateway, and he said it was like finding yourself in another country. Such trees, that must have been brought from the end of the world: there were none like them in England, though one or two reminded him of trees in Kew Gardens; deep hollows with streams running from the rocks; lawns all purple and gold with flowers, and golden lilies too, towering up into the trees, and mixing with the crimson of the flowers that hung from the boughs. And here and there, there were little summer houses and temples, shining white in the sun, like a view in China, as he put it.'

Harliss did not fail with his response, 'I tell you there's no such place.' And he added:

'And, anyhow, it all sounds a bit too flowery. But perhaps your cousin was that sort of man: ready to be enthusiastic over a patch of dandelions in a back garden. A friend of mine once sent me a wire to "come at once: most important: meet me St John's Wood Station." Of course I went, thinking it must be really important; and what he wanted was to show me the garden of a house to let in Grove End Road, which was a blaze of dandelions.'

'And a very beautiful sight,' said Arnold, with fervour.

'It was a fine sight; but hardly a thing to wire a man about. And I should think that's the secret of all this stuff your cousin told you, Perrott. There used to be one or two big well-kept gardens at Stoke Newington; and I suppose he strolled into one of them by mistake, and then got rather wildly enthusiastic about what he saw.'

'It's possible, of course,' said Perrott, 'but in a general way he wasn't that sort of man. He had an experimental farm, not far from Wells, and bred new kinds of wheat, and improved grasses. I have heard him called stodgy, though I always found him pleasant enough when we met.'

'Well, I tell you there's no such place in Stoke Newington or anywhere near it. I ought to know.'

'How about St James's Market?' asked Arnold.

Then, they 'left it at that'. Indeed, they had felt for some time that they had gone too far away from their known world, and from the friendly tavern fires of the Strand, into the wild no man's land of the north. To Harliss, of course, those regions had once been familiar, common, and uninteresting: he could not revisit them in talk with any glow of feeling. The other two held them unfriendly and remote; as if one were to discourse of Arctic explorations, and lands of everlasting darkness.

They all returned with relief to their familiar hunting grounds, and saw the play in theatres that had been pulled down for thirty-five years or more, and had steaks and strong ale afterwards, in the box by the fire, by the fire that had been finally raked out soon after the new law courts were opened.

III

So, at least, it appeared at the time; but there was something in the tale of this suburban park that remained with Arnold and beset him, and sent him at last to the remote north of the story. For, as he was meditating on this vague attraction, he chanced to light on a shabby brown book on his untidy shelves; a book gathered from a stall in Farringdon Street, where the manuscript of Traherne's *Centuries of Meditations* had been found. So far, Arnold had scarcely glanced at it. It was called, *A London Walk: Meditations in the Streets of the Metropolis*. The author was the Reverend Thomas Hampole, and the book was dated 1853. It consisted for the most part of moral and obvious reflections, such as might be expected from a pious and amiable clergyman of the day. In the middle of the nineteenth century, the relish of moralising which flourished so in the age of Addison and Pope and Johnson, which made *The Rambler* a popular book, and gave fortunes to the publishers of sermons, had still a great deal of vigour. People liked to be warned of the consequences of their actions, to have lessons in punctuality, to learn about the importance of little things, to hear sermons from stones, and to be taught that there were gloomy reflections to be drawn from almost everything. So then, the Reverend Thomas Hampole stalked the London streets with a moral and monitory glance in his eye: saw Regent Street in its early splendour and thought of the ruins of mighty Rome, preached on the text of solitude in a multitude as he viewed what he called the teeming myriads, and allowed a desolate, half-ruinous house 'in Chancery' to suggest thoughts of the happy Christmas parties that had once thoughtlessly revelled behind the crumbling walls and broken windows.

But here and there, Mr Hampole became less obvious, and perhaps more really profitable. For example, there is a passage – it has already been quoted, I think, by some modern author – which seems curious enough.

> Has it ever been your fortune, courteous reader [Mr Hampole inquired] to rise in the earliest dawning of a summer day, ere yet the radiant beams of the sun have done more than touch with light the domes and spires of the great city? . . . If this has been your lot, have you not observed that magic powers have apparently been at work? The accustomed scene has lost its familiar appearance. The houses which you have passed daily, it may be for years, as you have issued forth on your business or on your pleasure, now seem as if you beheld them for the first time. They have suffered a mysterious change, into something rich and strange. Though they may have been designed with no extraordinary exertion of the art of architecture . . . yet you have been ready to admit that they now 'stand in glory, shine like stars, apparelled in a light serene.' They have become magical habitations, supernal dwellings, more desirable to the eye than the fabled pleasure dome of the Eastern potentate, or the bejewelled hall built by the Genie for Aladdin in the Arabian tale.

A good deal in this vein; and then, when one expected the obvious warning against putting trust in appearances, both transitory and delusory, there came a very odd passage:

> Some have declared that it lies within our own choice to gaze continually upon a world of equal or even greater wonder and beauty. It is said by these that the experiments of the alchemists of the Dark Ages . . . are, in fact, related, not to the transmutation of metals, but to the transmutation of the entire Universe. . . . This method, or art, or science, or whatever we choose to call it

> (supposing it to exist, or to have ever existed), is simply concerned to restore the delights of the primal Paradise; to enable men, if they will, to inhabit a world of joy and splendour. It is perhaps possible that there is such an experiment, and that there are some who have made it.

The reader was referred to a note – one of several – at the end of the volume, and Arnold, already a good deal interested by this unexpected vein in the Reverend Thomas, looked it up. And thus it ran:

> I am aware that these speculations may strike the reader as both singular and (I may, perhaps, add) chimerical; and, indeed, I may have been somewhat rash and ill-advised in committing them to the printed page. If I have done wrong, I hope for pardon; and, indeed, I am far from advising anyone who may read these lines to engage in the doubtful and difficult experiment which they adumbrate. Still; we are bidden to be seekers of the truth: *veritas contra mundum.*
>
> I am strengthened in my belief that there is at least some foundation for the strange theories at which I have hinted, by an experience that befell me in the early days of my ministry. Soon after the termination of my first curacy, and after I had been admitted to Priest's Orders, I spent some months in London, living with relations in Kensington. A college friend of mine, whom I will call the Reverend Mr S——, was, I was aware, a curate in a suburb of the north of London, S.N. I wrote to him, and afterwards called at his lodgings at his invitation. I found S—— in a state of some perturbation. He was threatened, it seemed, with an affection of the lungs and his medical adviser was insistent that he should leave London for awhile, and spend the four months of the winter in the more genial climate of Devonshire. Unless this were done, the doctor declared, the consequences to my friend's health might be of a very serious kind. S—— was very willing to act on this advice, and indeed, anxious to do so; but, on the other hand, he did not wish to resign his curacy, in which, as he said, he was both happy and, he trusted, useful. On hearing this, I at once proffered my services, telling him that if his Vicar approved, I should be happy to do his duty till the end of the ensuing March; or even later, if the physicians considered a longer stay in the south would be advisable. S—— was overjoyed. He took me at once to

see the Vicar; the fitting inquiries were made, and I entered on my temporary duties in the course of a fortnight.

It was during this brief ministry in the environs of London, that I became acquainted with a very singular person, whom I shall call Glanville. He was a regular attendant at our services, and, in the course of my duty, I called on him, and expressed my gratification at his evident attachment to the Liturgy of the Church of England. He replied with due politeness, asked me to sit down and partake with him of the soothing cup, and we soon found ourselves engaged in conversation. I discovered early in our association that he was conversant with the reveries of the German Theosophist, Behmen, and the later works of his English disciple, William Law; and it was clear to me that he looked on these labyrinths of mystical theology with a friendly eye. He was a middle-aged man, spare of habit, and of a dark complexion; and his face was illuminated in a very impressive manner, as he discussed the speculations which had evidently occupied his thoughts for many years. Based as these theories were on the doctrines (if we may call them by that name) of Law and Behmen, they struck me as of an extremely fantastic, I would even say fabulous, nature, but I confess that I listened with a considerable degree of interest, while making it evident that as a Minister of the Church of England I was far from giving my free assent to the propositions that were placed before me. They were not, it is true, manifestly and certainly opposed to orthodox belief, but they were assuredly strange, and as such to be received with salutary caution. As an example of the ideas which beset a mind which was ingenious, and I may say, devout, I may mention that Mr Glanville often dwelt on a consequence, not generally acknowledged, of the Fall of Man. 'When man yielded,' he would say, 'to the mysterious temptation intimated by the figurative language of Holy Writ, the universe, originally fluid and the servant of his spirit, became solid, and crashed down upon him overwhelming him beneath its weight and its dead mass.' I requested him to furnish me with more light on this remarkable belief; and I found that in his opinion that which we now regard as stubborn matter was, primally, to use his singular phraseology, the Heavenly Chaos, a soft and ductile substance, which could be moulded by the imagination of uncorrupted man into whatever forms he chose it to assume. 'Strange as it may seem,' he added, 'the wild inventions (as we consider them) of the Arabian Tales give us some notion of the powers of the homo protoplastus. The prosperous city becomes a lake, the carpet transports us in an instant of time, or rather without time, from one end of the earth to another, the palace rises at a word from nothingness. Magic, we call all this, while we deride the possibility of any such feats; but this magic of the East is but a confused and fragmentary recollection of operations which were of the first nature of man, and of the fiat which was then entrusted to him.'

I listened to this and other similar expositions of Mr Glanville's extraordinary beliefs with some interest, as I have remarked. I could not but feel that such opinions were in many respects more in accordance with the doctrine I had undertaken to expound than much of the teaching of the philosophers of the day, who seemed to exalt rationalism at the expense of Reason, as that divine faculty was exhibited by Coleridge. Still, when I assented, I made it clear to Glanville that my assent was qualified by my firm adherence to the principles which I had solemnly professed at my ordination.

The months went by in the peaceful performance of the pastoral duties of my office. Early in March, I received a letter from my friend Mr S——, who informed me that he had greatly benefited by the air of Torquay, and that his medical adviser had assured him that he need no longer hesitate to resume his duties in London. Consequently, S—— proposed to return at once, and, after warmly expressed thanks for my extreme kindness, as he called it, he announced his wish to perform his part in the Church services on the following Sunday. Accordingly, I paid my final visits to those of the parishioners with whom I had more particularly associated, reserving my call on Mr Glanville for the last day of my residence at S.N. He was sorry, I think, to hear of my impending departure, and told me that he would always recollect our conversational exchanges with much pleasure.

'I, too, am leaving S.N.,' he added. 'Early next week I sail for the East, where my stay may be prolonged for a considerable period.'

After mutual expressions of polite regret, I rose from my chair, and was about to make my farewells, when I observed that Glanville was gazing at me with a fixed and singular regard.

'One moment,' he said, beckoning me to the window, where he was standing. 'I want to show you the view. I don't think you have seen it.'

The suggestion struck me as peculiar, to say the least of it. I was, of course, familiar with the street in which Glanville resided, as with most of the S.N. streets; and he on his side must have been well aware that no prospect that his window might command could show me anything that I had not seen many times during my four months' stay in the parish. In addition to this, the streets of our London suburbs do not often offer a spectacle to engage the amateur of landscape and the picturesque. I was hesitating, hardly knowing whether to comply with Glanville's request, or to treat it as a piece of pleasantry, when it struck me that it was possible that his first-floor window might afford a distant view of St Paul's Cathedral; I accordingly stepped to his side, and waited for him to indicate the scene which he, presumably, wished me to admire.

His features still wore the odd expression which I have already remarked.

'Now,' said he, 'look out and tell me what you see.'

Still bewildered, I looked through the window, and saw exactly that which I had expected to see: a row or terrace of neatly designed residences, separated from the highway by a parterre or miniature park, adorned with trees and shrubs. A road, passing to the right of the terrace, gave a view of streets and crescents of more recent construction, and of some degree of elegance. Still, in the whole of the familiar spectacle I saw nothing to warrant any particular attention; and, in a more or less jocular manner, I said as much to Glanville.

By way of reply, he touched me lightly with his fingertips on the shoulder, and said:

'Look again.'

I did so. For a moment, my heart stood still, and I gasped for breath. Before me, in place of the familiar structures, there was disclosed a panorama of unearthly, of astounding beauty. In deep dells, bowered by overhanging trees, there bloomed flowers such as only dreams can show; such deep purples that yet seemed to glow like precious stones with a hidden but ever-present radiance, roses whose hues outshone any that are to be seen in our gardens, tall lilies alive with light, and blossoms that were as beaten gold. I saw well-shaded walks that went down to green hollows bordered with thyme; and here and there the grassy eminence above, and the bubbling well below, were crowned with architecture of fantastic and unaccustomed beauty, which seemed to speak of fairyland itself. I might almost say that my soul was ravished by the spectacle displayed before me. I was possessed by a degree of rapture and delight such as I had never experienced. A sense of beatitude pervaded my whole being; my bliss was such as cannot be expressed by words. I uttered an inarticulate cry of joy and wonder. And then, under the influence of a swift revulsion of terror, which even now I cannot explain, I turned and rushed from the room and from the house, without one word of comment or farewell to the extraordinary man who had done – I knew not what.

In great perturbation and confusion of mind, I made my way into the street. Needless to say, no trace of the phantasmagoria that had been displayed before me remained. The familiar street had resumed its usual aspect, the terrace stood as I had always seen it, and the newer buildings beyond, where I had seen oh! what dells of delight, what blossoms of glory, stood as before in their neat, though unostentatious order. Where I had seen valleys embowered in green leafage, waving gently in the sunshine and the summer breeze, there were now boughs bare and black, scarce showing so much as a single bud. As I have mentioned, the season was early in March, and a black frost which had set in ten days or a fortnight before still constrained the earth and its vegetation.

I walked hurriedly away to my lodgings, which were some distance from the abode of Glanville. I was sincerely glad to think that I was leaving the neighbourhood on the following day. I may say that up to the present moment I have never revisited S.N.

Some months later I encountered my friend Mr S——, and under cover of asking about the affairs of the parish in which he still ministered, I inquired after Glanville, with whom (I said) I had made acquaintance. It seemed he had fulfilled his intention of leaving the neighbourhood within a few days of my own departure. He had not confided his destination or his plans for the future to anyone in the parish.

'My acquaintance with him,' said S——, 'was of the slightest, and I do not think that he made any friends in the locality, though he had resided in S.N. for more than five years.'

It is now some fifteen years since this most strange experience befell me; and during that period I have heard nothing of Glanville. Whether he is still alive in the distant Orient, or whether he is dead, I am completely ignorant.

IV

Arnold was generally known as an idle man; and, as he said himself, he hardly knew what the inside of an office was like. But he was laborious in his idleness, and always ready to take any amount of pains, over anything in which he was interested. And he was very much interested in this Canon's Park business. He felt sure that there was a link between Mr Hampole's odd story – 'more than odd', he meditated – and the experience of Perrott's cousin, the wheat-breeder from the west country. He made his way to Stoke Newington, and strolled up and down it, looking about him with an inquisitive eye. He found Canon's Park, or what remained of it, without any trouble. It was pretty well as Harliss had described it: a neighbourhood laid out in the twenties or thirties of the last century for City men of comfortable down to tolerable incomes.

Some of these houses remained, and there was an attractive row of old-fashioned shops still surviving. Again, in one place there was the modest cot of late Georgian or early Victorian design, with its trellised porch of faded blue-green paint, its patterned iron balcony, not displeasing, its little garden in the front, and its walled garden at the back; a small coach house, a small stable. In another, something more exuberant and on a much larger scale: ambitious pilasters and stucco, broad lawns and sweeping drives, towering shrubs, and grass in the back premises. But on all the territory modernism had delivered its assault. The big houses remaining had been made into maisonettes, the small ones were down-at-heel, no longer objects of love; and everywhere there were blocks of flats in wicked red brick, as if Mrs Todgers had given Mr Pecksniff her notion of an up-to-date gaol, and he had worked out her design. Opposite Canon's Park, and occupying the site on which Mr Glanville's house must have stood, was a technical college; next to it a school of economics. Both buildings curdled the blood: in their purpose and in their architecture. They looked as if Mr

H. G. Wells's bad dreams had come true.

In none of this, whether moderately ancient or grossly modern, could Arnold see anything to his purpose. In the period of which Mr Hampole wrote, Canon's Park may have been tolerably pleasant; it was now becoming intolerably unpleasant. But at its best, there could not have been anything in its aspect to suggest the wonderful vision which the clergyman thought he had seen from Glanville's window. And suburban gardens, however well kept, could not explain the farmer's rhapsodies. Arnold repeated the sacred words of the explanation formula: telepathy, hallucination, hypnotism; but felt very little easier. Hypnotism, for example: that was commonly used to explain the Indian rope trick. There was no such trick, and in any case, hypnotism could not explain that or any other marvel seen by a number of people at once, since hypnotism could only be applied to individuals, and with their full knowledge, consent, and conscious attention. Telepathy might have taken place between Glanville and Hampole; but whence did Perrott's cousin receive the impression that he not only saw a sort of *Kubla Khan*, or Old Man of the Mountain paradise, but actually walked abroad in it? The S.P.R. had, one might say, discovered telepathy, and had devoted no small part of their energies for the last forty-five years or more to a minute and thoroughgoing investigation of it; but, to the best of his belief, their recorded cases gave no instance of anything so elaborate as this business of Canon's Park. And again; so far as he could remember, the appearances ascribed to a telepathic agency were all personal; visions of people, not of places: there were no telepathic landscapes. And as for hallucination: that did not carry one far. That stated a fact, but offered no explanation of it. Arnold had suffered from liver trouble: he had come down to breakfast one morning and had been vexed to see the air all dancing with black specks. Though he did not smell the nauseous odour of a smoky chimney, he made no doubt at first that the chimney had been smoking, or that the black specks were floating soot. It was some time before he realised that, objectively, there were no black specks, that they were optical illusions, and that he had been hallucinated. And no doubt the parson and the farmer had been hallucinated: but the cause, the motive power, was to seek. Dickens told how, waking one morning, he saw his father sitting by his bedside, and wondered what he was doing there. He addressed the old man, and got no answer, put out his hand to touch him: and there was no such thing. Dickens was hallucinated; but since his father was perfectly well at the time, and in no sort of trouble, the mystery remained insoluble, unaccountable. You had to accept it; but there was no rationale of it. It was a problem that had to be given up.

But Arnold did not like giving problems up. He beat the coverts of Stoke Newington, and dived into pubs of promising aspect, hoping to meet talkative old men, who might remember their fathers' stories and repeat them. He found a few, for though London has always been a place of restless, migratory tribes, and shifting populations; and now more than ever before; yet there still remains in many places, and above all in the remoter northern suburbs, an old fixed element, which can go back in memory sometimes for a hundred, even a hundred and fifty years. So in a venerable tavern – it would have been injurious and misleading to call it a pub – on the borders of Canon's Park he found an ancient circle that gathered nightly for an hour or two in a snug, if dingy, parlour. They drank little and that slowly, and went early home. They were small tradesmen of the neighbourhood, and talked their business and the changes they had seen, the curse of multiple shops, the poor stuff sold in them, and the cutting of prices and profits. Arnold edged into the conversation by degrees, after one or two visits – 'Well, sir, I am very much obliged to you, and I won't refuse' – and said that he thought of settling in the neighbourhood: it seemed quiet. 'Best wishes, I'm sure. Quiet; well it was, once; but not much of that now in Stoke Newington. All pride and dress and bustle now; and the people that had the money and spent it, they're gone, long ago.'

'There were well-to-do people here?' asked Arnold, treading cautiously, feeling his way, inch by inch.

'There were, I assure you. Sound men – warm men, my father used to call them. There was Mr Tredegar, head of Tredegar's Bank. That was amalgamated with the City and National many years ago: nearer fifty than forty, I suppose. He was a fine gentleman, and grew beautiful pineapples. I remember his sending us one, when my wife was poorly all one summer. You can't buy pineapples like that now.'

'You're right, Mr Reynolds, perfectly right. I have to stock what they call pineapples, but I wouldn't touch them myself. No scent, no flavour. Tough and hard; you can't compare a crabapple with a Cox's pippin.'

There was a general assent to this proposition; and Arnold felt that it was slow work.

And even when he got to his point, there was not much gained. He said he had heard that Canon's Park was a quiet part; off the main track.

'Well, there's something in that,' said the ancient who had accepted the half-pint. 'You don't get very much traffic there, it's true: no trams or buses or motor coaches. But they're pulling it all to pieces; building new blocks of flats every few months. Of course, that might suit your views. Very popular these flats are, no doubt, with many people; most economical, they tell me. But I always liked a house of my own, myself.'

'I'll tell you one way a flat is economical,' the greengrocer said with a preparatory chuckle. 'If you're fond of the wireless, you can save the price and the licence. You'll hear the wireless on the floor above, and the wireless on the floor below, and one or two more besides when they've got their windows open on summer evenings.'

'Very true, Mr Batts, very true. Still, I must say, I'm rather partial to the wireless myself. I like to listen to a cheerful tune, you know, at teatime.'

'You don't tell me, Mr Potter, that you like that horrible jazz, as they call it ?'

'Well, Mr Dickson, I must confess . . . ' and so forth, and so forth. It became evident that there were modernists even here: Arnold thought that he heard the term 'hot blues' distinctly uttered. He forced another half-pint – 'very kind of you; mild this time, if you don't mind' – on his neighbour, who turned out to be Mr Reynolds, the pharmaceutical chemist, and tried back.

'So you wouldn't recommend Canon's Park as a desirable residence.'

'Well, no, sir; not to a gentleman who wants quiet, I should not. You can't have quiet when a place is being pulled down about your ears, as you may say. It certainly was quiet enough in former days. Wouldn't you say so, Mr Batts?' – breaking in on the musical discussion – 'Canon's Park was quiet enough in our young days, wasn't it? It would have suited this gentleman then, I'm sure.'

'Perhaps so,' said Mr Batts. 'Perhaps so, and perhaps not. There's quiet, and quiet.'

And a certain stillness fell upon the little party of old men. They seemed to ruminate, to drink their beer in slower sips.

'There was always something about the place I didn't altogether like,' said one of them at last. 'But I'm sure I don't know why.'

'Wasn't there some tale of a murder there, a long time ago? Or was it a man that killed himself, and was buried at the crossroads by the green, with a stake through his heart?'

'I never heard of that, but I've heard my father say that there was a lot of fever about there formerly.'

'I think you're all wide of the mark, gentlemen, if you'll excuse my saying so' – this from an elderly man in a corner, who had said very little hitherto. 'I wouldn't say Canon's Park had a bad name, far from it. But there certainly was something about it that many people didn't like; fought shy of, you may say. And it's my belief that it was all on account of the lunatic asylum that used to be there, a while ago.'

'A lunatic asylum was there?' Arnold's particular friend asked. 'Well, I think I remember hearing something to that effect in my very young days, now you recall the circumstances. I know we boys used to be very shy of going through Canon's Park after dark. My father used to send me on errands that way now and again, and I always got another boy to come along with me if I could. But I don't remember that we were particularly afraid of the lunatics either. In fact, I hardly know what we were afraid of, now I come to think of it.'

'Well, Mr Reynolds, it's a long time ago; but I do think it was that madhouse put people off Canon's Park in the first place. You know where it was, don't you?'

'I can't say I do.'

'Well, it was that big house right in the middle of the park, that had been empty years and years – forty years, I dare say, and going to ruin.'

'You mean the place where Empress Mansions are now? Oh, yes, of course. Why they pulled it down more than twenty years ago, and then the land was lying idle all through the war and long after. A dismal-looking old place it was; I remember it well: the ivy growing over the chimney pots, and the windows smashed, and the "To Let" boards smothered in creepers. Was that house an asylum in its day?'

'That was the very house, sir. Himalaya House, it was called. In the first place it was built on to an old farmhouse by a rich gentleman from India, and when he died, having no children, his relations sold the property to a doctor. And he turned it into a madhouse. And as I was saying, I think people didn't much like the idea of it. You know, those places weren't so well looked after as they say they are now, and some very unpleasant stories got about; I'm not sure if the doctor didn't get mixed up in a lawsuit over a gentleman, of good family, I believe, who had been shut up in Himalaya House by his relations for years, and as sensible as you or me all the time. And then there was that young fellow that managed to escape: that was a queer business. Though there was no doubt that he was mad enough for anything.'

'One of them got away, did he?' Arnold inquired, wishing to break the silence that again fell on the circle.

'That was so. I don't know how he managed it, as they were said to be very strictly kept, but he contrived to climb out or creep out somehow or other, one evening about teatime, and walked as quietly as you please up the road, and took lodgings close by here, in that row of old red-brick houses that stood where the technical college is now. I remember well hearing Mrs Wilson that kept the lodgings – she lived to be a very old woman – telling my mother that she never saw a nicer-looking, better-spoken young man than this Mr Valiance – I think he called himself: not his real name, of course. He told her a proper story enough about coming from Norwich, and having to be very quiet on account of his studies and all that. He had his carpetbag in his hand, and said the heavy luggage was coming later, and paid a fortnight in advance, quite regular. Of course, the doctor's men were after him directly and making inquiries in all directions, but Mrs Wilson never thought for a moment that this quiet young lodger of hers was the missing madman. Not for some time, that is.'

Arnold took advantage of a rhetorical pause in the story. He leaned forward to the landlord, who was leaning over the bar, and listening like the rest. Presently orders round were solicited, and each of the circle voted for a small drop of gin, feeling 'mild' or even 'bitter' to be inadequate to the crisis of such a tale. And then, with courteous expressions, they drank the health of 'our friend sitting by our friend Mr Reynolds'. And one of them said:

'So she found out, did she?'

'I believe,' the narrator continued, 'that it was a week or thereabouts before Mrs Wilson saw there was something wrong. It was when she was clearing away his tea, he suddenly spoke up, and says:

'"What I like about these apartments of yours, Mrs Wilson, is the amazing view you have from your windows."

'Well, you know, that was enough to startle her. We all of us know what there was to see from the windows of Rodman's Row: Fothergill Terrace, and Chatham Street, and Canon's Park: very nice properties, no doubt, all of them, but nothing to write home about, as the young people say. So Mrs Wilson didn't know how to take it quite, and thought it might be a joke. She put down the tea tray, and looked the lodger straight in the face.

'"What is it, sir, you particularly admire, if I might ask?"

'"What do I admire?" said he. "Everything." And then, it seems, he began to talk the most outrageous nonsense about golden and silver and purple flowers, and the bubbling well, and the walk that went under the trees right into the wood, and the fairy house on the hill; and I don't know what. He wanted Mrs Wilson to come to the window and look at it all. She was frightened, and took up her tray, and got out of the room as quick as she could; and I don't wonder at it. And that night, when she was going up to bed, she passed her lodger's door, and heard him talking out loud, and she stopped to listen. Mind you, I don't think you can blame the woman for listening. I dare say she wanted to know who and what she had got in her house. At first she couldn't make out what he was saying. He was jabbering in what sounded like a foreign language; and then he cried out in plain English as if he were talking to a young lady, and making use of very affectionate expressions.

'That was too much for Mrs Wilson, and she went off to bed with her heart in her boots, and hardly got to sleep all through the night. The next morning the gentleman seemed quiet enough, but Mrs Wilson knew he wasn't to be trusted, and directly after breakfast she went round to the neighbours, and began to ask questions. Then, of course, it came out who her lodger must be, and she sent word round to Himalaya House. And the doctor's men took the young fellow back. And, bless my soul, gentlemen; it's close on ten o'clock.'

The meeting broke up in a kind of cordial bustle. The old man who had told the story of the escaped lunatic had remarked, it appeared, the very close attention that Arnold had given to the tale. He was evidently gratified. He shook Arnold warmly by the hand, remarking: 'So you see, sir, the grounds I have for my opinion that it was that madhouse that gave Canon's Park rather a bad name in our neighbourhood.'

And Arnold, revolving many things, set out on the way back to London. Much seemed heavily obscure, but he wondered whether Mrs Wilson's lodger was a madman at all; any madder than Mr Hampole, or the farmer from Somerset or Charles Dickens, when he saw the appearance of his father by his bed.

V

Arnold told the story of his researches and perplexities at the next meeting of the three old friends in the quiet court leading into the inn. The scene had changed into a night in June, with the trees in the inn garden fluttering in a cool breeze, that wafted a vague odour of hay-fields far away into the very heart of London. The liquor in the brown jar smelt of Gascon vineyards and herb gardens, and ice had been laid about it, but not for too long a time.

Harliss's word all through Arnold's tale was:

'I know every inch of that neighbourhood, and I told you there was no such place.'

Perrott was judicial. He allowed that the history was a remarkable one: 'You have three witnesses,' Arnold had pointed out.

'Yes,' said Perrott, 'but have you allowed for the marvellous operation of the law of coincidences? There's a case, trivial enough, perhaps you may think, that made a deep impression on me when I read it, a few years ago. Forty years before, a man had bought a watch in Singapore – or Hong Kong, perhaps. The watch went wrong, and he took it to a shop in Holborn to be seen to. The man who took it from him over the counter was the man who had sold him the watch in the East all those years before. You can never put coincidence out of court, and dismiss it as an impossible solution. Its possibilities are infinite.'

Then Arnold told the last broken, imperfect chapter of the story.

'After that night at the King of Jamaica,' he began, 'I went home and thought it all over. There seemed no more to be done. Still, I felt as if I would like to have another look at this singular park, and I went up there one dark afternoon. And then and there I came upon the young man who had lost his way, and had lost – as he said – the one who lived in the white house on the hill. And I am not going to tell you about her, or her house, or her enchanted gardens. But I am sure that the young man was lost also – and for ever.'

And after a pause, he added:

'I believe that there is a perichoresis, an interpenetration. It is possible, indeed, that we three are now sitting among desolate rocks, by bitter streams . . . And with what companions?'

The Dover Road

The disappearance of Sir Halliday Stuart, the well-known antiquary, was really a very puzzling affair. And even the solution of it is in itself something of a puzzle.

Some of the circumstances that surrounded and involved this singular business were recalled by the painstaking though futile attempt undertaken by the B.B.C. to pin down a ghost that was supposed to haunt an old manor house in an out-of-the-way part of Kent. The B.B.C. people, it will be remembered, put themselves in the hands of a recognised expert. This gentleman took the precautions which considerable experience of sprites, some of them exceedingly tricky, suggested as necessary. He sealed the doors with a special seal, he established microphones at critical points. In that quarter which was supposed to be afflicted now and again by icy draughts of air he set up an automatic temperature registering instrument. A watch went on guard outside the house, and patrolled the ground from eight o'clock to a quarter to twelve. Then the expert and four or five others sat down to watch and listen.

Everything, in short, that could be done was done. And nothing, or next to nothing, happened. The instrument that registered the temperature showed some odd alternations, moving up and down within four or five degrees Fahrenheit, but there was no indication of the blasts of ice-cold air of which the legends spoke. Beyond this, there was nothing, and the expert and his assessors broke off the enquiry, observing very sensibly that the local ghost in particular and ghosts in general had neither been proved nor disproved by the proceedings of the night.

Very much the same kind of thing happened at an earlier investigation of a supposed case of haunting, which was conducted without the aid or countenance of Broadcasting House. In this case, the building supposed to be haunted was an old manor house called Morton

Grange, situated in Essex, fourteen or fifteen miles from London, to the north-east. In those days, it might fairly be said to be in the country, but now it stands, if it does stand at all, in the very middle of the Morton Grange Estate, a sad grey rock in a red suburban sea. At the time of the experiment in ghost-detection, the Grange was not only in the country, but lonely – for a house within reasonable distance from Liverpool Street. Following the main road, dotted here and there with pleasant old cottages, and not unpleasant oldish villas – the sort of villa that has a trellised porch, a verandah, and a curving penthouse over a window here and there – one came to the hamlet of Morton; a whole row of cottages, a Queen Anne house for a doctor, a public house with dim green seats and tables before it, the rectory, with a drive, behind shrubs and elms, and a small, unrestored church. At the end of all this, a yellow-washed farmhouse, with famous barns, red brick, half-timber, and dipping roof trees, and a bare quarter of a mile farther, on the other side of the road, and some way from it, where the land rose up in a slope, Morton Grange, a confused appearance of buildings, part stucco and part stone, and altogether of a neglected aspect.

It was approached, in spite of what must have been its former dignity, by a lane that could hardly have been a formal drive in its best days, since it had rough high banks with old timber growing on them. Then, a stone wall with good ironwork gates, beginning to rust away, and a grove of dark ilexes. Before the front of the house, a lawn sloped down to a sunken fence or ha-ha: there were remnants of flower beds, their edges vague and overgrown with grass and weeds, remnants of a rosary, in which the suckers of the wild stock had overpowered the cultivated flowers, and grown into matted and thorny thickets. A leaden statue, with one arm missing, stood in the midst of a stagnant pool; some grey stone urns on pillars showed vague and mouldering indications of stone garlands.

Where the stucco had begun to peel away on the right, as you faced the house, the architecture looked early Georgian; the left, the grey stone portion, was a good deal older, though the mullions had been knocked out of most of the windows. At the back: kitchens, pantries, butteries, brewhouse, and the rest smacked of the sixteenth century; low, solid, cavernous places. The living rooms were dank and damp; the gorgeous Chinese paper of the drawing room was smeared with grey shapes of rising wet, the heavy crimson flock paper of the dining room was beginning to peel and rip from the sweating wall. In three or four of the rooms there was a skeleton furnishing: cheap modern stuff, shabby after forty, fifty years of little use and long neglect. And the usual story was told about the house. It was empty because no one could live in it. It was haunted.

Of course, there was a legend; and here again it was the usual legend; more or less. I believe there was a Monk who was looking for treasure, and might have had some difficulty in explaining his *locus standi*, if he could have been brought to book, since the Grange had never been a religious house. There was a Priest, who had been stifled in his hiding-hole, contrived in the hall chimney. And there was a Cavalier, who perished in some very unhappy manner. These three stock phantoms hovered about the legend of the Grange; now one troubled the peace of its inhabitants, now another. There was every reason to suppose that all three of them were invented some time in the 'thirties or 'forties of the last century, together with the Mysterious Terror of Glamis Castle, and the *chère reine* of Charing.

Yet, though the Monk and the Priest and the Cavalier were, doubtless, idle and late inventions; there was a certain remnant of strangeness about Morton Grange, which, it seemed, could not be explained as the result of natural and normal causes. Andrew Lang, if I remember, was taken into counsel over the place, and on hearing of some of the alleged abnormal phenomena, was inclined to suggest rats and defective waterpipes. There was also a singular moaning sound, distinct and different from the whine of the wind in the chimneys; and Lang advised a close structural examination of the other parts of the house; it was possible, he thought, that there might be a tunnel or vent in the thickness of the walls, which might catch the wind blowing from a particular quarter.

This surmise, I believe, was justified on examination; such a tunnel was found in the old brewhouse at the back of the Grange. But beyond the moans and whines and sighs, there were other manifestations of a more difficult order. There was a cellar door which persisted in staying open, whatever you did with it. A new lock was affixed, the bolt turned, and the other two keys taken away in the occupant's pocket; but when he came back from London in the evening, the door was wide open. The man, not to be beaten, had another and a very special mechanism, with an alphabetical combination, affixed, but again the door was opened – somehow. Lang confessed that he could not account for this circumstance; and there the matter rested until Professor Warburton took the Grange in hand ten or a dozen years ago.

Warburton was a distinguished man of science, and a strong exponent of the purely materialistic theory of the universe; he was even reckoned by some of his own school as a little old-fashioned in this respect. I am not sure that the particular instance applied in his case; but he was certainly with the older men who held that the stigmata – for example – were lies and impostures and didn't happen, rather than on the side of the younger scientists, who would discuss cases of the stigmata that they had observed in the hospital wards, and show that they had no more spiritual significance than carbuncles.

Somehow, this very valiant and determined man heard of the Morton Grange puzzle, and felt certain that either trickery or a purely mechanical cause was the only agent. He made up his mind to investigate, not without hesitation, since he held that the man of science should hardly partake so far of the evil thing – which he sometimes called Mysticism and sometimes Spiritualism – as to admit that it required investigation. However, in this case, the end seemed to justify the means; and the professor began to make his arrangements. The then occupant of the Grange, who seldom occupied it, made no difficulties; and Professor Warburton chose as assistants three or four friends and acquaintances: Rodney, the biologist, W. K. Forster, a Chancery barrister, Sir Charles Lemon, the throat specialist, and Ian Tallent, who was supposed to have inherited a good share of the Andrew Lang mantle, and had a very ingenious hypothesis as to the firewalking problem.

The night of the inquest was fixed, the caretaker and his wife were warned to get in sufficient fuel and have a fire burning all day in the room nearest to the cellar stairs, and to await the party at eight o'clock, thereafter to betake themselves to the village inn, where a room had been ordered for them. On the morning of the appointed day, Professor Warburton was sitting in his study at his house in Philpot Crescent, Kensington, contemplating the campaign of Morton Grange, when his servant announced a caller. The Professor knew the name, Sir Halliday Stuart, the famous antiquary, very well, though he had never met the man. Sir Halliday was asked to come up, and the two eminent personages met with grave courtesy. After a phrase of apology, the caller came directly to his point.

'I understand,' he said, 'that you are going down this evening to investigate certain phenomena which are alleged to take place at Morton Grange, in Essex. Well, if I may venture, I would put it that you would do me a very great favour, if you would allow me to be of your party. Do you think you could stretch a point?'

Warburton was agreeably impressed by the antiquary. He was of a dark, agreeable presence, and his face lit up with a very engaging smile, as he made his apology and petition.

'We shall all be most pleased, I am sure,' he said, 'and honoured too by your company. But I didn't know that Spiritualism was much in your line.'.

'It's not, not a bit of it,' said Sir Halliday. 'And if you'll forgive me, I've always understood that it was still less in yours.'

The Professor explained.

'You're perfectly right. Thirty years ago I shouldn't have dreamed of having anything to do with such unmitigated nonsense. There were exceptions, of course – there was Crookes – but men of science wouldn't hear of such stuff or of any approach to it. They didn't refute it. They didn't know it was there. And any scientist who was suspected of having any kind of interest in all this mystical humbug would have forfeited the respect of his colleagues.

'But the War had changed everything. It was, no doubt, a very severe national shock. It has had all sorts of bad effects and repercussions; and one of the worst, in my opinion, is this hysterical credulity that one sees everywhere. There's no tale too monstrous to be believed. We're threatened with the return of the most childish superstitions of the Middle Ages. Here's an instance: this tale of a door that can't be kept shut whatever locks you put on it. And there are people of supposed intelligence who are ready to discuss this nonsense seriously! I feel it's my duty to expose the trick, whatever it is. It will be "doing my bit", as the men used to say in the War.'

'I quite understand,' said Sir Halliday, 'and I may as well explain my interest in the matter. I made a study of Morton Grange some years ago and included it in my *Essex Manor Houses and Halls*. There are some extremely interesting features in the building. The vaulting in the cellar is, in my opinion, unquestionably Roman, though Markham won't admit it. I think there is a very strong evidence that the Grange cellar was, originally, a Mithraian temple. I should like to have the opportunity of making a re-examination. And it also occurred to me that my knowledge of the structure of the place might possibly be of some service to you in your investigation.'

Sir Halliday Stuart was cordially included in the party of ghost-hunters. He refused with thanks the offer of a seat in Warburton's car: he was going down earlier, he explained, as he wished to have another look at the very singular squint in the Grange brewhouse: an undoubted thirteenth-century building, he explained, the original lancets having been replaced by square headed windows of 1530–40.

'And for this I shall want daylight. So you will find me at the Grange when you arrive. It is extremely kind of you to let me join your party.'

Warburton was pleased with this addition to his committee of investigation. There was a genial gravity about the antiquary that won favour; and he was evidently a man of an accurate habit of mind, accustomed to careful observation, a minute weighing of evidence, the very man for the occasion. The Professor told the others about the inclusion of Stuart, when they all met at his house in the late afternoon, and they agreed he would be valuable. They all knew him by reputation, and Tallent had read his revised edition of *Isca Silurum* with very great interest. When the cars drew up before the door of Morton Grange that evening, Stuart was waiting on the steps. He was mildly excited.

'I've examined that squint very minutely,' he said to Warburton. 'I have Markham at my mercy.'

The introductions were made, and the party entered the house. Warburton had brought down flasks of strong coffee, and the caretaker, having set cups and saucers on the table, departed with his wife. Warburton locked the front door, the back door, and the door communicating with the brewhouse, and put the keys in his pocket. A systematic tour and search of the mouldering and desolate house was made. The cellar came last in the inspection, and Professor Warburton pointed out the bolts he had added to the alphabet lock.

'One top, one bottom,' he said. 'The best steel, fitted under my supervision.'

The door stood open; a powerful lamp was fixed above it, and another on the other side, within the cellar. Sir Halliday Stuart went in eagerly, and peered about him.

'Look at the entablatures,' he said. 'There's no room for doubt.'

Warburton called him out, adjusted the lock, and shot the bolts. The party went up the steps of the winding stair, and sat down to their hot coffee, while Warburton explained his plan.

'One of us,' he said, 'is to be on guard at the bottom of the cellar stair, by the door, the whole evening from eight to twelve-fifteen. The watch will be for an hour; I will take the first watch, and Rodney will relieve me at nine. The door at the top of the stairs will be open, and the door of this room will be open. The instruction to the man on guard is: to call out at the top of his voice if he sees or hears anything in the least out of the way. That is understood? Very good. It is now half-past seven; perhaps Sir Halliday will tell us something about the history of Morton Grange while we are drinking our coffee?'

Sir Halliday cordially assented, and proceeded to deliver a bristling lecture. He merely touched on the evidences for stone and bronze age occupation, was diffused and elaborate on the Roman period; thinning again with the Saxon invasion; but becoming merciless from Doomsday Book to the end of the seventeenth century. Strange terms and allusions were heard; *inquisitis post mortem*, Fine and Recovery, *diem clausit extremum*, *mortuus sine prole*, Pipe Rolls, vert, a *chevron or*. Some of these terms awoke memories in Forster, the barrister; to the rest they were as the hooting of owls. The Monk, the Priest, and the Cavalier were mentioned only to be puffed away like thistledown.

'So you see,' said the antiquary, 'the place has a very ordinary history; the typical history, in fact, of the East Anglian manor house. So far as I know, apart from certain remarkable features in construction, which I have explained to you as well as I can, the only point of interest I can recall in the history of the Grange is the discovery, a few years ago, of a hiding place in the chimney of the great hall, used from 1690 onwards as a brewhouse. A workman employed in putting right some loose bricks, found a small oak chest in a place contrived in the thickness of the chimney. The contents were legal documents, of the late sixteenth and early seventeenth centuries, relating to the passing of the manor and estate from the Mullins Moleyno family to the Roches.'

At eight o'clock, punctually, the watch was set, Warburton went down, impressing on the others that they were to join him at top speed if he called out. The two doors, the sitting room door, and the door at the top of the stairs, were left open as arranged. The party in the room broached another flask of coffee, smoked a little, and talked a little in low tones. Some of them thought they were making fools of themselves, and were sorry they had come.

The hours went by without event. The antiquary, having delivered his lecture, seemed to sink into a gentle abstraction, from which he roused himself now and again to make remarks which seemed to be dictated by a sense of conversational duty, rather than by interest in the (possible) ghost. He pulled out his watch, looked at it and observed with bland satisfaction, 'We are keeping good time, I think.' Warburton, who had just come up from his turn at the door, assured him that the timetable was being strictly adhered to. Sir Halliday nodded, and again became quiescent.

Nothing happened. Rodney had crept like a snail down the stairs on hearing Warburton's summons. The barrister, Forster, succeeded the biologist. Sir Halliday, brightening once more, said it was a calm night, at all events, 'and that's in our favour'. People were puzzled for a moment, and then concluded that he meant that their observations were not to be confused by the noises of high wind and restless trees. Sir Charles Lemon took up his position at the bottom of the stairs at eleven. The low-voiced conversation flagged. Most of the men looked tired and bored to the extreme. Sir Halliday's head shook and nodded, not with sleep, but rather as if he were following a train of reasoning, an argument with an imaginary opponent, dissenting and agreeing by turns. Finally, as Lemon's watch drew on and midnight was at hand, the antiquary, feeling, perhaps, that he had cultivated silence at the expense of courtesy, remarked in a very amiable manner:

'Well, I suppose Dover *is* rather a hole. But I must say I've always liked it; Strond Street and the old harbour; all that part, you know.'

The company in general, who were longing to make an end of a tiresome and futile sitting, as they considered it, looked up crossly, and wondered what on earth Stuart thought he was talking about. Tallent chuckled quietly; the key word of Sir Halliday's sentence, and its lack of precise relevance to the business in hand, had reminded him of a certain immortal axiom relating to milestones on the Dover Road, but he speculated also as to whether Sir Halliday's intellect was quite the keen instrument of their belief.

It was on the first stroke of twelve that at last something happened. Lemon, who had by this time quite made up his mind that he had wasted the evening, was just calling on Ian Tallent to take his place, when the summons changed to a dismal sound, something inarticulate, between a croak and a cry. The whole company in the sitting room jumped up and pelted out of the door, and jammed in the narrow stair. Sir Charles, gasping, with a grey-white face, was hauled up, on the verge of a fainting fit, to the higher region. Brandy was administered, and he was soon able to say, rather tartly, that beyond damned foul air, he had nothing to report. They were all yawning and looking at their watches and agreeing that there was nothing to be done but to go home, when Warburton, glancing from one to another, said with a jerk:

'Where's Stuart?'

And, in a second or two, it was evident that he had asked a question that nobody could answer. Sir Halliday Stuart was not there, nowhere in the room at all. They bustled into the passage, went again, not quite so madly, down the stair to the cellar; presently explored every room in the house with the aid of electric torches, returned, looking helpless, to the room where they had held their session. They had not found a trace of the antiquary. And Warburton, who had the keys of every exit in his pocket, knew perfectly well that he must be in the house – somewhere. Then a notion struck him.

'Will you all stay in this room?' he said. 'I should think it would be as well if you sat down. It has just struck me as possible that Sir Halliday is in the cellar, examining those accursed entablatures of his. I can't think how he can have got there, if he is there, without knowing the lock combination – but perhaps there is some trickery about that door which circumstances have prevented us from detecting so far. At any rate, I am going to make sure that Sir Halliday has not been caught in some sort of trap. May I ask you again to keep your positions exactly as you are at present?'

Warburton was absent for seven or eight minutes. His face was blank when he returned.

'I've been over every inch of the cellar,' he said. 'There's no one there. I've put out the lights and refastened the door. We mustn't leave a bolt hole. Not that I would suggest for a moment that Stuart could or would desire to bolt; of course that's absurd. Still . . . what on earth can have become of the man? I was standing just behind him when the doctor gave the alarm, and we all ran down. Did anybody else notice him, then or afterwards?'

Nobody had. They were all staring at Sir Charles Lemon. They saw nothing else during the critical moments.

'There is nothing to be done,' concluded Professor Warburton after some minutes of perplexed meditation, 'but to make a thorough and systematic search of the whole house. Perhaps we were a little haphazard before. I will take Forster with me, and we will go over every room in the house.'

The two went off with their torches. They were away for half an hour. They had failed to discover Sir Halliday, or any trace or hint of his presence. It was evident that there was nothing more to be done. Tallent put the position of affairs to himself that Sir Halliday was both in the Grange and not in the Grange at the same time; he remembered having seen something of the kind in Eastern philosophy. But he kept the contradiction to himself, not thinking it suitable for the company. He substituted the sagacious and commonsensical remark:

'A difficult thing to be sure you've gone into every nook and cupboard of an old place like this. A little chap of Stuart's build could pack himself away in a very small space.'

'Little chap?' said Forster. 'I should have said that Sir Halliday was above the average height.'

Finally, they all returned to town in a condition of stupefied bewilderment.

The first thing, the next morning, Professor Warburton found out Sir Halliday Stuart's address. He had a place in Oxfordshire, it appeared, but when in town he occupied a suite of rooms in service chambers near St James's. Warburton went there at once and saw the management. Sir Halliday had been in residence for five or six weeks, the manager told him.

'Yesterday morning, soon after twelve, he came round to the offices and handed in his key. He said he might be away for some little time. I was not at all surprised; there was nothing unusual in the proceeding. Sir Halliday often went away without giving us notice in advance. He would be out of town for a week, a month, even three months. Sometimes he would send a postcard announcing his return; but as a rule he merely walked in and asked for his key.'

'And there is no address to which I could write?'

'You might try Sir Halliday Stuart's Oxfordshire address. I can give you that: "Campden House, High Street" – the name of the village, I understand – "Oxfordshire". It is possible that Sir Halliday is there.'

The professor went home and wrote two letters. One to Sir Halliday, politely begging to be reassured as to his safety, asking no questions, going into no detail. This letter he put into a small envelope, which was enclosed in a large envelope, addressed 'Occupant', with a letter begging for Sir Halliday's present address. The large envelope, marked 'Urgent Immediate', was despatched by registered post. There was an answer by return. M. Timpson begged to say that Sir Halliday Stuart was at present residing in his London chambers, the address of which was enclosed.

Meanwhile, Professor Warburton had taken counsel with the friends who had been with him in the strange adventure of Morton Grange. They had all agreed together that it would be well to keep the whole affair in strict secrecy. It was clear, they decided, that in some way or another, Sir Halliday Stuart had contrived to get out of the house in the midst of the confusion over Lemon's collapse. Nobody could suggest how he made his exit or why he made it; but it was evident that he *had* made it. One of them, given on the quiet to the reading of very old-fashioned fiction, babbled of sliding panels and secret passages. But Warburton, who had reluctantly thought of this, had paid another visit to the Grange, going there in broad daylight, and taking with him an expert with a foot rule, who tapped and measured and surveyed within and without, and gave it as his technical and considered opinion that in this case, at all events, the notion of sliding panels, hidden doors, and secret passages was bunkum. There was nothing to be said; they all felt that they had come to a blank and intolerable wall. And if, by some unconjectured way and dark passage, Sir Halliday had got out of Morton Grange, where was he?

No doubt they all tried their best to keep the secret, but Sir Halliday, it seemed, had an aunt, very old and energetic, and this lady, hearing that her nephew was not to be found, went to the police, and the constables of Essex called in Scotland Yard, which was interested by the peculiar circumstances of the disappearance.

Now, there is nothing illegal about disappearing. Hundreds, or dozens at any rate, of people disappear every year, and nobody bothers about them. Night by night, 'Time, Weather, and News', on the wireless is prefaced by one, two or three S O S's: 'S O S Lawkins. Will Thomas Lawkins, last heard of about five years ago in Dulverton, go to Hampstead Heath Hospital, Hampstead, London, where his father Albert Lawkins, is dangerously ill.' Clearly, Thomas Lawkins disappeared five years ago or more, and did so in perfect peace. A few years since, a man was found murdered in a car on the highway; and even the violent notoriety of his death did not suffice to identify him; he also must have disappeared, leaving neither trace nor enquiry behind him. But, presumably, Lawkins and the murdered man and men like them have been undistinguished and obscure people, who for one reason or another have shed relations and connections, and have left no great curiosity as to their whereabouts behind them. But Sir Halliday Stuart was none such: he was highly distinguished, a figure in his own world, a man of many friends and colleagues. Moreover, there were the peculiar circumstances, and other people, also well-known, were, one must not say involved, but at any rate present on the occasion when Sir Halliday, as it appeared, was last seen by his fellow men. Ten days after this event, Professor Warburton received a call from a high official of Scotland Yard, purely in search of exact information. The Professor gave it, told the whole story, gave the name of the men who were associated with him in the affair, and at the end said very frankly:

'And I should be very much obliged to you, sir, if you would tell me what has happened to Sir Halliday Stuart.'

The Scotland Yard man said that that was a question which could not be answered offhand. Enquiries of the most searching nature would be made: there must be a flaw somewhere, a weak spot, in the statement he had just heard, and, no doubt, a trained man would be able to put his finger on it – in time. They would send their own experts to make a special examination of Morton Grange; they might find something.

'Here's a possibility, now, that has just occurred to me. It's not uncommon to come across old, disused wells in such houses as Morton Grange. They are sometimes in the most unexpected places; at the end of dark passages, in a corner at the bottom of a staircase: you never know where to look for them. And the covering, the trap at the top, has sometimes gone rotten. The solution may lie in that direction; though I sincerely hope it doesn't. And in the meantime, would you give me the addresses of your friends who were engaged with you in this business? They may give us some help; you never know. And would you let me have the best description you can manage of Sir Halliday Stuart's personal appearance? Height, fair or dark, colour of hair and eyes, fat or thin, any peculiarities, facial or otherwise; scars; you know the sort of thing?'

The four men were run down at once; they were all Londoners. Each had been asked to give the best description he could of the missing man, together with his account of what had happened, as each had observed the events of that singular night. By the evening, the shorthand notes had been transcribed, and were laid before the personage at the Yard.

'Now, look here,' he said to his lieutenant. 'This is going to be a very complicated business. For the moment we won't bother about the accounts of the proceedings at this dam' silly business of theirs. I've run through them and compared them with what I got from Professor Warburton this morning, and as far as I can make out they all agree as to the main facts. There are no important discrepancies, anyhow. It's these descriptions of Sir Halliday's personal appearance that are bothering me. Here, you see, is the stuff we got from two of his most intimate friends: Dr Manning, of Brasenose, and Lord John Ashley of Queen's Row. You see they agree practically in every particular: height, about 5 ft. 7 ins; hair, dark brown, thinning; eyes, grey; – Lord John Ashley says blue – nose aquiline; short upper lip – Manning doesn't mention that – thin; white scar on forefinger of right hand; chestnut eyebrows; and so forth and so forth. As I say, the two descriptions agree.'

'By the way,' said the lieutenant, 'no photographs?'

'He hasn't been photographed for twenty years. There's a sketch in black and white, but I don't think it's going to be of much use. But here's the important point. Look at these descriptions of Sir Halliday by Professor Warburton and his four friends: you see, they don't agree. One man says short, another tall; the professor says hair black; Forster, light brown. They're all at odds. Yet by their own account they were sitting with Sir Halliday and talking to him for four hours on end. What do you make of it?'

The other man studied the documents carefully.

'It's a pity,' he said, 'that detective fiction is so seldom of much use to detectives. You remember, "The Murders in the Rue Morgue", the witnesses differing about the language which they had heard the unseen murderer speaking? The Frenchman thought it was English – he didn't know any English. The overwrought Dutchman held it to be Russian; the Englishman, who was ignorant of French, was sure it was French. The deduction to be drawn was that the murderer wasn't speaking any language at all; that he was an ape, and merely gibbering. But I don't see how we can apply Poe's invention to our difficulty.'

'No, I don't think we can,' said the chief with some dryness and a touch of impatience.

'Unless,' said the lieutenant, 'we argue that there was nobody there –

no Sir Charles Halliday, I mean. That seems the legitimate conclusion; and, obviously, it won't do.'

Then the chief said that it was a serious business and they must go about it seriously. He had put a man who knew his job into the Grange, and had told him to go over every inch of it. And if he wanted to do any digging outside, he was to telephone for help.

'You don't think so?'

'No, I don't; but it may perhaps be as well to make sure.'

The problem remained the secret of Scotland Yard, and of a circle that was moderately small, considering all things. It was kept out of the Press; and the enquiries went on without result for a month, less three or four days, when a solution was given in a very singular manner. The scene returns to Professor Warburton's study. The Professor is discovered at his bureau, trying hard to occupy himself with his proper business, but wondering at intervals when he would be arrested for the murder of Sir Halliday Stuart. That was what he told his friends later, as a matter of fact he was not beset at all by any such nonsensical fears; but he was still intensely puzzled by the antiquary's disappearance, and intensely curious to know what had really happened. And while he was in this state of mind, his man brought in a card. Warburton took it impatiently; he didn't want to be bothered by anybody. He read: Sir Halliday Stuart.

He stared at the servant with an expression that the man found dreadful in its sheer amazement. He gave the necessary order with difficulty, and got up from his chair and stood waiting, in such surprise and confusion of mind as made him realise for the first time that he had never thought to see Sir Halliday again amongst living men.

The door opened, and the servant announced the visitor. A middle-aged, baldish man with a beaky nose entered the room, and, smiling, confronted the bewildered Professor.

'I gather that you wish to see me, Professor Warburton,' he began. 'When I got back to High Street yesterday, my housekeeper handed me this envelope, with the enclosure addressed to me. You ask' – he took out his glasses – 'to be reassured as to my safety. I hope you will excuse me: but I assure you that I haven't the remotest notion of what you mean.'

Warburton feebly motioned the visitor to a chair, and sat down himself, so far incapable of coherent speech.

'You see,' Sir Halliday went on, 'I don't think I've had the pleasure of meeting you till the present moment, and I, naturally, feel a little puzzled. Is it possible that there has been some mistake, some confusion possibly on the part of your secretary? Were you by any chance mixing me up with Mackinlay Stuart, the Science Don? You know him, no doubt?'

Warburton felt that he was sinking into yet deeper and dimmer depths of confusion. 'Not had the pleasure of meeting you till the present moment,' he quoted helplessly to himself, and though not deeply versed in Holy Writ, he thought of somebody who could have roared for the very disquietness of his heart. He gaped at the man sitting before him, amazed at his barefaced denial of their former encounter, and of the hours they had spent together at the Grange. 'Is it possible,' he asked himself, 'that he doesn't recognise me as I recognise him?'

He scrutinised Sir Halliday's features more intently, and then realised, astonished, that the Sir Halliday of a month ago compared with the Sir Halliday now in presence, was rather like an old, yellowed, and blurred photograph in an ancient album, put beside a clean, recent likeness; or, one might say, a first sketch contrasted with the finished drawing. One saw the resemblance, of course, but the Sir Halliday of the Grange had been, as it were, faint.

But how did that help? Not in the least. It rather added confusion to a business that was already utterly confounded. But after a long silence, Warburton struggled from his morass of dazed perplexity and climbed his way into speech. On the whole, he did not do badly; he told Sir Halliday the story of his morning call and evening's occupation, finishing with his mysterious disappearance from Morton Grange.

'And at the present moment,' he ended, 'Scotland Yard are looking for you. Unless, of course, they have heard of your return.'

And it was hard to say which of the two were the more astounded. Warburton, by telling it, had revived all his first amazement when Sir Halliday could not be found. Sir Halliday could not control himself as he heard an account of his movements on a particular day in October which he knew to be at total variance with the facts. He looked hard at Warburton. There is always a certain way of escape open, when a man is confronted with an incredible and intolerable statement. That is, to hold the person who makes the statement to be a liar. And, undoubtedly, this is often the right solution of such problems. But the antiquary, scanning the visage of the man of exact science, measuring the manner of his utterance, felt that, in this case, mere lying was not the required answer to the riddle. And, besides . . .

'There were four men with you, you said. Who were they?'

Professor Warburton gave the names.

'They're responsible men,' he said. 'All of them of a certain distinction.'

'And they all share your impressions of what happened that night?'

'Absolutely. We are all agreed; I think I may say in every detail.'

He suppressed the fact that there had been some discussion and divergence in the party as to Sir Halliday's build and appearance; firstly, because it seemed personal, and then, because he thought very few men were capable of exact observation and subsequent description, and lastly, because he was still puzzled by the difference he had just observed between the look and show of Sir Halliday on his former and his latter visits, and didn't know what to say or think about it.

Sir Halliday pondered. He knew the names of the people who had been associated with Warburton, and, as the professor had observed, they were responsible men. None of them was at all likely to conspire in the concoction of an aimless and preposterous fiction. To believe that would be simply to substitute one incredible story for another. He would take it, then, that the whole five of them supposed that they were telling the truth. He broke his silence.

'I really don't know what to say. The absolute antinomy between your statement and what I know to be the facts as to my doings on the day in question is quite overwhelming. But I'll tell you what really happened, so far as I am concerned, and I hope you'll forgive the small quantity of shop I may have to introduce.

'Well, then. You may be aware that a few years ago there was a good deal of discussion in the press as to certain discoveries in Central France of objects in baked clay which were said to belong to a very remote period. There were considerable names in favour of their antiquity. However, in the long run, evidence of a destructive character was produced, and in spite of a very spirited defence, the verdict was that the supposed prehistoric pottery was nothing more or less than a modern forgery. Naturally, therefore, we were inclined to treat reports of similar finds with a good deal of distrust, and it was some time before I paid any attention to accounts of discoveries of very early pottery at a place near Loches, in the department of Indre-et-Loire. However, on the morning of October 13th last – your date, I think, Professor

– there was an article in *The Times*, which seemed to leave no room for suspicion. I felt I must see for myself: the occurrence of the maze of labyrinth pattern on Neolithic objects struck me as of very great significance and importance.

'I left my chambers late in the morning, took a long walk out into the country, dined in some strange place in Soho, and left London by the night service. I got to Paris the next morning, caught the *Rapide* to Tours, and stayed the night at Loches. Next day, I walked through the forest to the village of Genille, and through the courtesy of M. Pic-Paris, the distinguished French antiquary, whom I had met before, I was able to make a thorough examination of the objects discovered in the rock caves, a short distance from the village. In this case, I may say, I am convinced of the entire genuineness of the find – but that doesn't concern our present purpose. After a week of very close study and of conferences with M. Pic-Paris and other French colleagues, I went on to Tours; a most agreeable city. I left Tours for England a couple of days ago. I should be glad to show you my hotel bills.'

There was a pause. Very evidently and certainly Professor Warburton considered within himself, the man was telling the truth. Then Sir Halliday began talking again, with a sudden plunge.

'But here's a very odd thing, which has just struck me. It is the case that some years ago Morton Grange engaged a good deal of my attention. I made a special study of it for a book of mine, called *Essex Manor Houses and Halls*.'

Warburton interrupted, 'You told me that before – the last time you were here.'

Sir Halliday choked down an inarticulate noise in his throat.

'And you were a good deal interested in something you called a squint in the brewhouse at the Grange. Also in the vaulting of the cellar. You said, I think, that you were convinced that the cellar had been originally a temple of Mithras.'

The effect of this utterance on the two men was tremendous. It was the great name of Mithras that produced this effect. Sir Halliday had been shaken by Warburton's, 'You told me that before.' He took his host for a truthful man; his familiarity with the *Essex Manor Houses* title was, therefore, not a feigned one. And it might be taken as certain that this physiologist, or physicist, or whatever he was, had never so much as seen the publication in question – a subscription book issued to the members of a learned society – and yet he talked of the cellar vaulting and the brewhouse squint. But the matter of Mithras! That was a secret, held in reserve, not breathed to his nearest associates. The evidence for the Mithraic origin and use of that Morton Grange cellar, drawn from many sources and accumulating for years, was almost ready to be welded into a demonstration. Other affairs had pressed on Stuart, and he had not been able to bring this matter to an absolute conclusion; he had been waiting for time and opportunity to make one more visit to the Grange, to satisfy himself by a final and meticulous examination of certain details that his theory was well-founded and assured. And here was this man speaking as easily of the great secret of Mithras as of cucumbers in June. He was astounded and confounded: and he looked it.

And Warburton on his side marked the effect he had produced. He did not altogether understand the full force of his own words, but he noted the shock, and interpreted it in his own manner. He thought that the antiquary must be one of those unfortunate people who suffer from lapses of memory; that he had honestly forgotten his call of a month ago, and his subsequent visit to the Grange; and that the mention of his researches and theories had suddenly recalled the lost memories. The next thing would be that he would explain how he got away, unobserved, from the Grange; very likely it would turn out to be quite simple. Very possibly, he had really been to France on the business he had specified; he had merely antedated his journey by a day. Warburton was going to hint, very gently, something of all this to Sir Halliday, but his guest forestalled him.

'You will excuse me, I am sure,' he said, 'but I think I had better leave you. I do not think that we can do any good by discussing this subject further. I do not know how you feel, but to me it is intolerable. Something very awful must have happened. I do not dare to think what it can have been. I am afraid – I am afraid that I must be on the other side of death.'

He stumbled out of the room. Warburton, going to the window, saw the unfortunate man swaying and staggering like a drunkard, as he picked his blind way along the pavement.

The Professor went down thoughtfully to his lunch. He felt sure that he had been right in his theory. Loss of memory; or perhaps it might be a case of double personality. He had heard, somewhat doubtfully, of such cases. It had struck him as rather fanciful, but men of good scientific repute were said to have been convinced, and to have undoubted evidence in favour of the doctrine. Well, one or the other, at all events he was afraid that Sir Halliday had been very much upset.

Warburton, on the other hand, was immensely relieved by the solution he had propounded to himself. He was an extremely worthy man, but a materialist and a rationalist to the core; the determined and unrelenting foe of all mysteries. If you had told him that a man of sense passes his whole life in wondering awe and amazement before the mysteries which perpetually confront him, he would have thought you either a madman, or else an intolerable and pretentious humbug. He dismissed the whole affair from his mind, and lived in extreme comfort for the remainder of his days.

It was Ian Tallent who provided an hypothesis, extravagant and improbable in the highest degree, no doubt, and yet the only tolerable solution of a most difficult problem. He conferred with Professor Warburton, and had the story of his conferences with Sir Halliday out of him, noting his point of view, the loss of memory or if you like – double personality – theory, and leaving him to enjoy it. He had more trouble with Sir Halliday Stuart, who had gone down to his retreat in Oxfordshire in sorry condition, and was making a slow recovery there, restoring himself to a normal state by degrees as he found that the common processes of life still continued in their usual order. At first, Sir Halliday refused Tallent's petitions for an audience with the driest negative; he said that he wished to dismiss 'the wretched business' entirely from his thoughts. But Tallent persisted. He had got from Warburton an account of the shattered condition in which Sir Halliday had left him; but, naturally, Warburton had given his own reasons, as he had conceived them, for the shock which the antiquary had very evidently received.

'You see,' Warburton had explained, 'my reference to the conversation we had had together on his former visit brought the whole thing back to him. It made him aware that for a whole month there had been a lapse in his personality; the transactions of a day and a night had been blotted out as if they had never existed. He was prepared to deny, as he did deny, that he had ever seen me before, that he had visited Morton Grange in our company, and had somehow or other succeeded in avoiding our observation and getting away from the place. And it was then, in my opinion, that the break in consciousness occurred. He got home to his chambers, I don't pretend to say how, in a dazed, confused state, went to bed, and woke up next morning – with the whole of the previous day missing from his memory. And it was no doubt a very startling and a very painful shock when he realised from my remarks the true state of the case.'

Tallent heard all this and seemed to accept Warburton's theory. Indeed, it might be true; but he did not think so. He had a dim glimmering in his mind of possibilities far stranger than this; but he felt that he must talk to the antiquary, with whom the secret must rest. He saw that Warburton, pleased with his solution of the problem, was willing to treat the manner in which Sir Halliday had withdrawn himself inexplicably from their midst as an affair of secondary importance. But to Tallent, this appeared of vital moment: he could not let it go by as a trifle. And if it had happened as he began to dream it might have happened: then, by all means he must see Sir Halliday. But he let him rest a little, and gather his broken forces together, and refit. Then, in a couple of weeks, he wrote again, urging a meeting which might do a great deal, he said, to clear up a very obscure business.

After a few days, he got a letter of reluctant consent, and Tallent went down to High Street, and found Sir Halliday obviously in much better condition than that described by Warburton. And Warburton, it should be said, had not mentioned the odd impression he had received on the antiquary's last visit; the feeling that his visitor's aspect was more fully defined, more sharply 'bitten in' than before. This circumstance had become negligible; indeed it was dismissed as a passing fancy – since it did not minister to the master theory of the loss of memory and the consequent annihilation of a day. But Tallent in his turn was impressed in much the same fashion. Sir Halliday looked worn and anxious; but he was distinct and present, as he had not been at the Grange. As Tallent put it to himself: a faint mist seemed to have cleared away from before him.

There was something of a nervous air in Sir Halliday's welcome; a suggestion of disquiet and almost of fear, as if he dreaded a renewal of the very painful and terrifying sensations that had sent him trembling from Warburton's presence a few weeks before. Tallent moved tactfully; he had come prepared to avoid any rough-and-ready handling of this very delicate and difficult case. He made no secret of his interest in the affair, he admitted that there were extraordinary complications and obstacles in the way of a clear issue.

'But before we go down into the deep waters,' he added, 'there are one or two trifling matters that I believe you would be able to clear up without any trouble. I don't know that they're of much consequence; still, it's as well to start fair. Now, Warburton tells me that on the night of October 13th you went to Paris?'

'I most certainly did,' said Sir Halliday, with the strongest emphasis.

'By what route? Dover–Calais?'

'By Dover–Calais. I'm an extremely bad sailor, and I always shorten my discomfort as much as possible. Luckily, it was a calm night. I remember remarking on that fact with considerable satisfaction to a fellow traveller.'

Tallent all but smacked his lips. He remembered the sentence: 'It's a calm night, at all events; and that's in our favour.'

'Well,' he said, 'you're meeting me halfway. All these little impressions and recollections of the journey down to Dover: that's exactly what I want you to tell me, if you will. They're trifles, no doubt, but we may possibly find a use for them. Go ahead, sir.'

'Really, there's very little to tell: London – Dover isn't generally very eventful. There were two other people in the carriage with me; a middle-aged man and a youngish man. For a good part of the way, I was reading some papers that I had brought with me. And that does remind me of something: I found myself distracted to a certain extent in my reading – somewhat technical matter, I may say – by what struck me as a hum of low-voiced conversation. An odd effect; as if one were listening at one end of a large room to three or four men talking quietly together at the other end. I could just distinguish, as I thought, one man speaking and then another; but I couldn't make out a word they were saying. It quite worried me at last. So far as I've observed, I don't think one hears one's neighbours in the next compartment talking; but I supposed that that was where the sound came from. So, at last I got up from my place and strolled up and down the corridor for a few minutes; and the queer thing was that one of the compartments next to us was empty, and in the other there were two men fast asleep. So I went back to my place and shut the door after me. I took up my papers again, but the hum of talk went on, and it bothered me so much that I gave up the attempt, and began to talk myself to the young man opposite me – the youngish fellow.'

Tallent heard Sir Halliday intently.

'And where were these people talking, do you think?' he asked.

'I haven't a notion. I know nothing whatever about acoustics, and I may be talking great nonsense; but I wondered whether by any possibility the sound may have been somehow transmitted from a remote carriage to my own. Sound does play very odd tricks sometimes.'

'Whispering galleries? Echoes? That kind of thing, you mean? Well, I don't know. But . . . did you distinguish one voice from another? Do you think you could recognise them if you heard them again?'

'I don't know about that,' said Sir Halliday, doubtfully. 'But, as you ask me, I must say that your own voice reminds me a good deal of one of these unseen conversationalists. One of them spoke on a slightly higher pitch than the others; and really, the tone was very like yours.'

'That's odd, indeed. So you gave up trying to read, and began talking to one of the men in the carriage. Just about the weather and the news, I suppose; things in general?'

'That sort of thing. Then, if I remember, he propounded his solution for the unemployment problem; he would provide work for the workless by pulling down all the old buildings in the country and running up new ones, constructed on purely functional lines, and adapted to the needs of the age. As you may imagine, I don't often hear that sort of talk at the Antiquaries, and I was a good deal amused. I tried to argue with him. I asked him if he didn't take a certain pleasure in looking at an old church or an old house.

' "No more pleasure than you would take," he replied, "if you were speeding and saw a heap of old stones and rubbish in the middle of the road, right in front of your car. Old churches, old houses, old castles; they're obstructive rubbish, nothing more or less."

'Well, he went on at a great rate in this style, and I put in an objection now and again, without any effect, I must confess. We were getting near Dover by this time, and the young iconoclast began to abuse that harmless old place; he said it was a hole. I stuck up for it, and told him that I liked Dover, especially Strond Street and the old harbour.'

Tallent remembered this utterance very well.

'And that's all, I suppose. You got out of the train and got on board the boat – and I hope you had a good crossing?'

'Perfectly calm, I am glad to say. But, since you mention it, getting on board was not quite so quiet a business as usual. There seemed a good deal of pushing and excitement; I am sure I don't know what about. There was plenty of time, of course; but people positively plunged down the gangway; it was almost an ugly rush. But I am afraid I have bored you terribly with all these trivial details. Still, I warned you that you can hardly expect very exciting adventures on the Dover boat-train.'

Then the wild hypothesis stood fully confirmed; so Tallent murmured in his mind. 'And now,' he said to himself, 'for the deep waters.' He had not only obtained matter of extraordinary value and significance from Sir Halliday's recital of his traveller's trivialities – as he thought them – but the simple story of the Dover boat-train had been soothing to the teller of it. Tallent put his question:

'Professor Warburton,' he began, 'gave me to understand that you seemed a good deal put out when you left him, after your talk together a few weeks ago. Now, we want to clear things up; and I feel quite sure that it would help very much if you would tell me the exact reason of the distress which I am afraid you experienced.'

Sir Halliday Stuart rose from his chair and began to pace slowly up and down the room, evidently in deep and perplexed consideration. At the end of a few minutes, he stopped and faced Tallent.

'I think you are right. Apart from any question of clearing or elucidating a most perplexing business, which I am sure is most desirable, I feel that I shall be the better for plain talk. At the moment, I certainly received a hideous shock.'

Tallent perceived that the hour of the forceps had come.

'Tell me exactly what it was.'

'It was this. I knew and I know exactly how I had spent that particular day. I knew and I know how every hour of it had been occupied. I knew and I know that I had never set eyes on Professor Warburton before the visit I paid him a few weeks ago. But . . . from certain things that he said, I also knew and know that I had seen him before and told him my most reserved secrets.'

He sat down, and covered his face with his hands, bowing his head. Then Tallent said:

'Do you know that your casual remark about your liking for Dover was heard that night in a room in Morton Grange, where Warburton and the rest of us were sitting? And do you know that you, to all appearance, were sitting also in that room, and that we saw you as you spoke? So it was.'

He was met by a blank stare; uncomprehending, utterly incredulous.

'That is quite impossible,' said Sir Halliday, quietly and finally.

'There are very few things that are impossible,' Tallent replied. 'In pure mathematics, perhaps, there may be; though I believe that of late even these eternal canons – as we used to think them – have begun to admit of doubts and uncertainties. Still, I hope we shall not be required to admit the possibility of three-sided squares and two-sided triangles. But, once outside these regions, can we dare to talk of impossibility at all? We can use the word, of course, and I have no doubt that we shall continue to use it; but I think we shall all have to recognise the fact that when we say any event is impossible, we merely mean that we've never heard of such a thing before, and that we don't begin to understand how it can happen so. That is very well, and very applicable to your own case, for I don't think I have ever heard of anything quite on all fours with the extraordinary manifestation in which you were concerned. And I certainly don't begin to understand how it could happen so.

'But, look here; I've just remembered something. I mentioned mathematics just now: I take it you believe there are such things as lines, don't you? Well, have you ever seen one? If so, I should be interested to hear how *that* happened; how length without breadth became visible to the human eye. If you think it over, I believe you will recognise that there are more evident impossibilities lurking in this elementary axiom of geometry than in your own – adventure, shall we call it?'

Sir Halliday was dazed and amazed, and yet attentive. Tallent thought he could hold him, and went on:

'As I said, I think that there are circumstances in your case that are unique; but in the main outlines it falls under a well-ascertained category. There have been many instances of what used to be called Doubles, but are now generally known as Apparitions of Phantasms of the Living. In its early years, the Society for Psychical Research published a thick volume of such cases, all carefully examined and well attested. If I remember, a number of these appearances were of people at the point of death, and the large majority of them were, so far as can be seen, purposeless.

'I remember one case, which might be called typical. A Berkshire farmer, coming down to breakfast one morning, sees on the stairs a Buckinghamshire miller, a market acquaintance, no more, coming up to meet him. The farmer is astonished to see him; and as he stares, the miller is not there. The miller, it was found, was dying at the time, but nobody could guess why he had projected this image of himself into the consciousness of a man with whom he had been barely on nodding terms.'

'But, you see,' broke in Sir Halliday, 'I wasn't dying, or anything like it. I was perfectly well at the time, and that must be seven weeks ago.'

'Quite so, but these appearances are by no means invariably the images of the moribund. Indeed, I think that the most remarkable case I know of is a man who was perfectly well and at ease when he became apparent – can we say? – where he was not. This is not one of the Psychical Researchers' cases, it is recorded by Charles Dickens. I have it in my notebook, and here it is –

'"I once saw the apparition of my father at this hour (the early morning). He was alive and well, and nothing ever came of it, but I saw him in the daylight, sitting with his back towards me, on a seat that stood beside my bed. His head was resting on his hand, and whether he was slumbering or grieving, I could not discern. Amazed to see him there, I sat up, moved my position, leaned out of bed, and watched him. As he did not move, I spoke to him more than once. As he did not move then, I became alarmed and laid my hand upon his shoulder – as I thought – and there was no such thing."

'You see? There you have the apparently purposeless projection of the image of a man in good health. And I think I may say that in the Psychical Research records, there is hardly a single case – if there is such a case – where the apparition was anything but purposeless. To quote a passage from one of the publications of the S.P.R.: "One has to admit a total absence of any apparent aim or of any intelligent action on the part of phantoms." We may venture, then, to say that this is the rule: that the apparition or projection of the image is not (in our modern jargon) a "wish-fulfilment" on the part of the projector. The miller did not want to see the farmer; old Mr Dickens did not want to see his son.

'Here is where your case parts company from all the others on record. We know that you had made a special study of Morton Grange, and I gathered from Warburton that for some time you had wished to revisit the place, to make a further examination of certain details of importance. That is so, isn't it?'

'Yes, that is quite true. There were points on which I wished to satisfy myself by a second inspection, before finishing some work I had in hand.'

'Exactly; and there, I believe, we have the distinction between your particular case and all the others that we have been considering. You say you had a fixed purpose to revisit Morton Grange, in order that you might satisfy yourself finally on certain matters which to you were of the first importance? Good. Then, I think, having established that distinction – the purpose behind the projection – we come, not unnaturally, to the other distinction or difference – the superior intensity of the image projected. The normal phantasy of the living manifests and vanishes. It does not speak, it does not abide our question, its visibility is its only energy, and that is rapidly exhausted and dispersed. In your case, on the other hand, the phantasm was in all respects like an ordinary human being; it was both persistent and energetic; to all apparent intents and purposes it was yourself as you sit there before me.

'Beyond the extraordinary character of the whole manifestation, there are one or two very curious points. For instance. While the phantasm was with us, we saw nothing, as I have just intimated, at all peculiar or out of the way about it. But when it had disappeared, and we were wondering what on earth had happened, it came out accidentally that the figure – I was going to say, "you" – had not impressed us all in the same way. One man thought Sir Halliday was short and small, another described him as above the average height. And another thing: when I came into this room about an hour ago, I noticed at once the difference between Sir Halliday of Campden House and the Sir Halliday of Morton Grange: the former figure was by far more definite and vivid than the latter. You know in the old Christmas Ghost stories, the apparition is often described as "a shadowy figure". A traditional phrase, no doubt, and an instance, as I think, of the fact that tradition often tells the truth under the form of a picturesque symbolism. We couldn't see the furniture through the phantasm of Sir Halliday; but, in a sense, the image was certainly shadowy, indeterminate.

'And again: here is a puzzle. As you sat in the train on the way to Dover, you heard the murmur of the conversation in the room at Morton Grange. You recognised my voice just now. And, on the other hand, we heard some – not all – of your remarks to your fellow travellers in the carriage. Of course we thought you were speaking to us. These are difficulties which I do not attempt to explain. But I hope that on the whole you are relieved.'

Sir Halliday Stuart had listened in a deep, meditative silence; assenting, now and again, with a nod of the head, when Tallent appealed to him.

' "Journeying very far, I found what I had not sought",' he murmured to himself, sighing, in great wonder.

'Well, yes,' he said aloud. 'In a way, I suppose you have relieved me – of the sense of an intolerable contradiction.'

'Well, I am glad,' said Tallent, rising. 'Though I believe it may be held at last that true wisdom consists in accepting contradictions and rejoicing in them greatly.'

Ritual

Once upon a time, as we say in English, or *olim*, as the Latins said in their more austere and briefer way, I was sent forth on a May Monday to watch London being happy on their Whitsun holiday. This is the sort of appointment that used to be known in newspaper offices as an annual; and the difficulty for the men engaged in this business is to avoid seeing the same sights as those witnessed a year before and saying much the same things about them as were said on Whit Monday twelvemonth. Queuing up for Madame Tussaud's waxworks, giving buns to diverse creatures in the Zoo, gazing at those Easter Island gods in the portico of the British Museum, waiting for all sorts of early doors to open; all these are spectacles of the day. And the patient man who boards the buses from suburbs may chance to hear a lady from Hornsey expounding to her neighbour on the seat, an inhabitant of Enfield Wash, the terrible gaieties that Piccadilly Circus witnesses when the electric signs are fairly lit.

On the Whit Monday in question I saw and recorded some of these matters; and then strolled westward along Piccadilly, by the palings of the Green Park. The conventional business of the day had been more or less attended to: now for the unsystematic prowl: one never knows where one may find one's goods. And then and there, I came across some boys, half-a-dozen or so of them, playing what struck me as a very queer game on the fresh turf of the Park, under the tender and piercing green of the young leaves. I have forgotten the preliminary elaborations of the sport; but there seemed to be some sort of dramatic action, perhaps with dialogue, but this I could not hear. Then one boy stood alone, with the five or six others about him. They pretended to hit the solitary boy, and he fell to the ground and lay motionless, as if dead. Then the others covered him up with their coats, and ran away. And then, if I remember, the boy who had been ritually smitten, slaughtered, and buried, rose to his feet, and the very odd game began all over again.

Here, I thought, was something a little out of the way of the accustomed doings and pleasures of the holiday crowds, and I returned to my office and embodied an account of this Green Park sport in my tale of Whit Monday in London; with some allusion to the curious analogy between the boys' game and certain matters of a more serious nature. But it would not do. A spectacled Reader came down out of his glass cage, and held up a strip of proof.

'Hiram Abiff?' he queried in a low voice, as he placed the galleyslip on my desk, and pointed to the words with his pen. 'It's not usual to mention these things in print.'

I assured the Reader that I was not one of the Widow's offspring, but he still shook his head gravely, and I let him have his way, willing to avoid all *admiratio*. It was, I thought, a curious little incident, and to this day I have never heard an explanation of the coincidence – mere chance, very likely – between the pastime in the Park and those matters which it is not usual to mention in print.

But a good many years later, this business of the Green Park was recalled to me by a stranger experience in a very different part of London. A friend of mine, an American, who had travelled in many outland territories of the earth, asked me to show him some of the less known quarters of London.

'Do not misunderstand me, sir,' he said, in his measured, almost Johnsonian manner, 'I do not wish to see your great city in its alleged sensational aspects. I am not yearning to probe the London underworld, nor do I wish to view any opium joints or blind-pigs for cocaine addicts. In such matters, I have already accumulated more than sufficient experience in other quarters of the world. But if you would just show me those aspects which are so ordinary that nobody ever sees them, I shall be greatly indebted to you.'

I remember how I had once awed two fellow citizens of his by taking them to a street not very far from King's Cross Station, and showing them how each house was guarded by twin plaster sphinxes of a deadly chocolate-red, which crouched on either side of the flights of steps leading to the doorways. I remembered how the late Arnold Bennett had come exploring in this region, and seen the sphinxes and had noted them in his diary with a kind of dumb surmise, venturing no comment. So I said that I thought I understood. We set out, and soon we were deep in that unknown London which is at our very doors.

'Dickens had been here,' I said in my part as Guide and Interpreter. 'You know *Little Dorrit*? Then this might be Mr Casby's very street, which set out meaning to run down into the valley and up again to the top of the hill, but got out of breath and stopped still after twenty yards.'

The American gentleman relished the reference and his surroundings. He pointed out to me curious work in some of the iron balconies before the first floor windows in the grey houses, making a rough sketch of the design of one of them in his notebook. We wandered here and there, and up and down at haphazard, by strange wastes and devious ways, till I, in spite of my fancied knowledge, found myself in a part that I did not remember to have seen before. There were timber yards with high walls about them. There were cottages that seemed to have strayed from the outskirts of some quiet provincial town, off the main road. One of these lay deep in the shadow of an old mulberry, and ripening grapes hung from a vine on a neighbouring wall. The hollyhocks in the neat little front gardens were almost over; there were still brave displays of snapdragons and marigolds. But round the corner, barrows piled with pale bananas and flaming oranges filled the roadway, and the street market resounded with raucous voices, praise of fruit and fish, and loud bargainings, and gossip at its highest pitch. We pushed our way through the crowd, and left the street of the market, and presently came into the ghostly quiet of a square: high, severe houses, built of whitish bricks, complete in 1840 Gothic, all neat and well-kept, and for all sign of life or movement, uninhabited.

And then, when we had barely rested our ears from the market jangle, there came what I suppose was an overflow from that region. A gang of small boys surged into the square and broke its peace. There were about a dozen of them, more or less, and I took it that they were playing soldiers. They marched, two and two, in their dirty and shabby order, apparently under the command of a young ruffian somewhat bigger and taller than the rest. Two of them banged incessantly with bits of broken wood on an old meat tin and a battered iron tea tray, and all of them howled as barbarously as any crooner, but much louder. They went about and about, and then diverged into an empty road that looked as if it led nowhere in particular, and there drew up, and formed themselves into a sort of hollow square, their captain in the middle. The tin pan music went on steadily, but less noisily; it had become a succession of slow beats, and the howls had turned into a sort of whining chant.

But it remained a very horrible row, and I was moving on to get away from the noise, when my American interposed.

'If you wouldn't mind our tarrying here for a few moments,' he said apologetically. 'This pastime of your London boys interests me very much. You may think it strange, but I find it more essentially exciting than the Eton and Harrow Cricket Match of which I witnessed some part a few weeks ago.'

So we looked on from an unobtrusive corner. The boys, evidently, agreed with my friend, and found their game absorbing. I don't think that they had noticed us or knew that we were there.

They went through their queer performance. The bangs or beats on the tin and the tray grew softer and slower, and the yells had died into a monotonous drone. The leader went inside the square, from boy to boy, and seemed to whisper into the ear of each one. Then he passed round a second time, standing before each, and making a sort of summoning or beckoning gesture with his hand. Nothing happened. I did not find the sport essentially exciting; but looking at the American, I observed that he was watching it with an expression of the most acute interest and amazement. Again the big boy went around the square. He stopped dead before a little fellow in a torn jacket. He threw out his arms wide, with a gesture of embrace, and then drew them in. He did this three times, and at the third repetition of the ceremony, the little chap in the torn jacket cried out with a piercing scream and fell forward as if dead.

The banging of the tins and the howl of the voices went up to heaven with a hideous dissonance.

My American friend was gasping with astonishment as we passed on our way.

'This is an amazing city,' he said. 'Do you know, sir, that those boys were acting all as if they'd been Asiki doing their Njoru ritual. I've seen it in East Africa. But there the black man that falls down stays down. He's dead.'

A week or two later, I was telling the tale to some friends. One of them pulled an evening paper out of his pocket.

'Look at that,' said he, pointing with his finger. I read the headlines:

MYSTERY DEATH IN NORTH LONDON SQUARE

HOME OFFICE DOCTOR PUZZLED

HEART VESSELS RUPTURED

'PLAYING SOLDIERS'

BOY FALLS DEAD

CORONER DIRECTS OPEN VERDICT

APPENDIX

Introduction to 'The Bowmen'

From *The Angel of Mons: The Bowmen and Other Legends of War*, 1915

I have been asked to write an introduction to the story of 'The Bowmen', on its publication in book form together with three other tales of similar fashion. And I hesitate. This affair of 'The Bowmen' has been such an odd one from first to last, so many queer complications have entered into it, there have been so many and so divers currents and cross-currents of rumour and speculation concerning it, that I honestly do not know where to begin. I propose, then, to solve the difficulty by apologising for beginning at all.

For, usually and fitly, the presence of an introduction is held to imply that there is something of consequence and importance to be introduced. If, for example, a man has made an anthology of great poetry, he may well write an introduction justifying his principle of selection, pointing out here and there, as the spirit moves him, high beauties and supreme excellencies, discoursing of the magnates and lords and princes of literature, whom he is merely serving as groom of the chamber. Introductions, that is, belong to the masterpieces and classics of the world, to the great and ancient and accepted things; and I am here introducing a short, small story of my own which appeared in *The Evening News* about ten months ago.

I appreciate the absurdity, nay, the enormity of the position in all its grossness. And my excuse for these pages must be this: that though the story itself is nothing, it has yet had such odd and unforeseen consequences and adventures that the tale of them may possess some interest. And then, again, there are certain psychological morals to be drawn from the whole matter of the tale and its sequel of rumours and discussions that are not, I think, devoid of consequence; and so to begin at the beginning.

This was in last August, to be more precise, on the last Sunday of last August. There were terrible things to be read on that hot Sunday morning between meat and mass. It was in *The Weekly Dispatch* that I saw the awful account of the retreat from Mons. I no longer recollect the details; but I have not forgotten the impression that was then on my mind, I seemed to see a furnace of torment and death and agony and terror seven times heated, and in the midst of the burning was the British Army. In the midst of the flame, consumed by it and yet aureoled in it, scattered like ashes and yet triumphant, martyred and for ever glorious. So I saw our men with a shining about them, so I took these thoughts with me to church, and, I am sorry to say, was making up a story in my head while the deacon was singing the Gospel.

This was not the tale of 'The Bowmen'. It was the first sketch, as it were, of 'The Soldiers' Rest'. I only wish I had been able to write it as I conceived it. The tale as it stands is, I think, a far better piece of craft than 'The Bowmen', but the tale that came to me as the blue incense floated above the Gospel Book on the desk between the tapers: that indeed was a noble story – like all the stories that never get written. I conceived the dead men coming up through the flames and in the flames, and being welcomed in the Eternal Tavern with songs and flowing cups and everlasting mirth. But every man is the child of his age, however much he may hate it; and our popular religion has long determined that jollity is wicked. As far as I can make out modern Protestantism believes that Heaven is something like Evensong in an English cathedral, the service by Stainer and the Dean preaching. For those opposed to dogma of any kind – even the mildest – I suppose it is held that a Course of Ethical Lectures will be arranged.

Well, I have long maintained that on the whole the average church, considered as a house of preaching, is a much more poisonous place than the average tavern; still, as I say, one's age masters one, and clouds and bewilders the intelligence, and the real story of 'The Soldiers' Rest', with its *sonus epulantium in æterno convivio*, was ruined at the moment of its birth, and it was some time later that the actual story got written. And in the meantime the plot of 'The Bowmen' occurred to me. Now it has been murmured and hinted and suggested and whispered in all sorts of quarters that before I wrote the tale I had heard something. The most decorative of these legends is also the most precise: 'I know for a fact that the whole thing was given him in typescript by a lady-in-waiting.' This was not the case; and all vaguer reports to the effect that I had heard some rumours or hints of rumours are equally void of any trace of truth.

Again I apologise for entering so pompously into the minutiæ of my bit of a story, as if it were the lost poems of Sappho; but it appears that the subject interests the public, and I comply with my instructions. I take it, then, that the origins of 'The Bowmen' were composite. First of all, all ages and nations have cherished the thought that spiritual hosts may come to the help of earthly arms, that gods and heroes and saints have descended from their high immortal places to fight for their worshippers and clients. Then Kipling's story of the ghostly Indian regiment got in my head and got mixed with the mediævalism that is always there; and so 'The Bowmen' was written. I was heartily disappointed with it, I remember, and thought it – as I still think it – an indifferent piece of work. However, I have tried to write for these thirty-five long years, and if I have not become practised in letters, I am at least a past master in the Lodge of Disappointment. Such as it was, 'The Bowmen' appeared in *The Evening News* of September 29th, 1914.

Now the journalist does not, as a rule, dwell much on the prospect of fame; and if he be an evening journalist, his anticipations of immortality are bounded by twelve o'clock at night at the latest; and it may well be that those insects which begin to live in the morning and are dead by sunset deem themselves immortal. Having written my story, having groaned and growled over it and printed it, I certainly never thought to hear another word of it. My colleague 'The Londoner' praised it warmly to my face, as his kindly fashion is; entering, very properly, a technical caveat as to the language of the battle cries of the bowmen. 'Why should English archers use French terms?' he said. I replied that the only reason was this – that a *Monseigneur* here and there struck me as picturesque; and I reminded him that, as a matter of cold historical fact, most of the archers of Agincourt were mercenaries from Gwent, my native country, who would appeal to Mihangel and to saints not known to the Saxons – Teilo, Iltyd, Dewi, Cadwaladyr Vendigeid. And I thought that that was the first and last discussion of 'The Bowmen'. But in a few days from its publication the editor of *The Occult Review* wrote to me. He wanted to know whether the story had any foundation in fact. I told him that it had no foundation in fact of any kind or sort; I forget whether I added that it had no foundation in rumour but I should think not, since to the best of my belief there were no rumours of heavenly interposition in existence at that time. Certainly I had heard of none. Soon afterwards the editor of *Light* wrote asking a like question, and I made him a like reply. It seemed to me that I had stifled any 'Bowmen' mythos in the hour of its birth.

A month or two later, I received several requests from editors of parish magazines to reprint the story. I – or, rather, my editor – readily gave permission; and then, after another month or two, the conductor of one of these magazines wrote to me, saying that the February issue containing the story had been sold out, while there was still a great demand for it. Would I allow them to reprint 'The Bowmen' as a pamphlet, and would I write a short preface giving the exact authorities for the story? I replied that they might reprint in pamphlet form with all my heart, but that I could not give my authorities, since I had none, the tale being pure invention. The priest wrote again, suggesting – to my amazement – that I must be mistaken, that the main 'facts' of 'The Bowmen' must be true, that my share in the matter must surely have been confined to the elaboration and decoration of a veridical history. It seemed that my light fiction had been accepted by the congregation of this particular church as the solidest of facts; and it was then that it began to dawn on me that if I had failed in the art of letters, I had succeeded, unwittingly, in the art of deceit. This happened, I should think, some time in April, and the snowball of rumour that was then set rolling has been rolling ever since, growing bigger and bigger, till it is now swollen to a monstrous size.

It was at about this period that variants of my tale began to be told as authentic histories. At first, these tales betrayed their relation to their original. In several of them the vegetarian restaurant appeared, and St. George was the chief character. In one case an officer – name and address missing – said that there was a portrait of St. George in a certain London restaurant, and that a figure, just like the portrait, appeared to him on the battlefield, and was invoked by him, with the happiest results. Another variant – this, I think, never got into print – told how dead Prussians had been found on the battlefield with arrow wounds in their bodies. This notion amused me, as I had imagined a scene, when I was thinking out the story, in which a German general was to appear before the Kaiser to explain his failure to annihilate the English.

'All-Highest,' the general was to say, 'it is true, it is impossible to deny it. The men were killed by arrows; the shafts were found in their bodies by the burying parties.'

I rejected the idea as over-precipitous even for a mere fantasy. I was therefore entertained when I found that what I had refused as too fantastical for fantasy was accepted in certain occult circles as hard fact.

Other versions of the story appeared in which a cloud interposed between the attacking Germans and the defending British. In some examples the cloud served to conceal our men from the advancing enemy; in others, it disclosed shining shapes which frightened the horses of the pursuing German cavalry. St. George, it will be noted, has disappeared – he persisted some time longer in certain Roman Catholic variants – and there are no more bowmen, no more arrows. But so far angels are not mentioned; yet they are ready to appear, and I think that I have detected the machine which brought them into the story.

In 'The Bowmen' my imagined soldier saw 'a long line of shapes, with a shining about them.' And Mr. A.P. Sinnett, writing in the May issue of *The Occult Review*, reporting what he had heard, states that 'those who could see said they saw "a row of shining beings" between the two armies.' Now I conjecture that the word 'shining' is the link between my tale and the derivative from it. In the popular view shining and benevolent supernatural beings are angels, and so, I believe, the Bowmen of my story have become 'the Angels of Mons.' In this shape they have been received with respect and credence everywhere, or almost everywhere.

And here, I conjecture, we have the key to the large popularity of the delusion – as I think it. We have long ceased in England to take much interest in saints, and in the recent revival of the cultus of St. George, the saint is little more than a patriotic figurehead. And the appeal to the saints to succour us is certainly not a common English practice; it is held Popish by most of our countrymen. But angels, with certain reservations, have retained their popularity, and so, when it was settled that the English army in its dire peril was delivered by angelic aid, the way was clear for general belief, and for the enthusiasms of the religion of the man in the street. And so soon as the legend got the title 'The Angels of Mons' it became impossible to avoid it. It permeated the Press: it would not be neglected; it appeared in the most unlikely quarters – in *Truth and Town Topics*, *The New Church Weekly* (Swedenborgian) and *John Bull*. The editor of *The Church Times* has exercised a wise reserve: he awaits that evidence which so far is lacking; but in one issue of the paper I noted that the story furnished a text for a sermon, the subject of a letter, and the matter for an article. People send me cuttings from provincial papers containing hot controversy as to the exact nature of the appearances; the 'Office Window' of *The Daily Chronicle* suggests scientific explanations of the hallucination; the *Pall Mall* in a note about St. James says he is of the brotherhood of the Bowmen of Mons – this reversion to the bowmen from the angels being possibly due to the strong statements that I have made on the matter. The pulpits both of the Church and of Non-conformity have been busy: Bishop Welldon, Dean Hensley Henson (a disbeliever), Bishop Taylor Smith (the Chaplain-General), and many other clergy have occupied themselves with the matter. Dr. Horton preached about the 'angels' at Manchester; Sir Joseph Compton Rickett (President of the National Federation of Free Church Councils) stated that the soldiers at the front had seen visions and dreamed dreams, and had given testimony of powers and principalities fighting for them or against them. Letters come from all the ends of the earth to the Editor of *The Evening News* with theories, beliefs, explanations, suggestions. It is all somewhat wonderful; one can say that the whole affair is a psychological phenomenon of considerable interest, fairly comparable with the great Russian delusion of last August and September.

*

Now it is possible that some persons, judging by the tone of these remarks of mine, may gather the impression that I am a profound disbeliever in the possibility of any intervention of the super-physical order in the affairs of the physical order. They will be mistaken if they make this inference; they will be mistaken if they suppose that I think miracles in Judæa credible but miracles in France or Flanders incredible. I hold no such absurdities. But I confess, very frankly, that I credit none of the 'Angels of Mons' legends, partly because I see, or think I see, their derivation from my own idle fiction, but chiefly because I have, so far, not received one jot or tittle of evidence that should dispose me to belief. It is idle, indeed, and foolish enough for a man to say: 'I am sure that story is a lie, because the supernatural element enters into it;' here, indeed, we have the maggot writhing in the midst of corrupted offal denying the existence of the sun. But if this fellow be a fool – as he is – equally foolish is he who says, 'If the tale has anything of the supernatural it is true, and the less evidence the better;' and I am afraid this tends to be the attitude of many who call themselves occultists. I hope that I shall never get to that frame of mind. So I say, not that super-normal interventions are impossible, not that they have not happened during this war – I know nothing as to that point, one way or the other – but that there is not one atom of evidence (so far) to support the current stories of the angels of Mons. For, be it remarked, these stories are specific stories. They rest on the second, third, fourth, fifth hand stories told by 'a soldier,' by 'an officer,' by 'a Catholic correspondent,' by 'a nurse,' by any number of anonymous people. Indeed, names have been mentioned. A lady's name has been drawn, most unwarrantably as it appears to me, into the discussion, and I have no doubt that this lady has been subject to a good deal of pestering and annoyance. She has written to the Editor of *The Evening News* denying all knowledge of the supposed miracle. The Psychical Research Society's expert confesses that no real evidence has been proffered to her Society on the matter. And then, to my amazement, she accepts as fact the proposition that some men on the battlefield have been 'hallucinated,' and proceeds to give the theory of sensory hallucination. She forgets that, by her own showing, there is no reason to suppose that anybody has been hallucinated at all. Someone (unknown) has met a nurse (unnamed) who has talked to a soldier (anonymous) who has seen angels. But that is not evidence; and not even Sam Weller at his gayest would have dared to offer it as such in the Court of Common Pleas. So far, then, nothing remotely approaching proof has been offered as to any supernatural intervention during the Retreat from Mons. Proof may come; if so, it will be interesting and more than interesting.

But, taking the affair as it stands at present, how is it that a nation plunged in materialism of the grossest kind has accepted idle rumours and gossip of the supernatural as certain truth? The answer is contained in the question: it is precisely because our whole atmosphere is materialist that we are ready to credit anything – save the truth. Separate a man from good drink, he will swallow methylated spirit with joy. Man is created to be inebriated; to be 'nobly wild, not mad.' Suffer the Cocoa Prophets and their company to seduce him in body and spirit, and he will get himself stuff that will make him ignobly wild and mad indeed. It took hard, practical men of affairs, business men, advanced thinkers, Freethinkers, to believe in Madame Blavatsky and Mahatmas and the famous message from the Golden Shore: 'Judge's plan is right; follow him and stick.'

And the main responsibility for this dismal state of affairs undoubtedly lies on the shoulders of the majority of the clergy of the Church of England. Christianity, as Mr. W.L. Courtney has so admirably pointed out, is a great Mystery Religion; it is *the* Mystery Religion. Its priests are called to an awful and tremendous hierurgy; its pontiffs are to be the pathfinders, the bridge-makers between the world of sense and the world of spirit. And, in fact, they pass their time in preaching, not the eternal mysteries, but a twopenny morality, in changing the Wine of Angels and the Bread of Heaven into ginger beer and mixed biscuits: a sorry transubstantiation, a sad alchemy, as it seems to me.

ARTHUR MACHEN